Garmelia Edgar 9-8-2012

Hope Rekindled

Striking a Match, Book 3

Hope Rekindled

Tracie Peterson

Bethany House Publishers
Minneapolis, Minnesota

Hope Rekindled

Cover design by Jennifer Parker
Cover photography by Kevin White Photogaphy, Minneapolis

Published by Bethany House Publishers
11400 Hampshire Avenue South
Bloomington, Minnesota 55438

Bethany House Publishers is a division of
Baker Publishing Group, Grand Rapids, Michigan.

Printed in the United States of America

Library of Congress Cataloging-in-Publication Data

Peterson, Tracie.
Hope rekindled / Tracie Peterson.
p. cm. — (Striking a match ; bk. 3)
ISBN 978-0-7642-0891-1 (hardcover : alk. paper) — ISBN 978-0-7642-0614-6 (pbk.) — ISBN 978-0-7642-0892-8 (large-print pbk.)
I. Title.
PS3566.E7717H66 2011
813'.54—dc22

2011008203

To Dr. Peter Kelleher
with thanks for your
generous heart and fantastic
surgical skills.

Books by Tracie Peterson

www.traciepeterson.com

A Slender Thread • *House of Secrets* • *Where My Heart Belongs*

BRIDAL VEIL ISLAND*
To Have and To Hold

SONG OF ALASKA
Dawn's Prelude • *Morning's Refrain* • *Twilight's Serenade*

STRIKING A MATCH
Embers of Love • *Hearts Aglow* • *Hope Rekindled*

ALASKAN QUEST
Summer of the Midnight Sun
Under the Northern Lights • *Whispers of Winter*
Alaskan Quest (3 in 1)

BRIDES OF GALLATIN COUNTY
A Promise to Believe In • *A Love to Last Forever*
A Dream to Call My Own

THE BROADMOOR LEGACY*
A Daughter's Inheritance • *An Unexpected Love*
A Surrendered Heart

BELLS OF LOWELL*
Daughter of the Loom • *A Fragile Design* • *These Tangled Threads*

LIGHTS OF LOWELL*
A Tapestry of Hope • *A Love Woven True* • *The Pattern of Her Heart*

DESERT ROSES
Shadows of the Canyon • *Across the Years* • *Beneath a Harvest Sky*

HEIRS OF MONTANA
Land of My Heart • *The Coming Storm* • *To Dream Anew* • *The Hope Within*

LADIES OF LIBERTY
A Lady of High Regard • *A Lady of Hidden Intent*
A Lady of Secret Devotion

RIBBONS OF STEEL**
Distant Dreams • *A Hope Beyond* • *A Promise for Tomorrow*

RIBBONS WEST**
Westward the Dream

WESTWARD CHRONICLES
A Shelter of Hope • *Hidden in a Whisper* • *A Veiled Reflection*

YUKON QUEST
Treasures of the North • *Ashes and Ice* • *Rivers of Gold*

*with Judith Miller **with Judith Pella

TRACIE PETERSON is the author of over eighty novels, both historical and contemporary. Her avid research resonates in her stories, as seen in her bestselling HEIRS OF MONTANA and ALASKAN QUEST series. Tracie and her family make their home in Montana.

Visit Tracie's Web site at *www.traciepeterson.com*.
Visit Tracie's blog at *www.writespassage.blogspot.com*.

Chapter 1

East Texas, March 1887

"You . . . you can't marry him," Jake Wythe declared, taking Deborah Vandermark by the arm. He swayed for a moment, then pulled her with him to the far side of the porch. "You can't."

Deborah broke loose from his hold. "Jake, don't be ridiculous. We've been through this. I love Christopher. This is a celebration of my upcoming wedding, and I will thank you not to embarrass me by making a scene." Deborah hoped her words would somehow sober him a bit. "Let's return to the others."

"You only wanna . . . wanna marry him because he's a doctor. You want to be a doctor and figure this is . . . is the way to get that done."

"Nonsense," Deborah said, putting her hands on her hips.

"If I only wanted to train to be a doctor, there are other ways to accomplish the task without committing my life to someone. Now, if this is all you came to tell me, I'm going back inside to be with my guests."

"He's an Irishman!" Jake declared, stumbling forward.

Deborah stopped and looked at him. The fact that Christopher Clayton was truly Christopher Clayton Kelleher was well-known in her family and circle of friends, but why Jake thought it important to bring it up now was beyond her.

She shook her head. "I'm sorry, Jake. You've saved my life more than once, but I don't love you. We're just good friends."

He pushed her back against the house. "But I love you. Don't you understand? I want to marry you. It should be me." He took hold of her face rather roughly and covered her mouth with his own.

Deborah fought against his hold. His breath reeked of beer as he sought to deepen his kiss. She tried to claw at his face, but Jake quickly pinned her arms.

"I can make you . . . happy," he murmured against her lips.

"Stop or I'll scream!"

She didn't need to. In a flash, G.W. had yanked Jake away from her and onto his backside. Standing over the smaller man, Deborah's brother shook a fist at him. "Of all the dumb things. What in the world is wrong with you, Wythe?"

"I love her. She shouldn't . . . shouldn't marry the doc. She . . . she . . . she should marry me."

"You're drunk." G.W. reached down and pulled Jake to his feet. "You're drunk and you attacked my sister. Get out of here and don't come back. You're fired."

Jake looked at him, confused—as if the words didn't make

sense. He stumbled back against the porch rail, then lurched toward Deborah.

G.W. grabbed him and threw him off the porch. "I said to get on out of here. We don't tolerate drinkin', and we sure don't allow for drunks to attack our women."

Jake landed in a flurry of dust. "I didn't mean to hurt you, Deborah. I love you."

Christopher came to her side. He put his arm around her shoulder and gave her a quizzical stare. "What's this all about?"

"Jake wants me to marry him instead of you. He's been drinking and he . . ." She paused a moment, unsure of what to say. "Well, he forced a kiss on me." She tried to sound casual, but in truth it had really shaken her.

Christopher frowned and looked to where Jake was just picking himself up off the ground. "Are you all right?" he asked, his hand stroking her arm in concern.

"I'm fine. Let's just go back inside." Coming alongside her brother, Deborah put her hand on his shoulder. "Thank you, G.W." She refused to cast even the briefest glance at Jake, which only caused him to call after her.

"Do you hear me? Deborah? I love you, Deborah. I love you."

Mercifully, as she drew nearer to the house, the music drowned out Jake's pathetic cries. A little band of local talent played while others danced and laughed in celebration of her upcoming nuptials. Apparently Jake had decided to forgo making merry, preferring to numb his pain and bolster his courage with liquor. She glanced around the room, wondering if others were also imbibing.

"Why were you outside?" Christopher asked.

She shrugged. "Jake asked me to step onto the porch with

him so he could tell me something. I had no idea that he'd been drinking."

Christopher led her to where the refreshments were laid out and poured her a glass of punch. "I'm sorry I wasn't with you."

"There was no reason to believe you needed to be." Deborah took the glass from him. "It's best we put it behind us now."

He narrowed his gaze and tilted her face to the light. "You may have a bruise."

She touched her free hand to her jaw. "Oh, bother. Well, it's a week until the wedding, so it should fade."

"Just a week," he said with a grin. "Seems like an eternity."

Deborah laughed. She sipped the punch and gazed out at the people who'd come to her family's home to share their revelry. Mother and Arjan were dancing, as were others. G.W. and Lizzie stood to one side. As Lizzie drew her husband's hand to her lips, G.W.'s deep scowl softened. No doubt his thoughts were still on Jake Wythe. At Lizzie's kiss, however, his outlook appeared to change. Deborah could see that her friend had a soothing effect on G.W. Lizzie motioned to his leg and he rubbed it, but nodded. G.W. had nearly lost the limb and his very life when he'd fallen from a tree over a year ago. He'd worked hard to recover, although he still was not up to dancing.

"Would you like to waltz with me?"

Deborah looked at the man who would soon be her husband. "I would like that very much." She allowed Christopher to take the glass from her and place it on the table. He extended his arm and she smiled. They might live in the seclusion of the Big Piney Woods, but they were still quite civilized when it suited them.

Christopher placed his hand upon her waist, and Deborah found girlish joy bubble up from within as they swayed to the music. She remembered the first time she'd been at a barn dance—the first time she was actually allowed to stay up for the dance itself. She had been fourteen and quite enthralled to discover what went on at such events. Her steps had been more awkward back then, and she'd mashed and bruised her fair share of toes. The gangly girl she'd been had grown up, however, and she easily kept stride with her husband-to-be. She had never been happier.

"I wish we could bring your family here for the wedding."

Christopher shook his head. "It's far too costly. I promised my mother we would come for a visit in the summer if all went well."

The music ended and the fiddle player declared he needed a break to smoke his pipe. The band disbursed and the dancers headed for the refreshment table.

"I can hardly wait to meet your mother. She sounds like a wonderful woman," Deborah whispered as Christopher led her to the side of the room.

"You two are very much alike," he replied. "You are both very intelligent, although my mother never had the chance for school—at least nothing more than grade school. But she's a determined soul, nevertheless, and taught her children to read and encouraged them to attend school. She would appreciate your stance on education being of the utmost importance." Christopher leaned closer. "It looks as though there are ladies who would like to speak to you. I'll go talk to G.W. and thank him again for rescuing you."

Before she could reply he was gone, and Deborah found herself half circled by several women. Mrs. Perkins and Mrs. Huebner were on her right, while Mother and Dinah Wolcott were on her left. Lizzie and the pastor's daughter, Mara, made their way to join her, as well.

"So is your gown finished?" Mrs. Huebner asked. "I understand you're reworking your mother's wedding dress."

"Yes," Deborah replied, giving her mother a quick smile. "Mother's gown was designed in the late 1850s, and as you know, the fashions have changed considerably. I have to admit, however, my contributions have been minimal. Mother and Sissy have been the ones to transform it."

"Have you changed it to a great degree, Euphanel?" Mrs. Huebner asked.

"Yes. You must remember, I married in Georgia. The skirts then were quite voluminous. We have been able to drape the tiered flouncing up and back over a bustle. Sissy is a genius when it comes to such handwork."

"She is," Deborah agreed.

"We need to hem it, but otherwise, we're very nearly done," Mother added.

Mrs. Perkins glanced around the room. Her husband founded the little sawmill town of Perkinsville, which left Mrs. Perkins as its unofficial matron. "Oh, a wedding is just the thing to cheer up our little town. Look what this party has done for our spirits." She continued, "I'm certain you have more than enough flowers for the wedding, but should you need any additional blooms, please feel free to visit my garden. You are free to take anything you need."

"That's so kind, Rachel," Mother replied before Deborah could answer. "We will keep that in mind. I have to admit, however, that I've been far more concerned about getting everything to the church in one piece. I'm beginning to think we should have just planned to have the wedding here."

"It will all work out, you'll see." Mrs. Perkins patted Mother's arm. "So will you and the doctor take a wedding trip?" she asked Deborah.

"We're planning a brief trip to Galveston," she replied. "Neither of us wants to be gone for too long, however. Just in case someone needs a doctor."

"Galveston is lovely. The water is so refreshing." Mrs. Perkins looked around the room. "It's such a pity that there aren't more folks in town these days." She shook her head and gave a *tsk*ing sound. "Since the mill fire, so many have left to find work elsewhere, and who can blame them? Mr. Albright and Mr. Longstreet will not give my husband any definitive terms for rebuilding. I wish he'd never taken on partners. In the old days, we could just assure folks that they'd still have a job and that the mill would be up and running before they knew it.

"Remember the early days of our little town, Euphanel? We weren't much of a community, and certainly the mill was very small, but each of our men ran their own business affairs. Now we are dependent upon others to let us know what the plan will be."

"Have they given no indication?" Mother asked.

"None. When Mr. Perkins confronts them, they merely tell him that he is a lesser partner and that they will be the ones to make the decisions about rebuilding. Mr. Albright did say he was seeking advice on whether the current location was most advantageous or if he should build elsewhere."

"Seems going somewhere else would be foolish," Lizzie threw in. "The rails are here—the town's already in place."

"That's exactly what Zed told them, but they weren't very inclined to concern themselves with such things. Mr. Albright said that the town could be disassembled and rebuilt."

"Seems like a lot of work when a little could suffice," Mrs. Huebner declared.

Deborah agreed. The entire matter seemed to be nothing more than a delaying tactic to torment her family.

"Miz O'Neal will no longer run the boardinghouse," Mrs. Perkins added. "She said without guests, there's really no need for her to stay on, and Zed can't afford to pay her out of his own pocket."

"When does Mary plan to leave?" Mother asked. "Where will she go?"

"Plans to join her sister in Ohio. I heard her say that she'll stay on until after the wedding. She wanted to see Deborah married."

Mrs. Huebner nodded. "I told Curtis the same thing."

"Surely you'll stick around until the school term is concluded," Deborah said. She was surprised the Huebners were considering a move, but if Stuart and Mr. Longstreet were not inclined to get the mill up and running again, what choice did they have? Perkinsville would simply continue to diminish until no one was left—not even its founding family. Those in need of a school would simply have to send their children to the county school some distance away.

"I heard that your sons moved their families elsewhere, Mrs. Perkins," Lizzie said as if reading Deborah's thoughts.

"Yes, it seems things will never be the same again. I never thought to leave this place, but now . . ."

"Surely Zed isn't going to pull out." Mother looked at her friend, as if to ascertain the truth in her eyes.

"He said it will completely depend on the decisions of Mr. Albright and Mr. Longstreet."

Deborah saw Lizzie clench her jaw and look away. Deborah recognized the emotion on her face, for she, too, had her own moments of guilt. After all, she had encouraged her friend to leave Mr. Albright at the altar, and in turn, Lizzie had left her home in Philadelphia to come to Texas with Deborah. Then Lizzie fell in love with and married Deborah's brother. It was hard not to feel at least a bit responsible for the fact that Stuart Albright wished to make them pay for the embarrassment he'd endured.

But it had never been about embarrassing Stuart. It wasn't even about denying him the inheritance that they later learned he would have received upon wedding Lizzie. Deborah had never wished Stuart harm; she had only wanted to see her dear friend happy.

And Lizzie could never have been happy married to Stuart—of this Deborah was certain. But now the price being imposed was not only intended for the Vandermarks, but for all of Perkinsville. Stuart was hurting them all because his pride was wounded.

"He didn't even love her," Deborah muttered.

"What was that, my dear?" Mrs. Perkins asked.

Deborah realized she'd spoken aloud and shook her head. "It was nothing. I'm sorry. I'm just pondering the past again." She gave a smile. "I hope very much to forget that which is behind me."

Mara Shattuck nodded. "There is great wisdom in that Bible encouragement." The pastor's daughter was often compared in looks to Deborah, but tonight they were nothing alike. Mara had pulled her hair into a tightly coiled knot at the nape of her neck and had dressed in quite a sedate fashion. It was a concession that she'd even come to the party. Deborah understood that when Mara had lived with her grandmother in New Orleans, they had observed the Lenten period with reverence and piety. They weren't of the Catholic faith, but even so, they took the opportunity of those weeks preceding Maundy Thursday, Good Friday, and Easter to remember the poor and needy and reflect on

God's ministry. Mara had come to the party only after spending the day helping the people of color who remained in Perkinsville.

Deborah admired the young woman who she was quite sure would one day marry into the family. Rob Vandermark, Deborah's other sibling, had set his sights on Miss Mara Shattuck, and once he concluded his studies at the seminary in Houston, she felt certain they would wed.

The musicians began to return to their instruments. "It looks like we'll soon be dancing again," she said with a smile. "My feet already ache, but I have to say, you've all made this one of the happiest nights of my life."

Mother gave her a hug. "I'm sure it's just the first of many."

Christopher made his way to Deborah as she bid the last of the guests good-bye. It was getting quite late, and he would have to leave, as well. He leaned against the wall and watched his fiancée, amazed at her ease. She was so accomplished, and not only in this. He'd seen her stitch up a wound or help set a bone without a moment's hesitation. He'd always hoped to marry a woman who was as capable as his mother. Deborah Vandermark was certainly that and more.

Her grace and calm soothed him in ways he didn't fully understand. And tonight, she was radiant in her joy. He couldn't help but admire her fine figure and stylish attire. Just seeing her stirred his blood. He longed to pull her into his arms and spend the rest of his life in her presence.

"You look spent," Euphanel Vandermark told him. "Are you sure you wouldn't just as soon spend the night here? You are welcome to sleep in Arjan's old cabin."

Christopher was more than a little tempted. He suppressed

a yawn. "No. I need to head back to town. I'm trying to inventory everything for Stuart Albright. He wants a complete list by Monday, and I figured all week to devote Saturday to it. If I stay here tonight, I won't want to leave in the morning."

Euphanel smiled. "Just another week—and then you two will have the rest of your lives together."

He nodded. "I hadn't known a week could last so long."

Arjan moved to Euphanel's side and put his arm around her shoulder. "We'd best let these two say their good-nights, Wife."

She smiled up at him and nodded. "I suppose so. Be careful on your ride home, Christopher. I wouldn't want anything happening to you."

He chuckled. "If I get hurt, I understand there is a fine woman doctor in these parts. Well, I suppose she's not a full-fledged doctor . . . yet," he said loud enough to catch Deborah's attention, "but I understand she's quite capable."

"That she is," Euphanel said with a quick glance over her shoulder. "That she is."

Christopher waited until Euphanel and Arjan had gone before approaching Deborah. He pulled her into his arms without warning and captured her lips in a lingering kiss. Deborah melted against him and sighed. Just another week and she'd be his. A few more days. Part of him longed to change his mind and stay the night—if only to be that much closer to her.

He felt Deborah's fingers on the nape of his neck toying with his hair. He would have to get a trim before the wedding, he thought. He touched the soft skin just under her ear and thought of what it would be like to place kisses there.

Pulling away, he grinned like a mischievous child. Deborah arched a brow in question, but he only laughed and dropped his hold. "One week, Miss Vandermark. A week from tomorrow—you will be mine."

"Why did we decide to wait so long?" she asked with a pout.

He roared with laughter. "The date was your idea. As I recall you wanted spring flowers and warmer weather." He walked to the door and lifted his hat from a nearby peg. "I would have married you last fall without flowers or warm weather. I would have married you during the awful cold months of the winter when all of the plains states were buried in snows and hideous cold. I'd marry you tomorrow if you'd just say the word."

For just a moment, he thought she looked tempted. Then she squared her shoulders and stepped forward. "Good evening to you, Dr. Kelleher. I will see you in one week, at which time I will say the only words necessary to seal our arrangement. Until then, enjoy your inventory."

He shook his head. "You're a cruel woman."

She gave him a wink. "I promise to make it up to you."

Chapter 2

Deborah stood on a dining room chair while her mother and Sissy pinned a hem in the white silk of her wedding gown.

"I can hardly believe it's the same dress," Mother declared. "I remember when the huge hooped skirts were all the fashion, and now this." She motioned to the straighter sleek lines of the gown.

"It was made good," Sissy commented. "Easy 'nuf to work with quality."

"I'm still amazed. It looks so much like the one in the magazine," Deborah commented, gazing down at the delicate silk.

The original gown had been skirted with three tiers of lace flouncing over white China silk. Mother and Sissy had crafted those flounces into a waterfall draping the bustled back. They modified the belled skirt to fit with the fashion of the day, which gave women a sleeker, more slender appearance—at least in the front. The back was another story. Voluminous amounts of material were fashioned over what seemed to be larger and larger bustles. Deborah was glad they'd chosen only a modest bustle. Anything bigger would have made her feel even more self-conscious. Still, she would have worn a bustle three times larger if required. She was marrying Christopher, and the gown was perfect. She felt like royalty—at least what she imagined royalty would feel like.

Deborah had always planned to wear her mother's wedding gown, and with the need to conserve money these days, it fit their plans all the better. Thanks to her mother's and Sissy's skill and the latest copy of *Godey's*, the masterpiece looked as if it had come from an expensive shop in Paris.

"Now turn and let's see if we have the hem pinned straight," Mother commanded.

Deborah took hold of her mother's hand and carefully turned on the chair. She let go and gripped the back of the chair as she made a full circle.

"It looks perfect." Mother sounded quite satisfied. "The train is so lovely."

"Won't be no problem to finish it up in time," Sissy said.

Deborah allowed them to help her from the chair. She ran her hands down over the overlaid bodice and basque waist. "I feel like a queen." She went to the cheval mirror they'd brought into the dining room.

Gently plucking a piece of lace that had twisted on the sleeve, she set it right and smiled. "I have never seen anything more beautiful, and just knowing that you wore this gown first . . ." Tears came to her eyes as she turned to face her mother. "I'm so very blessed."

Mother embraced her gently. "As am I. I can hardly believe this day has come."

Deborah pulled away and gave a light-hearted laugh. "Neither can I. It seemed forever in arriving." She gently touched the modest sweep of the scooped neckline. In just a couple of days, she would be Mrs. Christopher Kelleher. Dr. and Mrs. Kelleher. She giggled. One day it would be Dr. and Dr. Kelleher. Or maybe just "the doctors Kelleher." She giggled.

"You are getting giddy," her mother teased. "Let's get you out of the gown before you do something foolish."

"I wouldn't be so silly."

"Oh, look at you!" Lizzie and Jael declared as they entered the room, each carrying one of Lizzie and G.W.'s twins. Rutger wanted out of his mother's arms the moment they stepped into sight of his grandmother, however. At nine months of age, Rutger and Emily Ann, or "Annie" as she had quickly been dubbed, were getting into everything and charming everyone.

"I swear, they grow by inches each and every day."

"I agree with that," Lizzie said, wrestling her son. "Especially now that they eat from the table, as well as nurse. I can hardly believe they'll soon have their first birthday. Here it is the end of March; June isn't that far off."

Jael cuddled the calmer Annie. "I certainly wish I had a baby so sweet." Annie laughed and reached up to take hold of Jael's chin.

"Maybe you and Deborah both will have a baby this time next year," Lizzie said, her face revealing her delight at such a thought. "Then all of our children could be close in age and play together."

"I doubt we'll even be in the area," Jael said sadly. "Stuart doesn't like the influence you have over me. He's jealous of how close we are." She sighed. "He wouldn't be if it weren't for all his revenge nonsense." She shook her head and shifted Annie in her arms. "Sorry. I shouldn't have said that."

"But it's the truth," Lizzie said. "I'm afraid our lives will never be the same because of my bad decision to leave him."

"Leaving Stuart at the altar wasn't a bad decision," Deborah countered. "You should never marry someone you don't love, and I know you don't regret doing otherwise." That comment brought to mind the fact that Jael had married Stuart for less than love. She hurried to redirect the conversation. "Are you both as impressed as I am at what Mother and Sissy have done with this gown?"

"It's remarkable," Lizzie said, walking a few steps to see the back. "I can scarcely believe it's the same piece."

"We have the hem and waxed orange blossoms yet to sew," Mother said, "but I'm quite pleased with how it's turned out."

"Did the waxed blossoms survive the train trip?" Jael asked.

"They looked perfect," Mother replied. "The florist in Houston packed them quite carefully. They will make a grand finish to the dress."

A loud knock on the front door caught everyone's attention. Rutger immediately wanted to investigate and Lizzie battled to keep him in her arms.

"I'll get it, since Rutger seems to insist," she told them.

"Come, let's get you out of this gown," Mother said to Deborah.

Deborah nodded and followed her mother from the dining room. They were in the hall near the front foyer when she recognized the sound of Christopher's voice. Sissy turned, eyes wide.

"Groom ain't supposed to see you in your weddin' dress afore the ceremony."

Deborah froze in place, uncertain what to do as Christopher came into the room. Sissy tried to shield Deborah from sight. "Bad luck for you to be here, suh," she told Christopher.

"I'm afraid bad luck has preceded me."

Deborah moved from behind the older woman. "What is it? What's wrong?"

He noticed her gown and his frown deepened. "I'm so sorry."

She touched his arm. "What is it, Christopher? What has happened?"

Holding out a telegram, Christopher's gaze never left her face. "I've had bad news. Apparently something has happened to my family."

Deborah took the telegram and read it. The message was short and yet sent a wave of icy cold through her body. " 'Family tragedy.' " She looked up. "What kind of tragedy? It says nothing about the cause—about what's happened."

"I don't know. It was sent by the neighbor who lives across the street from my family. She and my mother are good friends."

Glancing again at the telegram, Deborah suddenly grew fearful. The second part of the message was simple.

Come quick.

Mother came to her side. "Do you have any way of contacting the woman to learn what has happened?"

"No. Not really. I could send her a reply, but I'm certain this must have cost money she didn't have. Even if she got the money from my folks, telegrams aren't cheap. They could never afford to send a lengthy explanation."

Something in his expression caused her to tremble. He was going to postpone the wedding. He was going to leave her and go to his family. She braced herself and waited.

"I . . . I have little choice . . . but to go." The look on his face seemed to plead with her to understand. "I . . . I'm so sorry."

Light-headedness washed over her. She wondered if Christopher would change his mind if she fainted dead away.

The twins began to fuss, and Deborah heard Lizzie suggest that she and Jael take them to the kitchen. Mother and Sissy offered to help, and before she knew it, Deborah was alone in the foyer with Christopher. A part of her wanted to break into tears and cry aloud at the unfairness of it all. Here she was, just days away from her wedding, and the groom was leaving her at the altar. Well, not exactly.

She thought of Stuart Albright and how he would most likely find this news quite satisfying since she'd played such a big role in ruining his wedding. Perhaps it was justice. Perhaps God was getting her attention—reminding her of the pain she'd caused when she encouraged Lizzie to leave Stuart.

That's not how God works, she told herself, trying to gather her wits. *God is just and righteous, and even now, I must see that He is in control of the situation.*

"Deborah?"

She lifted her chin ever so slightly. "When will you leave?"

Christopher reached out and cupped her quivering jaw. "I'm hoping to catch the train tomorrow. If not, I'll take my horse to Lufkin and catch another there."

Deborah nodded. "I understand."

He studied her intently. "Do you?"

She blinked several times, hoping to keep her tears at bay. "Your family relies upon you. What choice is there?"

"You could come with me to town. We could have Brother Shattuck marry us now," he said. "I'm not running out on you. I will return as soon as humanly possible."

His words offered little comfort; dread gripped her like talons. She wanted to believe that everything would be all right, but nothing seemed further from the truth.

She toyed with the idea of a rushed ceremony, then dismissed it. Mother and Sissy had worked so hard on the dress and other preparations. Surely the wedding would only be delayed a short time—a week, maybe two. It would be pure selfishness to demand Christopher marry her in a rush.

"You won't be gone for long," she said, trying to convince herself more than him. "I can wait."

He shook his head. "But you shouldn't have to, Deborah. I feel that I've put my family before you, and that's not at all what I want to convey. If I thought I could easily exchange telegrams with Mrs. Maynard, I would. It's just that I know the financial situation—my mother barely runs the household on what she gets. There's no money for such things."

"I understand."

"And I don't know anyone else who could afford to act as messenger and shoulder the cost until I could reimburse them."

"I understand," she repeated softly.

"I've thought about this all the way out here, and I don't know what else to do but go and see for myself. Perhaps my father has died—or maybe one of the children. If that's the case, then I'll have to help with the funeral expenses, and that will take the money I've put aside for our trip to Galveston."

Deborah lifted her finger to his lips. "Christopher. You must go. It's all right."

He pulled her into his arms. "But I don't want to. I've looked forward to our wedding day, just as you have. I've longed to make you my wife, to share my life with you."

"And you will . . . we will," she murmured. Deborah held

back her tears. She had to show Christopher that she could be the strong woman he needed.

She let him hold her for a few moments, then pulled away. Stepping back, she held up her hands, as if to ward him off. "You'd better go."

Christopher looked at her for a moment. "You look beautiful. I can hardly wait to see you in that gown again."

She smiled, but felt no joy. "That day will come before you know it. Just hurry back to me."

He nodded. "May I kiss you good-bye?"

She winced, but ducked her head quickly so he wouldn't see. "I think it might be better if you just went. I have no desire to ever bid you good-bye."

"Deborah . . ." He let her name fade without saying anything else.

She looked up and could see the battle raging inside him. "I'll tell everyone that you had to go to Kansas City. Please let us know as soon as you can what has happened. And be confident that we will be praying for you and for your family."

"They are soon to be your family, too," he said.

"Yes. In many ways, they already are. I know that if the situation were reversed, you would understand. Family has always been important to us—and always will be. That's one of the things I love about you, Christopher."

He stepped forward and pulled her back into his arms. He gave her a brief but sound kiss. "That wasn't good-bye," he said, turning to go. "That was a promise of my return."

Deborah kept a brave face all through supper and into the night, even while her family plied her with questions she could not answer. Now, however, in the quiet of her room—away from everyone else—fear overcame Deborah in a way that she had not anticipated.

What if the tragedy were such that he couldn't return?

What if it wasn't his father who had died, but rather his mother? After all, the neighbor had sent the telegram. Perhaps she had to do so because Mrs. Kelleher was dead. If that had happened, Christopher would be forced to make some sort of arrangement. After all, his father's injuries from an accident in a rail yard kept him from working and Christopher's younger siblings certainly couldn't fend for themselves.

Deborah rolled restlessly to her side and tucked her knees up to her chest. What if he had to stay there and help his family for an indefinite period of time?

What if he never came back?

Overwhelmed by the weight and fear that had settled squarely on her chest, she muffled her sobs against her pillow and tried to pray. Words failed her, however. And the comfort she often found in talking to God remained elusive.

"Deborah?" her mother's soft voice called out.

She hadn't heard the door to her room open—hadn't seen the glow of her mother's lamp. Mother put the light on the dresser, then sat beside Deborah on the bed.

"I'm so sorry that this has happened, honey. But take courage. Christopher loves you dearly. He will be back—of that I'm certain."

Mother stroked back damp hair from Deborah's face. "I don't know why it had to be like this, but the world is full of heartache and tribulation, just as Jesus said it would be. Yet He reminds us that He has already overcome the world."

Deborah shook her head. "But that's because He's the Lord. What does that mean for us? For me?"

"I believe that because He lives within our hearts—because we belong to Him—we have victory. Satan would steal everything from us. He would take our joy, our hope, our contentment. He desires to destroy us, and what better way than by interfering in our lives and loves?"

"But God has more power than the devil. You've often reminded me of that," Deborah replied. "Why doesn't God keep these bad things from happening to us?"

Mother gave a sad smile. "Oh, how many times I've asked that very thing. Why did God give Satan power in this world? Why does God allow evil to corrupt and destroy the things He's created?"

"And what conclusion did you come to?" Deborah asked, sitting up. "What peace can you offer me now?"

Taking Deborah's hand in her own, Mother sighed. "The same peace that brought me through those long nights after your father's death—the peace that comes in knowing that all of this is temporal. Nothing here will last forever. God gives us earthly life for a brief time, and while it is ours, we should cherish it as a gift. We should live life to His glory and love one another in the richness of the love He holds for us.

"Christopher isn't lost to you—he's merely delayed. His love for you goes on, as does yours for him. This time apart is temporary. Use it for God's glory and not your own sorrow."

Her mother's embrace reminded Deborah of being a young child again—a child that held no responsibility or worry.

O God, she prayed, holding fast to her mother, *would that I could trust you like a little child. Would that I could let go of my worry and fear and trust that you will hold me.*

Chapter 3

April 1887

Christopher glanced at the clock. It was still early, but not unreasonable for a house call. He wanted to let Zed Perkins know what was happening and why he was suddenly leaving again.

He made his way through the quiet streets. Perkinsville was hardly more than a ghost town now. Most of the families had moved on, for there was no sense in waiting around, hoping that the mill would be rebuilt. There were mouths to feed and children to clothe, and those things couldn't be done with hopes.

The unnatural silence only seemed magnified by the clear skies and clean air. When Christopher had first arrived, the mill smoke and dust put so much debris into the air that he was hesitant to even open the windows in his home and clinic. Now that was gone, but at what cost?

He made his way up the walk to Zed's house, stifling a yawn. He'd not slept much at all the night before, fears overwhelming his thoughts. Whatever had happened must be grave, or his mother would surely have sent word herself. Still, uncertainty baffled him and burdened him with a sense of dread. This, coupled with the postponement of his wedding, had left him unable to sleep.

Knocking on the door of Perkinsville's finest two-story house, Christopher was surprised when Zed himself opened the door. Apparently they had let their hired housekeeper go.

"You're just the man I wanted to see," Christopher declared, extending his hand.

Zed waved off the formality. "None of that. Come on in and have some coffee with me. Better yet, have you eaten breakfast yet?"

"No, I didn't want to heat up the stove."

"Then we'll just head back to the kitchen. I was finishing up, but there's plenty left."

They made their way into the tastefully appointed house. Christopher caught the sound of female voices arguing from one of the rooms as they passed. Zed led him to the kitchen and motioned him inside before offering an explanation.

"I'm afraid my daughters have it in their mind that we should move to Houston. They have been pleading their case to Mrs. Perkins."

Christopher could well imagine the spoiled Maybelle and Annabeth nagging their mother. Around town, those two were known to get their own way in most every matter, but perhaps this time would prove the exception.

"What brings you here today?" Zed asked. "Have a seat," he said as he pointed. "I'll grab you a plate and silver." He went quickly to the task and plopped the utensils in front of Christopher. "This is one of Mrs. Perkins's everyday dishes. She'll chide me for not breaking out the good china and serving you in the dining room, but I figure you won't mind." He put the plain white plate in front of the doctor and added, "Now help yourself to the food."

Taking up a platter of bacon, Christopher chose several pieces. Zed left him to fill his plate while he fetched a mug for coffee.

"We've got cream if you need it." Zed put the cup in front of Christopher and waited for him to comment.

"No, black is fine. This is really far more than I expected. I certainly didn't mean to impose."

Zed laughed and took his seat. "No imposition. It's always good to have the company of another rooster—especially when the hens are raising a squawk." He shook his head as one of his daughters protested loudly. "Those girls are spoiled by my own hand, and now I'm paying the price."

Christopher waited until Zed had a long drink of his coffee before replying. "I'm going to get right to it. I've had bad news from my family in Kansas City. I don't know much other than what the telegram told me, and that was only that tragedy had occurred and I was needed." He sipped the strong black brew and let the warmth steady him. "I'm leaving when the train comes through, and I felt you should know."

Zed put his own cup aside. "I'm sorry to hear about your family, Doc. I wish I could offer some sort of assistance. I feel bad that you've gone without wages the last two months."

"It couldn't be helped. You were good to keep me paid long after the mill fire. That and the money I've earned by riding around to the various folks in need of a doctor's skills have kept me well enough." It wasn't exactly the truth, but Christopher didn't want the older man bearing the guilt of what he couldn't help.

Christopher sampled a mouthful of cheese grits and reached for the salt. He seasoned the grits as well as the eggs before continuing. "I don't know when I'll be back."

Zed slathered butter on a piece of corn bread. "You were right to alert me. Knowing Albright, if he sees that you've gone, he'll either take over the clinic or sell off the furnishings."

"Albright had me inventory everything that belonged to the company. I gave him that information the day before yesterday. It came later than he wanted, but I got called out on an emergency before I could finish it." He took a long drink, then gazed into the cup. "I figure it's just a matter of time before Albright demands I vacate the house anyway."

"Not as long as I have any say!" Zed sounded quite angry, but he quickly sobered. "Although, to be honest, I have little leverage anymore. I never figured to find myself in such a predicament. Never thought the day would come when I wouldn't be my own boss."

They ate in silence for a few moments. Christopher felt sorry for the older man. To have a younger man—an Easterner, at that—sweep in and deplete you of your livelihood and all you held dear would be humiliating and heartbreaking. The town of Perkinsville was only a shadow of its former glory. At one point, the town was growing fast enough to rival nearby Lufkin. Funny how things had changed overnight. Life was ever-changing, and property and possessions were easily destroyed. Since the devastating fire, the few who remained were mostly black families that had no choice but to stay and try their best to survive. If you could call it that.

A handful of white families remained, but it seemed they had plans to leave soon enough. The Huebners would go since there was no money to pay a schoolmaster. Mrs. O'Neal had already made known her plans to leave. The Wolcotts, Greeleys, and Shattucks remained in town, along with Mr. Perkins and his family, but most of the other residents had moved on. Mr. Perkins's sons had even relocated to other cities. It was really no wonder his daughters wanted to do likewise.

"Has Albright or Longstreet given any indication as to what they plan to do?" Christopher finally asked, pushing away the empty plate.

Zed shrugged. "They claim they will let me know when they have decided. They aren't even askin' for my opinion. I curse the day I ever took on a partner, much less two. If I hadn't gotten it in my head to expand, I wouldn't be in this position."

"I can't imagine that it's financially advantageous for them to do nothing," Christopher countered. "I suppose Albright could have felt the need to delay due to the bad winter. The plains states were devastated with the snows and cold weather. I read that hundreds of thousands of cattle and other livestock were lost. My guess is that buying extra building supplies isn't a luxury most can afford."

"That was just his excuse," Zed said, scowling. "Most of our buyers were back East." His expression changed almost instantly. "Say, what's this going to do to your wedding plans?"

"We're having to postpone. I spoke briefly to the pastor, and of course went out to see Deborah yesterday. She understands my need to go, although we both wish I could do otherwise. If only I knew the degree of the tragedy and whether or not a day or two would make a difference, I might simply stay until after the ceremony."

Zed nodded thoughtfully and rubbed his chin. "Well, these things have a way of workin' themselves out. I certainly didn't mean to burden you with my own troubles."

"Nonsense. Your troubles affect the entire community." Christopher placed a hand on Zed's shoulder. "I can well understand your concerns. You're a good man, and you care about your neighbors."

"Those folks trusted me for employment, and now that's been taken away. And for what? Albright somehow got the insurance company to agree it was an 'act of God.' The mill supposedly caught fire from a lightning strike, but I know different. That fire started from the inside. Someone set it—of that, I'm certain."

"I suppose without witnesses to say otherwise, money talked for Albright. He could have even offered to cut the investigator in on the deal." Christopher put his cup aside. "Well, I should head back to my place. Jude Greeley arranged for someone to send him a telegram when the train pulls out of Burke so that I can be ready. I told him I'd be at home. Thanks again for breakfast, and I'd appreciate it if you would keep Albright from throwing my things into the street."

"You have my word on it," Zed replied.

The two men got to their feet just as someone went wailing down the hall. Apparently one of the girls was quite distraught. Christopher turned to Zed with a hint of a smile. "If you need to stay at my place, feel free."

The older man laughed and slapped the doctor's back. "I just might take you up on that."

They were nearly to the door when Mrs. Perkins stepped into the hall. "Doctor Clayton—I mean, Kelleher. Goodness, but it will be hard to get used to that. Why you ever thought we would hold being Irish against you is beyond me."

Christopher gave her a slight bow. "I apologize for that, ma'am. It wasn't so much you and the folks of Perkinsville that concerned me. It was my decision long ago when I went east to medical school. However, you feel free to call me whatever you like."

"Oh, pshaw." She glanced back over her shoulder. "I'm the one who must apologize. If I'd known we had a guest, I would have put an end to the girls' fussing much sooner."

"Think nothing of it," Christopher replied. "But as I told your husband, I must be going."

"Oh, surely not. You should stay for breakfast."

"I've already fed him, Mrs. Perkins." Zed put his arm around her waist. "You have no need to fret."

"Indeed he did, and I must say, it was all quite delicious."

She smiled. "Well, you are welcome to stay and visit anyway."

Christopher shook his head and opened the front door. "I'm afraid I can't. Zed can tell you about my situation, but I thank you for the invitation." The last thing he wanted to do was spend additional time trying to explain.

"Do come back soon," Mrs. Perkins declared as she and Zed followed him out onto the porch. "You know you don't have to wait for an invitation."

"Thank you." Christopher made his way from the porch and had just started down the street when he caught sight of Pastor Shattuck.

"Good morning, Christopher. Do you still intend to leave today?"

Christopher nodded. "Just waiting for the train."

"Looks like you'll have a decent day for travel," the older man said as he looked upward. Overhead, the blue skies were void of clouds. "Hopefully the rain will hold off until you make it back."

"I hope so. What with the winter melt, I was told some of the tracks in the north are washed out and won't be repaired for some time to come. Hopefully it won't interfere with the line to Kansas City."

They climbed the steps to his porch and Christopher motioned. "Would you like to sit?"

"I would," Pastor Shattuck said, easing into one of the chairs. "I couldn't help but feel the need to come and just encourage you. I know this has been a difficult choice to make."

Christopher frowned. He never really felt there was a choice in the matter. He supposed there was, however. He could have refused to postpone the wedding in order to head north. Did it make him less worthy of Deborah that he didn't?

"Do you think I'm making a mistake?"

The pastor considered the question for a moment. "It doesn't really matter what I think. How did your bride-to-be take the news?"

Deborah's disappointed expression came to mind. "She understood, but I could tell she wasn't happy. What bride would be? They've all gone to so much work to arrange this wedding."

"And you think that's all she'd be worried about?" He threw Christopher a grin. "If you say yes, then I'm not gonna marry the two of you when you get back."

Christopher shook his head. "Of course that's not the only issue. I know Deborah loves me. I love her, too." He took the chair beside Brother Shattuck. "Did I do the wrong thing?"

"What do you mean?"

"All of my life I've had to be responsible for my loved ones. I was the firstborn and had to grow up quickly. It was impressed upon me that family came first—that my loyalty to them was a mark of my manhood. When I got the telegram, I never considered doing anything but going to them. Now I'm wondering if that was wrong. If I've somehow betrayed my love for Deborah."

"You're a good man, Doc. I can't fault you for caring about your folks. The delay is unfortunate. I suppose you two could have wed and she could have gone with you to help. There are always other alternatives."

"Maybe I'm not the man Deborah needs me to be." The thought troubled Christopher more than he cared to admit. He hadn't given her feelings nearly the consideration that he should have. Being a husband would be quite different than being a single man who watched over his mother's and father's needs.

"Well, the Word does say that you are to cleave unto your wife. Now, I realize you aren't married just yet, but that is something to consider. If you can't separate yourself from your mother and father, you won't be honoring the vows you make before God. Your wife must come first—not your mother and father. That doesn't mean you don't go on honoring them or caring about them."

"And if I can't put her first, then I shouldn't take a wife." Christopher stated matter-of-factly.

Brother Shattuck nodded. "That's about the size of it. Husbands are admonished to love their wives as Christ loved the church. He died for the church—for us. His heart wasn't divided."

Is my heart divided?

Christopher gave a heavy sigh. "I feel like I'm making a mistake, but I don't know what else to do. It's not like I can pick up one of those new telephones and call to see what the problem is."

The pastor smiled. "Those things surely are somethin' else, aren't they? I heard tell there are over a hundred thousand folks with telephones. I suppose someday everyone will have one, though I can't imagine they will ever take the place of speaking face-to-face."

"Neither can I," Christopher agreed. "Still, such a thing would certainly make occasions like this much easier."

"If it's any consolation," the pastor told him, "I've been praying for you through the night. I knew your heart was troubled, but you can trust God to direct your steps."

"I fear what awaits me," Christopher said, turning to the older man. "I feel like a coward."

"A coward wouldn't head into the heat of the battle. It's only natural that the unknown should offer some concerns, but you needn't let that build into fear. The Lord has promised to be with you wherever you go. He won't abandon you to face this on your own. I want you to know that I'll be praying for you while you're gone."

"The Vandermarks said they would do likewise," he admitted. "I can't say that I won't be thoroughly prayed over."

"Doc!" Jude Greeley called as he bounded down the street from the commissary. "Train's just left Rhodes." He stopped and shook his head. "No, I mean Burke. I can't get used to them changing the town's name. I mean, why was that necessary? Oh, and there's a rumor that they're getting a Farmer's Alliance store." He smiled and waved a piece of paper in the air. "But I digress. I got the telegram just now. You'd best get on out to the main track. They'll do little more than slow down for you."

Christopher got to his feet, as did Pastor Shattuck. "Well, I suppose I should make haste. I wouldn't want to make the train wait on my account."

Jude laughed. "Train makes everyone else wait on its account."

He turned and headed back down the dirt street. "Gotta get back. The missus hates it when I leave her in charge."

"I'll take my leave, too," Pastor Shattuck said. His expression softened with compassion. "There's no way of knowing at this point what you'll face in Kansas City, but you need to remember you won't face it alone."

Christopher drew strength from the words and stood a little taller. "I know you're right. I'll remind myself of that at every turn."

But deep within there was a nagging sensation that, in spite of the prayers and the knowledge that God would be at his side, Christopher was about to fall into a dark abyss—an abyss that promised to consume him, body and soul.

Chapter 4

G. W. Vandermark tied his horse to the hitching post outside the house Stuart Albright had taken for himself. The nervous bay sidestepped—almost sending G.W. to the ground—and he winced in pain. His leg injury was good to remind him of how quickly life could change. Who could tell? Maybe there would be another change after his discussion with Albright. The important thing was to keep a tight rein on his temper.

After regaining his footing, he stroked the horse's mane. "Easy, boy. There's no sense in either of us gettin' our head up."

Drawing a deep breath, G.W. gave the horse another couple of pats, then made his way to the door. He knocked and, while he waited, rubbed the tops of his boots on the back of his trouser legs just in case any dirt clung to them. No sense appearing shoddy.

A young Negro woman dressed in a simple black gown and white apron opened the door and smiled. "Mornin', Mr. Vandermark."

"Mornin', Essie. I'm here to see Mr. Albright. Is he in?"

"Yessuh." She stepped back and reached for his hat. "Please step inside and I'll fetch him."

G.W. entered the house, none too surprised at the extravagant decor. Statues and paintings adorned every possible space. While completely out of place in Perkinsville, no doubt Albright felt right at home.

Essie disappeared for several minutes and G.W. continued to study the interior of the entry. A marble-topped receiving table near the center of the room was graced with a stylish silver vase and a huge arrangement of flowers.

"Mr. Albright say you can come to his office," Essie said from the hallway arch.

G.W. squared his shoulders and let the young woman lead him. There would be nothing pleasant about this meeting—of that he was certain.

Lord, he prayed silently, *please go before me. Give me the right words to say.*

As they made their way, G.W. noted that the rest of the house was just as elaborate as the foyer. When Essie ushered him in to Stuart Albright's office, he noted the room boasted pieces of art, including a huge oil of Jael dressed in a daringly low-cut gown. Embarrassed at the risqué piece, G.W. quickly glanced at the book-laden cases that lined one entire wall.

"Do you not care for my painting?" Albright chuckled. "I believe beauty should be appreciated. You can hardly appreciate what you cannot see."

G.W. felt at a loss for words. He shook his head, but still couldn't find his tongue.

Albright was not a patient man. "Why are you here?"

G.W. turned to address the man. Stuart sat behind a massive mahogany desk that very nearly reached from wall to wall. Of course, the room wasn't all that big, but it was made even smaller by the ridiculous furnishings.

"We need to talk," G.W. finally said.

Albright's icy blue eyes seemed to lend a chill to the room. He motioned to the red leather chair. "Sit down, Vandermark, and tell me why you've come to disturb my day."

G.W. tried not to let his temper flare at his host's rudeness. He took his seat and folded his hands. For a moment, he wished he had his hat back so that he could twist the rim, as he often did when feeling edgy. Instead he rubbed his leg.

"I've come on behalf of Vandermark Logging. We want to know what your plans are for the future."

Albright looked at him for a moment, then shrugged. "I'm afraid there is little to tell. We have been trying to decide what is most advantageous to our associates. Obviously much of the work force has already left the area. Getting them back might be difficult. Building another mill here . . . well . . . I haven't yet been convinced that it would be to our advantage."

"Then I'm here to demand you release Vandermark Logging from our contract. If the sawmill isn't operating, we've gotta sell our logs to someone who *is* operating."

The man laughed. "Whatever makes you think I would release you?"

G.W. leaned forward and narrowed his eyes. "You seem to be concerned with what's best for you and yours. I'm thinkin' this would be one of those things."

"Is this your way of threatening me?" Albright fixed him with a hard stare. "Because if you think to intimidate me, you might as well give up. I've crossed better men and won."

G.W. eased back in the chair. "Without a mill up and runnin', neither of us are makin' money."

Stuart laughed. "You may not be making any money, but I'm doing quite well for myself. A wise man diversifies, Mr. Vandermark. It's hardly my fault you've failed to do so. You're the one who agreed to provide your logs exclusively to my sawmill."

It was hard to remain seated, but G.W. managed somehow. "You need to know that we've talked to a lawyer. He tells us we are well within our rights to sue for breach of contract. You've taken longer than needed to make a decision regardin' the mill. A court would most likely release us from the contract and allow us to team up elsewhere. We're willin' to take this as far as we need to if you won't see reason."

"My, my. You certainly get right to the point." Albright leaned back in his chair as if completely unconcerned. "I suppose you think this comes as a surprise to me. That I have failed to plan for this possibility."

"I don't reckon I care one way or the other. If you're surprised, then that's the way it is. We still plan to do what's necessary to take care of our business."

"I see. Well, let me assure you, Mr. Vandermark, I'm not a man to be threatened or forced. When I feel backed into a corner, I simply come out fighting."

G.W. shrugged and rubbed his leg. "That's your right. I've cornered many a wild hog that felt the same way. The results weren't in their favor."

Albright clenched his jaw and narrowed his eyes to mere slits. G.W. knew the man was trying to intimidate him, but the only thing G.W. feared from Albright was the way he was bent on hurting the Vandermarks. And even then, it wasn't so much fear as irritation.

"Mr. Vandermark, do you suppose that a country bumpkin such as yourself could best me at anything?"

G.W. couldn't resist. He grinned smugly. "I got the gal, didn't I?"

Albright's face flushed scarlet, and his eyes seemed to bug out of his head.

With nostrils flaring, Albright got to his feet. "You think you can throw that in my face and win? It only serves to strengthen my resolve to see you destroyed. You have no power to stand against me. I will crush you like so many ants beneath my feet."

G.W. crossed his arms against his chest and hoped he looked as though he hadn't a care in the world. "Seems to me, Albright, that you're the one without a leg to stand on. You're used to bullyin' folks to get what you want—includin' women. Folks out this way don't much appreciate that kind of thing. You might have all the power in the world back East, but here in Texas, things are done different and folks look out for one another. My suggestion is that you get over losin' Lizzie and love the woman you married. You'd think with all that money you're always braggin' about, you could afford to buy her whole dresses."

Albright rounded the desk and stared down at G.W. with intense hatred. "I will see an end to you and your family."

G.W. got to his feet and stood nose to nose with the man. "This is between you and me. It's got nothin' to do with my family, and I'd thank you to leave them out of this."

"Your family took in Elizabeth when she ran away from me. They deserve to pay for their part—especially that sister of yours. If she hadn't interfered, Elizabeth would never have changed her mind. Your sister is as much my enemy as you are."

"I'm warnin' you, Albright. Leave Deborah out of this. You have a problem with me, then deal with me. Otherwise, back off."

Stuart's face seemed to relax and to G.W.'s surprise, he smiled. "You really have no idea what I'm capable of doing. I find it rather amusing."

"I hope you're just as amused when I beat that smirk off your face." G.W. felt a hint of satisfaction as Albright took a step back. "You've threatened my family and imposed your will on the good people of this community, but I'm gonna see that it comes to an end. Hopefully, I can do it with legal means, but if not . . ." He let the words hang in the air before turning for the door.

"Your threats mean nothing! Nothing!" Albright yelled after him. "I have more friends and power than you can even imagine. I'll see you destroyed if you dare try to break this contract."

G.W. paused at the door and shook his head. "Don't seem I have much to lose then, seein's how your actions threaten to destroy us if we sit idle. I'd rather go down with a fight. We've got a saying around here when things seem darkest. 'Remember the Alamo!' "

Stuart took three steps forward. "As I recall, Mr. Vandermark, your precious Texans lost that fight."

With a smile, G.W. nodded. "But I reckon we redeemed ourselves at San Jacinto. You mighta won the first battle, but you only managed to get our dander up to win the war."

༄

"I can't help but feel like all of this is my fault," Lizzie said, tears forming in her eyes.

Deborah embraced her. "Now, we've had this talk before. Stuart Albright is a vindictive man, and he is the only one to blame."

G.W. placed Rutger on the floor and came to stand beside

his wife. Deborah backed away to let her brother take charge. She knew his love for Lizzie ran deep and he would protect her and their family no matter the cost. Would Christopher offer her the same support? He gave it readily enough for his family.

"We're not gonna let him win, Lizzie." G.W. stroked her cheek. "We've got the Lord on our side. His evil ways won't stand against God's truth."

"Oh, G.W., you don't know how Stuart can be. He has all the money he needs to ruin us."

Annie started fussing, as if sensing her mother's fear. Deborah went to the little girl and picked her up. "There, now, you mustn't fret. Your mama and papa are right here." She bounced the child on her hip and looked to Lizzie. "G.W. is right. God is stronger than any Albright. We need to put this to prayer and trust that God will help us. It's not like we're seeking to hurt Stuart; we simply want what's right."

Lizzie took her daughter from Deborah and hugged her close. "I wish that I had your faith, but I don't." With that, she all but ran from the room.

Deborah looked to her brother and sighed. "She has no blame in this, but only time and the Lord will convince her."

Rutger crawled to his father and began to whimper, pulling himself up by G.W.'s pants leg. G.W. lifted the boy and rubbed his head. "I think it's nap time. I'll take him in and help Lizzie get them to sleep."

She smiled. "You're a good father, G.W. I always knew you would be."

He shook his head. "Sometimes I question whether I am or not. It seems Pa would never have allowed Albright to have this kind of control over us. I wish I had his wisdom."

"You can have the wisdom you need, G.W. The first chapter

of James says that if anyone lacks wisdom they have only to ask God and He will give it freely."

G.W. put Rutger to his shoulder. "Maybe I should spend a little bit of time in that book."

Deborah patted his shoulder. "It couldn't hurt."

She waited until he'd left the room to let down her guard. Her shoulders slumped. "I would do well to take my own advice."

Christopher's absence weighed heavy on her mind even though it had only been a few days. She tried not to let her heart lose hope. Surely everything would soon be back to normal.

"You certainly are deep in thought," her mother said from the door.

Lifting her face, Deborah gave a brief nod. "That I am."

"Christopher?"

She crossed her arms against her chest. "I can't help but worry. I try not to, but with something like this . . . well . . ." She shrugged. "I suppose times like these are meant to grow my faith."

Mother crossed to where Deborah stood. She pushed back an errant strand of her daughter's dark hair and smiled. "He's a good man who loves you. He'll be back before you know it."

"It seems like he's been gone months instead of days. I can't help but feel that Christopher's family troubles are going to be more than either of us can deal with."

"Nonsense. There is nothing the two of you can't face with God's help."

Deborah wrapped her arms around her mother's waist. Mother hugged her close. "I just hate not knowing what the future holds in store."

"Oh, my darling girl, it's not necessary for us to know the future. All that matters is that we know the One who holds it. God has already made provision—you'll see."

Chapter 5

Arriving in Kansas City three days later than he'd hoped due to heavy rains that had washed out part of the tracks, Christopher immediately hired a cab to drive him to his parents' home in the poorer section of town. The ramshackle dwellings where the more unfortunate residents lived were poorly constructed—some looking as if a good wind would surely cause their collapse. His overriding impression of his parents' house from his last visit was that it was in need of demolition more than anything. Perhaps if the present complications weren't too grave, he could help his mother spruce up the place a bit.

Christopher winced as the carriage found every rough spot on the road, and he banged from one side to the other. Hopes of comfort abandoned, he instead fought sleep as the driver continued through the city. It had been a long time since he'd been this tired. It was almost as if someone had placed a heavy weight atop him. He told himself it was just the humidity and threat of rain, but he knew different.

He closed his eyes and saw Deborah's dark eyes filled with sorrow. She had tried so hard to be assuring when he'd delivered the news of leaving her. Her willingness to support his decision only served to remind him of how much she loved him.

And I love her. I love her more than I ever thought possible to love another. She is everything to me.

Leaving her that day had been so hard. He pounded his fist against the carriage in a series of frustrated strokes—or at least he thought he had. Startled by the noise, he sat up and opened his eyes. Somehow, he'd dozed off. The carriage had stopped and the cabbie or someone was pounding loudly on the roof. He hadn't thought it possible to sleep, but apparently his body could simply take no more. Opening the carriage door, Christopher felt like his legs were leaden. His body rebelled at the interruption of rest and he hit the ground with a groan.

"Are you sure you want me to leave you here? Looks like rain," the driver told him. Christopher nodded, suppressing a yawn, and took the single suitcase the man handed down.

"I can wait for you, if you like?" the man added.

"That won't be necessary." Christopher settled the price of the ride and waited until the cab pulled off down the street before turning to face his family's home.

But it wasn't there.

He stared in shock at the charred frame. Brick chimneys rose out of the remains like strange sentinels guarding what had been left behind. Christopher dropped the suitcase. A fire had destroyed not only his family's home but the homes on either side. Family tragedy, indeed. This was a complete catastrophe.

He twisted around to see if the Maynard house was still standing. It was. He started for the door, then remembered his case and went back to retrieve it. Christopher couldn't keep his gaze from the blackened debris. How had the fire started? Was anyone hurt? Were they all dead? He felt sickened as the breeze blew the undeniable scent of destruction his way.

"Dr. Kelleher! I thought that was you," Mrs. Maynard called from her now-open front door.

Christopher forced himself to turn and face the thick-waisted woman. "What happened? Where is my family?"

Stuart Albright was sulking. At least that's what Jael called it. He was clearly miffed about something. Probably the fact that G. W. Vandermark didn't roll over and play dead at his threats. She smiled and gave a slight shrug. Her father had tried to warn Stuart. He told him some men would not be motivated by intimidation, and clearly he had met his match.

"Have you decided when we are going back to Houston?" she asked with only a brief glance up from her needlework.

"No."

He didn't offer another word, and Jael allowed the silence to continue for a good ten minutes before pressing another question. "Have you decided to rebuild the mill?"

"No."

She frowned and fixed him with a look. "So you won't rebuild?"

He glowered. "It's none of your concern. Stick to your sewing."

Clearly agitated, he got to his feet and retrieved his newspaper. "I'll be in my office."

Stalking from the room, Stuart left Jael to wonder if this was the way her future would always be. She hadn't married for love, she reminded herself. Love wasn't real—not for her anyway. The man she'd given her heart to so long ago had also given her that realization, just before he deserted her and left her to carry, and later lose, his unborn child. Promises made in the heat of passion were seldom trustworthy, she supposed.

The needle pierced her finger, causing Jael to jump. She hurried to suck the droplet of blood to keep it from staining her work. Putting the hoop and threads aside, Jael got to her feet, still nursing her finger. She walked to the window and pulled back the heavy drapery to stare out into the night.

With so many people having left the town, there were very few lighted houses. She wondered why Stuart had allowed this abandonment of Perkinsville. He would stand to lose a great deal of money, and that was truly the only thing he cared about. This thought gave her resolve to seek him out once again. She wasn't afraid of his pouting and belligerence. In fact, she wasn't afraid of much anymore. Living without love had been her worst fear, and since that had been realized, nothing else seemed all that important.

She entered his office without knocking. Her gaze immediately went to the awful painting he'd demanded she pose for. He'd picked out the most scandalous dress, not caring at all that it made her feel immodest and uncomfortable. The memory only served to bolster her resolve. Jael fixed him with a silent stare.

"What do you want now?"

"I want answers, Stuart. I want to know why you insist on

tormenting the Vandermarks and the people of Perkinsville—at least those few who are still around to be tormented."

"As I've said before, my business is my business. Stay out of it and you'll be much happier."

"I didn't marry you expecting to be happy." The words dripped sarcasm. She crossed the room and put her hands on his highly polished desk. She knew the action would irritate him, but she didn't care.

"If you are so lovesick for Elizabeth Decker Vandermark, why do you even bother to keep up the pretense of devoted husband?"

He smiled. "Because you are so charming, of course."

Jael straightened. "Stuart, we both know what a farce our marriage is. I didn't ask you to pretend to love me or even care for me. It's just as you told me when we agreed to this arrangement—this marriage was for the sake of convenience and nothing more. Oh, I'll admit I fooled myself into believing that love might grow, but now I see it cannot, for the soil is poisoned."

"And what of it? I have not played you false."

She looked at him and shook her head. "I suppose you haven't. You said there would be no love and that is certainly true."

He pounded his fists on the desk. "And why should there be? You came into this marriage carrying another man's brat in your belly. You were just as desperate to save face as I was to reap my inheritance."

Stuart's words had the impact of a slap on the face. Jael steadied herself by taking hold of the back of the chair. "I want a divorce."

"No." He stared at her as if daring her to challenge him.

"I'm sorry, Stuart, but I was a fool to marry you. I should have faced my father's wrath and dealt with the consequences. I could have come to Deborah. I suppose I always knew that. You were simply a convenience."

He jumped to his feet. "As were you. And now you are an inconvenience."

"Then let me go. Give me a divorce."

"I will not, and you will not pursue this subject any further. In fact, should you dare to bring it up to your father or the Vandermarks, I will make you pay."

His words seemed suspended in the silence that followed. For just a brief moment, Jael had hoped he would agree to end their marriage and let her go on her way—perhaps even settle a small amount of money on her. But it was clear he would not.

"Why, Stuart? Why do you insist on remaining in a marriage where there is no love?"

"Marriage was never about love, and those fools who think otherwise are as simpleminded as you." He crossed to where she stood. "Marriage is nothing more than an arrangement to benefit those joined together."

"But I'm not benefiting."

He grabbed her roughly and forced Jael against him. She fought to free herself, but Stuart buried one hand in her hair and wrenched her head back to expose her face. Kissing her hard and without feeling, he pulled her head until Jael thought her neck would snap. Perhaps that was what he had in mind. Perhaps he would kill her and put her out of her misery—tell everyone she had fallen down the stairs. She went still in his arms and waited for the end. When it didn't come, she opened her eyes to find Stuart staring at her with an odd expression such as she'd never seen.

"Well? Why don't you finish it?" she taunted. "Kill me now so I might at least be free of you that way."

He let her go as if she'd suddenly become painful to touch. He staggered back, looking like he'd been gut punched. Jael righted herself. "I will have my divorce, Stuart. You won't stop me."

She turned and walked out the door. Her only thought was to pack her things and go to Deborah. The Vandermarks would take her in. She knew they would.

Jael had made it to the stairs when Stuart caught up with her. "If you dare to try leaving me—divorcing me—your beloved Deborah will pay with her life."

The words froze her in midstep. Could he possibly be serious? Jael turned and faced him. Evident satisfaction played across Stuart's expression.

"I thought that might get your attention."

"You could kill another person?"

Stuart's maniacal laugh left Jael doubting his sanity, but his reply removed all doubt. "It wouldn't be the first time." He narrowed his eyes. "And I seriously doubt it will be the last."

"Sit and rest. You look quite weary," Mrs. Maynard said as she ushered Christopher into her sitting room.

The house was simple but clean. Christopher took a seat where the older woman pointed and waited to hear what was sure to come.

"The fire started in the middle of the night. The weather had been cold and fires were necessary to keep the house even slightly warm," she began. She sat nearby and studied him with a mother's gentle expression. "They believe the chimney flue got too hot and something caught afire."

Between his shock and exhaustion, Christopher could only

nod at the explanation. Thunder rumbled in the distance. The storm had finally arrived.

"Your mother, God rest her soul . . ."

"What?"

"Oh, my dear, I hardly know how to tell you, but they're gone. Your ma and da. They perished in the fire."

This wasn't happening. Christopher felt as if he might be sick. He forced back bile. "And the children?"

"The children? Oh, gracious me, they survived. Your ma saw to that. She got them out first and then went back for your da. Of course, the fire had grown by that time. Your brothers tried to go into the house to bring them both out, but the neighborhood men stopped them. They knew it was too late. The house began collapsing, and even the chief of the fire brigade said that nothing could be done but to try and contain it. As you can see . . . well, it claimed two other houses, but no other lives."

His mother was dead. His father, too. He had never once allowed himself to really consider the possibility. Oh, he had certainly expected his father to pass sooner than later. The man's health had been precarious, and the last time Christopher had seen him, it was clear to him as a physician that time would take its toll and Da's life.

"I wish I could have given you some forewarning," Mrs. Maynard continued. "The telegram took every free cent I had, and I couldn't afford to say anything more." She leaned forward. "As it was, they gave me the word *quick* for free. I told the telegraph operator what had happened, and he felt it imperative to get you here in a hurry."

Christopher could hardly believe what he was hearing. It seemed like a bad dream. Perhaps he had fallen asleep in the carriage and was even now simply caught in a nightmare. He looked up and refocused his eyes. No, this was happening. He was fully awake.

It just didn't make sense. He wanted to know so much more—wanted answers. How could this kind of thing have happened? Instead, he nodded, making a mental note to see that the woman was repaid for contacting him. "Where are . . . where are my brothers and sisters now?"

"They've been staying here with me, but at this moment, they're in school. I told them it was better for them to go than sit around here mopin'. Your ma and da were laid to rest day before yesterday. We considered waiting for you, but I had no way of knowing if you'd even received the telegram."

Burying his face in his hands, Christopher tried hard to think. Exhaustion clouded his thoughts and pain filled his heart.

"Why don't you take a rest? The children won't be home for another three hours. I have a room ready for you at the top of the stairs."

He looked up. "What? A room?"

She nodded and got to her feet. "I figured you'd need a place to stay."

"I can go to the hotel."

"Nonsense. I have the space and you needn't spend your coin that way. There will be plenty of other expenses. The accommodations ain't much, but the bed is comfortable. Now, come along. I'll show you the way."

Christopher looked at her for a moment and then got to his feet. "Are the children . . . were they hurt at all by the fire?"

"Only their hearts," she replied. "The wee ones, especially. They cry in the night, and though she won't say it, Miss Darcy frets about this house catchin' fire, too. I tried to comfort her, but she's a force to be reckoned with, that one."

"And the boys? Jimmy and Tommy?"

She nodded with a knowing look. "They're angry. They couldn't save their ma and da. They're madder than any two young men have a right to be. The days to come won't be easy for any of you."

Christopher was silent, for what could he say? Nothing made sense, no matter how hard he tried to force coherent thought.

"Come along, now. I'll fetch your suitcase later. You have a rest while you can." Her voice was soothing and gentle. "I loved your dear ma. Bertha was my best friend." She wiped at a tear as it trailed down her cheek. "The days are much darker now."

He nodded and followed her up the rickety wooden stairs. The polished finish had long since dimmed with continued wear; a clear path marked an outline on each step. At the top, Mrs. Maynard paused only long enough to regain her breath.

"I'm . . . getting too . . . old." She offered him a smile. "This is your room right here." She managed to cross to the door and open it. "Sleep and when you wake, I'll have something for you to eat."

"Thank you," Christopher said, barely able to form the words. He entered the room and turned in surprise at the sound of the door closing.

He stared at the wall for several moments trying to clear the cloudiness that dimmed his ability to reason. The truth wearied him. Christopher turned to take in the rest of the tiny room. A single bed had been pushed up against one wall. An open window displaced the musty odor of a room long closed and unused with scents of the pending rain. Christopher sat on the edge of the bed, pulled off his coat, and threw it over the footboard. He took off his shoes and eased back onto the bed. Mrs. Maynard had been correct—it was quite comfortable.

Christopher gazed upward at the unmistakable evidence of a leaking roof. The stains made strange patterns—hazy pictures, really. His vision blurred, and he blinked hard. He could make out what looked like a profile of Queen Victoria, and to her right, a rather sorry looking rabbit. But tears soon overwhelmed his eyes.

With a moan, he rolled to his side and drew the pillow to his mouth to muffle his cries. He was a grown man, but at the thought of his mother burning to death, he was once again a young boy. Why couldn't he have saved her?

Chapter 6

Lizzie's father, Brian Decker, sat across the dinner table and marveled at his grandchildren. "They are a perfect delight." He reached over to wipe a bit of applesauce from Rutger's mouth. "I must say, they remind me very much of you when you were small, Lizzie."

"I'm so glad you are here to share in our joy of them," Lizzie answered. "Oh, Father, they have been the biggest blessing amid this adversity."

Mr. Decker had only arrived that afternoon, and Deborah knew her brother and Lizzie were overjoyed and relieved to have him present. G.W. had been soliciting advice from his father-in-law, a lawyer, and now the man had come to share some answers with the family.

Lizzie handed Annie a small piece of buttered corn bread. "We've all been quite beside ourselves."

"I gathered as much from your last letter. It seems that Mr. Albright is refusing to yield any kind of advantage to you."

"I went to talk to him," G.W. interjected. "Just like you suggested in your telegram. He wasn't in any mood to discuss options."

Mr. Decker straightened. "I'm sorry to hear that. Did he say why?"

"No. He only told me that should we dare to sue him for breach of contract, he'd tie us up in court for years to come. Seein's how he's gotten his way in any other legal issues regarding the mill, I'm inclined to think he's got powerful friends and can do just about whatever he likes."

"Well, I reviewed the contract several times, as well as shared it with colleagues to get their professional opinion. The fact of the matter is, Vandermark Logging does have an agreement to sell your lumber exclusively to Zed Perkins's sawmill. Still, while there should have been some noted date on how long they could force you to remain idle due to their 'act of God,' it's water under the bridge. At this point, we need to find a way to make a mutual agreement benefit both sides."

Deborah immediately felt guilty. While the contract had been Zed's requirement, she had been the one to make many of the changes. She'd never thought to add any kind of time frame on such a matter. After all, they were dealing with a man for whom their father held nothing but the highest regard. A handshake had always been good enough in the past, but when Zed needed a signed contract in order to secure his bank loan, Deborah had seen no reason not to comply. Neither could the rest of the family. It wasn't their fault that Zed had found it necessary to take a partner at a later date. And it certainly wasn't their choice to have Stuart Albright involved in any part of the business. Still, guilt gnawed at Deborah's conscience. If she had been more knowledgeable about contracts, perhaps she could have prevented this.

"I don't think you'll ever talk Stuart into doing anything beneficial for us," Lizzie replied. "He hates me, so he hates the Vandermarks. It's just that simple."

"Well, I will speak to him nevertheless," her father said as Rutger reached out to offer his grandfather a handful of mushed corn bread. Mr. Decker laughed and rubbed the boy's head. "No thank you, little one." He glanced to Annie and shook his head. "I can't get over how they look like you, Lizzie."

She smiled and glanced G.W.'s way. "So my husband continues to remind me. I suppose that isn't as surprising, however, as the unexpected arrival of two babies instead of one. This double blessing came as quite the shock."

"Oh, it shouldn't have," her father said. "You were, after all, a twin."

All gazes turned to Mr. Decker, and the room fell completely silent. Even the twins looked at him in noiseless wonder for several heartbeats, and then Annie let out a squeal of delight and Rutger followed.

"What?" Lizzie asked.

Her father blew out a long breath. "I thought your mother had told you."

"Told me what?" Lizzie looked most perplexed.

Lizzie's father put down his fork. "That you were the firstborn of two baby girls. You had a twin sister who died at birth."

"Why did no one tell me before now?" Lizzie asked. "Even when I wrote to Mother about the babies, she never said a word."

"I suppose I should have expected as much," her father answered. "You mother swore everyone to secrecy when the child died. The baby was taken away and buried without fanfare. It was as if there had never been a twin. Your mother refused to speak about her and forbade anyone else to so much as mention the situation of your birth. She wouldn't even let us name the child. The tiny gravestone I purchased simply says *Baby Decker*."

Putting her napkin to the side of her plate, Lizzie got to her feet. "How can this be? How could Mother do this to me? She had only to be honest. I asked her once if she'd ever had other children, and she told me no."

"The death of that baby really upset her, but she would never talk to me about it. I asked the doctor, but he said it was best to let her deal with it as she found fit."

"And what of you, Father?"

He shrugged. "Men are not encouraged to worry overmuch about such things, but it cut me deeply. I have to admit, I was quite upset with your mother's manner of handling the situation. For her sake, however, I said nothing."

"And my poor little sister didn't even have a name," Lizzie said, shaking her head. "Was she so unimportant?"

"Not to me." He glanced away for a moment. "I called her Elsa. I thought it went well with Elizabeth."

"I think I need to be alone for the moment." Lizzie hurried from the room and Mr. Decker gave G.W. a look of alarm.

"I never meant to upset her. I honestly thought her mother would have mentioned it at some time or another."

G.W. shook his head. "There never was any mention of it. Her ma seldom writes—especially now that she's gone to England to help the women with their cause. When she heard about the twins, she sent a short note and two silver rattles. She said nothin' more—certainly nothin' about the past."

"Leave it to Harriet to send something useless and hide the truth," Mr. Decker said.

Deborah could hardly believe the news. It shouldn't have been so startling. Everything she'd read about twins said that being one increased the chances of reproducing them. Even just having twins in the family seemed to strengthen the appearance of other sets. She frowned. There were twins in Christopher's family, too—his sisters Mary and Martha. She knew how busy the twins kept Lizzie. Had it not been for the help of Deborah, her mother, and Sissy, Lizzie would never have been able to manage.

What if I have twins?

The thought of just one baby was startling, but two babies? How would Deborah ever find time to further her medical studies and help her husband?

Deborah forced her mind to focus on the people at the dinner table. It was foolish to let such wild thinking discourage her. She and Christopher hadn't even wed yet.

"If you can talk him into such a thing, then could we act right away?" Arjan was asking.

"I don't know that we should even bother to approach Albright on the matter," Mr. Decker replied. "We can ask his intentions, talk about the possibility of a lawsuit for breach of contract, but as for the other, I don't believe I would even mention it. In fact, you would do well to hide it from him all together."

G.W. frowned. "That won't be easy."

Deborah realized she'd missed most of the conversation. "What are you saying?" she blurted out.

Everyone looked at her rather oddly at her outburst. "He's talking about trading logs for other things," her mother replied.

"You sure we wouldn't be in any kind of legal trouble if we decided to go that route?" Uncle Arjan asked.

Brian Decker leaned back in the chair and smiled. "Mr. Albright seems to be a man who twists the law to suit his needs. I'm not suggesting that we do anything that breaches the agreement. Your contract states that you will sell logs exclusively to the Perkinsville Sawmill. It says nothing about you giving logs to other mill owners. Nor does it prohibit them from gifting you in some manner."

Arjan considered this a moment and nodded. "I suppose you make a good point."

Deborah felt as if her head were in a cloud. "How would this work?"

"As I stated earlier, you could give a shipment of logs to another mill and the owner could in turn give something to you. He could give you goods such as food, material for clothing, lamp oil, equipment; he could even make a payment on your mortgage. No money need ever change hands directly. It wouldn't even be a formal barter. You would simply gift the mill owner. He in turn would give you a gift." Mr. Decker shrugged slightly. "There's nothing in the contract that even hints that gift-giving would be unacceptable."

G.W. exchanged a grin with his father-in-law. "It would be just the kind of thing Albright would do to us if the shoe were on the other foot."

"But that's not the attitude I want us to have in this," his mother chided. "We are Christian folk, and as such, we do not want to lie or cheat."

"I do not recommend either of those options," Mr. Decker agreed. "As I said, the contract has nothing in it to suggest this would be a breach. You agreed to provide Perkins and his mill with logs. There is no mill at this time, and Perkins's associates have not decided whether they will rebuild. To be certain, they have made it clear that they will not pay for log deliveries. Therefore, I see no reason that you cannot do as you like with your own timber. So long as you aren't selling, you should be fine. I've run this by the best legal minds."

"But that was back East," Uncle Arjan countered. "Texas isn't exactly known for doin' things like the rest of the country. I've seen the book of rules get thrown out more'n once."

"And that might very well work to your benefit." Mr. Decker paused and picked up his fork once more. "The most Mr. Albright could do is demand you begin log distribution to him again. That, of course, will mean he'll have to pay for those logs, and you will have the money you need. I do not see a problem with the situation."

"We've got good friends to the north who own mills and would probably agree to the arrangement," Mother said. "They go way back with this family."

"Why don't I go with G.W. and Arjan, and we'll visit these folks," Mr. Decker suggested. "I could assure them of the legalities and put to rest any concerns."

"We can use the excuse of picking up our horses in Lufkin. Jefferson Marshall was expecting us to fetch them most any day now," Arjan said. "And if anyone asks, we won't have to lie about why we're there."

G.W. nodded. "We can also pick up a few supplies."

Deborah could hear a collective sigh of relief from around the table. She certainly hoped this was the answer they were looking for. If not, G.W. had made it clear serious financial problems would soon befall them. She had offered the money she'd set aside, but G.W. refused it. He told her the day might well come when they'd have no other choice, but for now, there were still alternatives. It appeared Mr. Decker had just widened the possibilities considerably. Now, if Christopher would just return or telegraph to let her know what was going on, all would be well.

"We can leave tomorra," G.W. declared. "We'll start up in Lufkin. The logs won't even have to pass through town at all; no one even needs to know what we're doing." He got up from the table and looked to their mother. "Could you watch the babies for a spell? I want to make sure Lizzie is all right."

Mother nodded. "Of course. She needs you."

Deborah watched her brother leave, wishing she could go with him. Lizzie was her dear friend, and she wanted to offer her comfort. But Mother was right. Lizzie needed G.W. more than anyone else.

She let out a heavy sigh and picked at her food. If she didn't hear soon from Christopher, she might well go mad.

After sleeping a little more than two hours, Christopher arose and went quickly to work. He decided it would be best to be gone when the children came home. That way, Mrs. Maynard could let them know he was in town and that he would be back to speak with them. Christopher hoped it would allow them a little time to deal with the surprise of his presence, given that Mrs. Maynard had not mentioned to them that she'd sent a telegram. Not only that, but there was plenty to be accomplished.

First, he needed transportation, and Mrs. Maynard assured him a livery was just a few streets away. As he walked, Christopher made a mental list of what needed to be done. He should telegraph Deborah, then make his way to the funeral home to see what kind of debt was owed. Mrs. Maynard had also informed him that the children had little more than the clothes on their backs. Something would have to be done about that.

The livery was exactly where Mrs. Maynard had directed. A tall beanpole of a man welcomed him.

"Name's Rothberg. Need a saddle ride or a buggy?"

"A horse for now," Christopher replied. "I'm Christopher Clay . . . Kelleher. Mrs. Maynard sent me over."

The man nodded and sobered. "Sure was sorry about your folks." He motioned Christopher into the stable. "I have a gelding over here. One of my best."

"That will be fine." Christopher noted the sturdy-looking chestnut. He was a tall one, just like the man, and looked to have some Arabian blood.

"Your folks was good people." He quickly cinched the saddle. "Your brother Jimmy used to help me out during the summer. 'Course, when school began, he was only able to come for a few hours after classes. A smart one, your brother."

Christopher knew from his mother's letters that Jimmy was quite interested in his education. He hoped to promote that interest and keep his brother motivated to continue his education.

"Yes, sir. Good people. Your ma was one in a million."

"Thank you for saying so," Christopher said, the ache in his heart becoming more pronounced.

"She'd send over a loaf of just-baked bread from time to time. Probably the best I ever ate. And cookies as big as dinner plates." He smiled and shook his head. "Everyone in the neighborhood is going to miss her."

It touched Christopher to hear this tribute to his mother, but he felt as if his own emotions might boil over at any moment.

He paid the man for two days. "I don't know how long I'll need him, but I'll return and pay additional fees should it be longer."

"No problem. You're staying with Mrs. Maynard, and I can always check up on you there." He smiled and handed Christopher the reins. "Colleen owes me a hot meal. I think she's sweet on me anyway."

It was the first time Christopher had felt like smiling in days. He could well imagine the stocky Mrs. Maynard and the tall, skinny Mr. Rothberg. "Could you direct me to the closest telegraph office? I need to send a message to Texas."

Rothberg walked with him and the horse to the front of the stable. "Just turn right at the second street. You'll go down about six blocks and then you'll see a row of businesses. The telegraph office is on the corner."

"Thank you." Christopher stepped into the stirrup and mounted the horse. The gelding was well behaved and stood stock-still. "I'll be in touch."

The horse acted as if they were old friends. He quickly complied with Christopher's directions and seemed completely at ease with the city traffic. The area had changed a great deal since the last time Christopher had been back. Everything looked foreign to him—felt foreign, too. Of course, most of his adult life had been spent elsewhere avoiding his Irish heritage—avoiding the pain of seeing his father helpless.

"Helpless is exactly how I feel," he muttered.

His parents were dead. His mother gone—truly gone. He hadn't even been able to say good-bye. He thought about his last letter home. What had he told his mother? What kind of affection had he offered? His eyes blurred, but he refused to give in to the pain of his loss. He could grieve later. For now, there was work to be done.

He thought again of the children who barely knew him. It wouldn't be easy for them to see him as their authority or rescue.

"Nothing will be easy for them now."

"And this is your youngest brother, Jonah. He just celebrated his seventh birthday two days before the fire," Mrs. Maynard declared. She finished the introductions and took a seat beside the boy.

Christopher let his gaze travel over the ragged quintet. Jimmy and Tommy glared at him with expressions that suggested they wanted nothing he had to offer. They were angry and hurting, and the appearance of a big brother offered no comfort. Darcy, at the age of thirteen, was quite a young woman. She admonished nine-year-old Emma to sit up straight and reached over to straighten her sister's pigtails. The three youngest were quite petite—perhaps even underfed. No doubt they had less to eat than their older brothers. Christopher shook his head, feeling guilty for not having done more.

Jonah continued to watch him with wide eyes and a look that seemed almost fearful. The boy's intensity caused Christopher to rethink how he would approach them. Somehow he had to win their trust—had to help them to see that he was there to help.

"I realize that none of you know me very well, but I can tell you honestly that I grieve our mother's loss as much as you do." He paused and added, "Our father, as well."

"Mrs. Maynard said they went up to heaven," Jonah offered, then buried his face in the stocky woman's waist.

Christopher was rather at a loss as to how to deal with the situation. His discomfort stymied rational thought; he could have more comfortably performed surgery while wearing a blindfold.

Drawing a deep breath, Christopher knew he would have to be strong. Strong and firm. He'd already decided that he would take the children back to Texas with him. There was certainly nothing for him in Kansas City, and while it would be stripping away the last remnants of all that was familiar, a new start would be good for all of them. Of course, Jimmy and Tommy would have plenty to say on the plan.

"I asked Mrs. Maynard to gather you all here," he began, "because I wanted to explain what will take place in the next few days. Since the house has burned down and the landlord had no insurance to rebuild, you have no home here in Kansas City."

"We got a home with Mrs. Maynard," Jimmy said in a terse clipped tone. "I can see to it that we manage. I'm almost seventeen." He was clearly used to being in charge of his siblings.

Christopher met his brother's gaze. "I'm sorry, but I cannot allow that. You see, I know our ma wanted to see you continue your education. She was very proud of you—proud of each one of you. She wrote to me all the time about what you were accomplishing. I know she would want you to be happy, but she'd want you to be safe and cared for above all. Mrs. Maynard cannot continue to care for you—that isn't her job."

Jimmy folded his arms against his chest but said nothing more. Tommy, too, remained silent, while Darcy had little difficulty posing the questions they no doubt all had on their minds.

"So where are you gonna take us?"

He smiled, hoping it would ease their fears. "I'm going to take you back to Texas with me. I'm soon to be married, and I know my wife would love having each of you." At least he hoped she would. He hadn't been able to explain everything in the brief telegram he'd sent her and had already decided he would wait until they returned to let her know the full impact of the fire.

"I ain't gonna go," Tommy declared, getting to his feet. "You can't make me. I'll be fifteen in a couple of months, and that's old enough to take care of myself."

"Me either," Jimmy said, joining his brother. "You can't just come in here and expect us to leave. We've lived here all our lives. We'll go on livin' here."

It was just as Christopher had expected. "I'm sorry, but that won't be possible. You are underage and cannot fend for yourselves. You cannot earn a living to support the little ones, and even if you were allowed to roam off on your own, the county would come in and take the rest of your brothers and sisters."

Jimmy let out a breath that was something between a growl and a sigh before storming off upstairs. Tommy opened his mouth as if to speak but then closed it and stomped off. At this, the two youngest began crying and Mrs. Maynard gathered them in her arms.

"I'll tend them in the other room," she told Christopher.

That just left Darcy. The blue-eyed, redheaded girl looked at him rather matter-of-factly. "Looks like you got a big problem."

Chapter 7

On Saturday, Deborah accompanied her mother to the commissary. The building was poorly stocked and able to satisfy only the most basic of needs. Her mother hoped to purchase at least several spools of thread, and two or three bags of flour, cornmeal, and coffee.

Deborah walked the aisles, looking for anything useful. There had been a time when the place had been brimming with supplies and trinkets. Now it was just the basic needs, and hardly much of those.

She heard footsteps fall behind her and backed up to let the other person pass. To her surprise, Deborah was immediately taken in hand by Jael. Her friend hurried them to the far end of the store, catching her skirt for a moment on a rough spot on the wood floor.

"Oh bother." She tugged the material loose, not at all mindful of its delicacy. She pulled Deborah behind a stack of barrels. "Stuart is livid. He apparently had a falling out with G.W."

"I know about it. G.W. asked Stuart to let Vandermark Logging out of the contract since they aren't moving ahead to rebuild."

"But now Stuart has decided he will rebuild. He figures if he's rebuilding and your family files for breach of contract, he can get a judge to rule in his favor because . . . well, something about there being a tangible effort to rectify the situation." Jael rolled her eyes. "It was all rather muffled as I was eavesdropping on Stuart and my father."

"So he plans to rebuild?" Deborah questioned. "That's wonderful news."

Jael shook her head. "I don't trust Stuart to be doing a good thing in this matter. The man still hates you and your family. He even threatened you."

Deborah looked at Jael and shook her head. "What in the world are you saying?"

"I told Stuart that I wanted a divorce. He refused, of course, though I can't imagine why at this point. He has all that he wants—his inheritance, the ability to hurt Lizzie and your family. He's extremely wealthy. Anyway, when I mentioned that I wanted a divorce, he told me no. Then he added that if I dared to try to leave him or divorce him, he'd make you pay—with your life." Jael reached out and took hold of Deborah's arm. "He means it, too."

"I'm not afraid of Stuart Albright," Deborah replied. How dare he deliver such a threat!

"Perhaps you should be. Stuart made some comment about having killed before. I don't know exactly what it was all about, and he certainly offered no details, but Deborah—I'm scared of what he might do."

Deborah felt her brows knit together. "He boasted of killing?"

Jael nodded and glanced around to be sure no one could overhear. "When I asked him if could really kill another person, he said it wouldn't be the first time or the last. It might well have been nothing but lies—just words spoken in anger to frighten me."

Deborah shivered as if a sudden icy breeze had blown into the store. "What an evil man."

"I fear if I do not stay with him and cooperate fully, he will carry through his plans to harm you. I couldn't bear it if that happened."

"But if you left him, where would you go? Were you planning to leave Perkinsville?"

Jael looked toward the floor, then back to Deborah. "I thought I might stay a while with you."

Deborah could see what her friend had in mind. "Of course you would be welcomed. You needn't stay with him because of his threats. I'll let G.W. and Uncle Arjan know. Christopher, too, when he returns. Perhaps they will speak to the constable."

"Stuart probably has the man paid off. I wouldn't trust anyone but family at this point. Have you heard from Christopher? Do you know when he'll be back?"

"There was a brief telegram. He said he'd arrived safely and that his parents' home had been destroyed by fire, but little else. Certainly nothing about when he planned to return." She shrugged. "I suppose he will have to see them moved to new lodgings before he can leave."

"Stuart talked of us moving back to Houston, at least for the summer. He has no desire to be here, where he believes there is a greater chance of disease breaking out. I'm not sure why he believes this, but I think it would be good to get him away from here and your family. Especially from you. He still blames you for taking Lizzie from him."

At this, Jael's expression changed to one of betrayal and hurt. Deborah wanted to comfort her but didn't know what to say. Jael continued, however, before Deborah could offer so much as a single word.

"I knew he didn't love me when we married. I didn't love him, either, but I thought I might come to. Now I know that won't happen. It grieves me to know that I made such a hasty mistake."

"You did what you felt you had to."

Jael nodded. "And I'm paying the price for it." She squeezed Deborah's hands. "He's forbidden me to see you at all. I don't know what I shall do or if I'll even have a chance to say good-bye."

Deborah thought for a moment. "You can leave messages with Mara Shattuck. If you go to Houston, you can even correspond with me, through her. I'll speak to her today and let her know what's happening."

"I should be able to manage that," Jael agreed. She glanced around once more, fidgeting like a treed coon. "I need to go."

"Please be careful. We know now that Stuart is dangerous. We must be on our guard."

Jael nodded.

"Go out the back way and I'll keep watch."

"That's a good idea," her friend agreed. "Where is the door?"

Taking Jael by the hand, she led her to the storage room, careful that they should not be seen. "The door is there—to the right."

Deborah waited until her friend had fled and then went to find her mother. Whispering, she relayed the information Jael had shared—all but the threat on Deborah's life. She would talk to G.W. first. He wouldn't overreact, but her mother might be inclined to do something out of pure emotion.

"I need to speak with Mara," she told her mother. "Would it be all right if I did it now?"

Mother nodded. "I can visit with Rachel until you're ready to head back. Just come to the Perkinses' house when you're ready."

Deborah nodded and hurried out of the commissary, nearly colliding with the constable. She straightened just in time. "Mr. Nichols, good morning."

"Miss Vandermark," he said, tipping his hat. "It looks to be a mighty fine day."

"It would be finer if you would tell me you'd caught the men who beat up and hanged George and David Jackson. Have you any leads? Has anyone stepped forward, seeking the reward my mother and uncle—I mean stepfather—have offered?"

He frowned and looked quite sorry he'd even addressed her. "Miss Deborah, it's been over a year. Nobody's gonna say nothing about what happened. They're too afraid. The White Hand of God has folks runnin' scared. There were some lynchings up north not but a week back and some twenty folks witnessed the scene, but no one is talking."

"That's ridiculous. How can an entire community allow a mob of masked men to cause such disruption?" She fixed him with a hard stare. "It seems to me you aren't doing your job."

He took umbrage and struck a defensive pose. "Now, see here. I'm doing my best. What with the mill burned out and all, my guess is that anyone who saw what happened or heard tell of it is long gone. We simply gotta accept that this is one of those things that can't be resolved."

Deborah stiffened. "I refuse to accept that nothing can be done about murder."

"She makes a good point, Ralph."

Looking around the constable, Deborah could see Pastor Shattuck sitting at a barrel where an unfinished game of checkers awaited. She smiled sweetly. "Mornin', Pastor. I wonder, is Mara at home?"

"She sure is. I know she'd love to visit with you. Ralph and I are trying to solve the problems of the world over a game of checkers. I'm afraid you caught us right in the middle."

"Pardon me," Deborah said, glancing back at Ralph. "I can see more important things await you."

She hurried down the steps, narrowly missing one of the constable's hound dogs. Anger and irritation followed her all the way to the pastor's house, and while she wanted nothing more than to explode over the matter, Deborah held her tongue.

When Mara opened the door, she offered a smile and a warm greeting. Deborah gave Mara a brief hug. "I wonder if I might speak with you. I have a bit of a problem."

"Did she say when he plans to start rebuilding?" G.W. asked Deborah.

She shook her head. "No. Jael told me before she headed back to her house that she thought he was already arranging supplies and laborers."

"Well, that is good news," Mother said, crossing the room to where Uncle Arjan stood. They had been married less than a year, and their happiness and contentment in each other's company was evident.

"I'm going to go back to work in the kitchen. Give a holler if you need me, but Sissy has lunch nearly ready for us, so don't be long." She gave her husband a quick peck on the cheek and exited the room.

Deborah breathed a sigh of relief. "There's something more. I didn't want to say anything in front of Mother, but I feel I should tell you both."

G.W. frowned and rose from behind the desk. "What now? Albright go and threaten to tear out the train tracks?"

She shook her head. "No. Not that I know of, but Jael asked him for a divorce and he told her no. He was quite angry and added that if she tried to leave him or get a divorce, well . . . he would . . ." She hesitated and looked at her uncle, now stepfather. She had planned all along to let them know of Stuart's threat, but now it didn't seem like such a good idea. What would he say if he knew the truth? Would he and G.W. forbid her to leave the house? Would G.W. go challenge Stuart to a fight? She didn't want to lie, but neither did she want to be the reason that even more harm was done to her family.

"He would what?" her brother prompted.

Deborah didn't know what to say. She wanted someone to know the truth besides Jael, but what good would it do? It was only a threat, and nothing could really be done.

"What was it he said he'd do?" Arjan asked.

Deborah swallowed hard, her decision made. "He said he would make us pay." It wasn't exactly a lie.

G.W. shook his head. "Like he's not already doing that. I tell you, if Jael wants to leave the . . . the . . ." He blew out a heavy breath and held his tongue.

"I think what your brother is trying to say is that Jael would be welcome here if she needed help in getting away from Albright. We aren't afraid of him. What else could he possibly do to cause us harm?"

Deborah nodded and offered them a weak smile. "Indeed. What could he do?"

But Deborah knew Stuart Albright was a powerful man. He could do a great deal to cause them trouble. If he was willing to threaten her life—he would no doubt find it a simple matter to harm the others. And what if he decided to hurt the twins? She could never bear that.

What should I do? If only Christopher were there, she could confide in him. A thought nagged her. Knowledge was power, she'd always been told. Her family deserved to know the dangers that could be possible. They deserved to know the truth. Guilt coursed through her. Guilt for her part in developing the contract and not having the foresight to avoid such issues. Guilt for the harm that might come to her family. Guilt for not telling the truth.

The truth will set you free, a voice seemed to speak in the depths of her heart, but Deborah turned a deaf ear. The truth, in this case, seemed much too dangerous.

Christopher had delayed as long as he could before seeking out Jimmy and Tommy. He figured that waiting until Sunday after church should have given them ample time to consider the situation and let the news of the move sink in.

"We need to talk," he told them as soon as the noon meal was completed.

"I hope you can spare Darcy, Emma, and Jonah," Mrs. Maynard stated. "I need them to help clear the table and wash up the dishes."

She had promised this excuse to allow Christopher to speak with Jimmy and Tommy alone. Christopher nodded and smiled.

"Thank you for a wonderful meal. I'll sit with the boys in the front room."

He motioned them toward the archway that led into the hall. Tommy and Jimmy looked at each other for a moment, then got slowly to their feet. They seemed to realize that the discussion was inevitable.

Christopher waited until they were both seated before continuing. He lowered his voice. "We have to talk about Texas."

"I don't wanna go," Jimmy declared. "I have the highest marks in school and my teacher says I can graduate by next year—maybe sooner."

"And I have a job. I can't leave." Tommy looked at Christopher. "It's important I stay here."

He didn't want to remind them of their age and helplessness and chose another tactic. "What about the little ones? What about Darcy? Have you considered their needs? Would you have me split up the family and take them south while you—the only brothers they truly know—stay here?"

The boys looked at each other, apparently not having considered this possibility. Christopher shook his head. "I know you don't want to leave, but I need your help. I'm willing to make you both a deal."

"What kind of deal?" Jimmy asked.

"I want you to continue your education. I will see to it that you further your studies. I only ask that you give Texas—and me—a chance. Come with me and stay for a year. If you graduate and are ready for college, I will find a way to send you. And Tommy, I'm certain that my fiancée's family could help you find a job—maybe something to do with their logging company."

"Truly?" Tommy asked. "That would be great." He immediately regretted the outburst and gave Jimmy an apologetic look.

"Nothing has to be forever. I'm just asking that you come and help the little ones to adjust. You two can't take care of them. They need far more than you can provide. The girls need a woman's guidance, and Jonah needs mothering, even if you two don't. Please . . . help me out in this." He paused as he searched for what to say next.

"Even though I was gone most of the time you were growing up, you were never far from my thoughts. All of you were with me no matter where I went; I held you in my heart and mind. I prayed for you and did . . . well, whatever else I could." He fell silent, not wanting to boast of how he'd cared for them over the years. "You've always been important to me."

Jimmy looked to the ground as if ashamed. "I know. Mama told me how much you did for us."

"I believe God made us a family in order to help each other in times like this." Christopher placed a hand on each boy's shoulder. "You will grow up soon enough. You'll move off and marry and have your own little ones. But right now you owe it to them, as well as yourself, to take a little time to grow up."

Tommy frowned. "We're not babies."

"I never said you were," Christopher replied. "But I promised our mother that I would always be there for you, should anything ever happen to her. I promised her that you would finish school if I had anything to say about it."

The brothers exchanged a glance and then looked back to Christopher. Jimmy was the one to speak. "And if we don't want to stay after a year, you'll help us get somewhere else?"

Christopher breathed a sigh. "I will. You might even be able to go live with one of our sisters and their families, but I know money has always been difficult for them to come by, as well.

I'm not even all that sure where to find them these days. Perhaps you know?"

"They haven't moved," Jimmy said. He looked to Tommy and gave a brief nod. "But I don't think we'd be any better off with them. I guess we can go with you. If that's the only way."

"For now it is," Christopher said. "That doesn't mean God won't provide another at a different time."

"God?" Jimmy asked and shook his head. "I got no interest in Him. He's obviously not interested in us."

Christopher shook his head. "You know that's not true. God has always been there for this family."

Jimmy got to his feet. "Well, He sure has a funny way of showin' it."

Chapter 8

I can't say I've ever heard of such an arrangement," Bertram Wallace said, "but your family and ours go way back. I'll do whatever I can to help."

Wallace's family had once worked for the Vandermarks before heading out to start their own logging and sawmill company. G.W. knew they had long since cut out their acreage of forest, however, and now only managed the mill.

"We want to keep this fair, but not let anyone else know what's going on," G.W. explained. "Mr. Decker, my father-in-law, assures me that if we give you the logs you need and no money changes hands, we'll be legal."

Decker leaned forward. "It's true. The exchange of gifts should not create a problem of legal means; however, it would be better not to throw it in the face of Stuart Albright and his business associates. Their delay in deciding to rebuild the mill or move elsewhere has caused difficulty, but it is their right."

Wallace nodded. "I don't have a problem with the plan." The older man looked at Arjan. "We had plenty of secrets in the good ol' days, didn't we?" He gave them a broad smile. "Sounds like this Albright fella wants to see you folks on your face in the dirt. I can't abide that."

G.W. had known Mr. Wallace would feel that way. It was the reason he'd put the man at the top of their list to visit. "We thought," G.W. continued, "that we'd talk to Mr. Kealty and maybe Mr. Danview, too."

Wallace considered this for a moment. "There's talk that Kealty is selling, but he might be interested in hearin' what you have to say. He's a good man."

"I'd like to involve as few people as possible," Arjan added. "We just need enough to keep the mortgage paid and food on the table. We can live and have lived frugal. We know what's necessary."

"We all have had a taste of that. Don't want to go back to it, neither," Wallace replied. He held out his hand. "Let's shake on the deal. You write out the information for how you want things done, and I'll figure up what I can do for you from my end."

Later that day, as the trio sat down for dinner in one of Lufkin's nicer cafés, G.W. shook his head and smiled. "I'm thinkin' this is gonna work out all right."

"You've got a fine family reputation and folks seem to share a good history with you," his father-in-law replied. "I like the way people pull together out here."

"You can always join us out here," G.W. said with a grin.

"I know one little gal who would find that prospect awfully rewarding."

Decker laughed. "I'm sure she would. I was a little worried about her after unloading the news of her being a twin, but she seemed to bear it well."

G.W. picked up a spoon, intent on the bowl of chicken and dumplings the waitress had just brought. "We spoke for quite a while, and Lizzie said that learning about her twin explained so much. She always felt that there was something or someone missing in her life. She had thought it was just because of the way her ma treated her, but now Lizzie says she can finally understand why she's always felt that way."

Brian Decker shook his head slowly. "To think that I could have helped her long ago. I honestly figured Harriet would tell her; I mean, there was certainly no reason to keep it from Lizzie. I suppose the pain of remembering what had happened was something Harriet couldn't face."

"Lizzie plans to write to her ma and ask for an explanation. I don't reckon she'll reply if it's too much of a burden to bear," G.W. said and sampled more of his food. "This is mighty good."

Spying a familiar face across the room, G.W. waited until the man was nearly even with their table before addressing him. "Bart Perkins. I heard your father mention you were up this way."

Bart looked at the trio in surprise. "Well, I do say, this is a surprise. What brings you to Lufkin?"

"That sorry excuse for a train we have," G.W. said, laughing. "What about you? Your father said you were gettin' involved in politics, of all things."

Bart hooked his thumbs in his waistcoat pockets and rocked back on his heels. "That I am. I plan to be mayor of this town one day. The times have changed, and with it, we have many problems that need attending."

G.W. glanced around. "Seems like Lufkin is a well-managed town."

Bart leaned forward. "So long as we can keep the Negroes in their place. They are causing us all kinds of grief. I don't know why that pig Lincoln ever figured freeing them was a good thing. They're shiftless and lazy, uneducated and thieves—every last one of them."

G.W. frowned. He wasn't used to hearing friends speak so harshly about the blacks. "I'm sorry to hear you're having problems."

"Oh, there were problems in Perkinsville, too, but Father never wanted to deal with it in an appropriate manner. I reminded him on more than one occasion that he was letting the colored folks get away with too much. They weren't working anywhere near to capacity, but my father never wanted to interfere. That's as much why we're out of business today as anything."

"Well, the fire certainly put an end to production," Arjan said.

"It was set by the blacks."

"Do you have any proof?" G.W. asked.

"Well, I'm sure you know my father is certain the fire was set. No one but the blacks had any reason to set it afire."

G.W. leaned back to fix Bart with a hard look. "How do you figure that? Most of them worked at the mill."

Bart nodded enthusiastically. "Exactly. And everyone knows those people don't want to give an honest day's work."

"That crazy," G.W. said. "We have both blacks and whites working for us. They are all hard workers who give a good effort. George and David Jackson were two of the best workers we'd ever had before the White Hand of God killed them."

Bart shrugged. "They must have done something to offend. That's the trouble with colored folks—they just don't know enough to stay in their place and keep their mouths shut. We see it here, too, and they probably thought that if the mill was out of commission, they could laze about."

G.W. tensed and Arjan put his hand on G.W.'s knee.

Arjan looked to Bart. "We just got our food. Why don't you sit down and eat with us."

Bart shook his head but didn't lose the pose. "I've already eaten; besides, I have a business meeting to attend to. How long will you gentlemen be in town?"

Arjan answered for them. "I don't think it'll be much longer. We got what we came for."

"Which was what?" Bart asked.

G.W. slammed his empty mug down a little harder than he'd intended. "Horses. We came to pick up the team that we lent out last winter."

Arjan smiled and nodded. "Jefferson Marshall used them for freighting. He was waiting on a new team to be delivered from El Paso. Now they've arrived."

"I saw them," Bart said, looking glad to change the subject. "Nice looking pair." He glanced at his pocket watch. "Well, I must be going. Perhaps we'll cross paths again later."

G.W. watched as Perkins hurried from the café. "I wasn't exactly expecting his attitude."

Arjan looked to Brian Decker. "He's the son of Zed Perkins. We should have made introductions. I apologize."

"No need. The man sounds like he's the one who should apologize."

G.W. reconsidered the conversation. "You don't suppose he had anything to do with the lynchings in Perkinsville, do you?"

"I seriously doubt it, Son. Bart has always been good to go off at the mouth, but his follow-through leaves a lot to be desired. My guess is he's repeating somebody else's thoughts."

"Well, whoever they are, they're wrong," G.W. said with a glance at his father-in-law.

ꕥ

Christopher couldn't sleep, despite the bed's comfort. He got up and sat staring into the darkness. Now that he'd convinced Tommy and Jimmy of the need to keep the family together, the time had come to press forward.

He thought of Deborah and wondered what her reaction would be to the arrival of a ready-made family. She would no doubt be shocked—maybe even angry—that he'd not consulted her first. But if there had been any other way, he would have taken it.

"I'm not cut out for this," he whispered. How was he supposed to take over the care of these children?

A sound echoed from somewhere in the house. Crying—of that he was certain. Christopher got to his feet and pulled on his clothes. Without bothering to tuck in the shirt, he made his way to the door and opened it. He listened for a moment. Mrs. Maynard's room was downstairs, so it had to be one of his siblings.

He crept into the hall and the sound grew louder. It was coming from the left of his room, where Emma, Jonah, and Darcy slept. He eased open the door. The sobs were coming from the bed where he'd tucked in the two youngest earlier that evening.

Christopher couldn't see very well, but didn't want to light a lamp. He retraced the position of the room's furnishings in his mind and carefully made his way to the bed.

"Emma and Jonah, are you all right? Are you ill?"

The crying softened. "I'm a-scared," Jonah said, sitting up.

Emma sat up, as well, and fought to speak. "I want . . . want . . . Mama. I miss . . . miss her."

This sent Jonah into a new round of tears. There was nothing to do but offer what comfort he could. Taking the boy in his arms, Christopher sat on the edge of the bed. Emma quickly scooted across and crawled onto his lap beside Jonah.

"I miss her, too," Christopher said as the children calmed in his arms. He sighed and held them close. "I miss her more than I can say."

Emma lifted her head. "Can't she come back?"

If she could, it certainly would simplify things. But instead of voicing his thought, he shook his head. "Mama is in heaven now. Da too." At least he hoped his father had trusted his soul to Jesus. After years of anger and bitterness, it was hard to say if his father had put faith in anything other than the bottle.

Christopher didn't want to dwell on that possibility. "Would you like me to tell you a story?" he asked.

"What kind of story?" Emma asked, sniffing back tears.

"About when I was a little boy."

"You were little?" Jonah asked.

Giving a chuckle, Christopher rubbed the boy's back. "I was indeed. I looked very much like you."

"Tell us a story about Mama," Emma said.

"Well, you and Jonah get back under the covers, and I will do just that."

They seemed reluctant to leave his lap. "Will you stay here?" Jonah asked.

"Just until you fall asleep." Christopher glanced to where Darcy slept soundly on a narrow cot across the room. He couldn't really see the child, but he heard her deep breathing. "Now, we must be very quiet so we don't wake up your sister."

"She won't wake up," Emma said. "Mama always said Darcy could sleep even with a freight train coming through the middle of her room."

Christopher smiled. He could imagine their mother saying such a thing.

He helped the children snuggle back under the blankets and then surprised them, as well as himself, by reclining on the bed beside them. It was a good thing the narrow frame was up against the wall. Otherwise they might have all tumbled off the opposite side.

Emma and Jonah snuggled up close to Christopher. Up until this moment, they had kept him at a distance, preferring Mrs. Maynard. It touched him that they felt safe enough to rest in his arms.

"When I was Jonah's age," he began, "Mama would tell me stories at bedtime."

"She told us stories, too," Emma interjected.

"Did she tell you about the time when she rode a train for the very first time?"

Emma shook her head against his arm. "Never."

"I ain't never rode a train," Jonah said.

Christopher smiled to himself. "Well, in a couple of days, we're all going to ride a train, so I think it would be good to tell you about Ma's first train trip. You see, she was almost a grown-up lady before she got to ride the train. She thought they were smelly and noisy and they frightened her."

"Da used to work on the trains," Jonah offered.

"That's right, and that's where Ma met him. Da was working to build a railroad track out of Chicago—that's a big city up north where Ma and Da used to live." Christopher smiled to himself as he remembered the way his mother's face would light up when she told the story.

"Our mama used to help wash clothes for the railroad men. Da used to tease Ma for being afraid of the trains. He told her they were just like big carriages with iron horses instead of real ones. He told Ma if she ever rode on the train, she'd never want to ride in a wagon again."

"And did Da take her for a ride?" Emma asked with a yawn.

"He did, indeed. He told her if she would come and ride the train with him, he'd give her something special—a big surprise."

"A surprise? What was it?" Jonah murmured. He sounded even closer to sleep than his sister.

"He wouldn't say what the surprise was, but he told Ma she'd be sure to like it. So Ma finally agreed to ride on the train. At first she was afraid, but Da helped her by holding her hand and telling her all about how he'd helped to build the track that they were riding on. Before she knew it, the short ride was over and she liked the train."

Emma yawned and snuggled deeper in the covers. "But what was Da's surprise?"

"Da gave her a big kiss—her first kiss, and our mama said she lost her heart to him." Christopher felt tears come to his eyes. For so long now, he'd only thought of his father as callous and sour. The accident had made him that way—the prejudices of people toward his ancestry had taken their toll, as well. He'd almost let himself forget the good man their da had been—the deep love he'd shared with their mother, the love she'd held for him. Had Ma forgotten, too? Is that why she'd never told the little ones how she fell in love?

Neither child said a word. Christopher listened to their steady breathing. One more sorrow had been laid to rest, at least for the moment. Would that peace of heart and mind could be his as easily.

And Deborah. How could he bring this responsibility to her? She planned to be his bride, to share his life as a physician and helpmate. It wasn't fair to saddle her with five grieving children. Of course, Tommy and Jimmy were hardly little ones anymore, and Darcy was quite the independent thinker. She even reminded him of Deborah. Even so, they were all still in need of guidance and direction. They weren't old enough, any of them, to be left to their own affairs. At least as far as Christopher was concerned.

Oh, God, what am I to do? I won't let them be sent to an orphanage. I won't abandon my own flesh and blood. But what if Deborah wants no part of them? What if she tells me it's her or them?

As soon as the whispered words were out of his mouth, Christopher shook his head. Deborah wasn't like that. She would never want him to leave the children to strangers or to seek their own way. She was a compassionate and giving woman—that was one of the reasons he loved her so much.

He let go a heavy sigh and eased from the bed. He wouldn't solve anything here tonight. Soon enough, he'd come face-to-face with Deborah and explain the situation for what it was. He was now responsible for five children, and if that was too much for her to bear with him, then he would have to let her go.

The very idea left him feeling empty inside. Perhaps even more empty and alone than he'd felt upon the news of his parents' deaths. To lose Deborah was unthinkable. He pushed the thought aside. He would not lose her. He was determined. There would be a way to make all of this work. Of that, he was confident. God would surely show him the answer.

Chapter 9

Easter weekend had been a stormy one, but the Vandermarks didn't let that stop their celebration of the resurrection. As they gathered for dinner after Sunday services, Deborah could only smile at the animated conversations around the table. Mother had invited Mr. and Mrs. Perkins, along with daughters Annabeth and Maybelle, as well as Pastor Shattuck and Mara to join them. The house was overflowing with glad hearts and good will.

Deborah found the atmosphere helpful for letting go of her worry about Christopher. She'd heard nothing from him since that first telegram. She would just have to be patient. As her mother always said, "God will show you the answer in His good time."

"This is a feast fit for a king," Arjan told Deborah's mother and kissed her check.

Deborah could see the joy her mother took in his praise. She was so glad that her mother had married again. Their marriage had made the family whole again, and Deborah knew that her father smiled down approval from heaven.

"These are the best creamed peas and potatoes I've ever had," Zed announced.

Mrs. Perkins smiled at Deborah's mother. "I never had much luck with them. I always manage to get the sauce too thick or too thin."

"Sissy made these. She can show you her tricks," Mother offered, nodding toward the woman who sat beside Deborah.

"I shore can, Miz Perkins. Ain't no problem. No problem at all."

Rachel Perkins nodded. "And you can also teach me how you made those wonderful hot cross buns. I've never had anything that tasted so good—especially slathered in butter. I haven't had decent butter or yeast bread in weeks."

"Well, Lizzie churned quite a bit of butter last week," Mother said. "I'll send some home with you when you go."

"That would be wonderful." Mrs. Perkins cast a glance at her two daughters. "Perhaps Lizzie can share her secrets with you."

Annabeth frowned. "I hate churning. I'd rather buy butter ready-made."

Maybelle nodded. "In Houston, they have stores that carry all sorts of foods, ready for the eating."

"Seems a waste of money to me," their father said. "If a person can make their own, why pay someone else to do it for them?"

"Because sometimes the product is much better than anything you can make yourself," Maybelle declared.

"That has not been my experience," Pastor Shattuck threw in. "I cannot tell you how much more I appreciate a homemade meal, prepared by loving hands—just like this. Why, I've never had food this good from any restaurant or packaged item."

Maybelle sulked but said nothing. Deborah felt sorry for her. No doubt the sisters were still encouraging their parents to move. Mother said that Mrs. Perkins was beside herself from their nagging.

Annie let out a howl of protest as Rutger reached over to take a portion of her bread. She slapped at him, but her brother was too quick. He snagged the food and yanked his arm back just before her hand slapped the table. This caused her to cry all the louder.

Lizzie took the bread from Rutger and handed it back to Annie. "Now, Son, you need to learn to leave other people's food alone." The boy looked up at her with a pout. Lizzie ignored it and buttered another piece of bread for him. She handed it to Rutger and gave him a pat on the head. "Now you have your own."

Mara laughed. "I used to fight with my brother for food. He was older and ate everything that wasn't nailed down. Aaron considered my plate free range."

Pastor Shattuck smiled. "I remember your grandmother writing to tell me of his voracious appetite."

The conversation moved to comments and stories of other childhood pranks and games. Deborah was glad no one seemed to notice how quiet she was. She truly was doing her best to just enjoy the day and the company of good friends. She didn't want to be sad or troubled, for Easter was a time of renewal and hope. Pastor Shattuck had spoken to them about the Lord's resurrection in terms of a new birth. Coming from the tomb was much like a babe being born, he had said. Jesus overcame death to be reborn into glory. She liked that thought—liked, too, that Pastor Shattuck said each of them were also reborn into eternal life when they accepted Jesus as their Savior.

"Eternity starts when you ask Jesus to forgive your sins and come into your heart. What a lovely thought." She hadn't meant to speak aloud and looked up, rather startled. "Sorry, I was just thinking back on the sermon."

Pastor Shattuck smiled. "So many folks think that eternity is something they are waiting for, and while heaven is yet to come, eternal life is found in Jesus and our accepting of Him."

"I agree," Arjan declared. "I look forward to heaven one day, but until that time I need to remember that God has given me a life right here—that I need to live it for Him."

"Exactly," Deborah agreed. "Live for and with Him eternally. It's a very pleasant thought."

"It helps us not to miss out on the blessings He has for us," the pastor added.

Deborah smiled and nodded. "Yes. I very much appreciated your pointing that out. It made me more mindful of not only my behavior, but of the very gift God has given in salvation."

"Makes me feel so safe," Mother said. "So cared for."

"Amen," Sissy said. "I's also so grateful you allowed us black folk to come and share Easter service."

"Miz Jackson, there is coming a day when folks of all colors will sit side by side in church and elsewhere," Pastor Shattuck replied. "I very much look forward to that day."

"So, Mr. Perkins, tell us about the new mill," G.W. interjected.

Zed leaned back in the chair. "I don't know all that much myself. My partners don't seem to think it necessary to keep me apprised. I don't know if they plan to rebuild on the old site or somewhere new."

"How soon do you think you'll need logs brought in?" Arjan asked.

"I can't rightly say. I was surprised to hear that Mr. Albright and Mr. Longstreet plan to bring in finished lumber from other towns. I kind of figured we'd set up an outside mill like the old days and process enough of our own lumber to build, but they wanted no part of that. I'm not exactly sure when they'll expect a delivery of logs."

Arjan seemed perplexed. "But it would be less expense to process your own logs."

G.W. frowned. "Sounds like more of Albright's games."

"That it does," Mr. Perkins replied. "I figure it's his way of holdin' all the cards."

"If they just get the mill up and running again," Mother said, "it will be such a benefit to everyone. I cannot imagine Mr. Albright can go on losing money like he has and not suffer."

"Stuart has more than enough money. His desire to have his revenge is worth whatever price he has to pay," Lizzie stated.

"Hopefully the man will tire of his games," Pastor Shattuck said. "We will pray it is so and that our little community can be restored."

"Have you heard lately from Dr. Kelleher?" Mara asked Deborah.

"No, I'm afraid I only had the one telegram that let me know he'd arrived safely."

"Oh, I feel like ten kinds of fool," Zed said, pulling a piece of paper from his pocket. "This came for you late on Good Friday. I was rather surprised to see it. Just so happened I was dealin' with some old railroad papers and happened to be in the office."

He handed the telegram to Deborah and smiled. "It's from the doc."

She glanced at the brief note. "He's headed back." Her smile broadened. "He sent this just as he was leaving Kansas City."

"What does it say?" her mother asked.

"Hardly more than what I said." Deborah passed the telegram to Sissy, who handed it to Euphanel.

"He left Friday and hopes to be back sometime this week," Mother announced. "That is good news."

"We've been blessed that there haven't been any accidents or problems in his absence," Annabeth declared. Maybelle nodded and both girls fixed Deborah with a rather smug expression.

"If there had been," their father countered, "I'm guessin' Miss Deborah woulda handled things just fine."

"She's a woman, Pa. It's vulgar for her to do such things," Maybelle said.

"Vulgar to heal a person? Vulgar to keep someone from dyin'?" G.W. asked. "Like she did for me? I can't see it as such."

Deborah was grateful for her brother's support. She gave him an appreciative glance and turned her attention back to the food on her plate.

"I think we're doing more talking than eating," Mother said, getting to her feet. "Perhaps if I bring in dessert, you'll feel more motivated. I have some mouth-watering strawberry shortcake, just waiting for our attention."

"Is that with that buttery pound cake you make, Miz Vandermark?" the pastor asked.

"It is indeed. Would you care to indulge?"

He laughed. "I'll be happy to have my portion and anyone else's."

Laughter filled the room. G.W. shook his head. "Nobody's gettin' my share. Ma makes the best pound cake I've ever tasted."

"I agree," Arjan declared.

"Then I'll be right back, and we can all indulge together."

G.W. pushed back from the table some time later and patted his full stomach. "I could celebrate the Lord like that every day."

"Perhaps we should," Lizzie said with a grin.

"And we'd all weigh as much as Miz Foster's prized hog," Mother replied. "Now if you'll excuse me, I'm going to gather some of these dishes."

"No, Mother, I'll take care of them," Deborah said, getting to her feet.

Mara began gathering plates. "I'll help you."

"Well, Sissy, it looks like we get to retire with the others to the front room."

"Iffen you don' mind, I's gonna take me a Easter nap." Sissy got up from the table, a hand upon her back. "The weather's got my rheumatism actin' up sumpt'n fierce."

"By all means, go and rest. You've earned it." Mother motioned to the hall. "Why don't we retire to the living room, and I'll bring coffee."

"It's gettin' kind of late and the stormy weather has kept the skies overcast," Pastor Shattuck stated. "I believe once Mara is finished helpin' out, she and I will make our way back to town. I ought to go ready the buggy."

"We really should be going, as well," Mrs. Perkins said with a quick glance at her husband.

He nodded and stood. "Pastor makes a good point. Might even get back before the next storm moves in."

They heard the rumblings of thunder in the distance, and Mother moved to the end of the table. "I will miss your company, of course, but I completely understand."

Deborah looked to Mara. "I can handle this by myself."

The young woman inclined her head to the kitchen. "I'll . . . ah . . . bring these in and then go."

Something in her expression made Deborah realize she had something she needed to say. Deborah nodded and led the way with a stack of plates. She quickly discarded the dishes on the counter and turned to Mara.

"Has Jael sent word?"

"Yes. She sent this letter." Mara put the tableware down and reached inside her blouse. "I hid it so I could give it to you when we were alone."

"Probably a good idea. Maybelle and Annabeth have a tendency to run their mouths at the most inopportune times." Deborah took the letter. "Thank you for doing this. I know it's probably not the most comfortable thing. I certainly didn't want to put you in a compromising position."

"I don't feel that it's a problem." Mara smiled. "I also heard from your brother Rob. He hopes to come home for a visit this summer. Probably toward the end of next month. Won't that be wonderful?"

"Has he hinted about the two of you setting a wedding date?"

Mara blushed. "Not exactly. We both know that when the time is right, we'll wed. We're trusting God will show us when."

"I wish He'd show me when, as well," Deborah said with a sigh. "I don't understand this waiting, but I suppose in time God will reveal everything I need to know."

Mara leaned forward and kissed Deborah's cheek. "He will."

Long after everyone had gone, G.W. checked in on the sleeping twins, then headed back into the room he shared with Lizzie. She was already in bed, and he had to admit, she made a most fetching picture with her long blond hair brushed out around her shoulders.

"You're the prettiest gal around. You never fail to make my heart skip a beat." He grinned and sat to take off his boots.

Just then, he heard the mules fussing, which wasn't like them. Getting to his feet, he reached for his rifle. "Sounds like we've got a varmint causin' problems."

"Do be careful," Lizzie said, sitting up. "It could be one of those wild hogs."

He nodded and headed out. Reaching the back door, G.W. wasn't surprised to find Arjan on his heels.

"What's goin' on out there?" his stepfather asked, holding up a lighted lantern.

"I don't know, but the girls sound mighty upset." G.W. opened the back door to agitated braying. He could see movement in the distance. "They're out of the pen. Somehow they got the gate open." The two men moved out to round up the animals. It was strange, G.W. thought, that they should be having this kind of problem. The mules had been confined since Friday and there hadn't been any trouble with them.

Arjan picked up a bucket and tapped the lantern base against it. "Come on, you old coots, I'll give you some grain." Several of the nearest mules began to wander toward them.

Without warning, G.W. heard a man call out, "Just wanted to get your attention!"

Arjan stopped. "Who's there?"

Several mounted riders approached. There were five in total, and each wore some kind of sack over their heads. Holes had been cut out to let them see, but otherwise their faces were hidden. "We're part of the White Hand of God," the leader announced.

"This here is what we call a friendly warnin'. Mind your own business or there'll be trouble."

G.W. felt the reassurance of the rifle at his side. He didn't move to expose the weapon, but stood stock-still. "Who are you to threaten us?"

"You Vandermarks have been nothin' but trouble. You need to remember your own kind and leave the darkies to themselves. I'm here to issue a warnin'. Stop offerin' that reward your family posted and keep that nosy sister of yours from pesterin' folks for answers. Otherwise, you'll be forcin' our hand."

"Kinda like you're forcin' mine," G.W. said, raising the rifle to his shoulder.

The leader pulled back on the horse's reins and the beast took several steps back. "Friend, you don't want to be doin' this. You don't know me, but I know you. I know where you live, and I know your family."

"Don't you dare threaten my family," G.W. said, moving a step forward.

"Bad things are gonna happen," the man said, turning his horse. "If you don't do what we've asked, the blood will be on your hands."

He kicked his horse and gave a blood-curdling yell, echoed by the other men as they moved back to the road. G.W. started to follow, but Arjan took hold of his arm.

"Let 'em go. There's no sense in goin' after them. We need to get the mules back in the pen."

"They threatened our family. It ain't right to just let 'em go."

"Maybe not, but if you go after them, they'll hurt you or kill you. They have the lead, and setting up an ambush sounds like just the kind of thing those cowards would do. Stay here, G.W. There'll always be another day to fight."

G.W. looked at his uncle for a moment, then lowered the rifle. "I suppose you're right." But the idea of letting such men roam at will didn't set well. "This leaves a bad taste in my mouth," he told his uncle.

"It does in mine, too, but it can't be helped just yet. Not without risking too much . . . not without endangering those we love."

Chapter 10

Christopher had been completely exhausted by the time they reached Lufkin. Rather than wait for a train to take them south, Christopher arranged to rent a wagon and an ancient pair of horses to pull it. Even though it was late in the day, he felt it was important to get the family home. The weather was clear, the roads dry, and he longed for his own bed.

It was the middle of the night, however, before he was finally able to make his way to that bed. Even then, despite the ache in his back and weariness in his bones, Christopher found sleep hard to come by.

Because the hospital was the only place with enough beds, Christopher had settled them there for the night, but Jonah was afraid of the small infirmary, and only an hour after Christopher urged the boy to give it a chance, Jonah found his way into Christopher's room. Emma soon followed, declaring that there were scary noises coming from outside. She was certain that bad fairies were coming to hurt them. The comment had made Christopher smile. Despite their Christian upbringing, Ma had no doubt shared the mythical stories she'd known as a child. She had wanted to hide their Irish beginnings, but Christopher knew his ma had been steeped in such superstitious tales. It would have been hard to bury them away.

The children crawled into bed with Christopher and quickly fell asleep. Throughout the remaining hours of the night, Christopher tried his best to doze, but it was useless. Each time he started to nod off, he worried about crushing Emma or Jonah. Finally, he gave up altogether and got dressed. A quick glance at the clock showed that it was nearly five.

With a sigh, Christopher went to the stove and got a fire started. The idea of strong coffee gave him hope that he could make it through the day. He put the pot on the burner and went to check on what food he had in the house.

There wasn't much of anything he could feed himself, much less five growing bodies. The only solution that came to mind was to take them to the Vandermarks. Euphanel would be more than capable of helping him figure out a solution, and he was anxious to see Deborah. Maybe breaking the news to her with the support of her family would make the situation easier. Maybe.

Christopher knew the Vandermarks would be up with the sun, but he didn't want to wake his siblings. They might as well get some rest, even if he couldn't. To busy himself while the coffee brewed, Christopher went to his office and pulled out a ledger. He didn't have a lot of money left, and that was the most worrisome challenge of all. How was he supposed to support a family? He had nothing of value to sell. He needed his gelding to get around the area to see his patients, and the crude wagon and horses he'd rented in Lufkin would have to be returned within the week.

He buried his face in his hands. *God, I just don't know what to do. I didn't think this through, and I didn't make provisions. All I could think about was getting back here.*

Guilt washed over him in waves. He'd put his own desires first. The children would suffer because of his need to return to Deborah. But it wasn't just Deborah. Christopher couldn't stomach remaining at Mrs. Maynard's much longer. Every time he caught sight of the charred remains of the family home, he was tormented by images of his parents burning to death. He couldn't get out of there fast enough.

Besides, there is nothing for us in Kansas City, he thought.

Christopher got to his feet. He needed the counsel of someone wiser, and Euphanel and Arjan Vandermark would offer reasonable solutions and godly guidance. They could help him figure out what to do. Heading into the infirmary, Christopher found Jimmy was already awake.

"I figured you'd still be sleeping."

Jimmy shook his head. "I kept thinking about everything. I can't seem to make my mind relax."

Christopher nodded. "I've got the same problem. Let's get the others up. I want to take you all out to meet some friends of mine. They'll be able to give us breakfast, and maybe some advice as to what we need to do next."

"Who are these folks?"

"My fiancée's family. The Vandermarks own a big logging

company and live north of here. We passed their place on the way down."

Jimmy nodded. "Okay. I'll get 'em ready."

"Good. I'll go hitch the wagon. Emma and Jonah are sleeping in my room, just off the kitchen. Have everybody out front as soon as you can."

Christopher made his way back into the kitchen and moved the coffeepot from the stove. Next he went to the examination room and took up his medical bag, just in case anyone needed his skills along the way.

He slipped out the back door and headed to the livery, where he found Peter Garby singing and shoveling hay. The old black man straightened and smiled at the sight of Christopher.

"Doc, I figured it was you what left me this new business. Where'd you get these sorry old nags?"

Christopher smiled. "Now, Peter, those nags brought me and my family all the way from Lufkin."

"Well, that 'splains it, then. They was probably in their prime when they started the trip. That old cow path you traveled ain't fit to be called a road." Peter laughed at his own joke and pointed at the wagon. "Ain't never seen kindlin' fixed up like that."

Laughing, Christopher nodded. "I feared it might well fall apart beneath us, but it was all I could afford to rent out."

Peter nodded and put his hayfork aside. "You headin' off, Doc?"

"Yes. I need to hitch up the wagon. I want to take my family out to the Vandermarks."

"That's the second time you mentioned family. What you jawin' on about?"

"It's a long story. I'm afraid my parents were killed in a house fire."

The older man took the hat from his head and placed it over his heart. "God bless 'em. I'm sure sorry, Doc."

"I have three brothers and two sisters who were still living at home. I brought them back to Texas with me."

Peter put the hat back on his head and went to the stall Christopher had used the night before. "You's a mighty good man, Doc. I'll get your wagon ready."

"I'm going to have to get some work quickly in order to pay you, Peter." Christopher hadn't thought even as far as to how he'd manage to care for the team of horses before taking them back to Lufkin.

"Don't you fret none, Doc. I know you's good for it." Peter worked quickly to harness the team and get them secured to the wagon. He managed it in half the time it would have taken Christopher. "They's ready for you."

"Thanks, Peter. I appreciate your help."

The old man grinned, revealing several black holes where teeth were missing. "My pleasure."

Christopher led the team from the livery and across the street. He stopped in front of his porch and found his siblings waiting impatiently. Jonah jumped down rather than taking the stairs. He hurried to Christopher.

"Where are we goin'?"

"To see some friends of mine." Christopher helped him into the wagon and motioned for the others to come.

"I'm hungry," Jonah declared, leaning down over Christopher's shoulder.

"I am, too," Christopher replied. "My friends will have food for us."

At least he was pretty sure they would. Times were hard for everyone, and maybe this wasn't his best idea. Still, he knew the Vandermarks—especially Euphanel. She would be madder than a nest of wet hornets if he let his family go hungry.

Jimmy helped load the girls into the wagon before he climbed aboard himself. Tommy followed suit, yawning all the way.

"Don't know why you had to wake us up so early," Tommy complained. He plopped down in the bed of the wagon. "Sure ain't as comfortable as a bed."

Christopher decided to remain silent. Getting them on the road would be a smarter solution than spending time trying to convince them of the benefit. He climbed up and took a seat. To his surprise, Darcy climbed over the bench and eased down beside him. She looked up at him with a smile.

"Can I help?" she asked.

Releasing the brake, Christopher maneuvered the reins between them. "Sure. I'll show you how it's done."

"I never drove a wagon before," she said, awed by the leather straps he'd handed her. Christopher showed her how to raise the reins to lightly slap them against the rumps of the horses.

"Now tell them to 'get along.' "

Darcy did so and began to giggle as the horses pulled in unison against their load. "Look at 'em go!"

Christopher chuckled. The old mares were barely moving. He showed his sister how to turn the team when they came to the main road, and soon they were headed north out of town.

"That's not so hard," Darcy said, tiring of the game. She handed the straps to Christopher. "Can I learn how to ride a horse?"

"I would think so," Christopher told her. He glanced over his shoulder to see that Tommy and Emma had fallen back asleep despite the bumpy road. Jimmy had become a pillow for both of them with Emma sprawled across his lap. Tommy leaned at an awkward angle to rest his head on Jimmy's shoulder.

The trip to the Vandermarks passed without trouble, and Christopher was more than a little relieved to see Euphanel coming from the barn with a basket over one arm. He gave her a wave and pulled the wagon to a stop near the front porch.

She looked at him for a moment, and Christopher could see the confusion on her face. Walking toward them, Euphanel shifted the basket.

"Christopher, you're back."

"I just got back last night."

Darcy stood and eyed the woman. "Are you gonna marry my brother?"

Euphanel laughed. "No, darling. I'm already married." She looked back to Christopher. "This is your sister?"

"One of them." He pointed to the others. "Emma is back there with three of my brothers."

"I'm Jonah," the little boy announced. "I'm seven and I'm hungry."

She smiled. "Well, I believe we should feed you. Do you like ham and eggs?"

The little boy's eyes widened. "I ain't never had an egg."

Euphanel smiled and looked to Christopher. "Shame on you for not teaching this boy a love of eggs."

"Gotta have them to love them," Christopher replied.

Her smile faded. "That's true enough. Well, bring them all in. You know your way to the dining room."

Christopher stepped down from the wagon. "Mrs. Vandermark—"

"Now, I thought you were going to call me Euphanel." She raised a brow.

"Euphanel. I want to apologize. I had nothing in the house to feed them. Fact is, I don't know quite what to do—"

She held up a hand to silence him. "After we get everyone fed," she said.

Christopher had just helped Darcy from the wagon when he heard his named called. Deborah stood only a few feet away, a look of amazement upon her face.

"Christopher?"

His siblings were now standing beside him. "I want you to meet my brothers and sisters. Well, five of them anyway."

Deborah didn't know what to think. She looked at the children and assessed the situation. Christopher introduced each one.

"I'm pleased to meet you," she told them, then turned her questioning gaze back on Christopher. "How is it that they came to be with you?"

"Our ma and da burned up in the fire," Emma said matter-of-factly.

Putting her hand to her mouth, Deborah tried to hide her shock. She could see the pleading in Christopher's expression. "Well, come along and have something to eat. We can talk about what happened afterward."

Christopher led the way. Deborah watched as all but the one called Darcy followed him into the house. To her surprise, Darcy stood waiting for her at the door.

"Are you going to marry my brother?"

Deborah nodded. "I certainly plan to."

Darcy seemed to consider this for a moment. "Do we have to call you Mama?"

She couldn't hide her surprise at the child's question. "Are you going to call your brother Papa?"

The girl laughed. "Nope. He's Christopher."

"Then you should call me Deborah."

This answer seemed to appease Darcy. "I like that name. You can call me Darcy."

Deborah wasn't at all sure what had just happened. She followed Darcy into the house and motioned her toward the dining room. There they found her siblings already seated and waiting to be fed.

Hurrying past Christopher, Deborah went into the main kitchen to help her mother. There was very little left over from breakfast, but that was easy enough to rectify. Her mother was already slicing ham.

"Would you start frying the eggs? I'm going to get this ham on, then fetch Sissy to bring in some of the corn bread she's been baking this morning." Mother took up the largest of their cast-iron skillets and filled it with the meat. Setting it atop the stove, she checked the fire.

"I'll be back momentarily, but watch so that it doesn't burn." She was gone before Deborah could even comment.

Going to the basket, Deborah made quick order of things. She began breaking eggs and had them on the stove within minutes. Stirring in a little cream, Deborah tried not to let her emotions overwhelm her as she beat the eggs into a frothy mixture. She didn't know what to think or how to feel about this turn of events.

"I didn't know how to tell you," Christopher commented from the door.

She looked up. "I'm so sorry about your parents, Christopher." She knew he held a deep love for them—especially his mother. "I wish I could say something that would ease your pain."

He nodded. "Thank you. The children didn't have anyone else—no place to go. Mrs. Maynard had taken them in after the fire, but she couldn't afford to keep them."

Deborah stopped stirring. She put the spoon aside and slowly walked to where he stood. "They are your family. You had to see to their needs."

He pulled her into his arms. "I missed you so much." He buried his face in her hair.

Holding on to him tightly, Deborah couldn't help but wonder how their lives were about to change. Darcy's question came to mind and weighed down on her like a load of logs. Had she just inherited a family? Did Christopher expect her to mother his siblings?

She hated herself for feeling distress. How could she begrudge little children the comfort of their older brother after losing their parents? She drew a deep breath.

Lord, I'm going to need help with this. I don't know what you want me to do, but whatever it is, I know I'm going to need strength.

She raised her head and looked into Christopher's face. Seeing a glimmer of tears in his eyes, she knew it would be wrong to question the matter.

Leaning on tiptoe, she placed a gentle kiss on his lips instead. "Are you hungry?"

"Famished."

Deborah touched his cheek. "Then find a seat at the table, and we'll have the meal on in just a few minutes." She stepped away from him and hurried back to the stove as her mother came back to the kitchen with Sissy in tow.

"Welcome back, Doc," Sissy said.

"Thank you," he said, but his gaze never left Deborah.

She could see the unspoken questions in his eyes. There was no time to do anything other than offer him a weak smile before she turned her attention back to the food. He wanted to know that she was all right with the news. That she accepted his new responsibility. That nothing had changed between them. But in truth, everything had changed, whether she liked it or not.

Chapter 11

With Lizzie and Sissy busy helping Mother, Deborah decided to pull Christopher away from the table as soon as he'd emptied his plate. She needed to know how he was doing—what had happened, and what she should expect to come next.

"Could we talk for a moment? Alone?" she whispered in his ear.

Christopher nodded. "I want you all to mind your manners while I talk with Miss Deborah." He got to his feet and looked to Euphanel, who was cutting up pieces of ham for Jonah. "If that's alright with you, Mrs. Vandermark . . . Euphanel."

She smiled at him. "Go on. We're just fine here."

The other children were still busy stuffing food into their

mouths. Deborah thought they ate like they hadn't had a decent meal in months. From the look of how thin they were, they probably hadn't. She frowned at the thought of them being hungry.

"I hope that look isn't for me," Christopher said as they made their way outside.

"No, of course not. I was just thinking of how bad it must have been for your brothers and sisters . . . for you." She stopped on the porch and wrapped her arms around Christopher's neck. "I prayed so much for you, and now I see why. Perhaps it was God's prompting that kept me on my knees."

Christopher touched her cheek. "I never expected this to happen."

"Of course not. Who would ever imagine such a tragedy was possible? Can you tell me what happened?"

"The chimney flue got too hot and set the house ablaze. Mother got the children out, but she went back to help my father. They were trapped and burned to death."

Deborah shook her head and closed her eyes. She couldn't imagine a more horrible way to die. "And . . . were the children . . . hurt?" she forced herself to ask.

"No. They breathed in plenty of smoke but were otherwise fine. Mrs. Maynard lives just across the street, and she graciously took the children in."

"Thank God for Mrs. Maynard. I hate to think what might have happened if she'd not been there."

"I know. Jimmy and Tommy would probably manage all right, but the younger ones certainly would have been taken to an orphanage. I might never have found them."

Deborah hugged him close. "I'm so sorry."

"I'm the one who's sorry, Deborah. I never intended to impose a family on you like this." He pushed away from her and walked to the end of the porch.

"I spent every cent I had. Paying for the funeral expenses, reimbursing Mrs. Maynard, purchasing train tickets, and feeding them on the way down. Oh, and I rented that miserable excuse for a wagon and team," he said, pointing to where the horses still stood.

"I have some money," Deborah declared. "It's yours. I've saved it ever since coming back home and working for our business."

"I can't take your money."

"It's ours," she insisted.

"No. You earned it and put it aside for your own purposes."

Deborah put her hands on his shoulders. "And now that purpose is to help you."

He shook his head. "Look, there are some folks around here that owe me money. Let me see first if I can collect. If not, then we'll discuss your idea."

"What about our wedding?" she asked, almost afraid to hear his reply.

He sighed. "I don't know. I don't know what to do. I have to figure out how to arrange for my siblings first."

"I thought I might find you two out here," Mother said, coming from the house. She crossed the distance in a casual manner and smiled. "Solving the problems of the world?"

"Just my little corner of it," Christopher replied.

"I hope you won't think me interfering." She took a seat and motioned for them to do likewise. Deborah felt relieved at her mother's presence—her own thoughts were skewed with all sorts of ideas.

"Christopher," her mother began, "it's obvious that you need help with your family. We are more than willing to offer you that assistance. We have enough room for everyone—food, too. I'm sure Arjan wouldn't mind if you wanted your family to stay with us for a time."

"I'm ashamed to admit that I'd hoped as much. I've very little money—"

"Hush. We won't speak of such a thing. You're family, Christopher—or very nearly." She smiled. "Family takes care of one another—just as you have taken care of those children."

"I didn't know what else to do. I couldn't stay there; neither could I just leave them."

"Of course you couldn't."

"They have nothing," he added. "They got out of the fire with little more than their nightclothes. Mrs. Maynard said some of the neighbors offered up the articles you see them wearing now. But that's all they have."

"Well, don't you fret, Christopher. We have plenty of things around here we can use."

"I don't know how I could ever pay you. I just told Deborah that I need to go around and see what I can collect on debts owed me."

"You needn't worry," Mother reassured him. "Times are hard for everyone, but God has a way of working it all out. He multiplied the loaves and fishes in the Bible, and He will multiple the food and clothes here today."

"What's going on?" Jimmy asked as he stepped onto the porch. Tommy followed and let the screen door bang against the frame.

"We were just discussing how to keep you strapping lads fed and clothed," Euphanel said. "Why don't you come over here and tell us what you think of our plan."

Jimmy looked apprehensive. "What plan?"

"I have just suggested to Christopher that you could all stay here. There are lots of chores to be done and we could use the help. I have plenty of rooms in the house, and while we are a bit of a distance from town, there's no reason we can't arrange for you all to go back to school and finish up the term."

"I don't wanna live with strangers," Jimmy said, then looked to Deborah's mother. "No offense, ma'am."

"None taken," she assured him. "And we aren't really strangers anymore—are we? I figure it might feel awkward for you two, being the oldest, but the younger ones need to feel safe and protected. The best way I know to do that is by keeping their bellies full and their hands busy. That way they'll be too tired at night to worry overmuch about the past."

Jimmy seemed to think about this for several minutes. Tommy, too, seemed thoughtful on the matter, and Deborah couldn't help but feel sorry for them. How trapped they must feel just now.

"I need a job," Tommy finally declared. "I had one in Kansas City."

"We both need work so we can earn our keep and help support the others," Jimmy confirmed.

"Well, we can probably put you to work for Vandermark Logging. I can't promise, of course, but my husband and son will be back soon, and we can certainly ask them then. There's always something to do in the logging camps, and I believe it would make a good trade. However, there's also school to consider. I wouldn't want either of you forsaking your education. You can always help out after school and on Saturday."

"Sunday, too," Tommy offered.

Mother shook her head. "No, Sunday is the Lord's Day and

we rest. We refrain from working in order to honor Him for all that He's done for us."

Tommy and Jimmy exchanged a look. "Nobody works on Sunday?"

"Well, of course, some people do not honor the Lord that way," Mother replied. "And if there's an emergency, we do not hesitate to work. Even Jesus said it was good to help each other, even if it was on the Sabbath."

Deborah could see that Jimmy and Tommy were mulling over the idea. She leaned forward. "Mother, Christopher and I aren't exactly sure when we'll go ahead with the ceremony, but couldn't he stay here, too?"

Mother looked to the doctor and nodded. "I would encourage it, since the children are used to you. It might ease their fears."

"I . . . don't . . . I don't think I should," he said, glancing over his shoulder at Deborah. "I would still need to keep up my practice. Let me think on it."

Mother nodded and got to her feet. "I'll go see if Sissy and Lizzie need help."

"I'll come, too," Deborah told her mother. She had a feeling Christopher needed some time to talk to his brothers.

They made their way into the house, and Deborah reached out to touch her mother's arm. "Thank you for all you're doing to help him. He's so torn up by what happened, and caring for his siblings is a tremendous worry to him."

Mother nodded. "It's a huge responsibility, Deborah. You must also consider what it means. Perhaps you'll even desire to postpone the wedding."

Deborah squeezed her mother's hand to halt her steps. "Why do you say that?"

"Five children to oversee changes everything," her mother

said. "There's no shame in admitting that. Five children who are grieving the loss of their parents will be even more difficult. Grief makes folks act strange. They say and do things they don't mean because their pain is so great. You will have to have an extra measure of grace for each child."

"I am afraid," Deborah admitted. "I don't know if I can help them navigate their grief. I might be more trouble than help. They may see me as a threat—someone who is taking away their brother."

"They might. However, we must simply put this in God's hands, Deborah. We must trust Him to show us what we need to do and how we can best help Christopher and his siblings."

Deborah longed to say so much more. She wanted to tell her mother her true fears—feelings of how she wasn't at all certain she wanted children in her marriage. Of course, there was no possibility of avoiding that now once they were married. Perhaps they shouldn't marry if she was this confused.

"Mrs. Vandermark," Darcy called from the entryway to the dining room. "Emma's cryin' and she won't stop."

Mother looked at Deborah and smiled. "God will give you the answers you need, darling. Don't fret. He wasn't taken by surprise, and He has a plan."

Deborah watched her mother go and frowned. "I wish He'd tell me what it was."

"Wish who'd tell you what?" Darcy asked.

Deborah felt like a child caught sneaking something to eat. She thought for a moment to lie, but immediately put that idea aside. Darcy was a smart one. In many ways, the girl reminded Deborah of herself.

"I wish God would tell me what to do—how to help you and the others." She held Darcy's gaze. "I feel quite sad that you have lost your parents. It must hurt a great deal. My father died several years ago, and I still miss him."

Darcy nodded. "I don't miss my father, but I do wish my mama was here. My da was sick and in bed a lot, so I never spent much time with him."

"My father was very important to me," Deborah told the girl. "He taught me so many things."

"Like what?"

"How to ride a horse. How to cut wood. How to tend animals. Of course, my mother taught me some of those things, as well. But she also taught me how to sew and make clothes. Do you sew?"

"I do. My mother taught me."

Deborah smiled. "Then we already have something in common."

Darcy seemed to think of this for a moment, then looked at Deborah expectantly. "Do you think you could teach me to ride a horse?"

"I suppose I could. Of course, your brother will have to agree to it."

"I'll talk to him," Darcy said matter-of-factly. "I think he'll listen to me."

"But I don't want to live here," Jimmy said. "It's not our home."

"Neither is my place in town," Christopher replied. "The owner may kick me out any day. I believe this is the best answer." He pushed back his hair and stood. "I know this is hard for you, but I need for you two to help me."

Jimmy looked at Tommy and nodded. "I know it's not easy for you, either. I just . . . well, I hate it."

"I do, too," Tommy added.

Christopher studied his brothers. They seemed so young to

him. Were they really nearly grown? "Come on," he encouraged. "I'll show you around."

The boys ambled along beside him while Christopher told them about the Vandermarks. "They really are the very best people you could ever know. I used to write and tell Ma about them, and she said they were just the kind of folks she'd cherish knowing better."

"And Mrs. Vanermark did say that we could maybe have jobs," Tommy added.

Christopher smiled. "As you can see, there're plenty of ways to earn your keep here. The garden alone takes many hours of tending." He waved his hand toward the area where Sissy was working even now. "Then there's canning and smoking food. Hunting and fishing."

"Do you suppose we could learn to shoot?" Tommy asked.

Christopher stopped walking and faced his brothers. "There isn't a single thing you can't learn if you put your mind to it. The Vandermarks can show you how to shoot, how to log, how to hunt, and do just about anything else you're of a mind to learn. If you give them a chance and agree to stay here, I promise I'll work quickly to come up with a more permanent solution. If we need to move to a bigger city like Houston or Galveston, I will need some time to make arrangements."

Jimmy kicked at a rock in the path. "They won't laugh at us 'cause we're from the city, will they?"

"I've never known them to be unkind to anyone, Jimmy. They are good God-fearing folks who practice what they hear each Sunday. I know you're feeling a bit angry with God right now, but I believe He has given us this opportunity for the safety and well-being of everyone concerned. I'm just asking you to give it a chance."

Jimmy and Tommy exchanged a glance. "Guess there isn't much of any other choice," Jimmy said. "Just remember, I want to go to college."

"I also want you to further your education," Christopher replied. "I won't forget."

Stuart Albright looked at the figures his father-in-law had just handed him. "I suppose if we're to rebuild, we'll be best to keep the present location."

"It will cost three times as much—just for start up—if we move the mill elsewhere," Dwight Longstreet told him. "More than that if we have to run a new siding for the train."

"I can see that for myself." He pushed the papers away. They fluttered in the air momentarily and fell onto the massive desk. "So have you arranged for workers?"

"I've put out the word. We need men with experience; otherwise, it will take forever to get the mill operational."

Smiling to himself, Stuart shook his head. "No, I want the blacks working on it. They are taking up space on my land—in company houses. Have them begin the construction work."

"And if they do not know how?"

Stuart shrugged. "Hire a foreman who does. One white man can handle it."

Longstreet looked at him oddly. "I suppose it could work."

"It will. I'm not in any hurry to see this mill running—I only want to prove that I'm actively pushing forward. That way, the Vandermarks won't have a leg to stand on should they decide to pursue a lawsuit."

"They will also expect you to begin purchasing logs again."

"I'll delay that until I have no other choice," Stuart replied.

"I want them to suffer, Dwight. I want them to know that I'm not a man to be toyed with."

His father-in-law said nothing, but the disapproval lined his expression. Just like his daughter—no guts for making bold moves.

"What of Houston?" Longstreet asked. "Are you still of a mind to move there?"

Stuart was glad for the excuse to change the subject. "I am. I think that it will keep your daughter away from the bad influence of the Vandermarks. She doesn't understand my desire for her to abandon her friendship with Miss Vandermark." Stuart leaned back and laced his fingers together. "She is too emotional to make a sound decision on this matter, so I must make it for her."

Longstreet shrugged. "I've never known Jael to practice poor judgment."

Stuart thought of revealing the truth of Jael's pregnancy to her father, then decided against it. It was much more powerful as a sword he held over her head. He smiled. "Well, I have. So this is how I will handle the matter. You are, of course, welcome to reside with us once we find a suitably sized home."

Jael's father nodded and picked up his hat. "I have my own place there, and I must return. There are banking affairs to see to."

Stuart gave him a curt nod and turned back to a stack of papers at his right. "I don't anticipate you'll need to visit Perkinsville anytime soon. Find a foreman and have him brought to me. I'll instruct him on what we want."

Longstreet looked like he might comment, but said nothing. Stuart hated the man. He was a coward, ignorant of the way modern business needed to be handled. He cared too much about people and the details of their lives. Such a waste.

Still, Longstreet had his uses. When those ceased to exist,

then perhaps Mr. Longstreet would, as well. For now, Stuart would tolerate the man, as well as his daughter. His father had put a stipulation on getting his inheritance and keeping it. He had to remain married to the woman for at least six years. It irritated him to no end, but he would prove to Father that even this wouldn't hold him back. He would remain married to Jael, and when six years had passed, then he would decide what was to be done. Until then, neither her nagging for a divorce nor her desire to help the Vandermarks would deter him from his duties.

Chapter 12

"I thought you'd never get home," Mother said, pulling Arjan into a long embrace.

He gave her a quick kiss, then turned to G.W. "Tell her the good news."

G.W. stood with his arm around Lizzie and nodded. "We found enough folks to help us in our arrangement of tradin' logs. Longtime family friends, willin' to keep it to themselves. It won't be easy, but we'll manage. Mr. Decker made a good suggestion."

Deborah came alongside at this. "And what was that?"

"We'll abandon the current camp and set up to the far north," G.W. replied.

"It seemed to me," Brian Decker began, "that any travel done by Mr. Albright is usually to Houston. If that is indeed the case, he would most likely never pass this way for any reason. You can reduce the rail time by moving to the far northern reaches of your acreage, as well as keep it out of the sight of locals who might say something without realizing the harm."

"That will mean no more coming home in the evenings," Mother said with a frown.

"Maybe not every evenin', but we'll still make it home often enough," Arjan replied with a grin and a wink.

"And have you talked to the men about this?"

"We have," G.W. said. "Stopped at the camp for a brief time on the way down here. They understand what we're up to. I reckon those with families will move them north to live in tents at the loggin' site. Some will probably move on into Lufkin since it'll be close enough to get home at night."

"Well, if you're certain this is how it must be," Mother said. "It will be a great deal of work just getting the site set up. You'll probably need to build a corral and keep the mules there."

"True. We've been discussin' all of this," Arjan answered. "We have a plan."

"What will you need us to do?" Mother asked.

Arjan put his arm around her shoulders. "Keep us in grub and prayers."

Deborah looked to her mother. "You'd best tell him our news."

Mother nodded. "Christopher is back. He's brought us a bit of a surprise."

G.W. shook his head ever so slightly. "What kind of surprise?"

"Five of his siblings. A house fire killed their parents, and Christopher found himself in charge of the five youngest. They range in ages from seven to sixteen. The oldest two boys would like jobs this summer."

"Where are they now?" G.W. asked, looking around.

"Christopher took them to town to see about school," Deborah interjected. "He wasn't certain when Mr. Huebner was ending the term."

"I was hoping you wouldn't mind if they stayed here with us," Mother added. "Christopher certainly hasn't enough space or food. We can easily put them to work here. They can help in the garden and with other chores."

"They seem to be very well behaved," Deborah added.

"They are," Lizzie concurred. "Darcy is thirteen and very capable with the twins."

"I'd say you ladies have this worked out already," Arjan said, laughing. "I see no reason to interfere. How about you, G.W.?"

"It's fine by me."

"I did want to ask if you might be willing to let Christopher use the cabin." Deborah quickly added, "Christopher suspects that Stuart will force him to leave his house soon. I thought if you and Lizzie weren't planning to move into the cabin yet, it might make a good place for Christopher to stay and see patients."

"I have no objection to that," G.W. replied. He fixed Deborah with an ornery grin. "Just so long as you two aren't sneakin' around at night to meet under the moonlight."

Deborah felt her cheeks grow warm. Arjan and Mother laughed. If a hole in the floor would have opened to swallow her, Deborah wouldn't have minded. They had no way of knowing that such thoughts had crossed her mind. It would be wonderful to have Christopher just a short distance away. The cabin was where Uncle Arjan had lived for years, and it might even be suitable for Christopher and Deborah after their wedding.

"I guess we're all set, then. I'll look forward to meetin' the doc's brothers and sisters—and I'm sure we can find the boys some work. Pay might not be much at first, however. They'll have to understand that. And now," Arjan pulled Mother along with him, "how about tellin' me what kind of cookies you have in the tin."

Deborah smiled as the couple exited for the kitchen. Mr. Decker glanced at Lizzie. "Where are my grandbabies?"

"Napping," she told him.

"That sounds like a splendid idea." Mr. Decker looked to the trio. "If you wouldn't mind excusing me, I will join them—at least in napping. I believe I'll seek the comfort of the guest room rather than the nursery, however."

"You go right ahead," G.W. said. "I have some things to talk over with Lizzie."

Deborah made her way into the front room to allow them some privacy and took up her sewing. A million questions assaulted her peace of mind.

When would she and Christopher marry? What would they do for money? Would they have to relocate? She certainly didn't want to leave.

And then there were the children. What kind of needs would they present? How could Christopher possibly provide for them unless he secured another steady position as a doctor? Again, the idea of moving elsewhere crossed her mind.

"But Stuart is rebuilding the mill," she murmured.

But that didn't mean he would hire Christopher. Stuart hated the Vandermarks, and Christopher was clearly tied to the Vandermark he hated the most.

The most important question, however, was the one Deborah didn't want to ask. It frightened her. What if Christopher no longer wanted to marry her? Worse yet, what if she decided she couldn't marry him? No. She shook her head. She loved Christopher. A little bit of trouble wouldn't keep her from a life of happiness with the man of her dreams.

Of course, five siblings were hardly a little bit of trouble.

"Deborah?"

She jumped, startled by G.W. calling her name.

"I nearly forgot. I ran into Jake Wythe in Lufkin," G.W. said. "He wanted you to know how sorry he was. Gave me this letter for you." G.W. handed the envelope to Deborah.

She looked at the handwriting and then back to G.W. "Was he well?"

"He seemed to be. Better off than last time, for sure. He seemed sincerely sorry for the way he acted at your party and asked if there was any chance of getting his job back."

"What did you tell him?"

G.W. shrugged. "I figured it was up to you. You were the one most wronged. He said he's left off drinkin'. He realized his mistake there. Said he was mighty discouraged and never meant to cause you harm."

Deborah looked again at the envelope. "I'm sure he didn't. He's usually a very gentle man. I knew it was the whiskey that caused him to act as he did. I never intended to see him lose his job, but I also didn't want him taking liberties with me."

"Well, read your letter and let us know what you think," G.W. said, heading back to the foyer. "He's a good worker, but I don't want him back with us if he's gonna make you uncomfortable."

Once G.W. was gone, Deborah opened the letter and began

to read. Jake was full of apologies and regret. He assured her that he would never touch liquor again, and that he was quite disgusted with the way he'd acted.

She read his final words again. *I've been drawing closer to God, knowing that my behavior was in part due to having walked away from my faith. Please forgive me, even if you don't want to ever see me again. I know that you and Dr. Kelleher will be very happy.*

He seemed sincere, and she couldn't help but feel a sense of relief. As far as she was concerned, Jake deserved a second chance. She would ask Christopher what he thought, however, before giving G.W. an answer.

By the time Christopher and the children returned, Deborah had finished the final touches on a shirt for Jonah. She held it up and showed it to the little boy. "What do you think, Jonah?"

He looked at the shirt and then to his big brothers. Christopher smiled. "Tell her thank you, Jonah."

"Thank you," he said, still uncertain as to what he should do.

"Well, go and get it," Christopher added, laughing. "I don't think he's used to getting presents—especially new shirts. In our family, hand-me-downs were more common."

The little boy walked up to Deborah and gave a shy smile. "Is it really for me?"

"Only you," she replied. She could not imagine how these children must have lived in Kansas City. Christopher had told her how poor they were, but it was still hard to fully grasp.

"We also have a surprise for you girls." Deborah got to her feet. "Mother and I changed the furniture around from my room to yours. You will each have your own bed now."

"Our own bed?" Darcy asked in disbelief. "Emma and I used

to share before the fire, and at Mrs. Maynard's house, I just had an old cot."

"I hope that means you are pleased. We took the smaller beds from my room and put them in yours so that you and Emma wouldn't have to share the big bed. I will use your bed in my room."

"Can we go see?" Emma asked. "Right now?"

"I don't see why not," Deborah said, smiling. She looked to Christopher. "Is that all right with you?"

"Absolutely."

The girls shot out of the room without another word. Christopher shook his head and laughed. "You've made them very happy."

"It was an easy enough solution. Also, Arjan and G.W. are back with Lizzie's father. They are waiting to meet Jimmy and Tommy. I think they'll be happy for the extra help."

"We can help right away," Tommy added. "Mr. Huebner isn't gonna have but another week of school, so we're not gonna start until next fall."

"Hopefully, by next fall, the mill will be up and running. Did Mr. Huebner say whether they plan to stick around?" she asked, looking to Christopher for an answer.

"He mentioned the possibility. He plans to head down to Burke to see what kind of jobs are available there, as well. He needs to find work in case the mill isn't up and running by September."

"Surely it will be operational by then," Deborah said. "Most of the mills set up with an outdoor arrangement at first. If they build a covered area for the saws, then they should get workers back right away. If the same men bring their families back to Perkinsville, then Mr. Huebner will have more than enough students."

"I thought I heard voices." Uncle Arjan came into the room. "These must be the Kelleher boys."

"Yes, sir," Christopher replied. "This is my brother Jimmy. He's nearly seventeen and has a mind to go to college. This is Tommy, and he'll be fifteen this year." He put his arm around Tommy's shoulder. "The youngest is Jonah."

"I'm seven," Jonah offered.

"Well, that's half grown," Arjan said, ruffling the boy's brown curls. Jonah beamed. "Why don't you come with me into the office, and we'll talk with G.W. about puttin' you to work."

The boys followed Arjan from the room, leaving Christopher and Deborah alone. She saw the weariness in his expression. "What's wrong?"

He straightened and crossed to her. "First, this." He lowered his mouth to hers and kissed her with such passion that Deborah felt her knees give way. He caught her easily and pulled her against him. With a low chuckle, Christopher set her on her feet.

Breathless, Deborah opened her eyes. "Goodness . . ." She fell silent and pressed her hands to her chest. Her heart nearly pounded out of her body.

"Do you require a doctor's assistance?" he asked, grinning.

"I very well might." She shook her head. "I have to admit, I was sitting here contemplating whether or not we should move forward with the wedding right away."

He raised a brow and frowned. "You're having doubts because of the children?"

She shook her head. "I'm not having doubts after a kiss like that."

"But doubts, nevertheless," he said without smiling.

Deborah reached out and took hold of his arm. "Not doubts about my love for you. It's never been that. Neither do I doubt your love for me. I do admit, I am concerned about my ability to care for all of them."

"I have worried about putting this burden on you."

"Christopher, I want to share your burdens—your worries. The children need you, and I understand that. I feel . . . well . . . I don't know what to say." Deborah turned away, knowing it would be impossible to tell him about her fears. At least not yet—not before she could face them herself.

"What's wrong, Deborah?" He came up behind her. "Talk to me."

"I'm not sure I can. I feel . . . so . . . overwhelmed." She turned and he took hold of her. "I'm afraid. I know it sounds ridiculous, but I am."

"Afraid of what?"

"I don't feel I can say—not yet. Give me time to sort through my thoughts."

He touched her face. "Don't be afraid. We're together. We can figure this out, one step at a time."

Deborah wanted to tell him about her fears of motherhood. She wanted to explain that his siblings only served to remind her that a large family would need constant care. She could hardly be working at Christopher's side as a physician while mothering children. Mill town medicine was too demanding—too bloody. If emergencies came up, as they always did, she would have to be able to move on a moment's notice. There wouldn't be time to make arrangements for the children.

"You are fretting, and it's not necessary. If we love each

other and trust God to direct our steps, we needn't fear our future."

She knew the truth of what he said—at least in theory. In practice, it was something entirely different, and she wasn't at all sure how to make the two become one.

ꕥ

Euphanel giggled like a young girl as Arjan led her to the crate on the back of the wagon. "I'm so glad you were able to get two of them." Peering inside the wagon she was rewarded with a yipping sound.

"Oh, they're so cute. What fun they will be for the children."

Arjan nodded and lifted two puppies from the crate and put them on the ground by the wagon. "Folks in Lufkin said they were ten weeks old." The lumbering little fur balls were part bloodhound and part collie. A strange mix, but it made for a sweet-natured animal with distinctive bloodhound ears and collie nose, coat, and tail.

Reaching down, Euphanel picked up one of the pups. "Oh, they're so soft." The puppy licked her face and nuzzled up to her ear as if looking for food. "I'll bet they're hungry."

"Could be. Long trip." Arjan nodded toward the house. "You want me to fetch somethin'?"

"Well, since we plan to have the children take responsibility, let's call them out here and let them be surprised. We can instruct them then and the puppies will bond with them more easily."

"Sounds good." Arjan headed for the house. "I'll call them."

Euphanel put the first puppy down and lifted up the second. "You will be the best kind of healing," she said, kissing the animal on the nose. This puppy was less excitable and seemed content to just settle into Euphanel's arms. She checked to see if it was a boy or girl. "Oh, so you're the little lady. And such a calm disposition." She glanced down to see that the male pup was already chewing on a piece of wood he'd found.

At the sound of the children approaching, Euphanel put the female on the ground to join her brother. Jonah was the first one to spot the animals. He stared in surprise, coming to a dead stop. Emma saw them next.

"Puppies!"

The three youngest siblings ran forward to take the pups in hand. There was a great deal of squealing, chatter, licking, and yipping as the introductions were made. Euphanel smiled when Jonah asked what their names were.

"I thought maybe you three would like to name them. This is the boy," she said, pointing to the pup with a splotch of black covering his right eye. "And this is the girl. See, she's a little smaller and doesn't have the patch."

Darcy picked the female up and looked at her seriously. "I knew some folks once that had a dog named Lady. She's just a puppy now, but do you suppose we could name her a grown-up dog name?"

"Of course. She'll grow into it. In fact, I was just remarking that she was quite the little lady."

"I like that name, too," Emma said, reaching out to take the puppy from her sister. Darcy tried to act like she didn't mind, but Euphanel thought she looked rather disappointed.

"I know there aren't three," she began to tell them, "but two of the barn cats are about to have kittens, so I think you'll all have plenty of animals to spend time with."

"I like cats better anyway," Darcy said.

"We ain't never had a cat or a dog," Jonah said, his eyes as big as saucers.

"Never?" Euphanel questioned.

"Mama said we didn't have enough food for people," Darcy explained. "We couldn't be feeding a dog or cat. Mrs. Maynard had a cat and sometimes she came to visit us when the mice were bad."

Euphanel felt regret for the children who'd grown up in such poverty. "Well, you can definitely help to take care of these animals. They will need a lot of love, and right now I think they're hungry. At least this little pup is." She reached out to scratch the male behind the ears. "So what shall we call this little boy?"

"Let's call him Man," Jonah said. " 'Cause we got a Lady and this can be the Man."

"That's a silly name," Darcy said. "Man isn't a dog's name."

Jonah looked crestfallen. "Well, you named Lady. Me and Emma get to name this one."

"How about Buster?" Emma suggested. "You know like Mama used to call you when you'd get into things you weren't supposed to?"

Jonah smiled. "Yeah. Buster. I like that—it'll remind me of Mama."

Arjan joined them about that time. "Ready for me to put the crate in the barn?"

Euphanel knew the children would want to live in the barn with the puppies, but it was time to explain the rules. "The puppies will live in the barn, and at night we'll keep them locked up. This way, the wild hogs won't get them. They can be really mean to animals and people who can't defend themselves."

"Can't the puppies be in our room?" Jonah asked.

Emma looked at Euphanel with great hope. "Please?"

She was ready for this. "No. Cats and dogs stay outside. The only time we let one of the cats inside is when there's a mouse we can't catch. You'll have plenty of time to spend with them, so don't fret. Right now we'll let Arjan take the crate for us and you can bring the puppies. After we get them settled, I'll show you what to feed them and you can come back to the barn with the food."

The children were quite excited at this prospect and forgot their concern about the puppies not being allowed in the house. Euphanel could only smile at their excitement. Her prayer was that the pups would help them in their grieving process . . . and so far her prayer looked to be answered.

Chapter 13

May 1887

The first week of May brought gentle hints of summer. After a wet and stormy April, the weather settled and the skies cleared. Even the heaviness of the normally damp air felt less imposing and brought a riot of flowery scents. Deborah loved this colorful time of year, when everything around her seemed alive and vibrant.

"Here's the last of those roses, Miss Deborah," Sissy announced, putting two pots on the ground beside her. "Your mama said to tell you she'll be bringin' some cookies out for the lil'uns soon."

Deborah straightened and reached for the first pot. She looked to where Emma had just finished digging the hole. "Are you ready for this one?"

"Yes. You can put it right here, and I'll pack the dirt around it."

Working the rosebush from the pot, Deborah maneuvered the plant into the hole. While Emma took care of securing the dirt, Jonah called Deborah's attention to the hole he'd dug.

"See how deep it is, Miss Deborah?"

She could see he was quite proud of his accomplishment. "It's very fine. I'm sure this plant will grow strong there."

"It's the best I ever dugged," Jonah said, rubbing his hands together to get some of the dirt off. "I never planted nothin' before."

Deborah thought of their life in the city and nodded. "I'm sure there wasn't much of an opportunity, living in town."

"Jonah, you've got to wash up before you can have something to eat," Darcy announced. "You too, Emma."

With the older two boys living at the lumber camp, Darcy took it upon herself to mother and direct Emma and Jonah, assuming the responsibility without it ever being suggested. She seemed to believe that her attention was not only needed, but expected.

She's so much like me, Deborah thought for about the hundredth time that day.

"Emma, if you're done, let's go wash." Directing her younger sister to the pump, Darcy helped Emma to get the water started. Jonah joined them, none too happy.

"I don't like to wash up."

Deborah smiled as she planted the second rosebush. She tapped down the dirt and dusted off her gloves. Standing, she watched Darcy help Jonah with the towel. They worked well together, and Deborah couldn't help but admire Darcy's patience.

"Can we play with the puppies now?" Emma asked, returning to where Deborah was getting to her feet.

"I'm sure that would be fine. Why don't you bring them up on the porch? That way we'll be ready when my mother brings out our treats."

"I'll help, too!" Jonah's enthusiasm sent him running for the barn. It was only a matter of seconds before the children came running back, arms full of roly-poly squirming delight.

Emma settled on the porch floor and let her puppy loose. She giggled when the animal climbed back up on her lap and licked her face.

"She sure likes the new puppies," Darcy said, coming to stand beside Deborah.

"I like them, too," Deborah admitted. "Don't you?"

Darcy shrugged. "I like horses better. Do you think we could have a lesson today?"

She looked so hopeful that Deborah couldn't resist. "Why not?"

Clapping her hands, Darcy all but danced away. "I'll change my clothes." She disappeared into the house without another word.

"Lady, stop!" Emma rolled to her side as the puppy held fast to one of her braids. "Lady!"

Jonah giggled hysterically at the sight. "She's gonna eat your hair." He turned to find his own pup about to wander down the porch steps. "Come back, Buster."

He rolled Buster on his back and scratched the pup's belly. Deborah sat down on the porch steps near Emma. "He definitely likes that," she told the boy.

Emma finally had Lady interested in something other than her hair. The pup sat calmly, chewing on the tip of the little girl's well-worn boot. The soles appeared paper thin and the leather was cracked and scuffed.

"We're going to have to get you another pair of shoes," Deborah said.

"Mrs. Maynard found them after the fire," Emma told her.

Deborah frowned. "Were they in the fire?" That would explain a great deal.

"No. They were somebody else's shoes. They gave them to Mrs. Maynard for me to wear."

"I see." Deborah glanced at Jonah's shoes and saw that they too were hardly worth wearing. "Well, tomorrow we will do what we can to get some new ones. The commissary might still have a few pairs. If not, then we'll order some."

"New shoes?" Emma looked at Deborah as if she were speaking another language. "I've never had new shoes."

"No? Well, it's about time, then." She smiled at the little girl. It made her feel good to know they could bless the children with a better life.

Mother came out on the porch with Darcy in tow. They carried refreshments and Deborah jumped up to help.

"We've got it all under control," Mother said. "I thought you might enjoy some cookies and milk," she said to Emma and Jonah.

The puppies were momentarily forgotten as the youngest Kellehers hurried to the table where Mother placed her tray. Darcy in turn added a plate of cookies and smiled.

"I helped bake these this morning," she announced proudly.

"Then I must have one," Deborah declared. "Oh, I see you've been practicing Mother's sugar cookie recipe."

Darcy nodded. "She said it was the easiest of them all. I got to mix the butter and sugar together. Then I added the cream and the eggs."

"I remember doing that myself," Deborah told her. "Did you roll out the dough, too?"

"Yes. My mama taught me to roll out crust a long time ago and it was just like that."

Deborah took up one of the cookies. She sampled it and feigned deep consideration. Darcy regarded her with wide, hopeful eyes. "Yes. It's as good as any I've ever tasted. You are a good teacher, Mother. And you, Miss Darcy, are an excellent student."

The young girl smiled with pleasure, then helped Jonah reach the cookies and waited for his approval, as well. When he reached to get a second treat, Darcy all but danced a jig. "He must like them."

"They are very good," Emma said in a most adultlike manner. She sat back down with her cookie and tears touched the corners of her eyes.

"Are you all right?" Deborah asked.

"I just miss Mama. She sometimes baked us cookies."

"Not very often," Darcy said. "We didn't have enough money for sweets."

Emma nodded and repeated her sister's words. "Not very often."

Darcy came to where Emma sat. "Stop crying. Do you want Miss Euphanel to think we aren't grateful?"

Emma wiped at her tears while Mother came to sit beside the little girl. "It's all right. Tears are perfectly fine. Your mama was a good woman and you loved her a great deal—just as I'm sure she loved you. You miss her, and that's only natural."

Mother hugged Emma to her side. The child relaxed against her, calming at the maternal touch. Deborah wondered if she would ever be able to offer similar comfort to a child. She did her best to be friendly and loving with the children, but could she really help to mend their hurts the way Mother had always helped to mend hers?

Jonah occupied himself once again with the puppy, while Darcy chose to indulge in another cookie. Deborah caught her mother's eye and motioned to Emma's feet.

"We need to get them some new shoes. These were given by neighbors after the fire."

Mother looked at the pair and nodded. "They look a little too small. Do they pinch your feet?"

Emma nodded. "But they was all we had."

"I'm sure we can find something else. Tomorrow, we can take the wagon and go into town to see what they have at the store."

Deborah smiled. "That's what I told them. I have some money set aside. We can use it and get what we need. Darcy, do you need a new pair, as well?"

The thirteen-year-old pulled up the hem of her dress and nodded. "These are too big."

The strange-looking brogans were indeed too big. Why hadn't Deborah or someone noticed it before now? She felt guilty for worrying about how to coexist with Christopher's siblings instead of truly recognizing their needs.

"We can take care of all of that tomorrow," Mother said with a smile.

Just then Lizzie came to the door. "I'm ready to pick herbs—Darcy, can you come and keep the twins out of trouble?"

Darcy looked at Deborah. It was clear that she was torn between playing with the babies and having a promised horseback riding lesson. Deborah waved her on. "If you want to help, we can always ride later. Just come find me when you're done."

Darcy darted for the door, forgetting all about the cookies. "Let's go," she said without so much as a backward glance.

Deborah had to laugh at the child's enthusiasm. "She certainly enjoys playing with the twins."

"Indeed. And I know Lizzie appreciates the help. Darcy can keep the children occupied and has more energy than we do," Mother replied.

"Can we go, too?" Jonah asked.

Mother shrugged and got to her feet. "I don't know why not. You and Emma, go put the puppies back in their pen, and wait for me by the well. We'll meet up with Lizzie and the others in just a minute." Jonah gathered Buster, while Emma wrapped her arms around Lady.

"Hurry, Jonah," Emma said, bounding down the stairs with her load.

"It takes so little to make them happy. I think of all they've gone through, and it amazes me they can find joy at all." Deborah sighed and looked off toward the mulberry trees.

"You seem troubled." Mother reached out to touch Deborah's chin.

Deborah lifted her gaze and met her mother's worried expression. "I'm really fine. I just feel a little confused. I don't know how to be a mother."

"Who has asked you to be one?"

She shrugged. "Well, the little ones need guidance and teaching. They need comfort when they get upset and cry. I feel completely inadequate to do that."

"But why? You have always had a compassionate heart," her mother chided. "I've never known you to be otherwise. You saw the need for new shoes; I certainly missed that. It's often the little things that offer comfort or distress. You are seeing to their needs in a practical, tangible way. If I had not been here, you would have offered Emma comfort and a kind word. Don't be so hard on yourself."

Deborah frowned and turned away. "I'm not like you, Mother, I don't know that I ever will be."

"What do you mean?"

Emotions threatened to strangle her. Deborah turned. "I don't know that I could ever be a good mother."

A gentle breeze blew across the yard, sending a sweet scent on the air, but even this had no calming effect on her spirit. "I try to imagine it," she continued. "I really do. But how in the world can I help Christopher and be a physician in my own right, plus have children to tend at the same time?"

"Are you saying you don't want a family?" Mother asked, her tone quite serious. "You do realize you don't get to decide about that fact. God is the one who creates life. If you marry Christopher, it will be God, not you, who blesses the union with children."

"Or not. Perhaps I cannot have children," Deborah replied. "Maybe the feelings I have are for a good reason. Maybe God has never intended for me to give birth to my own babies."

Her mother looked perplexed. Deborah immediately felt bad for even making such a statement. What was wrong with her anyway? What woman didn't naturally long to have a family of her own?

I hate the way I am, she said to herself. *I disgust even myself.*

She turned away and shook her head. "I'm sorry. I shouldn't have said anything."

"There's nothing wrong in speaking your heart, Deborah. Have I ever taught you otherwise?" Her mother took hold of her once more. "You don't need to hide your heart from me. I'm not appalled by such a declaration. I'm not troubled that you feel this way. Goodness, child, God has His own way for you. I wouldn't begin to tell you what that is."

"I find it hard to consider marriage knowing that Christopher probably wants a family," Deborah said. "I haven't had the nerve to even ask him about it. I mean, the fire happened and the children came, and well . . . it just seemed poor timing."

"No. Poor timing was that you hadn't discussed this long ago. Does Christopher know how you're feeling—even a little?"

"I don't know. He knows I love medicine, just as he does. He knows I love helping him treat patients. I worry he's brought his brothers and sisters here, expecting me to stop helping him and work with them."

"But why? Why do you think this?" Mother asked.

Frowning, Deborah raised her face. "He's not here asking me to assist. To me, his actions speak louder than any words. He's been heading out to tend patients for days now, and not once has he suggested I go with him." She drew a deep breath to steady her emotions. With very little urging she might burst into tears, and that was the last thing she wanted.

"Deborah, you must speak with him. This is not the way I raised you. If you are feeling out of sorts, then you must let Christopher know. He can't be expected to instinctively know your heart."

"I thought he already understood my heart." Her words were heavy with emotion. "I thought that was why we loved each other."

Mother embraced her for just a moment. "Oh, sweetheart, you need to tell him how you feel."

"But what if he doesn't want to marry me after that? What if we can no longer work together?" Deborah imagined all of her dreams suddenly dissolving before her eyes. "I don't know what I'd do."

"But you can't marry a man you don't trust."

"I trust him. I never said I didn't."

Mother pulled back and smiled. "If you trust him, then why

aren't you talking to him about this matter? Why are you bearing this alone—fearful of what the answer might be?"

Her mother's words hit hard. She *should* be able to sit down with Christopher and share her heart. She ought to be able to go to this man—the man she wanted to spend her life with—and explain her fears.

She nodded. "I'll talk to him tonight. If there's time and the children don't need him too much."

"You let me handle the children," Mother said. "I will have them help me with some task. You and Christopher need time to settle this. I don't want you to lose him out of fear—nor to marry him because of it. Fear is not a solid foundation upon which you can build a marriage."

"I know you're right."

Mother patted her cheek. "I must go now, but remember what I said."

"I will. I promise."

Deborah watched her mother leave and let out a heavy sigh. She made it sound so simple, and perhaps that was the truth of it. Maybe Deborah was just making it difficult. Either way, she couldn't be happy by settling for less than what she felt called to do. Christopher wouldn't want to marry her if Deborah was less than the woman God had created her to be.

"But what if I'm the one who's wrong?" she whispered to no one. "What if God is calling me to be a wife and mother—to raise a family and put aside all my book learning? What if I'm simply in rebellion against Him, and don't even realize it?"

Chapter 14

G.W., Stuart Albright just rode up. He's getting out of his buggy this very minute," Deborah announced. "You don't suppose he's heard about the trades, do you?"

Getting to his feet, G.W. shook his head. "I couldn't say, but I wish Lizzie's father had stuck around. I feel better when we have a scholarly man in our corner."

"Do you want me to stick around?"

G.W. considered this for a moment. His guess was that Stuart hated Deborah more than anyone—unless he counted himself. "No. I'll call for you if I think it's needed. Better let us men bang heads on this one."

Deborah nodded, but G.W. could see she was upset. He let her go without another word and looked down at his desk. He wanted to make sure there was nothing visible that might give away their secret dealings.

Sissy ushered Mr. Albright to the office and announced him. "Mr. Albright says he needs to speak with you."

"That's fine, Sissy." G.W. remained standing as Albright pushed the black woman aside and stalked into the room as if he owned it.

"Vandermark, I have a proposal for you."

"First, apologize to Sissy. You didn't need to be so rude. She's an older woman—please show some respect." G.W. knew he was setting the stage for Stuart's hostility to grow, but he didn't want Albright to think he could just barge in and treat people like that.

Albright cast a brief glance at Sissy. "I apologize." He turned back to G.W. "Will that suffice?"

G.W. looked at Stuart for a moment before taking his chair again. "Have a seat."

The man unbuttoned his suit coat and did as instructed. G.W. figured it was the last time Albright would do anything he was told. He decided that for now, he would hear the man out—then throw him out, if necessary. G.W. frowned and chided himself for his attitude. Maybe Albright had come to propose the start-up of log delivery.

"As I'm sure you've heard by now, we are arranging to rebuild the mill," Stuart began. He fixed his gaze on G.W. and settled back in his chair.

"I heard somethin' about that."

"It appears that the construction will take some time to complete."

"I suppose you'll set up saws out in the open and build around them."

Stuart shook his head. "You suppose wrong. There are far

more modern processes now for mills. We intend to have the latest equipment available. Steam power will cut costs, and I intend to see the latest innovations installed. However, such equipment is costly and requires a decent structure in which to house it."

G.W. ignored a wave of disappointment. If Albright was being truthful, it would no doubt be a while before he wanted logs from Vandermark Logging. "So why are you here today? I reckon you didn't come for logs."

"No, again you suppose wrong. I actually have come for logs."

"I see." G.W. tried not to sound hopeful. He took up a ledger and opened it. "How many do you want and when do you need delivery?"

Stuart gave a bit of a laugh. It wasn't one of joy, however, and G.W. closed the book and eased back into his chair slowly. "I suppose that was just your idea of a joke?"

"Not at all, but you misunderstand. I don't want a mere shipment of logs. I want to buy you out."

G.W. could hardly believe his ears. He narrowed his gaze. "I reckon you better explain yourself."

"Of course. Your company is completely tied to mine. I hold the key to your success or demise." He gave G.W. a smug smile. "You might say I control your destiny."

"You might, but it would be wrong. God alone controls my life." G.W. crossed his arms against his chest. "Vandermark Logging isn't for sale."

"Now, now. Let's not make rash decisions without hearing the details of what I am about to offer. I would like to present a legitimate business proposal. I will buy Vandermark Logging and all your land, houses, and equipment. You and your . . . family," he said, "can simply pack up your personal items and leave."

He made it sound like it were already a done deal. G.W.

shook his head. "You're barkin' up the wrong tree, Albright. Our company and land ain't for sale. Even if they were, we wouldn't sell to the likes of you."

"I hardly see how you have much of a choice," Stuart replied. "You have to be quite behind in your bank payments. I understand you received permission to sell off a small portion of land, but the bank will not allow further sale."

"And how is it that you know anything about our bank dealings, Albright?"

Stuart looked most satisfied, and G.W. regretted having asked the question. "I have my ways of knowing whatever I need to, Mr. Vandermark. I am a man of resources. I'm also a man of power."

"I suppose that's your way of sayin' that havin' money allows you to nose into other folks' business. Well, it won't do you any good this time."

"You can't hope to continue for long in this manner."

"I don't have to," G.W. said, taking a deep breath. "Our lawyer, my father-in-law, has it under control for us. I reckon he's just as smart as you when it comes to business dealin's."

"I seriously doubt that." Albright touched a hand to his impeccable suit. "Were he as capable as you say, Vandermark Logging would hardly be in this position."

"Albright, I didn't ask you here today, and I'd appreciate it if you'd state your business and go."

Stuart's icy blue eyes bored holes into G.W. "You are in a bad way, Mr. Vandermark. You are at my mercy. If I choose to, I can drag out the rebuilding of the mill until your family is dead in the dust."

"You do what you feel you have to," G.W. said. "I doubt Zed will be all that happy with it, however. He'll have something to say about all of this."

"Hardly. I'm buying him out, as well. He has no more say over anything."

G.W. couldn't hide his surprise. "Buyin' him out? It's his company."

"No, Mr. Vandermark. It is my company. Mine and Mr. Longstreet's. I hold the controlling interest. Mr. Perkins owes me a great deal of money. He had no insurance on his business, and no means to support himself apart from it except for the company stores—which are also now mine."

"So you're just gonna ruin the man? I guess I should have figured on that. It seems that stirrin' up trouble and makin' folks miserable is what you do best."

Albright shrugged. "It's a gift." He laughed and got to his feet. "I came in good faith to offer you a decent price on the business. It seems to me, a mill owner should handle his own logging. If you aren't of a mind to cooperate, I'll simply wait until the bank takes over your property, and then I'll buy it for a pittance of its former worth."

G.W. fought the urge to jump to his feet. He didn't want Albright to see that he was upset. He pretended to busy himself with the papers at hand. "I'm sure you know the way out."

Without another word, Stuart exited the office, leaving G.W. to contemplate the situation. He wished his father-in-law could have been there to help, but he figured he'd handled the situation well enough. G.W. really wanted to talk to Zed and find out what was going on. He couldn't imagine Zed had wanted to sell out. The longtime family friend would no doubt be devastated. With a sigh, G.W. pushed the papers aside and bowed his head. Prayer seemed the only hope any of them had.

Lizzie sat on the porch, glad that the twins were off with Euphanel and the others. It would give her a few free moments to confront the man she'd nearly married.

When Stuart bounded out the front door, a scowl on his face, Lizzie knew her time had come. She stood and faced him. "Why are you here?"

Stuart stopped in midstep, unable to hide his surprise. He quickly recovered and masked any emotion in his expression. "You know full well."

"You once said you loved me, and now you treat me this way."

He shrugged. "I lied. I never loved you or anyone else. I wasn't raised to love—I was raised to prosper. You nearly cost me everything. Had Jael not needed my help as much as I needed hers, I might have seen the end to my fortune. All thanks to you."

"I couldn't marry a man I didn't love," she countered. "It wasn't my intent to hurt you—neither in leaving you on our wedding day nor going through with the marriage." She softened her tone and took a hesitant step forward. "Stuart, I didn't want us to live in misery."

He laughed, causing her to step back again. "I would not have been in misery. You wouldn't have had to be, either. I told you as long as you presented yourself in a positive manner socially, I would give you the freedom to live as you wished. You could have had everything your heart desired."

"Everything but love." She shook her head. "I feel sorry for you, Stuart. At first I worried about causing you pain, but now I just hold pity for you. You have no idea what real love is all about. I'm blessed to know it for myself, and there is nothing so wonderful."

Her words hit their mark. Stuart paled slightly and shook

his head. "I will crush you. You and your precious family. Mark my words, I will have my revenge."

"The world is full of folks who are seeking the same," Lizzie said sadly. "I thought you to be smarter and definitely more secure in your position than that. Seems to me you've been running scared most of your life."

His face contorted in anger as he took a menacing step forward. "Watch yourself, Lizzie. It would be a pity if something happened to you—or one of your children."

She closed the distance between them and narrowed her eyes. "You'd do well to watch yourself, Stuart Albright. If you ever open your mouth to threaten my children again, I'll . . . I'll. . . ."

He laughed. "You'll what? You can't hurt me."

Lizzie regained her composure. "I'll have my father help Jael get a divorce." She smiled at the look of surprise on Stuart's face. "That's right. I know Jael wants to leave you. I knew it from the first moment when I learned the truth about why she married you. Mark my words, if one of my children so much as scrapes their knee, I'll be eyeing you first to ascertain whether or not you pushed them."

Stuart opened his mouth to speak, then turned instead. He stormed from the porch and into his buggy, barely releasing the brake before applying a whip to the back of his horse.

Feeling rather strengthened by Stuart's reaction, Lizzie squared her shoulders. It felt good to stand up to the man who'd so often manipulated her in the past. She felt a sort of quiet resolution in their exchange. He would know now that she was not a weakling. She was a woman who loved her family. A mother who would guard her children with her life.

Lizzie shook her head and wished that things could have been different with her own mother. She couldn't imagine how different their relationship might have been had her mother been more interested in Lizzie than in working for women's rights. She was so disinterested in motherhood that she didn't even tell Lizzie about her twin sister.

Taking a seat on the porch, Lizzie felt tears form. How she longed for her mother to come and see the twins and explain about the sister she'd never known. She wanted her mother to tell her how sorry she was for the wasted years—that she wanted a new life with Lizzie and the others.

"But that won't ever happen," she whispered with a sigh. Regrets wrapped themselves around Lizzie like iron bands. For all the joy she knew now—for all the love—she couldn't find a way to put the demons of the past at bay.

"Are you all right?"

It was Deborah, returning from teaching Darcy about the horses. Lizzie forced a smile. "I'm fine. Stuart came for a visit with G.W." She wiped away a tear. "How was your ride?"

Deborah shook her head and came to sit beside Lizzie. "Only Darcy rode. I observed and counseled, but that isn't important. What happened with Stuart?"

"I stood up to him. I waited for him out here and when Stuart concluded his business I cornered him about why he was here—why he was determined to make us suffer."

"He wants to make you suffer for the sake of suffering."

"And he's accomplishing it," Lizzie replied.

"Don't allow him the upper hand, Lizzie. You know that he's cruel and has proven himself to be underhanded in his business dealings. There is no shame in putting such a person from your life. No fault, either. The Bible says we are to resist the devil and he will flee from us."

"Instead, I resisted and the devil hunted me down."

Deborah put her arm around Lizzie's shoulder. "Well, he may know where you are, but he cannot have you. You belong to God, and He will not tolerate this torment forever. God will not be mocked, and that is exactly what Stuart Albright is doing. He's mocking God and seeking to harm those whom God loves. You'll see. God's hand will reach down and destroy Stuart and all he's built for himself."

Lizzie shrugged. "But you know as well as I do that evil men prosper all the time. Wickedness abounds and the weak suffer."

"Yes, but we are not weak. We have Jesus and the armor of God. Remember those verses in Ephesians six that Pastor Shattuck spoke on several weeks ago? The armor of God will protect us. And above all, the Scriptures say, we need to take up the shield of faith in order to deflect the darts of the wicked. God has made provision for our protection. We simply need to trust Him."

"When Stuart threatened the children, I found more strength than I knew I even had."

"He threatened the twins?"

Lizzie nodded. "He threatened me, as well, but I told him if he ever so much as caused one of my children to scrape their knee, I'd have my father help Jael get her divorce."

"You should let G.W. know that he threatened to do you all harm," Deborah said. She looked away. "Stuart told Jael he'd hurt me if she tried to leave him. I should have said something sooner about it to G.W. and Arjan, but I was afraid of what kind of trouble it might stir up. Now, I know."

It was Lizzie's turn to offer comfort. "It wouldn't matter, Deborah. Stuart is a cruel man. He will do his worst, but as you said—we have God's protection. We must rest in that and trust Him to keep us from harm."

"We must also be as wise as serpents, the Bible says." Deborah gazed down the road. "That's especially true when it's a snake in the grass that's threatening to bite."

ꕤ

"He honestly thought he could just waltz in here and buy us out?" Arjan asked.

G.W. nodded. "That's what he said. Said he knew we had to be gettin' desperate. He has no right to know anything about our business, but apparently he has his sources."

Deborah left the room and discussion in order to find Christopher. She had promised her mother she would speak with him about her fears. Something deep within her mind warned her to remain silent, however. She loved this man, and surely she would love his children.

"I can be a good wife and mother," she murmured. "I know I can. I've always been able to do whatever I set my mind to."

Christopher was outside talking to Jimmy and Tommy. The boys had come back with Uncle Arjan, full of stories and excitement. She held back, not wanting to disrupt their obvious enjoyment of the evening.

Mother had taken Jonah and Emma with her to work in the garden, and Darcy was mucking out stalls in the barn. Deborah decided a walk might do her better for the moment. She needed to understand her own heart. After all, how could she talk to Christopher about her fears when she wasn't even willing to face them herself?

She slipped down the stairs and headed off toward the woods. There was still enough light, and perhaps Deborah could spend that time in prayer. She thought of the words she'd just shared with Lizzie.

"Here I am again. Why can't I follow my own advice? Why can I speak of hope and safety in God to others, but not grasp it for myself?"

Gazing heavenward, Deborah looked up through the boughs of a longleaf pine and sighed. There was such beauty here. Such peace. Why could she not find it within?

Father, I don't know what to do. I love Christopher and want to marry him, but I'm afraid. She startled at the thought. Was it merely fear that kept her from feeling at ease—from taking delight in the idea of marriage and motherhood?

Chapter 15

With Christopher away on a medical call, Deborah took the opportunity to ride into town with Arjan and G.W. the next day. They had decided to see Zed Perkins and discuss the situation with Stuart Albright. Deborah wanted to check in with Mara to see if Jael had sent a letter. She hurried to the preacher's house and found Mara eager for a visit.

"I had a letter from Rob. He plans to come home at the end of this month and stay for several weeks. I'd like to surprise him with a party for his twenty-fifth birthday.

"I think it would be great fun."

Deborah took off her straw bonnet. "I think that would be wonderful. Mother would be thrilled to have you come by the house to discuss it." Deborah glanced around the house and lowered her voice. "We can certainly talk more about the birthday plans, but I was wondering if you'd heard from Jael."

"I have." Mara hurried to a small desk across the room. She slid open a drawer and removed a piece of folded paper. "She gave me this just this morning. I was planning to give it to you at church tomorrow."

Deborah took the paper and opened it. She scanned the lines and shook her head. "Stuart plans to move Jael on Monday. He's making her stay with her father in Houston so that she won't have any opportunity to be around me." She looked up at Mara. "She says we must speak before she leaves."

"How will you arrange it?" Mara questioned, then answered before Deborah could speak. "I could invite her here."

"No. Stuart might insist on coming, too." Deborah considered the problem for a moment, then tapped the side of her temple. "G.W. and Arjan are visiting Mr. Perkins at this very moment. They are discussing business. It would be quite appropriate for them to include Mr. Albright. Let me go speak with them and see if they would do this for me."

Mara followed her to the door. Deborah stuffed the paper in her reticule and then re-affixed her bonnet. "Pray that this works," she told Mara before leaving.

ꕤ

"I'll fetch him right away," Zed told Deborah. "I'll say it's urgent and cannot wait."

"Thank you so much, Mr. Perkins. I can't tell you what this means to me." Deborah turned to her stepfather and brother. "Thank you, as well. I know his company is not desired."

"That's all right, Deborah. A discussion between us all is needed," Arjan assured her. "This is the perfect excuse."

"I'll take the long way around to their house. I can slip in right after you and Stuart head back here," she said, nodding at Mr. Perkins, who was already reaching for his hat.

Once outside, Deborah lost little time. She hiked her skirt just enough to give her legs the freedom she needed, then half walked, half ran to the northern edge of the town. She hurried toward the railroad tracks, doing her best to keep careful watch down the open roads for Mr. Perkins and Stuart. At one point, she heard them before seeing them and barely managed to dart behind one of the houses as they passed along the road just to the south.

With Stuart on his way to meet with the men, Deborah picked up her pace. She didn't hesitate before knocking on the door. To her surprise, it opened right away and Jael stood in welcome. "Come in quickly. Mr. Perkins managed to tell me what was happening."

The two women embraced briefly before Jael closed the door. "Essie is gone for the morning. We're alone. Stuart was quite angry to be disturbed. I doubt he'll stay long."

"Then we must hurry," Deborah declared. "Your letter said it was urgent we speak."

Jael nodded. She looked gaunt and pale. "Stuart is forcing me to go to Houston. He wants me to stay with my father until he can arrange a house for me. Oh, Deborah! Stuart is acting so strangely. I came across some letters he received, and I believe he has someone at the bank who is giving him information on your family. When advised that money appeared in Vandermark Logging's account, he ranted around here like I've never before seen. I'm not sure what he plans."

"Oh, Jael, I am so sorry. Are you sure you wouldn't want to come back to the house with me?"

The young woman shook her head. "That would only make him angrier. I am, after all, his wife." She frowned and looked away. "And there's another thing. I think I might be with child."

Too stunned to speak, Deborah waited until Jael turned back to face her. "I don't want to be. Please don't think badly of me, but I asked Stuart for a divorce and he refused. If I'm carrying his child, there will be no possibility that he'll change his mind. What will I do?"

The hopelessness in her voice caused Deborah to reach out and take her in her arms. Holding Jael close, Deborah let her friend cry. Nothing she could say or do would make this better.

Jael suddenly pulled away. "There isn't time for this. Stuart told me he wasn't about to stay for long. He'll be back before we know it. Deborah, I feel so desperate."

"Go to your father. He loves you and will keep you safe. Tell him what is happening between you and Stuart."

"I can't. If I do, Stuart has threatened to tell Father about my indiscretion with Ernest Remington and pregnancy prior to our marriage."

"What if he does? It's in the past, Jael. Your father will not hate you. The family name wasn't dragged through another scandal. He will see your sacrifice and hopefully feel bad for it."

Jael considered this for a moment. "He might at that." She wiped her tears. "But if he doesn't . . ."

"Why would he not? I think he's endured enough of Stuart to know what kind of man he's dealing with. If you are the one to tell your father, then Stuart loses his power over you. He's convinced you won't be truthful—that you're too afraid of the consequences. I, on the other hand, know you to be quite strong and capable. The truth will set you free, just as the Bible states."

"I fear Stuart, Deborah. I fear what he might be capable of doing to . . . you. He's already tormenting your family."

"Don't you fret over us. God is our stronghold. Stuart has caused problems to be sure, but our hope is in the Lord."

"I wish I knew more about such things. My family was never all that religious."

"You don't have to be religious. Just know that God loves you—that He gave His Son, Jesus, to die for you. He wants to be there for you—to comfort you and encourage you. Trust Him, Jael. He will be faithful to you."

Her friend shook her head. "I don't know how God can help in this when Stuart is so very evil."

Deborah touched Jael's shoulder. "God is more powerful than the devil. He may have allowed him a certain amount of control over this world, but God will defeat Satan when all is said and done. We need only to stand fast. Don't be afraid to put your confidence in Him, Jael."

They both startled at the sound of footsteps on the porch. Jael grabbed Deborah. "The back door—hurry!"

They fled through the house and into the kitchen. "God be with you, Jael," Deborah said, giving her friend a quick embrace. "Write to me through Mara."

"I will. I promise."

Deborah heard Stuart bellowing his wife's name as she hurried out the back door. She ran from the house, turning to dodge behind one of the other houses and a small stand of trees. Deborah felt the pounding of her heart and paused a moment to settle herself. There was no sense in returning to her family in a panic.

She was focused on heading to Zed Perkins's house when she saw that Christopher's door was open. He was back. She knew he planned to come out to the house that evening, but she wanted to have some time alone with him first. Speaking with Jael about talking to her father made Deborah realize that facing her fears was the best advice she could give herself. It was time to be honest with Christopher—to explain her concerns, even if she wasn't entirely sure what they meant. Making her way across the road, Deborah knocked on the examination room door and opened it.

"Christopher?"

He looked up from restocking supplies in his bag. "What a pleasant surprise."

"I came into town with G.W. and Arjan. They're with Mr. Perkins. I wondered if we might talk."

Christopher came to her. "What's wrong?"

Deborah closed the door and leaned against it. "Why do you never ask me to join you on your medical calls?"

"What are you talking about? I didn't ask because . . . well, I presumed there was more than enough work to be done, what with my brothers and sisters at your place."

"And does that mean you expect me to remain there to take care of them?"

Christopher looked uncomfortable. "I . . . uh . . . well, I don't know what I expected. You know how worried I've been, trying to determine how I can provide for them. It's my responsibility."

Deborah felt sorry for him. "Christopher, my mother loves having the children there. This is something she has taken on and enjoys."

"And you want no part of it?"

"I didn't say that," she quickly countered.

Christopher reached for her hand. "I'm sorry if you felt slighted. I don't seem to be able to do anything right these days."

"Nonsense. It's not about me feeling slighted." Deborah drew a deep breath. "Christopher, I want to be a physician. I love medicine—you know that. I love you, as well. I just need to know that I can manage both at the same time."

"Why would that be difficult?"

"Children." She felt her chest tighten. "Ever since you returned home with the children, you've not asked me even once to accompany you. In fact, you've hardly said much of anything to me."

She could see the regret in his expression and held up her hand. "I didn't say these things so that you would apologize. I am saying this because it will affect our life together. If you expect me to stay at home and care for your brothers and sisters, then I can hardly be out there assisting you."

Christopher pulled up a stool and sat. "And what about after we're married?"

"I understand that your siblings will be a part of our future. They must have a home and care—especially the younger ones. In the fall, however, school will start and they will be busy with that."

"I see. And what about any children we might have?"

Deborah straightened her shoulders and tried to firm up her determination, but to her surprise, she broke into sobs. Knowing she'd completely ruined any chance to explain this without emotion, she buried her face in her hands.

Without a word, Christopher pulled her close. Deborah hated the way she was acting. How could she hope for him to take her seriously about helping him when she couldn't even discuss this openly without tears?

After a few moments, Christopher lifted her face to his. "Deborah, are you trying to tell me that you don't want my children—our children?"

"I . . . I . . . don't know." She gasped for breath. "I love you.

I know I . . . would . . . love our children. I . . . oh, I don't know what I'm . . . trying to say." She tried to pull away, but he held her fast.

"Deborah, calm down and listen to me. You can't turn away from me. We have to talk about this."

"I know." She drew a deep breath and tried her best to settle her nerves. "I'm so sorry. This has been troubling me for so long now."

Christopher looked at her oddly. "You've held this in all along while planning the wedding?"

She felt horrible. Nodding, she reached out to him. "I'm sorry. I was wrong. I was swept away in my desires and dreams. You're the reason I love medicine. I love you, Christopher. I don't want to lose you."

"Who said you would?" He shook his head. "Deborah, we can't keep such things from each other."

Deborah sniffed and he handed her a handkerchief. "I'm sorry. I know I was wrong. My mother told me that I couldn't even think of marrying you if I didn't trust you with the truth."

"And what is the truth?"

"I want to use my knowledge and training. I want to continue to learn from you, and I want to marry you. I'm afraid, however, that once we marry and I have a baby, it will all end. I can hardly follow you around to the mills and logging camps with a baby on my back."

He smiled. "If anyone could, it would be you." He reached up and pushed back damp strands of hair.

For several moments, neither said a word. They stood quietly gazing into each other's eyes. Deborah fought back her doubts. "When I left to attend the university, I did so out of a love for learning and a love for my family. I wanted to help with the business, and my father often said that it would be wonderful to have the help. I thought that meant that it was expected of me. Here I am again putting thoughts and feelings into your heart and mind that may or may not be true. Please forgive me."

He smiled. "Only if you forgive me first. I knew it was going to be a shock to bring home the children. I wanted to consult you—to figure it out together, but there was no time to contact you. I was uncertain as to how you might react. I knew five children would be rather daunting. Of course, Jimmy and Tommy don't need our attention like the others do. Even Darcy is pretty self-sufficient."

Deborah thought of the thirteen-year-old. "She's very much like I was at that age."

"You said," Christopher began thoughtfully, "rather . . . your brother said that I could stay in the cabin on your property."

"That's true."

"Would it be possible for us to stay there after we marry?" he asked.

"I believe so. At one time Lizzie and G.W. had planned to move into it, but Lizzie prefers the big house, and Mother loves having them there, as well. Since they added on, there's really no need to move into the cabin."

"Then perhaps we could live there. I don't know how big it is or if we could add space for the children, but if we could, perhaps we could open an office there. We could put out word that people could come and be treated there for their ills and injuries. If we have a baby, you could run the office when I need to go out to the mills. Would that be acceptable?"

"And I could continue to train and attend patients with you until we started to have children?" she asked, feeling her cheeks grow hot. Talking about marital intimacy was hardly something a proper lady did.

"Exactly. And perhaps by that time, the mill here will be reopened and the area will need a full-time doctor again."

Deborah nodded. "I would think so. Goodness, but I never considered that." She looked at him. "And you wouldn't mind? Are you sure?"

He pulled her back into his arms. "I'm quite certain. Marriage is about compromise and working together. It's also about being honest. Please don't keep things from me, Deborah. We can work through anything . . . together."

She relaxed against him and sighed. "I'm so sorry, Christopher. I'm going to do better, I promise. I've been so afraid that perhaps I didn't even want to be a mother—that I would be awful at the job."

He laughed. "You would make a remarkable mother, and if God blesses us with a child, I've no doubt you will love him or her just as you love me. Right now you're afraid, but I intend to help you get over your fears." He drew her fingers to his lips and kissed them gently. "I can be most persuasive." He kissed the back of her hand and glanced up.

Deborah felt her breath catch. Goodness, but he was so very handsome, and he loved her. She felt her heart skip a beat as Christopher touched his lips to hers. Deborah wrapped her hands around the back of his neck and sighed. Her mother was right. Honesty and openness was much better than holding secrets and fears in silence.

Chapter 16

Christopher handed Euphanel some money. "I want you to have it for the children. Deborah and I talked, and we're putting off the wedding trip."

Euphanel shook her head. "I wouldn't hear of it, Christopher. We're getting by just fine. We've been remaking old clothes and using up material on hand to see to their needs. The garden is producing in abundance, and G.W. and Arjan killed two hogs just last week and you brought in food not long ago. We have plenty to feed them and they're earning their keep—believe me." She threw him a broad smile. "You hang on to this money in case you need something."

"But you bought them new shoes. Those didn't come free. I

should have seen that they needed them, but it didn't even cross my mind."

Euphanel led him to a chair. The summer kitchen was hot and steamy from cooking, but Christopher barely noticed. He had far more on his mind. He'd tried everything he could to get a nice sum of money together, but folks were bad off. Those who could pay usually did so in trade—a chicken here, a sack of pecans there.

"You seem worried." Euphanel went back to the oven and peeked at her bread.

Christopher wasn't sure how to broach the subject of his fears with this woman. She would be his mother-in-law soon—at least he hoped she would—but Euphanel Vandermark was also strong and capable. She'd endured far more than taking on someone's orphaned children.

"There isn't much money to be made in this area," he finally said. "If the mill were back up and running, and if Albright hired me on to be the company doctor, then things would be better. Still, I can't see that happening."

Euphanel listened and nodded. "And it's hard to take on a wife and family without an income."

"Exactly. Deborah loves it here and I know she would hate to move, but it might be necessary."

"It happened that way for me, as well. I loved Georgia, and the last thing I wanted to do was move to Texas. Still, it was necessary for many reasons." She lifted a pot lid. Steam roiled from the pan and filled the air with the undeniable scent of molasses and brown sugar.

"Smells good," he told her.

"It's my special beans." She gave the pot a stir, then replaced the lid. "Secret recipe." She smiled and sat beside Christopher.

"Deborah will do what has to be done. My daughter is strong and knows that life is unpredictable. She is also determined to overcome obstacles."

"I know, but I don't want to be the one to take her from her family and all that she loves. It's bad enough I'd be saddling her with an instant family. She worries about how that will affect her ability to help me."

"I know. We talked. Christopher, you and I both know that life doesn't always look the way we think it should, especially when you're out of step with the times. Deborah has always been that way. She wants to be the Proverbs thirty-one woman—doing it all—working hard—providing for her family—using her mind. Yet society today puts many obstacles in her way."

Christopher worried the brim of his straw hat. "I want to give her a good life. I want to make her dreams come true. I know she longs to practice medicine and that she loves helping people. We talked about this the other day, and I was confident things would work out."

"But now you're not?"

"Well, there isn't enough work to keep me busy. If I can't earn a living here . . . well . . . we'll have to move to a bigger town."

Euphanel reached over and patted his arm. "I'd hate to see you go, but you have to do what's right for you and your family."

"But you don't understand. If we moved to a bigger town, then I'd definitely need Deborah to take care of the younger children. I had a solution in mind if we stayed here, and part of that depended on having family nearby. I knew you and Lizzie would help Deborah out if we were to have children—especially if Deborah continued to practice medicine. Moving away wouldn't allow for that."

"I see your point." Euphanel leaned back and wiped her face with the hem of her apron. "Have you prayed about this?"

"Until I'm all out of words." He turned to face her. "I love your daughter."

Euphanel smiled. "I know that full well."

"But I cannot condemn her to a life that she would hate, just to marry her. That would be a more selfish act than I could live with."

"Christopher, you need to let her be the judge of that. Lay out the situation and let her know what has to be. If she decides to walk away, then that's her choice."

He shook his head and dropped his gaze to the floor. "I just don't know if I can live without her."

On Saturday evening, when everyone was gathered informally in the living room, Jimmy announced that he'd arranged with Mr. Huebner to take a test to show that he qualified to graduate from high school. The discussion about the week had already been lively, but when Jimmy told them about his plans, the conversation took on a whole new enthusiasm.

"Your folks would no doubt be mighty proud," Arjan said.

Jimmy nodded. "Ma wanted me to go on with my studies like Christopher did." He looked to his brother and grinned. "Of course, I don't have plans to deal with blood and guts."

"Can we go outside and play with the puppies?" Jonah asked.

"Please? It's still light," Emma added.

Mother checked the clock on the wall. "You can go for just a few minutes. I'll send Darcy to come get you when your bath water is ready. Remember, tomorrow is church, and we need to look our best."

"I hate havin' a bath," Jonah said, shaking his head as he stalked toward the door. "I'm not that dirty."

Mother and Lizzie exchanged a smile with Deborah. The boy was so covered in dust he might very well turn the bath water to mud.

"Have you thought about what you want to study if you go on to college?" G.W. asked Jimmy once the younger children were gone.

"I love numbers. Anything to do with mathematics," he replied.

"And you just have to pass a test in order to move ahead?" Arjan asked.

"Yes. It'll show that I've learned all that I need to know in order to go to the university. Mr. Huebner said he's more than confident I'll pass. Especially in mathematics. He says I'm well ahead of him in that." Jimmy's smile revealed his pride. "He said if the test shows I've done just as well in my other subjects, I can attend a university next fall. Of course, dependin' on the college, I'll probably have to take a test for them, too, but Mr. Huebner said if I pass one, I can prob'ly pass the other."

"That's wonderful news," Deborah said. "I am so happy for you. I know you'll enjoy college—I certainly did, and the test I had to take was not all that difficult."

"Mr. Huebner says there are some great schools here in Texas, but I think I'd like to go back East. Those schools have been around for a lot longer and have more to offer. I want to teach college one day."

"That's an admirable career," Mother said.

Christopher remained silent, and Deborah found that strange. "What do you think of all of this?" she asked him.

All attention turned to the doctor. Christopher looked almost startled by the question. "I am very happy that Jimmy is of a mind to follow his dreams." He looked to Tommy. "I'm proud of what Tommy has accomplished, as well."

"I sure don't want to go to college. I just want to work in logging. I like working outside—it's so much better than the work we had in town. In fact, I don't want to go back to school at all. I was told that here, I don't have to. Besides, with a job I can help take care of the family."

"We will discuss that later," Christopher told him. Tommy shrugged but said nothing more.

Deborah knew Tommy's idea wouldn't bode well with Christopher. The younger Kelleher had spent only a short time in the logging industry and had no idea of the dangers involved. Christopher, on the other hand, knew them only too well. She tried to give Christopher a smile, but he wasn't looking at her. In fact, despite the fact he was sitting beside her, Christopher was quite far away. He seemed troubled; maybe he was worried about Jimmy leaving. Maybe he thought his brother wasn't ready to face the world.

Mother got to her feet. "I'm going to get the bath water ready. Darcy, would you please go call Jonah and Emma back to the house?"

Darcy had stretched out on the rug to study an atlas. She glanced up with a yawn. "Yes, ma'am," she answered and closed the book. She got to her feet, mindful of the new skirt she'd actually helped to make. "But they won't like it."

Everyone chuckled. Deborah knew the girl was right.

"Christopher, why don't you spend the night here? Use the cabin. I know you prefer to go back to town and keep an eye on what's yours, but one night surely won't be too great a risk," Arjan told him. "We could all head in to church together in the mornin'." He smiled at Deborah. "And if you had a mind to do a little spoonin' on the front porch, well, we'd make sure to keep the lights down low."

Lizzie giggled and G.W. nudged her. "If they don't take up the offer, we just might. Since the twins are already asleep, we could use a little spoonin'."

Deborah got to her feet and held her hand out to Christopher. "Oh, no you don't. The porch is ours. Go find another place to court your wife."

One by one, the family dispersed. Deborah waited until the silence hummed in her ears. "Are you coming?"

He looked up and nodded. Without a word, he got to his feet and took hold of her hand. Deborah drew him out to the porch. "Are you going to tell me what's wrong?"

Christopher looked at her for a moment, then let go his hold. Walking away a few paces, he planted his hands on the porch rail and stared off into the growing darkness.

Deborah followed. "Christopher, what's going on? Why are you so distraught?"

He heaved a heavy sigh. "I just don't know how to make it all work."

"What are you talking about?"

"Jimmy and school. The family . . . us."

She grasped his arms and forced Christopher to face her. He didn't resist, but she could see by the look on his face his reluctance to discuss the matter.

"I'm not sure I understand, but I do know that secrets between us are no good."

He nodded. "I know, and maybe that's why this is so hard."

"Please sit with me. No harm can come from discussion."

Christopher allowed her to lead the way again and took a

seat beside her on the swing. "I'm afraid harm might come from this one. Or at least disappointment."

Deborah shuddered and rubbed her hands against her arms. Christopher didn't seem to notice, however, and for that she was glad. Was he upset with her? Was he only now really thinking about what she'd said regarding children and her desire to be a doctor? Did he regret having asked her to marry him?

She tried to ease into the conversation. "Jimmy seemed quite excited about attending a university."

He nodded. "But I don't know how I could ever afford to send him—and yet, I promised."

"That's what this is all about?" she asked, trying not to sound too hopeful.

"Partly." He leaned back against the wooden frame of the swing. "I can't seem to make any money. Folks around here—what few there are—want to trade goods for doctoring. They're as bad off as the rest of us because of the mill being destroyed."

"But I thought you were having a better time of it, riding out to the surrounding areas."

He shook his head. "Folks are suffering, Deborah. The bad winter up north helped some of the cattlemen to sell their stock, but many did so either in trade or selling on agreement. Not much cash actually changed hands."

A sinking feeling came over Deborah. He wanted to leave this area—to move elsewhere. He knew she wouldn't like it, and he was anticipating the conflict. For a moment, she felt guilty. This was because of her, not Jimmy. She was the one who'd made it clear she didn't want to leave Perkinsville again. She was the one who wanted to practice at his side when there wasn't enough work for one doctor, much less two.

"And now Jimmy wants to go to school back East. How

could I ever help him with that when I can't even afford to take care of food and clothes—or put a roof over their heads? I was almost relieved that Tommy wanted nothing more than to go to work and help with expenses."

Questions wormed their way to the front of her thoughts, but she dared not give them voice: Was he going to tell her they needed to leave Perkinsville? Would he suggest they all move east so that he could practice medicine and Jimmy could attend school? Did he want to forget about the wedding—put aside their love until the financial issues could be resolved?

She longed for answers and feared them at the same time.

"I don't know what we're to do, Deborah. I can't rely upon your folks' charity forever. The children seem happy—happier than I figured they'd be having just lost Ma and Da." He shook his head. "I know that has to do with the love your mother has given them. They need someone like her—not me."

"Are you actually thinking of giving them up to be adopted? You would send them to an orphanage?" Deborah asked. While she didn't particularly relish the idea of the responsibility right now, she certainly didn't want the family split up or sent to strangers.

"I don't know. I don't know what they need."

"They need you. They need each other. You can't send them away," she said, sounding harsher than she'd intended. She reached out to touch him, but he surprised her by pulling back and getting to his feet.

"That's the problem. Don't you see? There is no answer here. Nothing that will satisfy everyone. You don't want to move away. The children don't want to be separated. Jimmy wants to go to college, and there is nothing here to help with any of our needs.

Tommy is only fifteen, yet he has better chances at making a living than I do!"

He stormed off the porch, leaving Deborah to stare after him, her mouth open. She'd never known Christopher to act in such a fashion. She wanted to run after him, but perhaps it would be better to wait until he cooled off. He probably just wanted to take a walk and think through matters.

Instead, she was shocked a few minutes later when Christopher came riding past the house, headed for town. He was leaving. Without saying a word to her or anyone else, Christopher was going back to Perkinsville.

Was he giving up? Did he just need to be alone?

Deborah walked to the edge of the porch and hugged her arms close. What was happening to her perfect dream—the dream of practicing medicine at her husband's side? The dream of living in this community and helping the people she loved? Hope flickered like a dying ember.

She felt rather ill as answers crept into her mind. She had deluded herself. There was no dream. Her desires were too many, and she could not have them all.

Foolish woman, a voice condemned from within. *You refused to stay in your place and do what was expected. You had to have an education and take on more responsibility than anyone wanted you to have. People tried to advise you, but you wouldn't hear them, and now you'll have no chance for happiness unless you are willing to give up your own way.*

"But can I be happy in compromising what I believe to be so very important?"

She stared into the darkness, her gaze still fixed on the road. There was a slim chance that Christopher might come back. But even if he did, what could she say? What could either of them do to make this right?

Chapter 17

Although Stuart and Jael were in attendance at church the following morning, Deborah had no chance to speak to her friend. Stuart ushered Jael in after the singing began, and as soon as Pastor Shattuck said the last amen, the Albrights quickly walked from the building. Deborah found it curious that they should even be there. After all, neither were particularly interested in church, and Stuart even boasted of despising religious practices. Their presence had taken Deborah's focus all morning, along with her worries about Christopher. He hadn't even shown up for the service.

"Where's Christopher?" Darcy asked as they left the building.

"I don't know," Deborah admitted. "I thought he would be here."

"Maybe he's sick. You should go check on him," the astute thirteen-year-old suggested.

Deborah wanted to do just that, but thought better of it. "I'll have Jimmy and Tommy go see if he's at the house. Could be he was called out to attend to someone who's sick."

Darcy nodded. "I'll get the boys." She took off before Deborah could change her mind.

Fanning herself against the growing heat of the day, Deborah watched Zed Perkins talk in low hushed tones with her brother and stepfather in the shade of a tree. His brows were knit together and his head downcast. Arjan put his arm around the older man's shoulders. No doubt this had to do with Stuart and his plans to buy out Perkins's interest in the sawmill town.

"Here they are," Darcy said, pointing to Jimmy and Tommy. "I told them we were afraid Christopher might be sick."

Deborah looked to Jimmy and smiled. "Could you two just go over to his house and check? He might have gone out on a call, but if he's not feeling well, then I want to be able to help him."

"Sure. We'll go," Jimmy declared. "Come on, Tom." They made their way through the folks lingering in the churchyard.

Looking up, Deborah saw G.W. motion her over. Deborah crossed the space and joined her brother and the other men. "What's wrong?" she asked at the sight of their somber faces.

"Albright is forcing Zed out," Arjan said in a whisper. "It's worse than we figured."

Deborah could imagine that anything having to do with Stuart would only benefit one person—Stuart. "How so?"

Zed shook his head. "Albright says I owe more than I have assets to support. He says there's not much I bring to the table anymore." He looked to the ground. "He says he's taking over the business affairs, the buildings and inventory that's remaining, and that he'll give me only a small amount of money in return. This is because of all the money I owe him for the loan on the mill."

"But I thought," Deborah interjected, "that he had insurance on the mill and had already been reimbursed for the costs involved. He should have paid the loan off with that money."

"It was his insurance though," Arjan replied. "Not Zed's. He can do with it as he pleases."

"But surely the bank would expect him to repay them," Deborah countered.

"The loan wasn't through the bank," Zed explained. "It was a personal loan between me and them—Albright and Longstreet. They took on the amount I owed the bank and paid it off. That's why they have the controllin' say over what happens now."

Deborah looked to her brother. "We should get ahold of Lizzie's father and let him know what's happening."

Zed shook his head sadly. "I already talked to a lawyer in Lufkin. He said that Albright has some big city lawyers handlin' things for him and that they've got folks runnin' scared—seems politics are involved. It's pretty well figured that he's got some of the judges in his pockets, too. That's why he's not afraid to do whatever he wants. It's why he's treatin' you folks like he is—he ain't afraid of being told no."

"I can believe that just from what he said when I mentioned the idea of us suing him for breach of contract," G.W. affirmed. "He made it clear that we'd be the ones regrettin' it."

Deborah fanned herself all the more furiously. "It's not right. This state used to be better than that. You could count on folks to do what was decent and lawful."

"Money makes folks whistle a different tune," Arjan said in disgust.

"And not havin' money leaves you with no choice but to

dance to the song bein' whistled," Zed said with great sorrow in his voice. "I never thought I'd see this day. Rachel and me . . . well, we figured we'd be passin' the business on to our boys about now. We figured that we'd be takin' life a little easier. That's not even possible now. We'll have to move, and I'll have to find work. Sawmilling is all I know."

"What about startin' up again?" Arjan asked. "If you're free of Albright, then you could put your own business together, and he'd have no say in the matter."

"I don't have the money for it. Once Albright is done with me, I'll be lucky to have the clothes on my back."

Deborah felt consumed by sadness and guilt. Her stomach tightened. If she hadn't encouraged Lizzie to leave Stuart, none of this would be happening. "I'm so sorry, Mr. Perkins. I still say we need to talk to Lizzie's father. He might have some suggestions."

"You can talk to him if you'd like," Zed said, "but I figure the answer will be the same. Now, if you'll excuse me, I reckon I'd best collect Rachel and head home. We need to spend some time in prayer about what to do next." The man headed for his wife after shaking hands with G.W. and Arjan, shoulders slumped forward in defeat and his head down.

"That poor man. I cannot believe Stuart will be allowed to get away with this," Deborah said, pushing down her anger. "Can't we do something?"

"You know we can't. Our hands are tied," her brother replied. "Albright knows that better than anyone 'cause he's the one who tied 'em."

"But surely we know some honest people who could help. Not everyone can be bought."

"Christopher isn't at the house," Jimmy said from behind

her. Deborah turned and met the boy's shrug. "Guess he's out doctoring like you said."

Deborah hoped that was all he was doing. She had a bad feeling about the way things had been left between them. It wasn't like Christopher to lose his temper and leave without a word.

She thanked Jimmy and made her way out of the church. Outside, the slight breeze made things marginally cooler than inside. Deborah was grateful she'd worn her lightest gown. The yellow gingham had been sewn into a fetching creation that brought many compliments, but at this moment Deborah would have just as soon jumped into the millpond—dress and all.

"Goodness, but if it's this warm in May," Olivia Huebner said as she joined Deborah, "imagine what the rest of the summer will hold in store."

"I'd rather not," Deborah replied. "I was just thinking of how nice it would be to go swimming."

Mrs. Huebner nodded. "I remember days when I was just a girl. We would slip off—just me and my sisters—and strip down to our unmentionables and go swimming in the creek by our place." She gave a nervous laugh. "I don't suppose I would want to share that with just anyone."

Deborah smiled. Mrs. Huebner was the epitome of propriety and, no doubt, figured such a comment might ruin her reputation. "Your secret is safe with me. I've been guilty of the very same thing, only it was girlfriends instead of sisters."

Over by the wagon, Mother laughed and chased after Jonah. Olivia and Deborah seemed to catch sight of her at the same time. Mother had never seemed happier—at least she hadn't laughed this much in a long time.

"You know, I think those children have taken twenty years of longing off your mother's age."

"What do you mean?" Deborah asked. She had never thought of her mother as longing for anything.

"Well, you know she always wanted more children. She could only have the three of you—oh, there was the other baby that died before you were born."

Deborah nodded. "Yes, our sister Janna." The infant had been stillborn, and Mother seldom talked about her. In fact, it wasn't until Lizzie found out that she had been the twin of a stillborn child that Mother spoke openly of the matter.

"Well, she couldn't bear any more children after you were born, and I know it bothered her a great deal. She wanted a large family, and for many years, it tormented her. I suppose now with Dr. Kelleher's siblings, she can enjoy mothering young ones again."

Deborah turned her attention back to where her mother was now swinging Jonah by the arms. She twirled in a circle; both of them laughed.

"I never knew," Deborah murmured.

Mrs. Huebner waggled her finger at Deborah's face. "Well, don't you be tellin' her that I told you. I wouldn't want her to think I was gossiping."

"No, ma'am. I won't mention it."

"She does seem mighty happy," Mrs. Huebner added. "Oh, there's Curtis. I must run along now. Try to stay cool."

"You, too, Miz Huebner."

Deborah watched Mr. Huebner take his wife by the arm and walk down the road toward their house. She then returned her attention to Mother. She wasn't that old. *Goodness*, Deborah thought. *Mother will be but forty-five at the end of June.*

"You looks to be ponderin' deep thoughts," Sissy said, coming to stand beside Deborah.

"I was just thinking about Mama and how she'll be forty-five next month."

Sissy nodded. "Have to have a nice party for her. 'Course, I was reckonin' we'd have a weddin' in June."

"I don't know if that's going to happen."

"Is there troubles betwixt you and the doc?" Sissy asked.

With a sigh, Deborah found herself explaining to the older woman what had happened. "I think he's more worried about my feelings than anything. He knows I have no desire to leave this place."

"Women go where they men go. That be the way of things. Iffen you ain't of a mind to be a wife and let him lead, you best not marry."

Her words hit Deborah hard. "I suppose I'm afraid," she said honestly. Speaking the truth aloud didn't come easy. "I love him so much, but I worry that I won't be a good wife. Especially since I'm such an unconventional woman."

"Bah! You follow the Lord, and you be good 'nuf. It be God's way what matters—not ours. The good Lord ne'r said you couldn't work with your hands; fact is, He 'spects you to. But He 'spects you to trust Him first."

"I know you're right," Deborah said. She gave Sissy a brief hug. "You always seem to know the right thing to say. Sometimes I feel so foolish. Here I have all this book knowledge and yet I struggle."

"Book-knowing and heart-knowing be two different things, Miss Deborah. Bein' smart ain't the same as usin' your smarts." Sissy gave her a big smile. "I had to learn that the hard way—sounds like it be the same for you."

Deborah nodded. "I guess so, but I'm hoping to change for the better."

"The good Lord be all about that." Sissy pointed. "Looks like your mama is loadin' up."

"Deborah!" Mara called, making her way from the church. "Hold up, please."

"You go ahead, Sissy. I'll be right there." She crossed the distance to meet Mara. "What's wrong?"

"Nothing. I just wondered if it would be all right to pay you all a visit tomorrow and discuss the plans for Rob's birthday party."

"Mother is just over there at the wagon. Why don't we go ask her?"

Mara leaned closer as they walked. "I saw that Mr. Albright pulled his wife out of church before she could speak to anyone. Such a pity he's so harsh with her."

"I know. I'm praying things might change for the better. Jael wants a divorce, and you know what kind of ostracizing that could bring. She doesn't even care, she's so miserable," Deborah said, careful to make sure no one else overheard. "Please pray for her. I don't know for sure what God would have her do, but she's so very unhappy."

"We're nearly ready," Mother announced as Arjan helped her into the wagon. "Are you riding with us or G.W. and Lizzie?"

"I'll come with you," Deborah replied. "However, we have a question for you. Mara wants to know if she might visit us tomorrow and discuss ideas for throwing Rob a surprise birthday party."

Mother beamed. "I would like that very much. Please do come whenever is convenient."

"Thank you, Mrs. Vandermark. I'll speak to Father and see when he might be available to bring me out."

"You are both more than welcome to join us for dinner. We'll eat around noon."

"I'll tell him. I'm sure he'd enjoy that," Mara said. "Until tomorrow."

Deborah gave her a brief hug, then climbed into the back of the wagon unassisted and took a seat beside Darcy. "God go with you," Deborah told Mara.

"And with you."

Darcy looked up at Deborah. "Do you really think God goes with us when we say that?"

The question was simple enough, but it took Deborah by surprise. "I do," she said as the wagon began to move out. "In fact, I think He goes with us whether we say it or not. Don't you?"

Shrugging, the girl looked away. "Who can say? We can't order God around like that."

Deborah smiled. "I don't think I've ever considered it ordering God around, but I can understand why you might. Truly, we're just reminding each other to walk in God's ways, and if we do that—we know He's with us."

Chapter 18

Christopher looked at the note left at his door. He had presumed it would be from Deborah; instead, he found it a summons from Stuart Albright. Christopher figured Albright was going to demand he clear out. Zed had warned him to expect it, and so Christopher had already been hard at work, crating up his personal effects. Nevertheless, he left his horse hitched outside the office and made his way to hear what the man had to say.

As he arrived at the Albright house, Christopher found Stuart sitting on the front porch. He appeared to be engrossed in a handful of papers. He glanced up and greeted Christopher with an expression void of emotion.

"Dr. Kelleher, I'm glad you could finally make it over."

"Had to set a broken arm. What did you want to see me about?"

"I would like you out of the infirmary by tomorrow evening."

"All right."

Stuart's face pinched, as though he sought to identify a foreign odor. "All right? No questions? No complaints?"

Christopher shrugged. "Would it help if I did?"

Laughing, Stuart shook his head. "No. It wouldn't change my mind, if that's what you wonder."

"Is that all you wanted?" Christopher asked, turning to move back down the steps.

"As a matter of fact, it's not. I have something else to discuss—an offer, actually."

Christopher could hardly imagine what Albright would want to propose. "What did you have in mind?"

Stuart gave a smug smile. "Why don't you take a seat and I'll get right to the point."

Apprehension washed over Christopher. He briefly reconsidered. But the worries of the future compelled him to weigh all possibilities. All night and morning he had prayed that God would show him an answer. He tried not to look too eager, however, and ambled casually over to where Albright sat.

Sitting, Christopher raised a brow in question. "So?"

"I have in mind to give you a great deal of money." Stuart put his papers on the table between their chairs. "Does that surprise you?"

"Do you have to ask? Of course it surprises me," Christopher replied. "You give me twenty-four hours to vacate my residence, and now you want to give me money. Why shouldn't I be surprised?"

"Well put," Stuart said. "I like a man who isn't afraid to

speak his mind. My proposal will make you as wealthy as you are forthright. Given that you have five other people dependent upon you for their well-being, I think you'll find this most lucrative. Perhaps one could even say an answer to prayer."

Suspicion tensed Christopher's muscles. Stuart Albright had proven himself to be a man who did nothing out of the goodness of his heart. Albright wanted something—wanted it badly enough to subject himself to this conversation.

"What is it you want, Albright?"

"It's very simple, really. I will pay you two thousand dollars to do exactly as I say."

Christopher couldn't imagine ever having that much money in his hand at one time. He knew the deed Albright would request for that amount would, no doubt, be dear. "Get to the point. What is it you want?"

Stuart gave a small chuckle. "Leave this area and never return."

The demand confused Christopher. Albright had to know that with no steady work to be had, such an idea would have already surfaced in the doctor's mind. Christopher needed to make a living now more than ever.

"And where did you have in mind that I should go?"

"I don't care," Stuart replied. "Take your siblings and go back to Kansas City, for all it matters."

"And if I do that, you'll give me two thousand dollars? Just for taking my family away from here?"

"Well, there is one other requirement."

Of course. Christopher nodded and looked Albright in the eye. "And that would be what?"

"Break your engagement with Deborah Vandermark. Leave her and agree to never marry her."

The words fell like a lead weight, crushing any hope that

Christopher might have taken the man up on his offer. Christopher rose and walked down the porch steps. He had reached the walkway when Stuart finally called out to him.

"Two thousand dollars cash is a lot to walk away from."

Christopher turned. "You're quite mad, Albright. If you honestly think to buy me off so that you can perpetuate your vengeance on the Vandermark family, you have another think coming."

"Three thousand." Stuart's voice bore no hint of anxiety.

"No." Christopher started walking toward home.

Albright came to the side of the porch. "Five thousand dollars. That's my final offer."

It was a great deal of money, more than Christopher could ever have imagined. He looked hard at Albright and shook his head. "I'm glad it's your last offer, because my honor and love aren't for sale."

Deborah had returned from swimming with the children only a few moments earlier and was still trying to fix her wet hair into a long single plait. Her heart leapt and sank when she saw Christopher ride into the yard, two large carpetbags hanging over his saddle horn. With nimble twists and tucks, she finally secured the braid and got to her feet to go to him.

Arjan greeted Christopher first and offered to take the horse to the barn for him. Deborah was glad when Christopher agreed. He took the bags from the saddle and dropped them on the ground. She wanted to ask about them immediately, but she remained silent.

He turned and gave her a sheepish smile. "I'm back."

"I see that," she said, returning his grin. "I missed you at church."

"Had a broken arm to set."

Deborah nodded and cast a glance at the bags, then back to his face. Christopher shrugged. "Albright kicked me out. I'm supposed to vacate the property by tomorrow."

"Oh, Christopher, I am sorry. G.W. is more than willing for you to take over the cabin. You can let folks know that you're setting up there. We'll get the word out."

He stepped forward and reached up to touch her cheek. "I'm sorry for the way I behaved."

"I know. I'm sorry, too. You've been carrying the weight of all this responsibility and I've done nothing to relieve your mind. I haven't been a very good example."

"In what way?"

She sighed. "I haven't exactly been allowing you to lead in our courtship. A wife should be obedient and let her husband direct their plans. I didn't do that."

"You aren't yet a wife," he replied.

"Are you rescinding your offer?" she asked, surprising herself.

Christopher appeared just as surprised. In fact, he looked almost like he'd been caught doing something wrong. Was he contemplating that very idea? Had she forced him to comment on it before he was ready?

"I see I've perhaps touched on a nerve." She started to go, but he took hold of her arm.

"Don't go. If I seem awkward in dealing with your question, it's just that . . . well, Stuart Albright asked me to do just that not even an hour ago."

"What?" Deborah could scarcely believe her ears. "Stuart asked you to end our engagement?"

"He did. In fact, he offered me five thousand dollars," Christopher said, grinning. "I should have thanked him, because, frankly, it put me in a much better frame of mind."

Deborah didn't know whether to be offended or happy. She looked at him and shook her head. "Five thousand dollars?"

Goodness, but that would resolve a world of problems. It would be enough to set up house elsewhere and establish his medical clinic. Why, with that much money, he could afford to send Jimmy to the university of his choice.

"He must really hate me."

"Not as much as I love you," Christopher said. "He helped me to realize that my moping about money was foolish. Money certainly isn't anything compared to love. Oh, a person still needs to make a wage and support his family. But I can do that without worrying about the amount of cash it yields."

"But that's a great deal of money, Christopher." What if they married and he later regretted not having taken it? Dread snaked through her veins like ice water. It left her feeling rather cold and clammy. She wasn't a woman given to fainting, but suddenly it seemed like a possibility.

As if reading her mind, he steadied her shoulders. "Deborah Vandermark. You surprise me. You're the one who has been trying to get me to see how God handles all things—even our financial needs."

She drew a deep breath to clear her head. "I know. I suppose it's just that . . . well, you were so angry at me last night."

"No I wasn't. You had nothing to do with it—well, very little. I was upset with myself. I was frustrated that I couldn't seem to find a way out of this. I spent most of the night praying and asking God to reveal the truth to me—and when Stuart Albright gave me his proposal, it was like God had done just that.

"I could see the matter clearly, Deborah. It was such a freeing moment. I was wrestling with the wrong things. Remember those verses in Ephesians? The ones Pastor Shattuck preached on here a while back?"

She remembered them very well. "Ephesians six."

"Yes, it says we aren't wrestling with flesh and blood, but with the powers of darkness." He shook his head. "I don't remember the exact words, but the principle is fixed in my mind—at least it is after dealing with Albright. My battle isn't for money or patients or a nice place to set up an office. It's about putting the future in God's hands and trusting that He will supply our needs."

Deborah knew that what he said was right, but she couldn't shake the feeling that she was keeping Christopher from a much-needed answer to his prayers. She looked at the ground to hide the tears that came to her eyes.

He put his arm around her. "Besides, five thousand dollars would never come close to the value of the love I feel for you. Now, if he'd offered ten . . ."

Deborah snapped her head up to meet his grin. How could he tease about something so important? Albright offered no mere pittance. Five thousand dollars was more money than most folks ever saw.

"How can you—" she started, but Christopher put his finger to her lips.

"Nothing equals the love I feel for you. I'm sorry I ever acted in a way that suggested otherwise."

It wasn't easy to remind herself that she'd been the one who'd had misgivings about their love—all based upon her fear of how children might interfere with her plans. What a fool she'd been.

"I love you, Deborah. I want you to be my wife—to share my life," he said, tracing the line of her jaw.

"I want that more than anything," she replied, finally knowing that it was the absolute truth. "I love you, too. I guess we've both allowed our fears to cast a shadow on our love. Oh, Christopher, I am so sorry for the way I've behaved."

He kissed her with such tenderness that Deborah felt lightheaded and swayed in his arms. Perhaps it was just the heat, but there was no denying this man had power over her.

"Mama Euphanel, can I have another piece of chocolate cake?" Emma asked.

Jonah nodded in a most enthusiastic manner. "Me too, Mama Yoonell. With lots of gravy on top."

"It's not gravy," Emma corrected. "It's toffee sauce. And her name is Yoo-fan-el—Mama Euphanel."

Mother looked at the children and then to Christopher. "I . . . uh . . . I don't know what to say. I never . . ." She stammered into silence and a dark shade of crimson flooded her cheeks.

Deborah thought it charming that Emma had addressed her in such a manner, but she could understand her mother's surprise. Christopher, too, seemed to understand.

"I would suggest just a little piece—perhaps they could share another piece of cake." He gave Mother a wink. "That way, Mama Euphanel, I can have another whole piece to myself."

"Me too," Jimmy chimed in.

"Well, you don't get it all," Tommy declared. "I want more, too."

It was wonderful how easily the situation resolved itself. Mother got up without another word and brought the cake plate into the dining room. She began slicing additional helpings while the others passed their plates to her.

Deborah reached over to squeeze Christopher's hand, but got his thigh instead.

"What!" he fairly yelled, and gave a start as if he'd sat on a hot coal. The plate he was planning to hand to Mother was all but thrown into the air.

Deborah nearly upended her chair in backing away. Now everyone turned to look at them, only making matters worse. She stared in silent horror that they should all know what had just taken place.

"What's wrong?" Arjan asked.

Christopher quickly recovered. "It's nothing. I was just startled. Thought maybe a spider had come to share my cake."

"You scared of spiders, *too*?" Jonah asked. "Just like me?"

"And me," Emma said, shuddering for emphasis.

"Not me," Darcy declared. "I think they're amazing. I saw a really big one the other day in the barn."

"Well, you need to be careful," Mother chided. "There are a great many poisonous insects and snakes here in Texas. I wouldn't want you to get sick from a bite."

"She's right. Spiders can be very dangerous," Christopher said, catching a sidelong glance at Deborah. "Often they appear without warning."

Deborah thought she might well die of embarrassment. She stared at her hand, still feeling the touch of his thigh beneath her fingers.

"Did you get bit?" Emma asked. "You keep looking at your hand."

Snapping her head up to meet everyone's intent stare, Deborah shook her head. "No. No, it's fine."

"I should probably check it," Christopher said, reaching over to take hold of her.

He was only making this that much harder. Deborah squirmed in her seat, but Christopher refused to let go of her.

"There are jumping spiders," Tommy offered. "I heard about them at school last year."

Christopher nodded. "Perhaps that was what I was thinking of just now."

Deborah wished she could find some excuse to leave. Of course, that would only serve to bring more unwanted attention.

"So when are you two gonna get around to havin' that weddin'?" G.W. asked, putting his arm casually around Lizzie's shoulders.

"That's a very good question. In fact, it's one that I was kind of hoping to resolve myself." Christopher turned to Deborah. "Why don't we take a little walk—check out my new home?"

"Be sure and look for spiders," Jonah instructed.

Christopher gave Deborah a wicked grin. "I would very much like to look for spiders."

Deborah felt her eyes widen and her throat tighten. Goodness, but would he ever stop teasing her about this?

Mother gave the final piece of cake to Arjan. "The cabin is all aired out, and I took fresh linens and bedding out there. I doubt you'll see any spiders. You, of course, will take your meals with us, Christopher."

"I'd like to see anyone stop me," he said, finishing the last bit of cake on his plate.

Deborah had never seen anyone gulp down food so fast, but even now, Christopher was pushing back his chair. "Will you accompany me? We can pick our wedding date."

"Now, I don't want to sound harsh," Arjan said, picking up his fork, "but if she's not back here in fifteen minutes, I'm gonna send the children over to see what's keepin' her."

"If there are spiders," Darcy said, "I can help you kill them. Just come and get me."

"I will do that, sister of mine." Christopher got to his feet and extended his hand to Deborah. "Fifteen minutes is more than enough time. If she can't make up her mind on a date in that span, I'll fix it myself."

Arjan laughed and nodded. "Go on, then."

Deborah had no chance to refuse. Christopher quickly hurried them out of the dining room and into the kitchen. From there, they slipped out the side door. By the time they cleared the back of the house and were half way to the cabin, Christopher burst into laughter and lifted Deborah to whirl her in a circle.

"You are quite the catch, Miss Vandermark."

Deborah felt her cheeks grow hot again as Christopher returned her to her feet and pulled her close. "I think you are the most charming woman I've ever met."

"Because I grabbed your leg instead of your hand?"

He laughed again and kissed her nose. "No, because you were so embarrassed by it. For a physician well acquainted with the anatomy, I am rather surprised, however, that you should mistake one part for the other."

"You moved your hand to pick up your plate. It's a wonder you didn't drop it," she said, clinging to what little self-respect she had left. "And then you start speaking about spiders, of all things."

"Would you rather I had pointed out your firm hold on my thigh? Of course, I could have told the family that you couldn't help yourself—that you were quite overpowered by your attraction to me." He put his finger to his chin. "No, I don't suppose that would have gone over all that well. Your brother would probably have refused to let me stay anywhere on this property if he'd thought that was the case."

"Oh, you are impossible," she said, moving away from him to head back to the house.

Christopher moved quickly, however, and pulled her back against him. "Darling, you need never be embarrassed around me. I might tease you, and I might correct your medical skills, but I would fight to the death to defend you and keep you from shame."

Deborah felt his arms tighten around her and leaned back against him with a sigh. How she loved this man. "June the eleventh," she said in a barely audible voice.

"June eleventh? What about it?"

"That will be our wedding day."

He loosened his hold and turned her to face him. "But that's over three weeks away. Do we have to wait so long?"

She smiled and gently brushed his lips with her finger. "The time will fly by. You'll see."

He sighed and nodded. "I suppose if that's the way it must be." He paused and cocked his head toward the cabin. "In the meantime, we could look for spiders."

Deborah pulled away and started back for the house. "I'll get Darcy to help you." His laughter rang in her ears, and Deborah couldn't help but smile.

Chapter 19

Deborah stood back as Zed and Pastor Shattuck loaded the last crate of Christopher's books onto the wagon. Mara strolled out of the house with a heavy brown coat and came to Deborah.

"Dr. Kelleher asked that you pack this in the wagon. He doubts he'll ever need it down here, but figures it's too good of a coat to leave behind."

Deborah laughed and took the piece. "Is that everything?"

"It's just down to a bit of cleaning now, and I told Dr. Kelleher I would handle that for him."

"How kind. You certainly don't have to, though. I offered to stay behind and handle it." Deborah tucked the coat into an open crate half filled with books. "There, that ought to ride all right."

Mara nodded. "I didn't have anything special going on today and figured you would have plenty to do at the other end, setting things up."

Deborah considered the idea for a moment. "You're probably right. I suppose if Christopher is all right with it, then I certainly will not argue." She smiled. "Have you heard that we set the wedding date—again?"

"I was going to ask."

"June the eleventh," Deborah said without further prompting. "I figure Rob will be home and that will make it all the more special."

"Oh, that is wonderful. Do you suppose . . . I mean . . . would you be offended if we also celebrated his birthday that day—after the wedding sometime?" Mara toyed with a single long black braid of hair. "I suppose that was really brash of me to ask."

"Not at all. I think that would be great fun. Folks will already be gathered," Deborah said. "You wanted it to be a surprise, so how about this—we will have the wedding and then I can turn to the congregation and announce that we're celebrating Rob's twenty-fifth birthday a few days early. That will be such a shock to him."

"You don't think he'll mind, do you?" Mara questioned. "I feel like I know him better and better with each letter he writes, but I also realize there is much to learn."

"I think he'll be quite embarrassed and unsure what to do. But I figure that's what will make it the most fun. Look, you get the word out to anyone and everyone that we're going to do things this way. Your father is going to announce the wedding date at church on Sunday, so you can let other folks know then."

Mara smiled and hugged Deborah. "Oh, this will be so much fun!"

"What will?" Christopher asked, coming up behind Deborah.

She let go of Mara and turned to him. "I'll tell you on the way home. Mara tells me she's going to clean up for us here."

"Yes, she said she would like to do it for us, and I yielded to her persuasion."

Deborah nodded. "As did I, but I've also arranged to compensate her in another way. That's what I have to explain on the way home."

"Are you two ready?" Arjan asked as he and G.W. climbed into the first wagon.

Jimmy and Tommy jumped onto the back of Deborah's wagon since it held less, and Deborah allowed Christopher to help her up. She took her place on the seat and waited for him to join her.

"I think we're set to go," he told Arjan.

"Thanks again for the help, Pastor. You, too, Zed."

"Glad to do it; sorry about having to do it under these conditions," Zed replied.

"God will work it all out," Christopher said.

His confidence made Deborah smile. She found strength in his words. God would work it all out—of this, she was certain.

Euphanel finished sewing a sleeve onto the dress she'd made for Darcy. Sissy was working feverishly on hemming Emma's smaller matching gown.

"I think this sprigged muslin is perfect for the girls. The light blue will go perfectly with Lizzie's gown. Her dress is the color of a brilliant summer sky and has that lovely white lace and ribbon. It will look like we planned it all along." Euphanel held the gown up to better see the bodice. "I'm glad they'll have a part in the wedding. That will help them to feel a part of their brother's new life."

"I reckon so," Sissy said, stopping her labor. " 'Course, maybe it don' matter much to them one way or t'other. Young'uns always have their own notions 'bout such things."

"Yes, I'm sure you're right about that." Euphanel looked at her friend. "I've sure become quite attached to the children."

Sissy nodded. "I reckon you have."

Smiling, Euphanel could see the unspoken question in Sissy's face. The woman's dark brown eyes seemed to demand an answer. "I haven't mentioned it to Arjan, if that's what you're wondering."

"Don't you reckon it's time?"

"I do. I had planned to talk to him today, since I knew he'd be home to help Christopher get his things. The only problem is, he's been gone all day." She shrugged. "Maybe tonight."

"You best get it talked out afore the weddin'."

"I will," Euphanel promised. At the sound of the wagons pulling into the yard, she smiled at Sissy. "I'll see if I can't manage some time with him before supper."

Euphanel gave the men a half hour before she went in search of Arjan. She had practiced what she wanted to say and hoped—prayed—that he would understand and agree. Of course, he could be dead set against it, too, but she wouldn't know until she told him what was on her mind.

When she reached the cabin, she found Arjan getting ready to lead the first team back to the barn. "May I accompany you? There's something I'd like to discuss."

"I can take the horses," G.W. announced. "Why don't you two go ahead."

Arjan seemed surprised, but made no objection. "What did you have in mind?"

"How about a little time by the creek," she said, taking his hand.

They walked down the path toward the water, where Euphanel knew it would be cooler under the thick shade of the pines and hickory.

"Have a seat first," she said once they'd reached their favorite spot. "This might take a little explaining."

He raised a brow. "You been plottin' somethin', Wife?"

She smiled and allowed him to help her to sit on the grass. "You could say that, I suppose. Truth is, it's not so much plotting as . . . longing."

Arjan joined her on the ground and leaned on his elbow as he reclined. "All right, let's hear it."

Euphanel felt a rush of doubt. What if this wasn't a good idea? What if Christopher objected? What if Arjan thought her senseless? *Now I sound like Deborah. I should just follow my own advice*, she told herself.

"I want . . . well . . . let me start at the beginning." She twisted her hands in her apron. "As you know, I couldn't have any more children after Deborah. The doctors weren't really sure why, but it just never happened."

He nodded. "I know that grieved you. Grieved me, because of the hurt it caused you."

She smiled at his tenderness. "I know. Anyway, it's just that I've very much enjoyed having Christopher's little brothers and sisters here. I've enjoyed being a mother again."

"You never stopped being one of those," he replied. Then his voice filled with regret. "Wish I could have given you a child."

She reached over and touched his face. "I wish I could have done the same for you."

"I sure hope you know that I'm not holdin' that against you," he said, sitting up. "Were you thinkin' that?"

"Of course not. You've never made me feel that way. It's just me. I've always wanted more children, and having Christopher's family here only served to remind me of how much I love caring for a child."

"I've grown pretty fond of Jimmy and Tommy, to tell you the truth. Tommy and I actually had a long talk out at the camp a few days back. He told me he'd learned more from me than he'd ever learned from his pa."

"Then maybe it won't come as a shock to you."

"What won't?"

"What I'm about to say." She smoothed her apron on her lap. "I'd like to talk to Christopher about letting us adopt the children. My sister has even mentioned being willing to let Jimmy come stay with her like she did Deborah. He could attend the university there in Philadelphia."

He grinned. "I see you've given this some thought."

She felt her cheeks flush. "I have. It's been on my mind—day and night of late. Ever since the youngest children started calling me Mama Euphanel, I just felt a tug to give them my full time and attention."

"What if the boys aren't of a mind to go changin' their name to Vandermark? They may not have gotten to learn much from their pa these last years, but he was still the one to give them the Kelleher name."

"I thought of that, too," Euphanel said. "I guess what I mean by adopting is that we would take on the responsibility of seeing that they're raised right. A guardianship might be a better way to suggest it. It would also free Christopher and Deborah from having to deal with a ready-made family."

"What if they want that responsibility?"

"Then we just offer our support and perhaps we could look at finding some children to adopt elsewhere." She looked at him with a questioning gaze. "Would you consider that?"

"Nell, there isn't much I wouldn't consider for you. God knows I've wanted to give you a much better life than we've known these last couple of years."

"Oh, go on with you, Arjan Vandermark. We've had a good life and don't you go forgetting that. God has given us many blessings. Sure, things are rough right now, but God has made a way even in that. I'm truly a happy woman." She paused and gave him a smile. "I've just been thinking that I could be happier."

He laughed. "Well, I suggest we pray about this and then talk to Christopher and the others. If the children aren't of a mind to be cared for by us, then we sure don't wanna go imposin' such a thing on them."

"No indeed. I would not want that." She leaned over and kissed him lightly on the lips. "Thank you for your understanding."

He surprised her by pulling her down on the grass beside him. Wrapping her in his arms, Euphanel lost herself in the moment and the warmth of his touch.

Jael looked across the table at her father. "I'm so sorry, Father. I never wanted to shame you like Justine did." She could see him wince at her sister's name.

"I was wrong, Jael. I was wrong for how I treated her. I was a proud and boastful man, and the price was the life of my child."

"No, Father. Justine's death was her own choice. Certainly she was saddened by the things that happened, but the responsibility was hers. She loved the wrong man and he was a scoundrel for deserting her."

He shook his head and dabbed the napkin to his lips. "That much is true, but I acted wrongly. And now you're telling me you married a man you did not love—one who has left you to fear what he might do."

"I asked him for a divorce." She bowed her head. "Not just for that, but . . . well . . . there were other women. I've never confronted him about it, but I knew that he'd had his way with my lady's maid back in Philadelphia. It was one of the reasons I didn't want servants when we came here. He insisted, however. I don't know if he's bothered any of them or not, but it wouldn't surprise me."

"This is outrageous," her father said, slamming his fist on the table. "No daughter of mine deserves to be treated in such a fashion. How can I help you?"

Jael breathed a sigh of relief. Her father understood. He loved her enough to put aside his fears of scandal and offer his support. "I don't exactly know. I cannot abide how Stuart has treated the Vandermarks. I wish you could do something about that before we even consider what I need. They are good people, Father. The very best, in fact. Deborah says it is because God guides their steps. I'm thinking perhaps it's time I considered His place in my own life."

"Well past time for the both of us. When your mother died, I did you girls a great injustice in turning away from God." Remorse rang in his words and echoed in his sorrowful expression.

"I don't know what can be done," Jael continued. "But I know you are a thoughtful and wealthy man in your own right. Since you are in partnership with Stuart, I thought perhaps you could influence him to do better by the Vandermarks."

"He's determined to have his revenge. I don't know what I could do. However, I will look over the contract we have with Vandermark Logging, and I will ask my lawyers to do the same. Perhaps there is a way to nullify it and start over."

Jael looked at the food on her plate and pushed it back. She was still uncertain as to whether or not she was pregnant, but just discussing her poor choices and husband's hard heart was enough to leave her unable to eat.

"If you don't mind, I believe I'll retire for the evening. This conversation has robbed me of my strength."

Her father nodded. "By all means. And Jael . . . please promise me that you won't keep such things from me in the future. I want to make a better life for us, but I need the truth to be spoken."

She gazed across the table to see his eyes were filled with tears. "I promise. I will be truthful with you, even if it's painful."

Chapter 20

Rob arrived home on a sweltering Sunday evening, the twenty-second day of May. Mara had already been invited to spend the evening at the Vandermark home, just in case Rob arrived. He had actually planned to be home on Saturday, but something forced the delay, though Deborah hadn't yet heard what that something was. She smiled at the way her brother had changed as she observed him and the rest of the family relaxing on the lawn. He no longer swaggered like a young dandy seeking female companionship, but rather walked with the confident air that their father once used. Still, his whimsy popped up from time to time, like when he teased Mara or told stories of when he and G.W. had been young. His eyes would almost twinkle in delight as he confessed his childish adventures.

"They make such a nice couple," Deborah murmured. She looked at Christopher and smiled. "Do you suppose folks look at us and think the same thing?"

He chuckled and put his arm around her shoulder as they enjoyed the porch swing. "No, they probably say, 'What in the world does that sensible Vandermark woman see in that Irishman?' "

She elbowed him ever so slightly. "You know that no one around here cares about that. And those who pay a mind to such things are too busy hating the black folks to worry over an Irishman or two."

"Or six," he said, motioning toward his brothers and sisters.

Deborah nodded. "Or six."

"Wouldn't you agree to that, Deborah?" her mother called from the yard below.

"What was that?" she asked. "I didn't hear your question."

"I was just saying it would certainly be a shame if Rob couldn't be here for the wedding, and that perhaps you would agree to move up the date."

"To when?" she asked. "And why can't Rob be here on the eleventh? I thought he was staying several weeks."

Rob clasped Mara's hand. "I wanted to do just that, but in order to finish my studies sooner, I agreed to take on some work this summer. I reckon I'll have to head back to Houston by the first."

"But that's just a little over a week," Deborah said, looking to Mara, then to Christopher and back to her mother. "Are you suggesting we move the wedding up to this Saturday—the twenty-eighth?"

"Well, why not? Everything is ready, and Pastor Shattuck has no other plans."

The pastor nodded. "It's true. I'm as free as a man can be."

Deborah turned to Christopher. He was already grinning from ear to ear. "So I take it that you like the idea?"

"I didn't want to wait until the eleventh anyway, if you'll recall. Six days from now suits me just fine. Fact is, the pastor's here now—we could just get the formalities out of the way."

The men laughed, but feminine sensibilities prevailed. Mother was the one to put everyone in their place. "Deborah deserves a nice wedding. We'll move it up to Saturday. That will be soon enough."

A million butterflies seemed to release at once in Deborah's stomach. She put her hand to her waist to try to vanquish the feeling. Christopher didn't help matters at all when he leaned forward and whispered in her ear, "Just six days and you'll be mine."

"You should give a maniacal laugh and twist your mustache when you say that," Deborah teased, trying not to show how nervous she felt. "I remember the villain doing that once in a play I saw in Philadelphia."

Christopher feigned distress. "I'm the villain?"

Deborah put the back of her hand to her forehead. In the voice of a pathetic damsel in distress, she stood and pleaded, "Oh please, sir! Do me no harm."

"You are mine, dear lady. No one can save you now," Christopher declared, jumping to his feet to pull her close.

Her family laughed at their antics and Rob even clapped. "You two really should work on the stage."

Deborah shot him a scowl. "Don't encourage him. Next thing I know, he'll have some plan for us to perform scenes for patients."

"Well, we have a full day ahead of us tomorrow," Arjan said, nodding to Jimmy and Tommy. The trio got to their feet and

Arjan continued. "I asked Jack to stop the train here in the morning at five. We'll head up to the camp and get done what we can." He looked to Rob. "Don't suppose you'd like to dirty your hands."

Rob didn't get a chance to speak. "If you don't mind, Mr. Vandermark," Mara interceded, "I have plans for him."

The men chuckled and whistled, but Mother quickly agreed. "Rob is resting this week. We will let him court his girl and enjoy our celebrations and food, but he will not work."

"Wish somebody would let *me* rest for a week," G.W. said, getting to his feet. He rubbed his thigh gently. " 'Course, my leg would really stiffen up if I just sat around—like that could ever happen. These rowdies of mine keep me busy day and night." He hoisted a child under each arm and turned to Lizzie. "What say we clean these two up and get them to bed?" The twins squealed in protest.

"Yes, it's well past their bedtime. I should have had Sissy take them inside earlier."

"Oh, it did them good to be up, and who knows? Maybe they'll let us sleep past five-thirty."

"If they do, then you'll have cold breakfast," Mother threw out.

"There truly is no rest for the weary," G.W. said. "I reckon we'll be to breakfast on time."

"They sure are a precious pair," Rob said as the little family started for the house. "I'll enjoy being an uncle and spoilin' ever' last one of your children."

"You do, and you'll answer to me," G.W. called over his shoulder. "My children ain't gonna be spoiled. They're gonna be well behaved and brought up in the way they should go—just like we were."

"Whoever said you two were well behaved?" Deborah asked.

G.W. grinned as the twins giggled in his arms. "There are some things a fella just knows."

Now it was the women who laughed. Mother, in particular, seemed amused as she came up behind Lizzie and G.W. "Come along," she told Lizzie. "I shall tell you a few stories about your well-behaved husband."

"Now, Ma, that ain't exactly fair," G.W. protested as the women sidestepped him and headed for the door.

"We're heading to bed," Jimmy announced, giving Tommy a poke. "He's already half asleep."

Tommy yawned and nodded. "Been a long day. Even for a Sunday." The boys headed for the house.

"Well, I should be getting back," Pastor Shattuck told Arjan.

"Are you sure you don't want to just stay the night? Awful dark without the moon to lead you back."

"I'll be fine, Arjan. Thanks for the invitation. I'd actually like the time to just pray and think on the Lord."

Arjan got to his feet. "Well, let me bring your buggy around."

"Much obliged," the pastor told him.

Deborah came to the rail of the porch. "So when are you two going to tie the knot?" she asked Rob and Mara.

Rob grinned. "Well, if I have my way, it'll be as soon as I get this schoolin' out of the way. I'm just as anxious to marry my gal as you are to marry your fella." He put his arm around Mara's shoulder. "I reckon the time can't pass fast enough for either of us. Now, if you'll excuse Miss Shattuck and me, we're gonna go see what's left to eat. I'm starvin'."

"You just had supper three hours ago," Deborah reminded him.

"No wonder I can feel my stomach pressin' against my backbone," he replied. "We'd best hurry, Mara, before I plumb fade away."

"Mara, before you go, did you have some special time I needed to pick you up tomorrow?" her father asked.

Rob answered for her. "If you'll allow me, sir, I'll bring her home in the afternoon."

"I think that would work out all right."

"I was also hopin' you and I could spend some time discussin' a few things," Rob told him. "Things regarding ministry work. I'd like to have your opinion on my future plans."

Pastor Shattuck appeared quite pleased. "I would like that very much."

"And I'll fix supper for us," Mara declared.

"Maybe you can get my brother to talk serious about marriage," Deborah said, smiling.

Rob turned. "Whoever said I wasn't serious about marriage? Mara knows exactly how I feel. She's also got more sense than to go marryin' a man who doesn't even have a job or home of his own."

Christopher stiffened beside her, and Deborah put her hand on his arm. "Maybe she's just heard from Lizzie and Mother how difficult it is to be married to a Vandermark man."

Pastor Shattuck surprised them all. "I've actually been meaning to talk to young Rob about how stubborn and ornery we Shattucks can be. Especially the womenfolk."

Everyone laughed at this. Mara gave a slight rise of a dark brow and batted her eyelashes. "Why, Papa, whatever do you mean?" She took hold of Rob's arm in a possessive manner. "We Shattuck women are docile, reserved, and obedient."

The pastor gazed heavenward. "I'll say nothing further on the matter."

Deborah loved the merriment and wished it could go on and on. Just then, however, Arjan led the horse and buggy around the corner of the house. The dapple gray gelding seemed almost ghostly in the pale light of the lantern Arjan had hung from the frame.

Pastor Shattuck climbed up and bid them good-night. "I shall see you both tomorrow, then. Arjan, please thank Mrs. Vandermark for another delicious meal." He snapped the reins lightly and the horse moved forward.

"Well, I reckon I'd best get to bed. You sweethearts behave yourselves," he directed. "I don't want to have to come lookin' for you."

"We have patients to see in the morning," Deborah stated, "so we won't be out here for long. Besides, the mosquitoes are biting something fierce."

"Is that what it was?" Arjan teased. "I thought it was your mother pokin' me with her knittin' needles." He opened the screen door. "See you in the morning."

"Good night," Deborah and Christopher said in unison. Rob and Mara were already well on their way to the kitchen.

Turning to face Christopher, Deborah gazed deep into his eyes. "Six days. Are you sure you don't mind?"

"I told you, woman—I would have married you long ago if you'd just said the word." He bent his head to touch his lips to hers. "I would still marry you tonight. All we have to do is catch up to the pastor."

Deborah felt a delicious shiver run up her spine. The thought was tempting, and no doubt, Christopher would have had the preacher back before she could so much as tell the others. But reason and sense surfaced.

"Saturday is soon enough," she told him. "It's only six days."

"Only?"

The look in his eyes—the desire in his expression—caused

Deborah to take a step backwards. "Yes . . . only." She felt her backside come in contact with the porch rail.

Christopher stepped forward like an animal cornering its prey. "God created the world in six days. That's a long time, as far as I'm concerned."

Deborah's breath caught in her throat. Christopher wrapped her in his embrace and began kissing her. His lips first touched her forehead, then trailed down to her eyelids. Deborah sighed and sank against him. He kissed her nose, her cheeks, and earlobes. Deborah raised her mouth to meet his, but instead Christopher began to kiss her neck. She couldn't help the gasp that escaped or the trembling that began in her knees and ran up her body.

Christopher moaned softly against her ear just before claiming her mouth in a hungry kiss. Deborah had never known such passion. She felt as if her skin were afire under Christopher's consuming touch.

"Oh, Deborah." He spoke her name as if it were a secret.

All rational thought lost, she tightened her hold on his neck, encouraging his lips once again to take hers. He eagerly complied; then without warning, Christopher stepped back and dropped his hold. Deborah thought she very well might have sunk to the floor had she not quickly grasped the porch railing. She looked at him in question and saw the burning desire in his eyes.

"I think six days will be very long," he said, turning to leave. "I'm going to the cabin. Good night."

Deborah fought the urge to follow him. "He's right," she said rather breathlessly to the night. "Six days is going to seem like an eternity."

"You do look thinner," Mara told Rob as he cut himself a hunk of ham.

"I don't eat as well there as here. Of course, no one there cooks as well as the ladies of Angelina County. And besides, I don't do anywhere near the amount of physical labor. Although I have become quite handy at tending the grounds and gardens."

Mara poured him some buttermilk. "I can scarcely allow myself to believe you're really here." She handed him the glass. "I've missed you."

He grinned and put the ham aside. Rob took the buttermilk and placed it with the ham. "I missed you, too. I haven't had a chance to tell you that you're the prettiest gal in all of Texas." He touched a curl of her ebony hair. "I think about you nearly as much as I ponder the Scriptures."

She smiled. "I don't suppose the teachers appreciate that."

Rob shrugged. "They don't seem to mind. I get my work done, and that's what matters. One of my instructors reckons I have a unique way of lookin' at life. He said I have a way of talkin' and thinkin' that reaches the common man. He thinks I'll do well in small towns with everyday folk."

Mara couldn't help but nod. "I agree. That's one of your charms."

Laughing, Rob picked up the glass and downed about half of the buttermilk. "I didn't reckon I had any charms."

"Oh, you have them all right. I have to say, I've heard plenty of stories about you from some of the other young women in the area. You were quite the charming suitor, as I hear it told."

Rob sobered and shook his head. "Those times seem like a long ways back. Fact is, sometimes I can't rightly believe that was me. I'm not that man anymore."

"Thank God for that," Mara said most sincerely. "I could not have loved that man as I love you."

He studied her face for a moment. "I know. I'm just glad God showed me in time. I can't imagine my life without you in it."

She smiled and gave him a nod. "Just don't be reckoning it any other way, because I don't intend to let you get away."

Grinning, Rob picked up the ham. "Honey, you'd be hard-pressed to get rid of me now."

"Mama Yoonell?" a faint voice questioned from the doorway.

Euphanel bounded out of bed as if it were afire. "What's wrong?" she asked, finding Jonah standing in the hall.

"Emma's crying," he told her. "I think she needs you." His voice trembled as if he, too, might start in with tears.

"Let me get my robe." She hurried back to the end of the bed as quietly as she could. Arjan's steady snoring let her know she'd not disturbed his sleep.

Making her way back into the hall, Euphanel pulled on her cotton robe and tied the sash. Jonah looked at her and motioned to her head. "You sure got pretty hair, Mama Yoonell."

She smiled. "Why, thank you, Jonah. What a kind thing to say. I'll bet your mama had pretty hair, too."

"It was real long. She would braid it and wrap it around her head sometimes. I liked it that way." His voice dropped. "I don't like to think about her. It makes me sad."

"Well, that's all right. I'm sure that God understands how you feel."

"God? He knows how I feel?"

Euphanel heard the longing in his voice. "He truly does,

Jonah. He loves you. He knows that you're sad to lose your mama. He knows each tear you cry."

"And Emma?"

Euphanel paused as they reached the upstairs. "God knows how each of you feels. He wants you to remember that you are never alone. He is with you always."

"Truly?"

She smiled. "Truly."

Jonah surprised her by wrapping his arms around her legs. "I love you, Mama Yoonell."

Her heart swelled with joy. "I love you, Jonah. I love you very much."

Chapter 21

Zed. G.W." Bertram Wallace extended his hand and took a seat opposite the two men. "Thanks for the invitation to breakfast. Seems like a long time since I've seen you, Zed. It'll be good to catch up."

G.W. motioned to the table. "We knew that you'd want coffee, but they have two specials and we didn't know what you'd like to eat."

"Hello, Bert," the middle-aged waitress said as she brought platter-sized plates of food to Zed and G.W. "You want the regular?"

"Yes, ma'am," he said, grinning. "Cheesy grits and ham."

"Comin' right up." She looked to G.W. and Zed. "And do you gentlemen have everything you need?"

G.W. looked at the mound of scrambled eggs, potatoes, and bacon. "Yes, ma'am. I reckon we've got enough and then some."

"That's for sure," Zed said, digging into the pile of fluffy eggs.

She wasn't gone but a few minutes before returning with another large plate for Bert. "I had Cook give you a nice thick slice of ham."

"You're mighty good to me, Mabel." He gave his coffee a sample. "Strong . . . just the way I like it."

Mabel smiled. "You boys let me know if you need anything. I'm gonna go clean up a couple of tables."

G.W. glanced across the room. Several of the tables were in need of her attention. He figured it would give them plenty of time to talk without interruption.

"Zed, I heard what Albright has been up to," Bert began. "Your son told me he plans on buyin' you out."

"You can't exactly call it 'buying him out,'" G.W. interjected. "More like stealin' him blind."

"Do tell." Bert sliced into the ham. "Why don't you explain it to me?"

Zed nodded. "I'm much obliged to you for listenin'."

Bert listened patiently, and G.W. focused on his food. He knew Zed was proud, and begging a job wasn't easy for him. G.W. finished his coffee and lifted the cup to motion to Mabel. She was there without a word, filling mugs and scanning the table like a watchful mother. Seeing nothing amiss, she moved on.

"Seems like there ought to be a law against what he's doing," Bert said, shaking his head. "Have you signed any papers yet?"

"No, but it won't be long. Albright plans to have his father-in-law handle the matter in Houston and then bring the papers back to Perkinsville once everything is finalized," G.W. declared. "We've got good lawyers lookin' into it, but apparently Albright's put money in the right hands. So far he's managed to get folks doin' things his way."

"I'm mighty tired of them Easterners comin' in here, makin' changes," Bert growled. "I've seen it happen more times than I care to say. You know the old Carreston cotton plantation northeast of here?" The men nodded in unison and Bert continued. "Easterners bought 'em out and ruined the place. It's happened all across the South—I don't reckon I should be surprised by your news."

"You can see why I brought him here," G.W. said, lowering his voice. "You were good to help us in our time of trouble. We just wondered if you could recommend someone who might hire Zed on for a time."

"You're lookin' for a job?" Bert asked in surprise. "Well, I'll be. This must be what my wife would call one of them fortuitous moments."

G.W. shook his head. "How so?"

"My mill foreman up and quit yesterday. I've been tryin' to figure out who to put in his place. Zed, the job is yours for as long as you want it."

Zed reached out his hand. "I'll take it."

"We can discuss the particulars over at the mill," Bert said, pushing back his plate. "Why don't you come on over with me, and I'll show you around."

"Thank you kindly, Bert." Zed shook his head. "Don't know what I'd've done otherwise. I haven't even told the boys yet. They knew things were bad—just didn't know I'd gone and lost their inheritance."

"Things have a way of workin' out," Bert said as he got to his feet. "Breakfast is on me, boys." He fished out several coins. "Come on now. Let's make us a plan."

ᘓᘐ

"Father," Jael said, holding out a recently delivered telegram. "Deborah's wedding has been moved up to this Saturday. I must be there. I can't allow Stuart to force me to stay here in Houston when my dearest friend is getting married."

"I will accompany you," he said, looking over the message. "I have some business to discuss with Stuart, and I'm sure he wouldn't like you being left alone in the city anyway. If the wedding is Saturday, we would be wise to get up there as soon as possible."

"The housekeeper can have me packed up in twenty minutes," Jael said with a smile. "Can your butler do the same for you?"

Her father seemed more than a little amused. "I'm sure he can." He put the telegram aside and rose. "I'll send the driver around to the train station to see when the next train will be heading north."

Jael wasted little time making her way upstairs. Her father's house wasn't all that big, though there was certainly enough room for the two of them. She felt a sense of relief knowing Father would accompany her to Perkinsville; she had grown quite close to him since her arrival in Houston. They had talked about the past—about her sisters and the death of their mother. Jael had never known her father to be so free with his thoughts, and it truly blessed her to hear his heart. It blessed her even more to have learned the week prior that she was not with child. There was nothing holding her back from doing what needed to be done.

"Mrs. Lee," Jael called, spying the woman dusting at the end of the upstairs hall, "I need your assistance."

"Yes, Miz Albright?" the sturdily-built woman asked.

"Father and I are traveling to Perkinsville as soon as he can arrange passage. My dear friend is getting married on Saturday," Jael explained. "I'll need for you to help me pack."

The woman put her dusting rag in her apron pocket. Following Jael into the bedroom, Mrs. Lee went to the window and raised the sash. "It's going to be another hot day," she said, as if Jael had asked after her actions. "The weather will most likely make things miserable for travel."

"I won't take a great deal with me," Jael said, trying to think through her plan. She would love nothing more than to tell Stuart she was leaving him, but she didn't want to ruin Deborah's wedding. It would be bad enough to have her sulking husband at her side during the wedding. Of course, he might yield and allow Jael to be accompanied by her father. That would be much better.

Mrs. Lee opened the armoire, then went to the dresser. "I'd advise you take only your lightest gowns. The cottons and muslins will serve you better than silk. The silks tend not to breathe as well."

"That's quite true." Jael began sorting through the dresses. "Of course, I can't wear cotton to the wedding. I shall have to take at least one silk gown."

Just then, the butler appeared with Jael's trunk. "Mr. Longstreet said you would have need of this."

"Oh, thank you, Mr. Adams." The man was older than her father, yet seemed to have the strength of someone half his age. He placed the trunk at the foot of the bed and straightened. "I must now help your father to pack, but should you need anything, simply send Mrs. Lee to find me."

Jael nodded. Adams had been with her father for over twenty years. The two had a wonderful relationship that sometimes mimicked father and son, with Adams offering her father advice or comfort. Other times, they seemed like two friends. Never did they really appear as employee and employer.

Mrs. Lee came to the armoire. "You look lovely in blue, Miz Albright. It goes so nice with your red hair. I knew a redheaded woman who attended our church long ago. She would never wear any color but brown. Such a pity."

"Then we shall take this one," Jael said, pulling out a peacock-blue silk. "I've always been partial to this gown, even though it has to be cinched up extra tight. I think it will be perfect for the wedding, and it does have the removable sleeves."

"What about this one, as well?" Mrs. Lee asked, holding out a creation of white sprigged muslin.

"Yes, that one is definitely good for the heat. So is this green batiste." Jael held up the gown of pale sage. "Have you seen the underdress that goes with it?"

"I believe so." Mrs. Lee moved to the dresser. After several minutes of rummaging through the drawers, she managed to locate it. "You'll have to have it pressed."

Jael nodded. "We can round things off with several blouses and the plum-colored skirt. That should suffice."

"I'll put in two nightgowns. That way if one gets too dirty, you can use the other while it's being washed." The housekeeper pulled the nightclothes from the bottom drawer. "I'll see to it you have an extra corset and other undergarments."

"I will put some personal items in my small carpetbag," Jael said, pulling the luggage out from under the bed.

"It won't be pleasant traveling in this heat. Miz Buckley—the neighbor two doors down—fainted dead away in the middle of the street." Mrs. Lee was already packing the peacock-blue silk between paper. "You'd best make sure to take extra fans, and your smelling salts, of course. And what do you plan to wear?"

Jael looked down at her simple day dress. "I suppose I should change." She rummaged through the ensembles available to her.

"Why not just wear a muslin gown," Mrs. Lee asked. "No one's gonna mind. Your lilac one is plenty modest and will afford you the benefit of keeping cool. At least, as cool as is possible."

Jael pulled the gown from the armoire, held it up, and nodded. "It seems rather informal, but I think you're right. I have never cared all that much for what is said about me. If they post an article in the paper about my risqué attire, you will simply have to cut it out and show me later."

"Goodness, if they post an article on that, I'm bettin' they'll hear an earful. Newspapers ought to be for more important things than what a lady wears on a hot day."

"I think you look quite lovely," Mrs. Lee announced after she'd helped Jael change into the lilac-colored gown and arranged her hair. She went back to the trunk and closed the lid. "Everything is ready. I'll summon the groomsmen to come fetch this."

Jael glanced at the ring on her finger and couldn't help but think of Stuart. What would he say when she told him she intended to see Deborah wed?

He would forbid it, of course. But she refused to be intimidated. He would threaten to reveal the shameful impetus of their marriage to her father, but now the upper hand belonged to Jael. The truth had set her free.

"He could threaten Deborah again," she said aloud without thinking. She glanced up, relieved to see that Mrs. Lee had already gone from the room. It wouldn't be good to have the older woman asking questions. Mrs. Lee was a woman who thought it her business to know everything about everybody. Especially if the people involved were other than Texans themselves.

Jael walked to the open window. The air sagged with moisture.

The stifling heat was not unlike that which she'd known during Philadelphia summers, but this was only late May. What would July and August be like?

"Jael?"

She turned to find her father standing in the open doorway. "Did you manage to get us tickets?"

He nodded. "But we will have to hurry. There isn't much time before the train will arrive and be ready to depart."

She pointed to the trunk. "I'm ready to go. Mrs. Lee has gone to bring the groomsman to carry my things to the carriage. I have only to secure my bonnet and take up my parasol." She beamed him a smile. "Stuart won't be happy to see me, but with you by my side, I feel I can face just about anything."

"A letter for Stuart arrived just this morning. It's on the front table. You might want to take it with you. It's from his father, and perhaps that will put him in a better state of mind upon seeing you again."

Jael doubted that anything would cause Stuart to approve of her, but it was worth a try. "I'll get it before we leave."

Rob strode up to the pastor's door and rapped on it. He gave Mara a lazy grin when she opened the door. "You get prettier every time I lay eyes on you."

"You've just been in the heat of the sun too long, Mr. Vandermark." She looked past him to the wagon. "I see you've brought some of the wedding food. Why don't you drive the wagon around back so we can unload it easier?"

"I reckon I can do that," he said. "I hear tell you're makin' the weddin' cake."

She nodded. "I am. I'll bake it today, and tomorrow I'll

decorate it before the service. I have a garden full of budding roses, and I plan to use them on the cake."

He frowned. "Can't eat roses."

"Well, actually you can," she chided, "but these will simply be for show. I plan to sugar them so they'll sparkle."

"You gals sure dream up a lot of work for yourselves. Sparkly roses aren't exactly what I call worth the effort."

She giggled. "Then I suppose you won't be wanting them on our wedding cake?"

"I don't even care if we have a cake, to tell you the truth. And I'm mighty fond of cake." He leaned down to whisper in her ear. "But I'm even fonder of you. Perhaps you could share a kiss with me before I get to work."

She let him give her a brief kiss before stepping back. "You, Mr. Vandermark, are becoming quite talented in the art of persuasion. They must be training you well in the seminary."

He laughed. "I was always good at talkin' folks into things. It's just now, I'm using it for the Lord."

Mara looked past Rob and frowned. "What does *he* want?"

Rob turned and found Stuart Albright approaching the house. Rob positioned himself between Albright and Mara. From the stories he'd heard of late, this man's appearance could only spell trouble.

"Mr. Vandermark," Stuart said as he came up the steps. "Miss Shattuck. I'm here to see the pastor."

"He's not at home, but I expect him back soon," Mara replied. "He went to see a family across the tracks. I'm sure you could locate him there."

Albright glanced over his shoulder and then back to the couple. Rob didn't care for the look in the man's eyes. With the pastor out, Rob felt quite protective of the woman he loved.

"I would just as soon leave a message. Tell your father that I am closing the church, effective immediately."

"What?" Mara exclaimed, coming out from behind Rob. "You can't do that. We're having a wedding tomorrow."

"So my wife tells me. She insists she attend the wedding, but I have no intention of setting foot at such an affair." Stuart pretended to dust something off of his tan linen coat. "But the fact of the matter is, I can close the church. It's my property. There will be no wedding held there on Saturday or any other day. Nor will there be Sunday services. In fact, you can tell your father that I want the two of you to vacate this property by Monday."

"How very generous," Mara said. "You only gave Dr. Kelleher a day."

Stuart shrugged. "I have a soft spot for beautiful ladies."

Rob restrained his urge to punch Albright in his smug face. "You sure you wouldn't like to reconsider?" he asked, taking a step toward the smaller man.

Albright backed up but didn't retreat in full. "If you think to threaten me—"

"I haven't threatened anything, Albright. I just asked if you wouldn't like to rethink this. What's it gonna hurt you to allow for the weddin' to take place as planned?"

"Hurt?" He shook his head. "I don't imagine it would hurt anyone if I allowed the wedding to go on, and that's the problem. I *intend* to hurt you and your family. I intend to make you all as miserable as you have made me. After all, this ordeal started with a wedding." He turned to leave and called over his shoulder, "Good day, Miss Shattuck, and thank you for relaying my message to your father."

Rob started to go after the man, but Mara took hold of his fisted hand. "Don't. It will serve no purpose. He's hoping to make people miserable—it feeds his evil nature. Let's not allow him any foothold in our happiness."

"What do you propose we do about the weddin'?"

She smiled. "You Vandermarks have the most beautiful grounds around. Why not hold the wedding there? Father and I will come out and help you set up. When Father returns, I'll explain the situation. We'll pack our things and"—she shrugged—"who knows? Maybe we'll move to Houston."

Rob glanced around for a moment, then pulled her into his arms. "I've probably just ruined your reputation, but you, Miss Shattuck, are a very smart young woman and you deserve to be kissed properly."

He kissed her with as much restraint as possible, then put her an arm's length away. "Maybe we should plan a double weddin'."

"That would not hurt my feelings in the least, Mr. Vandermark," Mara said, grinning. "Not even the tiniest bit; however, your sister has worked hard to bring this day about. I say we let her have her moment to shine."

"I suppose if you reckon that's for the best." Rob shook his head. "I don't know, though. Seems to me it would only make sense to take care of two birds with one weddin'."

"That phrase is 'to kill two birds with one stone,' Mr. Vandermark, and frankly, I'd just as soon not have my marriage to you associated with such a thing."

He laughed and jumped from the porch, not even bothering with the steps. "Mara Shattuck, I am crazy about you. I hope you know that."

She laughed. "I do, Mr. Vandermark, and I'm just as crazy about you."

Chapter 22

"Oh good, it looks like Rob is back from town," Mother said, heading to the door. "I'll get him to take the smoked pork and corn bread along with the dishes on his next trip."

Deborah wiped the sweat from her forehead with the back of her hand. She had insisted on helping prepare the food for their wedding feast, deciding it would be better to keep herself occupied. Christopher requested she stay home these last two days while he rode off to make his rounds. Today he would visit the Vandermark logging camp, and he didn't want her to have any last-minute upsets with Jake Wyeth. Deborah had supposed it really was for the best. While Jake hadn't tried to see her or send her any other letters, Christopher had told her that a man like that would hold out hope to the bitter end when it came to loving someone.

"Ma, we've got problems," Rob said as he bounded into the summer kitchen. "Whew, it's hotter in here than out there."

"That tends to happen when you light a stove," Mother replied. "Now, what's this about problems?"

Rob turned to Deborah. "I'm sorry to be the one to tell you this, but the weddin' can't take place at the church."

Deborah looked at him in disbelief. "But why?"

"Albright." Rob let the word linger on the air a moment before explaining. "He's closed down the church and said it wasn't to be used anymore. He's also demanded that Mara and her pa get out of their house by Monday."

"The very idea," Mother said, shaking her head. "That man is heartless. What could it possibly hurt to at least allow them to remain in their home?"

Lizzie stepped forward. "Stuart is about causing pain, not preventing it."

"Funny, he said very nearly the same thing," Rob said. "So I brought the food back here. Mara suggested something, and I think it's a good solution. She said we ought to hold the weddin' here in our yard. What with the flowers and newly painted fence and porch, it ought to be a right perfect place for a weddin'."

"You're the bride," Mother said to Deborah. "What do you say?"

"Well, it's not exactly like Mr. Albright gave us a choice." Deborah shook her head and looked at Lizzie. "I'm so glad you didn't marry him. I feel so sorry for Jael."

"Speakin' of which, she's back in town. Albright made a comment about that and how she's insisted on bein' at the weddin', but that he doesn't want any part of it. I saw her pa on the porch of Albrights' house as I headed home. Maybe he'll bring her."

"Well, if we don't get this matter resolved, there won't be

any wedding to attend," Mother said. "Deborah, we can make a lovely wedding for you here. Will that be all right?"

She was angry that Stuart Albright should have any chance to disrupt her wedding. Angry, too, that he should force Mara and her father out of their home. When would this madness stop? She looked to Lizzie and could see that she was close to tears. Forcing a smile, Deborah turned to her mother.

"I think it's a wonderful idea. I wish I'd thought of it first. A wedding here will be all the more special. We'll need to get word out to folks."

Mother looked to Sissy. "Later today, you and I will go to town and spread the news about the change of location. For now, let's get the food inside."

Deborah let her mother and the others head to the wagon. She was surprised that Rob waited behind.

"I'm really sorry, Deborah," he told her. "I tried to reason with him, but Albright wouldn't listen."

"I don't doubt it. Thank you for trying to help."

"I never said this about anyone before, but I'm inclined to believe the man is just pure evil. He seems to be full of demons."

Deborah leaned back against the wall and sighed. "Rob, he's not going to stop until he destroys everything and everyone I love."

"Now, Sis, you know God is stronger than the devil. He won't let Albright win—at least not for long."

"I wish I could believe that, but as Lizzie has said over and over, the world is evil and bad things happen all the time. I know one day God will put everything in order, but for now we must endure the misery caused by Satan."

Rob nodded. "I know it seems that way, but you know the Bible says we aren't to fear those who can only kill the body.

Albright can take all we have, and it won't matter. Not truly. Pa started with little of nothin' and if need be, we can, too."

"I just can't believe one man can be so completely controlled by the devil."

"You know, I saw a puppet show in Houston. It was very entertaining, but the one thing that I thought about most was how those puppets couldn't do anything without the puppeteer controllin' them." Rob mimed having a puppet on each hand. "Folks who do evil are just like that. They wouldn't do a thing on their own, but when the devil gets to controllin' them—pullin' the strings—they come to life, doin' his work for him.

"Albright's no different. He's allowed the devil to harden his heart and pull the puppet strings that control his thinkin' and feelin's. There will always be folks who give the enemy power over them, and yet we don't need to be afraid of those folks. God will see to us. His love is more powerful."

Deborah reached out and embraced her brother. "You certainly have gotten a whole lot smarter since you went to Houston."

He hugged her and kissed the top of her head. "It's amazin' what happens when a man is willin' to listen to God."

Deborah considered his words and nodded. Stepping away, she drew a deep breath. "We'd best help the others, and maybe while we're at it, I'll work at listening to God at the same time."

After supper, Euphanel shooed Deborah and Christopher from the dining room. G.W. and Rob took Jimmy and Tommy to play horseshoes while it was still light.

"All right, whose night is it to clear the table?"

Emma and Jonah held up their hands. Euphanel smiled. "Then let's get to it."

Jonah jumped up and started picking up silverware while Emma reached for the plates.

"Don't forget to save the scrapes for the dogs," Euphanel instructed. She leaned forward to retrieve an empty platter.

"What do you want me to do?" Darcy questioned.

"Darcy, if you wouldn't mind watching the twins," Lizzie said, "I'll help Sissy wash."

"Oh yes! I'd *much* rather play with the babies," Darcy said, jumping up. She went to where Rutger and Annie were straining to be set free from their chairs. "Come on, you two. Let's go wash up and play."

Annie clapped her hands and Rutger fought a little harder to get loose. Euphanel had to laugh. How she loved her little family.

"Mrs. Vandermark, if you wouldn't mind," Arjan said, coming to Euphanel's side, "I'd like a word in private."

Euphanel nodded eagerly, hoping he'd brought some good news.

They moved through the house to their bedroom, and Euphanel quickly closed the door behind them. "So, what did he say?"

Arjan laughed. "I'm amazed you could sit through dinner without asking."

"Don't tease me. What did he say?"

"He was surprised to begin with."

Euphanel pulled him to where two chairs flanked the fireplace. "Come sit and tell me everything."

She settled into the seat on the right and waited for Arjan to speak. Her stomach felt as if it were doing flips.

"Well, Christopher seemed open to the idea. 'Course, he said it was ultimately up to the children. He planned to talk to the boys later tonight—well, at least Jimmy and Tommy. He wants to see how they feel about it first. Then he suggested we could talk to the others together."

"So he said yes?" she asked, clasping her hands to her chin.

Arjan held up his hand. "In a manner of speakin'. But he said that while he felt we could offer the children a more beneficial home, he would leave it up to them. He didn't want them—'specially the younger ones—to feel yet another sense of loss."

"But surely you told him that he and Deborah could stay on here for as long as they liked. That way, no one need feel a loss of any sort."

"Of course, but Christopher also knows that various issues of parenting and discipline will come up. He don't want there to be any confusion on that."

"But if we explain to the children, they will understand," Euphanel replied. "They are very smart."

"Yes, but they're still children, Nell. We don't want to hurt them no more. We've shown them love and kindness, but we ain't their blood kin."

Euphanel smiled. "There are ways to be family that have nothing to do with blood." She felt so very hopeful. "Love knows no boundary of blood or location. This will work. I know it will."

"So the wedding will be here tomorrow instead of the church," Christopher said. "Are you sure you won't regret that?"

"The building doesn't matter to me. What matters is that my family and friends will be with us, and God will join us together. What more could any bride want?"

Christopher looked at Deborah and thought she'd never been more beautiful. He loved the way her dark eyes seemed to dance. She was both little girl and woman grown, but most of all, she was his.

"Tomorrow you will become my wife."

She sobered and fixed him with a gaze. "You aren't having second thoughts, are you?"

"Good grief, no, woman. I'm beside myself with anxiety that you will change your mind."

Deborah looked surprised at his comment, then gave a brief laugh. "You needn't worry, my dear doctor. I am most assuredly yours." She leaned forward and rose up on tiptoe to touch his lips with her own. Christopher didn't move. He didn't so much as twitch.

"I will always be yours."

Christopher felt her breath against his lips. He wanted nothing more than to lose himself in her gaze, her touch. His heart quickened, and he knew that if he wasn't careful, he'd soon find Deborah back in his arms. He took hold of her shoulders.

"Wait, there's something I wanted to say."

She looked at him with her dark passionate eyes. "Is something wrong?"

He wanted to explain Deborah's mother's and Arjan's plans to take on his siblings. He wanted to tell her about his desire to give them a better life—a family. He hoped that she would agree and approve.

"Christopher! Come quick!" It was Darcy, and she sounded frantic. "Jonah cut his hand!"

Christopher and Deborah both turned at the same time and hurried for the house. Christopher beat her to the kitchen by only a step.

"What happened?" he asked, hurrying to where his brother sat crying on Euphanel's lap.

"He broke one of the dishes."

"It . . . it . . . cut me bad," Jonah said, sobbing.

"Let me see," Christopher said, taking hold of the little boy's hand. He examined the wound on Jonah's palm.

Deborah brought a warm wet cloth and gave it to Christopher. "I'll get your bag from the cabin."

"Thank you." He looked back to Jonah and smiled. "Now, I'll just wipe the blood away."

Jonah began to howl again, and Euphanel whispered in his ear. The boy immediately calmed.

"Are you sure?" he asked.

"Quite sure. Your brother would never hurt you. He needs to clean the cut so he can see how deep it is. When he's done, I'll give you a cookie."

Christopher wiped at the cut and could see it wasn't all that bad. "You're very lucky, Jonah. I won't need to stitch it up."

Deborah soon returned with his bag. Handing him the carbolic acid, she waited patiently at his side. Christopher appreciated the ease with which they worked together.

"This might sting just a bit, but don't worry—it won't last long."

Jonah leaned his head against Euphanel's shoulder. "I'll be brave."

Before Jonah could fret too much, the task was done. It touched him the way Euphanel comforted the boy. His brother obviously felt reassured in her arms. It made him all the more certain his siblings would be well cared for by Euphanel and Arjan. Perhaps he should forget about discussing the matter with the children and simply announce that the Vandermarks were going to raise them as their own.

"All done," he announced.

"There, you see," Euphanel told the boy, "it wasn't so bad."

"No," Jonah said, smiling. "Now can I have a cookie?"

Euphanel laughed and helped the boy from her lap. "Yes, indeed. Let's go right now and get you one."

Christopher gathered his things as Euphanel led the others from the summer kitchen. Only Deborah remained. He pulled his pocket watch and glanced at the time. Nearly nine. In fourteen hours, they would marry.

She looked up and smiled. "You seem very deep in thought."

He gazed into her eyes. "I am. I'm thinking of tomorrow."

Deborah stopped and put her hand on Christopher's chest. He took hold of her hand and pressed it to his lips. "I can hardly believe the day is almost here. When I first arrived in Perkinsville, I wasn't at all sure that I was doing the right thing. I knew my family needed support and felt that this was the best I could do for them. Now I see it was really the best for me—God's very best for me."

Chapter 23

Rob could hardly believe his eyes when he found Mara at the breakfast table with his family on the day of Deborah's wedding. She looked radiant—angelic, even—all dressed in a pale pink gown. He smiled and took a seat beside her.

"I gotta say, this is quite a surprise." He looked to his mother. "Sorry I'm late. Guess I overslept."

"We just went ahead and started without you," she replied. "I figured you could use the rest."

"I was perty tuckered, to be sure." He turned to greet Mara. "Nice surprise to find you already here. I figured I wouldn't see you until closer to the time for the weddin'."

She squeezed his hand. "I had to come early so I could take

care of the cake. I just brought everything with me and Father delivered me."

Rob looked around for the pastor, but Mara quickly added, "He'll be back in time for the wedding."

"I should hope so," Arjan said with a wink at Deborah. "So are you gonna eat or just stare at the food?"

Deborah shook her head. "I'm not hungry. I'm too nervous." The clock chimed half past five and her eyes widened. "Five and a half hours are all I have to get ready."

"Goodness, child," her mother said, patting her back, "why don't you go back upstairs and try to relax. I'll bring you a tray in a little while."

Rob heard his sister protest and his mother respond, but it was Mara who held his attention.

"Is there anything I can do to help?" Rob asked.

"You can help me by carrying the cake once it's finished," Mara said. Rob found himself mesmerized by her lips as she spoke. "And you may keep me company while I work—if you like."

"I have plenty for the boys to do," Arjan interjected. "I know we said no work for Rob, since he just got home and all, but this is just for an hour or two. We have to build a few benches so our weddin' guests won't have to stand. We're just gonna use simple planks of wood and supports, but they'll do the job. And then we'll need to haul them up from the barn."

"Of course I'll help. I'll do whatever needs to be done to help make this day special for Deborah." He looked for his sister only to find that she'd slipped from the room.

"She's got the jitters somethin' fierce," G.W. said, laughing.

"As I recall, Mr. Vandermark, you were none too calm yourself on our wedding day," Lizzie said, wiping Annie's face.

G.W. shrugged. "I figured grooms were always nervous.

Brides, on the other hand, have planned out all the details. They're the ones in charge, so I reckoned they weren't that jittery."

Lizzie rolled her eyes and picked up her fork. "I was so nervous I could hardly make sense of anything."

"You sure didn't seem like it," he said, grinning. "I figured you were completely at ease, havin' caught me and all."

"Me? Caught *you*?" she asked in surprise. "It was really the other way around."

Arjan laughed. "Ladies always figure to let us chase them until they want to be caught. By then, it's too late for us to do anythin' else. We're completely taken in by their beauty and charm." He winked at Mother and shrugged. "I don't reckon I minded bein' caught in your spell."

"Me neither," G.W. said, locking his gaze on Lizzie.

Rob couldn't help but turn back to Mara. He lowered his voice. "I know I don't mind." She blushed, and Rob thought it only added to her beauty.

After breakfast Rob followed Mara to the summer kitchen and watched in silence as she went to work. He marveled at her ability to create a thing of beauty out of cake and icing. She was skilled in so many things, and it only served to remind Rob of what a good wife she'd make.

"You're mighty good at that. 'Course, I haven't seen much you ain't good at."

Mara looked up and smiled. "I have my flaws same as everyone. I just happen to enjoy baking and decorating cakes."

She squeezed some icing in a scalloped pattern. "Say, aren't you supposed to be helping with the benches?"

"Yeah, I'll get out there to help soon enough."

The time seemed to fly by and before he knew it, Rob realized she was finishing up. And as she did, he knew it was time for what he'd truly come home for. He'd thought about this moment for a long time—and truth be told, he hadn't figured it would happen over sugared roses and icing. But his mind was made up. Pulling a ring from his pocket, he took hold of her hand and pulled her away from the cake. Dropping to one knee, he held up the ring like an offering.

"Mara Shattuck, will you marry me?"

Her mouth dropped open in stunned amazement. He couldn't help but chuckle at the look on her face. "Didn't you think I meant it when I said I love you?"

She nodded and tears filled her eyes. "I knew you meant it. It's just . . . well . . . I wasn't expecting this. Not today. Certainly not here."

He frowned. "I hope I didn't disappoint you. I just couldn't wait any longer. I've been wantin' to make it official ever since I came home. It's the reason I was late gettin' in. I was buyin' this ring and missed the train." He stood and placed the ring on her finger. Drawing her hand to his lips, he kissed the ring in place. "I pray you'll never take this off."

Mara stared at her hand for a moment. Without warning she hugged Rob close. "I'm so happy. Of course I'll marry you. I've always known I would marry you."

He laughed and lifted her face to his. "I'm glad God let you in on it first. If He'd told me, I'm sure I would've just made a mess of things." He kissed her ever so gently.

"I have work to do," she said, pulling back just a bit. "It's nearly eight o'clock. I have to finish up here and then change my clothes for the wedding."

"What do you mean change? You're beautiful, and that gown is quite fetching."

She laughed. "And dotted with bits of frosting and sugar. I

have something else to wear to the wedding. First, however, I need to put the last of the roses in place."

With great reluctance, Rob released her with a sigh.

She gazed down at the ring on her finger. "Leave me. Go help the men. I can't seem to concentrate while you're in the same room."

Rob laughed, but nevertheless headed for the door. "I reckon that's only fair. You distract me all the time when you're not even in the same room. When I'm reading the Bible, I think of you and how blessed I am that God gave you to me. When I'm studying how to help folks, I can only think of how much you've helped me. You're never far from my thoughts—even when we're in chapel, singing—"

"Robrecht Vandermark, you need to go . . . now." She pointed to the door. "This minute."

"I'm goin'. Mercy, but you sure can be bossy." He turned at the door and grinned. "I reckon we'll need to think about settin' a date for our weddin'."

She glared at him and picked up a wooden spoon and hurled it at him. Rob only laughed and quickly ducked from the room. Yes, sir—this was shaping up to be a fine, fine day.

Deborah could scarcely breathe as Lizzie finished cinching her corset. "Not too tight," Mother admonished. "We don't want her swooning before she says 'I do.' "

Lizzie let the ties release just a bit, then secured them. "Besides, she doesn't need much corseting. I think she's lost weight since this dress was first made," her friend declared. "Probably just in this last week. I don't think I've seen you take more than a few bites of food at any given meal." Lizzie brought the bustle and quickly tied it around Deborah's waist.

Deborah's head was spinning with concerns. "Oh, Lizzie, Mother—I pray I'm doing the right thing. I'm so anxious that I won't be the wife Christopher needs. I don't know anything about raising children, and Jonah and Emma are still so young."

Lizzie continued dressing her while Mother took hold of her shoulders. "Deborah, I want you to listen to me. God has a future—a wonderful future—for you and Christopher. Never doubt it, and don't bring it grief by worrying about what might or might not be. I had hoped Christopher would mention this to you first, but I think I'd better say something to put your mind at ease."

"What?" Deborah asked hesitantly.

"Arjan and I asked Christopher if we could take over guardianship of the children. He was very positive about the idea. He knows how attached Emma and Jonah have become—especially to me. The older boys are very fond of Arjan, and whether they want to be formally adopted or not, we want to raise them. I've even shared letters with your aunt Wilhelmina. She is open to the idea of Jimmy coming to stay with her and attend university. That just leaves Darcy. She's a mighty independent little miss, much as you were, but I have a soft spot in my heart for her, as well."

Deborah looked at her mother in disbelief. "I don't know what to say. I can hardly . . . well . . . I presumed in marrying Christopher that I would also . . . well, in a fashion, marry his siblings, as well. I figured mothering them was a part of my promise for better or worse."

Mother put her hand to Deborah's cheek. "There will be time enough for you to be a mother. Be a wife first."

"If we don't get her in this dress," Lizzie said, holding up the wedding gown, "she's going to have to get married in her undergarments."

Both Deborah and Mother giggled at the thought. Deborah savored the release of tension as she imagined walking down the aisle in her petticoat and chemise. That would definitely get tongues wagging for years to come.

Raising her arms, she let Mother and Lizzie settle the gown over her head. Deborah was surprised by the coolness of the fabric. The morning had dawned bright and beautiful, but the air felt dryer than it had in days and the silk slid against her skin like a breeze. Perhaps the mild temperatures were a wedding gift from the Lord.

Lizzie did up the thirty-some tiny back buttons and stepped aside when Mother brought the veil and headpiece. There hadn't been time to get waxed orange blossoms, but Deborah didn't care. Her mother had fashioned a circular crown of white roses and ribbon, and the dress was perfect even without the extra adornment. After carefully arranging the veil on Deborah's beautifully styled ebony hair, Mother leaned forward and kissed her on the cheek.

"Your father would be so proud. You are a beautiful bride."

"I wish he could have seen this day," Deborah whispered.

"I do, too. He would have loved Christopher. He's just the kind of man your father would have hoped for you to have as a husband."

Deborah grasped her mother's hands. "I love him so."

Mother smiled and nodded. "I know you do. And I know that he loves you. Just remember that with God, there is nothing you cannot overcome. Don't let the sun go down on your anger, and always be willing to forgive and try again."

"I will do my best," Deborah replied. "I promise I will."

A knock sounded on the door, and Lizzie went to open it. "We're nearly ready," she told Arjan.

Deborah looked to her uncle-stepfather. Dressed in his only suit, he looked very dapper. He'd seemed quite honored when she'd asked him, instead of G.W., to give her away.

"I reckon it's time," he told the ladies. "The bridegroom is gettin' mighty antsy."

"He's waited this long," Lizzie chided. "He can cool his heels just a little longer." She smiled at Deborah. "Best he learn how to wait patiently, eh?"

Deborah had never known a man with more patience than Christopher. She couldn't imagine that he was all that concerned with the time. He knew she would be his by the end of the day, and that they would have the rest of their lives together.

Mother pulled Deborah's veil in place to cover her face, then Lizzie helped Deborah into delicate white lace gloves. With this accomplished, Lizzie handed Deborah a bouquet of pink and white flowers that Sissy had put together.

"Sissy said she prayed over each flower as she picked and arranged them," Lizzie said. "She said to tell you that you should let these flowers remind you never to fret about what you'll wear or eat. Consider the lilies of the field and the birds of the air. God doesn't forget them, and He certainly won't forget you."

Deborah looked at the flowers in a new light. What a precious blessing. Mother pressed a fine white lace handkerchief into Deborah's gloved palm.

"This belonged to my mother and her mother before her. We've each carried it on our wedding day, and I'm hopeful you will continue the tradition. My mother told me that this handkerchief is for tears of joy and sorrow. The two mixed together represent all that a good life offers—for without the times of struggle, we cannot truly appreciate the times of rest. Without the moments of pain, we do not realize the blessing of its absence."

Deborah nodded. She was afraid to speak for fear she might cry. She caught her reflection in the mirror and was startled. She couldn't help remembering that she'd felt this same way on that day, two months earlier, when they'd been making the final adjustments to the gown. She felt like a queen, all garbed in silk. It was all the more special because this was the gown, albeit remade, that her mother had worn to wed her father. It was more precious to Deborah than she could ever express.

Arjan came to her side. "You make a beautiful bride, Deborah. I'm right proud to give you away."

Deborah tucked the handkerchief around the flower stems and placed her hand in the crook of his arm. "Thank you. I'm so blessed." She looked to her mother and then to Lizzie. Drawing a deep breath, she smiled and gave a nod. "I'm ready."

They made their way downstairs and out the side door. When she'd dreamed of this day, the wedding service had always been in a church with hundreds of people in attendance. But instead, it was in her mother's own beautifully cultivated yard with just a few friends and family. Yet Deborah forgot all about that when they rounded the corner and she saw Christopher standing beside Pastor Shattuck.

She felt light-headed as G.W. nudged him and Christopher caught sight of her for the first time that day. The look on his face told her everything she needed to know. He loved her. It was all she could do to keep from running to cross the distance. A nervous giggle escaped her at the thought. What would they all say if she hiked her skirts and dashed for the porch steps?

"Are you all right?" Arjan whispered.

"I'm fine. I'm just fine."

Deborah caught a whiff of honeysuckle from the bush near the porch. In a flash of blue and white, Emma and Darcy came rushing around the corner of the house. They looked quite dainty and stylish in their new gowns.

"Is it time?" Darcy asked, looking up expectantly. "Emma and I are all ready."

"It's time," Lizzie told them.

Jacob Wythe stood at a distance, obscured from view by the trunks of longleaf pines. He'd told himself he wouldn't come to the wedding. He'd convinced himself that it wasn't something he should do—that he would only regret it and cause others pain. And still, he couldn't help himself.

He'd very nearly convinced himself to leave when he caught sight of Deborah coming from the side of the house. He couldn't take his gaze from her.

She might have been mine, he thought. He watched Lizzie and Mrs. Vandermark fuss with the skirts of Deborah's wedding gown while Arjan patiently waited until the women finished.

Two young girls came bounding up as the wedding party reached the front yard. Jake supposed they were the doc's sisters that he'd heard so much about from Jimmy and Tommy. They danced around Deborah in their excitement.

He remembered days long past when he had known a family's joy and celebration. Everything had changed with the drought and his father's decision to sell the ranch. If he'd only been able to hold on a little while longer, he might have found himself in a good position after the horrendous loss of the previous winter. Many Texas ranchers were making good deals on their cattle because of the thousands of head lost to the blizzards.

Jake watched Deborah for a few more minutes and realized that his sense of loss wasn't in her—but in her family. He wanted to be a part of something. When his family headed to California, it was as if he'd lost his history.

"Why did I stay?" he questioned, shaking his head. He remembered the anger he'd held toward his father. He'd argued with the man for not having the courage to stand fast through the drought. Jake sighed. He'd put up a wall of separation with the only two people he truly needed in his life. Maybe, he thought, it was time to apologize. He could send a telegram to California. The idea encouraged him. He cast one final glance at Deborah and smiled. She was beautiful. Kind and loving. She'd make a good wife—just not his. And for the first time in many, many months, Jake felt that he could accept and live with that fact.

Chapter 24

Do you, Deborah, take this man, Christopher, to be your lawfully wedded husband—" Pastor Shattuck threw her a smile—"to have and to hold from this day forward, for better or for worse, for richer, for poorer, in sickness and in health, to love and to cherish?"

Deborah looked through the fine netting of her veil and nodded. "I do."

Christopher, having already agreed to the same, took hold of her hand. He carefully removed the glove and slipped a simple gold band onto her finger. "With this ring, I thee wed." His gaze rose to meet hers, and he tightened his hold on her hand. "May it be a symbol of all that we've pledged today."

She fought back tears of joy and managed a nod. Pastor

Shattuck closed the Bible. "It is my joy to pronounce you husband and wife. You may kiss your bride."

Christopher lifted the veil. He smiled at her. "We finally managed to see it through," he teased. Then with great tenderness, he drew Deborah into his arms and kissed her.

Deborah heard the applause and shouts of congratulations, but it was Christopher who held her attention. "I love you," she whispered as he pulled away.

"Good thing, too, for I love you with all my heart."

"I think this was the perfect setting for your wedding," Lizzie said, handing Deborah back her bouquet.

"I agree," Pastor Shattuck said. "Perhaps my next church will have some lovely gardens in which I can marry folk."

"I'm hopin' your next wedding will be mine and Mara's," Rob declared, coming to congratulate Deborah. He looked to Mara's father. "Thank you for giving us your blessing."

"So it's official now?" Deborah asked.

Mara held up her hand and revealed the small pearl that adorned a simple gold band. "He asked me this morning."

Mother seemed nearly ready to dance at the news. "And have you set the date?"

Rob and Mara exchanged a glance. "No, but we'll work on it," Mara replied. She motioned to the table where Sissy and Mrs. Perkins were already helping to ready the food. "A great deal of work went into this feast, and I suggest we celebrate."

"I couldn't agree more," Arjan declared. "I'm very patient, but that roasted pork is hard to ignore. The aroma just about caused me to make a scene."

The gathered well-wishers laughed at this comment. Christopher, however, appeared to feel the same way. "Let us lead by example, Wife." Mara came to Deborah's side and whispered in her ear. Deborah smiled and nodded.

"Ladies and Gentlemen, I have an announcement to make. Today we are not only celebrating my wedding, we are also celebrating my brother's birthday." She looked at Rob and her smile broadened. "Surprise!"

His expression was one of confusion. Glancing to Mara and his mother, Rob shook his head. "But it isn't my birthday."

"It will be soon enough," Mara declared. "You're the one who forced us to move up the date."

Deborah crossed to where Rob stood. "And if we'd waited until the actual day, it wouldn't have been a surprise. Now come along and let us celebrate."

Christopher joined his wife and gave her a wink. "I'm gonna waste away if we don't get to eating soon."

Everyone laughed, but Deborah's expression was serious. "I suppose you only married me for this feast."

He chuckled and leaned close to her ear. "If you would allow me some privacy, I'd explain in great detail why I married you."

"Dr. Kelleher!" she exclaimed, pulling back. "Mind your manners."

He only laughed and took hold of her arm. Deborah allowed him to guide her to the main table. Arjan and the others had put together several tables to accompany the newly made benches. Mother and Lizzie had, in turn, covered those with tablecloths.

"I'd much prefer privacy . . . with or without food," Christopher whispered in her ear.

Deborah felt her face flush. She looked toward the ground to avoid anyone seeing her embarrassment. Christopher hugged her close, then assisted her onto the bench. She worried that her wedding gown would be snagged by the wood, but someone had thoughtfully put a small covering on her seat. Her bustle neatly collapsed as she took her place. Deborah carefully arranged the skirt of her gown to allow Christopher room to sit at her side.

The party spirit grew as the minutes passed by. Zed Perkins shared stories about his wedding day, including his last-minute stop on the way to the church to shoot a ten-point buck.

"Grandest deer you ever saw," he said, laughing. " 'Course, I doubt Rachel saw it the same way. She was less than impressed when I told her we'd be cleaning it later that night."

"How awful, Zed," Mother said, shaking her head. "That's no way to treat your bride."

"Well, as luck would have it, our friends took pity on me," Zed replied. "They told me they'd gut it and hang it, in return for a dance with Rachel. Of course, I complied."

"He knew better than not to," Rachel countered. "Otherwise, that deer would have been his only companion that night."

Laughter filled the air, and Deborah said, "I was afraid my new husband would be off delivering babies or setting bones."

"The day's still young," her uncle declared. "You can never tell what might happen."

Jake had taken his time lumbering down the road to town, planning in his mind exactly what he would say in the telegram. He didn't have a lot of ready cash, so it would have to be short, but he wanted to apologize and let them know that he wished to come back to live with them. Of course, there was the possibility that his folks wouldn't want him to come to California. They might hold him a grudge.

Jake shook his head, as if trying to dislodge the fear. He wouldn't know the truth until he sent the telegram and heard back from his folks. It didn't make sense to give credence to such ideas before their time.

A sound caught his attention and he paused at the side of the road. Riders were approaching. A good many riders, from the sound of it. They were headed north toward the Vandermarks'. He didn't know why, but something told him to head back into the woods. He slipped behind several hardwoods and waited to see what was going on.

The sound grew louder and now he could hear voices. Horses and riders came into view, and Jake's blood ran cold at the sight of them. Flour or gunny sacks covered every head. Holes had been cut out for the eyes, but otherwise, nothing hinted as to who they were. There wasn't any need. Jake clearly recognized the uniform of the White Hand of God.

The horses slowed as the man in the lead held up his hands. "Reload. We don't wanna get caught on empty chambers."

The men allowed the horses to walk on at a slow pace while they loaded their pistols and rifles. Jake walked quietly through the trees, pacing the riders—backtracking toward the Vandermark place. He had to strain to make out what they were saying.

Jake edged back toward the road to see if he could figure out how many there were. Looked to be at least fifteen, and the one in front appeared to be the leader.

"You done good back there, boys. Now we'll take care of this last little bit of business and head home."

"I heard there was a weddin' goin' on at their place," someone said.

"I heard that, too," the leader answered. "I figure it's the best place to lay down the law. Every white man and woman in the area 'ceptin' us is gathered there to watch that Vandermark gal get hitched. I figure it makes the job all the easier. We go there and tell them all how it's gonna be. I don't wanna hurt no white man, but I guarantee we'll get their attention. Sometimes you have to discipline a wayward child."

That was all Jake needed to hear. He knew that if the men moved into a full gallop he'd never be able to reach the Vandermarks first. Unconcerned with whether the men heard him, Jake lit out through the forest, praying that they would be far too consumed by their plans to even notice him.

He felt a burning in his legs but pressed on. His lungs were aching from the exertion of running, but Jake couldn't slow. He knew if he did, the others would reach Deborah first. He saw the cutoff that would bring him around to the railroad tracks and decided to take it. The horses and riders would no doubt stick to the main road. The Vandermark place was more easily reached that way on horseback. Jake angled off toward the tracks, and only when he was certain the road was clear of any possible observer did he dare to dash across the open path.

Plunging into the woods that ran alongside the tracks, Jake was grateful that the forest ground had been burned off earlier in the year. The distance was fairly easy to cover, and he knew he'd soon approach the Vandermarks' southern property line.

All he could think of was that those men meant to cause harm. Harm to Deborah and anyone else who got in their way. He prayed, pleading with God to protect the woman he loved and the family and friends she cherished.

He was completely exhausted by the time he reached the clearing. Jake could hear the laughter and joy of the celebrators. They would, no doubt, be surprised by his intrusion, but they'd be grateful, too.

The guests were sitting at tables, enjoying dinner, and waiting for Rob to cut a large cake, when Jake stumbled out across the yard. G.W. and Arjan were first to get to their feet, but it didn't take long for the others to gather round him.

"Riders . . . White Hand riders . . . comin' this way." He gasped for air and Arjan directed Rob to bring water. He dropped the knife and grabbed a pitcher.

"Take it easy, son. Get your wind and then tell us what's goin' on," Arjan instructed.

"No. No time. Riders comin'." Jake pointed toward the road. "There's . . . gonna . . . be trouble."

He sank to his knees and took the water Rob offered him. Gulping it down, Jake struggled to control his breathing. They didn't understand. They just stood there, looking at him like he was crazy.

Just then, however, the sound of horses moving in at a full gallop drew G.W.'s attention. "He's right—someone's coming."

"They're armed," Jake said, getting back on his feet.

"Well, we can be, too," G.W. said, running for the side of the house. "Christopher! Rob! Help me out."

The men bounded up the porch stairs. Arjan motioned to Deborah and her mother. "Nell, you and Deborah get the women and children inside."

But it was too late. The first of the riders could be seen on the road, and that was when guns started blazing. Jake did the only thing he could. He ran for Deborah and put himself between her and the gunmen.

Deborah could scarcely believe what was happening. The riders stormed the yard like soldiers taking a battlefield. Jake shoved her behind him, but she couldn't register the words he was saying over his shoulder. Shock made her deaf and nearly void of rational thought.

The riders circled them, upsetting the tables of food. They fired their guns into the air, and one particularly large man cocked the hammers of his shotgun as he aimed at the wedding cake Mara had made. Cake and sugared roses splattered out across the yard.

Deborah turned slightly to see her mother forcing the younger children and Lizzie into the house. There was no hope of making it there herself. She wondered where Christopher was—if he would know to sneak around from the back of the house rather than rush out through the front door. He would be worried about her, just as she was concerned about him.

Calm yourself. Calm down, or you'll be no use to anyone. G.W. and Rob will help him.

All at once, the riders came to a stop. It was very nearly like a well-planned dance. The horses settled and the shooting stopped, but the leader pressed forward and pointed his long-barreled pistol directly at Jake and Deborah.

"I'm here on account of the bride," he declared. The masked men snickered, and Deborah couldn't help but look around Jake to get a better view. It wasn't like she could see their faces, but even so, she had to look.

Jake pushed Deborah back behind him again. "You'll have to shoot me to get to her."

"That doesn't bother me one bit." He lowered the gun to aim at Jake's chest.

"No!" Deborah shouted. "What do you want?" She side-stepped Jake, but he took hold of her arm.

"That's just what I was gonna ask," Arjan said, moving in front of Jake and Deborah.

The man on the lead horse stared in silence for several

minutes. The eerie face covering gave him a surreal appearance—not quite human, not quite apparition.

Arjan crossed his arms. "I asked what you wanted, mister."

"I heard you. I reckon I'll answer you when I'm good and ready."

"Well, get ready," G.W. called from the side of the house. "I have a rifle fixed right between your eyes."

"Well, ain't you the brave one," the man replied.

Deborah glanced across the yard to the other side of the house and saw Rob and Christopher. "We have a bit of a standoff here, fellas," Rob declared. "I'd suggest you put away your guns."

"I don't reckon I'll do that," the leader said. "And further, I don't figure you'll do anything about it. You might shoot me, but my men will kill this pretty bride deader than Mr. Lincoln."

"So tell us what you want and get off our property," Arjan demanded.

"Well now, I'm figurin' you already know full well what we want. After all, we paid you folks a little visit not so long ago. Y'all've been stirrin' up trouble and takin' up the cause of the colored folk. We've decided to put an end to that. First, we took care of the situation in town, and now we're takin' care of you. You Vandermarks need to realize that there are far more of us that hate the Negroes than those of you who appear to love 'em."

Deborah could see the strained expression on Christopher's face. She feared he might well charge across the yard to reach her. Shaking her head, she mouthed just one word: *No.*

"We aren't the kind of folks to run scared," Arjan said. He nodded to the pastor and some of their other friends. "We're Texans, and we don't take kindly to threats."

"This ain't just a threat, Mr. Vandermark." The man nudged his horse a little closer and pointed the pistol at Arjan. "This is a bona fide promise. Let our example speak for itself. If you don't stop tryin' to interfere, you and yours are gonna end up like the folks in Perkinsville. We'll burn this place to the ground—just like we did that shantytown."

"What?" Deborah found it impossible to remain silent. "You burned them out?" The breeze had been westerly all day and no doubt that was why they hadn't so much as smelled the burning wood.

The man laughed. "Burned 'em and beat 'em. There ain't much left, and there'll be even less of this place if you don't yield."

"You had no right!" Deborah started for the man, but Jake held her fast. It took only that action to cause Christopher to rush across the yard.

"Stay there, Doc. You don't wanna make her a widow before she gets a weddin' night. Worse yet, you don't wanna be a widower." He turned the pistol again on Deborah and Jake. The men around him laughed and threw out vulgar comments. "Now, I ain't in the habit of shootin' white folks, but I'll do what I need to do in order to get my point across."

"Please, Christopher, don't move." Deborah felt a sense of dread like she'd never experienced in her life.

Arjan shook his head and stepped forward as if to take hold of the leader's horse. "This has gone on long enough. I answer to a higher authority. God Almighty directs my steps."

The pistol rang out without warning. The man had moved his aim so quickly that Deborah actually found herself waiting to feel the bullet pierce her. Instead, she watched Arjan crumple to the ground. The horse reared up beside him, but miraculously missed coming down on the injured man by only inches.

"See if you can walk His way with a bullet in one leg." He repositioned the pistol on Jake and Deborah. "Now, unless you want the next one to cut down this heroic young man, and then the bride . . . I'd suggest you all put down your guns."

For several minutes, no one did anything. Deborah strained to see if Arjan was all right, but she couldn't tell.

"We're puttin' 'em down," G.W. announced, his words surprising Deborah.

"That's a wise choice. Now, like I said, today is your last warnin'. The law won't help you because *we* are the law—the new law of the land. You'd do well to understand that fact right now." He backed the horse up with the slightest pull of the reins.

"I want five of you boys up on the road, holding guns on these kind folks." Without questioning the request, five riders headed off toward the main road. The leader waited for them to be in position.

"I never intended to shoot you, Vandermark, but it's enough for you to know I'll do what I have to. The boys and I are gonna leave you to your weddin' party, but in the future, I'm hopin' you'll remember this and realize that the times have changed. Mr. Lincoln's war may be over, but Southerners everywhere are regaining their legs—we're gonna rise again, and that's a fact. Best you figure out which side you'll be on."

He reined the horse hard to the left and gave him a kick. "Yah," he cried and the other awaiting riders did likewise.

Deborah didn't wait for the men to clear the yard. She rushed to Arjan's side, mindless of her wedding dress. She reached out to steady the leg. "Hold still." She waited for Christopher to join her. He gave her a look that said far more than words.

"Let's get him inside."

G.W., Jake, and Rob came to help, as well as Jimmy and Tommy. Mother appeared at the door. "I saw it all," she said, biting her lower lip. "Is it grave?"

"I don't know yet," Christopher told her.

Sissy already had an oiled canvas atop the dining room table and the men lowered Arjan onto it. Christopher wasted no time tearing away the man's trouser leg. He assessed the wound and motioned to Deborah. "Get my bag."

She hurried through the kitchen and out the door. The shock of what had happened kept her from breaking into tears. She had to do what was needed. She had to help Arjan.

To her surprise, the cabin had been decorated for their wedding night. Someone had brought in flowers and candles. But there was no time to take any pleasure in the setting. Deborah went quickly to where Christopher had begun to set up a small examination room. She grabbed the bag, bandages, and several other items before heading back to the house.

"Oh, God, please help us. Please help Uncle Arjan."

"Is there anything I can do?" Jake asked, appearing on the path.

Deborah nodded. "Pray, Jake. Please pray."

Chapter 25

It's not much more than a flesh wound, shot clean," Christopher told them. "It didn't hit the bone or major blood vessels. Take it easy for a while, and I think it will heal up nicely." He washed his hands and looked to where Deborah was applying the final bandages to Arjan's leg.

Euphanel shook her head. "I can't believe this has happened. What in the world are we going to do?"

"Well, Christopher and I are going to head into town and see how we can help the people there," Deborah announced.

Christopher glanced at the clock and nodded. It was just after one o'clock. "Can I borrow a wagon?"

"You know you can," Arjan said, struggling to sit up.

Deborah gripped him firmly at the shoulders. "You need to

rest. G.W. and the others can put you to bed for Mother. Then they should probably come help us."

Zed and Rachel headed for the door. "I think we'd all best get back to town."

"I'm so sorry for all that's happened," Jael said, coming to give Deborah a hug. "This certainly wasn't what any of us would have wished for your wedding day."

Deborah embraced her friend. "I didn't even have a chance to realize that you were here until we were gathering to eat. I'm sure Stuart was livid about your coming."

"He'll get over it, I assure you," Jael said with a weak smile. "You'd best go. We can talk later."

"Yes." She looked down at her clothes. "I need to go change."

When Deborah turned back from Jael, Christopher frowned. The front of her wedding gown was saturated with blood and dirt, ruined. There would be no passing it down to their children. No beautiful memento of their joyous day.

Some joy, he thought. He just couldn't shake the picture of that horseman holding a gun to her.

"Doc, you'd best change your clothes, too," Sissy said. She gestured to his instruments. "I can boil these things for you. I has the water hot on the stove."

"Thank you, Sissy. Boil them for exactly five minutes, then dry them and wrap them in a clean towel. We could also use any spare bandages or sheets."

Euphanel waited until her sons had carried Arjan from the room before moving. "Tommy, run upstairs to the attic. There's a stack of old blankets and sheets. If those men burned the town down as they said, then those folks will need all the extra supplies we can spare." She turned to Jimmy. "Take Darcy and the little ones and go to where we keep the canned food. Start packing crates with whatever you can."

Christopher shook his head and headed for the door. "I'll gather my things from the cabin. Perhaps we can talk Mr. Albright into sharing goods from the store." He doubted that Stuart would consider it, but it was worth a try.

Making his way to the cabin, Christopher felt a heaviness settle over him. As much as he longed to see an end to prejudices and negativity, he knew they would go on. People were people, with their own opinions and desires. Some were productive and useful to society. But with the hatred and bitterness of racism, the bad seemed to outweigh the good.

He rushed through the cabin, peeling off his wedding clothes. Like Deborah's, they were stained with blood. How much more blood would he have on him before the day was over? He gathered his things and headed back to the house, not even bothering to tuck his shirt in.

G.W. stood ready with the wagon and Christopher's horse, while Rob helped Mara into her father's carriage. "I'll head in with them," he told G.W. and jumped up to join the Shattucks.

Deborah and her mother were bringing out baskets of food. "I'll be here with Arjan and the children," she told Deborah. "Send word if you need anything."

"I want to help," Darcy said, coming to stand by the women. "Can't I go?"

Christopher couldn't help but think of the ugliness that awaited them. "You'd be more of a help here keeping the little ones busy. I'd like Sissy to come with us. Mama Euphanel won't have anyone else."

Darcy met his gaze and seemed to understand. "I'll stay."

"Thank you." He mounted his horse.

Sissy came from the house with the doctor's bag. She handed it up and motioned to where Jimmy and Tommy were climbing into the back of the wagon. "I figure to go along."

He nodded. "I hoped you would. I know you'll be a comfort and help."

The rest of the wedding guests had already headed back to Perkinsville. Christopher kicked his horse into action and headed down the road at a full gallop. He passed Jael and her father, giving only a nod as he rode on. His mind was on the tragedy at hand. How much time had passed? How bad would he find things? The men had said they burned out the shanties. Would any structure remain to shelter those who had survived?

Deborah wasn't surprised to find Stuart Albright doing nothing. He was sitting on his porch, casually watching the chaos with disinterest. How could he be so heartless? Deborah wanted to climb from the wagon and rail at him for his lack of Christian charity toward the less fortunate. She wanted to call to mind that these people were, in every way that mattered, his responsibility.

Instead, she held her tongue. Stuart wouldn't care. In fact, he'd probably laugh at her, and that would only anger her more. As G.W. drove the wagon across the tracks, Deborah cast a brief backward glance and saw that Mr. Longstreet had brought the Albright carriage to a stop in front of the house. Perhaps as his business partner, he could talk some sense into Stuart.

The smoke hung heavy in the air, as some of the houses were still afire. The school for the colored children was now completely gutted, as were the houses nearest the railroad tracks. Men and women were struggling to pull bodies of the unconscious to safety.

"Oh, Lord, have mercy. Have mercy," Sissy said, weeping. She didn't wait for anyone to help her from the wagon and nearly fell as she jumped from the back. Hurrying across the ground, she came to where several women were heating kettles of water over fires. "Let me help you," she commanded.

Deborah looked out across the destruction. The charred, smoldering remains bore witness to the violence—the broken bodies, along with the screams and moans of the wounded, assaulted her like a slap across the face. What kind of monster did such things?

She knew the answer. She'd dealt with those monsters face-to-face. Well, not really. They hid behind masks, and she understood why. If she'd ever done something so heinous, she would hide her face, as well.

"Well, they did exactly as they said," Christopher said, helping her from the wagon. "Are you ready?"

"I don't really have a choice, do I? Helping the sick and injured is what I want to do—what God has called me to do."

He nodded. "We need to open the hospital. Do you suppose we can talk Stuart into that?"

"I don't plan to talk him into anything," Deborah declared. "We will simply tell him that's how it's going to be. After all, there are more of us." She crooked her finger to G.W. "We need to open the hospital," she told him as he approached.

"I'll take care of it."

Christopher reached for his bag. "I'll leave it in your capable hands. Come along, Deborah. We need to see whose injuries are the worst."

She started to follow him, then noticed the trees near the edge of the clearing. "Oh no!" Her gasp caused Christopher to take note.

Deborah thought she might vomit. At least seven swinging

bodies, lynched. A couple of young boys were struggling to bring down the dead. Several bodies were already on the ground.

"I'll take care of that," Rob said, coming alongside them. "I'll take Jimmy and Tommy. It's hard for a boy to become a man this way, but we have no choice."

"I'll help you," Pastor Shattuck declared.

Deborah and Christopher made their way to where the injured were gathered. Many had been shot. Some would make it; others were certain to die. Deborah watched as Christopher assessed each man, woman, and child.

One little girl had been shot in the face. It was a glancing blow, but she would be marked for life—if she lived.

G.W. came running—his limp hardly noticeable. "I've got the hospital ready."

Christopher looked from his patients to the wagon. "We need to get the worst of them to my examination room. Take these folks first. I'm going to have to operate. Arrange them as best you can in the front room. We'll move as quickly as possible."

"What do you want me to do?" Deborah asked her husband.

"I'll need you to assist me in surgery," he told her. "Sissy!" The black woman came running.

"Yessuh, Doc?"

"I need you to tend those whose wounds are less severe. Deborah and I are going to be operating over at the hospital."

"You jes' leave it to me," she assured him. "I'll get hot water to you, too."

He nodded and turned back to G.W. "Let's get the wagon unloaded at my place, then you can use it as an ambulance."

"Sounds good." The two men jumped into the wagon.

Deborah motioned them on. "I'll be there shortly. I'm going to see if Jael can help."

She crossed the tracks and made her way to the Albright house. Stuart and Mr. Longstreet seemed to be arguing. She didn't have to explain her presence, however. Jael bounded out of the house, her arms full of sheets. She had changed her clothes and now wore a full apron.

"What can I do?" she asked Deborah.

"You'll do nothing," Stuart said, coming between them. "I will not have my wife acting in such a manner."

"What manner, Stuart?" she asked. "That of a compassionate human being? No doubt that is foreign to you, but I will not be stopped." Jael looked to her father. "We could use help from both of you. After all, you're the ones who own this place. At least that's what you're always boasting. Have you no concern for your people?"

"They aren't *my* people. The land and the buildings that have been destroyed are mine, but the people were set free—or have you forgotten?"

She shook her head. "Sure doesn't look that way to me."

Deborah wanted to applaud her friend, but instead reached out to take some of the bedding from Jael's arms. "Come. We need to hurry. I hope you aren't squeamish."

Jael gave Deborah a look that said it all. "I'm stronger than you think."

As night closed in, Deborah had never known such exhaustion. She remembered briefly when Sissy had sent someone with food and instructions that Deborah and the others were to eat or she would come and feed them herself. Deborah paused long enough to grab a piece of bread and ham. She downed it without even tasting it. Christopher and Jael did likewise, and by then, Mrs. Perkins and Mrs. Huebner had come to assist in the infirmary. They had agreed to stay through the night and attend the wounded. As Christopher explained, there was little else he could do at this point but wait.

Most of the injured were treatable. Those who weren't had died fairly soon after being brought to the examination room. Deborah wept silently as she covered the body of a ten-year-old boy. Someone had bashed in his head. He had struggled to live, but he had lost too much blood. It was just as well, she supposed. His mother and father were both dead.

Christopher once spoke of a certain ability with which God blessed medical folks. It was a kind of separation—a numbness that allowed them to see the most horrific sights and still function. His words proved true this day. But now, as the urgency passed and the moments settled into routine, emotion overwhelmed Deborah. Scenes revisited her thoughts—gashed heads, gunshot wounds, burns, and the ever-present odor of burnt flesh and death. When Mr. and Mrs. Perkins came forward to tell them to go home, she nearly cried with relief.

"You've done all you can, Doc. Why don't you go on back home and get a good night's sleep. We can handle these folks tonight. Rachel here is quite good at nursing, and Sissy won't be far."

Christopher seemed torn in regard to his duty. "I can sleep in my old bed."

Zed led him to the door, taking Deborah along as he walked by. "We took that bed into the infirmary for a patient. You two were just married, and already you did more than anyone had a right to ask."

"He's right," Jael said, coming alongside Deborah. "You two need to rest or you'll be no good to us tomorrow."

Deborah looked to Christopher. He nodded and put his arm around her. "I suppose we can bring back more supplies in the morning."

"Take our carriage," Jael offered.

"That's all right. We can ride back with G.W." Deborah had seen her brother only ten minutes earlier. He and Rob were going to finish up the remaining burials and then head home.

"I'll go let them know," Christopher said, heading toward the railroad tracks.

"I hope your work here hasn't caused you too much trouble," Deborah said to Jael. "I know we couldn't have helped as many without you."

Jael smiled. "I will be fine. Sometimes God brings about answers we don't expect."

"So you're feeling less inclined to ignore the Lord?"

"I realized that doing things my way wasn't exactly accomplishing a whole lot of good." She smiled. "I'm new at this praying thing, but I asked God for His help and promised to do whatever I could to live a life He would find worthy of saving."

"Just remember that salvation is a free gift. We can't earn it, Jael. We aren't any of us worthy in and of ourselves. We only find value in God's eyes when we accept His Son as Savior."

"Then that's what I want," her friend assured her.

Deborah embraced Jael. "I'm so glad. You won't regret it."

Jael pulled away and nodded. "I have already had answered prayer."

The look on Jael's face piqued Deborah's curiosity, and apparently the question was fixed in her expression.

"I'll tell you all about it later. Your brothers and husband are coming back this way." She kissed Deborah's cheek. "I'll see you soon—I promise."

ꕥ

Jael looked at Stuart and crossed her arms against her chest. Her father had long since gone to bed, but she wasn't going anywhere until she had settled some issues.

"I do not intend to return to Houston until after I see this matter resolved with the Vandermarks."

"Do you suppose to order me around—tell me how it will be?"

Jael took a seat opposite Stuart's desk. "I had hoped we could work amicably together. Reach a compromise, if you would."

"What makes you think you have anything I want?" He sneered. "You satisfy my needs quite well already, and as my wife you will continue to do so. There is no compromise to be had."

"Ah, but there is."

"If this is about a divorce, I have already told you no. We are married and will stay that way."

"Not unless there are some changes." She fixed him with a hard look. "You see, I know the truth."

He looked around the room for a moment as if someone else had joined them. "What is this about?"

"I know you had to marry me to obtain your inheritance. We were both in need of marriage, and together we helped each other. I had hoped love would grow between us, Stuart, but I'm not sure that you are even capable of such emotion."

"This is nonsense, Jael. Of course you knew the situation when we married. Now, leave me be and stop with any further thought of making demands. Or have you forgotten my previous threats? Miss Vandermark—excuse me, Mrs. Kelleher—may be married, but she could still meet with an accident." He shrugged. "Things like that do happen." He appeared to focus on the ledger before him.

Jael refused to be moved. "Of course I knew that you needed a wife to obtain your inheritance." She waited until he raised his gaze to her before continuing. "What I didn't know then was that you needed to remain married for a certain time period or your father would fail to release the final fortune to you. He would also cut you from his will irrevocably."

Stuart tried to hide his surprise, but he was unable to mask his expression. "What are you talking about?"

Jael smiled and held up a letter. "I found this from your father. It was waiting for you in Houston."

"You had no right to open that." He pounded his fist against the desk. "No right."

She shrugged. "Be that as it may, I read the contents and must say, they were quite liberating. You need me to remain married to you."

Stuart appeared most uncomfortable. He pulled at the neck of his shirt and fell back against the chair. "What are you proposing?"

"I will stay with you, Stuart. I have spoken to my father about the matter, and while he is appalled at my being in a loveless marriage, I assured him that I could be content. We will live as man and wife in name only—perhaps even in the same residence, so long as we maintain separate living arrangements. You have your mistresses and liaisons anyway. I doubt you'll be that inconvenienced."

"And what must I do in return?" he asked, leaning forward.

She could see she had his utmost interest. "I think you already know the answer to that. Tear up your contract with the Vandermarks. Free them to do business elsewhere and stop this childish determination to get revenge. Do that and I will stay with you. Refuse and I will have lawyers draw up papers immediately for a divorce. My father will wire your father and explain, and your inheritance will be forfeited."

"You tramp. You think you have me where you want me."

Jael got to her feet. "No, because that place would be six feet under."

"Speaking of which, I could simply do away with you," he threatened.

She smiled. "But you won't. The proviso of your father's instructions stipulates that if I should die in any way other than during childbirth, he would immediately withdraw your funds until such time as you were able to remarry and remain that way for . . . what was it—ten years? Yes, I believe it was to be increased to ten." She narrowed her eyes. "Since I do not intend to bear your children or share your bed again, my death in childbirth is clearly not going to happen."

Stuart jumped to his feet. "I could force you! I could have my way with you here and now."

She stood her ground. "You dare to try, and our divorce will be imminent. You see? I now hold the winning cards. You have tormented and tortured my friends for long enough. Resolve this matter immediately or lose it all."

Chapter 26

June 1887

Stuart was not pleased to see his wife and father-in-law enter his study. "I'm very busy." He looked at Longstreet. "It's been over a week since you arrived—don't you have business to attend to back in Houston?"

"I do, but I also have affairs that need my attention right here," Longstreet replied. He seated Jael and pulled up a second chair for himself. "As your partner, I figure we need to talk."

Stuart looked at Jael, and the rage brewing within him since her proclamations the week before threatened to boil over.

"With all that has happened," Longstreet began, "we need to figure out what is most beneficial and productive for this town. I have arranged to have the blacks moved into the houses on the north side of town."

"What? Those are quarters for whites. This isn't their side of town," Stuart protested.

"That was once the case, but now there is no other alternative. They cannot be expected to live without shelter. The thunderstorms of the past few days should prove that if nothing else. Then there are the sick to contend with."

"I already allowed the infirmary to be reopened. Dr. Kelleher has used up most of the inventoried supplies, and I haven't even charged the people for their care."

"Nor will you," Jael declared.

Stuart was not used to being ordered about—especially not by a woman. He glared at her. "I may have money, my dear wife, but I won't have it for long if I give charity to everyone."

"You are the reason this town is in ruins," she countered. "I've overheard your conversations with the insurance inspector. Whether you set the mill on fire yourself or hired it done, it was still your doing. You have a grudge against the Vandermarks and anyone who cares for them."

"You can never prove that," Stuart said without thinking. He fought to regain his composure, adding, "Because it isn't true."

Dwight Longstreet raised his hand. "It isn't important. We need to turn things around and see this town rebuilt. Until new quarters can be constructed to house the blacks, they will stay in the ones already in place."

"No white man will put his family in a house where former slaves have lived. Your knowledge of whites in this part of the country may be limited, but I've made it my duty to understand." Stuart crossed his arms. "We'll only end up having to tear those houses down or drag them to the other side of the tracks."

"If it comes to that, then we will do what must be done," Longstreet replied. "In the meanwhile, I intend to speak to Zed about setting up an outdoor mill. I'm going to instruct him to order the things he needs and get at least a minimal mill operation going. That will give people work to do and provide the needed lumber for the reconstruction."

Stuart jumped to his feet. "You overstep your bounds, Longstreet. You forget that I am the controlling partner in this business."

Jael stood to face her husband. "And you forget that I know full well about your father's requirements for your inheritance. Your days of revenge and control have come to an end. You are no longer going to do these people harm."

"Me? I didn't burn down the shanties. I didn't shoot up the town." He was annoyed that she should even imply such a thing. Certainly he'd done nothing to stop it, but he was only one man against fifteen or twenty. Lying low in the house was far wiser until he could learn to what extent the riders intended to cause damage.

"Have you torn up the Vandermark Logging contract yet?" she asked.

Stuart knew that he had to reclaim control over the conversation. He drew a deep breath. "I have considered it, but given what your father is demanding of me, I cannot." She frowned and he continued. "We must have logs in order to create lumber. I will let the Vandermarks know that we need to immediately resume deliveries."

Jael considered this for a moment, then retook her seat. Instead of looking to Stuart, however, she turned to her father. "Would that be helpful to them—to rebuilding?"

Stuart wanted to throw something at her. How dare she look to her father for answers? He held his tongue, however.

Longstreet was already assuring her that it would be a good arrangement.

"The Vandermarks will get paid, and we will have immediate product. Stuart has already had some lumber brought in, as well as milling equipment. I'm certain that if we get Zed Perkins back on the job, we can see progress within a matter of weeks."

Jael nodded. "And what of the people, Father? They've lost everything. They have no food or other necessities."

"I have already placed an order for the commissary to be restocked in full. We will give the people company tokens for working to help us clear the debris and rebuild the mill and houses. Women will be hired, as well as youngsters. I'll have Zed get word out that we need workers."

"You take too much upon yourself." Stuart all but growled out the words.

"When will you let the Vandermarks know about bringing in the logs?" Jael asked, turning back to Stuart. "Today?"

Stuart looked at the two people. Was it possible that he now hated this pair more than he did G.W. and Deborah?

A thought came to mind. Perhaps he could still have his revenge. If things went his way, he might even own Vandermark Logging before it was all done. Of course! Why hadn't he considered this before?

"I will go today," he told them. He searched around the desk and pulled up several pieces of paper. "I will see what we are entitled to and request it all. They will make a small fortune, and I will have the necessary wood to begin rebuilding."

Jael smiled. "That sounds wonderful. Come, Father. Let's go talk to Mr. and Mrs. Perkins."

"I thought they'd returned to Lufkin," her father replied.

She frowned. "I'd forgotten that. Let's send them a wire,

then. We need to get them back here immediately. They can bring others with them." She waited for him to get to his feet. Glancing at Stuart, she gave him a curt nod. "Thank you, Stuart. I'm glad you've decided to cooperate."

"Deborah, you in here?" Arjan called from the cabin door.

Coming out from the small room they'd made into an examination area, Deborah smiled. "Goodness, you gave me a start. I was just putting away some supplies."

Arjan entered the house, cane in one hand and a very pale Jake helped along by the other. Jake held his left arm close to his body. Someone had wrapped his hand and forearm in a bandage, but blood was seeping through.

"What happened?" she asked. "Bring him in here."

Deborah led the way to the examination room. She motioned for her uncle to assist Jake while she lit the two bracketed wall lamps at the head of the table and angled their reflectors to give her maximum light.

"Christopher isn't here right now, so I'll have to take care of you," she said, looking at the solemn-faced Jake.

"I'm all right with that. I know you're good. I've seen you work."

His face was a pasty white, and Deborah feared he might well faint. "Why don't you lie down here on the table and tell me what happened."

Arjan leaned the cane against the wall, then helped ease Jake into position as best he could. "Saw slipped. He just happened to have his hand and arm in the way."

"Hurts like the devil," Jake said.

Deborah unwrapped the bandages. Caked blood and dirt

would need to be washed away before she could tell exactly how bad it was. "I'll need to clean it. This won't be pleasant, but you'll be glad for it in the long run."

"If you don't need me," Arjan told her, taking up his cane, "I'll go let your ma know what's happened."

"That's fine. Jake will hold still." She looked at him and smiled. "Won't you?"

Arjan laughed, but Jake only gritted his teeth as Deborah began to wash the wound. "I'll be back shortly to check in on you," her stepfather told her.

Taking a good look at the damage, Deborah could see that the wound was far deeper toward the center of the hand. The gash ran along the lower edge of the forearm and right between the line of tendons that connected to his thumb and index finger.

"I think that if an injury could be called lucky, this would be the one. If you'd been sliced the other way, you probably would never be able to use this hand again."

"Sure don't know why it had to happen."

"Who can say? I'm going to have to stitch you up between your finger and thumb, but the rest isn't so deep. I don't think this is going to give you too much grief. You'll have to take it easy for a while, though, and keep it clean so infection won't set in. I don't know that you can work."

Jake opened his eyes and smiled. "I was going to be quittin' at the end of the week anyway."

"Truly? But why?"

He grimaced as she examined the wound further. "I sent my folks a wire. I want to join them in California."

"That's wonderful, Jake. I'm so glad you felt you could."

"I came to realize something," he said, fixing his gaze on her face. "I do care about you, but I care just as much about your family. What I was lookin' for was that sense of belonging. I just figured it meant that I needed to take a wife and that she ought to be you."

Deborah was touched by his confession. "Jake, I'm so blessed to hear it. Thank you for telling me."

"I miss my folks. We were always close, but the drought and the loss of the ranch changed my father. Changed me, too. I wasn't kind to him. I was angry and I blamed him for losin' what had been in the family for some time." Jake's expression saddened. "I have a great deal of apologizin' to do."

She reached for her needle. "The important thing is that forgiveness is something we do for ourselves as well as the other person. If you forgive your father, you will feel better in your own soul. If your father forgives you—who knows? It may well set matters aright and find him able to move forward. I'm sure the loss of the ranch was hard on him, as well."

"I know it was," Jake said. "Knew it then, too, and I hate myself for being so heartless."

"But hate won't serve any good purpose. Look what it did in town. Look what it's done to this country. We won't ever be without it, but we can do our part to lessen it."

"I heard that Arjan talked to the law about the White Hand of God."

Deborah nodded. "Not that it will resolve the problems here, to be sure. Some folks will support ugliness as well as beauty. We talked long and hard with Pastor Shattuck, and he said that it will take time to change the hearts of folks who are steeped in such a desperate desire to punish others. I have to have hope that God can do it, though. If not, then I would truly be lost in despair."

Jake glanced down at his arm. "So you really gonna stitch me up or just sit there and jaw with me?"

She laughed. "Believe me, by the time I finish, you'll be beggin' me to just talk."

He drew a deep breath. "Well, give me something to bite down on. I don't want no one hearin' me holler."

Deborah glanced across the room for something to give him. She spied a towel and went to fetch it. Fixing it into a tight roll, she handed it to Jake. "This ought to help muffle your protests."

He took the towel and brought it to his mouth. "Let's get this over with, then."

It was bad enough being forced to do something he'd never intended to do, but Stuart hated wasting his time even more. After making excuses for several days, he'd finally ridden up to the Vandermark logging camp only to find it deserted. Now it was late afternoon and he was finally reaching home, but he had no answers to give his nagging wife. He'd considered stopping at the Vandermark house on his return, but with the light fading and his mood definitely darkening, as well, he decided against it. If Jael asked him about it, he would simply let her know that he'd try again the next day.

It was clear they'd moved the camp, but Stuart had no idea where they'd gone to or why. He would ask around and see if anyone could tell him. If that failed, he'd have no choice but to go to the Vandermark house and inquire there. He didn't want to do that if he could help it. He despised seeing G.W. and Lizzie together. They were happy, in spite of the problems he'd created for them. It didn't make sense, but Stuart supposed it didn't have to. It frustrated him, nevertheless.

When he rode up to his house, Stuart could see that Jael was serving a guest on the front porch. He frowned. Who had come to plague them now? He dismounted and tied the horse off at the post near the front steps.

Jael came to the rail. "Mr. Jennings from Houston has come to see you," she said as any dutiful wife might. "Since it was cooler out here on the porch, I thought to serve him some chilled lemonade. Would you care for a glass, also?"

Stuart shook his head and tried to recall who Jennings was. The name was vaguely familiar. He climbed the steps and extended his hand to the older man. Getting to his feet, the man gave a hint of a bow.

"Mr. Albright, I'm from your bank in Houston. I have some business to discuss, if you can take the time."

He remembered the man then. He was one of the lesser bank officers who kept an eye on the Vandermark accounts for him. Stuart turned to Jael. "Thank you for seeing to our guest in Essie's absence. I do need to speak with him privately, however."

Jael nodded. "Then I will go check on supper." She smiled at Mr. Jennings. "I hope you'll find our guest room to your liking. I'll see to it that you have fresh water in the pitcher. We'll dine at six-thirty."

"Mrs. Albright, you are a delightful hostess. I'm certain that I will sleep like a babe in the arms of his mother," the man said, bowing lower than he had for Stuart. "And if the aroma of that food is any indication, supper will be a culinary delight."

"Thank you, Mr. Jennings. I will allow you to reserve judgment until you've sampled the meal."

The interaction irritated Stuart, but he said nothing. He waited until Jael had returned to the house before motioning the man back to his seat. Pulling up a chair to sit directly in front of the man, Stuart gave his guest a sober gaze. "So tell me what has caused you to come all this way."

❧

The last person G.W. had expected to see that Saturday morning was Stuart Albright. Even so, there the man stood, filling the office doorway with a scowl as dark as the growing clouds outside.

"What can I do for you, Mr. Albright?" Thunder rumbled in the distance, making the moment feel even more ominous to G.W.

Stuart's expression changed to one of smug control. "It's more what I can do for you. I tried to let you know about it yesterday. I made my way out to the logging camp but found it deserted."

"Camps move from time to time. You have to go where the trees are," G.W. replied, hoping he sounded convincing. "Turpentiners finished up in one section, so we wanted to get those trees down before a strong storm came along." He'd certainly not expected Albright to venture anywhere near the camp, but now that he had, it would be up to G.W. to make it seem irrelevant.

"And where are you now located?"

"Well, we have one camp up on the northern edge of our property. There's another we've started just east of here. Why do you ask?"

G.W. could sense that the man was up to something, but he was still uncertain as to what that was. Albright could not be trusted—that much G.W. knew.

"I'd enjoy seeing it sometime, especially now."

"Especially now?" G.W. questioned. "What's that supposed to mean?"

Albright laughed, but it sounded hollow and devoid of any real amusement. "It means that I have come to reinstate our logging contract. My father-in-law has convinced me that we can do better for ourselves by processing our own lumber for the rebuilding of the mill. Of course, that also means we must act fast."

G.W. found it hard to believe the man was serious. This couldn't be boding well with Albright. He meant to force Vandermark Logging out of business. He wouldn't do anything to benefit them.

"So when would you like delivery to start?"

"Immediately," Stuart replied. "Of course, I realize that may tax you somewhat."

"Tax us? I don't reckon I understand."

"Then perhaps I'd better explain," Stuart said, finally taking a seat in front of G.W.'s desk. "I want what is owed to the Perkinsville Sawmill, the full amount. Of course, I will also be paying you in full, you understand."

G.W. did understand. Albright wanted Vandermark Logging to supply them with the quota of logs that they'd agreed to under contract. That would entail thousands and thousands of board feet, but it would bring them a nice tidy sum and put the family business back on its feet.

"I reckon we can to do that." G.W. took up a piece of paper. He figured it would come to Albright as a surprise with what he was going to say next. "We can have the first delivery made on Monday. Do you want 'em dumped in the millpond like before or just stacked?"

"I want them stacked. I want all of them stacked and ready by June twentieth."

G.W. wasn't sure exactly what Albright meant. He looked at the man and shook his head. "I said I could have them on Monday. You want me to wait till the twentieth? That's two weeks from Monday."

"You're right," Stuart replied, pressing his fingers together.

"So you don't want a delivery on Monday?"

"I didn't say that. What I want is what is owed me—in full—in two weeks."

It began to dawn on G.W. exactly what Stuart was implying. "You want delivery of all the logs we would have brought into the mill since it burned down? And you want them in two weeks?"

"Exactly," Stuart said, his smug smile broadening.

"That's impossible," G.W. said, shaking his head. "We can't cut that fast."

Stuart shrugged. "You should have been cutting all along."

"We have been, but we can only stockpile so many logs. You wouldn't want the quality jeopardized."

Stuart didn't seem to even hear him. "It's legally owed me, and if you do not comply, then you will be in breach of contract. I will see to it that you are forced to forfeit your land in payment." Getting to his feet, Stuart headed for the door. "Perhaps if you'd seen fit not to go behind my back and arrange for your logs to go elsewhere, you'd have enough stockpiled to meet my needs."

He was gone before G.W. could respond—not that he knew what to say. G.W. thought of going after Albright and telling him they had done nothing illegal, but he figured Albright already knew that. In fact, it was probably the very reason he'd come with the demands he'd just made. He couldn't punish the Vandermarks for giving away their logs, but he could penalize them by forcing them to meet an impossible deadline.

G.W. glanced at the clock on the wall. His mother, Arjan, and the children were out checking on the black grapes. Mother always liked to get them picked early, and even though they mostly ripened in July and August, she kept a close vigil. Arjan could get around with a cane but Mother wouldn't yet let him return to the logging camp, so he busied himself the best he could by helping where she'd allow for it. Lizzie and the twins were out in the garden. His son and daughter would celebrate their first birthday on the sixteenth—just four days prior to Albright's newly imposed deadline.

He rubbed the long healed injury to his thigh and wondered how they could make it all work out. G.W. had never been as good with figures as he would've liked to be, but a fella didn't need a higher education to know that the logs they owed Albright were more than they could hope to cut with the small crew employed by Vandermark Logging.

"We're gonna need your help on this one, Lord," he said, looking to the ceiling. "And we're gonna need it by the twentieth."

Chapter 27

Deborah sat beside Christopher and listened as her brother and Arjan laid out their plans for the two weeks to come. She and Christopher had agreed to come and help at the logging camp. Christopher felt that with her there to tend the injured, as well as help with the cooking, he could lend a hand in the actual logging. The idea made Deborah smile. He had no idea what he was in for. Logging was not for the faint of heart, and while her husband had great stamina and strength, he was used to tending patients.

"We've got to get the word out that we'll take any and all workers," Arjan said. "I figure with my leg the way it is, I can at least take care of that much."

Mother shook her head. "You shouldn't even be up and

around, but like my mama used to say, 'You can't harness the wind.' "

Arjan laughed. "Is that your way of declarin' I'm full of hot air?" He smiled and continued. "I'll send out a wire, then head up to Lufkin and see if I can round up some men. We've got friends all around us, and hopefully they'll lend a hand."

"I'll help Deborah at the camp," Lizzie announced. "Mother has already agreed to keep the children here with her."

G.W. nodded. "Havin' you gals there to cook and clean up will be a great help. Those fellas are gonna need hardy helpin's of food. Jake, you sure you don't mind stayin' here to lend Ma a hand?"

"I don't mind at all. In fact, I'll come back to work if Mr. Vandermark will just let me."

"No, Son. Havin' you here will put my mind at ease."

"Mine too," Mother said, giving Jake a reassuring nod.

"I'll go to the commissary and see what can be had," Arjan promised. "I'll be headin' there to send the telegram anyway."

"I'll go with you," Deborah interjected. "There are cots at the infirmary. We could use them for the workers. Stuart Albright may not like it, but I don't intend to ask for his permission."

"Sounds good. I know any extra tents are bein' used to help shelter the folks who lost their homes," Arjan replied. "I'll see what's to be had later in Lufkin. We'll get what we can and get back here as soon as possible. By then, you oughta have the rest of the gear loaded and ready to go."

Mother nodded. "Sissy and I will pack the other wagon with dried beans and cornmeal." She looked to her friend. "We're running low after taking so much into town after the fire, but we'll get by."

"The garden is producing, and with game and such, we can

surely get by until Albright pays us on the twentieth," G.W. said. "We'll need to work around the clock at the camp, so we're gonna need a lot of lanterns and kerosene."

"I'll add that to the list," Arjan said.

"Can we really do this?" Mother asked.

Deborah hated the way her voice sounded—so uncertain, weary before they even attempted to accomplish the goal.

"It'll be close. We'll have to work every day," G.W. said.

"We aren't working on the Lord's Day," Arjan declared firmly. "Your pa and I had a long-standin' agreement that we would always honor the Lord by keepin' that day holy. I don't intend to break with that now."

Deborah looked at him in surprise. "But it's just this once, and the circumstances are critical."

"Either we believe God will see us through this or we don't," Arjan replied. "God certainly expects us to work and do our part, but He won't be replaced by a false idol—even one as honorable as meetin' our contract obligations."

"He's right," Mother said, glancing at her husband with a smile. "We put God first. He will provide what we need."

Deborah fully believed in having faith, but this surprised her. Surely God allowed for extenuating circumstances. Jesus was even confronted by the Pharisees about healing on the Sabbath. What was it He said?

" 'Wherefore it is lawful to do well on the Sabbath days,' " she murmured, remembering the twelfth chapter of Matthew.

Her stepfather met her gaze. "What was that?"

"I was just remembering that Jesus said it was lawful to do well on the Sabbath. He said it just before healing a man."

"And I suppose we must reckon what the Lord meant by doin' well," Arjan said. "Like healin'. I figure selfless acts that keep a fella or animal from starvin' or dyin' are doin' well. Earning a livin' can't hardly be the same difference."

Deborah knew she wouldn't convince him otherwise and only nodded. She supposed he made a good point. Their dilemma was one that, when resolved, would provide them with monetary gain.

"Don't fret, Deborah," her stepfather added. "God ain't forgotten about us in all this time. I don't reckon He's gonna start anytime soon."

She smiled, knowing he was right. She pushed back her fearful thoughts and settled on revisiting such issues at a later time. "Well, we'd best get to town. There's no tellin' what we'll find. Stuart Albright may well have shipped the commissary off to Houston by now." She got to her feet.

"Let's pray first," Arjan said, standing.

The others rose and joined hands. Deborah bowed her head and closed her eyes. *Father, this seems to be more than we can bear*, she prayed even as her stepfather began his petition. *Please go before us.*

Deborah was surprised to find the commissary very nearly emptied. Arjan stood at the counter, shaking his head as Jude Greeley explained.

"Mr. Longstreet came in here with the black folks and set them up accounts to get the things they needed. He moved them over to the row of empty houses on the north side of town and said they could stay there until new places could be built. He figures to get the mill going mighty quick—even put in a big order of supplies to come up from Burke and any place else he could get 'em."

"Do tell," Arjan said, shaking his head. "Well, it would seem

Mr. Albright and Mr. Longstreet have had a change of heart in matters regardin' Perkinsville."

"It would seem that way," Jude admitted. "I still have some bags of beans and meal, though. Just not a great deal. I'll give you what I can and then you come back next week and we should be restocked. Mr. Longstreet wired for the new supplies to be sent right away."

"Guess that'll have to do us," Arjan replied. "How about kerosene and some lanterns?"

Jude shook his head. "I have some kerosene left, but they cleaned me out of lamps and lanterns. Why don't you take a look around and see what's left. If you can use it—take it. Say, you oughta check over at the livery. Maybe they could spare a few lanterns for you to borrow."

"It's worth askin' after," Arjan agreed. "We may just have to make some smudge pots."

"Or some good old-fashioned bonfires." Deborah touched his arm. "I'm going to go over to the infirmary and get the cots."

"I'm sorry, Miss Deborah—I mean Mrs. Kelleher," Jude interjected, "but they took those, as well."

She looked at him in disbelief. "All of them?"

" 'Fraid so. Those folks lost everything, as you know."

"Looks like we'll be sleeping out under the stars," she told Arjan.

"Reckon so. Guess we'd do well to finish up here and get on our way."

G.W. loved being out in the woods again. He relished the smell of pine and earth. Watching the men at work, he found he even missed the hard labor of swinging an ax. His father had taught him at a very early age how to cut wood for the hearth. Later, he instructed G.W. how to cut a wedge to fell a tree. So many lessons he'd learned from his father. And in times like this, G.W. couldn't help but think of them. His father had been a good man—loving and generous. How he missed him.

An approaching wagon drew G.W.'s focus. He figured Arjan and Deborah were returning with the commissary purchases and left his things to go greet them. Not seeing any telltale evidence heaping the back of the wagon, he frowned.

"What happened?" He saw only a few bags of beans, cornmeal, sugar, and salt. There were also half a dozen other items, including some extra axes and saws and tins of kerosene.

"Apparently, Mr. Longstreet and Albright practiced generosity on the black folks. The commissary was pretty bare by the time we got there." Arjan climbed down, accepting G.W.'s offer of help. "The ride put me to achin', but don't tell your mother or she'll be fussin' over me."

G.W. nodded. "We can make do. I'll send a couple of the boys out to shoot a rabbit or two. Maybe a squirrel. We'll get by."

"They took all the hospital cots, as well," Deborah said, coming from the other side of the wagon. "I can't fault them for doing such a kindness, but it does change things for us a bit."

"Not to worry," Arjan said. "I'm gonna head right up to Lufkin. If I get a move on, I can get there by dark. I'll attend church with Bertram Wallace in the morning and return on Monday."

Deborah reached into the wagon bed and took up several small sacks of flour. Smiling at her stepfather, she said, "We'd best get you on your way."

Within a matter of minutes, Arjan was back in the wagon

seat. "I'll see you on Monday." He snapped the reins and moved the horses out.

G.W. turned to Deborah. "Lizzie has been workin' to expand the cooking area. I'm gonna send Jimmy and Tommy down to bring up the tables and benches we made for your weddin'. I reckon they'll serve us pretty well."

"Where's Christopher? I need to let him know that I couldn't bring much of anything from the old house. It was pretty well stripped."

"He's actually gettin' a lesson on the two-handed saw. I have a feelin' your husband is in for blistered hands and a sore back before this is all said and done."

"There are worse things," Deborah replied. "Where did he set up?"

"Right over there. We doubled the boys up in the other tents, and you and the doc are in the one by mine and Lizzie's." G.W. pointed to where two tents sat apart from the others. "You'll be closer to the creek that way. I told the boys to just figure on bringin' up two pails of water every mornin' to help you ladies get it heated for coffee and anything else you need. After that, you'll pretty much be on your own. The men are gonna be too busy."

She laughed. "Gijsbert Willem Vandermark, we are fully capable of doing our part. Hard work never hurt anyone."

"I beg to differ with you," he said, grinning. "Hard work just about kilt me when I fell out of a tree."

"I can see your point, but unfortunately there's no more time to chat. There's a lot of work to be done. I've got to get the beans soaking for tomorrow and help Lizzie figure out how we're going to manage everything."

"Oh, Sis?"

She turned back to face him. With a rise of her brow she questioned him without a word.

"You use my full name again, and I'm gonna tell doc about the time you tried to hatch that nest of eggs by sittin' on them. Then I'm gonna tell him about the time—"

She held up her hand. "Point taken, G.W. It won't happen again."

ꕥ

Nearly a week later, Jael was happy to see a noticeable change in the town. The remaining debris from the mill site had been cleaned up and cleared away. Zed Perkins had returned to town, along with two of his sons, and with them came several other men from Lufkin. Apparently, Arjan Vandermark had found Zed before he and Rachel had even received the telegram Jael had sent. Zed was more than happy to return to town, and happier still when her father explained that he intended to take over Stuart's supervision of the town and send his son-in-law back to Houston. At least that was the plan.

Jael tried not to think about Stuart. She knew he was unhappy, being forced to adhere to the demands she and her father had given him. He'd barely said two words to her on any given day that week, although she'd heard more than one yelling match between her father and Stuart behind closed doors. He'd made it clear that he was enraged at being ordered about. He accused her father of going behind his back and spending money that should have been spent elsewhere. Jael had been proud of her father's willingness to stand his ground, however. He was no pauper, and in his own right, he could very nearly match Stuart's financial success. He, however, could boast that his money had been earned—something that was now more respected than it used to be. Stuart felt his wealth was more impressive because he'd inherited it, even if it came by deception and cruelty.

Jael made her way to the commissary and walked in to find several black women helping to put away supplies. Jude Greeley was telling one woman where to place the cast-iron pots while another waited patiently to be shown what to do with a box of thread.

"This is certainly a fine change," she said as Jude pointed the last woman in the right direction.

"It is indeed. Reminds me of when we first set up business, only then it was just the missus and me puttin' away stock. It's good to see the place up and runnin' again."

"There will be a great many more people coming back to Perkinsville," she told him. "My father and Mr. Perkins intend to see the mill operating, at least in part, by the middle of next week."

"I heard that, as well, Mrs. Albright. What was it that changed your husband's mind?"

Jael smiled. "I suppose he saw the value in moving forward."

"Jael!"

She turned to find Deborah rushing across the store. "I can scarce believe my good fortune. I had heard you were far to the north at the logging camp." She embraced Deborah. "Goodness, but you're thin as a rail."

"I don't think I've ever worked harder in my life," Deborah said with a laugh. "G.W. and I came down to the house to see how Mother and Sissy were doing. We heard the supplies had come into the store and thought to take a load back up with us."

"You look exhausted," Jael said, taking Deborah aside, "but how marvelous that Stuart finally honored his contract."

"He honored it all right. Honored it with his demand that

we meet an impossible goal by June twentieth or he'll sue us and take our land." Deborah frowned. "Hardly a victory."

Jael could hardly believe what she was hearing. "I don't understand."

Deborah cocked her head to one side. "Don't you know?"

"I can't imagine what you're talking about."

"Stuart demanded the full quota of logs owed him by Vandermark Logging—the amount we would have provided from the time the mill burned until now."

"How can that be legal?" she asked in disbelief.

"It's within his rights, despite the absurdity of his demands. As usual, he's found a way to manipulate the legal aspects to his benefit—and our detriment. Lizzie's father told us that Stuart apparently has several judges eating out of his hand. He has an entire team of lawyers who do his bidding, and apparently owns the bank—or at least some of their people—where Vandermark Logging has borrowed."

Jael felt her ire rise. "I knew it was too good to be true. Stuart has been far too quiet. I demanded he tear up the contract with Vandermark Logging, but he said he had a better idea—he would get you back in business. My father even thought it sounded like a worthy idea."

"It would be, except for the deadline and quota of logs." Deborah shook her head. "We've hired on as many men as want work and have experience. The job is getting done, but we still don't know that we can meet Stuart's demands."

"Leave that to me."

"What can you possibly do?"

She wasn't exactly sure. She could only push Stuart so far, but given all that he'd done, Jael figured he still owed her. "I'll do what I can. When is the deadline?"

"Monday the twentieth. We're to have the logs stockpiled by the tracks or already delivered here to the mill. I'm not sure Stuart understands exactly how much ground that's going to take up, but I figure that's his concern."

"And it will be the least of them." Jael took hold of Deborah's arm. "I'll speak to Father. He may have additional ideas."

"Thank you. You have been a good friend to me." Deborah caught sight of the clock as it chimed two. "I need to run. G.W. and I have to get the wagon loaded and delivered yet this afternoon." She leaned forward and kissed Jael on the cheek.

Jael watched her friend head to the counter and contemplated what she should do. She thought about just confronting Stuart and decided against it. She would talk to her father first. He had proven himself more than capable of handling Stuart and the business of Perkinsville's rebirth.

Deborah awoke Sunday morning to the sound of rain pelting the tent. Thunder rumbled overhead and left her feeling more discouraged than she'd thought possible. The summer storms were wreaking havoc on their ability to harvest trees. Ever since the week before when she'd run into Jael at the commissary, the weather had been unpredictable. There had been no word from Jael or her father, not to mention Stuart. Deborah had hoped that one of them would arrive to say the deadline was extended—especially since it had rained off and on most every day.

Christopher stirred, but he was still asleep. She smiled and scooted closer to her husband. What would they do if the deadline wasn't met? Would Stuart really find a way to take their land? She sighed. Why were there no answers?

Christopher opened his eyes and smiled. "What time is it?"

Lightning flashed and thunder boomed right behind it. Deborah wanted to bury herself in her husband's protective embrace. The storm was apparently right on top of them. "It doesn't matter. We can't leave the tent."

He held her tight. "Pity."

"That was exactly my thought," she said, giggling.

"I've got things pretty well figured out now," Christopher declared.

She looked at him oddly. "What things?"

"Well, I now know that I don't want to be a logger. I don't want to work with mules, and I definitely prefer houses to tents."

"I'm glad, because I'm of the same mind. My back is sore from sleeping on the ground."

He slid his hand down to the small of her back and rubbed it gently. "I found myself wishing for one of the infirmary cots."

The rain grew heavier and beat out a rhythmic beat on the canvas tent. "I'm glad I left the lids off all the pots. That rainwater will come in handy," Deborah said, snuggling close.

After a few moments of silence, Christopher sighed. "The deadline is tomorrow."

She leaned up on her elbow. Doubt and worry etched her husband's features. "I know. I was thinking about that before you woke up."

"We aren't doing too bad," he added.

"We don't have enough to meet the quota," she reminded him. "I doubt Stuart is going to give us an extension. Jael had thought she could help, but I'm guessing that was just wishful thinking. Otherwise we would surely have heard something by now."

The wind picked up and pummeled the tent walls. Deborah dropped again to the crook of Christopher's arm. "I hope the storm will pass quickly."

"Arjan said the storms have been unusual for this time of year."

"Well, at least this many in a row and this strong," Deborah agreed. The fury of the weather kept them from working in any consistent fashion. "Just when I thought we had a chance . . ."

"Hey, that doesn't sound like my ever-optimistic wife," Christopher said, gently stroking her cheek. "You aren't giving up, are you?"

"I don't want to give up, but . . . I feel depleted of hope." Lightning illuminated their tent. The thunder seemed to rumble the ground around them. Deborah shuddered. "I've never had to be out in a storm like this. I'm afraid."

"Don't be," he said. "We're going to make it through this." He grinned and placed a kiss on her nose. "I kind of like being here with you. It's not the wedding trip I would have planned for us, but I'm content. I think I will always be content, so long as you're at my side."

The storm inside Deborah began to abate, even as the one raging around them lessened. Nestling down in her husband's arms, she listened as the storm began to slowly move off. Little by little the rain diminished to a gentle rhythm as the storm played out. In the distance, she heard someone singing and smiled.

It was Lizzie. The tune was more than a little familiar, the words so very appropriate for the moment.

" 'The raging storms may round us beat,' " Lizzie sang, " 'a shelter in the time of storm. We'll never leave our safe retreat, a shelter in the time of storm.' " Deborah couldn't help but smile. It was a fairly new hymn that her mother had found for the sacred-harp singing. Deborah felt peace wash over her as Lizzie's voice lingered in the air.

" 'O Rock divine, O Refuge dear, a shelter in the time of storm. Be thou our helper ever near, a shelter in the time of storm.' "

Chapter 28

The storm dissipated and the warmth of summer returned. The sun steamed the air, making everything feel heavy and sticky. Since it was later than usual, Deborah decided to do what she could to hurry breakfast. Taking dry wood from the tent, she worked quickly to get the fire going. Despite having been sheltered, the wood was still rather damp and the fire didn't want to catch. Coaxing it with dried bits of pine straw, Deborah finally established a tiny, but growing, flame. She soon had the fire built up and burning nicely.

Lizzie brought two coffeepots to hang over the fire. "I'll get some water on to boil."

"Thanks. I'll start slicing the ham."

The others emerged from their tents, rather like she imagined

Noah and his family had from the ark. They looked hopeful, but hesitant.

"Breakfast will be ready in about twenty minutes," Deborah told them as Lizzie put a large kettle of water on beside the coffee and threw more logs onto the fire.

G.W. pulled up his suspenders as he walked toward the women. "Lizzie and I talked about it last night and plan to go home after the Sunday service. We're missin' the little ones, and I reckon Ma could use the rest. Woulda headed there last night, 'cept for that storm."

"I'm sure Mama didn't mind. She loves those babies," Deborah replied, focusing her attention back on cutting the ham. She figured there would be at least twenty of them for breakfast. When they'd finished working near eleven-thirty the night before, many of the men had decided to ride to Lufkin with what little pay Arjan could amass. Those who remained were mostly young men who had come west looking to make their fortune, only to find that life on the frontier didn't come easy. Arjan had promised each a bonus if he would willingly work for no pay until the twentieth. Most had originally agreed, but after a week of battling the weather, over half of the men had decided to head to where they could get a hot bath and a comfortable bed. Deborah could only wonder if they'd made it home ahead of the storm.

"I figure with the deadline loomin' over us tomorrow, Lizzie and you might as well stay home anyway. Either we'll make the number or we won't. No need to keep you gals workin' here," G.W. said. "The train will be haulin' in logs all day and there's nothin' you can do to help with that."

"We can still cook and clean," Deborah replied. "Lizzie can stay home and maybe Mama would like to join us here."

Lizzie returned to put two more coffeepots over the fire

before checking the water in the pot. "It won't be long before it's boiling."

"It would do us all some good to go home," Arjan declared, joining them. "We could enjoy a nice restful Sabbath there just as well as here."

"That would be fine by me," Deborah agreed. "But I plan to return in the morning. If Christopher's going to work here, then I am, too."

"I think that's just fine, but you'd both better be willin' to take your pay, just like the others." Arjan grinned and gave Deborah a wink.

Deborah heard movement behind her and saw that her husband had finally moved to join them. "What do you think?" she asked Christopher, who sort of duck walked out of the tent.

"About what?" He straightened and grimaced. "I think the ground is getting harder."

She laughed. "Arjan was just suggesting we all head home for the day after breakfast. So many of the men left last night for their homes in Lufkin. Those that remain can come to the house and enjoy some time in out of the rain." With the water finally boiling, Deborah stirred in grits and covered the pot with a heavy iron lid.

"I'd be happy to sleep in my own bed, even for a few winks." Christopher suppressed a yawn and stretched. "Coffee ready yet?"

"Not quite. Soon." Deborah collected the plates. She motioned everyone to the tables. Thunder rumbled from far away.

Deborah glanced at the skies overhead. The clouds churned and thickened once again. "Hopefully we can eat before the next storm moves in."

"We haven't had a run of weather like this for years," Arjan declared.

"It's actin' like spring instead of summer," G.W. threw in.

Lizzie brought out two jugs and plopped them down on the table. The men were notorious for eating their grits with equal amounts of the thick molasses sweetness. Hopefully two jugs would be enough. It wasn't long before Deborah was ladling the food into large serving bowls. Jimmy took the first one to the table, and Lizzie took the second. Tommy and Arjan took the next bowls, and G.W. and Christopher helped by taking the platters of ham and leftover corn bread. Lizzie and Deborah brought the coffee at long last, and Arjan offered the blessing.

"Lord, we thank you for your many blessin's. We ask that you would guide us on this, your Sabbath. Help us to remember that you gave us this day of rest to think on you and your goodness. Bless this food. Amen."

"Amen," the men murmured around the table.

Arjan stood and began to speak again as the food was passed. "You men are welcome to come back to our place for the day. Looks to me like it will rain and storm into the night. You can get in out of the weather, though you may be sleeping on the floor."

There were some chuckles over this. "Hard floor, hard ground—take your choice."

"One's dry and the other's wet," Jimmy added.

Deborah watched her stepfather nod and smile. "He speaks the truth. Still, you're welcome to it. We'll leave just after breakfast and return tomorrow mornin' to finish what we started."

"We haven't made the number yet, Mr. Vandermark," one of the men declared. "Won't make our goal for tomorrow iffen we don't keep workin' today."

Arjan nodded. "Son, as I've said before, this is God's day. I know we could work it, but I believe we'll honor it instead. God multiplied the loaves and fishes for the crowds of hungry folks in the Bible. I reckon He can multiply logs if need be."

In the end, about half the men decided to go home with the Vandermarks while the others decided to stay put. Arjan had led them all in prayer and Scripture reading before announcing that they could further their time with the Lord once they were safely inside with a roof overhead.

Sprinkles of rain had started to fall by the time they reached the house. It appeared, however, that the worst of the storm had passed them by. Deborah was certainly glad about this. The children and Mother came bounding out from the house as the wagons came to a stop near the barn.

"You boys help me turn the mules loose in the corral," Arjan instructed. "Tommy and Jimmy, you throw them some feed."

"We've got kittens!" Emma declared to the new arrivals.

"Truly?" Deborah smiled. "Who's the proud mama?"

Her mother held Jonah back to keep him out of the way of the mules. "It was the long-haired gray."

"And how many babies are there?" Deborah asked, getting down from the back of the wagon with Christopher's help.

"Five. There are five kittens and five of us children. Mama Euphanel said that's just like God to provide exactly what we need," Emma announced.

Deborah laughed. "I believe she's right."

"She also said we can't be pickin' them up yet," Jonah said. "Else their eyes won't open."

"That's very wise. The mama cat knows best what they need right now," Deborah told him. "Soon enough those kittens will be scampering all over the place. How are the puppies?"

"They're getting big," Darcy replied. She was dressed in her Sunday best and looked like quite the young lady.

"What are you all gussied up for, little gal?" Arjan asked. "You look right pretty."

"Pastor's coming for dinner," she told him. "He was here yesterday, and Mama Euphanel invited him and Miss Mara."

"I'm right glad she did. Maybe he'll preach us a sermon," Arjan said, taking Mother in his arms.

Deborah smiled as he gave her mother a big kiss. "I missed you, Wife."

"Not half so much as I missed you." Mother kissed him right back.

Deborah turned to Christopher. "I'm going to have a bath before the pastor arrives."

"I could use one, too."

Jonah pulled on his brother's coat. "You can't both take a bath at the same time. Mama Euphanel says it's not fittin' for girls and boys to take a bath at the same time, so I know she won't let you grown-up folks do that."

Deborah saw her mother's eyes widen in alarm while Arjan coughed and sputtered as he did his best to keep from laughing. Pretending she hadn't heard, Deborah left Christopher to handle the comment.

"I reckon I can wait until she takes her bath first," Christopher replied. "I don't want Mama Euphanel mad at me. I haven't had her dessert in nearly two weeks."

Jonah nodded. "That'd be good, 'cause today we're having pie."

Arjan regained control of his merriment and motioned to the family. "We'd best stop jawin' out here in the rain."

"It's barely a sprinkle, but I agree," Mother said. "Come along, little chickens, let's get in the house."

Deborah headed for the cabin, knowing that Christopher

was right behind her. She didn't say a word until they were inside with the door closed, then she burst out laughing.

"You . . . you nearly . . . caused a scene," she sputtered.

"I thought your ma would have kittens," he replied, grinning.

Tears came to her eyes as she fought to get her breath. She hadn't laughed this hard in years. She fought to sober herself as she listened to the rain begin to fall in earnest. "I guess I'll get a rainwater bath. The barrel is bound to be full."

"Why don't you light the stove, and I'll drag out the tub." He tossed his bag and coat onto a nearby chair. "Then I'll bring the water in for you. It shouldn't take too long to warm up."

Deborah nodded. It was just good to be home. Good to be able to soak in a tub and rest in bed. She hurried to light the stove. Time was a-wasting.

After the evening meal, Pastor Shattuck stood to offer a reading from Psalm ninety-one. " 'He that dwelleth in the secret place of the most High shall abide under the shadow of the Almighty. I will say of the Lord, He is my refuge and my fortress: my God; in Him will I trust. Surely he shall deliver thee from the snare of the fowler, and from the noisome pestilence. He shall cover thee with his feathers, and under his wings shalt thou trust: his truth shall be thy shield and buckler.' "

"What's a buckler?" Jonah asked, a little louder than intended.

"That's a very good question," Pastor Shattuck declared before Mother could hush the boy. "In the old days, when men fought with swords instead of guns, a buckler was used as a small shield. But it was decidedly more than that."

Lightning lit the room, seeming to come out of nowhere.

Thunder cracked shortly thereafter, but Pastor Shattuck continued without concern.

"A buckler had five main uses. The warrior would hold it in the hand opposite his sword. It was often round and made of strong metal. It wasn't all that big, but it didn't need to be for what it was intended. You see, a buckler was a weapon of close combat. The kind of fight you would have face-to-face with your enemy."

Deborah could see that Jonah was completely captivated. So, too, were most of the young men who'd come home from the logging camp to share the Vandermark hospitality.

"A buckler's first job was to act as protection for the hand," Pastor Shattuck told them. "The grip that allowed the warrior to deflect the blows of his attacker. Thus, the second job—deflecting. Because it was lightweight and small, it was easier to use than a large shield.

"Third, a warrior could use his buckler as a blinder. He could hide his sword momentarily from view and strike his opponent unexpectedly. He could also reflect the sun into his opponent's eyes."

The pastor's words fascinated Deborah. She had always enjoyed learning the deeper meaning of scriptural details. Knowledge of God's word was precious to her, and this explanation made a most beloved psalm all the more meaningful.

"The buckler could also be used as a metal fist to the face or body of the enemy," Pastor Shattuck continued. "Soldiers punched at their opponents and drove them off balance while wielding their sword to strike.

"And lastly, the buckler was used as a binder. A soldier could trap a man's sword arm against him, binding him from further attack. It offered a means of controlling one's enemy." He smiled at Jonah. "Now, I can tell you something else about this. I once had a very learned friend who knew the language of the Old Testament—Hebrew. I learned that the word used here for 'shield' was *tsinnah*. This was a shield so large it covered a man's entire body. Only his head would be exposed. The word for 'buckler' in the Hebrew was *cocherah*. I'm told that this verse is the only place in the entire Bible where this word appears. Of course, I couldn't tell you for sure that this was true, but I've tried to explore that for myself and haven't yet seen it elsewhere.

"*Cocherah* actually means something that wraps up a person. So perhaps God desired to show us in this verse that His truth is a shield that surrounds us completely. A protection, as well as a weapon. You see, God has given you weapons to fight the devil, your enemy. The truth of God is your shield and buckler. You are not to fight without a means of defense *and* offense. God has provided for all our needs." Jonah nodded with great enthusiasm.

Pastor Shattuck picked up his Bible once again. As he spoke, the winds outside seemed to calm. " 'Thou shalt not be afraid for the terror by night; nor for the arrow that flieth by day; nor for the pestilence that walketh in darkness; nor for the destruction that wasteth at noonday. A thousand shall fall at thy side, and ten thousand at thy right hand; but it shall not come nigh thee. Only with thine eyes shalt thou behold and see the reward of the wicked. Because thou hast made the Lord, which is my refuge, even the most High, thy habitation; there shall no evil befall thee, neither shall any plague come nigh thy dwelling.' "

He paused and smiled. "It doesn't mean we won't face the enemy or that adversity won't threaten, but God has assured us that we *will* be delivered. We rest in His protection. He will completely surround us."

"Like a sucker-raw!" Jonah exclaimed.

Pastor Shattuck laughed and nodded. "Exactly right, young Jonah. And well pronounced."

Deborah heard the train approaching in the distance and frowned. If Jack had found it necessary to put the old engine in motion today, it could only mean some problem. Perhaps someone needed the doctor. She glanced toward the door and decided to see for herself. She slipped out of the room and pushed back the screen door.

The air suffocated her with moisture and warmth. Arjan joined Deborah on the porch as the sound of the train grew louder.

"I wonder why Jack's coming," she said looking toward the track. "You don't suppose there's been another attack by the White Hand?"

Arjan's eyes suddenly widened as the wind once again began to pick up. "It's not Jack or the train. It's a twister. Get inside—we have to take cover!"

Chapter 29

I never seen a storm the likes of this," Essie told Jael. "Turned day to night and threw down hail like stones."

Jael was still battling her rattled nerves. The wind had blown so hard that she'd feared the walls would come down. "Do you suppose there has been a lot of damage?"

"I figure there is, iffen a tornado dropped out of them clouds."

"We had a few bad storms in Philadelphia, but nothing like that." Jael walked to the porch to survey the surroundings. Tree limbs littered the tracks, making it look as though the workers had never gathered up the White Hand's debris. Where were Stuart and her father? When the clouds rolled in, thick and black, they had headed over to get Zed Perkins and help secure the mill supplies. They hadn't returned.

The skies overhead cleared, making it appear as if nothing had happened. An eerie calm settled over the world. Only a short while ago, Jael had feared they could lose their lives; now, everything seemed again at peace.

She saw her father coming down the street and hurried to meet him. "Where is Stuart?"

"He and Mr. Perkins are checking out the mill. I wanted to make sure you were safe."

Jael hugged her father close. "It was terrifying."

"I know. I'm so sorry you were here alone."

"Essie was with me," Jael said, pulling back. "She knew exactly what to do. We hid in the hall at the very back when we heard the hail."

"We did the same at the commissary. We never even made it over to Zed's place until after the storm."

"Has there been a lot of damage?"

Her father shook his head. "I don't know. I only wanted to make sure you were all right."

She smiled. "Too bad my husband didn't feel the same." She walked away, telling herself that it didn't matter. Though she held no affection for Stuart, she did care if he'd made it through the storm. Stuart only cared about his investment.

"Essie said there may have been a tornado," Jael said, heading back to the house.

Her father reached out to stop her. "Do you suppose the Vandermarks were in the path of the storm?"

Jael felt as if she'd been slapped. She looked at her father in horror. "I . . . I don't know." She knew that Deborah and the others had been working at the logging camp. Living in tents, they wouldn't have had any place to take refuge from the violent winds.

"We need to go to them," Jael told her father. "We can at least go to the house."

"I'll get the carriage."

Grateful that he didn't question her suggestion, Jael hurried into the house. "Essie!" The young woman appeared with a quizzical expression. "Father and I are going to drive out to the Vandermarks'. Will you let Mr. Albright know where I've gone, if and when he comes home?"

"Sure will, Miz Albright." Essie looked at the clock. "Gettin' late . . . will you be back tonight?"

"I don't know." Jael took up her parasol. "I suppose we'll know better after we make certain the Vandermarks are safe." She didn't want to think what she'd do if they weren't. The house might have been directly in the path of the storm, and the logging camp might have been destroyed, as well.

Her new faith in God was being sorely tested. What was she supposed to do at a time like this? Jael looked at Essie.

"Are you . . . do you . . ." She wasn't even sure what she wanted to say. "Essie, I'm worried about Deborah and the others. I haven't learned very much about praying, but I'm sure we should pray."

"Oh, absolutely, Miz Albright. I been prayin' all along."

Stuart watched his father-in-law drive the carriage around to the front of the house. Where were they headed at this hour of the day? He crossed the road, his boots sinking deep in the muck. He'd had just about all he could take of this town. Nothing was going right. Now that Jael had let her father know about her reasons for marrying him, Longstreet treated him with contempt. The man no longer regarded Stuart as being in charge. He'd taken many decisions into his own hands without so much as a discussion. Just like now.

"Where are you going?" he asked as Longstreet got down to help Jael into the carriage.

"To check on my friends," Jael declared. "Essie said there may have been a tornado, and I intend to make sure that Deborah and her family are all right."

"But they're up at the logging camp. You can't possibly hope to make it up there before the light is gone. And even if you did, you'd still have to drive back in the dark. The roads are certain to be difficult, if not impassable, from the heavy rain."

"We only intend to get as far as the house. Hopefully they will have gotten word to Mrs. Vandermark and she can let me know. Then Father and I can simply return."

"Not before the light is gone. I won't have you out there on the road given the problems we've had in the area."

Jael looked at him oddly. "Why, Stuart, you almost sound as if you care about our well-being."

Her sarcasm irritated Stuart to no end. "I don't need the expense of a funeral."

To his surprise, she laughed and settled into her seat. Longstreet looked at Stuart and shook his head. "This is a most unholy union. If I can convince my daughter to leave you, I will."

"We're partners, you and I. Or have you forgotten?" Stuart fixed the man with a scowl. "We stand to lose a great deal of money and land because of your daughter's interference."

"You know, I never came here to seek revenge on anyone. That's probably why I feel capable of walking away from this ordeal without making a profit. I would rather lose money than friends."

"Then you're a fool!"

Longstreet shrugged and climbed into the carriage. "At least I realize my foolish doings. You seem blind to yours."

Stuart watched the carriage pull away and cursed them both. The same kind of helplessness he'd known the day Elizabeth had married G. W. Vandermark crept upon him. She had ruined all his plans, and now Jael and Longstreet were attempting to do the same thing.

He stormed into the house, mindless of the mud he tracked throughout. Stomping out his frustrations on the stairs, he made his way to the bedroom he'd once shared with Jael and began tearing at his clothes. They were filthy and he hated being dirty. Dirty like a common laborer.

"The world will judge you by your appearance," his father had always declared. *"You can hide what you're really thinking—what you plan to do in order to have your way—but you cannot hide your appearance."*

Stuart threw his shirt aside. Such advice had served him well over the years. Pleasing his father by keeping a well-dressed, fashionably groomed appearance had allowed Stuart to conceal his true feelings of hatred toward the man who had never shown him the slightest consideration.

"Essie!" He bellowed from the door and waited for some response. There was none. Jael had probably let the woman leave.

He railed at the air, cursing his wife and everything around him. Nothing was going his way. Not even something as simple as a bath.

Deborah felt Christopher loosen his hold on her as the winds died down and the rains ceased. She had scarcely been able to draw a breath at the height of the storm, and now she gasped to fill her lungs.

Jonah cried in Mother's arms while Emma and Darcy clung to either side of her. Deborah felt a sense of relief and regret. She prayed that she would one day be able to offer such love and peace to her own children.

"We'd best check out the damage," G.W. said, pulling Lizzie to her feet. They each reached down to pick up one of the sleeping twins. "I swear these guys could sleep through anything."

Mother smiled. "They felt safe in your arms."

Deborah remembered the comfort of Christopher's arms around her. Better still, their time of prayer through the storm and the sense of being wrapped in God's protection. Just like the cocherah Brother Shattuck had mentioned.

"I'll take that boy," Sissy said. She lifted Rutger from his father's arms. "Me and Miz Lizzie can tend them."

Lizzie nodded. "You probably have more than enough to deal with outside."

They had taken refuge down the main hall and under the stairs, far away from any windows. A good idea, too—Deborah had heard glass shattering through the wind's roar.

The family slowly made their way outside to survey the destruction. The house, except for some missing shingles and broken panes, had come through the storm without much noticeable damage. Deborah noted with relief that the barn was untouched.

"I ain't never been this close to a twister's path," Arjan said, looking across the vast cut of destruction.

The tornado had taken a sharp turn to the north after narrowly missing their house. Downed and twisted trees were left in its wake. Worse still was all the debris slung across the railroad tracks.

"The train ain't gonna be able to get us to the camp," G.W. said, following his stepfather's gaze.

"If there's a camp left to get to," Arjan said, shaking his head. "Unless that twister took another turn, it looks to have headed straight on to our site."

"Surely it would have lifted by then," Deborah said. But in her heart, she couldn't help but fear they were right. Why had God let this happen? They had honored Him by resting on the Sabbath. They had blessed His name for the safety and harvest. They had kept their faith. And still, they'd suffered the storm.

Mother came alongside them. "We are so blessed that it didn't hit our house or the barn and outbuildings. The animals all seem fine. We're all safe."

Deborah didn't have the heart to remind them that it might be only a temporary blessing. If the storm had destroyed the logging camp, they would lose it all on the morrow.

Arjan put his arm around Mother's shoulders. "We are blessed. Indeed, we are. We're alive, and no one was hurt."

"Do you suppose it hit town?" Mother asked.

"Can't say for sure. Looks like it was hoppin' and skippin' around. See over there? No damage. But then it touched down over here, just beyond the tracks, and cut a path as far as you can see."

Pastor Shattuck and Mara walked over with Jake. "We can stay and help," the pastor declared. "Since Mrs. Albright managed to get her husband calmed down about forcing us to move, we haven't a care in the world." He grinned. "Just tell us what we need to do."

"We'll have to clear the tracks," Arjan said, leaning hard on his cane.

Deborah knew her stepfather was probably in pain, but he refused to let on. It wasn't the Dutch way to make a fuss.

"It's the Sabbath," G.W. reminded them. "There's time enough to work tomorrow."

"But we won't be able to get the logs down to the mill unless the tracks are clear," Mother reminded him.

G.W. nodded. "True enough, but I reckon God will work all of this to His good. Ain't never seen Him fail us yet."

But Deborah knew he didn't feel as convinced as his words indicated. Maybe God didn't want them to supply Stuart Albright with logs. Maybe God didn't want Perkinsville to revive. Who could say for sure?

Pastor Shattuck rolled up his sleeves. "I believe we can honor God even in our labor. Miz Euphanel, why don't you start us in some hymns of praise?"

Jael had been more than a little frustrated that wreckage on the road kept them from reaching Deborah's house. She and her father had turned back only a mile or so down the road. Stuart looked pleased at their return. He said finally something was going his way.

On Monday morning, Jael tried again. This time she donned her riding habit. Without sitting down to breakfast, she announced to her father and husband her intention to ride out to the Vandermark place.

"I'll take the black gelding from the stable. He'll be able to jump anything too big to ride around."

"You shouldn't go alone," her father said, getting to his feet. "Stuart, why don't we both accompany her. Today is, after all, your deadline for the logs. It would do you well to see if that quota has been met."

Jael frowned. She wasn't at all sure why her father had said such a thing. It would have been far better to say nothing and hope that Stuart would just let the matter go. Of course, now he wouldn't.

"I suppose you are right," Stuart said.

Jael looked at her husband and then to her father. "I'll let the stableman know to saddle three horses."

She wasn't surprised to see most of the townsfolk out working to clear the yards and streets. The wind had done some damage, but upon further inspection in the light of morning, Jael could see that the town hadn't suffered too greatly.

The horses were saddled and ready to go by the time her father and husband finally made their way to the stable. Jael sat impatiently atop her mount. She saw that her husband held something in his hand.

"What have you there?" she asked.

Stuart gave her a smug smile. "The Vandermark contract." He folded it and put it in his pocket. "I intend to see that they live up to every word."

Maybe it wasn't such a good idea to head out to the Vandermarks' after all. Stuart would show no mercy whatsoever if things were bad. That could only lead to problems. But she had been the one to insist on the journey; it would only cause him more reason to be ruthless should she suggest they forgo the venture.

The road was far from easy to manage. From time to time large branches blocked the main part of the path, forcing her father and Stuart to get down and move the ones they couldn't jump. It took nearly an hour to cover what should have taken less than half that time.

"The house is still standing!" Jael announced, urging her horse past her father and Stuart. She thought for a moment the place was deserted, but then heard the sound of mules, somewhere beyond the house.

She maneuvered her horse toward the railroad tracks, where she found the entire Vandermark family working to uncover the tracks. Deborah pulled a long, skinny branch to one side and let it drop. Straightening, she noticed Jael and waved.

"Oh, you are all right!" Jael declared, quickly jumping from the gelding's back. "I was so worried." She dropped the reins and ran to embrace her friend.

"We worried about you, as well. How are things in town?" Deborah asked.

"Nothing quite this bad." Jael looked at the path the twister had eaten. "Oh, it must have been quite frightful."

"It was," Deborah admitted. "I suppose Stuart has come to see about his logs."

"Oh, bother," Jael said. "He surely can't expect you to provide logs when the tracks aren't even passable."

"He has a way of expecting a great many things."

Jael's father and Stuart came to join them. Deborah turned. "G.W., we've got company."

Every last person, including Pastor Shattuck and Mara, congregated to where Deborah and Jael stood with the two men. Jael knew the questioning looks were all for her husband.

"Mr. Albright, Mr. Longstreet," Arjan said. He turned and tipped his hat to Jael. "Ma'am."

"I'm come to find out if my logs will be delivered in time to meet the deadline," Stuart said in an almost amused fashion. "But I can see for myself that things do not look hopeful for that."

"No, I s'pose not," Arjan said. "We made a trip up to the

camp, and truth is . . . the storm destroyed most of the waiting logs up at the camp. At least it disbursed them. I imagine your logs are all over Angelina County."

"Well, that's a pity. It would seem you have broken our agreement."

"Now, just a minute," Jael's father said. "Do you mean to tell me that you are going to hold the Vandermarks to every point of the contract?"

Stuart smiled and gave Jael a smug look of satisfaction. "I do."

Her father then turned to Mr. Vandermark. Jael saw Mrs. Vandermark grasp her husband's hand in support. Deborah went to stand beside her mother, and Jael felt tears come to her own eyes at the sight of them offering each other comfort.

"You cannot do this," Jael told Stuart. "You are being cruel in their time of need."

He said nothing, and Jael's father continued. "Mr. Vandermark, has it been your intention to honor the contract in full?"

"It has."

The simple statement seemed to boom across the short span of space. Jael was surprised to see her father smile. "Mrs. Kelleher, I wonder if you would be so kind as to read the last paragraph of the contract."

Deborah frowned but stepped away from her mother. "I'll have to go retrieve it from the office."

"Oh, don't bother," Jael's father said. "I believe my son-in-law brought his copy along."

Stuart pulled the folded papers from his pocket and handed them to the older man. "I did, indeed. I wanted to make certain that you would not attempt to dupe me with a different contract."

"Of all the low-down—" G.W. was silenced as his stepfather put his hand out to hold him back.

"We are men of honor," Mr. Vandermark declared.

"I'm quite glad to hear you say that," Jael's father said. He handed the contract to Deborah. "Please, read it aloud for us—just the last paragraph."

Deborah seemed none too happy to do so, but nodded. " 'The terms of this contract are to be strictly met and fulfilled until the termination date given. However, the contract will be set aside should any act of God cause either party to forfeit their responsibilities to the other.' " She looked up and smiled. Turning back to her mother and stepfather, she repeated one phrase. "Any act of God."

"Well, there's no denying the destruction of our product was at the hands of the storm, which I believe would be deemed an act of God," Jael's father said, turning back to his son-in-law. "Just as you claimed the fire that burned the mill to be such an act. As I recall, the judge allowed you to set aside the contract terms until the insurance company could assess and determine the cause."

"I . . . that isn't . . ." Stuart narrowed his eyes. "It doesn't change anything."

"Oh, but it does," Mr. Longstreet countered. "Read the final line, Mrs. Kelleher."

Deborah looked back to the contract. " 'Should said "act of God" interfere with the continuation of the agreed upon terms, such terms will be open for renegotiation and new dates of delivery and quotas set.' "

"But you couldn't possibly have met the terms to begin with," Stuart declared. "It would have been impossible for you to supply me with what you owed my mill."

"I hardly believe that is the issue now," Jael's father said, taking the contract back from Deborah. "The fact of the matter is, these good people did attempt to deliver the intended product. The ongoing rains slowed them, and a tornado made it completely impossible. I would say that the terms make it clear. The contract is open for renegotiation."

The Vandermark family and workers broke into cheers. G.W. hugged Lizzie with such enthusiasm that Jael couldn't help but laugh and clap her hands. She met Deborah's smiling face. Apparently prayer did work. So many times of late, God had helped her in times of trouble. Jael's faith had grown in each situation.

Stepping forward, Jael took the contract from her father's hands. "I suggest that this contract be completely dissolved." She tore the papers in two. "That way you can sell whatever you like elsewhere."

"You can't do that," Stuart protested. "My lawyers will see to it that you honor the terms. It changes nothing."

She smiled and handed him the pieces. "Oh, but it does . . . *Husband.* It does." Stuart clearly noted her emphasis. He looked at her for a moment, then drew a deep breath and nodded.

He turned to look at his father-in-law and then Arjan. "Very well. Let us start anew."

Jael smiled. "I think that would benefit everyone."

Chapter 30

September 1887

Summer's end brought many changes. Deborah and Christopher moved back to the doctor's house in town and received provisions to reestablish the infirmary. This was thanks to Jael's father, who had forced his son-in-law to sell his shares of the mill town. Together with Zed Perkins, who was back at the helm, Mr. Longstreet promised to make Perkinsville even better than before. To honor this pledge, the people voted him mayor.

"He's never been happier," Jael told Deborah.

"You seem quite happy yourself."

"I am, Deborah. I truly am happy."

Deborah knew the reason for this. Jael had been quite pleased when Stuart announced that his father needed him back East. Deborah had been there when Jael had told him firmly that she would stay in Perkinsville. Stuart hadn't been surprised, but he did seem concerned. Jael promised him that she would remain his faithful wife. She would write to him, so his father would see that they remained wed. Deborah argued that he didn't deserve her generosity, but Jael told her she desired to forgive Stuart the past and move forward. Her words humbled Deborah—Lizzie too.

"Who knows," Jael had told Deborah. "If God is as powerful as you say He is, then He can bring love even to our hard hearts."

Many of the families returned to Perkinsville. Margaret Foster came back with one of her sons and his wife. Their young children quickly befriended the Kelleher siblings. Little by little, many of the other regulars came home, as well. Zed reinstated each crew member with promises of a bigger and better mill. He split the workers between rebuilding the black town and getting the mill up and running. The progress lifted everyone's spirits.

Perhaps the greatest joy, however, had been the well-attended wedding of Robrecht Vandermark to Miss Mara Shattuck. Only an hour earlier, Deborah had stood at the depot with her family, waving good-bye to the couple as they caught the train to Houston. Rob had agreed to pastor a church in the area, and Mara had great plans for the Sunday school. Even Pastor Shattuck was delighted with the couple's plans, although Mara was worried he would grow lonely.

"I do fear he won't eat properly," she told Deborah as they bid each other farewell. "You will look in on him, won't you?"

"Of course," Deborah assured her. "And you can bet that my mother will, as well. She isn't about to see anyone go hungry."

But with everything falling back into a normal routine, Deborah couldn't help but wonder if that might allow for her and Christopher to have a little time to themselves.

"Haven't you finished in here yet?" Christopher teased.

"I'm daydreaming," Deborah said, glancing over her shoulder. "I often do so when I'm cleaning the examination room."

"And what are you dreaming about?"

She halted her work. "You do realize that we've never had a proper wedding trip? I thought that with Miz Foster back in town, perhaps we could get away for a week or two. She would surely be willing to treat folks while we were away. Wouldn't it be great fun to go to Galveston?"

"Goodness, woman, you think I'm made of money?"

Deborah put her hands on her hips. "I happen to know that my family paid you quite well for your service before and after the storm. And they paid me for my work. If you would check the new bank at the commissary, you would find that we have quite a nice bit of savings."

He laughed. "And it's burning a hole in your pocket—is that it?"

"Not exactly, but I think it would be awfully nice to be alone with you." She put down the cleaning cloth and walked toward him with a provocative smile. Reaching up, she trailed her fingers against his cheek and down to where a hint of chest hair peeked out from his unbuttoned shirt.

"Just imagine it. We could stay at the Tremont Hotel. I've heard it's absolutely beautiful since they rebuilt it. We could have a lovely suite and order room service." She stretched on tiptoes to brush his lips with a kiss. "Just imagine—an entire week alone."

He took hold of her. "Go on."

"Of course, there's also something else that might hold your interest."

Nuzzling her ear with kisses, Christopher shook his head ever so slightly. "That isn't possible."

"Oh, but I think it could be." She pulled away and smiled.

"They are building a new hospital, and rumor has it that a new medical college will be established. The paper noted that several lectures were going to be given next week. One is on the repair of compound fractures."

He laughed. "You don't want to get away with me—you just want to attend lectures on medicine."

Deborah feigned shock. "How could you say such a thing? You know perfectly well that I am the kind of gal who wants it all. Why couldn't we have both? After all, lectures only last an hour or two at the most. We needn't leave our room for much longer than that."

"You are positively scandalous, my dear." He drew her back into his arms. "And that's what I love most about you. You are a woman without boundaries. No one tells you no and gets away with it."

She shrugged and smiled. "At least not for long."

"Docs! Come quick!" someone yelled from outside.

They went quickly to the door. "What's wrong?" Christopher asked, pushing open the screen door.

"There's been an accident at the mill. Otis done cut himself up on that new-fangled saw," one of the young Foster kids declared.

"I'll get the bag and bandages," Deborah told her husband. "You go on ahead."

He nodded and shot out the door. Deborah hurried to grab what they would need. This was indeed the life for her—the life she loved. Working alongside her husband to help others. There was no way of knowing what the future held, but her hope had been rekindled and her heart overflowed with joy. And that—for now—was entirely enough.

Letter to the Reader:

Dear friends,

So many struggles plague people these days. From time to time, my readers write to tell me about a particularly difficult time or heartbreak that they've endured, reaching out to share when the world seems to turn a deaf ear to their pain.

My heart has been touched so many times by your letters, and I felt it was only right to share my heart with you now. I pray that the books I write will encourage you to lift your eyes to Jesus. That your hope will be rekindled in the promise of God *to never leave you or forsake you.* If you haven't yet put your hope in Him and accepted His free gift of salvation, then I encourage you to do so now.

The world tries to convince us that it is no simple process to yield your heart to the Lord. The world tries to tack on all sorts of other requirements, but the Bible makes it clear in Romans 10:9–13 that receiving salvation in Jesus is quite easy:

That if you confess with your mouth, "Jesus is Lord," and believe in your heart that God raised Him from the dead, you will be saved. For it is with your heart that you believe and are justified, and it is with your mouth that you confess and are saved. As the Scripture says, "Anyone who trusts in him will never be put to shame." For there is no difference between Jew and Gentile—the same Lord is Lord of all and richly blesses all who call on him, for, **"Everyone who calls on the name of the Lord will be saved"** (NIV, emphasis added).

I'm praying that these verses will bless your heart and bring you to a richer life in Christ Jesus. God bless you!

Tracie Peterson

9-9-2012

Garmelia Edgar

Hearts Aglow

STRIKING A MATCH, BOOK 2

HEARTS AGLOW

TRACIE PETERSON

BETHANY HOUSE PUBLISHERS
Minneapolis, Minnesota

Hearts Aglow

Cover design by Jennifer Parker
Cover photography by Kevin White Photography, Minneapolis

Published by Bethany House Publishers
11400 Hampshire Avenue South
Bloomington, Minnesota 55438

Bethany House Publishers is a division of
Baker Publishing Group, Grand Rapids, Michigan.

Printed in the United States of America

Library of Congress Cataloging-in-Publication Data

Peterson, Tracie.
Hearts aglow / Tracie Peterson.
p. cm. — (Striking a match ; bk. 2)
ISBN 978-0-7642-0868-3 (hardcover : alk. paper) — ISBN 978-0-7642-0613-9 (pbk.) — ISBN 978-0-7642-0869-0 (large-print pbk.)
I. Title.
PS3566.E7717H43 2011
813'.54—dc22

2010041185

To Jonathan Gerlund and the folks
at the Diboll History Center,
Diboll, Texas,
with gratitude for your help
with this project.

A special thanks to Emily
for reading the story for accuracy.

Books by Tracie Peterson

www.traciepeterson.com

A Slender Thread • *Where My Heart Belongs*

SONG OF ALASKA

Dawn's Prelude • *Morning's Refrain* • *Twilight's Serenade*

STRIKING A MATCH

Embers of Love • *Hearts Aglow* • *Hope Rekindled*

ALASKAN QUEST

Summer of the Midnight Sun
Under the Northern Lights • *Whispers of Winter*

Alaskan Quest (3 in 1)

BRIDES OF GALLATIN COUNTY

A Promise to Believe In • *A Love to Last Forever*
A Dream to Call My Own

THE BROADMOOR LEGACY*

A Daughter's Inheritance • *An Unexpected Love*
A Surrendered Heart

BELLS OF LOWELL*

Daughter of the Loom • *A Fragile Design* • *These Tangled Threads*

LIGHTS OF LOWELL*

A Tapestry of Hope • *A Love Woven True* • *The Pattern of Her Heart*

DESERT ROSES

Shadows of the Canyon • *Across the Years* • *Beneath a Harvest Sky*

HEIRS OF MONTANA

Land of My Heart • *The Coming Storm*
To Dream Anew • *The Hope Within*

LADIES OF LIBERTY

A Lady of High Regard • *A Lady of Hidden Intent*
A Lady of Secret Devotion

RIBBONS OF STEEL**

Distant Dreams • *A Hope Beyond* • *A Promise for Tomorrow*

RIBBONS WEST**

Westward the Dream

WESTWARD CHRONICLES

A Shelter of Hope • *Hidden in a Whisper* • *A Veiled Reflection*

YUKON QUEST

Treasures of the North • *Ashes and Ice* • *Rivers of Gold*

*with Judith Miller   **with Judith Pella

TRACIE PETERSON is the author of over eighty novels, both historical and contemporary. Her avid research resonates in her stories, as seen in her bestselling HEIRS OF MONTANA and ALASKAN QUEST series. Tracie and her family make their home in Montana.

Visit Tracie's Web site at *www.traciepeterson.com.*
Visit Tracie's blog at *www.writespassage.blogspot.com.*

Chapter 1

Angelina County, Texas
February 1886

Deborah, wake up! Deborah, hurry!"

At the sound of her mother's frantic voice, Deborah instantly awoke, bolting up from her bed as if the quilt itself were on fire. Her mother crossed the room—a lamp in one hand, Deborah's robe in the other.

"Sissy needs you."

"Sissy? But why? What's wrong?" Deborah pulled on the old dressing gown and tightened the sash.

A moment of silence hung heavily between the two women. "She's . . . been attacked."

Deborah met her mother's worried expression, illuminated by the lamp she held. The single light gave Euphanel's face an eerie, unnatural glow. "Attacked? By animals?" Deborah felt her heart pick up its pace; dread pulsated through her veins. "What time is it? When did this happen?"

"Two, or thereabouts. Just come with me and you'll see for yourself. She's been wounded, and since you've been studying with Dr. Clayton, I thought you could help."

Deborah nodded and followed her mother. Downstairs she could hear Sissy wailing and the voices of Lizzie and G.W. trying to calm her. What in the world had happened? Deborah saw her brother's form heading out the back door just as she arrived in the kitchen.

Sissy sat on a ladder-backed kitchen chair. Her normally rich brown skin was now a sickly sort of gray, and blood streaked her skin and clothes. Deborah rushed to her side and assessed her wounds. The worst was a deep gash on the side of her head.

"What happened, Sissy?"

The woman rocked back and forth while Deborah carefully examined her. She noted a swollen eye, cut lip, and numerous scratches. But it was the nasty head wound that held Deborah's attention.

Her sister-in-law brought a basin of warm water and several towels. "Best as we've been able to understand, some men came to the house threatening David and George. I sent G.W. for the doctor. They're going to stop by the Jackson cabin first and then come here," Lizzie said.

"They said . . . blacks had to be taught their place . . . that they was . . . the White Hand of God," Sissy choked out the words. "Said they . . . was sent to do . . . God's will."

"The White Hand of God?" Deborah asked, looking to her mother.

"G.W. said it's a group of white men who go about with their faces covered so no one knows who they are. They cause trouble for folks of color, but of late it's gotten more violent."

Deborah shook her head and took up a towel. Dipping it in the water, she began to clean the head wound. "How did they do this to you, Sissy?"

"A big fella done hit me with the butt of his rifle," Sissy said. She looked to Deborah's mother. "You s'pose Mr. Arjan and Mr. Rob will get there in time to he'p my boys?"

"I'm sure they'll do what they can," Mother replied. She looked over Sissy's head to Deborah. "For now, let us tend to your wounds and get you safely in bed."

Deborah nodded and rinsed the bloody towel in the basin. "Mother, please get me the scissors. I need to trim back some of Sissy's hair from the wound site." She looked at the older woman and bent close to her face. "I'll not cut away too much of your covering glory." She gave the woman a sad smile. Sissy had helped Deborah dress her hair many times, always reminding her that Brother Paul in the Bible called a woman's hair her covering—her glory. Sissy didn't so much as try to respond.

Mother handed her the scissors and shook her head. "I just don't know what kind of men would do such a thing."

"Hate-filled ones," Lizzie replied. "Only bitter and hateful people could even consider hurting another human being in such a way."

"Right after the War Between the States, there were such heinous groups—men who would kill Negroes just for the right to say they'd done it," Mother replied. "The government had to step in and make laws to keep such things from happening—not that it was very effective in some areas. I have often prayed that such things would come to an end, but I suppose they never will—at least not in my lifetime."

"It is hard to rid the world of hate," Deborah said, carefully trimming the wooly hair. The wound was deep and splayed out in jagged tears. Sissy had lost a lot of blood; no doubt the woman was in shock. "I think it would be best if we could put Sissy to bed and get her feet up. I can tend her there." Deborah stepped back and seriously considered whether the older woman could even walk.

"No, I don' wanna go. I need to be here for George."

"Sissy, you can't do anything down here that you can't do upstairs in bed. Prayer is the best thing any of us can do." Euphanel gave the woman a tender smile. "Your husband wouldn't want you refusing treatment on his account."

"Mother is right," Deborah replied in a soothing fashion. She gave Sissy's head a gentle stroke as she looked for any wounds she might have missed.

"Let's put her upstairs in my bed," Mother declared. She reached for her friend's left arm while Deborah put the scissors aside and put her arm around Sissy from the right. A moan escaped the injured woman's lips.

"I'm feelin' a mite poorly," Sissy murmured. Her knees seemed to buckle with every step. "They kicked me pretty good."

"Oh, Sissy! What a horrible way to treat such a gentle soul," Mother said, tears running down her cheeks.

"They weren't thinkin' of me as havin' a soul, Miz Euphanel—they said I was no better than an old cur. An old cur . . . what had turned on his master."

She staggered and fell against Deborah, exhausted. She'd walked the entire way from her cabin to the Vandermarks', in the deep of night, injured. The poor woman likely struggled through the woods to reach them, for she would have been too afraid of her attackers to take the easier roadway.

Lizzie led the way with a lighted lamp, while Deborah and

Mother mostly carried Sissy up the stairs. Lizzie opened the door to Mother's bedroom and they guided Sissy to the recently vacated bed. Mother left to light another lamp. "It's cold in here," she said with a backward glance. "I'd best stoke up the fire."

"I wish you wouldn't fuss so," Sissy said, looking to Deborah. "It's George and David I's worried 'bout. These old scratches ain't gonna hurt me none."

"Your wounds are more than mere scratches," Deborah told the older woman.

"I'm sure the men will help them," Mother said in confidence. But Deborah could see her mother's concern for the men's safety. Trouble had been brewing for months in their little community, and stories from surrounding counties didn't sound much better. It was hard to imagine where it was all headed.

"The boys are in God's hands," Mother added, but Sissy never heard. She had mercifully surrendered to unconsciousness.

By the time Arjan and Rob arrived at the Jackson cabin, the attackers were long gone and the house was on fire—clearly too far gone to save. Rob immediately caught sight of the ghostly apparitions hanging from the front oak tree.

"They hanged 'em," he said, urging his horse forward. He came to where David's body swayed ever so slightly from a hastily fashioned noose. Flames from the burning cabin gave enough light to show that the man had been badly beaten before being strung up. David's arms hung at awkward angles, leaving little doubt they'd been broken. Just beyond David was his father. The place where his face once had been was now nothing more than a mass of blood and mangled flesh.

Rob looked away as his stomach tightened. His uncle said

nothing, but it was clear he was equally disturbed. There was no shame in being sickened over such a sight. He was glad supper had been some hours before, or he'd certainly have lost it at this scene. Surely only the monsters who'd done this evil could look upon it and not feel the effects.

"Let's get them down. We can't save the house," Arjan said, coming alongside Rob. He handed Rob the reins to his horse and climbed down. "Thankfully the cabin is in the clearing and there isn't any wind. I'm thinkin' it won't catch to the trees."

"I ain't never seen anything like this," Rob admitted.

Uncle Arjan took his horse and tied him to the hitching post in front of the house. Rob dismounted and asked, "Why would a fella want to hurt George and David? They were good people."

"Good people with the wrong color skin," Arjan replied. "At least wrong in the eyes of those that done this."

Rob secured his horse and followed his uncle back to the oak tree. The older man reached for the rope that held George. It had been tied off at the base of the tree—knotted in such a fashion to allow quick release. He gently lowered the former slave to the ground while Rob guided George's body into a position on his back.

"Look, there's some kind of note," Rob declared, reaching for the bloodstained paper. The scrawling was poor, but legible.

"What's it say?"

"Ephesians 6:5."

Arjan nodded. "I heard it used often during the war."

Rob shook his head. "Do you remember what it says?"

"'Fraid so. 'Servants, be obedient to them that are your masters according to the flesh, with fear and trembling, in singleness of your heart, as unto Christ.'"

The verse chilled Rob to the bone. "It's signed, 'The White Hand of God.'"

They said nothing more, but instead went to where David's body swayed. Working together as they had for George, they lowered David to the ground. Another note had been tacked onto David's bloody shirt.

" 'Let others be warned.'" Rob shook his head and reached out to remove the paper, only to realize that it had been affixed with a nail—a nail driven into David's chest.

He covered his eyes with his hand. "They were good men—good workers, willing to help anyone who needed it. This oughtn't have happened," Rob said.

"It's gonna keep happenin' as long as decent folks let it," Arjan replied.

They heard a wagon approaching and turned to see two men seated on the buckboard. G.W. had finally arrived with Dr. Clayton. Another man approached on horseback. As he drew closer, Rob could see that it was Ralph Nichols, the town constable.

Arjan stepped forward. "They're dead."

Dr. Clayton jumped down from the wagon and went to the bodies as if to confirm the statement. Rob went to where G.W. stopped the wagon. He couldn't contain his sorrow.

His voice broke. "We were too late. Too late." He shook his head. "Just ain't right."

"Who did this? Did you see them?" G.W. questioned.

"They were long gone when we got here. The cabin was burning and the men were . . . were . . ." He fell silent and regained his composure. "They were hangin' from the oak."

G.W. glanced past his brother but said nothing. The constable walked up to the brothers and pointed over his shoulder. "Doc confirmed they're dead."

Anger coursed through Rob at the matter-of-fact statement.

He turned and glared at the man. "Of course they're dead. The question is, what are you gonna do about it?"

ꕥ

The minutes ticked by ever so slowly, worry and fear taking each moment captive. Though Deborah was relieved to see that the bleeding had stopped, she still worried about the degree of damage done to Sissy's head. The swelling in her face had increased, making her nearly unrecognizable. She'd balanced precariously between wakeful moanings and unconscious peace ever since being placed in the bed.

When they finally heard the wagon pull into the yard, Deborah breathed a sigh of relief. Mother hurried to the door. "That will be G.W. with Dr. Clayton!"

Sissy stirred but didn't open her eyes. "Mebbe my men, too."

"I'll bring them right upstairs." Mother left Deborah with Sissy.

Deborah patted the woman's leathery scratched and scarred hand. She pressed a kiss on her cold fingers, pleading silently with God for good news. The older woman struggled to open her eyes. "Sissy, stay awake. Look at me—it's important you not sleep. We need Dr. Clayton to examine you first."

"I's tryin', Miss Deborah."

Soon she heard the sound of boots in the hallway and Dr. Clayton strode into the room. "How is she?" Christopher asked, meeting Deborah's gaze. He put his bag aside and began to take off his coat.

She raised a brow. "Very weak. I've cleaned the head wound and managed to stop the bleeding, though she's not able to stay conscious. There's fresh water in the basin by the bed."

He nodded and rolled up his sleeves. Next he took up the bag and drew out a brown bottle of carbolic acid. She waited as he washed his hands, then handed him a clean towel. His handsome face contorted in worry.

"Bring me more light."

Deborah did as he instructed. Shining the lamp just right, the wound was quickly revealed. Seeing that Sissy had once again passed out, she asked softly, "What about George and David?"

He said nothing as he studied the wound. Finally he glanced up momentarily, but his look told her everything. Deborah felt a sob catch in her throat and bit her lip to keep from crying out. She fought back tears and forced her mind to focus on the matters at hand. Steadying her voice, she pointed out the obvious.

"She has a swollen eye and . . . and . . . lacerations. She . . . well . . . they hit her with the butt of a rifle."

Christopher nodded and threw her a brief but compassionate look before retrieving several things from his black bag. "You did a good job here. The wound is extensive, but the skull appears intact. A miracle, to be sure."

"Sissy would tell you that she's hardheaded," Mother announced from behind Deborah.

Christopher looked up. "Sometimes that benefits a person, eh?"

Deborah saw her mother nod, but the look on her face revealed that she, too, was overwhelmed with grief. Straightening, Deborah took hold of her mother's hand. "We have to be strong for Sissy."

Her mother nodded. "I know."

Sissy remained unconscious for most of the doctor's ministrations. As Christopher and Deborah worked together to close the gaping wound, Euphanel maintained a hold on her friend's hand.

Deborah couldn't help but think of the years the two women shared. Sissy had once been the property of Deborah's grandparents. Mother, however, had been happy to see the slaves set free and had welcomed Sissy into her own home as a paid worker. But more important—as a friend.

They had gone through so much together. Sissy had been there for the delivery of each of the Vandermark babies. Mother, in turn, had helped Sissy deliver David. They had doctored and cooked, cleaned and gardened together for so long that each woman could very nearly guess the next move of the other. The color of their skin had never been important. Mother always said she'd never had a friend so dear as Sissy.

Moaning softly, Sissy opened her eyes as the doctor moved to exam her ribs. "Doc Clayton?" she asked. She struggled to focus.

"I'm here, Sissy. Rest easy now."

"My men. Where's my George? My David?"

Euphanel interceded. "Now, Sissy, you know we can't be worrying about that just now. You're hurt mighty bad and we have to get you mended first. Arjan and Rob are taking care of George and David."

This seemed to calm the woman. Both eyes were now swelling, making it difficult for her to keep them open. When Christopher touched a particularly tender area on her side, Sissy couldn't help but cry out.

"I would say you have some broken ribs," he told her.

"They was kickin' me and kickin' me. I . . . liked to . . . never got away."

Deborah frowned. "We will see to it that they pay for this, Sissy. It's hate, pure and simple—and it cannot be tolerated. Not by good Christian folk."

But Sissy never heard the words as she slipped back into sleep. Christopher straightened. "I'll keep watch. The next few hours will be critical. We'll pray there's no brain swelling, but it seems likely there will be. We may have to drill a hole through the bone to release the pressure."

"Now then, Dr. Clayton," Mother said with an edge of reprimand to her voice, "you either believe the Good Lord is faithful to answer the prayers of His children or you don't. We'll pray His will and trust that it includes Sissy's healing. I can see death being a more perfect way of meeting that, but I would be sorely distressed to lose my friend." Mother squeezed Sissy's hand one more time, then slowly released it. "I'm going to go start some breakfast. I'll bring you both a plate when it's ready."

"Thank you, Miz Vandermark," Christopher replied. He went to wash the blood from his hands as she exited the room.

Deborah stared down at Sissy's damaged body. The older woman had been a part of their family as long as Deborah had been alive. She had taught Deborah to weave baskets from reeds, to can her first batch of grape jam, to catch catfish in the river. The woman could truly do almost anything. At least she *had* been able to do those things. What would happen if she was unable to function normally?

Tears fell hot on her cheeks, and Deborah couldn't help but speak her thoughts aloud. "She's always been there for me . . . for all of us. I can't imagine losing her." Her voice cracked. "Sissy has always been family. She will always be family."

Christopher crossed the room and took Deborah in his arms as she began to sob. For several minutes, she found it impossible to compose herself. She shook from the intensity of her emotions. She could feel Christopher's hands on her head stroking her haphazardly fashioned hair. The ribbon that tied back the bulk of her tresses easily gave way under the new attention and Deborah's ebony locks fell about her like a veil.

"Life is hard, my dear. Injustice and misery will always be dreaded companions."

She tried to speak, but words would not come. Burying her face against his shirt, Deborah let out all of the fear and frustration she'd been feeling. How would she ever manage to help comfort Mother if Sissy died? She needed to bolster her strength, but Deborah felt as though she had none.

For a long while Christopher held her and let her cry. Deborah had never been so long in another person's arms—especially not a man. There had been times when her father had consoled her after a fall from a horse or the death of a beloved pet, but those times were never so lengthy. Aunt Wilhelmina had held her while she cried after learning about her father's death, and Mother had comforted her several times since. But this was different.

"You have the most beautiful hair," he whispered against her ear. "I've so often wanted to see it down like this—to touch it."

Deborah stilled in his arms. She allowed her mind to clear and her body to relax in his embrace. It wasn't in keeping with propriety that she should be here in her nightclothes with the man she hoped to one day marry, but at such a time as this, there was surely no condemnation. Or was there? Didn't the Bible speak about weak-willed women? Was this one of those moments?

Her conscience got the better of her, and Deborah straightened and pulled away. Here the worst thing possible had happened—good men had been murdered, Sissy had been beaten—and Deborah was thinking of romance. "I'm sorry. I didn't mean to fall to pieces. Maybe I won't make a good doctor after all."

Christopher shook his head and glanced back to where Sissy remained asleep. "You did all that was required. Do you suppose I never break down after dealing with folks? That's why doctors are better off not tending their own family members. It's often hard to be objective when the broken body before you is that of a loved one."

"It seems you would be most competent in dealing with those folks," Deborah countered. "Because you care more for them than anyone else."

"True, but emotions can blind you, paralyze you. I once saw a doctor back East unable to amputate the mangled arm of his son. The young man had caught it in a thresher, and in order to save his life, the arm had to be completely severed. The father knew it would cost his son's life to do nothing, but he couldn't bring himself to do the job."

"And so *you* did?" Deborah asked.

"Yes. I was but a student, with a great deal to learn. But under the circumstances, I had to do what I could." Christopher looked away. "Sometimes life is like that. The choices we must make are made of necessity—to do nothing would be far worse."

"Some would say otherwise. They would tell you that you acted above your station or your training. In my case, it's a matter of acting in an unladylike manner or interest. Doing nothing is often expected—especially of women."

He looked at her with great consideration. "I suppose you're right. I hadn't thought of it that way. It seems that sometimes doing nothing at all is the lesser of two evils, but it isn't. I have often heard people complain of having no choices, but I believe there is always some sort of opportunity we can take hold of."

"I hope choices are made to put an end to this injustice. I can't believe anyone could be so cruel." Deborah went back to Sissy's side. "Her family . . . George and David . . . they were both good people. Sissy would have taken in a complete stranger if there was need. She would feed any hungry soul, no matter the color of his skin or whether he was Christian or not."

"Hate grows where fear and misunderstanding thrive," Christopher replied.

Deborah looked at him and nodded. "That's it, isn't it? That's the reason behind this hatred of blacks. Fear—misunderstanding—a lack of knowledge. People are terrified of anything that seems different than what they're familiar with—anyone who threatens their beliefs and way of living."

"And knowing that should be the beginning of understanding." Christopher met her gaze. "But it seldom is."

Chapter 2

Shortly before breakfast, Deborah slipped back upstairs to dress. She donned a simple brown calico gown and pinned her hair back in a serviceable knot, then tied an apron around her waist. She smiled, remembering that in Philadelphia she had never once worn an apron. It wasn't acceptable for women of society. Aprons were worn by servants.

"Well, I'm a servant now," she said aloud. With a quick upward glance she offered a silent prayer that she would be a useful one.

She rejoined Christopher in her mother's room and noted that Sissy's coloring looked a bit better. "Perhaps it's wishful thinking, but she doesn't seem so pale."

He nodded. "There's some improvement. Her pulse is stronger.

Your mother brought some ice for the swelling. It should continue to help."

Deborah took a seat beside the bed. "I'm sorry for the way I acted earlier. Falling apart and all."

Christopher squeezed her shoulder. "Don't be so hard on yourself," he said, his voice soft and warm.

Deborah felt almost lulled to a rest by his smooth, comforting tone, then realized she was letting herself get carried away again. *Why am I being such a ninny?* She stood in an attempt to shake off the emotion of the moment.

"I tried to speak with the constable about what happened. He's out there investigating right now, but he says little can be done. The White Hand of God is comprised of men from several counties. They wear masks and cannot be identified. They claim they are doing God's work—righting a wrong done by the emancipation of slaves. They use the Bible as a basis of support for slavery, declaring that anyone who would go against such a thing is going against God himself."

Christopher shook his head. "It's ignorant."

"But the Bible does approve slavery," she replied. "The very verse that was left behind on George speaks to that issue."

"I wouldn't exactly say it's an approval of all slavery," Christopher said thoughtfully. "The Bible does speak to the attitudes and issues of slaves and masters, but does that really suggest an approval? I hardly see slavery as God's institution. Doesn't the Bible speak about Jesus coming to set us free? That we are all slaves to sin?"

Deborah considered his words for a moment. "That's really the first sensible thing I've heard yet in regard to slavery."

"Not only that," Christopher continued, "but while the Bible does give guidelines to slaves and owners, it also quite readily speaks out against one man stealing and selling another. It says that such a man should be put to death."

Her eyes widened. "Truly? I never read that verse."

"It's in Exodus. Of course, we also have to remember that slavery was not the same in the Bible as what we saw here in America. On occasion, people in the time of the Bible put themselves into slavery to pay a debt. Some even chose to be slaves, for if they had a master, that person would clothe and feed them and keep them housed. It left the untrained and those without kin or other means of support with hope for a future. Some servitudes were only for a set number of years—rather like some apprenticeships or indenturements here in America."

"I never knew that," Deborah replied. "But given what you've just said, most slavery here in America was wrong."

"Absolutely." He felt Sissy's brow. "Much of the slavery here was born of man-stealing. People were torn from their families and homes, often stolen by enemy tribesmen to be sold. There was corruption at every level and from every society."

Deborah shook her head. "But to commit such heinous crimes and further that corruption . . ." She sighed. "It's beyond anything I can understand."

Sissy stirred and opened her eyes as best she could. "Miss Deborah?"

"I'm here, Sissy. Dr. Clayton is here, too. We've stayed with you—Mama, too."

"My head's 'bout to burst. What happened?"

Deborah looked at Christopher and then back to the older woman. "What do you remember?"

Sissy closed her eyes, and for a moment, Deborah thought maybe she'd fainted again. But the woman's eyes opened once more.

"I know there was trouble. Some men comed to the house." She shook her head. "I don't 'member much more. Where's George?"

Deborah bit her lip and looked to Christopher for help. He seemed resigned to the job of telling Sissy the bad news. "I'm sorry, Miz Jackson."

"What are you sayin'?" The woman struggled to rise but had no strength and flattened back against the pillow.

Christopher put his hand on her shoulder. "You have a severe head injury. You must remain still. We can talk about everything when you are feeling better."

She gripped his hand with surprising strength. "No. Tell me now. Tell me everythin'."

Just then Deborah's mother stepped into the room. Rob and Arjan were with her. It was as if the trio had been summoned. Mother crossed quickly to Sissy's side.

"I see you're awake."

"Doc won't tell me 'bout George. You tell me."

"George and David have crossed over Jordan," Mother said softly. "Arjan and Rob tried to save them, but they were too late."

"No. No," Sissy moaned and shook her head ever so slightly. "Ain't true. Not my David. Not my George. Oh, Lord . . . oh, Father, he'p me."

Mother took hold of Sissy's hand and gave her forearm a gentle rubbing. "I know how terrible it is to lose your man, Sissy. I will stand by you through this pain. You will stay here with us, and I will see to your wounds."

"Can't be so," the woman sobbed. Tears oozed out from her swollen eyes. "Oh, Jesus, say it ain't to be this way."

Deborah turned away; it hurt too much to watch Sissy bear the news. She walked from the room without another word, only to find Zed Perkins waiting at the front door. The sight of the town's founder gave her new determination.

"I heard about the trouble at the Jacksons' last night," he said as Deborah let him into the house.

She nodded. "George and David are dead. They were hanged, and the house burned to the ground. Sissy was badly beaten but managed to run away. She made it here before collapsing."

"I am sorry." Zed took off his hat and bowed his head. "Will she live?"

Deborah shrugged. "God alone knows. She's suffered a tremendous blow to the head."

Zed nodded. "Seems our sorrows continue to grow."

"Sissy just learned the truth about George and David. Mother and the others are with her. You can imagine the horror of it all."

"Yes." Zed looked beyond Deborah. "Dr. Clayton . . . will she live?"

Deborah turned to find Christopher behind her. She felt a sense of relief at the sight of him.

"It's hard to say, but I have done all I can. I will remain here until I'm certain she is out of danger. If anyone needs me—you can direct them here or have Miz Foster see to them."

Zed gave a slow nod before adding another comment. "Ralph said murder was done."

"Two men were beaten and hanged," Christopher replied. "Mrs. Jackson is fighting for her life, but her husband and son are dead."

Mr. Perkins nodded. "I am sorry to hear that. Is there anything I can do?"

"You could catch the killers," Deborah said matter-of-factly.

Mr. Perkins met her stern expression. "I'd like to do just that. Seems hard to figure who's to blame, though."

"They claim to be part of the White Hand of God." Deborah put her hands on her hips. "Surely someone knows something about this if there are members in the area."

"You don't figure folks will just offer up such information, do you?" Zed Perkins questioned.

"What information?" Rob asked as he and G.W. joined the trio.

"Your sister suggested that we could nose around—ask folks to betray their loved ones and reveal who might have been involved in this mess."

Rob looked at Deborah and nodded. "And why not? Not everyone is going to agree with such actions. Laws were broken—lives were taken."

"But they were . . ." Mr. Perkins fell silent, but Deborah refused to let him off that easily.

"But they were black? Is that what you were going to say?"

Mr. Perkins looked uneasy. "You know how folks think."

"I do," she replied, "but that doesn't make it right. Surely if it is put to the people around here that this isn't a matter of skin color but of murder, then maybe we could catch those responsible."

G.W. seemed less convinced. "I think you would be hard-pressed to get folks around here to talk. There's a code of silence when it comes to such things. Remember a few years back, when all that thieving took place? A lot of folks knew who was responsible, but nobody was talkin'."

"Maybe we should offer a reward," Deborah suggested. She looked to her brothers. "Perhaps that would loosen tongues."

"Don't be so sure," Christopher said, surprising her. "My guess is that more people will stand in support of last night's activities than against them."

Deborah turned in disbelief. "How can you say such a thing?"

"Because this isn't the first time I've seen such things," he replied, turning away. "I'm going to check on Sissy."

Deborah wanted to question him further, but let him go. Instead, she turned to Mr. Perkins. "Couldn't you hire additional men to help keep order?"

"I've already mentioned that to Ralph. I can put additional men around town, but that won't help the folks who live away from the area, like Sissy's family."

Deborah glanced at G.W. "At least an additional show of force might quell the next act of violence. What if we hired some men to act as guards?"

"Guards for each of our black workers?" G.W. asked. "We can hardly afford that. We don't even have a guard on the campsite—we rely on the workers to keep order and watch over the equipment."

"I cannot accept that nothing can be done. Surely good people will rise up against such matters." At least she prayed it might be so. "I still think we should offer a reward for information revealing who was responsible."

"Let's see what Ralph can find out with his investigation." Mr. Perkins gave Deborah a weak smile. "Seems reasonable that we should let the law take charge to resolve the matter." He tipped his hat. "Please give my best to your mother. I'll be heading back to town now."

The threesome followed the older man outside. G.W. and Rob exchanged a few inaudible words with Zed while Deborah waited on the porch. She hoped they were stressing the need for action. If the good people of the area didn't take a stand, this kind of behavior would continue.

Euphanel sat beside Sissy long after Dr. Clayton had gone.

There was little anyone could do but watch and wait. Only time would reveal whether the injuries would take her friend's life.

Euphanel lifted Sissy's hand and held it tight. It was hard to see the once-vital woman so lifeless. Euphanel pushed down her anger. Why had God allowed such a horrible thing to happen? Why were good, God-fearing folks victims of such evil?

"I'm so sorry, Sissy," she murmured.

"Sorry?" The woman's barely audible voice caused Euphanel to open her eyes.

"I thought you were sleeping. I didn't mean to wake you."

"What you sorry for, Nellie?"

Euphanel smiled at her friend's use of her childhood nickname. "That this happened. That you have to endure such a thing."

"You ain't done nothin' to be sorry about," Sissy said, moving her head slowly from side to side. "Ain't fittin' for you to be sorry."

"You're my dear friend," Euphanel replied. "We've been through so many things together. When Rutger was killed, you never left my side. I wouldn't have made it through those awful days without you. I want to help you—like you helped me."

Sissy closed her eyes. "Ain't sure I wanna live in such a world."

Euphanel leaned closer. "Oh, my dear friend. I can't bear to think of my life without you in it. I know your pain is great, but God has kept you here. Surely there's a reason. We have to trust that He will show us that purpose."

"Ain't gonna be easy. I . . . " Sissy's voice faded into silence.

Clutching Sissy's hand to her breast, Euphanel began to weep anew. It wouldn't be easy. Loss never was.

Someone touched her shoulders and Euphanel looked up. Arjan gave her a sympathetic smile. "You need to get some rest."

"I can't leave her, even to just go next door to Deborah's room. I don't want her to be alone."

Arjan nodded. "I kind of figured you'd say something like that. I've brought one of the camp cots. I'll set it up on the other side of the bed."

Euphanel tucked Sissy's hand under the covers and got to her feet. "Thank you. You were good to think of such a thing."

"No problem." He paused, as if trying to figure something else to say, then nodded and walked from the room.

Euphanel glanced back at Sissy and felt a helplessness she'd not known since the logging accident had taken Rutger. God seemed so far away—so silent.

Chapter 3

Sissy remained too ill to attend the funeral services for her husband and son. Dr. Clayton was encouraged by her strength and signs of recovery, but he forbade her to move from bed. Mother decided to remain at the house and care for Sissy, while the rest of the family attended the burial.

Deborah looked at the plain wooden coffins. They were simple and sturdy—much like the men who filled them. These had been good men—dependable, trustworthy—and now they were gone.

She felt great comfort that Pastor Artemus Shattuck had offered to lead the services. The black church was currently without a minister and relied on the elders to take charge of the services. It was a bold statement to the community that a white minister would think this a serious and important enough matter to officiate.

The black community stood to one side, while the whites were on the other. The two groups seemed in opposition to each other—just as the world would have it be. There were looks of accusation and anger on the faces of some of the blacks. Others bore tear-stained expressions.

Deborah had learned that some of the former slave women had dressed the bodies, and the men had put together coffins with wood supplied by Mr. Perkins. Thankfully, the coffins had been closed to hide the hideous damage done to the men. Deborah had no desire to remember George and David as the nightmarish image she'd overheard her brothers describe. Instead, she forced herself to remember the men as they had been in life.

A group of women began to sing. Deborah recognized most as former slaves who had been good friends to the Jackson family. The women had strong voices and the words of the song rang out, demanding her attention.

"Steal away, steal away, steal away to Jesus!
Steal away, steal away home, I hain't got long to stay here."

A chorus of "amens" and "glory be's" rippled through the congregated blacks. But it was only when the verse was sung in the powerful, mournful wail of the women that the crowd was really stirred up.

"My Lord, He calls me, He calls me by the thunder;
The trumpet sounds within my soul, I hain't got long to stay here."

Deborah felt deeply moved by the emotion of the song and its singers. These were people who had seen so much oppression, had endured great pain and misery. Their freedom had come at a high price—a price that left many bitter and angry. George and David had died because of such animosity.

The haunting melody and lyrics reached deep into Deborah's heart. She closed her eyes as voices from the congregation joined the singers. The music bound them together in a way that nothing else could.

> *"Green trees are bendin', Poor sinners stand a-tremblin';*
> *The trumpet sounds within my soul, I ain't got long to stay here.*
> *Steal away, steal away, steal away to Jesus!*
> *Steal away, steal away home, I hain't got long to stay here."*

The voices faded and muffled sobs took their place. Deborah opened her eyes and swayed ever so slightly. The moment—the deep spiritual intensity—overwhelmed her. Uncle Arjan put his arm around her shoulders as if to steady her. She glanced up to meet his concerned face, but said nothing.

"There is great sorrow in our community," Pastor Shattuck began. "Great sorrow in the death of good men—good men who were undeserving of such punishment."

Deborah looked around at the handful of whites in attendance. She was rather surprised to see Margaret Foster and some of her family. The Fosters had never been overly friendly with the former slave population, and in fact had spoken out against the blacks being given jobs that should go to whites first. Perhaps it signaled a change of heart. Deborah hoped so.

Christopher was there, along with her brothers, Uncle Arjan, and some of the men who had worked alongside George and David at the logging camp. Other than that, only Mr. and Mrs. Perkins represented the town officially. Constable Nichols was nowhere to be seen, and neither were the Huebners or Greeleys. Deborah frowned and lowered her head.

God, are you here?

The prayerful question nearly brought her to tears. How could God allow such pain? Surely He loved His dark-skinned children as much as He loved those with fair complexions.

You do love them, as you love me—don't you?

She glanced skyward as if expecting a booming reply, but God was silent.

"So often we are faced with adversity and conflict. We are left to wonder where God is when such things happen to the innocent."

Deborah started and raised her face to stare hard at Pastor Shattuck. It was as if he had read her mind. Could he possibly understand her feelings of confusion?

"Evil reaches out to quell the happiness of good people—God-fearing people who would do acts of generosity in the name of Jesus. Where is God when that evil overcomes as it did with George and David Jackson?"

The gathering was strangely quiet. It seemed as though everyone was silent with anticipation, awaiting the pastor's words.

"In the Psalms, David cries out to the Lord." He lifted up his well-worn Bible. "The thirteenth psalm speaks thus, 'How long wilt thou forget me, O Lord? for ever? how long wilt thou hide thy face from me? How long shall I take counsel in my soul, having sorrow in my heart daily? How long shall mine enemy be exalted over me? Consider and hear me, O Lord my God: lighten mine eyes, lest I sleep the sleep of death; Lest mine enemy say, I have prevailed against him; and those that trouble me rejoice when I am moved.'"

Pastor Shattuck paused to look across the sea of faces. " 'But I have trusted in thy mercy; my heart shall rejoice in thy salvation. I will sing unto the Lord, because he hath dealt bountifully with me.'" He lowered the Bible and closed it gently.

"We have trusted in God's mercy. We rejoice in His salvation. He has dealt us great bounty—great love. We do not face this sorrow alone. We do not put our eyes on the enemy at the door, but instead keep our vision fixed on God alone. This world will pass away and with it will go the sadness and injustices that Satan has imposed. God will not be mocked—nor will He be ignored. David and George will have justice—the Lord will avenge their blood and comfort our hearts. We have only to trust in His mercy. Let us pray."

Deborah bowed her head but heard very little of the pastor's prayer. Instead, God's presence surrounded her like a comforting breeze on a stifling day, like a glass of iced lemonade to quench her thirst. Uncle Arjan's embrace supported her, but it was God's powerful presence that engulfed and strengthened her spirit.

You're all we truly have—the only constant in a troubled world. Yet the pain she felt seemed to smother that small flicker of peace. *Why did you let this happen, God? Why?*

Deborah took a deep breath and wrestled with her thoughts. God had not left them as orphans—He was here—He would always offer his comfort and strength. There was still a world of evil with which to contend, but they would not face it alone. She knew this somewhere deep in her soul . . . so why did it feel so hopeless?

After the service concluded, Deborah longed to get away. She had thought to start walking home but found that her brothers and even Christopher objected to the idea.

"You can't walk home alone," Christopher stated firmly. "After what happened to George and David, it would be too great a risk."

"Why in the world would you say that, Doc?" one of the Shaw brothers questioned.

G.W. answered before Christopher could speak. "Klem, it's not just the people of color who have to worry about the deeds of evil men."

"Seems to me, this was just a matter of dealin' with some old slaves."

Deborah's expression changed from peaceful to angry. "They weren't slaves anymore. They were free—just as we are."

"Besides," Christopher said, eyeing the man, "Miss Vandermark has dark hair and eyes. Her skin is tanned from the sun. Someone from the White Hand of God might mistakenly think her to be of mixed-blood or Mexican descent."

Christopher's words took Deborah by surprise. She'd never once considered that someone might think of her as anything but white.

"That's downright foolish," Klem's brother Kale declared. "Ever'one knows Miss Deborah. Ain't nobody gonna think her a Negro or Mexican."

"People make mistakes," G.W. said, drawing Lizzie close to his side. "Not every white woman sports blond hair and pale skin as my wife does. Seems to me, Doc makes a good point. In the heat of a moment—in the fading light of the forest—someone just might make such a mistake."

By this time, the few other white men had gathered around them. There was a general cry of disapproval at G.W.'s statement.

"Ain't no one gonna lay a hand on a white woman," Matthew Foster declared. "That ain't the way things are done around here."

"I wouldn't think that a woman, black or white, would have

to fear for her life in these parts," Rob threw in, "but we got proof that ain't the case."

Several of the men muttered curses under their breath. Their attitude took Deborah off guard. "I can't believe that you could be so callous. A woman lies near death in my home. A loving woman—a dear friend to my mother." Deborah pulled away from her uncle's side.

"I thought the men of this community to be honorable—to look beyond a person's skin color—but I see I was wrong. Perhaps some of you even participated with the White Hand of God to kill George and David." Her statement took everyone by surprise and seemed to momentarily stifle their ability to reply.

G.W. looked at her and then to Lizzie. Deborah read fear in her brother's expression. Did he also think there were people here capable of doing such heinous acts?

"I believe it does little good to speak in anger," Pastor Shattuck said, coming to intervene. "We are all disturbed and wounded by what has happened. The attack on one family from our community is an attack on all. No matter the color or gender." He offered Deborah a smile, then turned back to the men who seemed none too happy with her comments.

"Let us retire to our homes and pray for wisdom. Our town has suffered enough. It's time for forgiveness and peace."

For a moment, no one uttered a sound or moved to go. Then the crowd dispersed in an eerie solemnity.

Christopher watched the Vandermarks depart the funeral service and felt an immediate sense of loss. He longed to follow them back to their house, knowing he'd be welcome to do so, but he fought the urge. He would call on them later and check on Sissy.

Otherwise, it seemed only right to allow them some privacy in their mourning.

He crossed the railroad tracks and walked slowly back to the white side of town. There was an unusual stillness in the air; Mr. Perkins had actually closed down the sawmill for the afternoon funeral, a rare occurrence. A dozen or so men were gathered on the porch of the still-open commissary, while a great many others milled around the hardware store.

At home again, Christopher poured a cup of lukewarm coffee and served himself the last slice of pecan cake. Mrs. Perkins had sent the cake as a gift, by way of her two silly daughters. It was clear that the girls thought him a good catch, and it didn't seem to discourage them that he was paying court to Deborah. Of course, he hadn't exactly gone out of his way to make his intentions clear. He supposed they might, in fact, question the validity of the courtship since Christopher had done nothing overtly public to inform the community. Perhaps the girls thought him only casually interested in Deborah. Maybe they thought if they were coy and flirtatious, he might well change his mind and court one of them instead.

He settled down to the table and picked rather absentmindedly at the cake. He supposed he had no one but himself to blame. Even though he and Deborah had agreed to court with an intent to one day marry, they had agreed to keep their courtship rather casual. The townsfolk were used to seeing them together, but then, too, they knew of Deborah's interest in medicine.

Not that this interest had been well received. It was one thing for a middle-aged healer to be a woman, but for a young, vibrant, unmarried lady to take up doctoring met with some discomfort in the little town of Perkinsville.

Christopher had said nothing to Deborah about the comments, but he was somewhat concerned. He'd had more than one family tell him that they did not wish to have Deborah involved in their medical needs. As the only doctor in the town, he felt he had to honor their desires, but it grieved him. Deborah was a quick learner and her passion for science knew no bounds. He hated to stifle her interests.

"Maybe I was wrong to come here," he said, pushing the cake aside. He gave a heavy sigh and abandoned the coffee, as well. Getting to his feet, he decided the best thing he could do was head on out to the Vandermarks' after all. He wouldn't have any peace of mind until he did. Whether that stemmed from his concern for Sissy or his desire to be close to Deborah, he couldn't be exactly sure.

He thought of his family as he crossed the road to the livery. He hadn't seen his mother in some time. Her last letter had been full of worries and woes. She wrote of his younger brothers, fearing friends were leading them astray. His father remained distant and withdrawn. He'd never been the same after the accident that had left him paralyzed.

Despite his turmoil he forced a smile and motioned to a young boy who worked at the stable. "I need my horse. I have to make rounds." He tossed a coin to the child.

"Yes, sir." The boy easily caught the money and smiled. "I'll be real quick."

Christopher waited patiently while the boy went to the back of the livery to collect the doctor's mount. The heady smell of horses, manure, and straw mingled in the air, which today was strangely lacking the normal smoke and dust from the mills. The air wasn't of good quality on most days, and Christopher was glad to see that prevailing winds took most of the fumes away from the town.

"Here ya go, Doc," the boy announced, leading a sturdy sorrel gelding. "He's all ready for a run."

Christopher thought the boy reminded him a bit of his youngest brother, Thomas. "How old are you, Robby?"

"Thirteen. Be fourteen next month."

Smiling, Christopher nodded. "I have a brother just your age."

"Truly? Does he have a job?" The boy pushed back his shoulders and eyed Christopher quite seriously. "Pa says by my age a boy needs to be workin'."

"I haven't seen him in a while," Christopher replied, "but last I knew he was in school."

Robby spit and shook his head. "Pa says there ain't nothin' I can learn in books what will beat life itself."

Christopher knew that was the attitude of half the men in the county. There was no use demeaning the boy's father and suggesting he was wrong. "Say, it's been kind of chilly out—where are your shoes?"

The boy laughed. "Don't wear shoes, lessen I have to. Ain't no shoes I like."

"Well, you don't want to catch cold or worse."

"Ma says I'm too ornery. My sisters both had scarlet fever and measles, but I ain't been a bit sick."

Christopher climbed atop the back of the horse and took up the reins. Without waiting for the boy to reply, Christopher urged the horse out of the livery and onto the road. The boy's zest for life again reminded him of his siblings.

Memories of his family washed over him and the image of his petite mother, standing over a steaming pot of dirty clothes, immediately came to mind. She was aged beyond her years and would no doubt die young, as most overworked women did. The very thought caused him great sorrow. Never once in her life had she had it easy. Never once had she known a carefree day of rest.

Even on the Lord's Day, there were children to care for and meals to put on the table. He knew the money he sent home helped, but it wasn't enough. Nothing would please him more than to hire a nurse or housekeeper to help his mother with the workload, but there wasn't any extra cash for such things. Not that his mother would ever allow for the frivolity.

He smiled and pressed on toward the Vandermarks'. Deborah reminded him of his mother. In fact, she reminded him of her a great deal. They were both hardworking and more than a little ambitious, and both had a special place in his heart.

Chapter 4

Pastor Shattuck called a community meeting at the church to discuss the Texas Independence Day celebration. The yearly event in March was anticipated very nearly as much as Christmas. Just thinking about the roasted meats and wonderful music put a tremor of excitement in Deborah's stomach. She hadn't been to an Independence Day celebration in some years and only now realized just how much she missed it.

"Before we finalize our plans for the Independence Day festivities," the pastor began, "I feel it's important we speak on the tragedy that has befallen our county."

There were murmurings and a barely audible curse. Stunned, Deborah turned to throw a disapproving glare in the direction of whoever might have said such a thing in God's house. Her mother did likewise, along with several of the other older women.

Artemus Shattuck let the matter go, however. He tucked his thumbs into his waistcoat pockets and rocked back on his heels. "I have a grave concern for this community. It seems to me that folks have closed their eyes to bad behavior in hopes that it will simply depart. I have rarely seen such a thing happen. It is important that we take a stand—together as a town—against the prejudices and injustices we've seen of late."

"I thought we were figuring out where to set up the judging booths for the quilts," an older woman declared.

"Yeah, I figured you were going to let us know what time the fiddlers and pickers were to commence playin'," a man in front of Deborah called out.

"All of that in due time. I hoped while I had your attention, it would be fitting to remind you of our recent tragedies so that we might prevent such things from happening again. After all, we wouldn't want such things to interfere with our preparations. I'm sure everyone here would agree that this is a community celebration. We wouldn't want anyone to feel left out or slighted. Given the problems we've seen of late, I fear that some of our black brothers and sisters might feel intimidated or fearful of attending."

"Long as they stay in their place, it won't be a problem." This came from Zed Perkins's eldest son, Todd. "We've always had a place where they could celebrate, as well."

"I had rather thought it might do us all well to include the black community in our own celebration. Unite the two parts of our town and get to know one another better," Pastor Shattuck declared.

A hush fell over the room. Folks grew uneasy. It was evident that they felt the pastor had lost his mind.

"We are all of different ancestry here. I'm of German and

English descent. The Vandermarks are Dutch. The Huebners are German. The Fosters have Scottish and English ancestors. Doc Clayton sports an English name, and the founder of our town told me not long ago that his family has roots not only in England, as the name Perkins suggests, but also he shares a connection with the French. We have our differences, but we all have one thing in common. We are Texans. Before we are Americans or anything else—we proudly bear the name Texan."

Deborah saw several people nod in approval. At least that much was well received. She met Christopher's gaze and smiled. She'd never thought of his name being English. The fact was, there was still a great deal she didn't know about the man. He spoke very little of his family except to say they needed his help. She would have to make a special point to get him to tell her more.

"Folks, what I'm trying to say here is that we're in a sorry state of existence when we focus on a man's skin color rather than his actions. The Good Book says God doesn't even see the outward appearance of man, but looks at his heart. Oughten we do the same?"

Pastor Shattuck came down from the pulpit and stood directly in front of the congregated people. "We want to celebrate our independence, but I don't see how we can do that by trying to restrict others. I'd like to suggest we start a new tradition. Let's have a black and white baseball game on our Texas Independence Day."

Deborah heard some grumbling, but then Zed Perkins stood and raised his hands. "Look, I think we need to get back to planning our festivities. I'm not opposed to a black and white baseball game. Seems likely they won't be very good, considering they don't get to play much, but I don't object." He looked to the gathered crowd.

Deborah thought his gaze lingered a little longer on some of the men. Perhaps he knew their hearts and wondered just as she did whether or not they had been involved. It was most disturbing to imagine that killers could lurk in their own little town. What if her friends and neighbors were amongst those who had killed George and David?

"Most of you know that I have my own issues with Injuns and Mexicans. Ain't necessarily somethin' I'm proud of, but it's just the way things are. I hire blacks, same as whites. I pay a fair salary for a fair day's work. I don't want to see any more killings in our town. I'd just as soon the White Hand of God not show itself around these parts anymore." He turned back to Pastor Shattuck. "But you ain't gonna change the way folks think overnight."

Pastor Shattuck smiled. "I didn't figure I could, but I do know that God is able to change the heart of any man or woman, and that is my prayer."

The discussion moved quickly after that to the original reason they'd gathered. When the plans were finally agreed upon an hour later, Deborah was more than ready to stand and stretch her legs. She looked at her mother and offered her a hand up.

"Seems like these issues should get a little easier to discuss each time they're brought up," Mother said, sounding bitter. "But they don't. Folks just seem unwilling to forget about the past and about our differences. Maybe it will never change. Maybe the color of a person's skin will always be the only thing people can see."

Deborah pondered her mother's words as Christopher came to join them. He appeared to have heard the latter part of the conversation.

"Introducing change is never easy," he said, nodding his head toward the two women. He then turned to Deborah's mother. "If it won't delay your departure, I have some medical journals your daughter should read."

"How soon do you plan to head home, Mother?" Deborah asked.

"Not for a little while. I have shopping to do, and G.W. and Rob were headed to the hardware store to pick up new saw blades. You go along. We'll come fetch you at the doctor's office when we're fixin' to go."

Turning to Christopher, Deborah smiled. "It seems I can manage a little time."

He nodded but didn't offer her his arm. Deborah walked easily at Christopher's side, keeping pace with his long strides. She liked the way he carried himself—so sure and confident.

"Before we talk medicine, I wondered if we might talk about you," Deborah said, smiling. "It seems you know so much about me and my kin. When Pastor mentioned you were of English ancestry, I realized that I knew very little about you. You have family in Kansas City, and you're the eldest of fifteen children, but what else?"

Christopher shrugged. "There's not all that much to tell. You know that my father is crippled and my mother does what she can to keep the family together. There are still five children at home."

"Tell me about them," she insisted. They walked to the doctor's office and house, and Deborah pointed to the porch. "Let's sit out here to avoid all suspicion."

Christopher chuckled. "You think that will reduce concern, do you?" He allowed her to step onto the porch first.

Deborah quickly took a seat and waited for him to join her. "I think it will help. Folks seem uncertain as to what our relationship constitutes. With me seeking to learn about medicine and our courtship arrangement . . . well, I believe we have quite baffled most of the community."

"How so?"

"Well, women do not seek out jobs, especially ones that require them to train with men. And we had no formal announcement of our courtship, so most folks believe us to merely be in the early stages of trying to decide if we want to court." She shrugged. "But let them guess. I've never been conventional."

"I'm sure you speak the truth." He grinned.

She leaned back and smiled. "So tell me about the children who are at home. How old are they and what are their names?"

He looked rather hesitant as he settled back against the wooden chair and rubbed his bearded chin for a moment. "Well, I suppose it's just as easy to start with the youngest. Jonah is five and a rascal. Emma is eight and a very serious young woman. There would have been a ten-year-old, but Daniel died at birth.

"Darcy is twelve. She's a feisty young lady who grew up with too many older, ornery brothers. She's a bit of a wild one at times."

"I know how that can be. I had only brothers," Deborah replied. "Go on."

"All right . . . next is Thomas—he's thirteen. I think I told you that. James is next. We call him Jimmy. He's fifteen and quite the scholar. He loves school and has fought hard to continue his education. He works selling newspapers at the crack of dawn and then again in the evening and attends school during the day. My da—father thinks it a waste of time, but I've encouraged Jimmy to continue."

Deborah couldn't help but wonder at his stumbled words, but said nothing. "Surely your father can see the good you made of your education," she offered.

Christopher frowned momentarily. "He thought I should have come to work with him on the railroad. He's never had much regard for doctors. He thinks us all nothing but killers who act with society's blessing."

"I'm sorry. That seems such a shame."

He shrugged. "He's known so many bad ones, I can't really blame him. Anyway, John would be next. He died when he was seven. Next come the 'the swing-gate boys' as my father nicknamed them. Calvin is nearly twenty, Andrew is twenty-one, and Benjamin is twenty-three."

"Why does your father call them 'the swing-gate boys'?"

"Because they used to leave home and return so much that my father says they should have a swinging gate on the front of the house instead of a door. They're always getting into trouble. They don't have much schooling between the lot of them—spent more time using their brawn than their brains. Andrew made money for a time in boxing, but Benjamin and Cal looked for easier means to make a living. They haven't been heard from in a while." He quickly moved on.

"Samuel would have been twenty-four—almost twenty-five had he lived. He died at the age of three after falling off a swing. The wooden seat hit him in the head and knocked him to the ground. That would have been bad enough, but he impacted his head on a rock. He lingered for several days but never regained consciousness. My mother was inconsolable."

"Goodness . . . that would be so very hard." Deborah shook her head. "Poor woman."

"It was a sad time for all of us. My father had been especially fond of Samuel. I think some of his love of life went into the grave with my brother. He was never quite the same after that. I tried hard to offer solace, but my father chose other means of comfort."

"Such as?" Deborah braved the question.

Christopher stiffened and looked toward the road. "It's not important now." He drew a deep breath. "Last of all are three more sisters. Mary and Martha are twins. They married and moved west with their husbands. We seldom hear from them, but last I'd heard, they each had a couple of children. Then there's Abigail. She's twenty-eight. She's married and lives back East with her husband. She has three children."

"That's an amazing brood," Deborah said, smiling. "I can't imagine how noisy your house must have been. Did you have a really large home when you were growing up?"

He shook his head and his gaze took on a faraway look. "No. We didn't have much money. The house was quite small until we moved to Kansas City. It was a little larger then because my father finally got steady work with the railroad. I remember that move well because we finally had enough bedrooms that the girls and boys could be separated. The more children came along, the more crowded it got. But about the time we found it unbearable, some of us started leaving home."

Deborah tried to imagine the little house and all its children. Would Christopher expect her to have as large a family, should they marry? Never one to keep her thoughts to herself, Deborah posed the question. "And do you want a large family?"

He gave her a wicked grin that left her rather breathless. "Why, Miss Vandermark, what a forward question."

She shrugged and hid her discomfort. "You know I speak my mind."

"Indeed, I do." He shifted in his seat; it was his turn to look uncomfortable. "I suppose I've never really thought the number mattered, so long as the father and mother loved each other and took good care of their offspring."

She nodded, still unable to look at him. "Sounds reasonable and wise."

"What of you? Have you given thoughts to such matters?"

Deborah shook her head. "No, not really. I always figured I'd be taking care of my mother and father and hadn't considered a family of my own. You have to remember, for most of my life, I thought that was my purpose."

"And now?"

"I have to admit, I'm still rather confused about that . . . in fact, I'm confused about a lot of things." She finally lifted her gaze to meet his eyes. "Even though you've said nothing, I know there are a great many people in this area who aren't fond of my getting involved with medicine. Sometimes . . . sometimes I think I should forget about it."

"Is that what you want?" His voice was soft and gentle.

"No. At least not yet. The truth is, I still remain confused about where God wants me and how He plans to use me."

Christopher looked at her oddly. "And does that extend to your relationship with me?"

She shook her head. "I don't think so. I enjoy my time with you." Her breath caught and she bit her lower lip hard to keep from saying more. Christopher seemed to realize her feelings and moved the conversation away from the topic.

"As I mentioned, I have some medical journals you may take back with you. *The Boston Medical and Surgical Journal* has several very interesting articles. You are, of course, familiar with the Gemrig bone forceps. One of the articles details information about the new Helmond bone forceps. I'm considering ordering a set, if they aren't too expensive."

"That's fascinating. I'll be sure to read the article."

Despite the conversation's turn to a comfortable topic, Deborah couldn't help but think Christopher seemed uneasy—as though he needed to say something else, but was trying to figure out how.

"Oh, there's also an article about a new medical concern—it seems a mania has overtaken our young people in America."

She looked at him oddly and found Christopher smiling. "Roller skating," he said without making her ask.

"Roller skating is a mania? I tried it myself in Philadelphia and found it quite delightful." Deborah couldn't help but smile. "Why does the medical world believe this is a mania?"

"They believe it to be a 'psychological contagium' and that the vibrating brain cells of the skater have something to do with it all. You'll have to read the article."

"I promise you, I shall." She started to ask him what people were saying to him about her interest in doctoring, but spied her mother coming from the commissary with G.W. They were heading for the wagon with an armful of goods. "It seems my family is packing to return home. I suppose I should take my leave."

"Let me retrieve the journals," he said, getting to his feet. "I wouldn't want you to miss learning about what you may or may not have done to your brain while roller skating."

Deborah couldn't suppress a giggle as she waited for him to bring the journals from the house. She felt as if his uneasiness had passed and he was more like his old self. Her mother started walking toward them as Christopher reappeared with his offering. She waved, and Deborah stepped down from the porch with the magazines in hand.

"Dr. Clayton, please feel free to join us for supper. I know you probably planned to look in on Sissy later, and we'd love to have you at our table."

"Oh, do come," Deborah agreed. "I'll try to get the articles read by then and we can discuss them."

He smiled. "I would find that very . . . um . . . worthwhile." He turned to her mother. "Might I bring something?"

"Not at all. Lizzie is already baking pies, and by the time I get home, Deborah and I will be able to handle the rest. We'll see you around five."

"I'll be there."

Deborah hugged the journals to her breast as she and Mother made their way back to the wagon, as if to contain the giddy sensations roiling in her stomach. She'd see Christopher again! She was losing her heart to him in a way she'd not expected, and if she were honest with herself, she was starting to regret their agreement to take their courtship very slowly.

"You look as though you have stars dancing in your head," her mother said as Deborah settled in the seat beside her.

Deborah smiled. "Sometimes Dr. Clayton has that effect."

Her mother laughed heartily. "So did your father."

Chapter 5

"I've been speaking to Arjan," Euphanel announced some days later. She'd asked her family to assemble in the living room and fixed each one with a gentle look before continuing. "I'd like to offer Sissy a permanent home with us. There's no way of knowing whether she'll make a full recovery or if she'll be left debilitated. I hope you won't have any objections to this."

"Not at all," G.W. replied.

Rob and Deborah nodded eagerly. "I think it's a wonderful idea," Deborah replied. "Sissy deserves the best of care."

"Dr. Clayton and I spoke about Sissy's recovery, and he believes she may continue to have difficulties for some time. She doesn't remember things like she used to and often gets frustrated by that.

She's spent her entire life taking care of others, and now I want to assure her that someone will see to her needs."

"I think we all feel that way," Deborah said. "Sissy is like family."

Euphanel gathered her thoughts and continued. "I think, in keeping with that, I want to expand the house. Arjan and I have discussed some ideas and I want your opinion."

"Tell us what you're thinking, Ma," said Rob.

She smiled. "Well, I'd like to change the office into Sissy's room and take back my old bedroom—the one G.W. and Lizzie are currently using. I'd like to add on to the front of the house, as it seems the most likely place to build. We could expand the living room, make a larger dining room and kitchen—oh, and add an office that could sit just off the house so that it can be more private. We can turn the old kitchen and dining room into bedrooms for G.W. and Lizzie, as well as a nursery. The old living room can be a sitting room for just the family."

"Sounds like you've given this a lot of thought," G.W. said, exchanging a look with Lizzie. "What do you think of this?"

Lizzie smiled. "I think the extra space would be very nice."

"I figure that one day, this will be your house," Euphanel said to G.W. Her husband, Rutger, had always planned to hand it down to G.W. He had intended to build Rob a house of his own elsewhere on their acreage, but the first son was entitled to inherit his father's place.

"It's gonna be a long time before we need to go worryin' over who owns what," G.W. replied. "But if we're gonna do this, we should do it right. If there's any other additions you want, we might as well include it all at the same time."

"Your ma gave it a pretty good piece of thought," Arjan explained.

"I might have contributed an idea or two, but she pretty well figured out what she thought would work."

"What about expanding the second floor, as well?" Rob asked. "Seems like it would make it easier to keep the roof one level. That way we wouldn't have to worry about makin' places where the water'll gather."

"I think that makes sense," Mother replied. "It would give the house additional bedrooms."

"And what about a proper bathing room downstairs?" G.W. suggested. "Those of us on the first floor would appreciate that."

It wasn't long before everyone was chiming in their ideas. Euphanel was glad they were of one accord. She hadn't been sure how the comment would be received, but Arjan had figured her children would go along with most anything she suggested. Euphanel was pleased to know her family enjoyed her company and considered this her home to do with as she pleased. No one ever said a word about it not being her place since her husband was dead. However, she had known plenty of widows who had suffered such attitudes and was thankful for the love of her family.

G.W. fetched a piece of paper and began sketching out the planned addition. It would be quite an undertaking, Euphanel knew, as it would nearly double the size of the house. Arjan said they could afford it, but she couldn't help but worry.

"If it's going to be too costly, we could wait a spell."

Her sons looked up and then to Arjan. "No, I think we can afford to move forward. It will take the bulk of our savings, but I feel confident we can make it back in a matter of months," G.W. declared. "Our accounts are in good order."

Deborah fixed him with a smile. "You've certainly picked up the bookkeeping quickly. Father would be proud of you."

G.W. rubbed his injured leg. The wound he'd received last

December bothered him from time to time; a fall from near the top of a tall pine had nearly cost him his life. He still walked with a limp and at times complained of a dull aching, but he was healing nicely. She knew he tended to rub the spot, however, when he began to feel embarrassed.

Euphanel got to her feet. "I'm going to go check on Sissy now. You boys can figure it all out with the help of Deborah and Lizzie." She slipped from the room.

I'm blessed, she told herself. *So very blessed.* The deaths of Sissy's husband and son had only served to bring back memories of her own loss. But how different life might have been had her husband been less generous in his attitude toward women and training of his sons. Her boys valued her opinion—Deborah did, as well. Where the fate of a widow was often tenuous, Euphanel's family had always made her feel useful and cared for.

She made her way upstairs and found Sissy awake, staring silently at the ceiling. She didn't bother to speak when Euphanel sat down beside her. Her pain and sorrow ran so deep that Euphanel couldn't help but take on a portion of it for herself.

"Some days, it feels as though this is nothing more than a bad dream," she whispered to Sissy. "But even in this, God has not left you nor forsaken you."

The woman nodded her head ever so slightly. "I never hoped to live this long—long 'nuf to bury my son—my man."

Euphanel nodded. "I know. I never thought to bury Rutger, either."

"I's sure sorry to be such a burden. Wish I were in the ground with 'em."

"Please don't say such things." Euphanel clutched Sissy's hand tight. "I can't bear the thought. I know this is painful, but our family loves you dearly. We want you to consider this your home now. We plan to make it larger so that everyone can live here comfortably for as long as they like."

Sissy finally turned to look at Euphanel. "Don't be doin' such things on my account. Ain't fittin'."

"What's not fitting is leaving you to fend for yourself when we have plenty and can aid you in your time of need. I don't want to make you feel that you have no choice, but I do want you to know how much we want you to be with us now."

Tears began to flow from Sissy's eyes. They slid back to her ears and wooly hair before Euphanel reached up to blot them with her handkerchief. "I ain't deservin' of such mercies," Sissy said, closing her eyes. "I's been layin' here, questionin' the Almighty. I don't deserve nuthin'."

"Oh, my dearest friend, you are deserving of this and more. The wrong done to you and your family should never have happened. It's only natural that you would have questions for God. I've been asking Him plenty myself—not because I don't trust Him, but rather because I just don't understand."

"Don't reckon we ever will."

Euphanel wiped again at Sissy's tears. "What's important now is that we figure out ways to keep it from happening again."

Sissy's head moved from side to side. "Ain't never gonna stop. Never so long as hateful folk live."

Euphanel knew Sissy was right, but she couldn't bring herself to admit such things. If she had anything to do with it—anything to say about such things—there would be a change. She would fight to keep anyone else from experiencing what her friend had been forced to endure.

The congregation took their seats after singing the last of their

Sunday hymns and waited as Pastor Shattuck took the pulpit. He looked rather grim this morning. There was no casual greeting or comment about the weather; instead, he set his Bible in place and lifted his hands in prayer.

"Oh, Father, we ask for your wisdom. Teach us to be merciful and forgiving, and help us to understand your precious Scriptures. Amen."

"Amen," the congregation murmured in unison.

Deborah wasn't sure what to expect from the minister, but she felt confident he would address the concerns of the community. When he opened the Bible and began to speak instead of Joseph and his brothers, she felt rather disappointed.

"The thirty-seventh chapter of Genesis introduces us to Joseph," began the sermon. "I will read to you now. 'Now Israel loved Joseph more than all his children, because he was the son of his old age: and he made him a coat of many colours. And when his brethren saw that their father loved him more than all his brethren, they hated him, and could not speak peaceably unto him.'"

He continued, but Deborah gave it less than her full attention. She had so hoped that Pastor Shattuck would make the people listen to reason—help them see that something had to be done about the recent murders.

" 'Come, and let us sell him to the Ishmeelites, and let not our hand be upon him; for he is our brother and our flesh. And his brethren were content. Then there passed by Midianites merchantmen; and they drew and lifted up Joseph out of the pit, and sold Joseph to the Ishmeelites for twenty pieces of silver: and they brought Joseph into Egypt.'"

The pastor looked up. "For twenty pieces of silver—only ten pieces shy of the price they gave Judas for our Lord. Jealousy led good men to make bad choices in this situation. Envy, jealousy, greed—all powerful influences when it comes to decision making."

There were a smattering of "amens" from amongst the listeners, but Deborah sensed the tension that ran through the entire gathering.

Pastor Shattuck stepped away from the Bible. "Evil wears many faces. Anger and bitterness—presumed wrongs, as well as those things I've mentioned—they all work together to send good men down bad roads.

"Not long ago, Mr. Perkins shared the story of his family's life in Texas. Having lived in the area for longer than I, it was fascinating to learn the experiences of others. Through his stories I came to understand him a little better. Stories are like that. We share information and learn the sorrows and woes of those around us, and it gives us insight into their hearts."

Deborah smoothed the skirt of her pale blue gown with her gloved hands and considered the pastor's words. She had heard the stories of Mr. Perkins's family but had no idea how it could possibly relate to Joseph and his brothers.

"I don't know if all of you are familiar, but Mr. Perkins has a past of great sorrows. It seems that members of his family—his grandparents and some of their children—were set upon by hostile Indians. The older folks were wounded or killed, while the children were stolen away. It was later learned that the Indians sold the children to wealthy Mexicans, but by the time those buyers were located—the children had been traded off and lost to the family."

Several people shook their heads. Some murmured derogatory remarks about the kidnappers.

"It is an awful thing to imagine, isn't it? Stealing a child and selling him. Just like Joseph's brothers. They sold their brother into slavery, just as Mr. Perkins's family members were sold. His own father only escaped the same treatment because he happened to have been in town with an older brother during the raid. Imagine his horror to return home and discover the truth."

There were additional comments and agreements. The atmosphere seemed to change from one of reverence and a routine Sunday sermon to an interactive discussion on the injustices put upon the white man by the Indians and Mexicans.

"Mr. Perkins tells me that the neighbors and townsfolk did what they could to find the children, but they were never recovered. It was years later that one of the boys managed to get away and return to the family. He told the story of what had happened, but he had no idea where his sisters and brother had ended up. He only knew that they had been sold along with him and sent to various places. Can you imagine such injustice? Such a horrible thing. Children snatched from the bosom of their family and taken against their will to work in a place where they couldn't even speak the language."

"Should have killed ever' last Injun and Mexican," a gravelly voice declared from somewhere behind Deborah.

She considered the comment for a moment, knowing that most everyone there felt the same way. Pastor Shattuck seemed to nod in agreement. His action surprised her.

"Would seem a just punishment. Kill those who killed and stole away the family members of innocent bystanders. Who among us would say such a thing was unjust?"

"The Good Book says, 'An eye for an eye,'" another man called out.

"It also says that stealing a man and selling him is punishable by death. Exodus 21:16 speaks to just such a thing, so it would only be fitting that those who stole the children and sold them should be put to death."

There ran a wave of agreements from the congregation that

increased in volume until the pastor finally held up his hands to continue.

"Joseph's brothers, by all rights, should have been put to death, but Joseph was full of mercy. He loved his family and he didn't want to cause them harm. He showed them mercy, even when they didn't deserve it."

Deborah felt a chill run through her body. Could it be possible that Pastor Shattuck would take his message even further? She leaned forward in anticipation.

"So I offer to you a question this day: Do you suppose the Negro came willingly to this continent? Or were they stolen by their enemies for whatever evil reason and sold to be slaves to those who needed workers—just as the Indians did with Mr. Perkins's family?"

The church went completely silent. There wasn't so much as a squirm from anyone in the pews. Deborah all but held her breath. The looks on the faces of the congregation conveyed stunned disbelief. They had been led where they did not want to go.

"We are so very quick to suggest that the Indian be killed for having stolen and sold slaves, but when it comes to people of our own skin color doing likewise, we are less inclined to see the wrongdoing."

He stepped down from the raised platform and gazed across the congregation. "We've witnessed many tragedies because of folks stealing other folks and selling them off. We've endured a war in this great nation because of such things. We've borne the agony of such injustice being done to people of our own skin color, and we stand up and cry out in anger at such wrongdoings. We raise a pleading hand to God to beg justice for our own, while pointing a finger of condemnation on the other hand at those whose skin is darker."

The congregation remained silent and fixed on Pastor Shattuck's every word. The man seemed to realize he had finally hit upon a chord they could all recognize. He tucked his hands in his pockets and stepped back to the pulpit and picked up his Bible. "I'll now close in prayer."

Deborah closed her eyes and felt a sense of elation. She had a new respect for Pastor Shattuck. He was much wiser than she'd given him credit for. He had found a way to get the people to listen to his heart and to the Word, even knowing they would never agree with what he had to share. He had addressed not the murders themselves, but the very origin of the problem.

Folks filed from the church in silence. Hardly a word was spoken as they departed. Pastor Shattuck extended his hand as he always did, and some folks took it while others passed by without even glancing up. A few, she was happy to see, thanked the preacher for his words. Her family was among those, as was Dr. Clayton.

But would the pastor's words only serve to put up walls of silence between those who agreed and those who disagreed?

Chapter 6

Word quickly spread that the Vandermarks were adding on to their house, and on the last Saturday in February, nearly half the town turned out to help. A palpable tension was evident, however. The ladies seemed to choose their words with great care as they shared the latest news, while the men spoke even less than usual. Deborah overheard several ladies ask her mother about Sissy. They approached her cautiously, whispering their questions. It was unfortunate that a community should be divided by something as heinous as the murders that had taken place; Deborah would have thought everyone could agree at least on the fact that the killings had been unjust. But apparently even that was too much to expect. There appeared to be an unspoken agreement to pretend that all was well, in order to accomplish what needed to be done.

Watching from the porch, Deborah marveled at how her mother moved among the crowd, making each person feel welcome. Mother was the consummate Southern hostess. She easily engaged their friends and neighbors, sharing a comment or asking a question. The tensions began to visibly ease, and finally people conversed, if not comfortably, then at least amiably. When Mother had finally made the rounds, she stepped to the porch.

"Friends, we're so glad to have ya'll here today," her mother told everyone. The crowd quieted down immediately. "Thank you so much for sharing your time and energy to help a neighbor. Arjan and my boys will direct you in what we're hoping to accomplish." She stepped aside to let Arjan take over, then held up her hand. "Oh, and of course the ladies and I will put together a wonderful lunch for you."

The men gave affirming comments and some even smiled. Perhaps they could put aside their troubled thoughts and disagreements for this one day. Deborah joined her mother to the side of the porch while her uncle took charge.

"We're thankful for the good weather and hopeful that we can raise the entire addition and roof it in one day. It's a big task, but I believe we Texans have always been up to big tasks."

This time the men raised an affirming cheer. In the distance, Deborah heard the logging train whistle. It would bring the last of the needed lumber and building supplies.

"Uncle Arjan seems to have a good way with organizing these kind of things," Lizzie whispered to Deborah.

She smiled and nodded. "Father used to say his brother could have been President of the United States with his ability to coordinate efforts."

Lizzie put her hand to her growing abdomen. "I'm sure the men in this family could be anything they set their minds to. G.W.

has taken to reading to me at night. Sometimes I have to help him, but he isn't letting his pride keep him from the task. I have you to thank for that, Deborah. It's given him something to live for since being injured."

Deborah considered her friend for a moment. "It always saddened me that my brothers held little value in book learning. Now it seems that both of them have a new interest, for Rob has actually begun to spend time reading, as well. I'd love to see the town's attitude toward schooling change . . . so many of the people are illiterate."

The men were beginning to break into teams as the logging train came to a stop. Arjan directed one of the teams to unload the new supplies, while the others immediately went to work framing up the walls.

"I suppose we'd better head to the kitchen," Mother said, joining them.

Mrs. Perkins approached and offered a basket. "I've brought three pies and five dozen cookies. I know they won't last long, but I figured it was a start."

Mother laughed. "We've been hard at it for days. We knew we'd have our loggers helping, and they can eat like an army. But what a pleasant surprise to have so many of our friends and neighbors join us."

"Your family is one of the most admired in the county." Mrs. Perkins lowered the basket. "Despite the recent troubles, I'm hopeful that perhaps this will afford us a coming together of hearts."

"That would be wonderful," Mother agreed. "Perhaps if there were more positive things to dwell on, folks would be less likely to cause harm."

"You know, I've been thinking that very thing," Mrs. Perkins replied.

"Oh, who's that with Pastor Shattuck?" Lizzie said, leaning toward Deborah. "She looks like she could be your relation."

Deborah followed Lizzie's gaze and saw the young woman at the preacher's side. She was nearly the same size and had dark black hair like Deborah, but unlike her, the stranger had arranged her tresses in a bevy of curls that gently draped her neck and shoulders. The young stranger carried herself in a very elegant manner, appearing to float across the yard on the pastor's arm, a sort of teasing smile upon her lips.

Looking back at Lizzie, Deborah leaned in to whisper. "I'm guessing it might be the pastor's daughter. He has two children who, as I heard it, lived elsewhere with their grandmother."

"Mrs. Vandermark, Miss Vandermark," Pastor Shattuck said as he approached and tipped his hat. He looked beyond them. "Mrs. Perkins, Mrs. Vandermark."

Mother stepped from the porch and extended her hand. "How are you, Pastor?"

He shook her hand, then stepped aside. "This is my daughter, Mara. Mara, these are the Vandermark women." He paused and smiled. "Of course, you've already met Mrs. Perkins."

"I'm delighted to make your acquaintances," Mara Shattuck said, offering a brilliant smile. "My father has spoken so highly of you."

Mother took charge. "Well, we are quite pleased to finally meet you. I understand you've been living in New Orleans with your grandmother."

She nodded. "But now it's time to help Father with God's work."

The comment surprised Deborah. She had thought Pastor Shattuck rather negative when it came to women. He never wished to discuss the Bible with her, at least, always making some excuse when Deborah asked him about certain Bible verses.

"I'm certain you will be an asset to him," Deborah's mother declared. "You must excuse us just now. We need to start putting together the noon meal."

"Truly? It's only just past dawn," Mara said, looking surprised.

Mother laughed. "True enough, but we will need to ready the food, nevertheless. The men will work hard and need coffee and doughnuts to sustain them until lunch. If you'd like to help, we'd be glad for the extra hands."

Mara looked to her father, who nodded. She looked down at her stylish suit. "Do you suppose I could borrow an apron?"

"Of course," Mother assured. "We have plenty. In fact, if you're worried about your clothes, Deborah would surely be able to loan you something."

Mara met Deborah's gaze and smiled. "I'm sure an apron will be sufficient. I wouldn't want to put anyone out."

"You wouldn't," Deborah replied.

The dark-haired woman smiled. "Then perhaps I will take you up on the offer. This suit isn't all that comfortable. Grandmother told me it was the height of fashion, but I find it less than serviceable for everyday."

Deborah's mother chuckled. "We'll fix you right up. Thank you for coming today, Pastor Shattuck. Perhaps you will offer grace at dinner?"

He nodded. "For now, though, I'll set aside my coat and roll up my sleeves. I'm quite good with a hammer."

Mother reached out to Mara. "Come along, ladies. We shall find something suitable for Miss Shattuck to wear."

"Oh, please call me Mara. I should like very much to be a good friend to each of you."

Deborah liked her immediately. She appeared so stylish and refined, but at the same time, Mara Shattuck held no pretense of airs.

"Mother!" Rob crossed the yard carrying a large lidded pot. "Miz Huebner asked me to fetch in this pot of chicken and dumplings." He stopped at the sight of Mara. His eyes widened slightly as a grin spread across his face. "I don't reckon we've met."

"This is Mara Shattuck, the pastor's daughter," his mother introduced. "Mara, this is my youngest son, Rob."

She smiled and nodded. "I'm pleased to meet you, Mr. Vandermark."

"Not nearly as pleased as I am." He stood fixed in place and might have remained there had Mother not broken the spell.

"Rob, Arjan is going to need you, so just go ahead and deliver the food to the kitchen."

"Maybe Mara could help me," Rob said in his smooth, practiced manner. His blue-eyed gaze was fixed on the younger woman.

"Help you carry the pot?" Deborah teased.

Rob looked almost confused for a moment. "No, silly," he finally managed. "I only figured maybe she could hold the door for me."

"I'd be happy to help, Mr. Vandermark." Mara climbed the steps and cast a quick glance over her shoulder. "Is this the door of which you were speaking?"

He quickly bounded onto the porch as if the heavy load weighed nothing at all. "That's the one, and please . . . call me Rob."

Deborah rolled her eyes and looked to Lizzie. "My brother can move fast when he needs to."

"To be sure," Lizzie whispered in reply.

They followed after the others, smiling at their exchange. Deborah knew her brother could be quite charming when he wanted to be. He'd paid visits to most of the eligible young women in the area, checking the potential of each with the same thoroughness he might use to select a tool with which to work. It wasn't surprising that he'd noticed Mara, although Deborah found the timing quite incredible—even for her brother.

The lunch hour approached and the men were signaled to stop work. Deborah was amazed at how much they'd already accomplished. The main framework of the first floor was completed and a good portion of the second floor was in place, as well. An entire team of men even worked on setting the interior walls in place.

Pastor Shattuck shared a blessing for the food and for the safety of the workers. So far the worst of the injuries had been when one of the children had fallen off the scaffolding. He looked to be sporting some bruises and a few scrapes but otherwise had been unharmed. Still, Deborah was glad to see Dr. Clayton show up just as the eating commenced.

Deborah went to where he secured his horse under the shade of a hickory tree. "Just in time for dinner."

He grinned. "That was the plan. Have you ever known me to pass up a meal cooked by the Vandermark women?"

She laughed. "Well, this meal happens to have been cooked by the entire community. We Vandermarks did plenty, but the ladies of Perkinsville have been most generous."

"I'm glad," he said, looking toward the new structure. "Looks like the men have been, as well."

Deborah followed his gaze. "It's amazing, isn't it? I remember when we raised the church in a day. . . . Of course, back then the entire town turned out. Here, not so much. We have a good number, don't get me wrong—but the tension at first was thick enough to cut with a knife. I figure there are still a good number of people here who don't agree with our thoughts on racial matters and stayed away."

Christopher looked back to her and nodded. "I just made the rounds in town, and believe me, there were plenty of folks more than happy to speak their minds." His expression darkened. "I've witnessed the damage that occurs when hatred and prejudice grows."

"Was it between blacks and whites?"

For a moment he said nothing, and Deborah thought perhaps he would refuse to continue their conversation.

"I'm sorry," she whispered, putting her hand on his arm. "You don't have to tell me."

He shook his head. "It's not that. It's just sad to remember. And I see it all happening here again. There were battles in Kansas City between the black and whites, of course. And there were white folks during the war who were proslavery, as well as against it. They fought amongst themselves almost more than they fought in the war."

"We had a lot of that here, as well," Deborah admitted. "Father called them guerillas. They were forever causing problems."

"Well, the same was true up north. They didn't call Kansas 'Bleeding' without due cause. Kansas and Missouri very nearly had their own little war within the war. But there were other problems, as well."

"Such as?"

He looked at her for a moment. "There were great prejudices among the whites toward other whites. For instance . . . the Irish. A great many folks take strong stands against the Irish. They dislike them for their fighting and drinking, not to mention their religious views. They dislike them for their culture—the way they speak—the things they love to eat. It doesn't seem to matter. They feel that the Irish take jobs away from others who were there first."

"But aren't the same problems true for the Italians and Polish?"

Deborah questioned. "I know in Philadelphia, there were problems also with those of Jewish descent. It was sometimes quite ugly."

He nodded, then looked up at the canopy of trees toward the cloudless sky.

"Well, are you going to let the doctor come and eat?" Deborah's mother interrupted.

Deborah hadn't even heard her mother approach. "I'm sorry, Christopher. I didn't mean to keep you from dinner."

He laughed and gave a brief bow to Mrs. Vandermark. "I don't miss too many meals, as you can see." He patted his stomach.

"Nonsense," Mother declared. "You are the very image of health. Fit as a fiddle, my mother would say. Can you stay for long?"

"I can. I finished my rounds, and now I'm yours for the day. I figured that a house raising would be the perfect place for a doctor. One can never tell what might happen."

"Truer words were never spoken," Mother replied. She entwined her arm with Dr. Clayton's. "Come. I'll show you where everything is."

Deborah followed behind as Christopher and her mother made their way to the luncheon table. Seeing that many of the men were out of coffee, she diverted to where Lizzie was already filling several pitchers.

"Let me take those," Deborah said, reaching for the full containers. "How are you feeling? Did you eat something?"

Earlier, Lizzie had suffered some nausea, but now she looked quite well. "I feel much better. It's G.W. I'm worried about. He seems so out of sorts."

"But why?" Deborah looked for her brother and didn't find him.

"He can't get up on the ladders and help. He feels that he's not able to do his part. I told him it was nonsense, but . . . well,

I'm wondering if you could speak to your uncle and maybe let him know what the problem is. He might have some idea for what G.W. could do to be useful."

Deborah nodded. "I'll mention it when I take the coffee. Don't you worry, Lizzie. My brother can be quite cantankerous at times, but he usually comes around." She smiled. "If not, I'll give him a good elbow to the ribs."

Lizzie laughed. "That's not exactly what I had in mind."

Pouring coffee as she went, Deborah greeted the workers and made comments about their progress. The men seemed pleased to hear her praise. A few of the single men tried to get her to stay and chat, but she made it clear that she had to be moving on so that everyone could have coffee while it was still hot.

She finally found Uncle Arjan and was happy to see he was just finishing. "I wonder if you could help me for a moment."

He looked at her oddly, but nodded. "What's the problem?"

She handed him the empty pitchers. "Follow me."

They went to where coffee was being poured into a large caldron to keep warm while more coffee was readied to perk in the pots. It had been like this all day, with Lizzie and a couple of other women focused on keeping coffee available to all the workers.

"Lizzie is worried about G.W. She says he's feeling rather useless. I was hoping you might have a special task for him." She took the pitcher from her uncle and handed it over to Lizzie, who nodded in agreement.

"His leg has been bothering him too much to get in there and really work," Lizzie admitted. "He doesn't like to favor it, but he can hardly do much else."

"I have the perfect solution," Uncle Arjan declared. "He can be in charge of positioning the interior walls. He knows exactly what we want. I'll tell him that since we've made such great progress, he can get the men to work inside while Rob and I get the upper floor finished and the roofing done."

Deborah smiled at Lizzie. "See—it's all resolved."

"I'll go find him and arrange things right now," her uncle said. "Thanks for a mighty fine dinner. A nap would suit me just fine, but I guess I'll get back to work."

ꕥ

The work continued until darkness made it impossible to see; the last of the shingles were put into place by lantern light. Those on the roof cheered loudly as Rob put in the final nail. He'd never been so tired in his life, but strangely, the action seemed to give him a second wind.

Climbing down from the roof, Rob immediately spied Mara Shattuck and made his way to where she stood. "Well, what do you think?" he asked her.

She smiled. "Looks like you won't have to worry when the rains come."

"If they come. Most of the state is sufferin' a horrible drought." He wiped sweat from his face with the back of his sleeve. The chilly evening air felt good. "So, do you plan to be around long?"

She looked at him and considered the question a moment. "I believe God brought me here, Mr. Vandermark. It seemed time to come and help my father with his ministry work."

"So is that a yes?" He gave her a broad grin.

She returned his smile. "I believe it is—at least for the time. I try very hard to go where God leads. What of you, Mr. Vandermark?"

"What do you mean?"

A coy look crossed her face. "Do you go where God leads?"

Rob felt a bit perplexed. He hadn't intended for the conversation to veer toward religion. "I reckon I try to. I don't suppose I've ever heard Him come right out and tell me exactly."

"Do you ask Him to speak to you?"

Her question took him off guard. "Am I supposed to?"

She gave a nod, her expression quite serious. "I believe we are. The Bible does admonish us to seek Him—to ask and it shall be given. It is of the utmost importance that we ask for His guidance. After all, surely we wouldn't want to go where He does not lead us."

"No, I reckon you're right on that." He grinned. "You know, for a pretty gal, you do a lot of deep thinkin'."

"Well, Mr. Vandermark, I am much more than my outward appearance." She turned to go, but stopped and gave him a smile. "Perhaps in time, you'll learn that for yourself."

Rob wanted to rush after her—to suggest he get started on his learning right away—but something held him in place. He was known in the community as something of a ladies' man. The family often joked that he had first spoken of marriage at the tender age of four when he spied a young neighbor girl at church and declared her just the kind of gal he'd like to get hitched with.

Since that time, there had been a great many young women who'd held his attention and his heart. Often when a new gal came to town, Rob would find himself convinced she was the one for him—at least until another young lady appeared to take his attention.

Now, however, he found himself feeling rather gut-punched. Mara Shattuck was unlike most of the other women he'd met. She seemed so sure of herself, and of course, she was easy on the eyes. But there was also something more. Something he couldn't quite explain. She had a way about her that left him feeling as though there was something more he needed to know—something that only she could tell him. Something that would complete him.

"She looks like Deborah," G.W. said as he joined Rob.

Rob looked at him and shook his head. "Who does?"

"Miss Shattuck. Don't you think she favors our sister?"

He shook his head, unable to imagine what G.W. was talking about. Sure, the beauty had dark hair and eyes, but she looked nothing like Deborah. "I think you need spectacles, brother of mine. Those two don't look a thing alike."

Chapter 7

March 1886

Frankly, I can hardly believe the celebration is tomorrow," Rachel Perkins told Euphanel. "Seems like this year has already gone by so quickly."

"I have to agree. It started with so many sorrows," Euphanel replied.

"Indeed it did. Speaking of which, how is Sissy?" Putting down the curtain she'd been hemming, Rachel reached for her cup of tea.

"She's much better. She likes to sit for a little while now. Her head will start paining her, however, so she doesn't spend too much time up. Doc says it will be a while before she's herself again. She might always suffer headaches."

"That must be so hard for her. I've never known Sissy to sit for long."

Euphanel nodded and tied off her stitch. "She's never even been one for standing still. I know it's hard for her to just rest, but I remind her that it's the only way to heal."

Rachel smiled. "And what does she say?"

Laughing, Euphanel put the finished curtain panel aside and picked up the next one. "She tells me that the Lord can heal her with a single touch, just like He did folks in the Bible. I agreed, but told her that until He decided to do that, she had to rest."

"I do wish Zed could find out who was responsible. I know he had our boys go to Lufkin to ask around there about the White Hand of God, but he told me that no one seems to know anything—or if they do, they aren't talking."

"That doesn't surprise me. Folks seem steeped in their secrets when it comes to such underhanded events. I do wish we could do something to bring the people together, though. I hate that we sit separately at any gathering—that we have our separate churches. I want to sit with Sissy in church, but she's hardly welcome in ours."

"I heard Pastor Shattuck say that if skin color were the basis for acceptance, then Jesus probably wouldn't be welcome, either."

Euphanel put her hand to her mouth and suppressed a giggle. "I'm sure," she said, lowering her hand, "that didn't go over well."

"No," Rachel agreed, smiling, "but I thought it made a whole lot of sense."

Euphanel began working on the next hem and shook her head. "Funny how folks always think of Jesus as blond-haired and blue-eyed. I suppose it comforts them to see Him in their own way."

"I would imagine so, but then, Sissy probably thinks of Him with skin as dark as hers."

Looking up, Euphanel grew thoughtful. "Do you suppose folks

all over the world think of God that way? Each in their own color and manner?"

"Seems reasonable," Rachel replied. "He is all things to all people."

"I'll have to ask Sissy sometime what color she sees our Savior."

Euphanel took careful stitches as she hemmed the heavy brocade fabric. Lizzie and she had found the dark gold and brown material at the commissary buried far beneath other more popular pieces. The price had been reduced because of a lack of interest, and Euphanel had taken the entire bolt. It seemed a nice heavy material to put up on the new bedroom windows.

"I just had a thought."

"About what?" Euphanel asked.

"You were talking about something to bring the people together. Pastor Shattuck suggested the black and white baseball game tomorrow, but what about the sacred-harp singing?"

Euphanel had once loved this community activity. Over the years, folks had gotten away from shape-note singing, or sacred harp, as others called it. "I think that's a wonderful idea. We could see if there was any interest at the celebration tomorrow—maybe in the evening, after the judging is announced. There are surely enough folks around here who've participated before that would want to do so now."

"We used to have quite a good group of singers," Rachel added. "Remember the old days when we would have gatherings on a Saturday after the mill shut down? We would sing all afternoon and into the night."

"Yes! I remember it well." Euphanel closed her eyes and could almost see the squared up formation. Altos facing the tenors, basses facing the trebles. "I enjoyed that so much."

"Then I think we should begin again. I don't know if the folks would feel comfortable asking the Negroes to join us, but it would be worth trying," Rachel said thoughtfully.

"Imagine using music to bring us all together."

Deborah closed the Bible and looked at Sissy. "Are you ready to lie back down?"

"I reckon so, Miss Deborah. I'm feelin' a bit poorly."

Getting to her feet, Deborah put the Bible aside and went to help Sissy from the rocking chair. "Dr. Clayton said it would probably be some months before you felt completely whole again."

She helped Sissy to the bed and gently eased the woman onto the mattress. Deborah removed Sissy's slippers and carefully helped her lift her legs.

Sissy moaned softly. It wasn't like her to complain, and Deborah knew that the fact she'd made any noise at all signaled she was in pain.

"Would you like some more medicine?"

"No, I cain't think clear when I takes it."

Deborah nodded and drew her chair closer to the bed. "Would you like me to sit with you awhile longer?"

"It's always a pleasure to have you near, Miss Deborah. You's good company."

"I don't know about that, but I know I enjoy our talks."

"Ain't much to talk about these days," Sissy said, her voice thick with sorrow.

"Oh, there's plenty," Deborah countered. "It's just not the most pleasant of topics. Still, I can share the news from town. The Independence Day celebration is slated to begin bright and early in the morning. Rob and Uncle Arjan donated six feral hogs for roasting, and several of the men have been hard at work to ready them. Mother is quite excited to try out a new recipe on the canning committee. She has perfected her piccalilli."

"Weren't nuttin' wrong with her old recipe," Sissy said with a hint of a smile.

"Oh, and they got Pastor Shattuck to agree to judge the pies along with Mr. Perkins, and Dr. Clayton will make the final decision. Lizzie has made several pies to enter. I hope she'll win a ribbon, since this is her first time to try."

"Miss Lizzie's turned out to be a right-fine cook."

"Yes, she has." Deborah folded her hands. "I can't say the same for myself. At least not where pies are concerned. I'm better at other things."

"We all gots our gifts. You makes a mighty good doctor." Sissy looked at Deborah. "I's been so proud of you."

"Thank you, Sissy. I'm very touched to hear you say so. It means a great deal."

"You's always been blessed by God."

Deborah considered that a moment. "Sissy," she began slowly, "have you remained close to God? I mean, in spite of what has happened, have you managed to keep your faith in Him?"

Sissy looked surprised. "What other choice we got, Miss Deborah?"

"Well, some turn away from God when things are bad. I can't say that I would blame you if your faith faltered. You've gone through more than anyone I know."

"I had a moment or two where I was hurtin' so that I couldn't hardly pray," Sissy admitted. "Your mama said that was the time when the Spirit hisself prays for me."

"Romans eight, verse twenty-six," Deborah said, nodding. " 'Likewise the Spirit also helpeth our infirmities: for we know not what we should pray for as we ought: but the Spirit itself maketh intercession for us with groanings which cannot be uttered.'"

"I shore 'nuf been groaning myself." Sissy smiled.

"It comforts me to remember that verse." Deborah reached out to grasp Sissy's hand. "So many times I don't know how to pray. . . . It just seems too hard, too confusing. In times like these when our lives seem so scarred by hate, I can't help but wonder what to even say to God. I know He hurts for us. I know it grieves Him that we act as we do."

"We's weak and sinful. Ain't no amount of good doin's gonna change that. Onliest thing what changes our hearts is Jesus."

"So you don't feel that . . . well . . . that God abandoned you?"

Sissy looked at her oddly. "Abandoned me? I'd sooner say I could fly. God ain't abandoned me. Evil comed into this world, and the devil, he done worked his miseries on us all. God's more powerful and God has His plan. I ain't thinkin' He's left me alone. 'Stead, He alone is with me." She closed her eyes.

"That's a wonderful way to look at it." Deborah got to her feet. "Sometimes it's really hard to remember that." She covered Sissy with the blanket. "I think it's time I let you rest. I'll check on you in a little while. If you need anything, you just ring the bell."

"You's mighty good to me, Miss Deborah." Sissy's words were barely audible.

Deborah pulled the curtains, then tiptoed to the door. With one final glance over her shoulder, she stepped into the hall to find her mother making her way to the room.

"Sissy is tired, so I told her I'd check on her later."

"I was just wondering if she needed anything. I didn't realize you'd been with her the whole time," Mother replied.

"We got to talking," Deborah said. "I don't know that I would have her degree of faith, had I gone through what she did."

"God doesn't call you to have Sissy's faith. He calls you to put your faith in Him. He'll grow and develop it from there."

"I know, but sometimes I feel that my faith must be as shallow as a river in drought."

Mother smiled and put her arm around Deborah's shoulder. "The rains will come. Trust Him. Just when you think you can't go on, they always come. In the meanwhile, why don't you join Rachel and me? We're hemming the curtains."

"I need to check on G.W.," Deborah said, inclining her head toward the door. "He wanted to make sure he was handling the inventory ledgers the right way."

"Well, if you finish, feel free to join us. I'm sure we'll be sewing for at least another hour."

"Deborah's not going to come?" Rachel asked as Euphanel took her seat.

"She has to oversee something in the office. G.W. is learning to take over the bookkeeping, but Deborah still has things to teach him."

"You should be proud of G.W., learning a new skill, despite his injury. I don't know if one of my boys endured the same kind of accident that they could make such drastic changes."

"It was God's hand that changed G.W.'s heart." Euphanel poured the last of the tea. "Would you like me to put on another pot?"

Rachel shook her head. "You don't need to for me. I'm fine."

Settling into her chair, Euphanel looked around the room. "I'll be so glad to get everything in the new addition completed. The boys have been working too hard. Arjan and Rob even took time away from logging. I know it makes Arjan feel rather out of sorts."

"Why do you say that?" Rachel questioned.

Euphanel shrugged. "He's always been more comfortable working outdoors. Rutger used to say that he was surprised Arjan would even live in a house." She chuckled. "He's a man of the land. I was really surprised when he stayed here after Rutger's death."

"Why should you be?" Rachel smiled and gave Euphanel a knowing look.

"What do you mean?" Euphanel shook her head.

"He stayed because of you."

Euphanel looked at Rachel to ascertain whether she was teasing. "You're serious? You think he feels responsible for me?"

"No, silly. I think he's in love with you."

Euphanel's mouth dropped open. She didn't even try to hide her surprise. "Rachel Perkins, that's ridiculous. He's an honorable man."

Rachel laughed. "Now, Euphanel, you know it's not ridiculous at all. Arjan cares for you. He always has. He acted quite noble, but now I believe he's just biding his time until you're done mourning."

The idea wasn't disagreeable to Euphanel, but it was totally unexpected. She tried to imagine Arjan declaring his love for her. What would she say? Could she allow herself to love again? What would the children think? This was their father's brother.

"I . . . well . . . I don't know what to say."

"You truly have never considered this before now?"

Euphanel picked up her tea and drank down the lukewarm liquid before returning the cup to the saucer. "I suppose I haven't. Rachel, please don't tease me." She leaned forward and replaced the china on the table. "Do you honestly believe that Arjan . . . that he . . ."

"Loves you? Yes I do. I've seen the way he looks at you, Euphanel. I believe he's been in love with you for as long as he's known you."

"But he's never said anything. He's never even hinted at having romantic notions."

"As you said, he's honorable."

Euphanel eased back against the chair and folded her hands. "What should I do?"

"Why do you have to do anything?" Rachel asked.

"I don't know, but I feel like I should do or say something."

Rachel leaned forward and patted Euphanel's knee. "Give it to God, as you do everything else. You once told me that God has perfect timing for everything. Allow God's timing for this."

Chapter 8

The day of the Texas Independence celebration dawned bright and clear and, despite needing more rain, the community was glad to have cloudless blue skies and low humidity. All of Perkinsville turned out for the event. Tables and booths were set up near the baseball diamond behind the church. Ladies assembled their canned goods, quilts, embroidery, and other fancy work on tables near the church, while the roasting pits and dinner tables had been positioned on the side of the clearing closest to Mr. Perkins's house.

The street had been roped off for horse racing, which would take place later in the day, as well as a parade of prized livestock that would be auctioned in the afternoon. It was unlike any other event the community held, and no one—regardless of skin color—would miss it.

Of course, Deborah thought, *there will be rules—for both the game and the social mingling.* Pastor Shattuck had convinced the town to have a black and white baseball game, but as was already in evidence, the people would still sit separately for the noon meal. And, in overhearing people talk, it wasn't just the whites who would want it that way. Many of the blacks wanted no part in comingling. Both sides displayed unspoken discomfort and evident tension.

Deborah moved among the people and exhibits looking for Christopher. They had agreed to meet at the festivities, and Deborah found herself anticipating the moment more than she'd expected. They would both be available to help should anyone get sick or injured, although Deborah knew there were few people who considered her an asset to the medical needs of Perkinsville. Folks in the area were more inclined to see her as fanciful, rather than useful. Thankfully, Christopher wasn't of the same mind. He appreciated her quick mind and desire to learn. The thought made her smile. She missed him more each time they were apart.

She'd just seen him at supper on Sunday, but his absences seemed more and more pronounced to her. Was that what it meant to fall in love? Many had been the night she'd lain awake, pondering the idea of marriage to Christopher Clayton. There were still so many mysteries about him, and she longed to know every one of them.

When she spied Christopher, he was standing beside Mara Shattuck. Dressed in his navy blue serge suit, Deborah thought the doctor cut a fine figure. The coat had been tailored to fit his broad shoulders and narrow waist, and the trousers were of the latest style. She couldn't help but believe him the handsomest man in attendance. Perhaps Mara thought so, too, for she leaned in closely and lifted her gloved hand to her mouth as if whispering a secret. The two seemed deep in discussion, and for a moment, Deborah experienced a twinge of jealousy.

The feeling took Deborah by surprise. Other women in the community spoke with Christopher on occasion, but something was different about this moment. Mara laughed and Christopher smiled. Deborah couldn't help but be drawn to them.

"Hello," she said, approaching the couple.

Christopher turned and extended his arm. "And here she is. We were just talking about you."

Deborah couldn't imagine what they'd said to elicit such laughter. "Oh, really?"

"Yes, from behind I mistook Miss Shattuck for you. I'm afraid I gave her a start."

All sorts of thoughts danced through Deborah's mind. Had he embraced her? Had he said something about her appearance that was much too personal?

"I told the good doctor that I had no idea what quinsy was, nor how to cure it," Mara added.

Deborah smiled. "He asked you that, did he?"

"He did indeed. When he learned I wasn't you, he was quite embarrassed."

Mara turned back to Christopher. "Now, if you'll excuse me, I need to see my father before he gets the baseball game started. However, if in the future one of you would like to explain the details of quinsy and the related healing methods, I promise to be most attentive."

She raised a pink parasol and swept gracefully across the grounds to join the pastor. Deborah shook her head. "I don't know how you could ever mistake her for me. She's far more elegant in her carriage and demeanor. I'll be brown as a berry in this sun—especially since I didn't see fit to bring an umbrella."

"Nonsense. You are just as elegant. I wasn't paying much attention when I approached her. I have to admit, your mother had just given me one of her orange spice doughnuts and I was deep in contemplation."

"Contemplation?" Deborah asked.

He laughed and leaned closer. "I was contemplating how to talk her out of another one."

She shook her head in mock disgust. Mother had always said that if she wanted to impress a man, it wouldn't be with how much knowledge she held but rather in examples of her cooking. Sadly, that had suffered over the years.

She feigned a pout. "I suppose you shan't want to court me unless I can make a doughnut as fine as my mother's."

"Don't be ridiculous," he said, taking hold of her arm. "I shall court you anyway. At least then I get to eat your mother's cooking."

She elbowed him just enough to get his attention and make him laugh. "I'm surprised you aren't more worried about the judging to come. I'm the one who will make the final decision on the pies. What if I'm swept off my feet by some wondrous creation?"

"What if I entered a pie?" she asked, brow raised slightly.

He looked at her and grinned. "Did you?"

Deborah shook her head. "No, but I might have."

"You'd be more inclined to enter your thoughts on curing quinsy." He stepped back a pace. "I must compliment you on your gown, Miss Vandermark."

She had hoped he might find the yellow crepe de Chine appealing. Her mother had worked hard to help her fashion it into a stylish gown that flattered her dark hair and eyes.

"I'm also quite glad you chose to leave off the elaborate bustles that so many find popular." He motioned his head toward the Perkins sisters, who happened to be strolling by.

"If you put them back to back, you could serve dinner atop their backsides," Christopher whispered against her ear.

Deborah shivered at the warmth of his breath on her neck. She giggled to conceal the effect, but found it impossible to speak. Christopher, however, seemed to have little trouble.

"Women and their contraptions shall always amaze me. I find a well-fitted corset to be advantageous to a woman's health, but bustles and the like are quite useless and sometimes downright dangerous."

"I find it rather amazing that we are standing here in broad daylight discussing women's undergarments," Deborah said, looking up at him.

Christopher's eyes twinkled mischievously. "Would you rather I wait until the dark of night?"

"Sir, you are positively scandalous."

He laughed. "Not at all. We are both interested in the medical well-being of women, are we not? Perhaps your delicate sensibilities are too fragile for a career in medicine."

She smiled. "Perhaps I shouldn't have agreed to court a physician. They seem to easily forget their manners." She started to walk away, but Christopher quickly pulled her in line with him.

"Oh no, you don't. I won't have you slip away from me that easily. Now come along. I want to watch the game."

He led her to one of the wooden benches that had been positioned for viewing the game. Deborah saw the pastor speaking to a collection of Negro players. The men were smiling and nodding at the minister. On the opposite side of the field, the white players stood with expressions that seemed mostly dubious. Deborah hoped her brother Rob would help keep the situation under control. He was to play second baseman, so he would be right in the middle of everything.

As the townsfolk assembled near the diamond, those of African ancestry took their place on the left side of the diamond toward third base, while the whites gathered more center and to the right. Pastor Shattuck climbed onto one of the benches and held up his hands. "Folks, it's time we got this game started. Let us have a word of prayer on this, our day of celebration."

A hush fell over the crowd. "Father, we commit this day to you. As we celebrate our independence, we recall that true liberty is found in Christ alone. May we, the people of Perkinsville, be mindful of your generosity to us and extend compassion and consideration to each person gathered here today. Amen."

He looked out across the flock of people, then turned to the players. "Let's commence the game!"

Cheers erupted from both sides, and Christopher settled in beside Deborah. "This should prove interesting."

"I was thinking much the same," Deborah replied.

The game started without conflict. Pastor Shattuck drew the two teams together. "For the sake of the day, we shall call this team the Perkinsville Razorbacks, as they have called themselves in the past." He nodded toward the captain of the white players. "And the other team will be called the Perkinsville Sawyers, since many of these men cut for a living."

"The Razorbacks will take their place in the field," Pastor Shattuck announced. "Sawyers—you're up to bat."

Deborah recognized the first player. "That's Abraham Garby," she told Christopher. "He works for us."

One of the many Foster cousins stepped to the mound to pitch. He threw the first ball, which was immediately declared a strike by the officiating umpire Mr. Huebner. As the local schoolmaster, Curtis Huebner had called many a ball game in the past.

The next pitch split the air with a loud crack as Abraham sent the ball slicing out across the open field. He ran for first base, then rounded second for third before the ball was retrieved. Picking up speed, Abraham slid into third while those gathered nearby cheered.

Deborah clapped, as did several of the other people around her, but most of the white people remained silent. The next two players were quickly struck out, but the third man managed to drive the ball into right field, allowing Abraham to reach home plate. The Sawyers were on the board.

For the next six innings, things went well, but when the seventh found the score tied four to four, conflict began to stir. Name calling, at first jovial and teasing, became more meanspirited and derogatory. Pastor Shattuck asked the men to put aside such comments, but the truce didn't last for long. Then when the teams changed places in the bottom of the inning and the Razorbacks stepped to the plate, a disaster struck on the first pitch. The ball slammed into the shoulder of John Stevens and knocked him to the ground. Although John did not see it as a personal attack, others on the team were livid and rushed to the pitcher's mound to see their form of justice done.

In turn, many of the Sawyers players came forward to assist their comrade and soon fists were swinging. Deborah watched in horror as Pastor Shattuck tried in vain to calm the men. It wasn't until Zed Perkins fired a shotgun in the air that some semblance of order settled upon them once again. By then, no one felt much like continuing the game.

"It's very nearly time for the dinner bell," Mr. Perkins announced. "I'd suggest we call this game a tie and begin eatin'."

Murmurs coursed throughout the crowd and a general consensus of approval was evident. The men separated hesitantly, each going to their assigned team places.

"I think I should see to the Sawyers and their wounds,"

Christopher told her as he got to his feet. "A couple of those men look to have taken the worst of it to their faces."

"Can I be of any assistance?" she asked.

He looked at her sadly. "It wouldn't be acceptable, Deborah. Why don't you go save us a place to enjoy our meal?" He gave her a weak smile before heading off.

Deborah frowned and let out a heavy sigh. Would this town ever see it as acceptable for a young, single woman doctor to tend a man—even in the open company of others?

"Why am I bothering to learn how to heal folks if they'll never accept help from me?" she muttered under her breath. Thankfully no one seemed to notice. The last thing she wanted was to stir up yet another controversy for the day.

Chapter 9

"Don't need you," a bloodied black man told Christopher. "Ain't needin' no white man's he'p."

"I'm a doctor. Your lip looks like it could use a stitch or two."

The man wiped his mouth with the back of his hand. "Don' need your he'p—just like I said."

Another man nodded. "We got womenfolk what can fix us up."

Christopher looked around the group of injured men. "And that's how all of you feel?"

"Tha's the way it be for all of us."

The statement was matter-of-fact, and none of the other men so much as met Christopher's gaze. One by one, they turned and walked away until only Abraham Garby remained. He finally looked up and shook his head.

"Sorry, Doc. Iffen we ain't careful, there'll be more trouble than this. Best you go back to your folks and we go back to ours." He turned and walked to where he'd left his hat. Picking it up, he knocked it against his leg and kept moving.

Christopher wanted to go after the men, but he knew it would do no good. There was too much anger on both sides of this situation. He blew out a heavy breath and shrugged. If they didn't want his help, he couldn't win their trust by forcing it upon them.

The aroma of roasted meat filled the air and drew his attention. Christopher marveled at the long line of makeshift tables laden with food. This was his first time to celebrate Texas Independence Day.

"Doc, if you're lookin' for my sister, she's over yonder," Rob declared and pointed toward a stand of trees.

"Thanks." Christopher started to head in that direction, but Rob stopped him.

"Was anyone badly hurt?"

"I don't really know. No one would let me tend them."

Rob shook his head. "I don't rightly know what got into folks. Seems to me it was just an accident."

"I think we can agree on that much," Christopher replied, "but apparently they can't. Sometimes I think people are just looking for an excuse to fight."

"Folks in these parts have plenty of excuses—leastwise, that's what it seems to me." Rob shrugged. "Guess it will always be that way."

"It shouldn't have to be." Christopher felt a heavy resignation wash over him. "But I suppose—at least for now—it will be."

"Ain't nothin' we can do by standin' here talkin' about it," Rob added. "If we don't get in line, we'll miss the white bread."

Christopher thought it ironic that even the color of the bread was of importance at this gathering. He understood that flour-based bread wasn't seen as often as corn bread, but another color-based preference was more than he wanted to face.

He found Deborah sitting alone and looking rather forlorn. This town wasn't interested in a woman doctor, but it was even less willing to accept an unmarried white woman working on the wounds of black men.

"Want some company?"

She looked up and studied him for a moment. "I didn't expect you to be back so soon."

"I know." He crouched down beside her. "They didn't want my help any more than they would have taken yours."

"Truly? But why?"

"Because I'm white."

"But you've helped them before."

Christopher looked out toward the muddy creek. There was only a minimal amount of water within its banks. They could certainly use some rain. He felt Deborah reach out to touch his hand. He turned back to see her worried expression.

"Will it always be like this?"

"So long as good men allow this to be the acceptable manner of behavior." He shook his head. "But let's try to put it aside. Today's for celebrating, right?"

She nodded. "But it doesn't seem folks truly understand. Texas was different back then, Mama says. Before the war, they didn't seem half so worried about the color of a person's skin. Before Texas became its own country, the Mexican government respected men of all colors. Seems we've lost something in our liberty."

Christopher stood and helped Deborah to her feet. "Hopefully we'll get it back," he said, escorting her to the food.

"Come on, you two," Lizzie said as she and G.W. neared the food tables. "I can hardly wait to try a little of everything."

Deborah laughed. "You'd be hard-pressed to sample it all. Mother said there were over two hundred dishes."

"Oh my." Lizzie looked to G.W. "I don't suppose I can."

"Well, I sure intend to give it my best," G.W. said, giving her shoulder a squeeze.

"I'm glad you're feeling better," Deborah added. She looked to Christopher. "Lizzie's been a bit queasy of late."

"I thought it would be behind me by now, but in some ways it seems worse."

"For how long?" Christopher asked.

Lizzie considered the question for a moment. "Probably the better part of the last month. Seems to strike without warning at most any time of the day or night. I've always had trouble with nausea since I learned I was in a family way, but it seems that lately I have more trouble than ever."

Christopher thought for a moment. "Any other problems?"

Deborah looked at him oddly. "Do you think something's wrong?"

Now Lizzie and G.W. looked alarmed. Christopher put up his hand. "Don't make more out of this than needs to be. I'm just trying to be thorough."

"I'm tired all the time, but you told me I would be," she replied with a smile.

"I'd like to examine you tomorrow," Christopher said immediately, holding up his hands. "Not because I think anything is wrong. Come with Deborah to the office, and I'll see if I can't find something for the nausea."

Lizzie and G.W. seemed to calm and exchanged a smile. "She'll be there," G.W. told Christopher. "I'll bring them both myself."

Christopher nodded. "Then we'll discuss this more at that time."

As G.W. and Lizzie strolled toward the food, Deborah tugged on Christopher's arm. "Do you think there's a problem?"

He chuckled. "You are definitely one for speaking your mind—still, it would serve you well not to say the first thing that comes into your head. Especially when standing right in front of a patient."

"Well, there's no patient standing here now. What is it you suspect?"

He grinned. "Well, consider this. Your sister-in-law is only about four and a half months along, but in the last month she's grown considerably in size. The nausea has been more severe than most women and even now is extreme. I'm thinking she might be carrying twins."

Deborah's mouth dropped open and her eyes grew wide. "Twins?"

"Don't say anything just yet. We should have a better idea tomorrow."

"Oh, there's Mother with our dishes," Deborah said, pulling Christopher along. "We have a plate and silver for you, as well."

Christopher liked that he'd been included in the family. When he'd first arrived in the community, few wanted to associate with him, much less allow him to practice his medical skills on them. Now more folks openly allowed his care—and his friendship.

"Well, you two look like you could use a good meal," Mrs. Vandermark said, holding a plate out to Christopher.

"Thank you, ma'am. I'm quite happy to put a dent in the food." Christopher glanced at the vast arrangement of dishes on the food table. "Where are yours?"

Deborah's mother laughed. "Why, do you plan to avoid them?"

"On the contrary, I intend to start with the best."

She smiled. "In that case, I'll let Deborah point them out. She knows exactly what we brought. Be sure you get a piece of her butter cake before it's gone."

He looked at Deborah in surprise. "You baked?"

Her right brow arched slightly. "Indeed, I did, and if you don't mind your manners, I won't tell you which cake is mine."

"Yes, ma'am," he said, nodding. "Thank you, ma'am."

Euphanel laughed and handed her daughter a plate. "You've got him well trained already."

Deborah rolled her eyes. "It's all just a show for you, Mother. Dr. Clayton has never listened to anything I've had to say. He thinks he already knows it all."

Christopher laughed and nudged Deborah forward. "What I really know is that I'm going to starve half to death if I stand around here waiting much longer. Come on."

Rob eyed Mara Shattuck trying to balance her plate and parasol and sauntered up to her as if he did this kind of thing every day.

"Can I be of service? Carry your plate?"

"Perhaps if you took the parasol," Mara said with a grateful expression.

Rob looked at the lacey pink thing and nodded reluctantly. No doubt he'd hear about this later if his brother caught sight of him toting the fancy umbrella around.

"Thank you." Mara handed him the parasol and focused on her choices of food. "Everything looks so good; it's hard not to take some of everything."

"I tried that once," Rob said, trying to decide if he should hold the parasol over Mara or just let it hang to the side. "It didn't work out so well. I got so stuffed, I was pert near sick."

"Gluttony is a sin, you know," she said sweetly.

"I suppose I do. Guess I'm just a regular old sinner."

"We all are sinners, Mr. Vandermark."

"Call me Rob. Mr. Vandermark is too uppity for me."

She looked at him, narrowing her eyes slightly. "It's a matter of etiquette and proper behavior, Mr. Vandermark. I am a single woman, and you are a single gentleman. We're only newly acquainted, and it would be unacceptable for us to pretend otherwise."

He looked at her and shook his head. "We might only be newly acquainted, but I'd like it well enough if we got to knowin' each other a whole lot better."

She stopped and turned. "To what outcome, Mr. Vandermark?"

Rob was momentarily stumped. "I . . . well . . . that is . . . I reckon I'd like for us to be . . . friends."

"I see." She shifted the plate from her left hand to her right. "I believe I'd like for us to be friends, Mr. Vandermark." She smiled. "Would you care to sit with my father and me at dinner? We're set up just over there by the church."

Rob followed her gaze and could see that Pastor Shattuck was already busily eating. He grinned. "I'd be mighty glad to join you."

She reached out to take hold of the umbrella. "Wonderful. I shall see you there." She walked away, parasol blocking any view of her face.

Rob smiled to himself and quickly retrieved a plate for food. He was making progress with Mara Shattuck, and it wasn't turning out to be as difficult as he'd thought it might. Joining the Shattucks on their blanket, Rob plopped down and extended a hand. "Pastor. Good to see you again."

"Rob, I'm glad you could join us. Mara said you were quite helpful to her just now."

He flushed slightly. "I don't know how helpful I actually was, but I have to say it was my first time to hold a parasol."

Mara's father laughed. "Oh, the things we men do for women. I was just commenting to Mara that she shares a resemblance to your sister."

"Deborah?" Rob questioned, shaking his head. "G.W. mentioned some likeness, but they don't look alike to me."

"Well, of course they don't look alike, but both have dark eyes and dark hair. They're even similar in size."

Rob glanced around as if looking for his sister, then settled his gaze back on Mara. "I reckon lots of folks can have some things in common. I think Miss Mara is much prettier than my sister, but don't tell Deborah." He grinned and picked up his fork. He quickly stuffed his mouth with some potato salad just in case someone wanted to ask him something else. This way he'd at least have a few moments to consider his answer.

"So tell me, Mr. Vandermark," Mara began, "where is God taking you on your life journey?"

Rob was momentarily mesmerized by the question. He finished chewing and swallowed before giving a shrug.

"I don't reckon I know for sure. I've been working in the family business since I was a small boy. My pa loved the forests, and logging became a way of life for our family."

"And now?" she asked, delicately picking at the food on her plate.

"Well, I guess there have been a few changes. My brother, G.W., got hurt last year. He took a fall out of a tree and injured his leg. Since then he's stayed at home to handle the office side of things.

'Course, he had to learn to read better. So my sister has been helpin' us both."

"So you're learning to read?"

He stiffened. "I could already read some; I'm just learnin' to do it better."

"But why?" she asked.

Her father saved him from having to answer. "Mara, I've never known you to be quite this inquisitive."

She shrugged. "People do not make changes without a good reason. I simply wondered what had prompted Mr. Vandermark to desire such skills."

Rob shrugged. "I don't rightly know. Strange as it sounds, I guess I just felt it was the right thing to do."

"God sometimes works like that," Pastor Shattuck said, nodding. "God will lay a matter on our heart, and we will find it impossible to rest until we act upon that urge."

Mara looked at Rob. "Was that how it was?"

He thought about it for a moment. "I suppose it was that way. Now I'm mostly readin' the Bible, and it's got me thinking more and more on God and what He wants from us."

"And have you learned what He wants from you?" she asked, her voice soft and appealing. "Did you try asking Him as I suggested?"

Rob contemplated the matter for a moment. "I've asked, but I don't reckon I've figured it all out just yet."

"But you do believe God has a specific plan for you—for each person?"

"Of course. I reckon I've known that since I was knee-high to a grasshopper." He grinned and picked up a piece of white bread. "Doesn't mean I know what it is—but I know He's got a plan."

"That's a good start," the pastor told him. "Some folks don't even know that much."

"What are you doing to figure out what it is that God wants of you?" Mara asked. Both Rob and her father looked at her in surprise. She smiled. "I'm sorry. Have I made this conversation too personal?"

"No, I don't reckon you have," Rob said, giving her a lazy smile. "I just don't have an answer for you. I guess I'm not sure how a fella goes about figurin' out what God wants."

"There is always prayer and meditation on the Word," Pastor Shattuck told him. "Psalm 119:105 speaks to God's Word being a lamp unto my feet and a light unto my path. It's not that you have a light the size of the sun showing all the details of the journey. Sometimes just a portion of the path is revealed at a time."

"That's good to know, Pastor. I guess I hadn't thought about it that way before, but I can see where it would make a good amount of sense." Rob stuffed some more food in his mouth, hoping it would signal that he was done answering questions. He wanted to get Mara to talk about herself so he could get to know her better. He couldn't very well do that if they just kept talking about him and what God wanted him to do with his life.

"Pastor, could I have a word with you?"

It was Zed Perkins. He stood directly behind Rob and nodded when Rob looked up. "Good to see you, Rob. I was just speakin' to your mother. Miss Shattuck, I hope you won't mind me borrowin' your pa for a minute."

"Not at all, Mr. Perkins. I assure you, I am in good company."

Rob smiled at this and tried not to act too pleased. Hopefully with her father gone, Mara would be willing to share something about herself. At least he hoped.

"So, tell me about your life in New Orleans," he said just before popping a piece of pork into his mouth.

Mara put her fork down and seemed to think about the question for a moment. Rob was about to give up on getting an answer when she finally began to speak.

"My father thought it important that my brother and I be raised with a woman's influence after our mother died. He sent us to New Orleans to live with our grandmother."

"I forgot you had a brother. How old is he?"

"He's four years older than me," she replied.

Rob shook his head. "That doesn't help me much. I don't know how old you are."

She smiled. "I suppose that was rather remiss of me. He's twenty-eight. We were both very young when we went to live with Grandmother. She was quite strict with her religious beliefs and saw that we received a complete education in the Bible."

"Did you go to a university like my sister?" Rob asked.

Mara shook her head. "No, I was never that good at my studies, and frankly, I had little desire to further my learning. I've known for some time what God's plan was for me."

Now the conversation was finally headed somewhere that Rob wanted to go. "And what'd God tell you?"

"Well, one of the most important things is that He wants me to share His love with the people I come across, so that they might know who God really is."

Rob didn't mean to, but he gave a bit of a chuckle. "Don't you think most folks already know about God and His love?"

"I suppose most everyone knows about God, Mr. Vandermark. But I sometimes wonder if knowing about Him is the same as knowing Him personally."

Rob considered her words. "I reckon there are folks who never really cared to know God."

"I've certainly known that to be true," she said softly.

"Well, what is it you think can be done?"

She appeared to consider this for a moment. "I think we should be a willing servant. Learn His Word—truly learn the Scriptures and what they mean. Know God in a more intimate way. As I do these things, I can better share His truth and love."

"And what will you do when you learn all of this? Ain't gonna work for a little gal like you to be a preacher. How can God use a woman, if you don't mind my askin'?"

She smiled. "God can use anyone, Mr. Vandermark. Even so, that's between Him and me for the time. When I feel He would have me share it with you, I assure you that I will."

Her response left him rather confused. Why had she been insistent on knowing what God wanted him to do, but when it came to returning the same information, she took quiet and refused to speak? Women were such queer creatures. Who could know their minds—much less their hearts?

Lizzie waited rather nervously for Dr. Clayton to finish his exam. She'd been terribly worried about her condition ever since their conversation the day before. She had fervently hoped he would tell her that there was nothing to worry about.

Deborah didn't seem overly worried, but then again, she was quite capable of hiding her feelings if the situation merited.

"Well, I can't be completely certain," Dr. Clayton began as Deborah helped Lizzie to sit up, "but I think I have some interesting insight into your nausea."

Lizzie extended her hand to Deborah. If something was wrong, she wanted to at least have her friend close. She swallowed hard. What would G.W. do? He was so excited about the baby. At times, the pregnancy seemed to be the only thing that kept him pushing his recovery.

Deborah scooted closer and took hold of her hand. Lizzie looked to the doctor and nodded. "Is it bad news?"

He shook his head. "Not to my way of thinking. I believe you're going to have twins."

Lizzie felt the impact of his statement as the breath caught in her throat. "Twins?"

"We will know better as the weeks go by, but I'm feeling rather confident that you carry two babies instead of just one. We'll watch you closely as time passes, and if you feel anything might be amiss, don't hesitate to let me know."

"Oh, this is so surprising." She put her hand to her stomach. "Twins."

Deborah patted her arm. "Let me fetch G.W. He will absolutely burst his buttons when he hears."

Lizzie shook her head. "Let's not tell him until Dr. Clayton is sure. I don't want to get him all excited and then disappoint him if it's not true." She looked to the doctor. "When do you suppose we can know for certain?"

"Probably in another month or so. Maybe less."

"That will be soon enough," Lizzie said, looking to Deborah. "We'll tell him only if we're certain. Agreed?"

Deborah smiled. "You're the patient. I will keep my mouth shut and wait for you to give me the word that it's all right to speak."

Lizzie nodded and let out a heavy sigh. Twins.

Chapter 10

Two weeks later, Rob found himself still considering his conversation with Mara. She made him look deep within his heart and mind. There were things about God that seemed simple and clear, while other issues were far more complex. Mara's comments challenged him in a way he'd never experienced before.

The evening was chilled, but not too humid. Rob found Deborah sitting on the porch quietly rocking. He hoped she wouldn't mind his intrusion. He thought with her being close to Mara's age, she might be able to help him understand the young woman's mind.

"Can I ask you some questions?"

Deborah looked up and stopped toying with her long thick braid. "Of course, you can. Have a seat and tell me what's bothering you."

"Did I say something was bothering me?" he asked as he plopped down on a three-legged stool. The seat rocked awkwardly as Rob worked to balance.

"You didn't have to. You only took two portions of Mother's lemon cornmeal cake and hardly poured any sweet cream atop."

He laughed. "That's only 'cause I'd already had three helpin's of her black-eyed peas and ate a whole fried chicken by myself."

Deborah nodded. "I suppose I should have taken that into account."

Rob sobered. "Still, fact is, I do have somethin' on my mind."

"Well, I hope talking about it might relieve your heart on the matter."

He thought for a moment. "Do you think God talks to each person?"

Deborah sat up and stopped rocking. "How do you mean?"

"Well, Mara Shattuck has asked me about where I figured God was directin' me to go. I don't think I've ever heard God talk out loud to me."

He watched his sister carefully. "I think God addresses each of us. Not always in the same way, but definitely with the same heart of love. He wants us to seek His will, but how can we if He doesn't speak to us? You grew up around folks who loved God—who revered His name. People in our family often talk about how God desires to guide us and have us walk with Him. A lot of folks in the world haven't the interest. A lot of people right here in Perkinsville probably think they know who God is but don't really have a clue."

"But have you heard God speak to you?"

Deborah eased back in her chair and started to rock again. "I believe I have. I think often when we get that nudge in our heart—when something keeps coming back to us in the Word or through the teachings the pastor gives or we hear wise counsel from someone who cares, those are the times God speaks to us. I think He can also speak to our hearts."

"And is that the way we can know Him better?" He couldn't hide the longing in his voice. He needed to know the truth.

"Some folks think just hearing about God means that they know Him. I think that really knowing Him requires we take an active role with Him."

"What do you mean?"

"As I said, we grew up with God-fearing parents. Our family has always talked about God and how we should respect and esteem Him. We were taught that the Bible is His infallible word to us—His inspired Word carefully written down by His faithful servants. There's never been a time in our lives when we didn't know who our parents believed God to be, and then to gradually learn who God was for ourselves."

"True enough."

A light breeze blew across the yard, rustling the trees and bringing hints of muscari on the air. Deborah pulled her shawl closer. "A great many people don't have it that way, Rob. I think having grown up as we did, it's easier to accept that God speaks to us. Some folks think God doesn't care—that He's just waiting to accuse us of our failings. I think God wants to talk to us like a Father—like our father used to talk to us. He offered us direction and encouragement. Why would God do any less?"

"I don't reckon He would."

She smiled. "I don't think He would, either. If you want to know what God is trying to say to you—ask Him to make it very clear. Ask Him to show you so there is no doubt the choice is right."

Rob nodded and mulled the matter in his mind. "Mara said a lot of folks know about God, but don't really know who He is. I guess if they never try to talk to Him or listen back, they won't get closer to Him."

"Exactly. They are just pretending so people will believe them to be good. Sometimes they really want to impress folks, and they memorize all sorts of Scriptures so they can spout them off whenever it suits them. Unfortunately, they don't always understand what they're quoting, and they use God's Word to hurt other people."

"I don't reckon God approves of that," Rob replied.

"Even pastors can be guilty of this. They are wolves in sheep's clothing, pretending to be holy and knowledgeable of God, but they don't know Him at all."

"You mean they preach and know about God's Word, but ain't accepted Jesus as their Savior?" Rob shook his head, trying to fully understand exactly what Deborah was saying.

"Sometimes," Deborah admitted. "Sometimes they don't even know what the Bible says. They have a form of godliness, but they really don't know God at all."

Something deep within seemed to call out to Rob. He found himself longing to know more—to understand what this might have to do with him and the future God had for him. He started to ask Deborah how he might learn more, but as if she'd read his mind, the solution was in her next words.

"If you want to better understand, I'd talk to Uncle Arjan or Pastor Shattuck. Either one is bound to offer you insight from a man's perspective—especially from that of a man who loves God and truly does understand, or at least seeks to understand, who God is."

"I'll do that," Rob declared. "Seems like a good thing." He got up and threw Deborah a wink. "Besides, if I go to talk to Pastor, then I'll get to see Mara."

Deborah smiled. "Somehow I doubt you'll have much trouble coming up with excuses to see Miss Shattuck."

Deborah finished reading the last of the books she'd borrowed from Christopher and looked rather sadly at the stack. Reading used to give her such joy, but the more she read about illnesses and cures, the more helpless she felt. How could she ever be of use in medicine if people wouldn't allow her to work with them?

A part of her could actually understand their fears and concerns. Women in medicine were usually relegated to working with other women or with children. Even Margaret Foster, the midwife and healer in Perkinsville, wasn't always allowed to treat the men. However, folks around here knew the ornery woman and most feared she'd put a curse on them if they didn't acquiesce.

"But she's a widow just turned fifty, and I'm young and unmarried." Deborah went to the dining room window and parted the curtains. The new dining room wasn't yet finished, so they were still using the old one. There were warm, comfortable memories in this room.

She thought of her father, sitting at the head of the table, reading the Bible to them. He had always helped each of them understand what the words meant and why they were important. Sometimes he'd share stories of when he'd been a boy and tell them something that reflected the same Bible lesson in real life. Mother called these his "walking the road" stories. It was all about applying the truth of God's Word to one's daily life. Deborah let the curtain fall back into place without really even seeing the outside. Her heart was turned inward, and that's where her vision remained.

"You seem awfully deep in thought," Mother said from the kitchen door.

Deborah looked up in surprise. "I thought you were with Sissy."

"I was for a spell. Then I went outside to work on a couple of the garden patches. I thought about putting some supper on to cook. You want to help me?"

She nodded. "I might as well. I don't seem to be of much use elsewhere."

Mother looked at her oddly. "Feeling sorry for yourself?"

Deborah laughed. Her mother knew her so well. "I suppose I was, in a way."

"Nothing to be gained from that." Mother motioned her to follow. "There's plenty of work to be done. It might not be exactly what you want to do, but it will be quite useful to me if you are of a mind to help." Mother took a large bowl of potatoes from the counter. "You can start by peeling these."

Deborah took up a paring knife and got comfortable. "Did you ever feel that God had somehow overlooked you, Mother?"

Pausing for a moment, the older woman cocked her head to one side. "Now your feeling of uselessness is about God forgetting you?"

"No. Not exactly. I just feel . . . well . . . confused. I always thought I was given the ability to easily learn from books because God wanted me to help with the business and keep the office. Now it seems really clear that G.W. is needed there. In fact, he and Lizzie often work together in the office, so he doesn't even need me to assist him."

Deborah paused as she began to cut away the skin of a potato. "Then there's my interest in medicine. As a young, single woman, I'm not allowed to see and treat men—especially if those men have black skin. Not only that, but I'm not really even desired by the women. I thought because Mrs. Foster was so accepted by them that I would be, too. After all, I grew up with many of the folks in the area."

"Perhaps it's your familiarity that makes them uncomfortable," Mother suggested. "Still, you won't always be a young, single woman. The woman part you can't change." Her tone was teasing as she continued. "But the young and single will pass away before you know it. Believe me. I've watched my youth flee before my eyes."

"Nonsense, Mother. You're still quite young," Deborah countered. "You're young enough that you really should consider remarrying."

The crash of metal pots on the floor caused Deborah to jump. She turned to find her mother staring at her in stunned surprise. "What did you say?"

Deborah put the knife and potato aside and went to pick up the pans. "You heard me. I said you should consider marrying again. It's not good for you to be alone."

"Have you seen me be alone lately? I have people all around me," her mother said, taking the pieces from Deborah.

"That's not the same, and you know it."

Her mother turned to put the pots away. "I thought we were talking about you and how God had forgotten you."

Deborah touched her mother's shoulder. "I hope I haven't upset you. I know you loved Father dearly, but you are still very young, compared to some widows. You're not even forty-four."

"That's decades past the age a man would want a woman for marriage," her mother said with a nervous laugh. "Most men are looking for women to share a lifetime and start a family. I have my family in place, and who knows how long I'll be on this earth."

"Mother, you have no way of knowing where God will lead."

"And you think you do?" Her mother turned to face her. Her cheeks were flushed.

Deborah wasn't used to seeing her mother like this. She seemed almost embarrassed. "Mother, has something happened? Something to do with this matter?"

Mother's eyes widened and she opened her mouth as if to give a quick retort, but then closed it and lowered her gaze. "I . . . well . . . I . . ."

Deborah took hold of her mother's hands. "Please tell me what's wrong."

"Well, it's just that," Mother said, lifting her head, "Rachel Perkins said something to me, and I have to admit I've not had a decent night's sleep since."

"Come and tell me what she said." Deborah pulled her toward the table. Mother sat and folded her hands together. She seemed so upset by the matter that Deborah wondered if she should just let it go. Still, her own curiosity was great. What could Mrs. Perkins have possibly said that would cause such a stir?

Waiting for her mother to speak was difficult. Deborah wanted to urge her to explain but knew Mother would tell her when and if she decided to do so. Picking up the knife and potato once again, Deborah thought perhaps the normalcy of the action would ease some of the tension. She peeled quietly and waited.

Finally, without warning, her mother blurted out the matter. "Rachel believes your uncle is in love with me."

Deborah's head snapped up. She quickly forgot the potato. "Uncle Arjan?"

Her mother nodded and fixed her gaze on Deborah's face. "It never even occurred to me, but Rachel thinks he's loved me for a very long time. Of course, he's never said anything, if he does. And he's certainly never acted untoward."

Deborah knew her uncle cared deeply about Mother's well-being. He was always very attentive and considerate of her needs.

Goodness, why hadn't I considered that before? He's never married, and he's always remained close to Mother.

Deborah smiled at the thought of her uncle and mother marrying. "I think it would be a grand idea for you two to be together."

Mother leaned forward. "Truly?"

"Of course. You know Uncle Arjan better than anyone. He's a good man, and he obviously loves you or he wouldn't care for you so earnestly. Perhaps that love is more than merely a brother for his sister-in-law."

"I truly had never considered it," her mother confessed. The words flowed more easily now. "When Rachel mentioned the possibility, I felt so strange. I tried to think back and remember if I'd ever done anything to stir his feelings. I certainly loved your father and never meant to give false hopes."

"Mother, no one could accuse you of being anything but faithful to Father. I've never seen two people who loved each other more. Even when you two would argue, I could always see that spark between you."

"I don't know what to do."

Deborah smiled. "What would you like to do?"

Mother shook her head. "I've been praying about the matter ever since Rachel brought it up. But I've felt completely out of sorts and have avoided being alone with Arjan for even a moment. I'm sure he thinks he's done something wrong."

"Well, I think you should simply ask him how he feels," Deborah suggested. "I mean, what if his love is limited to just being your brother-in-law? You have a right to know, either way."

"I would feel so odd, asking him."

"Perhaps. But I think if you pray about it, God can surely give you a sign or arrange the situation so that you can learn the truth."

Her mother nodded and got to her feet. "I know He can, and

maybe having Rachel say something was one of those ways. I just didn't expect such a thing at my age."

Deborah put the peeled potato aside and picked up the next. "Well, I think you're very deserving of love." She smiled and began to hum a tune often sung at weddings.

"Don't go marrying me off just yet." Her mother went back to the stack of pans and began organizing them. "I won't have you acting all silly about this."

Thinking of her mother and uncle together as husband and wife very nearly made Deborah giggle. There was no other man in the world she trusted more than her uncle. Perhaps God would even use her to help bring the couple together.

"Wouldn't that be something?"

"What?" her mother asked.

Deborah shook her head. "Oh, nothing. I was just thinking out loud."

Chapter 11

"You ladies have a nice time together," Pastor Shattuck bid as he headed for the front door of the parsonage. "I'm going to go visit the sick."

"We'll see you later, Father. I'll have a nice cake ready for your afternoon rest."

Pastor Shattuck smiled. "It's good to have a woman in the house again. My ministry has suffered without your mother."

After he was gone, Deborah couldn't help but question Mara. "I hope you won't mind my curiosity or find my words bold, but it seems odd to me that your father mentions his ministry suffering without your mother. I have asked on numerous occasions for him to clarify various things in the Bible, but he always directs me back to the men in my family. If the men in my family were knowledgeable, I would have asked them in the first place."

Mara smiled and poured Deborah a cup of tea. "It doesn't surprise me he should direct you in such a manner."

"So he doesn't believe women should study the Scriptures?"

Her new friend looked shocked. "Oh, it's not that at all. Father definitely believes women should study God's Word. He is of a heart that all people should."

"Then why wouldn't he be willing to speak to me? All I wanted to do was better understand, and oftentimes it had to do with his sermons."

Mara put the pot on the table and took her seat. "I will share something with you, because I believe I can trust you. However, I ask that this go no further than this room."

Deborah couldn't imagine what the young woman was about to say. Mara's tone was quite serious, and Deborah's imagination immediately conjured all sorts of thoughts. "I promise."

"Not long after my mother died, my father sent my brother and me to live with our grandmother. Father said it was because we needed a woman's hand, but I know that we reminded him of Mother, and he could hardly bear his sorrow.

"It was shortly after he sent us to live in New Orleans that a young widow in the church approached Father. Her family was quite wealthy. In fact, they pretty much owned the town. She told Father that she wanted to better understand God's Word. She opened her Bible and pointed to passages that were especially difficult. Father explained them to the woman and encouraged her to come to him anytime she felt confused."

"That would have been nice," Deborah said. She picked up the cup of tea. "He had no interest in doing the same for me."

"That's because as time went by, this woman came to him more and more. Soon she wasn't just coming to see him at the church; she was coming to the house. Then soon it wasn't just in broad daylight, but she began making evening calls, as well. Then without warning, she tried to seduce my father. She threw herself shamelessly at him and begged him to make her his wife. Father refused and forbid her to ever again come alone to the house."

"That must have been a very difficult situation."

Mara looked beyond Deborah at the fireplace where a small flame flickered. "It was devastating. The woman, like Pharaoh's wife with Joseph, told everyone she could that Father had taken indecent liberties. She had her family demand Father marry her."

"What did he do?" Deborah wondered how any woman could act in such a wonton, lying way. Why would she want to force a marriage that would surely leave her with a hateful husband?

"Father took his place in the pulpit on Sunday and announced quite clearly that nothing had happened. He told the people how he had done nothing untoward—he had in fact only answered the woman's questions about the Bible. He challenged them to seek the Lord to discern the truth of the matter. He further demanded that the woman stand before the church and God and tell the truth. She refused."

"What happened?"

"The woman's father came and offered Father a great deal of money to marry his daughter. He refused, of course, saying that his heart was still grieving for my mother and that he could not marry another. The man was furious. He felt his daughter's reputation had been damaged." Mara leaned toward Deborah. "Personally, we believe the man had endured such things from his daughter before this and merely wanted to make her someone else's responsibility."

"But why would any woman want a man who didn't love her?

Wouldn't a man, in fact, be more inclined to despise her for forcing such a situation upon him?" Deborah asked.

"I cannot say. There are a great many women in this world who cannot bear to live without a man. For whatever reasons, she appeared to be one of those. Father eventually had to step down and give up the church and leave town. He felt it necessary to keep the church from dividing in two, but it broke his heart, nevertheless."

"So this is why he won't spend time teaching women?"

Mara smiled and nodded. "Exactly so. He truly wants women to learn all they can about God and the Bible, but he cannot risk his ministry for God to do so. He wants to be above reproach in all things."

Deborah considered this new information and felt a peace wash over her. She had a newfound respect for her pastor. He hadn't been disinterested in her learning—only that they should not be alone for the teaching. "If I need to ask questions in the future, I'll take someone with me."

"I'm sure that would be acceptable. Also if I'm around, it shouldn't be a problem."

Mara sampled a cookie, then quickly put it down. "Father is also very worried about our town and the tensions that have risen up between the blacks and whites," she said out of the blue. "That grieves him most sorely."

"As it does a great many folks," Deborah countered.

"I know that your family has been personally wounded. I am sorry for that," Mara said. "Father hopes to continue to encourage the congregation to make changes—to recognize the wrong in harming each other."

"That will take a miracle."

Mara laughed. "Good thing God is in the miracle business, then, yes?"

Deborah smiled, grateful for her new friend. Mara had a way of putting her at ease, even when her worries took front and center in Deborah's mind.

"So if I might change the subject, I wanted to ask you about your family. Father said your family had been in Texas for a long while—even before the war."

"Yes, my mother and father came here right after marrying. Mother was only sixteen years old. I believe it was in February of 1858. Father wanted to start a new life here, and his younger brother wanted to come, as well."

"Your mother's people held slaves; is that not true?" Mara asked.

Deborah nodded. "Yes. Mother's family ran a large farm in Georgia. Sissy was her companion back then. When Mr. Lincoln set the slaves free, Sissy wanted to come west and be with Mother. Mother agreed, and Father hired Sissy to be our housekeeper and cook. Eventually, Sissy fell in love and married, but she continued to work for us."

"My grandmother owned slaves," Mara said rather thoughtfully. "For a long time she was convinced that it was her Christian duty to do so. She felt under her ownership she could guide them to a better spiritual walk. You must remember in New Orleans, there were a great many slaves who believed in superstitions and voodoo. It was quite frightening to see the effects of such beliefs. My grandmother was a strong woman of faith, however. She stood up to such things and, in doing so, taught me to make a stand, as well. She said that while she had no regrets in setting her slaves free, she had a great many fears for their well-being. Most couldn't read or write, and the animosity toward them made remaining in the South quite difficult. Your mother makes such a strong stand for better treatment of the former slaves, yet her own people were slaveholders. Was there anything in particular that caused her to believe slavery was wrong?"

"Mother once told me that she had never approved of slavery. She had seen too much cruelty. People often said, 'Oh, but the black man wouldn't even know how to dress himself without the white man to show him.' Mother thought it all hogwash."

Mara nodded. "I couldn't agree more."

"Now she still hears people making comments in regard to how the Negro will not understand the voting process or how to arrange for his own legal needs, and it causes her great frustration."

"Father says that the War Between the States ended only to have the War of Racial Antagonism begin. He believes this is something that will continue for decades, maybe even longer."

"I hate to think he's right, but I have little reason to doubt his judgment," Deborah replied.

"How is Sissy faring? Father said her injuries were terrible," Mara inquired.

"They were. She suffered a terrible head wound, but she is slowly improving. She's gaining strength every day, and while her full recovery is still some weeks away, we have hope that she will continue to do well." Deborah put aside her teacup. Mara offered her the plate of cookies, but Deborah shook her head. "Thank you, no. I shouldn't take much more of your day. I have some books to return to Dr. Clayton."

"Oh, might I come with you?" Mara asked. "I have a pie for him. It's cooling on the sill."

"Of course. That would be very nice," Deborah replied, though she had hoped for some time alone with Christopher. Yet she knew such privacy was frowned upon. They had, in fact, caused many raised eyebrows at the Independence Day celebration when Dr.

Clayton had taken hold of her arm at an unexpected moment. Such things were usually reserved for married couples.

Mara got to her feet and collected the cups and saucers. Placing everything on the tea tray, she excused herself. "I shan't be more than a minute."

Deborah took the opportunity to study the small sitting room. She had been here before with her mother, but now it bore a decidedly more feminine touch. She couldn't help but smile at the doilies that now graced the back and arms of a rather large cushioned chair. Mara's influence had obviously taken hold.

There were other things, as well. On the fireplace mantel there was a lovely vase of flowers, and framed photos of family members sat on either side of the arrangement. Beside these were small porcelain figurines of birds.

Mara returned with her basket and hat in hand. She placed the basket on the chair she'd just vacated and secured her stylish bonnet. Her long black curls had been pinned carefully at the back of her head, and her bonnet was snug against the thick locks, leaving little ringlets to peek out at the bottom.

"There, now I'm presentable," Mara said, adding short crocheted gloves to her hands. She picked up the basket, and Deborah took the signal as one for them to depart.

"I was just admiring your decorating ideas. You have given this home a much-needed feminine touch." Deborah moved to the door. "Let me get that for you." She maneuvered past Mara and reached for the handle. Before stepping through the door herself, she picked up the books she'd deposited on the foyer table.

The two ladies made their way across the street, past the church, and around the corner to the doctor's house. Deborah commented on a variety of things from the weather to the thick smoky air that reeked of coal and sawdust before they finally climbed the few steps to Dr. Clayton's porch.

Deborah didn't bother to knock. She opened the waiting room door and called out. "Dr. Clayton, you have visitors."

No one was in the outer room, so perhaps Christopher had gone to make calls on the area people. Just then, however, she heard a child crying from beyond the inner office.

"Ah, he must have a patient." She smiled and motioned to Mara. "Might as well have a seat. This could take some time."

Euphanel was surprised when Sissy announced she wanted to get up and walk a spell. The woman would simply not take no for an answer, so Euphanel helped her friend into a robe and steadied Sissy as she got to her feet.

"Feels good to be up," Sissy declared. "Me and that bed is gettin' to where we ain't such friends."

Euphanel smiled. "That's a good sign. Mother always said that when I was sick and tired of being sick and tired, I was on the mend."

"Dat be true." Sissy smiled and took an uneasy step. "Been lyin' there, feelin' sorry for myself, and the Lord done tol' me to stop. Said He got better things for me to do and so I's gonna do it."

"And did He tell you what it was you were supposed to do?"

Sissy smiled at Euphanel. "He just done told me to step out. So that's what I'm doin'. Jes' like Moses and the Israelites. I's bound for the promised land."

Euphanel put her arm around Sissy's waist and noted that the older woman had lost a great deal of weight. "I should think that some of what the Lord has in mind is for you to have a good meal. You're as thin as an old barn cat after having kittens."

Sissy chuckled. "Ain't never been called thin, afore now. I'm bettin' it won't last long. Don' you be a worryin'."

Euphanel shook her head and helped Sissy to a chair. "You should rest a bit before we move on. I'm quite happy to have you sitting in the front room, but I don't want you collapsing in the hall on the way."

"I's stronger than you know," Sissy said, meeting Euphanel's expression.

Euphanel grew somber. "I know you are my dear, dear friend. That gift from God has brought you through so far."

Sissy drew a deep breath and eased back against the chair. "George used to tell me I was stronger than any man he knowed, 'ceptin' for hisself." She grinned. "He jes' didn't know I was stronger than him, too. Had to be. The Good Lord done knowed what I would be up against, married to such a man."

Euphanel laughed and nodded. "Truer words were never spoken."

"I'm shore thankful for this family," Sissy said, growing more serious.

"And we're thankful for you. I'm glad you've decided to stay with us."

"Ain't a whole lot of choices, what since the house done burned down."

Euphanel shook her head. "You know that isn't true. We would have happily rebuilt your house. I would just rather you live your days with us. I don't care if you ever do another thing but sit and sing."

"Speakin' of singin', what did you and Miz Perkins decide about the shape-note singin'?"

"We have our first gathering next Saturday evening. It will be interesting to see who actually turns up. We might only have a handful of folks at best."

"And you plan to invite colored folk, too?"

Smiling, Euphanel sat on the end of the bed. "I do. Rachel and I have already discussed it. We had thought to wait until people were used to getting together and then start asking the blacks to join us, but Rachel decided we might as well just go for it straightaway. I think she's probably right."

"Won't be to the likin' of some folks. Might cause some trouble."

"We'll put that in the Lord's hands," Euphanel declared. "He holds the future for all of us—black, white, red, or brown. I can't see worrying about it until it's time."

Sissy smiled. "Even then, ain't no sense worryin'."

"You're right," Euphanel replied. "Now, come on. Let's get you up."

Chapter 12

"Well, this is a pleasant and fortuitous surprise." Christopher smiled at Mara and then turned to Deborah. "I have a case I'd like you to see."

"And what might that be?"

Christopher motioned. "Come and see for yourself."

"What about Mara? She's brought you something."

Christopher motioned them to follow. "You can both come. I'm sure the patient won't mind—she's only five."

He led them back into the examination room. "Miz Pulaski brought little Mary in with a sore throat and difficulty swallowing."

Deborah nodded at the young mother. "I remember speaking

with you at the Independence Day celebration. You are opening a new dressmaking shop."

The blond-haired woman smiled. "Mighty kind of you to remember me."

Moving to where the child sat on the examination table, Deborah reached out her hand. "Miss Mary, I'm sorry to hear that you're feeling bad."

"My froat hurts," the girl replied.

Christopher brought a lamp closer. "Pick up that mirror and you'll be able to angle the light down her throat." He waited for Deborah to get into position. "Now, Mary, I want you to open your mouth and say 'ahhhhh.' Can you do that again?"

The little girl nodded. "Ahhhhh."

Deborah peered into her mouth while Christopher depressed the child's tongue. "Can you see the problem?"

"Her tonsils are quite swollen. It appears that an abscess is starting to form." Deborah straightened. "Quinsy?"

He nodded. She was smart to be sure. He had figured her to easily see the enlarged tonsils, but the abscess was in the very early stages and not fully formed.

"What will you do to treat this?" Deborah asked.

Christopher smiled and replaced the lamp on the counter. "Well, I was just telling Miz Pulaski that since this is Mary's first time to have this trouble, we will treat it in the most widely accepted manner. Dover's Powder will help with the pain, warm apple cider vinegar gargles will hopefully eliminate any further development of the abscess, and plenty of fluids and rest will help with the rest of her miseries."

Deborah nodded. "I would have suggested the same thing. Maybe even a muellein poultice."

"I agree." He smiled and looked to where Mara had retreated

to a chair across the room. "Remember when I asked you about quinsy that day at the celebration?"

"Indeed. I, however, could never have known what to do for such a matter. Miss Vandermark certainly has a mind for such things."

"Are you a doctor?" the child asked.

Deborah looked at Christopher and then at the girl. "Not exactly, but I'd like to be one day."

"Ain't never heard of no lady doctors," Mrs. Pulaski remarked. " 'Ceptin' for midwives."

"Yes, well, times are changing," Christopher said. "There are many fine physicians of the female gender. The world is starting to see that women are just as capable of learning as men, and women are being admitted into more and more fields. One day maybe Mary will be a doctor."

Mary's eyes widened. She shook her head. "Ain't gonna be a doctor. I wanna sew dresses like my mama."

Mrs. Pulaski smiled and came to the child's side. "That would seem far more fittin' than bein' a doctor."

Christopher shrugged. "I think Mary should be whatever she desires. First, however, we need to get her well." He went and retrieved the medicine. After instructing the mother on how to measure out the medicine and administer it, Christopher sent the Pulaskis on their way.

"I hope that's her last bout," he said, coming back to where Deborah stood, "but I doubt it will be. She's at the right age to start having these problems, and it wouldn't surprise me if she hadn't already had several bouts of tonsillitis before now. She probably never saw anyone unless it was Miz Foster."

"No, the Pulaski family is new to the area," Deborah said,

shaking her head. "Mrs. Pulaski was mentioning that at the party. Her husband has been hired on at the mill with the expansion."

He nodded. "Just the same, I'm thinking it's possible the child has suffered this before. Either way, only time will tell if the tonsils need to be removed."

"Have you done that surgery before?" Deborah asked.

"I have on many occasions." He grinned. "But you haven't, so that will be something of an experience."

Mrs. Foster entered the examination room door without so much as a knock. She seemed surprised to find Deborah there and lost little time in commenting. "Are you sick?"

Deborah shook her head. "Not at all. We were merely discussing a case."

"Ain't no reason for you to be talkin' about patients," the older woman countered. "Doc has my help, and that's all he needs."

"Now, Mrs. Foster, I told you that Deborah wanted to train to become a physician."

"Deborah, is it? Seems like you two have gotten mighty familiar. I heard you was a-courtin'. Seems to me that workin' together would be uncalled for. Ain't right for you two to be alone together." She looked to Christopher and waggled her finger. "Things get out of hand mighty easy."

"Well, they weren't exactly alone, Miz Foster," Mara Shattuck said, standing to join the group. Margaret Foster seemed surprised to find the young woman present but said nothing. "I baked Dr. Clayton a pie, and Deborah was kind enough to accompany me here for the delivery." She smiled up at Dr. Clayton. "I do hope you like pie."

"Absolutely," he replied. "Deborah . . . ah, Miss Vandermark, would you show her where to leave it on my desk?"

"Certainly." Deborah led Mara back the direction they'd come.

Christopher looked at the accusing face of Mrs. Foster and smiled. "You really needn't worry. Nothing is amiss here."

"Still ain't fittin'."

"I find that strange coming from you. Didn't you tell me you trained early on to learn healing?"

The older woman's face contorted into a scowl. "I was in a healin' family. My granny and mama were healers. It were only right that I take on the chore. Miss Deborah ain't from such a line. She's got no reason to be workin' in such things."

"I beg to differ," Deborah said, returning from the delivery of the pie. Mara was close on her heels. "I loved my science courses at the university and believe that I have a gift for such things. I've helped on many occasions with sickness and wounds and I want to serve others by increasing my knowledge and skill."

"Folks round here ain't never gonna accept you doctorin' them."

"And why is that, Miz Foster?" Mara asked.

Christopher almost felt sorry for the older woman. With Deborah and Mara standing up to her, surely Miz Foster had met her match. Of course, not many folks had the guts to face the woman who was known to put curses on a fellow without warning.

But Margaret Foster was not to be bested by the younger women. She gave a jerk of her chin in defiance. "Ain't proper for her to be treatin' folks. She ain't even married yet and shouldn't have any knowledge of a man's body. What man is gonna marry her, with her knowin' such things?"

"I don't believe that is an issue here," Christopher declared.

He threw a wink at Deborah and found it most charming to see her blush.

"Papa says that men and women should do as God calls them," Mara countered. "Sometimes God calls us to tasks that seem unlikely, but He always has a reason. I think it's marvelous that Miss Vandermark would take on such an endeavor. I'd be pleased to have her for my physician. Seems a woman would better understand another woman's ailments."

"But it ain't needed here," Mrs. Foster declared. "I'm here to see to it."

"True for now, but that doesn't mean you will always be here. I think that anytime a person can increase their knowledge, it is good, don't you?" Mara questioned, looking to Christopher.

He crossed his arms and raised a brow. "I think that knowledge is always beneficial."

"I do, too," Mara replied, smiling as if the matter were completely solved. "I wonder, Miz Foster, if you wouldn't mind helping me with an herbal matter. I understand you have managed to grow butterbur. I think it's positively wonderful for headaches."

Margaret Foster seemed ready to speak on the earlier matter, then closed her mouth. She looked suspicious for a moment before finally nodding at the smiling young woman. "Come with me." She looked to Dr. Clayton and Deborah. "You two shouldn't be left alone. I'd get on home if I were you, Miss Deborah."

With that she marched to the door, Mara following quickly on her heels. Mara turned and gave a grin before following the older woman outside. Christopher let out a heavy breath and shook his head.

"That woman would try the patience of Job."

Deborah shook her head. "She makes me so mad sometimes. All I want is to do what I feel qualified and capable of doing. I don't mind studying until my eyes are blurry, but I have the right to be given a chance.

"How is it fair that she goes around turning people away from the idea of my becoming a doctor? It's not right." Deborah began to pace, waving her arms for effect. "It's pure jealousy. She's just out of sorts because she thinks I've taken something from her. But I haven't. And why is it not acceptable for a woman to treat an injured or dying soul, just as a man might do? I'm so intolerant when it comes to dealing with ignorance." She fisted her hands and let out a growl of frustration.

"Should I get the water pitcher?" Christopher asked casually.

"And another thing—" Deborah stopped and looked at him oddly. "What?"

"The water pitcher? Remember when you doused me to calm me down? I promised to keep it handy, and there it sits." He pointed to the table under the window. "I just wondered if I needed to retrieve it for the purpose of helping you to let go your anger."

"No. I'd rather not have to explain." She sighed. "I don't mean to be so volatile. It just crosses me wrong from time to time. I try so hard to do what's right, and then something like this happens. Maybe I should give up. Maybe it's not what God wants me to do. Maybe I just think it is."

Christopher heard her voice and figured a walloping dose of pity might be Deborah's prescription for dealing with the matter. Not that she didn't deserve to feel somewhat sorry for herself—but he couldn't allow it to steal her focus. "You might be right."

She looked at him oddly. "What do you mean?"

"Just what you said—you may not have understood God correctly. It might be best to stop what you're doing and go home to rethink and pray about the matter."

"But I have prayed. I pray about it all the time. I love learning how to help treat people. I've been so blessed to be able to help G.W. and Sissy. You said yourself that G.W. would have surely died had I not taken the measures I did when he was injured. I can't believe that God would give me such a desire and understanding if He didn't mean for me to use it."

"Then stop whining about what one backwoods woman thinks."

Deborah stopped and looked at him for a moment. She seemed to be considering his comment as if there were some great, hidden wisdom in the statement. Finally she nodded. "You're right. I guess I lost sight of the truth for a minute."

"You are going to be fighting an uphill battle when it comes to your desires to train in medicine," he told her. Reaching out, he pushed back a wisp of her dark hair, then let his finger trail along her jaw. "You have to stop worrying about what other people say and think. Focus on what you know to be right. You are gifted when it comes to medicine. You've learned more in the short time since I've been here than many people learn in years of study. You devour the journals and books that I have to offer, and you retain most of the information without error."

He felt her body sway ever so slightly as Deborah leaned into his touch. He wanted to kiss her, but it would be a mistake, as this was a very public place. Using every last ounce of determination, Christopher stepped back.

"Now, if we've resolved this crisis, I need to go. I have some folks to call on."

For a moment, she said nothing. To Christopher, it almost seemed as if she was battling within herself to either go or say something more. Finally she turned.

"Don't forget your pie," she told him. "Also, I brought your books back. They're on the desk, as well."

"I'll be seeing patients at the mill all day tomorrow. How about you join me?"

She whirled on her heel and looked at him in surprise. "Truly?"

He grinned. "I wouldn't tease about such a thing. It's about time folks get used to seeing you in this role. You won't learn any other way than to see and experience the variety of ailments and injuries. None of these visits require anyone to disrobe, so there should be no hint of impropriety. If a man is truly uncomfortable with your presence, I will trust you to have the goodness of heart to excuse yourself."

She nodded. "I promise."

Christopher could see the excitement in her eyes. "Good. Be here at ten sharp."

Euphanel was busy in the garden when Rob appeared seemingly out of nowhere. "What are you doing here? I figured you'd be some hours yet in the log camp."

"Uncle Arjan said my mind wasn't on my work and I was dangerous." He plopped down on the ground just beyond where she knelt.

"You troubled about something?"

He nodded. "I guess that's what it is. I don't rightly know, exactly. I find myself thinkin' about two things all the time. They're consumin' my mind."

"Let me guess," his mother said with a smile. "One of them is Mara Shattuck."

"I reckon that's easy enough to figure out." He grinned. "The other might surprise you."

"And what would that be?" She straightened and felt the stiffness in her knees. Funny, she used to be able to kneel for hours on end. She supposed it was just another flaw of growing old, and another good reason that it was silly to consider remarrying at her age.

"Well, you know I accepted Jesus as Savior when I was just a young'un?"

"Of course. I was there, praying with you."

Rob plucked a weed from the side of the plot and toyed with it while he continued. "I've been thinkin' that maybe God wants more from me."

"In what way?" Euphanel asked.

"Like maybe I should become a preacher or somethin'."

She hadn't expected this train of thought. "A preacher?"

"I know it's a surprise to you. I've always been the wild one around these parts. Folks would probably laugh out loud iffen they knew what I was ponderin'. But . . . well . . . it just keeps comin' back to mind."

Euphanel carefully considered her words. "You should always stand ready to answer God's call. If He is of a mind to make you a preacher—then that's what you should be."

"But what about the book learnin'? I ain't got a good education. That was never of interest to me. But now, what with Deborah teachin' me to read better, I guess I'm startin' to wish I'd gone to school more."

"It's never too late to learn, is it?"

He shrugged. "Can't hardly see myself sittin' in the Perkinsville School."

She smiled. "No, maybe not, but you could learn at home,

and there are numerous schools elsewhere or tutors that could be hired."

"But what about the company and Pa's dream for us boys to share it?"

Euphanel could easily remember the times Rutger had talked of just such a thing over the dinner table or after devotions. His vision for Vandermark Logging had definitely included his boys. But she also knew her husband would not have wanted any of his children staying with a job they felt was wrong for them.

"I believe your father would have wanted you to do what you felt was right. If God is directing you into the ministry, your father would have been the last one to stand in your way."

"I kind of thought that, too, but I figured it might be wishful thinkin'." He smiled. "You know how I like to do that."

She started to get to her feet, and Rob jumped up quickly to assist her. "Thank you, Son." She dusted the dirt off her skirt and straightened. "Your father . . . and I . . . would be proud to have a preacher in the family. We'd be even prouder to know that our son was willing to put aside his own plans and desires and follow God's voice. Never think otherwise."

Saturday evening, Euphanel headed to the church to meet with those who wanted to sing. She'd been a little uncomfortable when Arjan announced he would drive her into town and join the ensemble, but since Deborah and Lizzie couldn't come, it was a reasonable alternative. Even if the girls had come, Euphanel was certain Arjan would have insisted on accompanying them. It would be dark by the time they concluded, and he would never hear of them journeying home alone.

So she swallowed her fears and made small talk as Arjan drove.

Sissy joined them, although she sat in the back of the wagon and left Euphanel and Arjan to sit on the wagon seat together. Euphanel was startlingly aware of his presence—the warmth of his body next to hers, the scent of his cologne. Goodness, but she didn't even remember that he had cologne to wear.

"I'm lookin' forward to this evenin'," he told her. "I have the company of the best gals in the county, and while I won't promise to be all that good at singing, you'll have my undivided attention."

His words were still buzzing through her head as she stood in the center of the gathered singers. To her right were the sopranos or trebles, and opposite them were the basses. The altos were to their right and the tenors opposite them. This was the traditional setting, although Euphanel had, on rare occasion, seen it done otherwise. The trebles and altos were almost solely comprised of women, although a couple of young boys sat beside their mothers and would probably take on their part for the time being. These were the largest of the four groups, but Euphanel had been surprised to see at least twenty men show up to join them.

There were even a few blacks who'd felt brave enough to come, although they sat together and a bit apart from the others. Sissy sat in the alto section with some of her friends on either side. There were also two men who sat in the bass section with their gazes cast at the floor.

Euphanel raised her hand to quiet the group. "I'm so glad we've had this wonderful turnout. I want to start by explaining a few things and telling you my thoughts. I think that sacred-harp music is one of the finest ways to draw a community together.

"I arranged to obtain some books for us to use. This will help a great deal for those of you who are unfamiliar with the shape-note singing that we'll do."

Euphanel went to the first of two wooden boxes. "If a couple of you gentlemen would do the honors of passing the books around, I'll continue to explain."

Arjan and Mr. Greeley got to their feet and began to hand out the hymnals, while Euphanel took up her own copy. Walking back to the center, she shifted her gaze now to the tenors.

"This is the traditional setting for shape-note singing. As some of you probably know, there is no real leader to this group. We take turns announcing what hymn we wish to sing and then leading that song with an open hand. The first time through, we will sing the fa-sol-la's instead of the words."

She opened to one of the pages in the book. "You can see, when you get your hymnals, that on page three, it shows you exactly what is meant by that. Now, I know that some of you can't read, but we'll help one another, and you'll soon be able to understand exactly why this type of music is perfect for you.

"In shape-note singing, we use the fa-sol-la-fa-sol-la-mi-fa scale. If you look at the notes on the page, you'll see where the term 'shape-note' comes from."

She waited until the last of the hymnals were given out before continuing. "Each of the notes is a stemmed eighth, quarter, or half note, as well as a whole note. But instead of the circle of the note being positioned on the staff, there are various shapes relevant to the fa-sol-la scale. You will see for example that the fa is a triangle, the sol is oval like a regular note, the la is a rectangle, and the mi is a diamond." She looked up and smiled. "Any questions?"

When no one asked anything, Euphanel glanced around the group. "Let's see a show of hands if you've done this before."

Most everyone raised their hand. A few scattered here and there, however, including the blacks, were unfamiliar. Euphanel smiled. "I'm so glad to have the experience of this group. However, bear with me. For those who are not familiar, we will endeavor to make this easy."

She refocused on the hymnal. "Shapes and notes are designations of scale rather than a particular note or pitch. The leader will set the fa, hopefully at a comfortable pitch for everyone, but once that is set, then you will just join in with your harmony note. As that is established, we will begin to sing through the song. This will familiarize everyone with the tune, and hopefully allow you to read the music quickly and easily."

"Now, turn to page six. We'll start with something we all know. The title here is 'New Britain,' but many of you know it as 'Amazing Grace.' I will begin by making this quite simple. I happen to sing treble, but for this purpose will give you the tenor's part right now, as it sounds familiar and is the main melody of the tune. I'll do the first few bars in shape-note—and then in the words."

She cleared her throat and started to sing. "Sol fa la fa la sol fa la sol, Sol fa la fa la sol la sol. Amazing grace, how sweet the sound, that saved a wretch like me." She stopped and looked up to see most of the people nodding. "It's that simple—really."

One of the women raised her hand. "Why not just sing the words? Why worry about all the shape-notes?"

Euphanel smiled. "It's a simple way of teaching folks to read music and harmonize. If you can read the shape-notes, you don't worry about stumbling around for the right key or even version of the song. You can see by the shape-notes where your scale is taking you. That's why we get the leader to give one note and the rest join in finding their particular notes. This is important for the harmony, because it's all done without any musical instruments."

The woman seemed to understand and nodded. She looked back to the book, and Euphanel could see she was trying hard to silently mouth her own part. She turned toward the basses and found Arjan beaming her a smile. Her knees trembled slightly.

"Let's get started."

Chapter 13

May 1886

"Lizzie, you are positively glowing," Euphanel declared. She bent to pull a ham from the oven, but continued talking to her daughter-in-law. "I suppose it's because that baby has grown to be such a big one."

"It's probably the heat," Deborah said with a grin.

"It has been unreasonably hot," Lizzie countered.

The temperatures were already making it necessary to use the summer kitchen, and there was no hope that things might cool off and give them an easier season.

Christopher was beyond doubt now that she was expecting twins, and today Lizzie planned to share the news with the family. First she would go and tell G.W. in private, and then she would announce it to the rest of the family at supper. That was, if her mother-in-law didn't guess that something was afoot.

"Why don't you go on back in the house and rest?" Euphanel told her. "We've nearly got supper ready. Deborah and I can bring this in. You go ahead and check on Sissy for me."

Lizzie nodded. It would give her a good excuse to see G.W. "I'll do that. Seems Sissy is doing so much better. Each day she's more like her old self."

Euphanel nodded. "Indeed. I know she's still bearing a great sorrow, but her heart seems renewed almost daily. She's a good example of taking life day by day."

"You'll send Deborah for me if you need my help, won't you?" she asked as she headed toward the brick archway that led outside.

"We'll be just fine. You go ahead," Euphanel replied.

Lizzie labored under the growing weight of the twins as she made her way back to the house. Dr. Clayton had told her it wasn't at all unusual for women to give birth early when carrying more than one baby. He also told her that he wanted her to rest in bed for the final weeks. That concerned her somewhat. There was a lot of work to do around the house, and while they were all situated now in their new rooms, Lizzie still had things she wanted to do before the babies came.

Inside the house was only moderately cooler. How she longed for the heat to quell and the rains to come. There had been some rumors of storms building off the coast, but they hadn't had so much as a drop of rain in what seemed forever, and everyone longed for relief.

Making her way to the office, Lizzie paused outside the door and put her hand to her mouth to suppress a smile. She had wanted to tell G.W. about Dr. Clayton's suspicions, but she knew it had been wise to wait. Lately G.W. had been rather cantankerous. He was still limping badly enough to use a cane, and it was evident that he'd never again be able to climb up the huge longleaf pines. Lizzie hoped this news might take his mind off his problems and give him something new to think about.

"May I come in?" she asked from the open door.

G.W. looked up and nodded. He scratched his closely trimmed bearded chin and leaned back in the chair. "I'd be glad for the company." He got to his feet and hobbled to where she stood. Offering her his arm, he led her to the chair opposite his. "So to what do I owe this pleasure?"

"I have something to tell you," she said matter-of-factly. Taking her seat rather awkwardly, Lizzie tried to find a comfortable position. It was a moot effort, however, and she finally gave up and grew still.

G.W. wore a rather curious expression. "You look tired," she said to divert his focus. "I think you've been working too hard."

"Hardly. This work is nothing compared to the real work I used to do," G.W. replied. He came to stand before her and sat on the edge of the desk. "Now tell me what you want me to know."

She grinned. "Perhaps I should make you guess."

He shook his head, but smiled. "When it comes to you ladies, I wouldn't even venture one. Are you feeling all right?"

Lizzie nodded. "I feel quite well. Overburdened with this added weight, but well."

"My boy giving you a difficult time, is he?"

She laughed and tried again to shift into a more comfortable position. "You're so sure it's a boy?"

"Absolutely. We need more men around here."

"Then why not add two instead of one?" she asked casually.

He nodded. "In time, I'd be happy with a dozen boys. I suppose we could have a daughter or two for you."

"What if we have two boys right away?"

He looked confused. "Whatever the Good Lord decides is fine by me."

Lizzie took pity on him. "G.W., we're going to have twins. Dr. Clayton has thought this for some time now, but today he told me for sure."

G.W. stared at her with a blank expression. She couldn't help but giggle. He was positively struck speechless—a rarity for her husband.

"Apparently twins often come early," she continued, trying to sound nonchalant. "Dr. Clayton has ordered me to spend the rest of my confinement time in bed. I'm afraid my useful days are at an end for a while."

Still he said nothing. Perhaps G.W. was not pleased. She'd never considered the fact that he might not be happy with twins. "I'm sorry if this is disturbing news."

He shook his head and got to his feet. Practically lifting her from the chair, G.W. engulfed her in his arms and held her as close as the pregnancy would allow. "I'm not disturbed," he whispered against her ear. "I'm beyond words."

For several minutes, all he did was hold her. Lizzie relished the moment and sighed as she put her head against his chest. It was an awkward position, to be sure, but she longed for the tenderness of his embrace and prayed that it might go on.

G.W. seemed to feel the same and continued to hold her until one, or perhaps both, of the twins gave a mighty kick. He pulled back rather startled. "Was that . . . ?"

"The babies," she replied, not waiting for him to finish. She gently took hold of his hand and drew it to her belly. The activity continued, as did G.W.'s awed smile. It wasn't the first time he'd felt them kick, but it was the first time he knew there were two of them.

He looked at her and shook his head. "I don't know what to say. I felt so blessed that we were going to have a child, and now to know there are two . . . well, I guess I feel doubly blessed."

"I know. Me too."

"Do the others know?"

She shook her head. "Only Deborah. She was with me at the doctor's the first time he suspected. I told him I didn't want to say anything to anyone until he felt confident of it being twins. I figured I would announce it this evening at supper. Better yet, maybe you should be the one to share the news."

"I think I'd like that," G.W. replied. "It'll be right fine to share something good."

Deborah waited for the dessert to come, knowing that Lizzie had planned to announce her news at that time. She could hardly sit still for all of her excitement. Twins had never been born in Perkinsville, and once the news was out, folks would be sure to come calling. Twins were usually seen as a good omen, and with so many superstitious people in the area, Deborah had no doubt they would want to touch Lizzie's belly for luck.

"I have something to tell everyone," G.W. began.

Quickly, Deborah turned her gaze to the plate, lest she give away the news. She was tickled to hear her brother make the announcement. It would do him good; lately he'd been rather distant and quiet.

"Well, do tell," Mother said, putting aside her fork. "What is it that you want to share?"

Deborah looked up and found all eyes turned to G.W. Lizzie looked as though she might burst into song at any moment.

"Lizzie found out today that she's gonna have to be in bed for a time."

Mother frowned. "Is there a problem?"

G.W. shook his head. "Not unless you consider two grandbabies, instead of one, a problem."

Deborah clapped her hands at the stunned expressions around the table. "Isn't it grand news?"

Mother was the first to recover. "It's amazing news. Twins?"

Lizzie nodded. "Dr. Clayton has wondered for a time, but now he's sure. He said twins are likely to come early, so he wants me to spend these final weeks in bed."

Sissy, who sat beside Mother near the head of the table, leaned forward. "I was sure 'bout two babies a long time ago. Seems a doctor should'a knowed, too."

Deborah laughed. "I expected that you or Mother would figure it out before Lizzie made her announcement."

"We did discuss the possibilities," Mother admitted, "but I figured we'd know in time. Besides that, G.W. was a big baby, and I think I looked very nearly as large in my last months. Oh, this is grand news!"

G.W. smiled and put his arm around Lizzie's shoulder. "It's a double blessing from the Lord."

"To be sure," Uncle Arjan said, nodding. "Children are a gift from the Lord. The Good Book says so."

Rob nodded. "It does, at that. Guess you'll get your quiver full a little faster, havin' two at a time." He smiled. "Leave it to you to do things in a big way."

"Well, the first thing we need to do is double our efforts at making baby clothes and diapers," Mother said. "Of course, once word gets around, I know the women in this community will be coming forward with gifts and any of their extras."

"And lying about in bed will provide me ample time to sew," Lizzie said. She looked to Sissy. "Maybe you can teach me how to do that lovely smocking you put on the baby gown you made."

"I shore 'nuf can. Be my pleasure. You and me ain't much help otherwise."

"You neither one need to worry," Mother declared. "Deborah and I can manage just fine."

"And if we need an extra hand," Rob added, "I'm sure Mara would be right here."

Mother nodded. "So you see, it's all worked out."

Deborah thought of the time she'd been spending with Christopher helping on his rounds. The men at the mill had been hostile to her presence the first few times, but now they seemed to take her in stride, and a few actually seemed to welcome her company. Of course, they weren't willing for her to actually do much in the way of tending them. Other times, the women in the area seemed to accept her help without too much protest. As long as Christopher was there, they appeared to tolerate her quite well.

She wondered, though, if this news would put an end to her work with the doctor. Mother would need her here to help with the house and garden. Sissy was only just getting to a place where she could do simple chores like shelling peas and peeling potatoes without tiring too quickly. She had trouble remembering things, and often garbled her words, but Christopher said that in time it would either straighten itself out or not. There wasn't really anything they could do.

Tomorrow, she decided, she would go and speak to Christopher and let him know the situation. He would understand, and perhaps even have some thoughts as to how she could continue to work with him. Maybe on days when the men were home or Mara came to help, Deborah would be able to slip away and attend patients with Christopher.

To her surprise, however, Deborah didn't have to wait until the next day. A knock at the door soon revealed the doctor himself. He'd come to see Deborah, but she knew once he saw her mother's cobbler, he'd happily postpone their courting.

"We've just heard the good news about the babies," Deborah announced.

"And the bad news about me going to bed," Lizzie added.

"Ain't bad news if it keeps you and the babies safe," G.W. added.

Mother nodded. "That's right. Dr. Clayton, you just sit yourself down. I'll get you a plate," she said, getting to her feet. "I know you have a particular fondness for rhubarb cobbler."

"Yes, ma'am," Christopher agreed, taking a seat beside Deborah.

He was quickly rewarded with a heaping portion and smiled with great satisfaction as Deborah passed him the cream.

"If you'd timed your visit a little more carefully, you could have had supper with us, as well," Mother told him.

"I'll try to remember that next time," he said, pouring thick cream on the cobbler.

"We were mighty happy about the news," Arjan joined in. "Our Lizzie is having twins."

Christopher nodded. "That she is." He looked to G.W. "Many congratulations."

"Thanks, Doc. I have to say, the news just about made my whole year."

"I'm pleased to hear it." Christopher dove into the cobbler and smiled with great satisfaction as he enjoyed the first mouthful.

"We will see to it that Lizzie spends her remaining confinement taking it very easy," Mother added. "I hope you'll give us any special instructions we need."

"The important thing is the rest, which will lessen the strain on the uterus." He looked around the table rather quickly. "Excuse me for being so blunt."

"It's not a problem," Mother insisted. "We are all quite capable of hearing the truth. Rest assured, we shall watch over Lizzie with great care."

"I've no doubt about that." Christopher refocused on the cobbler.

Deborah watched him enjoy the dessert and took joy in his pleasure. It seemed it took so little to make him happy. She supposed that if she were to take her courtship seriously, it might behoove her to hone her cooking skills. Maybe staying at home was just the right thing to get Christopher more serious about their marriage. After all, he'd really not spoken of such things in months. Maybe he'd changed his mind.

She frowned. Would he tell her if he had?

Soon enough, the coffeepot ran dry and everyone, including Christopher, had enjoyed their share of dessert. Mother smiled as she got to her feet and suggested Deborah and Christopher might like to take a walk.

"Now that the sun is starting to set, the air won't be so heavy," she told them.

Christopher nodded and helped Deborah to her feet. "I had just such a thing in mind."

Deborah didn't even bother with a shawl. The heat would still be too much to have need of it. She made her way outside with Christopher and waited for him to point the direction.

They walked slowly, as if heading to town. Overhead, the large pines swayed in the light breeze. The air wasn't nearly so humid, and Deborah breathed deep of the heavy pine scent. She had missed such things when she'd lived in Philadelphia.

"What are you grinning about?" Christopher asked, smiling.

"I was just thinking of how much I love it here," she replied. "I missed my home when I was in Philadelphia. It can be overbearingly hot here, but so can the city."

Christopher said nothing, and Deborah wondered if she'd somehow caused him to think of his own home. She moved the conversation on. "I suppose you realize I'll be needed at home more now that Lizzie will be confined?"

"Yes, I suppose I do."

They continued walking in the fading light. Deborah longed to take hold of his arm, but refrained. It seemed every time they touched, something stirred deep inside that left her with even greater longing.

"We shouldn't venture too far," Christopher said, turning back toward the house. "You never know what kind of trouble might lurk."

"It's true," Deborah replied and quickly matched her steps to his. "But we needn't rush."

He smiled. "Trying to keep me out here, all to yourself?"

She felt her cheeks grow hot, but returned the tease. "Of course. Isn't that what courting couples do?"

He gave a low chuckle. "Some do much more than that."

Now she really felt the heat on her face. "Dr. Clayton, what a bold thing to say. You have me blushing."

Stopping, he stunned her to silence by taking her in his arms. "Then this should positively turn you scarlet." He lowered his mouth to hers and kissed her. For a moment, Deborah forgot where and who she was. She felt as if her heart was aglow—growing brighter by the minute.

Pulling away, Christopher had to steady her before she lost her balance. Looking up at him, Deborah could only stare open-mouthed. She tried to speak, but the words seemed stuck in the back of her throat.

"I hope I haven't offended you," he said with a hint of a grin. "I'm not the least bit sorry I did that, but I would hate myself if I upset you."

"I . . . uh . . . I just thought our first kiss would . . . well . . . be . . ."

"Be what?" He frowned. "Wasn't it good? I mean, I liked it very much."

"It was wonderful," she managed. Touching her hands to her cheeks, she couldn't imagine anything more delightful. "I suppose I didn't expect it to be so . . . stimulating."

He roared with laughter and swung her around in a circle. "You never fail to amaze me, Miss Vandermark. I've wanted to kiss you for a very long time, and while I know it's completely inappropriate with the standards of proper etiquette, I want nothing more than to do it again."

He stopped and lowered her back to the ground. His expression suggested he was seeking permission. Deborah nodded and closed her eyes. "Me too."

Chapter 14

Christopher looked at the letter once again and felt the same sense of discouragement. His mother wrote to give him the news as she did every month, and it only seemed that things were worse than ever. Two of his brothers were in trouble for fighting. They'd been expelled from school with the suggestion that they were incapable of learning. The youngest two had caught the mumps, but were recovering. His father was his usual angry self, insisting his wife bring him liquor instead of food.

Daily he curses God, his mother wrote. *He says such hideous things that I cannot bear to listen. I spend less and less time with him, and I know he hates me for deserting him. God is all I have to cling to these days.*

Christopher could just imagine his father's tirades. The man had given up what faith he'd had in God after the accident that crippled him; Christopher could still hear his father bellow, *"God clearly doesn't care about the likes of me and mine."*

He glanced back at the letter, and this time, his mother's voice drowned out the bitterness of his father. *I know these things will never change. I used to have hope that they would, but it takes too much of my strength.* Christopher hoped the money he sent would be enough to ease her burden, but that was foolish. Some miseries couldn't be alleviated with money.

He pushed the letter away and stared at his empty coffee cup. Maybe it had been a mistake to come to Texas. Perhaps his mother would have fared better if he'd set up practice in Kansas City. Of course, that would have brought its own share of difficulties.

Pushing back his chair, Christopher stood. He reached for the letter and folded it carefully before replacing it in the envelope. He'd reply later tonight. It would give him time to consider what he wanted to say.

"Hello? Christopher?"

He smiled and cast the envelope on the table. "I'm back here in the kitchen."

Deborah wasted no time in joining him. "How are you? I haven't seen you for so long. Lizzie is doing well, but we've been so busy."

Christopher picked up his coffee cup. "I think there's still some coffee, if you want a cup."

She shook her head. "No, I was just hoping to go with you on your rounds. In some ways, I feel like Lizzie's confinement is my own."

"It won't be long. Besides, this is good practice for you. For you to tend an expectant mother is something that women will not balk at. Tending a woman who is to birth twins will be excellent to add to your list of experiences." He put the cup on the counter. "Now, if you'll give me just a moment to gather my things, we'll head out." She followed him from the kitchen and back into the exam room.

"Is there anything I can do?"

"No, most everything is ready." Christopher went to the cupboard and pulled out several small bottles to put in his bag.

"I saw you had a letter on the table. News from home?" she asked.

He turned and looked at her with a frown. "Yes, but not as good as I'd hoped."

"Oh, I am sorry. Can you speak of it?"

Deborah moved toward him, then stopped. Christopher thought she looked genuinely concerned. No doubt, she would ask him questions. He probably should have remained silent.

"It most likely wouldn't help anything if I did."

Her expression changed from concern to frustration. "You never talk about your family. You know everything about mine, and I know very little about yours. Don't you trust me to be discreet?"

He considered her question. Perhaps now was the time to tell her the truth. "It's not a matter of trust," he began. "I suppose there are things about my family of which I feel guarded—though not because of any flaw of yours."

Deborah moved a bit closer. "Christopher, we all have our secrets. I'm sorry if I made you feel bad for yours."

Smiling, he reached out to touch her cheek. "I appreciate your understanding. In time . . . well . . . I want you to know."

"Doc! Doc! Come quick."

"That sounds like . . . " Deborah jumped back just as G.W. limped into the room.

"It's Lizzie. She's having pain, and Ma says it may be time for the babies."

"Goodness, she was just fine when I left to come here."

G.W. looked at Deborah. "It started just after you left. She thought at first she'd just turned wrong, but the pain continued."

Christopher grabbed his bag and motioned Deborah to the door. "Come on."

They raced to the wagon, with G.W. doing his best to keep up with them. Climbing into the wagon seat, Deborah moved to the far side to give her brother room as Christopher took his place in back. G.W. managed to take up the reins and release the brake very nearly at the same moment.

He quickly turned the wagon and headed the team down the road, ignoring the greetings of folks who walked along the way. Christopher took hold of the back of the seat, and Deborah glanced over her shoulder at him. She looked worried. Knowing the truth about medicine was that way. She would have to learn to conceal her fears, or her patients would suffer. If G.W. hadn't been there, he would have said as much, but the poor man was already a wreck.

The ride to the Vandermark place took less than half the time it would normally have taken. Despite the conditions of the road and other folks using the same path, G.W. managed to keep them moving. When they pulled up to the front of the house, he reined back the horses hard.

"Easy, G.W," Deborah said, climbing down from the wagon. "Don't take it out on the team."

Christopher followed suit with G.W. beating him to the porch by inches. "She's right, G.W. Don't give in to worry just yet."

G.W.'s piercing blue eyes fixed Christopher with a hard stare. "You will take care of her." It was more a statement than a question.

Giving the poor father-to-be a brief slap on the back, Christopher smiled. "Absolutely."

Rob had just finished loading the last of the logs onto the train car when he noticed Zed Perkins in the camp. Handing the mule team over to one of the other men, Rob went to where Uncle Arjan stood talking to the mill owner.

"Howdy," Rob said, joining them. "Good to see you, Mr. Perkins."

"You may not think so when you hear what I've come to say. I was just telling Arjan that my situation has changed, and I felt it important we discuss the particulars."

Rob looked to his uncle. "In what respect?"

Mr. Perkins looked uncomfortable. "Well, the fact is I've been having a little difficulty with the banks. The money promised for the final steps of my expansion has been refused."

"I'm sorry to hear that. Would you like to sit and have a cup of coffee?" Uncle Arjan asked.

"Sittin' in the shade would be good," Perkins replied. He took off his straw hat and wiped his forehead with the back of his shirt sleeve. "Mighty warm today."

"That it is." Arjan led the way to where they'd had lunch earlier. The few campstools made a decent place to rest.

"I know this comes as a surprise to you," Mr. Perkins continued, repositioning his hat. "It came as an even bigger surprise to me. I went to Houston, thinking I was securing the revenue needed for my mill, and instead, I found myself facing a bunch of two-timers."

"How will this affect your plans?"

Tucking his hands deep in his coat pockets, Mr. Perkins looked even more distressed. "Well, the thing is, the situation has forced me to take on some investors."

"Investors?" Rob questioned.

"Partners, actually. Look, I wouldn't have done this if I didn't have to. I want you to understand that up front. If there had been another way to manage things, I would have."

"Zed, what's the problem here? We have no say over whether you take on partners."

Rob could tell the answer wasn't going to be good. Mr. Perkins was nervous about the situation. He wouldn't have taken all the trouble to come clear out here if the matter weren't critical.

"I . . . well . . ." Perkins fell silent, then drew a deep breath. "The fact is, I was approached by someone who had been here before—last year. Mr. Albright."

Rob wasn't sure he'd heard him correctly. "Stuart Albright? The fella that was supposed to marry Lizzie?"

"That's right. He came to me with his father-in-law while I was in Houston. I don't know how he knew about my troubles, but he did. They came to my hotel and presented their proposition."

Arjan looked to Rob and then back to Zed Perkins. "Which was what, if I may ask?"

"They would provide the capital I needed for the final stage of my expansion."

"No chance Albright was doing it out of the goodness of his heart. What do they get in return?" Rob asked.

Perkins looked at the ground. "I had to make them partners."

"Partners?" Arjan questioned. "You mentioned that before. Are you saying they now own half the sawmill?"

"Only until I can pay back the loan. We agreed it would be a short-term scenario." Mr. Perkins seemed desperate to ease their minds. "I had no other choice. Without the expansion, I can't hope to produce the promised lumber. I'm sorry if this is going to cause problems between us, but I'm hoping you'll understand."

Arjan put his hand on Mr. Perkins' shoulder. "You did what you thought was best. I'm sure it will all work out."

"That's my prayer," the older man said. "I never wanted to compromise our business dealings, however. That's why I came to you today."

"We appreciate your openness, Zed," Arjan told the man. "I always like it best when folks deal honestly with me. We'll let the family know what's going on. I can't imagine that we have anything to worry about. Seems to me that Albright fellow was all about making a dollar. If he's that way, then your benefit will be ours, I'm sure. We'll keep providing all the logs you need. Just let us know if anything changes."

Rob heard the hesitation in his uncle's voice, but he waited until Zed excused himself and headed back to town before asking about it.

"You're lookin' a mite concerned. Do you think there will be trouble?"

Arjan shrugged. "I'm not sure. Seems strange that Albright would even concern himself with this part of the country. Maybe he was intrigued by Perkins's situation, but it just smells a bit sour to me."

Rob nodded. "I agree. G.W. ain't gonna like hearin' about this. Not one little bit."

"No, I'm sure he won't, but we have to tell him nevertheless." The train whistle blew and Arjan jumped up. "Come on. Let's hitch a ride."

Rob thought about Mr. Perkins's announcement all the way back to the house. Perkins knew there had been bad blood between the Vandermarks and Mr. Albright. Seemed to lack consideration for his friends and neighbors that he would partner with the man, but Zed Perkins was obviously concerned for his own business.

They were back to the house before they knew it. The train slowed but didn't stop. "You boys take care," Jack said as Arjan and Rob jumped off. Jack gave the whistle two brief toots and was out of sight.

"Look there," Rob said, pointing. "It's G.W. What's he doin' just sittin' around?" As the men drew closer, Rob could see his brother's pale face and strained expression. He looked almost ill.

"Son, you all right?" Uncle Arjan asked.

G.W. looked up in surprise. "It's Lizzie."

Rob shook his head. "Is she sick?"

"It's the babies. Doc and Deborah are workin' with Ma to deliver 'em."

"Kind of early, ain't it?" Rob regretted the question the minute it was out of his mouth.

"It's normal for twins to come early," their uncle interjected. "I'm sure everything will be just fine. You need not fret. This is an occasion for celebration."

"I know," G.W. replied. "I'm tryin' to remember that. It's just that I . . . well, I can't help worryin'. She's my whole world."

A baby's cry could be heard coming from the house. Arjan grinned and slapped G.W. on the back. "That world of yours is about to get a whole lot bigger."

G.W. jumped to his feet, but Arjan took hold of his arm. "Remember, there are two of them to be delivered. We might as well sit here and wait."

Reluctantly, G.W. retook his chair while Rob pulled up two seats so they could join him. "I don't know what I'll do if something goes wrong," Rob heard his brother murmur.

"Then let me help you get your mind off matters for a few minutes," their uncle began. "You're no doubt wonderin' why we came home early."

G.W. nodded. "I guess so. I suppose I was thinkin' you knew about Lizzie, but of course you didn't." He rubbed at his leg and began to rock.

"We had a visitor at the camp. Zed Perkins rode all the way out on horseback to come talk to us."

Rob could see that this only slightly interested his older brother. "The news wasn't good," Rob interjected. "Fact is, it's givin' us a bit to consider."

G.W. held his brother's gaze for a moment, then turned to Uncle Arjan. "What's he talkin' about?"

"Seems Perkins had trouble securing the money he needed for the last of his expansion. Apparently he can't hope to fulfill the promises he's made without it, so he felt he had to take on some partners."

"Partners?" G.W. shrugged. "I don't suppose that should be so bad."

"You ain't heard who he took on," Rob said. He caught a look of reproof from his uncle just as a second baby began to cry.

"There, you see. It all sounds as though things are well," Arjan announced. "They'll be comin' for you soon, so I might as well get the rest of this tale told."

"Rob seems worried about who Mr. Perkins took on," G.W. said, glancing anxiously toward the door.

"Seems Stuart Albright and his father-in-law are the new partners," their uncle said matter-of-factly. "Perkins thought we'd need to know right away. He doesn't expect it to change anything, but he knew we'd had some problems with the man."

G.W. frowned. "I'll say. What's Albright doing in Perkinsville, anyway?"

"He weren't here," Rob threw out. "Mr. Perkins said he was approached in Houston after the bank turned him down. He said he didn't know how they came by the knowledge that he needed help, but he felt he had to take it."

"Knowing Albright," G.W. commented, "he most likely arranged the matter. I wouldn't put it past him to do it, just out of spite. He knows we work with Perkins—probably wants to play boss man. Well, it ain't gonna work. He doesn't know how things are done down here. Albright won't have any say over Vandermark Logging. Ain't nothing he can do to change that."

Mother appeared at the porch door with a grin nearly as wide as her face. "G.W., come meet your children."

"Lizzie?" he asked, getting to his feet.

She nodded. "Doing just fine. So are your son and daughter."

"A boy and a girl?" Rob asked. "Now, how's that for fair and even?" He laughed and followed his brother toward the door.

Chapter 15

July 1886

The middle of the month arrived with no break in the heat. The twins were now clearly thriving, and in less than a week, they would be a month old and visitors would come to call on their presentation day. Deborah knew once that happened, the place would be pandemonium. She was thankful for the additions to the house, for the office was now slightly separated from the main living areas. It helped to keep the noise level at a minimum when she and G.W. were working together—although that happened less and less often.

Sissy was now fully recovered from her injuries and seemed to be regaining her old strength, doing the daily milking before heading to the garden. Mother was busy tending to her grandchildren and Lizzie; Deborah had never seen her happier.

Just after breakfast on the fifteenth, Christopher arrived to pay a visit to the new mother. Just the sight of his handsome form made Deborah's heart pound. She longed to find a moment of privacy where they might share another kiss. She giggled to think of how scandalous such a thing sounded, but couldn't help wishing for it just the same.

"There were rumors in town of storms off the coast," he told them. "Could be we'll have some rain soon."

"It would be most welcome if it ends this hot spell. There's been no relief from the heat! Let me take your coat. You know you don't have to stand on formalities here. You'll broil yourself to death if you stay in this," Deborah declared, taking the coat from him.

She herself had picked a lightweight cotton gown. It was an older dress and the once-vivid yellow was now a faded cream. The sleeves were unfashionably short, but Deborah didn't care. No one could survive Texas heat and worry overmuch about what the ladies were wearing in Paris.

"At least the air is clean here," Christopher said, wiping his brow with a handkerchief. "The mill is putting out so much smoke and dust you can hardly see across the road."

"We'll have to pray for a good stiff breeze," G.W. said, joining them. He extended his hand to the doctor. "You come to see Lizzie and the babies?"

"I did," Christopher replied. "They're coming up close to a month old. I presume they're doing well, or I would have heard otherwise by now."

"They're growing quite fat," Deborah replied before her brother could answer. "And, of course, we are spoiling them with a great amount of attention."

Christopher grinned. "I've no doubt about that."

"Lizzie's feeding them just now," Deborah continued. "Would

you like to have a cup of coffee and one of Mother's doughnuts?" She smiled sweetly knowing he would.

"Sounds good to me, but let's make it at least two. After all, I'm here to see twins."

Deborah laughed and led the way to the dining room. "Well, you're actually here to see Lizzie as well, so maybe we should make it three."

He nodded quite seriously. "I suppose that would only be right. It will be difficult, but I'll suffer through."

G.W. joined them but offered nothing to their banter. Deborah met his serious gaze. "Can I get you a cup of coffee, as well?"

He nodded and took a seat opposite Christopher at the kitchen table. Deborah went to the cold stove and picked up a pot. "I just brought this in from the outdoor kitchen a few minutes ago. Should still be nice and hot."

"It's surprisingly cool in here," Christopher said. He took up the cup after she placed it in front of him. "My house isn't as comfortable. Especially if I go lightin' the stove to cook anything. I'm starting to think it's better to just eat everything raw."

Deborah shook her head. "Now, you know what Mama said—you can eat your meals here three times a day." She poured G.W.'s coffee and brought a plate of doughnuts to the table.

"I was hopin' I might ask you about something," G.W. said without so much as glancing at the food.

Deborah wondered if he'd prefer her to go. "I can leave, if you like."

G.W. shook his head. "No. What I have to say might well involve you."

Deborah took a seat and waited for him to speak while Christopher downed his first doughnut. She knew G.W. had something on his mind and would share it when he was ready. He was never one to keep a matter to himself if it was important, but sometimes he could be irritatingly slow to deliver. It reminded her somewhat of the way one of her college professors had lectured. He would begin speaking on the topic of the day, then halt in mid-sentence. Sometimes he would pace a few moments; other times he would stare at the students as if trying to remember what it was he wanted to say.

Finally, G.W. piped up. "I want to know what can be done to help me regain full use of my leg. I mean so that I can mount and ride a horse, walk without a cane—maybe even run. I have two children now, and I want to be able to keep up with them."

Keeping her gaze on the table, Deborah remained silent. She was never so happy to hear anything. G.W. had been moody and difficult to live with ever since the accident, but now he found hope for the future in the form of his two babies.

"There are a number of things we can do to strengthen the muscle," Christopher said thoughtfully. "It's not going to be easy, of course. A lot of tissue was damaged. You may always have a bit of a limp."

"I can live with a bit of one, but I don't want to be kept from doing things for and with my family. I know I'll probably never work in the camps again, and I can accept that."

Deborah was glad to hear him say as much. It was a long time coming.

Christopher took a slow sip of coffee and continued to hold the cup as he began to speak. "My father was injured in an accident. It left him unable to use his legs at all."

G.W. shook his head. "I couldn't live like that."

"Neither can he. At least, not well."

Deborah perked up at this. Christopher shared so little about his family that, even though the conversation was more for G.W.'s benefit than hers, she wanted to hear it all.

"My father was always a very strong man—a laborer who knew his own capabilities and wasn't afraid to learn new skills. He was admired by many, but also scorned. There will always be men who are unable to accept that someone has a stronger back or can work without rest for longer periods of time. Those men are partly to blame for my father's accident."

"What happened?"

Deborah was glad G.W. asked the question. She figured Christopher would be more willing to answer—especially since he'd brought up the topic.

"For a variety of reasons, there was a fight in the train yard. My father was the object of disdain—along with a couple of his friends. A group of men took it upon themselves to settle a score that wasn't really valid. They ambushed my father and his friends at the end of the work night."

Deborah noted the pain in his expression, and she couldn't help reaching over to place her hand atop his. Christopher looked at her for a moment and gave her the briefest of smiles before continuing.

"The beating they received was brutal. In fact, my father's friends were killed. My father was thrown from the back of an idle train car. His back hit the rail and broke. It damaged his spinal cord and left him unable to use his legs."

"That isn't an accident," Deborah protested. "It was murder and assault. No doubt they intended to kill your father, as well."

Christopher nodded. "But I don't tell the story to dwell on the wrong done my father, but rather to encourage you, G.W. My father allowed his life to change in a most negative fashion. My hope is that you'll continue to desire and fight to make yours better. The things you'll have to do to strengthen your leg won't be easy. The pain of your injury is still fresh in your memory, but this will hurt like nothing you've ever endured. But I believe there is hope that you'll recover most—if not all—of your use."

"That's what I want," G.W. told him. "I don't want to give up, though I thought I did. I figured for a long while that my life was pretty much over. Deborah helped me to see that I could use my brain for something more than calculating board feet and where a pine was going to drop." He smiled. "She's a stubborn one, my sister."

"That she is," Christopher said before giving her a wink. "But I suppose we wouldn't want her any other way."

"So what does your pa do now?" G.W. asked.

"Mostly he makes life unbearable for my mother," Christopher replied without emotion. "He torments my brothers and sisters who are still at home, and he drinks. The latter is what he seems to do best. He says it's the only way he can deal with his miseries and pain."

"During really painful moments, I've considered it myself," G.W. admitted.

Deborah was surprised by her brother's words, but instead she addressed Christopher's comment. "Oh, your poor mother. How awful that must be."

"She gets by—barely," Christopher replied. "I suppose it's one of the reasons I've never been too anxious to talk about it."

"I can well understand," she answered, hoping her expression would convey her sympathy.

For several minutes, no one said a word. Christopher took up a second doughnut while G.W. nursed his coffee. Deborah had a million questions for Christopher, but she knew that now wasn't the time. There was no comfort in reliving such awfulness.

"Well, hello, Dr. Clayton. I didn't realize you were here," Mother said, coming into the kitchen. "Have you come to see my grandbabies?"

"I have," he said, getting to his feet. "And to eat your doughnuts."

She put her hands on her waist and eyed him quite seriously. "Did Deborah tell you that I was going to send her into town this morning with a batch for you?"

He looked at her as if he'd caught her walking out with another man. "She said nothing."

Deborah shook her head. "I would have gotten around to it. I figured you were more interested in eating than hearing about my plans for the day."

"If your plans involve bringing me your mother's doughnuts, it's only right that you share the news upon my arrival," he replied.

"Well, I'll certainly know better next time," Deborah said, then added with a teasing smile, "If there is a next time. One can never tell."

Deborah accompanied Christopher back to town, slowly driving the wagon while he let his horse amble alongside. She wanted to say something about what he'd shared earlier, but she didn't want to make him uncomfortable.

"Christopher, I'm sorry that things are so difficult for your mother. Is there nothing that can be done?"

He rode in silence for a moment, then looked at her. She had never seen such pain in his eyes. "She won't allow for anything to be done. My father is dying before her eyes, wasting away in a bottle of whiskey that, ironically, she supplies him. Yet, to refuse would be worse for her still. I can't imagine the dilemma she endures on a daily basis."

"I can see why you don't like to talk about your family, but I hope you know it does nothing to change how I feel about you."

He stopped the horse, forcing her to halt the wagon team. He drew up even with her and asked, "And how do you feel?"

She smiled. "I thought that was quite evident. I admire you greatly and enjoy spending time at your side."

"And that's all?"

Deborah grew a bit uncomfortable. "I try to guard my feelings as best I can."

His brow furrowed. "But why?"

"I suppose," she said, staring down the road, "that it's because of the agreement between us. Given your obligations to your family, I know that you do not intend to marry anytime soon . . . and I find that I am easily given to thinking on just such things if I'm not careful."

"I thought young women liked to dream about their wedding day."

She fought to keep tears from her eyes. He couldn't possibly understand how it was for her. She had come to love him so completely that to know she couldn't yet count on their marriage was the most painful thing she had ever endured.

"Deborah?"

She looked at him and offered a smile she did not feel. "I like to dream on things that I know will come about."

"You doubt that we have a future?"

A hint of breeze brought a bit of relief from the heat, and Deborah took the opportunity to take off her wide-brimmed hat and let the air dry her sweat-dampened hair. "A future with you still seems too distant to spend any time in speculation and dreams," she finally answered. "I'm a practical woman—you've always known that. Daydreaming and pretending that I can make things happen any sooner isn't a good way to spend my time."

"And what is?" He sounded almost hurt.

Deborah fixed her hat back in place and picked the reins back up. "Exactly what I'm doing. Learning everything I can. Growing closer to God and getting to know you better. I'm not unhappy, Christopher, if that's your concern."

He narrowed his eyes just a bit. "You wouldn't lie to me, would you?"

"Certainly not." She smiled, hoping it might relieve his mind. "I agreed to court you, knowing that your family had to come first. I spent a lifetime feeling much the same way about mine, so I understand your position. Please don't think I've changed my mind."

He smiled and eased back in the saddle. "I'm glad. I thought there for a minute, I might have to give you another kiss to persuade you."

She laughed and slapped the reins. "I'm already persuaded, but it never hurts to reevaluate my stand." Despite his laughter, a part of her said there were still too many secrets between them. Too many obstacles to allow for true love to grow. She prayed it wasn't so, but doubt still lingered.

Deborah had just finished her shopping at the commissary when she spied a young woman and older gentleman approaching from the boardinghouse. For a moment, she didn't trust her eyes. Perhaps she'd had too much heat for one day. She looked again, however, and could see that she'd been right.

She put the last of her packages into the wagon bed and hurried to greet the young woman. "Jael?"

"Deborah! How wonderful. I was just asking Father to find your house for me. He was going to check with the man at the store."

The two women embraced and drew apart once again to study each other. Deborah was amazed at how perfectly coiffed and gowned her college friend was. Of course, Jael had never been one for simplicity, but the pink-and-white bustled gown looked better suited for a party than a trip to a sawmill commissary.

"You look wonderful," Deborah declared.

"Are you terribly surprised to find me here?" Jael asked, laughing. "I can scarcely believe it."

"I am surprised, but I knew that your father and husband had become partners with Mr. Perkins. I dared to hope you might accompany them here one day, but hoping was as far as I got. I figured to mention it the next time you wrote."

"Which, I'm sorry to say, has been so infrequent," Jael replied. She looked at her father and smiled. "We've all been so very busy. Father and Stuart decided to make a trip to Houston, and I insisted they bring me along. I actually threatened to come on my own once they departed, if they didn't bring me."

Deborah looked to Jael's father, who nodded. "It's true; she did. I knew better than to threaten her or encourage Stuart to do likewise. Once Jael sets her hat for something—that's the last of it."

Jael patted the old man's face with her gloved hand before turning back to Deborah. "You look so slender and lovely. I am so jealous. I could never hope to have a waist as small as yours."

Deborah laughed. "It comes from all the bending I do in the garden." She smiled at Jael's father. "Mr. Longstreet. It's been some time since I last saw you." Deborah started to comment that it had been upon the occasion of Lizzie's intended marriage to Stuart, but she caught herself just in time. "Will you be in the area for long?"

"It will depend on how our business shapes up," he replied. "I've come to finalize some matters with Mr. Perkins. Most likely, it will take us a week or more."

"Then you must come and stay with us. We live several miles north on the main road. We're the only house out that far. We added on earlier this year, and there is more than enough room."

"Oh, Father, might we?" Jael looked at him, hopeful. "The bed at the boardinghouse is ever so hard."

He looked at his daughter, then back at Deborah. "I need to be here to oversee business. Miles away from town will do me little good."

"Well, it would definitely let you sleep in better air," Deborah replied.

"I have no objection to Jael going to stay with you."

Jael beamed him a smile. "Thank you, Father. I shall be so happy to be occupied while you are busy. I'm sure Deborah and Lizzie will happily fill me in on all the news."

"Starting with the fact that Lizzie was delivered of twins last month," Deborah replied.

"Twins? How marvelous. Oh, but I can hardly wait to see them."

"Come with me now, then," Deborah told her. "I was just heading home. We can stop by the boardinghouse for your things."

Jael smiled and pushed back her dainty reddish blond curls. "That would suit me just fine. You don't mind do you, Father?"

"Not at all," he said, seeming almost relieved. "I will take myself on to the mill."

"Do join us for supper, Mr. Longstreet. You can take this road and follow it north. You will come upon our place after several miles. As I mentioned, we're the only house that far out. Mr. Perkins can give you directions. The house is quite large with a huge porch, and there is a plain picket fence that skirts the roadside of the yard and across the front."

"What time should I come?" he asked.

"Six o'clock would be fine. We will most likely eat a little after that, and hopefully the temperature will have cooled some."

He nodded. "I would be quite happy to join you. Until then, ladies." He tipped his hat and turned to make his way to the mill.

Deborah looked at Jael and couldn't help but giggle. "It will be just like old times."

But Jael's face had sobered considerably with her father's departure. "I can't promise that, I'm afraid. My life is hardly the same."

Chapter 16

"We're fixin' to go to town. Are you sure you gals are gonna be all right?" G.W. questioned.

Deborah shooed him toward the door. "We'll be fine. Mother and Sissy need you much more than we will. We have to catch up on the past."

G.W. looked skeptical, but finally nodded and turned. "We'll be back before it gets too late."

"And be sure to remind Mama to have Mr. Longstreet come for supper," Deborah called after him, since business had kept him from joining them the night before.

Once G.W. was gone, Deborah turned back to Jael and Lizzie. Each held a baby and was happily engrossed in conversation. Now they could finally get down to hearing the details of why Jael had made the choices she'd made.

"So now that we're alone," Jael said without prompting, "I suppose you are both determined to know the reasons for my marriage to Stuart."

"Well, you have to admit, it was a rather shocking thing to spring on us," Lizzie said, putting baby Rutger to her shoulder.

"Yes, we were quite stunned," Deborah added. "You had tried to talk Lizzie out of marrying him, but we didn't think it was so you could catch him for yourself." She smiled to let Jael know she was just teasing.

Jael offered Deborah the baby girl before continuing. Deborah cuddled Emily close and took a seat near Lizzie. Jael smoothed the skirt of her stylish day dress and looked up to smile.

"Well, the story is not a very nice one. You know I had my heart set on Mr. Remington. And for a time I thought he, too, had his designs on me. Unfortunately, I gave of myself too freely and found myself in a family way."

Lizzie's eyes widened. "Oh, Jael, that must have been terrifying."

"It was. As you know, my oldest sister, Justine, found herself in the same situation, and Father dismissed her from the family for bringing them shame when the young man refused to marry her."

Lizzie and Deborah nodded. The story was indeed a sad one. When Mr. Longstreet had sent his daughter away in shame, Justine was unable to bear her grief and took not only her own life, but that of her unborn child.

"Well, I couldn't let that happen to me," Jael continued. "I knew Father would be livid, although I wondered if he might be more forgiving in order to avoid a repeat of what happened before. But

I couldn't work up my courage, and so I went to Ernest and told him I was expecting. At first, he was all compassion and agreed we would marry immediately. He said we would travel abroad and have the child there so no one would know exactly when the baby had been born. I thought it a perfect solution. Then the next thing I knew, he sent me a letter telling me he was on his way to England—alone—and was sorry that he couldn't bid me good-bye in person. There was never any mention of an engagement, because we never had formally announced such a thing. He merely escaped his fate and left me to mine."

"How hard that must have been," Lizzie said, shaking her head.

"Oh, Jael, you should have known you could have come to me—to us here in Texas," Deborah declared.

"I thought about that, believe me. I was preparing to consider just such a thing when Stuart returned from having seen you here. He stopped by to do business with Father, and when Father was called away for nearly an hour, I was left to entertain him. We talked about what had happened when you left him at the altar, Lizzie. I hadn't realized that his inheritance was tied up in marrying, but he was in great despair over what might happen. I took that moment to tell him that I, too, bore a great burden."

Jael let out a heavy sigh. "I told him about Ernest and the baby. He was livid that the man was such a cad. I told him his problem and mine were very similar, for once Father learned of my condition, he would disinherit me. Stuart was the one who suggested we help each other. Please understand—he was kind and gentle with me. He didn't pretend that he loved me, and neither did he expect me to pretend that I loved him. At least not privately. He asked that I be an attentive and loving wife in public, and that seemed easy enough. After all, he was coming to my rescue."

"Oh, but, Jael, to live in a loveless marriage . . ." Lizzie said with tears in her eyes.

Deborah could see that Jael wanted badly for them to understand, and she knew how that felt. Sometimes a person's choice never seemed justified until it received the approval of those around you—those you loved.

"Many people marry as if it were business, Lizzie. We cannot condemn our friend for her decision."

"But what now?" Lizzie asked. "What of the baby?"

Jael bit her lower lip for a moment. Deborah thought it looked like she might cry and reached over to pat her arm. Jael raised her head. "I lost it. After two months, I miscarried. Few people knew about it, and those that did thought it was Stuart's. You see, when Father returned that day, we told him our plans to elope. He was surprised, but not upset. He thought it very fine that I should marry into such a good family—especially to a young man with whom he did business and could trust implicitly."

"What happened between you and Stuart after you lost the baby?" Deborah asked.

"Really, he did nothing. He consoled me, told me how sorry he was that I should be inconvenienced, but added that we could one day have our own children." She looked at Lizzie and Deborah. "He was neither overly kind nor meanspirited about any of it. That, in fact, has been our marriage. We both needed each other in order to keep our reputations and social standing in place. I'm not sorry for my choice, but I am sorry that I did not consider how difficult it would be to live without love."

Tears ran down Lizzie's cheeks, and Rutger began to fuss as though he knew his mother was upset. Emily didn't like that her brother was unhappy and joined him. Deborah soothed her while Lizzie began to rock Rutger in her arms.

"I'm sorry. I didn't mean to be all weepy," Lizzie said, regaining control. "I feel that you have suffered—not only in marrying a man you did not love, but with the loss of your child. I would never have wished it on you, Jael, and yet I feel by rejecting Stuart, I have had a part in . . . well . . ."

"You had no part," Jael said firmly. "I made my choice based upon my need. If Stuart hadn't been agreeable and available, I still don't know what I might have done. Besides him, you two are the only ones who know the truth, and I'd like for it to stay that way."

"Of course." Deborah looked to Lizzie and then back to their friend. "It is your secret, and we shall keep it."

"I just wanted to explain my decision. I figured you both thought me quite out of my senses." She smiled. "I suppose there for a while, I was."

Lizzie relaxed, and so did Rutger. She seemed to choose her next words with great care. "So what . . . does the future hold . . . for you?"

Jael picked at the lace on her sleeve and refused to meet their gazes. "I'm not sure how to answer that."

"You mentioned that Stuart talked of having children together," Deborah threw out. "How do you feel about that?"

Jael finally looked up. "I want to have children. I'm hoping that somewhere along the way, Stuart and I actually might come to care for each other. Perhaps children would help that matter."

"Oh, Jael, do be cautious," Lizzie warned. "It's not a good idea to expect that a third person can spark affection between two people. Children often get used by their parents—look at what happened with me. My mother and father held no affection for each other and very little for me. Well, I suppose that's not fair. Father loved me, but he was unavailable to me. Mother loved her cause. Don't suffer a child to bring together a bad marriage."

"The marriage isn't so very bad," Jael replied. "It's more . . . well, it's rather boring. Stuart spends little time in my company, and I certainly haven't a mind for the things that hold his interest. I spend my days doing mostly as I please, and on occasion, Stuart comes to my bed." She blushed and added, "Although those occasions are infrequent, and always for his benefit."

Deborah could see that Lizzie was trying hard to hide her feelings. Likely they were both feeling the same emotions—sorrow . . . despair . . . grief—for their friend. The idea of being married to someone who so rarely shared one's company appalled Deborah. It only served to remind her of how much she wished she could be with Christopher. She thought of their conversation some time back when she'd assured him she was fine in waiting until the day he was free to marry her. That had been true at the moment, but sometimes it wasn't.

"As for the future," Jael said, seeming to lighten up a bit, "Father and Stuart are actually talking of moving to Houston. Business transactions here in the West have profited them greatly, and they are anxious to be near their investments."

"Houston isn't so terribly far," Deborah said. She couldn't begin to imagine what G.W. would have to say about it, but then again, perhaps Stuart and G.W. could now get along. Especially since losing Lizzie hadn't cost Stuart his inheritance.

Lizzie seemed to be on a different thought. "I am surprised you were allowed to accompany them."

Jael nodded. "I insisted. It was really the first time Stuart had seen me assert myself. I told them that since they were planning to be gone for a great many weeks, I should accompany them.

"Then I added that if they were serious about moving to Houston, it was only right I see the place that had so enthralled them. I also pointed out that I should have a say in the house we might purchase. After all, I would spend most of my time there."

"And so they were in agreement?" Lizzie asked.

"At first not so much, but when I threatened to follow the day after they left, they changed their minds."

"And what did Stuart say about your . . . uh, determination?" Deborah braved the question that she knew was on both her and Lizzie's mind. Stuart was not one to graciously consider challenges to his authority.

Jael eased back in the chair. "He came to me that night and told me he didn't like being forced into anything. I told him neither did I. I reminded him I had friends not far from Houston, and that frankly, I would enjoy a visit. He brought up that you were his enemies, but I told him that was nonsense—that just because Lizzie found someone to marry for love didn't mean he should condemn her for such an action. Not everyone was stuck in our situation."

She paused and shook her head ever so slightly. "I was actually surprised Stuart was taken aback by my comment. He actually asked me if I was unhappy."

"That is surprising," Lizzie replied. "Stuart never used to care whether I was happy or not."

"It's true," Deborah said. "Maybe Stuart has feelings for you, after all."

"I think he's grateful to me. He knows I helped him out of a difficult situation. I told him it wasn't so much a matter of true unhappiness, but rather discontentment—a sort of displacement. I felt a sense of loss from the baby and from ideals and dreams I had once believed in—a loss of innocence, if you would."

Deborah could hear something else in Jael's tone. Was it longing? Regret?

"But I mostly wanted to make sure my presence wouldn't make you uneasy, Lizzie," Jael said, changing the subject. "If it does, I'll go. My desire to see you both and enjoy your company is not nearly as strong as my need to make certain we remain friends. If distance is the only way to accomplish that, then I will regretfully go."

"No!" Lizzie declared, startling Rutger. He had just nodded off to sleep and for a moment stared up at his mother before closing his eyes once again. Lowering her voice, Lizzie continued in a calmer tone. "Our friendship is far more important than what's between me and Stuart. In time, perhaps we can meet socially and he will not be ill at ease, but even so, it would never have anything to do with you."

Deborah agreed. "She's right. We are more than friends—we are like sisters, and that bond will not be easily severed."

Despite G.W.'s misgivings, Euphanel and Sissy made their way to meet Zed Perkins at the sawmill. Euphanel assured her son she was going, either with him as an escort or without.

"Miz Vandermark, I must say this is a surprise," Zed said, coming from his office. "Won't you step in here? It's marginally cleaner and a little quieter."

Euphanel followed him into the office with Sissy and G.W. behind her. She took the seat Zed offered and smiled. "Thank you so much."

"It's a hot one today, and I had Miz Greeley bring me over some sweet tea and ice. Would you care for a glass?"

"That sounds wonderful," she admitted. Looking to Sissy, she asked, "What about you?"

Sissy glanced up to where Mr. Perkins stood. It was clear to Euphanel that she feared his reaction to the invitation. White women were offered refreshments, but black women were ignored. To ease the woman's concern, Euphanel spoke. "I'm sorry. Where are my manners? I presumed you would have enough for all of us."

"Of course," Zed said, not acting the least bit put out. "The invitation was extended to each of you."

Sissy seemed to breathe a sigh of relief. She nodded. "I'd be mighty grateful."

"Me too," G.W. said, limping over to his mother, "but I need to head on over to see the doc. Mr. Perkins, could I impose upon you to escort my mother and Sissy to the commissary after they conclude their business here?"

"Certainly," Zed replied. "It would be my honor."

G.W. excused himself, closing the office door behind him, while Zed went to get the ice and tea. Euphanel waited until he'd returned and she'd taken a sip of the tea before picking up the conversation. "This is quite good. Thank you so much. Now, I suppose you're wondering as to why we've come."

"I was rather curious," the older man admitted.

"It's been over five months since we lost George and David. In that time, no one has come forward to speak on the matter or offer any witness or hearsay on who the culprits might be. In my deep frustration over this matter, I've decided to offer a reward for information."

"Now, Miz Vandermark, I don't know as that's a good idea."

"Zed Perkins, you have had this matter in hand for all this time. I see no other ideas being shared or suggested." Euphanel's temper began to flare. "If this had been the murder of white men, the man or men would have been caught and hanged by now."

"Look, I know the unfairness of it all," Zed began. He hooked his thumbs in his vest pockets, which only served to draw attention to his pudgy midsection. "We have sought the murderers. We've asked questions of the law officials in the surrounding counties. Every county has had some sort of trouble from the White Hand of God, but no one seems to know who the men are or what they're planning next."

"Then our community is truly at the mercy of killers? This happened just after the war, and good men refused to sit still for it. It's a sin, and you know it. If we don't take a stand again, it will only continue. Money always loosens tongues with these sorts. I'll stake a twenty-dollar reward for information that leads to the capture of these men."

Zed frowned. He paced back and forth a moment, then finally took a seat behind his desk. "Miz Vandermark, I wish you wouldn't. I fear it will only stir up problems."

"Problems?"

He nodded and continued. "You go wavin' around that kind of money—especially in a company town—and there's going to be trouble. Folks will be inclined to lie about what they know."

"That's why the money is contingent upon the men being caught. If the information doesn't lead to such an arrest, the informant will not be paid."

"That's all well and good, Miz Vandermark, but the men who call themselves the White Hand of God are smart. They ain't been caught yet, and they've been practicin' their misdeeds for some time."

"And that is a good reason for moving forward instead of doing nothing," she insisted.

Zed scratched his cheek. "I think it will only bring more danger to our community."

Euphanel looked at him oddly. "How so?"

"Well, like I said, those fellas appear to be smart. What's to stop one of them from bearin' false witness—setting up a situation so it looks like an innocent man is to blame?"

That possibility had never occurred to Euphanel. "Well, there would have to be evidence."

"But don't you see? Who better to give evidence—or worse still, hide evidence—to support their claim? It would be simple enough for the White Hand of God to do something that underhanded and then the wrong person will hang."

"Ain't no white man gonna hang for killin' a black man, anyhow," Sissy muttered. "Miz Euphanel, this were a mistake."

Turning to Sissy, Euphanel shook her head. "It's not a mistake—or a lost cause. There has to be something we can do."

Zed got up and came back around. "We are keepin' our ears and eyes open to the matter, but frankly, I think you need to accept that we most likely won't ever know the truth of who killed those men."

A knock sounded from behind them. Euphanel turned to see a well-dressed man standing at the open door. "Pardon me if I'm interrupting."

"Mr. Longstreet, we were just concluding our discussion," Zed replied, looking quite relieved.

Euphanel got to her feet and Sissy did likewise. "Mr. Longstreet, you must be Jael's father."

He smiled and gave a bow. "I am indeed, but you have me at a disadvantage."

"I'm Euphanel Vandermark. Deborah's mother."

"Mrs. Vandermark, it is a pleasure." He once again bowed. When he glanced back up, Euphanel felt as though he were assessing her from head to toe. His study caused her cheeks to grow hot.

"I hope you will do us the honor of joining us for dinner this evening. Zed, you and Rachel are invited to come, as well."

"It's a rarity when I pass up one of your meals, Miz Vandermark," Zed replied. "We'll be happy to join you and will bring Mr. Longstreet. If that agrees with him."

Mr. Longstreet gave his hat a twist. "I'd be honored to share the company of such a beautiful woman."

Euphanel didn't know quite how to respond. She looked at Sissy and then Zed. "Well, I will expect all of you this evening around seven. Hopefully the house will have cooled somewhat by then."

"We'll be there," Zed told her.

Longstreet's grin danced all the way up to his cocoa brown eyes. "I will count the hours until then," he said in a husky voice.

Although the office was roasting in the July heat, Euphanel actually felt a chill climb her spine. The man was dashing and charming, unlike most anyone she'd ever met. She felt like a silly schoolgirl again.

"Let's be on our way, then, Sissy," she said, fighting her feelings of confusion.

"I'll walk you to the commissary as I promised." Zed motioned to Mr. Longstreet. "Please have a seat, and I'll be right with you."

As they crossed the street to the commissary, Euphanel dismissed Zed and took Sissy's arm. "Goodness, but it's a hot day."

"Ain't jes' the day what got heat in it," Sissy replied. "That Mr. Longstreet done put off his own sparks."

Euphanel looked at her friend in surprise. "I thought I was imagining that."

"No, ma'am. It were like the devil hisself offering Eve the apple." She smiled. "Best be warned—we know what done happened to Eve."

"We certainly do."

Chapter 17

Mother's announcement that their supper would include Christopher gave Deborah a reason to give special attention to her appearance. She decided to dress carefully in a beautiful gown lent her by Jael. Garner's extra fine sateen flowed in a regal waterfall over the small collapsible bustle Deborah had chosen.

"It's really designed for the larger bustles," Jael had told her, "but I think this looks just fine—it lays surprisingly well."

Giving a turn, Deborah praised the moderately low-cut gown. "I haven't worn anything this grand since Philadelphia." She gently fingered one of the lavender ruffles that had been trimmed in peacock blue. All of this had been set atop a white sateen foundation. "I'm also glad it has the shorter sleeves. I would surely have fainted from the heat if they were long."

Jael laughed. "I suppose the heat is something I shall have to get used to if we move to Texas. Of course, Philadelphia can be quite stifling. Father always had us go to Newport during the heat of the summer. I don't suppose he'll do likewise if we move here."

"That would be quite an expensive venture," Deborah said, still studying her profile in the mirror. "This makes me look so thin. I hope Mother won't be worried."

"And that's without having to even cinch up your corset very tightly." Jael assessed her friend. "You look beautiful, Deborah. Now come here so I can put the final pins in your hair. The curls we gave you are going to look lovely once we get them arranged."

Half an hour later Deborah walked into the front parlor. The men got to their feet, and Christopher gazed at her as if seeing her for the first time.

"Got yourself all gussied up, I see," Rob declared.

"You're gonna make the rest of us feel a bit shoddy," G.W. said, then noted his wife's transformation and nodded toward her. "'Cept for Lizzie, of course, and Miss . . . Mrs. Albright." The name came slowly, but nevertheless was acknowledged.

"Jael and Lizzie never look shoddy," Deborah declared. "Jael let me borrow this gown, and I must say, it feels quite wondrous. The material isn't as heavy as I thought it might be."

"It's the height of fashion," Jael commented. "I had it made not long before coming to Texas."

"It's quite grand," G.W. replied, "but probably a bit too formal for pickin' beans."

Jael seemed to think about this for a moment, then nodded. "But perhaps not too out of place for tomatoes."

The men chuckled just as Mother entered the room. "Supper is ready. If we are all assembled, I suggest we make our way to the dining room." She glanced at Deborah. "Goodness, but you girls look exquisite this evening. If I'd known, I would have gussied up a bit." She put a hand to her hair. The long braided coil suited her well.

"You are always beautiful, Mother," Deborah said, leaning over to give her a kiss on the cheek. "It is we three who aspire to reflect your gracious beauty."

Mother shook her head. "Flattery is the mouthpiece of the devil." She smiled and gave Deborah a kiss in return. "Now come along before everything gets cold."

"That'll be the day," Rob said with a hint of humor in his tone. "It's been hot enough to melt metal; I doubt the food will cool off even hours from now."

Mr. Longstreet hurried to Mother's side and offered his arm. "If I might be so fortunate, may I escort you?"

Mother looked rather shocked, but nodded. Deborah quickly caught sight of Uncle Arjan's frown. G.W. escorted Lizzie, while Mr. Perkins brought in his wife. Rob graciously offered his arm to Jael. Deborah stood, waiting for Christopher to offer to do the same for her, but he seemed strangely distant—almost disinterested.

"You'd better grab that little gal's arm before I do," Arjan told him.

Christopher seemed to snap out of his fog at this. "I do apologize. My mind was clearly elsewhere."

Arjan passed by him and spoke in a whisper loud enough for Deborah to hear. "Hard to believe with a gal lookin' that fetchin' that your mind would be anywhere but on her." He threw Deborah a wink, then made his way out of the room.

"You are quite lovely. I was completely taken aback. I've never seen you gowned quite this grand."

Deborah smiled. "I wanted to show you that I clean up good."

"That you do, Miss Vandermark." He came closer and offered her his arm. "Please allow me to escort you to supper."

She grasped the crook of his elbow and nodded. "I would like that very much, Dr. Clayton."

Deborah took her seat and suppressed a frown. Mr. Longstreet only had eyes for her mother, and it didn't bode well with Deborah. She had long been thinking on seeing her uncle and mother married. Now Mr. Longstreet's arrival was disturbing her plans.

Throughout the meal, Deborah could see that Uncle Arjan was also quite unhappy with Mr. Longstreet's focused attention. By the time dessert arrived and praises were sung for her mother's pecan pies, Uncle Arjan looked like he'd been sucking on a sour persimmon. Frankly, it made Deborah want to giggle. Her uncle must be in love to act in such a manner. Perhaps the arrival of another potential suitor would stimulate him to action.

"I am astonished to hear you say that you made this supper yourself," Mr. Longstreet told Mother. "At home, I have a staff of five in my kitchen who do not manage to turn out such delicious food."

"I had help. I have such a wondrous group of women in this house, and each is equally talented. We all had a hand in the creation of this meal."

"Well, not so much me," Lizzie added. "I was busy most of the time with the babies."

"I'm amazed that you don't have a full-time cook . . . and a nanny," Longstreet replied. "Such lovely ladies deserve to have help." He looked at Arjan and added, "Wouldn't you agree?"

"Euphanel's always had whatever she wanted—or needed," Uncle Arjan stated firmly.

"That's right," Mother agreed. "I've always wanted to tend my own home. And Sissy has been here to help. We hired her on long ago and since she's such a dear friend, she's now come to live with us after the death of her husband and son."

"I understand you're a widow, Mrs. Vandermark. I myself am a widower. Jael's mother passed on many years ago."

"And you never remarried?" G.W. asked.

He gave Mother a devilish grin. "I haven't yet found the right woman. Perhaps all of that will change with my move to Texas. I am coming to greatly appreciate Southern ladies."

"So you're for sure movin' here?" G.W. asked.

Deborah wondered if everyone could feel the tension as much as she did. She pretended to focus on the pie, but found it nearly impossible. She had a very quiet and distant Christopher on one side and her blushing mother on the other. At the head of the table, her uncle sat scowling, and beside him, the ever-flirtatious Mr. Longstreet. It hardly mattered where anyone else sat. At the moment, there was a sense of foreboding that things might not turn out well—especially for the latter three.

"I wonder if I might impose upon you for a tour of your property?" Jael's father asked Mother. "I realize it's growing dusky, so we could limit it to the area here around the house. I would love to hear why you chose this land to settle on."

"The boys and I would be happy to walk you around and tell you everything," Arjan said, getting to his feet. "Wouldn't we?" He looked to G.W. and Rob, who nodded in agreement.

"There you are," Mother said as she, too, pushed away from the table. "That will give me time to put things here in order. Deborah, I suggest you and Dr. Clayton enjoy the evening air, as well."

"I'm happy to change my gown and help you, Mother."

"Nonsense," Jael said quickly. "I will help your mother. Now go." She smiled knowingly at Deborah.

Deborah looked to Christopher. "Would you care to take a stroll with me?"

"I would," he said, helping her from the chair.

They made their way outside, pausing on the porch to enjoy the cool of the evening. It was still warm enough that Deborah had no need of a wrap. "Do you suppose we could just sit on the porch swing? I'd hate to get the hem of this gown dirty."

"Suits me," he said. "I rather like sitting beside you. I could detect your lovely perfume throughout the meal. It was intriguing."

"It belongs to Jael," she said, strolling across the porch. "Perfume seems like a senseless novelty for my life. Sateen gowns are much the same. I'm only put together tonight because of her help and mercy."

He helped her to sit on the porch swing, but looked at her oddly. "That bustle is a wonder."

She giggled. "Christopher, you are the most outspoken man. It collapses—if you were wondering. Now come join me."

He did as she commanded, but Deborah couldn't help but feel there was something pressing on his heart. "You've been very quiet all evening. Please tell me what's wrong."

"I didn't say anything was wrong." Bullfrogs and cicadas began a natural symphony of sounds.

"Maybe not in so many words." Deborah eyed him. "But I see it in your expression and feel it in your absence."

"Absence? I've been beside you all evening."

"Maybe in body, but not in mind." She took hold of his hand. "Christopher, what is it? More family trouble?"

He let go a sigh. "One of my brothers. I'm not yet sure what the trouble is, but my mother is worried. I suppose I shall know in due time."

"I am sorry. I know how hard it is when your loved ones are struggling."

Christopher put his hand atop hers and smiled. "You are always quite understanding. I like that about you, Miss Vandermark."

"Why, Dr. Clayton, are you paying me a compliment?"

He looked surprised. "I do so all the time, and well you know it. Do I not admire your ease in learning and retaining medical information? Haven't I spoken of how much I enjoy your company?" He paused. "Not to mention how beautiful you are. Though I might have a few criticisms on a profession level, of course."

"Of course," she said with a hint of laughter.

Across the yard, she could see her brothers and uncle showing Mr. Longstreet the chicken coop. "It would appear Mr. Longstreet is rather captivated by my mother."

"I think it goes without saying."

"I thought Uncle Arjan might well get up and punch the man square in the nose. But maybe it's good that Mr. Longstreet has arrived. After all, if my uncle loves my mother and wants to marry her, it's about time he spoke up."

"What?" Christopher looked at her as if she'd suggested someone commit murder.

Deborah put her hand to her mouth almost immediately. She hadn't meant to speak the latter part aloud. She shook her head and lowered her hands. "Oh, goodness gracious, I shouldn't have said anything."

"Well, you have now, so you might as well come clean. What's this about your uncle and your mother?" he whispered.

"Mother believes he's in love with her—at least that's what others have suggested to her."

"And why would anyone make that presumption?"

Deborah looked over her shoulder and lowered her voice even more. "Mother said that it was because Uncle Arjan has never married and yet has always stayed close to take care of her. Then it also has to do with the way he looks at her."

"But he's said nothing?"

"Not yet," Deborah replied. "But after tonight, it may come sooner than later." She smiled. "It would be wonderful to see my mother happily married again. Then I'd know she had someone to take care of her no matter what—someone to love her."

Christopher said nothing for several minutes, causing Deborah to look at him. "Did I say something wrong?"

He shook his head. "I was just thinking about how much I'd like that for my mother. I keep thinking my other siblings will come to her aid, and yet they don't. My sisters obviously have little say—the ones who are married must do as their husbands wish, the others are too young. My brothers who are old enough and making their own way in the world know how bad the situation is, yet they do nothing but cause grief." He blew out a heavy breath. "I just don't know where it's all headed."

"But God does, Christopher. He is faithful, and He won't leave you or your family. I'm going to be praying for you—that you will have peace of heart and mind. I'll pray, too, for your family." She paused for a moment. "I know it's not generally acceptable to speak of such things, but I have some money saved . . ."

He put his finger to her lips and shook his head. "No. I won't take your money."

She wanted to protest but held her tongue. Christopher got to his feet. "I should head back before it gets too dark."

"I thought you were going to follow the Perkinses' carriage." She stood. "I can't imagine they'll be much longer. Mr. Perkins said he wanted to head back to town early. Why don't I go and check on their plans." She started for the front door but came up short when someone called her name.

"Why, Miss Deborah Vandermark, if you ain't the purdiest gal in all of Texas."

She turned and found a familiar face gazing up at her. "Mr. Wythe. Whatever in the world are you doing here?"

Arjan was never so glad to see anyone leave as he was Mr. Dwight Longstreet. The man was annoying and definitely inappropriate in his conduct. He had flirted all evening with Euphanel and, even as he left, asked if he might come again to check on Jael's comfort. Euphanel didn't even realize his real intention was seeing her again.

The man had nerve, that was for sure. He would also have the freedom to visit while Arjan would be busy in the forest.

"What's eatin' you?" Rob asked as they checked on the mules before calling it a day.

"Oh, I didn't care for the way that Longstreet fella acted with your ma. He wasn't at all respectful."

Rob shrugged. "She didn't seem to mind the attention."

This further irritated Arjan. "She's a lady. Of course she didn't act as if she minded. He was a guest in her house, and she didn't want to make a scene."

"I ain't never known Ma to keep from puttin' a fella or lady in their place, if needed." Rob put the last of the mule harnesses on the wall.

This was the last thing Arjan wanted to hear—mainly because it didn't alleviate his concerns. Rob was right, and Arjan knew it as well as anyone. He'd seen Euphanel over the years stand up to any number of folks. If she had been annoyed by the attention and flattery given her by Mr. Longstreet, she would have made that clear. She'd have done it with grace and eloquence, but she'd have done it.

But she hadn't.

When he realized Rob was watching him, he grew embarrassed. "It's gettin' late."

"Wait a minute, Uncle Arjan. I . . . well, something ain't quite right."

"What do you mean?"

Rob stuffed his hands deep into his pockets. "I don't know. I just feel like something ain't right. I know you care about Ma. You've proven that over and over. Do you think something is wrong with this Mr. Longstreet fella? Are you worried that he might mean Ma harm?"

"Could be," Arjan said, then regretted the words. "I don't know. Maybe I'm just tuckered out."

"Why don't you stay home tomorrow? We're well ahead on our quotas, and I can oversee what has to be done. That way, someone will be here for Ma, just in case. I mean, G.W. is here, but he ain't strong enough to fight off a fella, unless he did it with a gun."

Arjan felt torn. He wanted to do just as Rob suggested, but at the same time, he knew it would look odd. Rob, however, was already assuming he would do as suggested.

"I know I'll feel a whole lot better if you're here, and you can finally have time to put in those shutters you promised Ma."

"Not another house in all of Angelina County has shutters, but if that's what your ma wants—then I figure that's what she should have."

Rob grinned. "It's always best to give Ma what she wants."

And without saying another word, the matter was resolved for him. He would stay home and do odd jobs and keep an eye on the person he cared about most of all.

Chapter 18

The sun wasn't even up when the Vandermark family sat down to breakfast. Arjan offered a prayer, then opened the morning's conversation by inquiring after Jacob Wythe.

"Seems you're a ways from home, Son. What brought you down here?"

Jake grinned and his expression grew mischievous. "Well, sir, I knew the purdiest gals in all the world lived here in this area."

Arjan laughed. "That they do, but ain't it gettin' kind of late in the summer for you to be gone from the ranch?"

The young man's expression quickly sobered, causing Deborah to take note. She'd never thought that something might be wrong. She'd just presumed that Jake had traveled south to secure cattle or do some other piece of business for his family.

"Fact is, my pa sold out. The drought killed off half the herd. There just wasn't water to go around. Grass ain't growin' and the cost of feed was gettin' so high, Pa said he'd had enough."

Deborah felt horrible for him. His mother and father had been born in Texas, and the ranch had been in the family since 1840.

"I'm surely sorry to hear that. What're your folks gonna do?" Arjan asked.

"They sold the land and the last of the cattle for what little they could get and headed to California. I didn't want to leave Texas, and so I'm trying to find a job. I remembered that you folks were running a logging operation and wondered if you might need an extra hand."

"It's mighty dangerous work," G.W. put in.

Wythe smiled. "So's ranchin'."

"He's got a point," Arjan replied. "Still, it will be different from anything you were doing on the ranch."

Deborah felt sorry for Jake and looked to her mother. "I'm sure he's a fast learner. And if you don't need him in the logging camp, then maybe we could put a good word in for him at the sawmill."

"That's a good idea," her mother answered. She turned to Jake. "We are good friends with the owner of the Perkinsville Sawmill. You might want to consider that before taking on logging."

"Pardon my sayin' so, ma'am, but I'd rather work outside. I've spent all my life either in the saddle or on the ground. I don't reckon I'd do so well inside a building."

"Well, I can definitely understand that," Mother replied. "What of it, Arjan? Surely we have need of another worker."

Arjan looked to Rob and G.W., who both nodded. "Seein's as how he's saved Deborah from harm more than once, I figure we owe him at least that much. Rob can show you around the camp today and discuss the various jobs. You may change your mind once you see how much work is really involved."

Mother passed a bowl of grits, and Jake smiled as he took them. "Thank ya, ma'am, and thanks to all y'all for givin' me a chance." He spooned grits onto his plate and passed them to G.W.

Sissy appeared with a huge platter of fried ham steaks and eggs. "Reckon these will fill you boys up." She put the food on the table, then took her seat near Lizzie.

Jake looked rather surprised at this move. He glanced at Deborah with his brows raised.

"This is Sissy. She's a part of our family. Sissy, this is Jacob Wythe."

"Most folks call me Jake or Slim." His words were stilted—almost awkward.

"Any friend of Miss Deborah's is surely my friend," Sissy said, taking the grits from Lizzie.

Mother started the platter around and followed this with a plate of biscuits. Deborah quickly picked up the bowl of gravy and offered it to Jake. "Mother's biscuits and gravy are quite delicious." He nodded and helped himself to a healthy portion.

"Mr. Wythe," Jael began, "Deborah tells me you attended university."

"That's true. But it wasn't for me. Like I said, I don't care to be fenced in. Sitting in classes day after day isn't very satisfying."

"I don't know about that," Deborah interjected. "It may not have been satisfying to you, but many of us quite enjoyed it."

He swallowed the big mouthful of grits he'd just spooned in and nodded. "I apologize if I made that sound as if nobody enjoys school. I forgot that you were quite fond of book learnin'."

"Deborah's definitely supportive of education," her mother said, "although many of our neighbors see no need for such things. We have a good school in town, but there are times when the older children are removed from class to work. Mr. Huebner is a dear friend and the schoolmaster in Perkinsville. He's often left with just a handful of the young girls to teach. We all think it's sad that the boys aren't encouraged to stay in school, but it's the way things are around here."

Mother smiled at Deborah. "However, Deborah has helped her brothers improve their reading skills. They are doing quite well at it, as I hear tell."

Jake looked at Deborah. "Well, if my teachers had been that purdy, I probably would have stayed in school."

Deborah felt her cheeks grow hot and focused on her plate. Much to her further embarrassment, however, Rob had to offer his thoughts.

"She may look decent, but she's a hard taskmaster. In fact, she can be downright mean if she thinks she won't get her own way."

Chuckling, Jake looked at Deborah. "I've seen her riled up a bit, so I don't doubt your words."

"I will not allow you to malign my dear friend," Jael declared. "Deborah is the most giving and compassionate person I know. She's training to be a doctor."

Lizzie leaned forward to look down the table at Jake. "That's right, and while we are quite grateful for the help you extended us in Houston last year, we certainly aren't going to allow you to hurt her."

He leaned toward Deborah and winked. "I had no intention of hurting you."

Deborah didn't want his attention and quickly dismissed him. "Apology accepted. Now, if you don't mind, I'd like to change the subject." She looked past Jake to her mother. "How is the sacred-harp singing coming along?"

Her mother dabbed the napkin to her mouth. "Well, so far it's going quite well. We have quite a few singers who have done this before, so that helps."

"I've even come to enjoy it myself," Arjan announced, looking at Mother.

She returned his gaze for a moment. "And he's been very quick to pick up the particulars."

Deborah wondered if she were the only one who saw the exchange. She glanced around the table, but no one else seemed to have noticed. Or, if they did, they didn't seem to think anything of it.

"I used to sing in the choir at church," Jake threw in.

Mother offered Jake another round of biscuits, but he declined. "Though we do sing hymns for the most part, this is mainly a social event. We get together and sing for the pleasure of it all. In the old days, we would sometimes sing for hours on end, with occasional pauses for food or fellowship. It's a wonderful way to draw a community together."

"We had quite a few square dances up around our place. Folks seemed to prefer dancin' for their entertainment," Jake replied.

"Well, if we know what's good for us," Arjan interrupted, getting to his feet, "we'd best get a move on."

"I thought you were going to stick around here today," Mother said, sounding slightly upset.

"I am," he said with a smile, "but I need to get to work. I know you want those shutters put in place before the next storm threatens to bust up the windows."

Deborah thought she heard a sigh of relief from her mother. The matchmaker within her begged to be given a chance to encourage the feelings brewing between the two.

"Mother," Deborah said, pushing back from the table. "Why don't you assist Uncle with the shutters? Jael and I can help Sissy with the kitchen and Lizzie with the babies. The sooner we get those shutters in place, the better you'll feel."

Arjan spoke up before Mother could respond. "I could use a hand, Euphanel."

G.W. looked at Deborah. She could tell by the look on his face that he was about to volunteer himself. She shook her head and jumped up. "G.W., I wonder if I might speak to you in the office before I get to work here."

His expression showed confusion, but he nodded as Mother agreed to help Uncle Arjan. Rob tossed down the last of his coffee and went to grab his hat. "Come on, Jake. We need to get up to the camp—the mules will be gettin' mean."

Deborah lost no time in heading out of the room. G.W. followed her into the office and closed the door. "What was that all about?"

She wasn't sure what to say. "Ah, I hoped to see Christopher this morning and wondered how your leg is feeling. I'll let him know so that he can evaluate the situation and decide if the exercises are working or if you're overdoing."

G.W. narrowed his gaze. "Deborah?"

"What?" She could see that her innocent tone didn't fool him. He fixed her with a look and crossed his arms, much as their father used to do when waiting for an answer.

Crossing to where he stood, Deborah lowered her voice until it was barely audible. "Mother and Uncle Arjan are in love."

"What?" His voice boomed across the sparsely decorated room.

"Shh." She put her hand to his mouth. "You heard me. Don't shout about it."

He lowered his voice as she took her hand away. "Where did you get that idea?"

"It's quite clear. Just the way they look at each other. Not only that, but haven't you ever wondered why Uncle Arjan never married? He is in love with Mother."

G.W. shook his head. "I can't believe we're having this conversation."

"Then let's not," Deborah replied. "But don't interfere. I think with just a little help, we might see a wedding before summer's end."

Rolling his eyes, G.W. shook his head again. "You need to stay out of it. If they are . . ." He paused and looked over his shoulder at the closed door. "If they are in love," he whispered, "they will figure it out."

"So you don't mind?" she asked, smiling. "Personally, I think it would be marvelous."

He laughed. "I do, too—if it's their idea and not yours."

With Jake close on his heels carrying a double-bitted ax, Rob led the way to the trees they would consider for cutting. The introductions had gone all around to the boys, except for the ones clearing brush near the cutting.

"It's the bull, look sharp!" one man called out to the others.

Jake looked at Rob. "The bull?"

Rob looked back and nodded. "The 'bull of the woods.' That's what they sometimes call the woods boss. I'm the boss today, since Arjan stayed home. 'Course, I'm often the boss for the likes of these fellas, even when he's here."

Jake nodded and Rob pointed the way with his measuring stick. "I like the looks of that big one over there. Let's get to it, boys."

Heading to a tall longleaf pine, Rob gave a look skyward and Jake did likewise. "I'm checkin' to see what the crown is like and what kind of toppin' we might have to be doin'. See, it's my job to figure out exactly where to make the undercut and such so that we can drop that tree down within inches of mark."

"Sounds hard."

"It takes practice," Rob admitted.

"Yeah, but he's the best there is . . . 'ceptin' for G.W.," another man announced.

"Jake, this is Warren Crandel. He's a sawyer. Practically can operate a two-man crosscut by himself."

Warren extended his hand. "You must be the new man."

"Name's Jake," he replied.

"Good to have you," Warren replied. "Days are long, usually ten to twelve hours. Iffen you git home afore dark, it's just 'cause you cheated the bull out of hours."

Jake grinned. "Since I'm temporarily living with 'the bull,' I won't have much of a chance to cheat him out of anything."

Rob shook his head. "We're gonna drop this one, Warren. Get Wolcott to top it off for me while I figure out the wedge cut."

"Will do, Bull."

Rob waited until the men were helping Ashton Wolcott with his gear before squatting down at the base of the tree to evaluate. Jake got down beside him, only to pop back up when Rob moved to the side of the tree and repeated the action. He gazed upward again, trying to tell the list of the trunk. This particular tree was just about as straight as a chopper could want.

Next he stood and walked several paces out from the tree. He glanced around gauging the other trees in the area and the lay of the land.

"We try to spare the seedlings and young trees," he explained. "Unlike some, we want to keep growin' this forest, so we are mighty particular about which trees we cut."

"But most aren't?"

Rob shook his head. "Most have what we call the 'cut-out-and-get-out' way of thinkin'. They are only tryin' to harvest the most wood in the fastest way possible; then they move on to another location, leaving a field of stumps behind. We clear the stumps—that's the reason I brought out the kerosene from the house. Once a tree is felled, we drill a hole as deep as possible and pour kerosene down it to kill the roots. After a while the thing just rots and we can pull out the stumps, easy-like."

He walked around the tree several times, then marked the trunk and walked out through several tall pines to pound a stake in the ground.

"What are you doing now?" Jake asked.

Rob grinned up at him. "I'm markin' where I want the tree to fall. The boys sometimes wager as to whether they can drive that stake into the ground. Mostly they do it, but sometimes they miss."

"Looks like an awful narrow place to put it down. You got trees all around it."

Rob straightened and handed him the mallet. "If they do it right, it won't be a problem at all. Once Wolcott gets the upper section of the tree cut off, you'll get to see firsthand how it works. I'm gonna let Warren show you how things are done."

Jake nodded. "Sounds good to me." He pulled on well-worn leather gloves and squared his shoulders. "I'm ready."

By the time the afternoon light was starting to fade, some ten longleafs had been cut and prepared. In all but one instance, the choppers were able to pound the stake into the ground, so Rob rewarded them with a short day.

"I feel like celebratin', boys. It's Friday and we're well ahead of schedule. I'm callin' it a week. Once we finish loading out the logs, you can head into town. We won't work tomorrow."

A rousing cheer went up from the men, who quickly stepped

up the process of skidding the logs to the train car. In another two hours they were done, anxious to clean up and get to town.

Rob himself was spruced up and standing at the door of the parsonage a short time later. He couldn't help but be unnerved by the beauty of the young lady who greeted him.

"Evenin', Miss Shattuck. I was wonderin' if you cared to take a walk with me, but I see it's gettin' pretty dark." Rob fought to keep his voice steady.

"I have a better idea," she said. "Why don't you come inside and have some cake and coffee. I just poured Father a cup and was getting ready to cut the cake."

He followed her into the house. "Thank you. Thank you, kindly. I reckon that would just about hit the spot."

"Father, look who's come to call," she said, leading Rob into the kitchen. The parsonage was much too small for a separate dining room, but Mara had made a lovely setting in the kitchen. The small table and chairs could manage up to four people and perfectly suited their needs.

"Welcome, Rob. Good to see you. What brings you around?"

To their surprise, Rob didn't reply as they expected. "I had a question about finding God's will."

Mara gave her father a brief glance before heading to the counter. "I'll get your coffee."

"Have a seat, Rob," the pastor directed. "I'll do what I can to help you in this matter."

Rob did as he was told but lost little time in expressing his thoughts. "I've been thinkin' a lot on it, and figure God is after me to do somethin'. I'm just not exactly sure what that is. I think I have an idea, but I want to know without any doubt that it's God's will."

Pastor Shattuck nodded. "I can appreciate that. It's only a fool who doesn't seek the Lord on such matters."

Mara came to the table with the steaming mug. "Would you care for sugar and cream?"

Rob shook his head. "I drink it black. The stronger the better."

She smiled. "I think you'll find this to your liking, then." She walked back to the cupboard and took down some small plates.

Rob turned back to the pastor. "My uncle told me—well, Ma and Deborah told me the same thing—that a fella ought to pray and read up on the Bible. I've been doing that quite a bit, and I'm still not sure."

"Some things take time, but you can rest assured that the Lord has thoughts on what He wants for you." He took hold of his Bible and opened it. "Here in Jeremiah, chapter twenty-nine, verse eleven, it says, 'For I know the thoughts that I think toward you, saith the Lord, thoughts of peace, and not of evil, to give you an expected end.'" Pastor Shattuck looked up. "Do you understand that passage?"

"I reckon so," Rob said. "Seems to me it means that God wants to make us hopeful about our days. He's tellin' us that He doesn't want evil for us—and that He has an expected way for things to turn out."

Pastor nodded as Mara put down plates of cake in front of them. "This is your mother's lemon cornmeal cake recipe," she told Rob.

"Thank you. It's one of my favorites."

She went back for forks and napkins, then joined them at the table. "Would you mind if I share this conversation?"

Rob shook his head and got to his feet to help her with the chair. "Not at all."

"If he doesn't mind, I surely don't," her father replied.

Mara situated herself and smiled. "One of my favorite verses is in the first chapter of James. 'If any of you lack wisdom, let him ask of God, that giveth to all men liberally, and upbraideth not; and it shall be given him.' He goes on to caution that we should ask in faith, believing that God will answer and that we not be wavering."

Rob considered the words. "I've been askin', that's for sure."

"And what is God telling you?" Pastor Shattuck asked.

"Well, that's the thing," Rob began. "I felt like He wanted me to learn to read better—maybe learn more than I already knew. So my sister has been helpin' me with such things. I've mostly been readin' on the Bible, and because of that, I feel sort of like maybe God wants me to do somethin' more than loggin'."

"Such as?"

Mara remained silent, but Rob could sense a quiet intensity in the way she listened. He shrugged. "Well, that's the problem. I'm not entirely sure. Sometimes I think maybe He wants me to become a preacher like you."

Mara gave a sharp intake of breath, but when Rob turned she looked perfectly at ease. She smiled and asked, "More coffee?"

Rob shook his head and rubbed his jaw. "I don't know how a fella tells what's God sayin' somethin' to his heart and what's just his own self wantin' such a thing."

"And have you long thought of becoming a pastor?" the older man questioned.

"No. Not a'tall. I figured to be loggin' all my life. My pa figured both of us boys would take over for him and Uncle Arjan. Now I don't feel at all certain about that. Ma says she'd be right proud to have a preacher in the family and that I should do what God's callin' me to do. I just want to be sure it's God doin' the callin'."

"And why would Satan benefit by having you study the Word of God and teach it to others? Seems to me the devil would rather put people away from such notions."

"Well, that's what I figured, too," Rob said. He took a long drink of the coffee.

"I find that fasting and prayer often help me to resolve matters," Mara said. "I will happily fast and pray for you, Mr. Vandermark."

He looked at her in disbelief. "You would? But why?"

She smiled. "Because you want an answer, and I care about you getting that answer."

"Mara's good about that," Pastor Shattuck said, patting her arm. "She's prayed and fasted many a time for me. She's a good woman."

Rob couldn't deny that—not that he wanted to. They finished their cake and coffee, and by the time Rob was headed to the door, Pastor Shattuck excused himself to head over to the church and followed Rob outside.

"Trust the Lord, Son. He will guide your steps," the pastor told him. "Mara, I'll be home in an hour."

Mara stood in the doorway to bid Rob good evening. The soft glow of lantern light cast elusive shadows around them, but Rob felt a nearly uncontainable urge to kiss her. He held back, though, and instead simply studied her for a moment. He had never met another woman like her. She made him feel . . . well, whole.

"I appreciate you bein' willin' to fast and pray for me. It's a kind and generous offer. I still don't understand why you would take on such a task."

Mara smiled and backed up to take hold of the door. "It's what we are to do for one another, Mr. Vandermark. And I have a vested interest. When God gets through showing you what all you need to do for Him, then I will benefit, as well."

"How's that?"

She began to close the door, but murmured, "Because then He will see us become man and wife."

Chapter 19

August 1886

On Sunday, the first of August, Deborah waited outside the church to speak with Christopher. She'd not seen much of him in the past few days, and though she had been free to assist him in his rounds, he had refused or simply not been available to explain.

"Are you avoiding me?" she asked as he started to head toward his house.

He looked at her, his expression rather pinched. "I'm sorry. I've just been dealing with several matters." He paused and shook his head. "Look, I can't explain just now, but I won't be able to use your help in the next few weeks."

"But why?" She crossed the short distance. "Have I done something wrong?"

He shook his head. "No. Certainly not." He glanced up and Deborah could tell someone was approaching. "I can't talk about it right now." With that he departed just as Jael came up to join her.

"What was that all about?" her friend asked.

"I honestly don't know." Deborah watched Christopher disappear from view. "But hopefully I'll soon find out."

She was still pondering Christopher's words the following Saturday. Deciding that enough was enough, Deborah told her mother she was going to take Jake into town to meet Mr. Perkins and also so that she could speak with Dr. Clayton about making rounds next week.

"Jake went to get the carriage ready," she told her mother in the summer kitchen. Sissy bent over a big mixing bowl and threw her a smile.

"Goin' a-courtin'?"

"Not exactly," Deborah replied. "I do plan to see Dr. Clayton, but it may not be all that pleasant."

"Well, if you're going to see Dr. Clayton, be sure to take him these corn cakes. Remind him they're awfully good with molasses. That should sweeten the matter."

Deborah took the cloth-wrapped bundle from her mother. "I doubt I'll have to remind him." She made her way to the barnyard and found that Jake was still harnessing the horses. The growing heat made Deborah irritable, and that, coupled with Christopher's strange actions and Jake's increasing attentions, made her want to run and hide in the forest.

Spotting her uncle inside the barn, Deborah climbed up on the carriage to set down the corn cakes. "I need to speak with Uncle Arjan for a minute. I'll be right back."

"I'll be fixin' to go when you are," Jake replied.

Deborah entered the barn and felt the temperature drop only

slightly. Her uncle was forking hay into the stall of one of the milk cows. They had just sold her latest calf, and the animal was rather forlorn.

"Poor Dottie," Deborah said, stroking the cow's face. The mother cow gave a mournful call for a calf that was long gone. "She sure misses her baby."

Uncle Arjan stopped what he was doing. "I see Jake's gonna drive you into town."

"Yes. He asked me to show him around. He wanted to see the sawmill, and Mr. Perkins said today would be best."

Uncle Arjan leaned on the pitchfork handle and smiled. "I suppose you'll be seein' that young man of yours."

"Well, I hardly know if he's mine," she snapped. Feeling rather embarrassed by her comment, Deborah smiled. "Sorry. I feel out of sorts today."

He nodded. "I can understand that. I feel that way a great deal of the time."

Deborah looked at him for a moment. For the life of her, she couldn't remember what she'd come to talk to him about. Frowning, she started to explain, but her uncle was already speaking again.

"I think each person has someone out there that the Good Lord intends to see them spend their life with. When the time isn't yet come and those folks are separated, I think there's a powerful longin' to set things right."

Deborah cocked her head and without thinking said, "Like you and Mother?"

Arjan straightened and looked at her as if he hadn't heard right.

"Uncle Arjan, I . . . well, most all of us can see that you love Mother. The thing is, I believe she loves you, as well. I do wish you two would stop being so respectful of each other and just get the words said."

"I . . . well, I guess I didn't expect . . ." He stopped and fixed Deborah with a narrowing gaze. "Do you really think she feels that way?"

Deborah laughed. "I do. Now, look—you did not hear that from me." She stepped forward and kissed her uncle on the cheek. "You've always been a part of my life, like a second father. Why not make it official? If you don't, it seems that Mr. Longstreet may well try to join our family."

She didn't wait for him to comment but hurried back to the carriage where Jake stood to assist her. Taking her seat, Deborah couldn't keep from grinning. She was rather glad her uncle's own words had opened the door for her to say what she did.

"You look like the cat what swallowed the bird," Jake said, taking up the reins.

"I'm just happy, is all."

"And is part of that happiness on account of your spending the day with me?" he asked hopefully.

Deborah could see that she needed to set yet another matter straight. "Jake, I'm courting Dr. Clayton. He's my beau."

"But you ain't engaged."

"No, we aren't, but our courtship is with marriage in mind."

Jake laughed. "Most are, aren't they?"

"Well, I just don't want you getting the wrong idea."

"I think until there's a ring on your finger, I have just as good a chance as he does in winning you over."

"That's a very bold thing to say. I think—" She fell silent at the sight of another buggy coming in from the road. "Oh my."

"What's wrong?" Jake looked at the well-dressed driver.

"Mr. Albright," Deborah said.

"I've come for my wife," he replied curtly. "Would you be so good as to get her?"

Deborah nodded, and Jake tied off the reins and helped her down. She heard Jake introduce himself to Stuart as she hurried toward the house. Jael wasn't going to be overly happy at this news. She had only said that morning what a peaceful blessing it had been to be with the Vandermarks and how she wished to remain here forever.

"Jael, you need to come quickly," Deborah called.

Her friend scurried into the foyer from the front sitting room. "What's wrong? I thought you were headed to town."

"I was, but Stuart's here. He said he's come for you."

Jael sobered and stiffened. "Very well. I knew it was only a matter of time. Tell him he may come get my trunk. I have it nearly ready. Father had already told me to expect him."

"Why did you not say anything to me?"

"I didn't want to spoil our time together. I was afraid you would fret and fuss over me." Jael took hold of Deborah's arm. "I'll be all right. In time, I truly believe love will grow and that Stuart will be an attentive husband." With that, she turned and headed up the stairs.

Deborah had no choice but to return outside and give Stuart his instructions. "She asked that you come and retrieve her trunk. She's just now finishing her packing."

Stuart nodded, his icy blue eyes narrowing slightly. "I understand Elizabeth has given birth to twins."

"Yes. Last June. They arrived early, as twins usually do, but they are quite plump and healthy now."

He said nothing for a moment, then secured the brake and climbed down from the carriage. "If you'll direct me."

Deborah led the way into the house but found it unnecessary

to go any farther. Jael was tying on her bonnet as she descended the stairs. "Hello, Stuart. My things are ready and waiting in the room just to the top right of the stairs."

She stepped into the hallway to give him access to the stairs. Without a word, Stuart left the women to their good-byes.

"I will come to call on you in town," Deborah promised. "Please feel free to send word if you need me for anything." She embraced Jael. "If you leave the area, please let me know."

"I promise I will." She smiled as they pulled apart. "Please tell Lizzie and your family good-bye for me and thank them. I have so enjoyed my stay and the hospitality. Hopefully I will be able to visit you from time to time. I know my father would certainly like to see your mother again." Deborah said nothing, and Jael continued. "If nothing else, I will see you in church tomorrow. I might have a better idea of what to expect after I have time alone with Stuart."

Just then Stuart came back down the stairs, a small trunk on one shoulder and a suitcase in the other. "Is this everything?"

Jael moved away from Deborah. "Yes. That's all I brought. The rest is with my father at the boardinghouse."

Stuart exited the house without asking for assistance. He had already secured the luggage and was back waiting to hand Jael up into the carriage when the ladies appeared on the porch. With another quick hug, Deborah let her friend go.

"I will see you tomorrow," she called after Jael.

Stuart turned the horses and headed back out of the yard almost before Deborah could descend the porch steps. The entire matter had taken less than ten minutes.

"You ready to go to town now?" Jake asked, drawing the buggy closer to the house.

Deborah nodded. "Yes, I suppose I am."

They followed Jael and Stuart to Perkinsville, taking care to keep far enough back so the dust could settle. The deeply rutted road was miserably dry, and it seemed all of the earth cried out for rain. Glancing upward, Deborah could barely see the skies through the thickness of pines, but it was clearly void of clouds.

"If you're thinkin' it might rain, I wouldn't get your hopes up. We spent much of the last year doin' that heavenward gawk. Didn't do us any good."

"I haven't had a chance to tell you how sorry I am about your ranch. I can't imagine how you must feel."

"Mostly angry," Jake said matter-of-factly. "Angry that I couldn't do anything to make it right. Angry that God didn't seem to hear our prayers."

"We can't always understand why things happen the way they do, that's for sure," Deborah replied. "Still, we have to have faith that God will keep us in His care—that no matter what happens, He is still in control."

"Sometimes I think that's askin' a lot."

Deborah didn't know what to say, and so she moved the conversation in a different direction. "I do wish it would rain. Uncle Arjan is very concerned about fires. One spark from the train or a carelessly tended fire, and we could have a disaster on our hands."

"That would surely trouble a great many folks."

"It's the dichotomy of living in the Big Piney. You want things damp and moist to keep the fire chances down, but you don't want the storms that bring the rain. If lightning comes with the rain, there's always the possibility that it will strike a forest fire."

"But you seem to really like livin' here," he said, keeping his gaze on the road.

"I do love it here. Texas is my home, and I know most every path and turn in these woods—where the rivers run and where the creeks twist off. When I was gone from here, it was all I could think on."

"I can see why. The forest has an appeal, just like the range. I miss it."

She looked at him in sympathy. "Goodness, but I don't know what I'd do if we had to give up our place."

"It ain't ever easy to lose what you love."

His words made Deborah uncomfortable, and so she settled back into the seat and said nothing more, pretending instead to be completely transfixed by nature. By the time they reached town, Deborah felt pretty certain that Jake's feelings for her ran deep. At one time she might have welcomed his attention. He was a very nice man—quite the gentleman for being raised on a ranch.

"Just stop over there by the commissary," she instructed. "I'll walk you over to the mill."

Once she had Jake tended to, Deborah made a straight path to Christopher's office. Entering the side examination room after knocking, she was surprised to find the room empty. She checked his office and the front waiting room, but there was no sign of him.

"Christopher? Are you here?"

Something drew her attention to the kitchen. It was just a hint of noise that sounded something like the fluttering of paper. Before she could go see what it was, however, Christopher emerged. He looked awful—as if he hadn't slept all night. There were dark circles under his eyes, and his face was pale.

"Are you ill?" she asked, crossing the room.

"Why are you here, Deborah?" His question was curt and to the point.

She stopped and crossed her arms. "Well, that's a fine way to greet someone—especially someone you supposedly care about."

He sighed. "It would be better if you go."

This made her angry. "So we're finished with the courtship? You've given up and are releasing me?"

"I didn't say that." He tossed the letter onto the exam table.

"No, you didn't. You don't say much of anything. I can't read your mind, and you won't share it."

He pointed to the letter. "Read that and then tell me how much you want me to share with you."

Deborah went to the letter and lifted it. "You could just explain what's in here."

"Better you read it for yourself."

Scanning the contents of the letter, Deborah could barely read the script. Apparently it was from someone in Indianola. The letter was brief and to the point.

> *You have been requested to support your brother Calvin Kelleher at his murder trial on the nineteenth of the month of August. He stands accused of killing a man in a saloon fight. Seemed to some to be a case of self-defense, but others are accusing him of provoking the attack. He says you are the only one who can come to his aid.*

She looked up and found Christopher watching her intently. She wanted to ask why Calvin's last name was different than his own but knew that now was hardly the time.

"So do you still see yourself in a courtship with a murderer's brother?"

"Your brother isn't you. You have no reason to bear his shame," she protested.

"You marry a man's family as well as the man," he countered. "My family has murderers and thieves, apparently. My mother tells me in another missive that two of my other brothers are in jail in

Springfield for attempting to rob a bank there." He began to pace and mutter inaudible things to himself.

"Christopher, you cannot let the misdeeds of your family cause you this grief. We must pray for them and do what the Lord would call us to do, but we needn't take it on our shoulders."

"He wants me to come to Indianola. No doubt he wants me to pay for him to have a lawyer and a fair chance. Maybe he even hopes for a character witness. Who can say? I've not seen Calvin in ten years. I went away to study when he was young and when I returned, he had left home with Benjamin and Andrew—the two in jail in Springfield."

Deborah moved toward him, but Christopher held up his hands. "Don't. Don't try to console me. I don't deserve it. If I'd been the man my family needed, I would have been there to see that they had a better time of it."

"You did what you could. They weren't your responsibility—that belonged to your father and mother." Deborah inched closer. "Christopher, you aren't to blame for this. Fact is, it really wouldn't matter who was in error of their upbringing; they are grown men. They make their own choices."

He seemed to calm a bit at this. "I know you're right, but it angers me to see the waste. They were good boys—they were smart. They had a future."

"They still do," she told him. "Maybe Benjamin and Andrew will use this time in jail to straighten out their lives."

"And what of Calvin? He's just twenty. His life has barely begun, and already he may lose it."

Deborah gently touched his arm. "Then you should go to him."

"This will kill our mother. She doesn't even know." His voice broke.

Taking him in her arms, Deborah pulled him close. Christopher buried his face against her straw bonnet and wept silently.

"I'm so sorry, Christopher, but we will see this through together. No matter what, I will be at your side in prayer, even when I can't be with you physically."

For several minutes, she simply held him. She remembered a similar scene many years ago when her father's mother had passed on. It was the only time she'd seen her father cry, and it frightened her. Christopher's tears didn't frighten her; they made her love him all the more. She longed to promise him that the world would right itself, that tomorrow he would awaken to find it all a bad dream. But, of course, that wasn't going to happen.

Deborah barely heard the door open behind her. When she glanced up, she found Maybelle and Annabeth Perkins staring at her with their mouths open. Christopher pulled away from Deborah and exited the room to compose himself. Deborah turned in greeting, as if nothing were amiss.

"Are one or both of you ladies ill?"

Maybelle shook her head, but it was Annabeth, the elder of the two, who spoke. "That was hardly appropriate for us to witness. You were in the doctor's arms."

"Actually," Deborah replied, "he was in mine. He received tragic news regarding family. I was merely offering consolation."

Maybelle giggled and Annabeth shot her a reproving glance. "No matter what his problems might be, it's totally unacceptable for you, a single woman, to be embracing a single man. Especially one whom everyone knows you are courting."

Deborah shook her head. "I'm sorry you feel that social rules should cancel God's. The Bible tells us to bear one another's burdens and offer comfort. I did no more or less, and for you to judge otherwise is wrong."

"We will see what Pastor Shattuck has to say about that."

Knowing the Perkins sisters, half the town would know what she'd done before the sun even crossed the sky. Deborah felt a pang of regret. She wasn't so worried about her own reputation, but Christopher had fought hard to win these people over. Her actions would put him in an unfavorable light, as everyone would assume he was the one to take liberties with her.

Shaking her head, Deborah tried hard not to show her irritation. "You will say whatever you see fit. I have done nothing wrong."

But what bothered her most was that she knew that was a lie. As far as she'd been taught, it was wrong for her to have been embracing Christopher—even in a moment of great sorrow. They weren't even to hold hands in public.

Christopher reappeared, his eyes still red-rimmed, but he'd managed to compose himself. "May I be of assistance to you ladies?"

Maybelle giggled again. "Mother wished for us to extend to you an invitation for dinner," Annabeth told him.

"I must go." Deborah felt more ill by the minute. The consequences of that one moment of oversight would no doubt haunt her for weeks to come. Reputations were easily lost in gossiping communities.

Christopher looked at her, but only nodded. Deborah hurried outside, the voices of the Perkins sisters prattling on about how their parents were entertaining the new partners and wanted Dr. Clayton to meet them over supper.

To her surprise, Jake was waiting for her at the carriage. "Did you have a nice visit?"

"Get in the buggy," she ordered, climbing up without assistance. She took up the reins. "Pull the brake."

He did as she instructed without questioning her actions. Turning the horses, Deborah caught sight of Maybelle and Annabeth standing just outside the doctor's office. Christopher stood behind them, his gaze fixed on Deborah.

"Are you all right? Is somethin' wrong?" Jake asked.

Deborah shook her head and urged the team to pick up speed. "Nothing I want to discuss. Nothing I think you'd understand."

Chapter 20

Rob couldn't shake the memory of the dream—or was it a nightmare?—that he'd awakened to that morning. In the haze of his sleep, he'd seen himself saying good-bye to his family, to Mara. Mother was crying, but he felt that he had her approval for whatever it was he was about to do. That was what bothered him the most. What was it he was doing? Why was he telling them good-bye?

He headed to church with the family. No one seemed to notice his silence, or if they did, they said nothing. He was grateful not to have to explain. How could he tell them when he couldn't figure out what bothered him so much? He'd had bad dreams in the past, but this one seemed different. This one seemed so real that he could almost recall the scent of the air—the feel of Mara's hair as she handed him a ribbon-tied memento.

Seeing her at church only stirred up the memory. He thought of the words she'd said to him—that they would one day marry. He wanted to know how she could just say something like that. They hadn't known each other long at all, yet there was something so unexpected about their relationship. He'd been the wild one—the guy who made himself available to all the girls. He'd had his share of stolen kisses and flowery words. Those kinds of things used to make for pleasant memories. Now, however, they didn't matter. He could think only of Mara.

Once they were back home and lunch had concluded, Rob decided to walk in the woods. Jasper and Lula followed after him. Lula was heavy with pups again but managed to keep up with Jasper just fine.

The day felt more humid than it had in the past months, and he could feel the perspiration form on his neck. A scant few clouds dotted the sky. Rob prayed it was a sign of rain. He hated working with the logs when they were slippery and wet, but the water was much needed. Besides, they were well ahead on their cuts. It wouldn't hurt to take a day or two for other chores. There were always axes and saws to sharpen, equipment to check, and a bevy of other menial tasks to see to that slowed them down when not tended to properly.

He breathed in deeply of the heady pine aroma. He was at home here, yet something seemed to be pulling him away. But where? Shaking his head, Rob studied the road ahead. The paths he walked were well-worn. His mother was always using them to gather herbs or bring the cows home.

Pausing, Rob caught sight of a rabbit scurrying amid the ramble ahead. Jasper and Lula raised a ruckus and took off after it. The rabbit hardly looked big enough to worry after, but that didn't stop the dogs from giving chase. Rob sat down beside a young pine and waited for their return. He had no real destination in mind, anyway. Resting here was just as good as walking deeper into the woods. He leaned back against the tree and gazed skyward. Up through the pine boughs he could see spots of blue with wisps of white.

Rob closed his eyes. *God, I don't know where you're taking me. I don't know for sure what I'm supposed to do, but I have some ideas. You're gonna have to show me, though, iffen for real it's your plan and not just my own.*

Of course the idea of becoming a preacher had never been one of Rob's dreams. Rob remembered breaking out in a cold sweat the first time it had come to mind, in fact. How could he, an unlearned man, share the Word of God?

"Saw you head out this way and figured to catch up to you," Arjan said as he came upon Rob.

Rob opened his eyes with a start. "Somethin' wrong?"

Arjan sat down beside him. "I was about to ask you the same thing. You ain't seemed like yourself for days, but today was particularly bad. I figure there's somethin' on your mind."

"I had a dream last night—kind of a vision," Rob admitted. "I was fixin' to head out—to leave the area. I was telling all y'all goodbye. Ma was cryin' and . . . well, I don't know where I was headed. And it really bothers me."

"Why?"

" 'Cause it felt like the Lord was showin' me somethin' I needed to know. I can't explain it, but when I woke up . . . well, now I think I'm supposed to do somethin'."

Arjan pushed back his hat and scratched his neck. "You've been thinkin' a lot lately."

"True enough. Seems like God's givin' me a lot to ponder." He turned and fixed his uncle with a questioning stare. "Do you believe God speaks to fellas like me? I mean, really talks to them?"

"I reckon so. Bible says that God doesn't change. He talked to men in the Bible, so why wouldn't He talk to us now?"

For several minutes, Rob said nothing. Then he leaned forward. "Mara Shattuck told me that God had plans for her and me to be man and wife."

Arjan grinned. "Well, I'll be. She said that, did she?"

"Yup. Then she closed the door on me and left me to figure it out for myself. Problem is, it just made matters more confusin'."

"So you came out here to sort your love life. I reckon I came out to do the same."

"Ma?"

The single word hung between them. Arjan nodded slowly. "I guess I can't deny my love for her."

"Why would you want to?"

Arjan laughed. "I don't. I guess I just want to ask your permission to ask your ma to marry me."

Rob grinned and raised a brow. "You promise to take good care of her?"

"You know I do—haven't I shown you that by now?"

"Of course you have." Rob got to his feet, and Arjan did likewise. "I'd be right proud to have you marry my ma."

"Think G.W. will feel the same way?"

Rob gave a whistle for the dogs. Arjan stepped in pace with him as Jasper and Lula came bounding out of the woods. "I reckon G.W. will want Ma to be happy, and I know Deborah does."

"Your sister has already given me her blessing," Arjan replied. "She's the one who really made me feel hope about the possibilities."

"When do you plan to talk to Ma?"

Arjan looked up. "I guess there's no time like now."

Rob caught the reason for his words. Ma was coming toward them just now—herb basket in hand, broad-brimmed straw hat on her head. She smiled and waved.

"What are you two doing out here?" The dogs rushed forward to greet her, then tore off in another direction when something caught their attention.

"Came out here to think and jaw," Arjan replied. "How about you?"

"I'm after herbs."

Rob nudged his uncle. Arjan looked at him for a moment, then turned back to Euphanel. "Would you care for some company?"

She smiled and lowered her gaze. "I'm always happy for a friend."

"I need to get back to the house," Rob said. He went to his mother's side and kissed her on the cheek. "Love you, Ma."

She smiled and patted his cheek. "I love you, too."

Euphanel looked after her son for a moment. "I wonder what he's up to?"

"Why does he have to be up to anything?" Arjan asked with a smile. He reached out and took the basket from her gloved hands.

"He's been acting strange. Ever since he started wondering about becoming a preacher. Seems like he's worried about leaving the logging business and home. I told him not to fret over it. Why is it so hard for my children to understand that I'd be proud of them no matter what they decide to do?"

"I suppose because Rutger made it clear to them that he had plans for them to take over the business."

"But he never intended for them to go against their calling," she countered. "If God wants Rob for a minister, then I want it for him, as well."

They continued down the path and Arjan fell silent. Euphanel wondered if she'd somehow upset him. Perhaps he, like Rutger, wanted the boys to stay focused on working for the logging company.

"I'm sorry if you think that's wrong. I know the company is something you two had a vision for." She smiled and looked down the canopied trail. "I always figured they would follow in Rutger's footsteps, but I won't force it. I hope you won't insist on it, either."

"I had no mind to."

"I'm glad." She rubbed her hands together. "You just seemed a bit put off by what I said."

He stopped. "Not at all."

When he didn't pick up walking with her again, Euphanel turned back. "Is something wrong?" She could see the uncertainty in his expression.

Arjan stepped forward. "Nell, I've long wanted to say somethin', but I haven't had the nerve."

Euphanel began to tremble. This was the moment she'd hoped would come—the moment she could speak of her heart and he would speak of his. Her knees quaked beneath her petticoat and skirt. She hoped he wouldn't notice the rustling of her dress. She met his eyes and knew that all she wanted was to spend her life enjoying his company. Why had she been so blind to this before now? Rutger had been gone for over four years now—it was time to move forward.

"I've had something to say to you, as well," she said in a quiet voice. "Something that I never thought I'd ever say."

He took a hesitant step, but kept his gaze fixed on her face. "Maybe you should speak first."

"I hardly know where to begin." She hadn't felt this nervous in ages. She tried to remember what she wanted to say—tried to remember what she'd said to Rutger when he'd declared his love for her. It was funny, but she couldn't bring any of it to mind. Looking into Arjan's eyes, she couldn't think of anything but him.

"Arjan . . ." She let the name linger on the air.

Without saying anything, he dropped the basket and stepped forward. Taking a hold of her, he whispered her name. "Nell."

She let him draw her into his embrace. Slowly she lifted her face to meet his. He hesitated only a moment, then lightly touched his lips to hers. Time seemed to stand still and Euphanel lost herself in the kiss. For so long, she had believed herself beyond love. When Rutger had died, she was sure that she had buried her heart in the grave with him. That her days of loving and being loved were over.

She'd been wrong, and she was glad.

The idea of giving her heart to a stranger was something she couldn't fathom, but loving Arjan was easy. She trusted him more than anyone. They shared the same history—they knew each other's likes and dislikes, fears and hopes.

He trailed kisses along her mouth and jaw. "Oh, Euphanel, you don't know how long I've wanted to do that."

She pulled back slightly. Her heart threatened to beat out of her chest. Putting her hand up to touch his cheek, she shook her head. "I don't know what to say—to do. This is unexpected to me . . . well, not completely. Seems like folks of late have been telling me how you cared for me. I guess I was the last to know."

A strange look crossed Arjan's face. "I never wanted you to know while Rutger was living. I never wanted him to know. It wasn't right to be in love with my brother's wife. I used to pray that God would take that feeling from my heart and for a long time I was able to keep my mind on my work. I wouldn't have ever done anything to dishonor you or him. I loved you both too much for that."

"I know. I never even suspected," Euphanel said. "I don't think Rutger knew, either."

"I only wanted to do right by both of you. I want to do right by you now." He covered her hand with his own. "Marry me, Nell."

She nodded. "I want to marry you."

He grinned. "Truly?"

Euphanel pulled away and reached down for the basket. She hadn't felt this good in a long, long while. Straightening, she smiled. "Truly. I might tease about a great many things, but falling in love for a second time isn't one of them."

"Well, look at that," G.W. said, nudging Rob. His brother had already told him what Arjan had planned. "Looks like he wasted no time." The brothers exchanged a grin at the sight of their uncle and mother walking hand in hand.

"What are you two prattling on about?" Deborah asked, coming to stand beside them on the porch. She looked around G.W.'s shoulder. "Oh, I see."

G.W. turned to her. "I guess there will be no livin' with you now."

"Why do you say that?" Deborah looked at him oddly.

"Well, you were the one who told me this was comin' our way. Rob said that Uncle Arjan meant to propose to Ma."

She gave a clap and giggle. "Oh, this is a wonderful day. What a grand celebration we'll have!"

Mother and Arjan approached and looked at the threesome on the porch. Arjan broke into a smile. "She said yes, if that's what you're wonderin'."

Deborah hurried down the porch steps. She went to embrace

her mother. "I'm so happy." She reached out to hug Arjan, as well. "We should celebrate."

"I'm glad you're pleased," Mother said, looking rather sheepish. "I don't suppose it will take long for everyone to hear the news."

"Not around here." G.W. gave Mother a kiss on the cheek and smiled back at Arjan. "Rob said you asked for our blessin', and you surely have it."

"I told your mother I wanted to give you and Lizzie my cabin. You don't have to take it, as there is plenty of room here, but I thought you might like the privacy."

"That's generous," G.W. replied. "I think we'd like that very much."

"When is the wedding to be?" Deborah asked. "We have to make you a dress and bake a cake and—"

"Now, hold on," Mother said. "There needn't be a lot of fuss. Arjan and I just plan to make it a quiet affair. We prefer it that way and hope you will understand."

G.W. took hold of Deborah's shoulders. "She understands and so do we. We'll do it your way."

"But we could—"

"Deborah, your ma wants it this way, and whatever makes her happy makes me happy." Uncle Arjan looked to G.W. and then to Rob. "I'm sure you boys understand, since you have gals you've come to care for."

G.W. saw a joy in his mother's eyes that he'd not seen since Father died. The pain he'd felt in his father's death—the way he'd blamed himself for the accident—seemed to fade a bit more. He felt a sense of peace in knowing that she would love again and be cared for.

He thought of Lizzie and the children. Life was good, and this only served to make it better.

Chapter 21

I'm so glad you could both come," Jael told Lizzie and Deborah. "I wasn't sure you could get away from the babies, and I knew Stuart would never approve of my driving out to see you."

"Mother is watching the twins," Deborah offered. "What's wrong?"

Jael motioned for them to have a seat and lowered her voice. "Shh." They were in the front parlor of the boardinghouse, and Mrs. O'Neal, the housekeeper, had a penchant for gossip. "I don't wish for us to be overheard. I told Mrs. O'Neal that we were going to have tea and discuss old times. Do you remember when we were in Philadelphia?"

Deborah looked to Lizzie and then back to Jael. "Of course. What about it?"

"We were happy and innocent then," Jael said rather sadly. "Life was different and we were different."

"That's true enough," Lizzie replied. "It seems like a million years ago."

Jael nodded. "There. That should suffice. I didn't wish to be a liar. We have discussed old times. Now we need to talk about the current state of our lives."

"Are you all right? Has something happened?" Deborah asked in a whisper.

"I'm not sure. I overheard Stuart and Father talking. I had hoped that Stuart was past his jealousy and anger toward your family, Deborah. He never speaks of it to me, so I presumed it had passed. I was wrong, however. I believe Stuart has underhanded plans when it comes to your family's well-being."

"But how could he possibly harm my family?" Deborah asked, looking to Lizzie. "Can you imagine anything he might do?"

"I can imagine a great deal," Lizzie replied. "I wouldn't put anything past him."

Jael moved closer to her friends. "I don't know what he has planned, but he was speaking to Father about some of their business dealings and how he never took on a project without a purpose. When Father asked him what his purpose was in coming to Texas, Stuart said he couldn't explain in full because a good part of it was personal."

Deborah felt her brows knit closer. "Personal? Did he say more?"

"Part of it I couldn't make out. They weren't exactly speaking freely. I pretended to be busy with something else on the far side of the room, hoping they would continue."

"And did they?" Lizzie questioned.

Jael looked rather worried and glanced around the parlor, as if the walls themselves had ears. She motioned for the girls to come closer. "I think Stuart means to exact revenge on your family. I don't yet know how, but the last thing I heard him mutter was something about how when he needed to teach someone a lesson, he very well knew how."

Deborah straightened. "That could mean almost anything. It certainly needn't be about us."

"Still, Jael is right. It could be, and for that reason we should warn the men," Lizzie replied.

There was wisdom in what Lizzie said. And Deborah worried about her as much as the rest of the family. Lizzie was the one who had rejected Stuart. If he was in the business of holding grudges, then Lizzie's name was no doubt at the top of his list.

A couple of men came into the parlor, deep in conversation. They didn't seem to notice the women at all as they headed toward the open French doors that led to the smoking porch.

"Seems to me that if the Negroes do not know how to mind their place in society, they deserve whatever punishment is meted out," the taller of the two men declared.

"I agree, Horace, but liquor was involved and that always serves to muddle men's minds."

"Where the black man is concerned, I agree. There is no call for the Negro to be drinking. He hasn't the constitution for it. Think of giving whiskey to a small child and there's little difference."

They exited the house, oblivious to the women. Deborah shook her head. "What was that about?"

Jael eased back in her chair. "Apparently some of the blacks were involved in an altercation at the white saloon. There was quite the fight, as I hear. The blacks were beaten severely and thrown unconscious onto the train tracks. Had someone not come along to find them, they might have been killed."

Deborah could hardly believe her ears. "That's hideous. How can good Christian people act in such a manner?"

"Perhaps they weren't good Christian people—after all, they were, as I heard it told, quite drunk."

"That's still no excuse to take a man's life," Lizzie said. "And just because they didn't die this time doesn't mean the next time won't prove fatal."

"I wonder if Christopher knows about this," Deborah said, getting to her feet. "I think I'll go check in with him and see what the extent of the injuries were. I'm sure if anyone knows, it will be the company doctor."

"I'll stay here and visit with Jael," Lizzie told her. She glanced at the grandfather clock in the corner. "G.W. will be back for us in less than an hour. Don't forget."

"I won't."

Deborah hurried from the room, nearly running Mrs. O'Neal over as she scurried to get away from the open pocket doors. "Good day, Mrs. O'Neal," Deborah called loudly. She hoped that would be enough to let Jael and Lizzie know the old woman was trying to overhear their conversation.

Crossing the dusty street toward the commissary, Deborah found several black women standing at the bottom of the stairs. The blacks were given certain hours when they could shop in the commissary, and the women were waiting for their turn. Deborah thought it all nonsense. Why should the color of one's skin dictate the ability to shop?

She maneuvered past a group of children who were busy chasing after a cat and approached the doctor's house. A strange feeling came over her as Deborah approached the front door. Something didn't feel right, but she couldn't put her finger on it.

"Hello? Christopher?"

She heard some shuffling and scuffing from the examination room. Mrs. Foster came through the door into the waiting room. "He ain't here."

"Oh," Deborah said, nodding. "I can wait."

"He ain't here. He's gone."

"On rounds?"

Margaret Foster shook her head. "He's gone to be with his brother. He left a letter for you. It's on his desk. I'll be handlin' the sick now."

Deborah quickly moved past Mrs. Foster and picked up the letter from his desk.

"When did he leave?" she asked, frustrated he hadn't said good-bye.

"Yesterday. Took the afternoon train out. Said he had business somewhere near Victoria."

"Indianola," Deborah murmured, opening the sealed envelope.

She moved away from the older woman and went to the window for better light. Christopher's neat and orderly script spilled out across the pages.

My dearest Deborah, I never intended to hurt you, the letter began. Deborah braced herself and continued to read.

> *There is never an easy way to tell someone good-bye, but I feel I must—at least for now. I am going to Indianola to see Calvin and offer whatever assistance I can. The situation does not look hopeful. If they hang him, I will need to go to my mother and give her the news. She will never be able to bear this alone.*

Deborah could feel a lump rising in her throat.

> *I have never cared for anyone as I have cared for you. It's because*

of my feelings that I know now that I must release you from any attachment or loyalty you may feel you owe me. You deserve so much better, and I long for you to be happy.

She slumped against the wall. Glancing up, she could see Mrs. Foster watching her. She quickly folded the letter and composed herself. "I need to go. My brother will be waiting to take me home."

Hurrying from the office, she found her vision blurred by tears. She wiped the dampness from her cheeks and went to where the family carriage awaited. G.W. was nowhere in sight, but she climbed into the back and opened the letter once again.

" 'There are so many things I wish I could have told you,' " she whispered, reading more of his words. " 'So many things I should have said. I know this will be difficult to understand, but in my mind I was protecting you from the truth. Now, however, I see that selfishly I was protecting myself.' "

Tears fell onto the page, causing the ink to run. Deborah held the letter away from her so that the wetness couldn't destroy the words. Once her tears abated, she continued.

I pray this letter will allow you to know that this decision was not easily made. I cannot hope that you will understand, but choices and decisions I've made make it impossible to continue our courtship. I don't know if I will return to Perkinsville or not. A great deal will depend on my brother's trial, but if I do not return, I want you to know that none of this was your fault. I accept full responsibility.

She turned to the second page, feeling a sense of desperation that would not be stifled.

When I saw the reaction of the Perkins sisters, I knew there would be trouble. Pastor Shattuck came to visit me shortly afterwards and told me that your reputation was threatened. I couldn't bear that.

Deborah felt livid. "Gossips. They had no right."

I never wanted this for you. I cannot be the cause of seeing your name smeared in gossip. I hope you will continue your studies in medicine. You have a gift that should not be discarded.

No matter what, please always know that my feelings for you will never change. I will never love another as I have loved you.

Christopher

She stared at the page shaking her head. He'd never uttered words of love before. She'd felt the passion of his kiss, had known his concern and tenderness—but he'd always held something back. Folding the letter, Deborah fell back against the leather carriage seat and closed her eyes.

This wasn't happening. It couldn't be. She'd known Christopher was troubled over the matter of his brother's incarceration—knew too that his mother's suffering was of constant concern to him. Still, she'd never expected him to just pack up and go without seeing her first—without explaining in person.

"Ah, I see you're here already," G.W. said, climbing up to the seat. "I heard something in the hardware store about the doc leavin'. You know anything about it?"

Deborah was grateful that he didn't bother to look around and study her face. "I just found out myself."

"Seems strange he would just up and leave. I was talkin' to some of the boys, and they said there was some kind of problem. Said the preacher was known to have gone and talked to him about some issue. You wouldn't know about that, would you?"

"I can imagine a lot of reasons the pastor would seek out Dr. Clayton." She said it in such a way that she hoped he wouldn't ask any more questions. She knew that Christopher didn't want anyone else to know about his family and their problems. "Oh, Lizzie is still at the boardinghouse."

"We'll pick her up on our way out." G.W. took up the reins, then released the brake. "Walk on," he called to the horses. "So what do you suppose the doc is up to?"

Deborah tried to maintain a hold on her emotions. "He told me he needed to help his brother. He got into some trouble down in Indianola. I'm not really at liberty to say more."

"He's a good man to go to the aid of his family."

Deborah did her best to wipe her tears and arrange her appearance. She hid the letter inside her blouse. There was no sense in having to explain it right then and there. Lizzie would suspect that something was wrong, but knowing her friend, she would wait to question her later or presume that Jael's worries were the reason for her concern.

G.W. brought the carriage to a stop at the boardinghouse walkway. Jael and Lizzie stepped from the porch and approached.

"Did you have a good visit?" G.W. questioned, hopping down to help his wife into the carriage.

"We did, but there is something we need to discuss," Lizzie said. She turned to Jael and kissed her cheek. "Thank you for letting us know. We'll talk soon—you must come for a visit."

"If I can get away," Jael said. She came to the carriage and looked up at Deborah. "Thank you for your visit."

Deborah nodded, not quite trusting herself to speak without giving away her pain. Lizzie took the seat beside G.W. Once she was settled, G.W. took his place. "Afternoon." He tipped his hat.

They were barely out of town when G.W. turned to Lizzie. "So what do we need to talk about?"

∞

At home everyone gathered around the dining room table to discuss the news about Jael's father and Stuart Albright. Deborah knew her brother's mood was dark. Lizzie had explained the situation to him on the way home. G.W. was livid.

"I should have known he'd try to do us harm," G.W. said, bringing his fist down on the table.

"There's no sense in letting anger lead your thinking." Arjan turned to Rob. "We've met all of our quotas on time, haven't we?"

"Yes, sir. We're ahead of schedule, in fact."

Arjan nodded. "That's what I thought. G.W., are the books in order? Are our debts being paid in a timely manner?"

"They are. Albright and Longstreet can't say otherwise."

"Then there really isn't any problem," Mother threw out.

"No, except that Albright wants to cause us harm. It ain't good for a man to have enemies, especially when those enemies can affect his livelihood," G.W. said, shaking his head.

"Maybe we could speak in private to Mr. Perkins and see if he's privy to anything that might explain what Stuart has planned," Deborah suggested.

Mother looked to Arjan. "That's a good idea," he replied. "Your mother and I had planned to speak to the preacher tomorrow after church. Maybe we could also have a talk with Zed."

"It certainly couldn't hurt. Zed would never do anything to cause us harm," Mother said. "If we explain our concerns, I'm sure he'll be willing to talk to us."

G.W. seemed to calm a bit, and Lizzie put her hand atop his fist. "I'm so sorry about this. I feel that it's all my fault. Stuart is taking his anger out on your family because of me."

"You had nothing to do with it," Mother interjected. "If Mr.

Albright is hateful and vindictive because a better man won your heart, that's something he'll have to deal with. We don't hold you responsible."

The babies began to fuss from the other room. No doubt, Sissy would soon pop out to say that they were hungry. Lizzie got to her feet. "I'd best see to them."

"I'll come and help you," Mother said, pushing back her chair.

Deborah looked at her brothers and uncle. "If you don't mind, I have some things I'd like to tend to." She got to her feet and hurried from the room. She'd not yet been able to think clearly about Christopher and longed for some time alone. Her hopes were dashed, however, when Rob followed her out the kitchen door.

"Wait up there a minute, Sis."

She turned at the door. "What is it?"

"That's what I want to know. Does this have somethin' to do with Dr. Clayton leavin' town, all quick-like?"

Deborah met his eyes and fought to control her emotions. She'd had a lifetime of teasing and joshing from her brothers, but she'd also known their protective attention. "I can't talk about it just yet—I promised Christopher. You understand, don't you?"

He gently touched her shoulder. "Just wanted you to know that I'm happy to listen."

She smiled, touched by his kindness. "Thank you, Rob. You've quite changed since I've returned home. I suppose it has something to do with growing up, but maybe also a bit with a certain preacher's daughter."

He laughed and backed away with his hands in the air. "If you ain't talkin', then neither am I."

Chapter 22

Deborah avoided going into town for the next week. The last thing she wanted was to face questions about where Christopher had gone and what she knew about it. Except for the understanding that Christopher's brother was in trouble, Deborah knew little else, and she couldn't admit to even knowing that much. She had no desire to share the news that the doctor had ended their courtship. She would never be able to escape the questions and suppositions should that information get out.

She tried to put the matter aside, telling herself that he hadn't really meant to end their courtship—that he had acted without thinking. He would come back. He had to. But just as she found the tiniest comfort in such an idea, reality would pour over her in waves.

Why did he do this? Why didn't he just come to me and tell me what was happening?

None of it made sense. She drew a deep breath and forced the truth to the front of her mind. Of course it made sense. There were far too many secrets between them. Christopher was never all that forthcoming with information regarding his life. He was a very private person, he had once told her.

"So private, in fact, that I haven't a clue who he really is," she muttered, attacking the hard ground with a hoe. She'd offered to weed the garden, and the task had at least kept her body busy.

Rob arrived home and, seeing his sister, headed her way. "I see you're out in the heat of the day," he said as he strolled up. "Good thing you're covered up. That sun's mighty fierce today."

Mother liked the weeding to be done in the heat of the day to ensure the deaths of the unwanted intruders. Deborah wore one of her father's old long-sleeved shirts over her lightweight cotton gown. On her head she'd secured a sunbonnet in the old-fashioned style her mother had once worn as a young woman.

"You're home early." She looked at the sky. "What time is it?"

"Only four. Uncle Arjan said it was too hot to keep workin'. He told the men to stay in camp but to quit for the day. Nobody argued with him. In fact, last I saw, several of the men were headed to the river to cool down. Not that they'll find an abundance of water there."

Deborah leaned against the hoe and prayed for a breeze. "So what are your plans for the rest of the day?"

"Well, I kind of figured to talk to you for a spell." He pushed back hair from his face. "Then I'm gonna see if Ma or Sissy can give me a haircut."

She knew her brother would probably want to talk about Christopher, but to her surprise, Rob began to speak on something else entirely.

"I know this is gonna sound abrupt-like, but I've given it a lot of prayer and thought," he began. "I believe God has a change planned out for my life."

Deborah straightened. "What kind of change?"

"Well, that's what I figured to talk to you about. See, I'm kind of worried that it's gonna upset Ma. Maybe Uncle Arjan and G.W., too."

"I can't imagine what that would be."

Rob hooked his thumb in his suspenders. "I'm gonna be leavin' this area."

His announcement took her totally by surprise. "I figured you were going to tell me that you'd asked Mara to marry you. I certainly didn't think you'd talk about leaving. Where did you have in mind to go?"

"Houston. There's a seminary there that I want to attend. I think my readin' and cipherin' has improved enough, not to mention that I've pert near read the Bible cover to cover. I don't figure it'll be easy, but I think God wants me to be a preacher."

"You seem quite certain."

"I am." He went over to the fence rail and climbed atop to sit. "I've been prayin' for God to show me, and He keeps bringin' me back to the same place."

"Have you talked to Ma about it?"

"Only the bit about thinkin' I might be called to be a preacher. She gave me her blessin'. She knows it would mean me leavin' the logging business, but she said she didn't want anything to stop me from my callin'. I haven't really talked much with anyone else. I wanted to talk to you, because I figured you'd understand. Sometimes the choices we make aren't that popular with other folk."

"To be sure," Deborah answered.

"I know Doc had something important to tend, but it seems to me he could'a come and said good-bye."

Deborah's gaze snapped up to meet Rob's. "He left me a letter." She knew her tone sounded defensive, so she added, "But I would have rather talked face-to-face. Christopher wanted privacy on the matter, but I need advice. He went to help his brother."

"What kind of trouble did his brother get into?"

She glanced around. "Please don't tell anyone else—promise? This town is so full of gossips."

"Of course I'll keep quiet."

"His brother Calvin has been arrested in Indianola for killing a man." Deborah stared at the garden patch and began to hoe again. "Some say it was self-defense, but others say it wasn't. If his brother hangs, Christopher said he would be obligated to return to his family in Kansas City."

"And what about you?" His tone wasn't accusing or otherwise harsh.

Deborah continued working, unwilling to meet his gaze. "He didn't want me to feel that I had to wait for him. He wasn't even sure he'd return to Perkinsville."

"Why not?"

She stopped and leaned the hoe against the fence. Pushing back her sunbonnet, Deborah wiped perspiration from her forehead. "His mother may need him to stay in Kansas City. His father is pretty useless. He's taken to drinking because he can't bear being an invalid. Christopher's mother suffers greatly."

"I see. Well, I reckon I can't fault a fella for somethin' like that."

"No." She gazed past him to the railroad tracks. She thought of Christopher leaving the town by means of the train. She couldn't help but wonder where he was now. Maybe he was sitting at his brother's side in some trial. Maybe he was pleading for his brother's life.

"I'm sorry he's gone," Rob said, drawing her attention back to him. "I reckon that must be powerful hard for you."

She nodded. "It is, but I'm trying to just put those feelings aside and focus on the work that needs to be done. Garden can't hoe itself and the clothes can't wash themselves."

"If it's any help," he said with a smile, "I feel pretty certain the doc will come back. You two are intended to be together."

"And how would you know about such matters?" she asked with a teasing smile.

"That's part of God's blessing on me, I guess," he said, his tone becoming serious. "I think on a matter long enough, and pretty soon, I'm not just thinkin' about ideas for fixin' the problem, but I'm seeing the problem already done in my head. It's like a vision or something."

"That sounds amazing." Deborah put her hand on Rob's knee. "You've picked up your reading so quickly, and just look at the gift you have for memorizing Scriptures. I think God has a definite path for you."

Rob nodded. "I do, too. Will you come see me in Houston?"

"Absolutely," Deborah promised. "However, I may well go off to get some training myself."

He looked at her oddly. "Like what?"

"Medicine. I'd like to continue my studies and become a real doctor. Since Christopher may not return for some time, I'll probably need to find another doctor to train me."

"I don't know that I like the idea. I hope you'll be givin' it a lot of prayer and thought."

"I will," she promised. "There might even be a doctor in Lufkin who would take me on once he knows about the details of my previous training." She gave a shrug as if it were all of no consequence. "We will just have to wait and see."

"Seems like you should give this a whole lot more thought."

"But don't you worry. I'll make sure the business won't suffer. G.W. now handles the office and business affairs quite capably. The exercises he's been doing to strengthen his leg have really improved his usage of the limb. It won't be long at all before he's fully capable of doing just about anything he wants. Uncle Arjan knows the logging business, and even with you off training to be a preacher, he'll hire the workers needed. Vandermark Logging will go on as it always has."

"Still, I'd hate to see you goin' away again. I know Ma would, too."

"I know. It's not ideally what I want," Deborah admitted. "I had planned that Christopher . . . Dr. Clayton would continue to train me. I suppose those who didn't feel it appropriate are happy now."

Rob studied her for a moment. "Just make sure your choices aren't about running away."

His comment took her off guard. "Why would you say that?"

"Seems to me you were quite content to be here until the doc up and left. I'd hate to see you change all your plans just because you feel out of sorts with him."

The conversation was taking a turn she'd rather not travel. She took the hoe back in hand. "But what about you? Have you thought to talk to Pastor Shattuck about being a preacher?"

"Yes. He's the one who told me about the seminary. We talked and prayed about it."

"What about Mara?" She knew her brother was more than a little sweet on the preacher's daughter.

"Well, she knew God had a plan for me before I did. Fact is, she told me that once I get done what God has for me to do, we'll get married."

Deborah laughed. "She did? Well, that's quite a proposal. I would never have expected Mara to speak so boldly."

"She's full of surprises," Rob admitted with a grin. "I can't say that I mind, though. I like a woman knowing her own mind and heart. I'm even happier that she looks to know God's, as well."

Deborah considered the young woman for a moment. "And have you asked her to wait for you?"

"Didn't have to," Rob replied. "She told me she'd be here waiting when I got back."

"Well, it sounds like you've truly considered all of this. I have to admit, I used to wonder if you'd ever settle down." She grinned. "I never figured you'd do it in such a big way."

He hopped down from the fence and gave her a hug. "I guess it's time I go talk to Ma and the others." He started to go, then stopped. "Say, you ought to know that Jake's pretty sweet on you. He's always askin' about you."

Deborah shook her head. "I know. I've made it clear to him that I have a beau." She frowned, thinking of Christopher's letter releasing her from their courtship. "But I guess that's changed."

"You think the doc will forget all about you?"

"Could be. He didn't ask me to wait for him. In fact, it was just the opposite." She moved back to the garden row.

"I'm sorry," Rob said. "Don't give up on him. You don't know yet what God has planned, but you two worked real well together. I can't believe God would just send you off in different directions. Findin' another person who understands your heart . . . well, it isn't easy."

"No, it certainly isn't," Deborah agreed. She looked at her brother. "Please don't speak to others about it. I'm not really ready to discuss it. Please just pray for me to know exactly what God has in mind."

ꕥ

"You were mighty quiet at supper," Jake said, finding Deborah alone on the front porch.

The last person she wanted to deal with was Jake, but she didn't want to hurt his feelings. Lifting her closed fan, she waved it from left to right. "It's so much cooler out here than inside—don't you think?"

He took the chair beside her and turned it around. Straddling it, he leaned forward against the back of the chair. "I suppose you ain't exactly wantin' to jaw with me."

She smiled. "It certainly isn't personal. I don't feel like speaking with anyone. I'm not good company tonight."

"I find that hard to believe," he said with a smile. "My granddaddy used to say that sometimes when a fella felt like he couldn't find the words, it was 'cause he needed someone to help him."

"And you're offering to direct me? Is that it?"

His smile broadened. "Sure, why not? You and me, we've been talkin' on and off for some time now. You know you can trust me. I'm the honorable sort."

Deborah couldn't help but laugh. "Yes, I suppose you are."

"So why not share your worries with me?"

She looked at him and had to admit she found his expression endearing. He tried so hard to impress. "It's not so much worries. I'm really not sitting here fretting as much as thinking. It seems my life is changing once again, and I just want to be sure I know where God wants me to be."

"Seems to me what with Him bein' God, He's able to put you where He wants you to be without you havin' to think overmuch on it." He sobered. " 'Course, my ma used to say that God didn't force us, so I suppose a fella could make a bad choice and go somewhere God didn't want him . . . or her."

"It's true," Deborah admitted. "My mother used to tell me that God has a perfect way for each person, but sometimes we don't care to know what that is. I honestly want to know, but it seems that just when I start to figure it out, everything changes."

"Like courtin' Dr. Clayton?"

Deborah stiffened. "I'd rather not talk about Dr. Clayton."

"Why is that?"

"Because it's a private matter. I wouldn't feel comfortable talking to you about it."

Jake grinned again. "Why, 'cause you know I'm wantin' to court you myself?"

Deborah looked at him and lowered her fan. "That's one very good reason for us to change the topic of our conversation."

"I think you're afraid to step out with me."

"I am not." Deborah hadn't meant to sound so indignant. She softened her tone. "So how are you enjoying your new job?"

He looked for a moment as if he wouldn't allow for the conversation to change course, then shrugged. "It's hard work. But I surely appreciate your family takin' me on."

"I wish things had gone better for your folks," Deborah said, thinking how sad it all was that Jake should have to leave the only home he'd known. "I know you must miss them."

"I do," he admitted. He got off the chair and walked to the end of the porch. "I always figured to take over the ranch when my pa passed on; instead, it's gone to strangers."

"Who bought your family's land?"

Jake shook his head. "I don't know. Some fella from up Chicago way. He was buying up a bunch of ranches. Told my pa the drought wouldn't last forever and when the rains finally came, he'd own a good piece of Texas."

"So he has the luxury of waiting for the rains, but your father didn't."

Frowning, Jake turned away. "No."

"I'm sorry, Jake. I really am. I can't imagine how I'd feel if we suddenly lost our land. For all the years I was away from here, I always knew I'd come home one day." She got up and walked to where Jake stood staring off across the yard. "Still, you did say that you believed God was able to put you where He wanted you. Maybe that's here. Maybe there's another kind of life God wants you to experience."

Jake turned and Deborah was more than a little aware of how close he stood. "Could be He sent me here because of you. Ever think about that? Maybe I lost one family—one home—because I'm gonna have another." He winked. "And maybe you're gonna be a part of it."

Chapter 23

On Saturday the fourteenth, Euphanel and Rachel decided to host a sacred-harp gathering for the community. They posted notices around town at the commissary, mill, and new dress shop encouraging everyone to attend, whether they could sing or not. The ladies felt that the heat of summer, coupled with the worry over drought was enough of an excuse to have a party.

Zed thought it was a good idea, as well. He talked of tempers running high at the mill and even some conflicts with his new partners. He donated scrap wood to build temporary tables and moved the benches from the ball diamond. By the time things were set in place in the grassy park area beside the church, it looked like the party might rival the Texas Independence Day celebration.

Most folks seemed happy to break their routine, as well, and by the time the singing began in the early evening, Euphanel was convinced that most everyone in the community was present. She was pleased to see that while some folks were surprised by the blacks joining in the sacred-harp choir, no one said anything to suggest it was inappropriate.

"My, you look lovely," Mr. Longstreet told her. He took hold of her hand and raised it to his lips. "I do hope there will be a chance to share a private moment." He kissed her hand, leaving the onlooking Rachel to gasp at his boldness.

"Euphanel, I need to see you about something," she told her friend.

Mr. Longstreet looked perturbed but said nothing as Rachel led Euphanel away from his company. Euphanel was more than grateful for her friend's attentive action.

"Thank you. I swear, the man has gone out of his way to charm me."

"Maybe he doesn't realize you've already been charmed elsewhere," Rachel smirked.

"How could he not know? This is a small town and gossip travels fast."

"I'm so excited that you and Arjan will be married tomorrow," Rachel gushed. "It's going to be a beautiful ceremony; I just know it."

Euphanel nodded. "It's definitely a new start for the both of us." Seeing that everyone was pretty much assembled, Euphanel motioned to Rachel that it was time to take their places.

After directing the first song, Euphanel took her seat and Rachel led the next. Folks seemed to settle in and enjoy the music, even if they didn't sing along. With an ever-watchful eye, Euphanel prayed the celebration would ease the racial conflicts they'd known throughout the year. She was especially prayerful that the folks of

Perkinsville would begin to see that skin color was not a barrier to friendships.

One of the tenors led them in a moving rendition of "How Long, Dear Savior." It only served to cause Euphanel to remember Sissy's husband. This was one of his favorite songs.

How long, indeed, she thought. *Dear Lord, how long must we suffer each other to such miseries and oppressions?* The war was years behind them, but the consequences seemed certain to carry on for generations.

Texas was different, she had to admit. Texas was mainly interested in what was best for Texas. It was a country unto itself, and Euphanel often wondered if it would go back to being a Republic instead of a state after the War of Northern Aggression. There had been talk in the early years following the war, when Texas was waiting to be officially readmitted to the Union. Many folks didn't want to be a part of the Union—not just because of slave issues, but because of Texas issues. They were quite happy to govern themselves and quite proud to stand on their own.

They sang another seven songs without a break before Zed Perkins stepped to the center and held his hands up to draw everyone's attention.

"I'm not gonna volunteer to lead you in a song," he said with a chuckle. "Instead, I've come to make an important announcement that has to do with a couple of special folks—folks most of you know quite well." He turned to Arjan and then to Euphanel. "You two might as well step up here, too."

Euphanel hadn't realized Zed was going to make their engagement a public announcement, but she didn't really mind. If it helped with the community spirit of things, she was more than happy to do her part.

She made her way to the center and stood beside Arjan as Zed continued. "Most of you know that we lost Rutger Vandermark many years ago to a logging accident. He and Euphanel had been married a good number of years and had three children together. Rutger and his brother, Arjan, started the Vandermark Logging Company, and some of you work for them."

He put his hand on Arjan's shoulder. "I just learned that Arjan and Euphanel plan to marry, and I felt this should be a time of celebration for our town. I know the ladies planned this to be nothing more than a summer gathering, but I hope you'll join me in extending your best wishes to the happy couple. They're plannin' to tie the knot tomorrow after church."

"Why not tonight!" someone called out from the crowd.

Zed looked to Arjan. "Indeed. Why not tonight? Why don't we make this a weddin' celebration?"

Euphanel did her best not to appear nonplussed, but she'd never been so stunned. The idea of turning the casual get-together into a wedding party had never once entered her mind. Why, she'd even made it clear to Deborah that she and Arjan planned a simple, quiet ceremony. She wasn't even going to make a special dress for the occasion. In fact, she'd probably wear exactly what she had on tonight. Her simple mauve gown with the cream lace edging was more than stylish enough for a second wedding.

Arjan looked at her with a devilish grin. "I'm ready for it—how about you?"

She felt a flutter in her stomach. She was really going to do this—remarry and have a husband—after all these years alone?

Is this all madness? Am I doing the right thing?

"Well, what do you say, Miz Vandermark? It's not like you have to change your name or anything," Zed teased.

Euphanel gazed about to find her children. Rob and G.W. were sitting with the basses. They nodded with big smiles, letting her know they approved. Deborah was off to one side with Lizzie and the babies. She, too, offered an encouraging smile.

"It seems everyone approves," she said. She hoped no one noticed the tremor in her voice. She licked her dry lips. "I suppose we might as well have ourselves a wedding."

Cheers went up from the crowd. Suddenly Euphanel felt like a young girl again. A moment of shy hesitation washed over her.

"Where's the pastor? Let's commence this joining here and now," Zed declared.

Arjan took Euphanel by the arm and whispered, "You're as white as a sheet. You sure you wanna do this?"

"I do," she said, nodding.

He grinned. "That part comes later."

She smiled. "I don't mind . . . truly. It's just a surprise. I had thought we'd have a very private ceremony. Now here we are, with the biggest wedding possible."

"But what better way to join our community together," he replied. "You can have Sissy stand up with you, and I'll have Zed. It'll be the first wedding in these parts to have both blacks and whites."

What he said was true. Euphanel had no better example to share with her friends and neighbors than to bring Sissy alongside as her witness. And if there was any question as to Sissy's legal ability to bear witness to the arrangement, well, nearly another hundred people could sign their names in her place.

Euphanel left Arjan's side to where her friend sat. "Sissy, will you stand up with me?" she asked.

The woman beamed a smile and got to her feet. "I'd be mighty proud."

They made their way back to the center of the gathering where Pastor Shattuck waited with Zed and Arjan. The two women took their place on the preacher's right, while Arjan and Zed stood to the left.

"Let us as one community—as one heart in the Lord—offer up our prayer of blessing for this couple." He bowed his head and Euphanel did likewise. She found herself praying privately as Pastor Shattuck prayed aloud.

Father, I know you've brought me to this place where I can love and be loved by a good man. I never thought it would happen again—I figured myself lucky to have found Rutger, but now you've given me Arjan, as well. I pray you will guide me—show me the way to be a good and godly wife.

"And give them your peace and blessing, Lord, we pray. Amen." The preacher looked at Euphanel and grinned. "Usually I add in a prayer for a healthy number of children to bless the union, but I wasn't sure you and Arjan would want me to do that."

The congregation roared with laughter, while Euphanel felt her face flush hot. Looking up, Arjan threw her a wink. Goodness, but was everyone determined to fluster her?

The ceremony itself was rather short and without pomp. Pastor Shattuck spoke the words Euphanel had heard at a hundred weddings before. Within a matter of minutes, he was offering a prayer of benediction.

Euphanel was so overwhelmed she didn't even think to close her eyes. Most folks looked happy for them. There would be many congratulations and even some teasing. Oh, but she hoped no one was of a mind to shivaree them. Nothing would be worse than to have the men hauling Arjan off or sneaking back to the house to put pinecones in their bed.

The thought of sharing her bed that night with Arjan was almost Euphanel's undoing. They had planned to stay in his cabin for a week or two, then move back to the main house. She'd been nervous about being alone with her brother-in-law husband before, but now it felt overwhelming. What if Arjan didn't love her as much as he thought he did? What if marriage proved to be a disappointment? She hated to think of their relationship turning sour. She'd depended on Arjan for comfort and help after Rutger's death. She certainly didn't want to lose that now.

" . . . and we commit this to your hands, Lord. Amen. You may kiss your bride," Pastor Shattuck announced.

For a moment, Euphanel couldn't even think of what she was supposed to do. Her knees began to wobble. Arjan took hold of her and steadied her.

"You all right?" he asked, looking deep into her eyes.

She swallowed hard. Her heart picked up speed. "Well . . . I thought I was." She gave an unexpected giggle. "Goodness, I feel just like a girl again."

He grinned and lowered his mouth to hers. The kiss wasn't long, but it definitely left Euphanel breathless. She vaguely heard the cheers and clapping of her friends and family, but otherwise, there was only Arjan.

Deborah felt both a sense of loss and joy at the marriage of her mother and Uncle Arjan. She had never thought to see her mother married again, much less before she herself had a chance to marry once. She knew it was a good thing—knew her mother would be well cared for and loved, but there remained that nagging reminder that love had once again passed her by.

"You must be pretty happy for your ma," Jake said, coming up from behind her.

She whirled around, nearly tripping on her dress. In a flash, Jake reached out to take hold of her arm.

"I am," she managed to say as she regained her footing. Jake dropped his hold. "Thank you for keeping me from falling on my face."

"My pleasure." His expression turned serious. "There's quite a bit of talk going around about Dr. Clayton . . . and some about you."

"I've no doubt about that," Deborah replied. "Folks are such gossips."

As if proof were needed, Mrs. Greeley and Mrs. Pulaski came up to speak to Deborah. "My dear," Mrs. Greeley began, "I'm so relieved that Dr. Clayton is gone. Your reputation was suffering greatly, and I feared for you."

"I did as well," Mrs. Pulaski added. "I heard it said that Dr. Clayton was the sort to take liberties with you."

Deborah shook her head. "Then you heard wrong, I'm afraid. Dr. Clayton was quite the gentleman—very conscious of proper etiquette."

"Well, I heard it said that you two were seen embracing in his examination room," Mrs. Greeley accused.

No doubt the Perkins sisters had been busy. Deborah nodded. "Indeed. Dr. Clayton had received bad news about a loved one. The embrace, however, was my misjudgment, not his. I saw his sorrow and couldn't help but desire to comfort him. Now if you'll excuse me, Mr. Wythe was just about to escort me to the refreshment table."

That was all the encouragement Jake needed. He smiled at the ladies and nodded as he and Deborah moved away.

"Thank you," she said, keeping her voice soft. "I'm sorry to have involved you. No doubt, you'll be the next to suffer their scrutiny and gossip."

"I can't say that I'd mind, so long as it includes you."

She looked at him and shook her head. "Believe me, you do not want to be the topic of the gossip this town is capable of delivering. They can cut deep when they want to, and the wounds are sometimes long to heal."

"Then I might need comforting," he said with a sly grin. "You could offer me the same sort of comfort you gave the doc."

Deborah stopped and fixed him with a hard stare. "That, Mr. Wythe, is totally inappropriate."

He laughed. "Don't worry. I'll mind myself. I wouldn't want the doc to come back and feel the need to teach me a lesson."

"I wouldn't worry overmuch about that. There's no telling if he is coming back," Deborah said, moving away from Jake. She hadn't meant to speak aloud—the words had just come and now she regretted them.

"What are you saying?" he asked, catching up to her with ease.

"Nothing that matters." She'd reached the refreshment table and glanced at the selections of cookies and cakes, pies and breads. She wasn't at all hungry, but figured occupying herself with food might hide her inner turmoil.

"You and the doc end your courtship?" he asked.

Deborah selected a cookie and started to walk away. Jake followed, much to her displeasure. She walked to the far edge of the gathering and waited for him to question her again, even while she prayed that he might simply drop the matter.

"You gonna answer my question?"

"It's hardly any of your business," she said a bit harsher than she'd intended.

"It is if I have my say about it. I'd like to court you myself."

Deborah had to think fast. "I have no intention of courting anyone else. I am . . . well, actually, I'm considering heading back East—to Philadelphia."

"Why?"

She drew a deep breath. "I feel that I should continue my

training in medicine. The college I attended there will allow for that. It is highly progressive and believes women should be allowed to be doctors in their own right."

"And you'd just up and leave?" he asked. "You wouldn't give me any consideration at all?"

"I must do what I feel called to do," Deborah told him. If only she knew exactly what that was.

"I was hopin' to talk to you for a minute," Rob told Mara. He'd never seen her more beautiful. She'd pinned her dark hair high atop her head, and he longed to pull out the pins and watch it cascade down her back. Though completely improper, he couldn't deny the thought was there.

She smiled and moved closer. "I would be happy to hear what you have to say."

"I don't reckon I know quite how you'll feel about this, but I figure it's best iffen I just say the words and then we can talk about 'em."

"Seems reasonable to me," she replied.

He noticed the necklace she wore. It was a small gold cross—a reminder of her faith and the sacrifice that was made by Jesus. It reminded Rob, too, of what he'd come to say.

"I'm gonna be leavin' in two days. I feel that God wants me to go to Houston—to the seminary there. I reckon it may seem strange, but I believe God wants me to be a preacher."

She smiled. "It doesn't seem strange at all, Mr. Vandermark."

He looked at her with great curiosity. "It don't?"

Mara shook her head. "In my prayers for you, I felt certain this was the decision you would make. Later, I cornered my father and spoke with him. He told me that he'd shared with you about the seminary his friend runs in Houston. It seems a very good place for you."

"And you aren't upset with me? I mean, what with . . . well, what you said . . . and . . ." Rob felt helpless to put it all in words. He wanted to challenge her comment—to ask her how she was so certain he was the one she would marry when now he was planning to up and leave.

"How could I fault a man for following after God's heart?" She glanced up, and Rob did likewise. Overhead the night skies were nearly as bright as day, lit by the full moon. "God has a plan and purpose for each of us. I would want only that you follow His direction for you."

"But what about us?"

She turned her gaze to his face. "It all works quite perfectly. You see, I always knew I would marry a preacher. The fact that you've only now come to this decision may seem surprising to you, but not to me."

"How is it that you knew these things?" he asked. "I reckon I'm hearin' God more than ever. I see things in my mind that reflect things He's showin' me through His Word. But you've acted like you've known about us since before you even got here."

She laughed lightly. "I suppose I have—at least, in part. I knew since I was young that God wanted me to be a preacher's wife. I have done everything in my power to work toward that day. I've studied the Word of God and obtained my education in a school run by the church. Everything about my life has revolved around learning to be a helpful mate to a pastor. When I felt the time was right to come and help my father for the purpose of furthering my training, God laid it on my heart that I would meet my husband here—that he might not seem at first like the man God was bringing into my life, but that I should trust and wait upon the Lord."

Rob shook his head. "That's mighty amazin'. I can't help but feel the hair on my neck give rise."

She nodded. "I felt the same way when I first met you. I knew that we would one day be together. I suppose that sounds very presumptuous, but it's the truth. I'm not prideful in this—merely firm in my faith. If God wants this marriage to take place, it will."

He reached out and put his hand on her cheek. "I will come back to you a better man. I promise that. Will you promise to wait for me?"

She surprised him by touching her hand to his cheek. "I will wait, just as I've been waiting. I am yours, Robrecht Vandermark. I will always belong to you."

Chapter 24

Rob had been gone only three days when word came that a terrible storm had hit the Gulf Coast. There was no way of telling exactly how powerful the hurricane was, but the information given the town of Perkinsville suggested it might well bring rain and wind their way.

"Arjan said the depot master said the telegram was brief but to the point. The storm looks to be heading this direction and it is still quite powerful. They're to get the trains north and out of harm's way," Mother declared.

"Did they say where the storm hit land?" Deborah asked. She couldn't help but think of Christopher and his brother in Indianola.

"No. Just that it hit and was moving fast. I'll feel better if we take precautions," Mother told Deborah. "I know Arjan thought me silly for wanting those shutters. I can still hear him saying that there wasn't another house in all of Perkinsville with such luxuries."

"He ought to be glad for them now," Deborah replied. "I remember once before when we had to replace nearly every window on the south side after a hail and windstorm."

"Oh, I know he's glad for them now."

Deborah helped her mother begin the task of closing the shutters. Uncle Arjan caught the train to the logging camp, and G.W. was busy securing the livestock and outbuildings. Lizzie and Sissy went to work preparing lunch.

The waiting was always the hardest part. The storm would never give them as much grief here as it did on the coast, but they could still experience tornadoes and wind damage, harming areas that weren't in the path of the original storm.

"Let's put Lula and her pups on the back porch," Mother told G.W. "That should keep them safe enough." G.W. nodded and headed back outside.

"I'll get the last of the second-floor shutters," Deborah told her mother. She hurried upstairs and went to the far end bedrooms first. The windows, being new, opened easily and Deborah was able to lean out and draw the shutters together without any trouble. As she progressed to the windows in the older part of the house, however, Deborah encountered more difficulty. She soaped a couple of the window's tracks to ease the tension; growing humidity had swelled the wood a bit and made for a tighter fit. At last she finished up in her own bedroom, grateful to have the task completed. The coming storm filled her with a sense of dread.

Christopher was in Indianola on the Matagorda Bay. While Deborah had no way of knowing exactly what the storm would do, she knew Christopher was at risk, simply because he was now on the coast. What if there had been no warning for him?

"Are you all right?" Lizzie asked from the doorway.

Deborah turned and met her friend's worried expression. "I'm afraid for Christopher. He's in Indianola, or I presume he's still there. Perhaps the trial has already taken place and he's long gone. I have no hope of knowing."

"I'm sorry. I know that must grieve you."

"It's the waiting and the not knowing," Deborah replied. She moved across the room and opened a blanket chest. "I know I must give it over to the Lord, but it's so hard."

"Out of your control, eh?"

Lizzie's comment didn't offend her; Deborah knew her friend was right. Taking a stack of blankets from the chest, Deborah straightened. "I suppose I always feel better when I have some hand in the solution." She shook her head. "All of my life I've been like that."

"Taking charge isn't always a bad thing, Deborah, but sometimes it's best to let others handle their messes. God will guide Christopher."

"I know He will." She let out a heavy sigh and shifted the bedding. "I just wish I could know what has happened. It's a terrible thing to be here safe and sound, knowing that Christopher and his brother might well be injured or even dead."

"Don't borrow trouble," Lizzie reminded her. "Give it over to God. He has a plan in all of this, and like you used to tell me, His plan is always better than those we have for ourselves."

Deborah tried to let the words calm her spirit. "I shall continue to pray and hope for the best."

"Do you need help with the blankets?"

"No," Deborah replied. "Mother wants them in the extra

bedrooms. The loggers will come and stay here until the storm passes. It wouldn't do for them to live in the tents during such a time."

"No, I can't imagine staying there in good weather, much less bad." Lizzie came to Deborah and smiled. "God is in control of everything. Here . . . in Indianola . . . in the middle of the storm, itself. He will see you through this. Dr. Clayton, too."

Deborah tried to take solace in Lizzie's words. "I know you're right. I know there is nothing I can do, but oh, how I wish it could be otherwise."

By noon the skies darkened and the air hung heavy, but so far there were no other signs of the storm. Deborah hugged herself and rubbed her arms as if chilled. She felt so anxious, and yet nothing had changed. The storm was not here—perhaps would never come—but she could sense the possibility of it, and that proved enough to make her uncomfortable.

Her life felt the same way right now. She could see the threat of turmoil on the horizon—feel the tension that came with the uncertainty—yet she was perfectly safe. Why couldn't she just rest in that?

"Would you help me make corn bread?" Mother asked.

Deborah put away the last of the dinner dishes before answering. "Of course. Are we making extra, in case the weather turns destructive?"

"Yes. I thought it would be a good idea. Arjan is concerned that we may lose a number of trees if the winds pick up. The turpentine harvest always weakens them, you know. If that happens, they'll have to strike camp where they're working now and head farther away to harvest any fallen pines. He wants to have plenty of provisions to take with them if that happens."

Sissy had already been hard at work on baking corn bread, but she happily relinquished the task to Euphanel and Deborah in order to help Lizzie with the children. By late afternoon, enough corn bread sat cooling that the men could easily be gone a week without needing additional provisions. "We have plenty of hams they can take with them, too," Mother said, bringing in a wooden crate. "Let's put the bread into the cloth sacks we saved and load it all in this crate to keep it from crumbling too bad. Don't bother to cut it into squares; the fellas can take care of that themselves."

The sweltering temperatures of the summer kitchen left Deborah damp with sweat. She assembled the sacks of corn bread while her mother checked the stew she'd prepared for supper. The first drops of rain began pelting the window as Deborah loaded the last of the bread.

"I guess it's starting," Mother said, looking out the door.

Joining her mother, Deborah watched the storm move in with thick and swirling clouds. The wind picked up, driving the rain down a little harder. Still, there was no real relief from the heat. "I guess we'd best get things into the house."

Lizzie came out the side door about that time. "Do you need help?"

Mother motioned her over to them. "You and Deborah take the bread in, and I'll get the stew for our supper. G.W. has already seen to bringing in some of the hams from the smokehouse."

Lizzie and Deborah each took an end of the crate and lifted. "Who knew corn bread could be so heavy," Lizzie said with a grunt.

By the time they had secured everything in the main house, the rain was beating down in earnest. Mother paced the floor until Arjan showed up with the loggers.

"I feel better knowing we'll all be under one roof," she said as the men started to file in, dripping wet.

Deborah handed out towels and couldn't help but smile at her mother's comment. *That must have been how Noah felt as he gathered his family in the ark.* The idea gave her a moment of amusement as she imagined their house turning into a large ship and sailing away.

"I ain't seen you smile since Dr. Clayton went away," G.W. said, coming alongside her.

"There hasn't been a whole lot to smile about. Still isn't, what with the uncertainty of this storm."

"Can't do anythin' more about the storm. As for the doc, I can't imagine he'll stay away long—not when I remember how he looked at you. He's just as gone over you as you are with him."

Deborah shrugged. "I thought so, too. Now I'm not so sure." She looked at her brother. "I can understand better than anyone the need to help your family. He knows that. But there were still so many secrets between us. I always felt like he was hiding parts of himself from me."

"Why do you reckon he would do that?" G.W. asked.

"I think . . . perhaps Christopher has fears."

G.W. looked at her oddly. "Fears of what?"

"Girls, would you set the table for supper?" Mother asked as she passed by. "Put out ten extra places."

"Of course, Mother." Giving her brother a shrug, Deborah followed Lizzie into the dining room and took out the plates and silver from the sideboard.

"What were you and G.W. talking about?" Lizzie questioned.

"He asked me about Christopher. The talk led to why I felt Christopher remained so guarded with me."

"And what conclusion did you arrive at?" Lizzie asked, arranging silver at each place setting.

"I think he was afraid of my reaction to the truth. Maybe he's afraid that if I know the details about him or his family, I'll want nothing more to do with him. After he told me about his brother's murder trial and the fact that two other brothers were in jail for robbery, he looked at me as if expecting me to flee any second."

Deborah paused for a moment to count the place settings. She needed two more and went to the sideboard for additional plates. "I haven't told anyone this, but when I read the letter asking him to come and help his brother, there was something that was most curious. His brother didn't have the same last name. Instead of Clayton, his given name was Kelleher."

"That is strange. Do you suppose his mother was married to someone else when she bore Christopher?"

"I thought of that possibility. He's never said anything, though. I suppose it's part of the mystery." Deborah stopped at the table and grew thoughtful. "That would make a lot of sense. If Christopher was the son of, say, someone disreputable—then he wouldn't want anyone to know about it. He might have never even known the man. Mr. Clayton could have married his mother later on and become a father to him."

"And it would be even worse if his mother and father divorced," Lizzie said in a hushed voice. "Think of the scandal."

Deborah nodded. "I'd never really thought of the possibility until now. It does make sense, however. He is the eldest."

Somehow, such thoughts served to comfort Deborah. Not because she wanted Christopher to have endured such a life, but if it were true, it would explain a great deal.

She pondered her discussion with Lizzie throughout supper and said very little. Deborah was so absorbed in her thoughts that even Jake gave up trying to talk to her. By the time supper had concluded, it had been raining for over an hour, the winds howling and the house nearly shaking at times.

"Guess this breaks the drought," Jake said, shaking his head.

"A little too late to help my family, but hopefully it'll be a blessin' to someone."

"It's a blessing here, for sure," Mother said. "The moisture will keep down the fire hazards with the trees, and we can definitely use it for crops and the animals."

"It'll make working tough," G.W. said. "The roads and paths are difficult enough, but when they turn to mud, it's nigh on impossible to travel 'em."

Arjan nodded. "Givin' a listen to that wind, I'm figurin' we'll have enough downed trees to keep us busy for a spell. We'll need to take all the mules with us when we head out. No doubt we'll have to skid logs back aways to reach the railroad siding."

"We can probably do some loads on the wagons—iffen the roads ain't too bad," Warren offered. " 'Course, G.W. may be right. They might be nothin' but mud by the time we get there."

"The storm should pass in the night, and tomorrow we'll be ready to face whatever comes," Arjan said. "Until then, no sense borrowin' trouble."

After the men headed out in the morning, Euphanel and Lizzie stood on the front porch with Deborah and surveyed the yard. There were a few downed branches, some shingles that had been torn off the barn roof, and a few outdoor articles that had been tossed around by the wind.

"It could have been much worse," Euphanel said, grateful that none of her windows had suffered damage. The cost of glass was nearly unreasonable, and she had no desire to go replacing windows after just a few months of use.

"Was Uncle Arjan going to send word back to let us know how bad the damage in the camp might be?" Deborah asked.

"He said he would try."

"I want to head into town and see how they are faring there. I'll bet Jael will be glad they all headed back to Philadelphia last Monday when she hears of the storm. She said they were planning to return in another month or so and stay in Houston permanently, but maybe after this, they'll change their minds. After all, Houston could have been hit quite hard," Deborah said, unfastening her apron.

"I pray not." Euphanel tried to conceal her concern.

"G.W. mentioned that Mr. Perkins is to have a house for Stuart and Mr. Longstreet in town so that when they come on business, they will have a place to stay," Lizzie added.

"They seem intent on becoming active partners in the sawmill." Euphanel didn't want to worry about the implications of such an arrangement. Arjan had told her that Zed was worried about some of the changes the two Easterners wanted to make. Apparently they each had equal votes on how things would be done, and with Mr. Longstreet and Mr. Albright agreeing on most things, Euphanel could only guess what might happen.

"Do you want to come to town with me, Mother?"

She looked at Deborah a moment, then nodded. "I believe I will. It would be good to check on folks and see how they fared. Good to let them know how we are, as well." She held her hand out. "I'll take your apron if you want to go hitch up the carriage. The boys took our wagon."

Deborah gave her the apron and headed down the steps. "Lizzie," she called over her shoulder, "if you need anything from town, just make us a list."

Euphanel smiled at her daughter-in-law. "Yes, we can pick up whatever you need—if the store is still standing."

On their drive, Euphanel could see that Deborah was fretful.

"I wish you wouldn't worry so," she told her daughter. "Worry won't change a thing."

"I know," Deborah said focusing on the road. "It's hard though. I have no way of knowing if Christopher is safe."

"But God knows, and He's with Christopher, just as He is with us."

"Do you suppose I could send a telegram to Indianola?" Deborah asked suddenly. "I mean, I could just send it to the sheriff there and ask that it be forwarded to Christopher. Since his brother is in jail, surely the law officials would know where Christopher was staying. It can't be that big of a town."

Euphanel could hear desperation in her daughter's voice. She put her hand on Deborah's arm. "I think that would be a good idea."

"Thank you for understanding. I can hardly stand not knowing."

"I do understand," Euphanel assured. "I've been wondering about Rob and whether Houston sustained damage."

Deborah pulled back on the reins. "I'm so sorry, Mother. I've been quite selfish in my concern. It never came to mind that Rob might be in danger, even when I mentioned Jael."

"We shall pray for both of them, Deborah. God has them in His hands, and I refuse to give in to the seeds of doubt the devil sows. In time, we shall know the truth, and when our answers come, we must know where our faith is fixed. Otherwise, we'll be tossed about, just like the tree branches in the wind."

Chapter 25

The air near town smelled of smoke, and while it was generally stale with dust and the scent of woodsmoke, this was different. A stiff breeze from the southwest moved most of the haze off to the northeast, but it was still evident that something was terribly wrong.

A great many people stood in the roadway near the boardinghouse, so Deborah turned the carriage down one of the side streets. She figured she could bring the horses around past the church and park alongside the doctor's office, avoiding the crowd. Doing even this, however, took some creative thought. Tree limbs littered the road, and she couldn't imagine why folks hadn't cleared them away. Studying the area around her, it seemed that no one had even bothered to begin their cleanup.

"You don't suppose the train jumped the tracks, do you?" Euphanel asked.

Deborah looked at her mother and shrugged. "Anything's possible. It's certainly notorious for that kind of thing, and the bulk of the people seemed to be standing near the depot office at the commissary. Still, I thought all of the trains were driven north yesterday."

Her mother nodded as Deborah maneuvered the horses onto Main Street. She gasped at the sight of flames that rose up from where the sawmill was positioned. "Oh no!" She pointed in the direction of the fire. "The mill!"

Her mother stared in disbelief. "It can't be."

Deborah hurried to park the carriage in front of the doctor's house. She climbed down from the wagon, then reached up to help Mother do the same. Many of the town's women and children were gathered by the commissary. The gathering spilled out, blocking First Street.

The two women hurried to join the others and learn what had happened. Deborah saw several women gathered around Rachel Perkins and moved that direction, with Mother on her heels.

"Rachel," her mother called.

Mrs. Perkins looked up. Her face was smudged from the ash in the air and streaked with tears. "Oh, Euphanel," she sobbed. "It's so awful."

"What happened?"

The women who had been standing with Mrs. Perkins moved away a bit to make room for Deborah and her mother. Rachel fell into Euphanel's arms. Deborah looked to Mrs. Greeley, who stood just to their left.

"We figure it must have been lightning," Mrs. Greeley whispered. "Fire started sometime during the storm. They've been trying to fight it all night—even in the fiercest winds."

"That must have been difficult," Deborah murmured.

Her mother pulled away from Rachel and lifted her friend's face. "Tell me, has anyone been hurt?"

"I don't know. The men have been gone for most of the night. Zed and my boys are all over there fighting the fire with the others. They are desperate to keep it from spreading. The women and children did what they could to water down the buildings nearby, as well as the stacks of lumber."

Deborah moved to get a little closer to the front of the crowd. To her surprise, Mother and Mrs. Perkins followed. She fixed her gaze on the front of the mill but could see very little through the smoke billowing out the open doors. Flames licked the already charred walls on the north side, however. Given the amount of smoke that clouded the sky, it was obvious that the fire had burned out a good portion of the roof.

Others in the crowd were crying. The children seemed uncommonly quiet and still. Perhaps, Deborah thought, they were thinking of what might be happening to their fathers and brothers. She felt sickened by the thought that some of the men might lose their lives fighting the flames. She wondered if she should volunteer to open the doctor's office, but realized Margaret Foster had probably already done so.

"I do wish Zed would come here and tell me what's happening," Mrs. Perkins said, taking the handkerchief that Mother offered her.

"No doubt he's much too busy, Rachel. Don't fret. I'm sure that with all the men helping, the fire will soon be out. Is there anything we can do to aid them?"

"No. Like I said, we were putting water on everything we could, but the heat got so intense, the men told us to wait over here. Zed got the bucket brigade going just after the pump was in position. The men are drawing water from the millpond. The pump can't put out a great deal, but it's better than nothing."

Mother nodded and looked at Deborah. "Why don't you go ahead and see about sending your telegram. The wires run along the other side of the tracks and shouldn't be burned."

Deborah hadn't even considered that possibility. She left her mother and the others and hurried to the depot office, hoping someone might be there to help her. Old Mr. Parsons sat at his post, ever faithful. She watched him as he wrote down a message to the clicking of the telegraph. He didn't so much as glance her way until the final words were given. Only then did he put down his pencil. Shaking his head, he looked up.

"Mornin', Miss Vandermark. Surely is a sad day."

She nodded. "It is indeed, Mr. Parsons. Mother and I just arrived and could scarcely believe that the mill was a-fire."

The smoke wasn't too bad, but the August heat warmed the room, making it quite stuffy. Deborah could see that the windows had been shut to keep out the ash and fumes. It was a wonder the old man could endure it.

"Ain't just the mill, neither," he replied. "Bad news comin' in from the storm. Seems it were a mighty strong hurricane. I've had word about damage in Houston."

She immediately thought of her brother. "How bad was it?"

"Well, it caused some destruction, but ain't near as bad as down the coast to the south. There's reports of towns bein' all torn up."

Deborah swallowed hard. "Can we send telegrams south?"

"Only for a ways. Some of the lines are still workin' and some ain't. Couldn't get word through to Victoria. Mrs. Greeley wanted me to send a wire to her ma to see if she was all right, but the lines are down. Seems the storm came right up the coast from that area. Galveston got through for a time. My daughter's family is down that way. I heard from the operator that the town took damage, but he didn't say how bad. Told me word came in that a lot of the towns on the Gulf are just gone—underwater. Wires are down and even the mail has stopped."

Deborah felt her stomach churn. Indianola was only about thirty miles from Victoria. If they had seen destruction that far inland, Indianola was bound to have met with a worse fate. It sat right on the water and rivaled Galveston for the busiest port in Texas.

"Have you heard . . . has there been word . . ." She stammered and looked to the older man for some kind of hope. "I wondered if there was word on Indianola?"

He shook his head. "Ain't heard a thing. I reckon once things settle down, the wires will get back in place and then we'll hear it all. 'Course, the newspaper folks down Houston and Galveston way will probably be gettin' any information they can, but it will most likely be weeks before we know for sure what's happened."

She couldn't help but detect the hopelessness in his words. Deborah fought back tears. "Thank you, Mr. Parsons." She started to leave, but remembered her brother. "I need to send a wire to my brother Rob."

"He's in Houston, ain't he? Gone off to be a preacher." The old man picked up his pencil. "We'll give her a go and see if it goes through. Never can tell."

Deborah arranged for Mr. Parsons to send a wire to Rob inquiring if he was all right and if he needed anything. The old man also promised to try and get a message through to Christopher, but he didn't hold out much hope. Deborah felt pretty deprived of it herself. Surely if Christopher were alive and well, he would have let her know. Wouldn't he? Of course, as Mr. Parsons told her, lines were down and the mail wasn't even getting through. How could he possibly hope to send word?

She rejoined her mother and was surprised to find a large gathering of black women crossing the tracks to join them.

Mother looked up to see them and smiled. Miriam, the wife of a one-time Vandermark Logging employee, came forward and Mother reached out to greet her. She took hold of her hand and squeezed it briefly. "It's good to see you."

"We comed to pray. Our men are over there fightin', too."

Deborah saw her mother nod and turn to Mrs. Perkins. "It seems," Mother said, "that the storm has done what we couldn't. Our men are all working together—side by side—no one caring what the color of the other man's skin might be."

Mrs. Perkins looked at Miriam and gave a weak smile. "You are very welcome to pray with us."

ꕥ

Hours later, the fire was finally out and the destruction evident. The mill was nearly consumed. Patches here and there were unharmed—stacks of lumber watered down enough that the sparks didn't catch it on fire. But little was untouched.

The men staggered back, blackened from head to toe with soot and ash. Their eyes were red-rimmed and watery from the acrid smoke, and most were gasping and coughing. Mr. Perkins and his sons came to join them. The Perkins boys looked for their wives in the gathering and quickly found them, while the elder Mr. Perkins pushed blackened red hair back from his face and fixed his gaze on Mrs. Perkins. They said nothing, but Deborah could see the unspoken relief between them.

"Is there anything we can do, Zed?" Mother asked.

He shook his head. "We kept it from burnin' down the town,

at least. Saved some of the equipment, but not much. Some was just too big to get moved in time."

"What will we do?" Mrs. Perkins asked.

"I don't guess I have an answer for that just now," Mr. Perkins replied. "If you don't mind, I just wanna bath."

She put her arm around his waist and nodded. "Come on. I'll see that you have what you need."

In similar fashion, other men appeared and rejoined their families. Very little was said as the couples moved off and headed home. Deborah watched as the crowd thinned until only she and Mother remained.

"This is surely a great tragedy," Mother said.

"It's only the start," Deborah replied. "Mr. Parsons said there are rumors of destruction all along the coast—some towns are underwater. He tried to send a wire to Victoria, but the lines are down. Galveston and Houston have both suffered damage."

"Houston?" her mother asked, her tone taking on an anxious edge.

Deborah squeezed her hands. "I sent a wire to Rob asking if he was all right and whether he needed anything. The wire went through, so hopefully we'll get a reply."

Mother's eyes filled with tears as she looked about. "Oh, this is such a nightmare. How could anything good come from it?"

Staring past her mother to the still smoldering remains of the mill, she shook her head. "I don't know. I honestly don't know."

That night the Vandermarks gathered around the dining room table and prayed. Word had come during the day that the turpentine harvesting area had been greatly damaged. Numerous trees had fallen in the wind, and Arjan figured they would be out restoring the area for some time. He would need for the women to keep an ample supply of food readied for them.

G.W. had seen to cleaning up the debris in the immediate yard, while Sissy and Lizzie had tried to right the damage to the garden. Everything had taken such a beating, it was unclear as to whether any of the vegetables would revive.

"We thank you Lord that we are alive and safe—that no loss of life was had in the fire," Mother prayed. "Guide us now and teach us what to do."

When she said nothing more, G.W. began to speak. "Father, we are troubled by what's happened. Ain't hardly words to explain."

He went on to ask God's mercy, but Deborah couldn't focus on his prayer. Instead she silently pleaded with God to bring her word from Christopher, to bring him home safely. She knew it was a selfish prayer, given all of the people who had been devastated by the storm. Word had come that the storm hadn't played out until it'd nearly reached the northern counties. It would, no doubt, go down in history as the worst Texas had seen.

Even that solemn thought didn't sway Deborah from her desperate longing to know of Christopher's safety. The entire state could lie in shambles, and she would still only have thought of the man she loved. And she did love him—loved him more than life itself. Nothing had made it more evident to her than the last twenty-four hours.

God, my heart is overwhelmed, she prayed. *I want so much to know that Christopher is alive and well. Rob, too, Father*, she added, remembering her brother. *Please, Lord, don't leave us without word. I can't bear the thought that I might never know. I can't bear that Christopher might be hurt and need me.*

She wiped away tears that spilled from her closed eyes. It was all she could do to keep from crying aloud. Lizzie seemed to understand her misery and reached over to squeeze her hand. Her touch was like a lifeline to Deborah—the only thread of support she could feel at the moment. Mother was worried about the men, about Rob. The others had, no doubt, forgotten all about Christopher.

Lizzie leaned close and whispered, "I've prayed for him, too, Deborah. God will surely hear our prayers."

She opened her eyes and met Lizzie's gaze. Nodding, Deborah tried to find strength in her sister-in-law's statement. Only God could intervene on Christopher's behalf.

Chapter 26

Weeks slipped by without much news. September brought relief to the heat, but not to Deborah's heart. She had tried unsuccessfully to get a wire to Christopher, and the rumors were more and more troublesome in regard to the damage done by the hurricane. Houston papers suggested that much of the coast between Galveston and Corpus Christi had been devastated by high winds and tidal waves. She couldn't bear the thought that Christopher might never have had a chance to escape. He wouldn't have left his brother, and since Calvin was jailed, she doubted he could have gotten away from the storm, either. Would they have moved prisoners inland? Had there been any warning? The questions tormented her.

She found no comfort in her routine chores. While helping her mother gather plums, Deborah prayed and prayed, but peace seemed far out of reach. How could there be no word? Surely Christopher would have known her worry, and even if he didn't plan to return to her, he would have let her know of his safety. Wouldn't he?

"I know you're fretting over the doctor," Mother said, pouring a basket of plums into a larger crate. "Your worry won't bring him back."

"It could be nothing will bring him back." She didn't want to believe that, but as the weeks passed, Deborah found hope a fleeting comfort. "But I can't help believing he'd at least let us know if he was all right. He knows folks here care about him."

"That's true enough. Still, he may not yet be able to get word out. If the devastation is as bad as some say, he may have no recourse."

"He also might be injured," Deborah said, unable to consider the extent to which this might be true.

"Who could that be?" Mother questioned, putting her hand up to shield her eyes.

Deborah heard the unmistakable sound of a horse approaching and ran to the edge of the road. She prayed it was Christopher but was further disappointed when the rider proved to be Zed Perkins.

"What brings you out our way?" Mother joined Deborah by the road.

Zed dismounted and walked with his horse to where the women stood. "I needed to talk with you and Arjan."

"He's still out working the fallen trees. Why don't you come on up to the house and have a cup a coffee? G.W.'s in the office and he can join us. Oh, we had word from Rob. He's safe and the damage was minimal in his area."

He nodded and they started up the road, toward the south side of the house. "That's mighty good news. I know Miz Greeley's news wasn't near as good. Seems Victoria bore a heavy blow from the storm." He turned and tipped his hat. "Miss Deborah—it's good to see you. You haven't been in town of late."

"Hasn't been much reason," she replied. "Margaret Foster made it clear she didn't want my help with the sick."

"Have you heard anything from the doc?" he asked.

She shook her head. "I had hoped maybe you had."

"No, there's been no word. 'Course, if Victoria was damaged, then Indianola must have been, too. Could be the doc is busy helping the hurt folks there."

Deborah could only hope that he was doing that, instead of being tended himself. She said nothing more, choosing instead to focus on the ground as they walked. There was nothing there of interest, but she didn't want her mother or Mr. Perkins to see her face and know how hard this was on her.

"I heard that a good number of people were packing up and leaving Perkinsville," Mother said. "Sissy was speaking to some friends of hers, and it seems this was the talk going around."

"Well, I reckon, what with the mill shut down, there are a lot of folks movin' on to other places. I'm offerin' what help I can, but there's very little I can do. All of my money was in the mill and the stores."

"What about the mill?" Mother asked. "Can it not be rebuilt? A good portion of lumber was saved, as I understand."

"It was and has now been sold. I've ordered some parts to start up small again, but I'm not sure where it's gonna take us. That's why I came out here today."

Mother waited for him to tether his horse before they headed together to the house. Deborah followed after. "I'll fetch G.W.," she told her mother and hurried to the office.

She found her brother deep in thought, ledger before him and a stack of papers beside him. "Mr. Perkins is here. He says he needs to speak to us about the business."

G.W. looked up. "I kind of figured he'd come callin' soon." G.W. closed the ledger and got up. The exercises Christopher had given him had done wonders to strengthen his leg. He still walked with a limp, but he was much faster now and had more endurance than even a few months back.

Deborah and G.W. joined Mother and Mr. Perkins in the front room while Sissy brought coffee and cookies. Deborah wanted neither and took a seat across from Mr. Perkins while he accepted a cup of black coffee.

"How's it going for your family, Mr. Perkins?" G.W. asked.

"It's been hard. I've got to say, there isn't a lot of happiness at my house these days. None of us is sure what to do. The boys all counted on the mill for their livelihood. They have families to feed and clothe so they'll need to do something—and soon."

"We'd be happy to help any way we can," Mother told him. "We've got plenty of smoked pork we could share."

"That's mighty good of you," Mr. Perkins replied. "I guess the worst of it is my girls. They want to leave right away and go stay with their grandparents back East. I can't say as I blame them, but that, too, will cost money."

"Perhaps they can be encouraged to bide their time here and be useful to your recovery."

"I'd like to see that happen, but I didn't do right by those gals. They're spoiled and used to havin' their own way. Not like your Deborah." He gave her a smile. "I'd be mighty proud if my girls were half as industrious as you."

Deborah was surprised by the praise and felt uneasy. "Tell us what's happening with the mill," she encouraged.

Mr. Perkins shrugged. "Nothing, unfortunately. Like I said, I've ordered a few parts in order to start back up on a small level. Mostly I need to cut lumber to rebuild. I have the logs in the millpond and figure to at least get a frame up in order to start over."

"Sounds wise," G.W. said. "What can we do to help? Do you want another load of logs right away?"

"That's why I've come out here, actually." He put the coffee aside. "I can't pay to bring in more logs just yet. I wanted to let you know that straightaway so you could sell your harvest to one of the other sawmills. I'm sure they'll take them in Lufkin."

G.W. nodded. "Probably will. I'll talk it over with Uncle Arjan."

"I hate doing this to you. I know you're counting on the income, just as I was counting on the mill to provide for me." Mr. Perkins sat back and shook his head. "My partners are set to arrive tomorrow. I suppose they will help me to assess the matter. I'm hoping they'll be willing to pour more capital into the business to see it rebuilt quickly. That would be to their benefit as much as mine."

Deborah frowned as she thought of Stuart Albright having any say in the welfare of Perkinsville.

"They certainly got word quickly," Mother commented.

"They don't actually know about the fire just yet. They'd already wired prior to the storm to say they were headin' back to Perkinsville."

"I reckon they'll be surprised to hear the news," G.W. said. "Especially since they were countin' on the mill to help them make their fortune."

"I'm deeply concerned. I'm trying to get as much accomplished as I can before they arrive, but the cleanup is still in progress. What few men I could afford to keep on are doin' their best to clear out the debris so we can get to rebuildin' right away."

"Do you know yet what started the fire?" G.W. asked. "Mother said it was rumored to be lightnin'."

Mr. Perkins looked up with a frown. "It wasn't lightning. I saw no sign of a strike. Fire started inside. Someone had to set it."

"Set it?" Mother asked in horror. "Surely not!"

"Some say the blacks set it as a means of avenging the deaths and beatings they've had in their number. Others say it was whites who done it—unhappy with me because I hired blacks instead of them. I can't say who exactly is to blame, but someone did it on purpose."

Mother shook her head in disbelief. "But no one benefits from such a tragedy. The entire town was dependent upon the mill for its existence."

"Well, someone figured to benefit somehow," Mr. Perkins replied. "Ain't never known a man to do much of anything without there bein' a benefit to it."

"We need to let Arjan know the situation as soon as possible." Mother looked to G.W. "I know it's nearly evening, but he should be here."

"I'll ride out to the camp where he's working," G.W. told them. "I'll bring some more food for them and let Arjan know what's happened." He got to his feet. "Do you want us to travel to town tomorrow?"

Mr. Perkins considered this for a moment. "I suppose it would be best. Albright and Longstreet should be here."

Deborah hoped that Jael would also travel with them. She couldn't imagine her friend allowing them to leave her behind—especially once they became aware of the hurricane and storms. She would want to see Deborah and Lizzie and hear all the news. Besides, Mr. Perkins said they'd settled their affairs. That surely meant they were making the move to Houston as planned.

"Mother, I'll bring Uncle Arjan back as soon as possible. It's late though, so we might just stay in camp tonight."

"I think that would be wise," Mother replied. "I don't want you pushing yourself too hard. You've done a wonderful job of keeping the supplies going to the camp, but I know your leg still gives you problems from time to time. There are also the hogs to contend with."

He bent down and kissed her head. "I'll be fine. Don't look for us until mornin'. Now, if you'll excuse me, I reckon I'd better let Lizzie know what's happening."

Deborah waited until he'd gone to voice her opinion. "It seems to me that the sooner the mill is back up and operating, the better for everyone. You mentioned folks were moving out—heading elsewhere for work."

Mr. Perkins nodded. "Some were leaving to be with family members who were hurt by the storm. Others were just needin' to keep wages comin' in to provide for their family. I hate to see them go; trained men are so much more valuable to me than greenhorns. When I do get the mill up and running, I'll be delayed as I train the new fellas."

"Well, hopefully we can work together," Mother said. "I'm sure God will provide."

Mr. Perkins picked up his coffee cup. "That's my prayer." He finished the contents and put the cup back down. Getting to his feet, he squared his shoulders. "I don't mind telling you, though, I'm pretty discouraged. I can't figure out why anyone would do a thing like this. I've tried to be a fair employer—always generous with my workers. I didn't figure I had any trouble with them."

Mother stood and Deborah did likewise. "It probably wasn't one of the workers," her mother told him. "A worker wouldn't risk losing his job. I'm confident this must have come from someone outside the company. Perhaps it's even the work of the White Hand of God. After all, you employ former slaves. Someone may be trying to prove a point."

"Yeah, but they're usually good about leavin' notes around after their deeds. This just doesn't add up."

"Let me get your hat for you," Mother said, moving into the foyer.

"I know this is gonna be hard on your family, as well," Mr. Perkins said as they stood by the front door. "I only hope Arjan and G.W. won't have trouble gettin' somebody to take their logs."

Mother smiled. "I'm sure they won't. Especially now with Texans working to rebuild the damaged areas, lumber will be in demand. Don't you fret about us, Zed. We'll be just fine. Please tell Rachel that if she needs anything—anything at all—she only has to call on me."

Deborah and her mother followed him outside and watched from the porch as he mounted and rode away. For a moment, neither said a word. Then Deborah voiced what had been on her mind the entire time.

"What if Stuart had something to do with this?"

Mother's concerned expression seemed to offer an unspoken question. Deborah hurried to explain. "You remember that Jael was certain he meant us harm."

"But why burn down your own investment—especially since it won't really hurt us at all? We'll simply load out the logs and send them elsewhere."

"I don't know," Deborah said, shaking her head. "It just seems like the kind of hateful thing he might do. I know it doesn't make any sense, but I can't help feeling there is something to this that involves him."

"I can't imagine it, but I suppose we shall know in due time."

Mother looked toward the plum trees. "We'd best get the fruit into the kitchen. I don't want to lose any more to the birds."

Night fell and it seemed particularly quiet without the men. Deborah and Lizzie put the babies to bed and found their way out to the front room, where Mother and Sissy mended shirts.

"Emmy and Rutger sleeping?" Mother asked as the girls joined them.

"They were quite worn out from their adventurous day," Lizzie told her. "I had them on a blanket in the middle of the floor while I worked on some new clothes for them. They seemed quite captivated with the new location."

Mother smiled and refocused on her work. "Hard to believe they are nearly three months old. Time goes by so quickly when they're small. Seems like just yesterday, Deborah was a baby."

"Shore do," Sissy said, nodding and rocking. Deborah could see that she'd been busy fixing a tear in one of Arjan's shirts.

"It's getting late," Deborah said suppressing a yawn. "I suppose I'll head up to bed."

"We should all get some sleep," Mother said, tying off her thread. "I've a feeling when the men get back, we'll have a busy day."

Deborah couldn't help thinking it wouldn't be busy as much as troublesome. "I'll see you in the morning."

"Good night, sweetheart." Mother got to her feet. "Come on, Sissy. We need to call it a night. I'll take this lamp, and you get the other."

The black woman put her mending in the basket at her feet and slowly rose. Deborah looked to Lizzie. "If you need help in the night, come get me."

Lizzie nodded. "I should be all right. G.W.'s never that helpful in the wee hours, anyway. He sleeps like a log whether the twins are fussing or cooing."

Mother laughed. "Rutger was the same way. Never did see a man who could sleep through such noise. The whole house could have fallen down around him, and he would have slept on."

Deborah readied for bed and slipped between the sheets, thinking of her father and days gone by. Her father would often take her on rides through the forest. She'd sit in front of him on his favorite horse and listen to him talk about the land.

"Land is good," he told her, *"but family is better. God gave us the earth to tend, but our families to love. Never forget that."*

"I won't," Deborah whispered to the air. "I won't forget any of the things you taught me, Papa."

An image of Christopher came to mind, and she couldn't seem to push it aside. He was all she wanted in a husband—everything except here and willing. He'd broken the courtship without even speaking to her. That served to anger as much as grieve her. She could never marry a man who refused to listen to her heart on matters.

"Of course, marriage isn't something I need worry about now," she muttered. Deborah snuggled beneath her covers and sighed. "Maybe I'll just always remain a spinster." She imagined herself earning her medical degree and spending the rest of her life alone. It was a daunting thought.

Deborah tossed and turned, unable to find rest. She was about to give up and light a lamp to read by when the dogs began to raise a fuss. She crossed to the window to see what the trouble might be—probably nothing more than an old coon or hog.

By the time she gazed out, the dogs had quieted. *That isn't typical,* she thought. Usually once they were riled, they continued to bark until someone demanded they stop. The blackness below her revealed little, though, and Deborah turned to go back to her bed just as the sound of broken glass came from somewhere on the main floor.

She pulled on her robe and got into her slippers. Making her way down the stairs, she saw that her mother was in the hallway. Lamplight revealed nothing immediately out of place.

"What was that?" Deborah asked.

Mother shook her head. "I don't know."

Sissy and Lizzie were soon at her heel. "Did you hear glass break?" Lizzie asked.

"I heard the dogs raise a ruckus and then the glass," Deborah replied.

Mother went to the door and opened it. She placed the lamp on a table behind the door, then tightened the belt on her robe. Peering outside for a moment, she stepped hesitantly onto the porch. The others followed suit.

"I don't hear anything," she said, turning to Deborah. "Do you?"

Deborah looked around and walked to the end of the porch. "Nothing."

"What's that? Is someone in the barn?" Lizzie questioned. "I see a . . ." She gasped. "Fire!"

Mother turned to follow her gaze. "Deborah, come help me." They rushed across the yard to the open barn door.

Inside, Deborah could see where someone had ignited straw in the corner of the empty front stall. She hurried to where a bucket of water sat. The fire had barely started, and she hoped to douse it before the flames could spread.

Mother followed right behind with a horse blanket. Together, they contained the fire with minimal damage to the area. Lizzie had come to the door with a lantern. With its soft glow, they surveyed the barn. Everything appeared normal.

The smell of burned straw was enough to drive them all back

out into the fresh air. Deborah looked at her mother through smoke-blurred eyes. She spoke the words they were all, no doubt, thinking. "Someone means to harm us."

"Someone," Mother replied. "But who?"

Deborah looked around for Jasper and Lula. She called for them, but they didn't come. "You don't suppose they ran off after whoever it was?"

Mother glanced around the yard. "I don't think they would have gone. You know how protective they are—especially at night."

Deborah motioned Lizzie to bring the lamp. "Maybe they're hiding in the barn. Could be they were frightened by the fire." They walked back into the haze and began to search the stalls. Fortunately, Dottie and Dorothy had been turned out to graze in the fenced pen to the north of the house. Since G.W. had taken the remaining horses, the barn was empty of life.

Moving to the far end of the barn, Deborah could see the carriage door was open. She hurried forward and Lizzie followed on her heels.

"Oh no," she moaned and fell to her knees. She touched Jasper's lifeless body. Lula lay just a few feet away, a pitchfork planted through her body. From the pooled blood around their heads, it was clear that someone had slit their throats.

"They killed them," Deborah said, a sob catching in her throat. "Someone has killed them both."

Chapter 27

In the humid dampness of the morning, Deborah wept and dug graves for the family dogs. She had heard the commotion that signaled her brother's return to the homestead, but continued to focus on the task at hand. She wanted to be alone with her grief, but it wasn't to be. In silence, Jake Wythe appeared. To her surprise he said nothing, but came up and took the shovel from her hands and began to make much faster progress.

Deborah carefully wrapped each of the dogs in an old bed sheet and squatted down beside their bodies. She buried her face against her knees and let out all the pent-up pain she held. She'd cried through much of the night and knew she looked a sight, but she didn't care. Someone's heartless ugliness had ripped away another piece of her comfort and security.

It wasn't long before Jake put the shovel aside and came to get the dogs. Deborah tried her best to regain control of her emotions. She stood and watched in silence as the graves were filled first with the bodies of the animals and then dirt. It was only after the burial was complete that Jake turned to look at her.

"I'm sorry we weren't here to stop this, but I promise you I'll find out who's responsible and see they pay."

She shook her head. "I wouldn't want you to get hurt. There's no way of telling who did this—it was dark and we didn't see anyone."

"There are always ways to learn the truth," he told her.

"Why should I expect to learn who killed my dogs, when we can't even figure out who murdered George and David?" Her anger seemed to boil over. "I can't believe how backward this part of the world can be. Folks will probably rise up in arms over the death of two hounds. I can just picture it now: Someone will probably form a posse to hunt the monsters down."

Coming to where she stood, Jake shook his head. "I'm so sorry, Deborah."

The gentle way he spoke her name caused Deborah to calm and dissolve in tears once again. She didn't try to hide her grief from him, nor did she push him away when he took her in his arms. He did nothing untoward; he simply let her cry. Yet despite his tenderness, Deborah wished it was Christopher's arms around her. She couldn't help but remember how she'd held Christopher and let him mourn the sorrow of his family's troubles not so long ago.

And then he left me.

"You'll make yourself sick if you keep goin' on like this," Jake said softly.

Deborah pulled away. "I am sick. Sick at heart. I don't understand why this happened. I cannot comprehend the heart of a man who acts in such a way—to kill people and animals." She wiped at her tears with the back of her sleeve before continuing.

"I don't understand why God has allowed this to happen." She knew she spoke of far more than just the deaths of Jasper and Lula. Why had God allowed her to lose her heart to Christopher and then taken him away from her? Why had the hurricane been allowed to wreak havoc all along the coast? Why had the mill burned down?

"I want answers." She looked at Jake, knowing he would have no solutions. Deborah turned to leave, but Jake took hold of her arm.

"Sometimes we don't get answers," he told her. "Leastwise we don't understand the answers."

Deborah knew his words were true, but they offered no solace. She looked at him hard for a moment, then relaxed. "I know you're right, but it hurts just the same."

She headed back to the house, aware that Jake followed just a few steps behind. Once she reached the back door, she opened it and stood to one side and glanced at the ground. "Thank you for your help with the dogs."

He paused and reached out to lift her chin to meet his gaze. "There ain't nothin' I wouldn't do for you, Miss Deborah. I know you love another, but maybe someday—if that love fades—you'll remember that someone else cares for you, too." He dropped his hand and stepped into the house.

Deborah stared after him for a moment. "That love will never fade, Jake. I have no hope of loving another," she barely whispered, knowing he couldn't hear.

In town, Arjan and Euphanel met with Zed Perkins at his house. Deborah had come along at her mother's insistence. Euphanel had been firm. She knew her daughter needed to put her attention on something other than her pain.

"You know Mr. Albright and Mr. Longstreet, of course," Zed said as he escorted them into his formal parlor.

Albright and Longstreet got to their feet at the sight of the ladies. They gave a brief bow of greeting but appeared otherwise disinterested. Euphanel thought Mr. Longstreet almost avoided her gaze altogether. Perhaps he was embarrassed now at the forward way he'd acted prior to her marriage to Arjan.

"I'm glad you could be here," Zed began. "I just wanted to make sure we could discuss any concerns or problems that needed to be addressed. Like I told Euphanel last evenin', I know this situation greatly affects Vandermark Logging, since you were under contract to us to provide logs." He motioned them to take their seats, then waited until everyone was settled before continuing. "I've no idea how long before we're able to produce lumber."

"Euphanel says that you're already working to get the mill back up and running," Arjan said. "We'd like to help anyway we can."

Zed nodded. "I appreciate that. I'll be usin' the logs I have in the millpond to begin the reconstruction. There ain't funds available just yet, but in due time, I hope to be able to receive your logs. I'm positive you'll have no trouble selling your cuttings to another mill in the meanwhile."

"No, I don't imagine so," Arjan replied.

"If I might interrupt," Stuart Albright said, leaning forward in his chair. "Selling to another company is not an option at this time."

Zed's puzzled look suggested he'd not expected this comment. Euphanel could see that Longstreet, however, was not surprised. He simply nodded and stroked his mustache a time or two.

"Then you'll need us to continue delivery?" Arjan questioned.

Albright's face took on a most menacing expression. "No. I have no interest in taking on additional wood at this time."

"Then what are you saying?" Zed asked before Arjan could get the words out.

"I'm saying that you will simply have to stockpile your logs until we decide what is to be done with the mill," Albright replied.

"Stockpile? But there's no reason for that," Zed interjected. "It'll be some time before we can start up production in earnest. They might as well make their livin' elsewhere. They have employees and debts to pay as much as anyone else."

Euphanel saw Stuart give Mr. Longstreet a quick sidelong glance before continuing. "It would seem that you have forgotten the terms of the contract. Let me bring to mind the paragraph that states Vandermark Logging will sell their cut pine logs exclusively to Perkins Sawmill."

"Yes, but that was before the fire," Zed countered. "They can hardly be expected to wait until the mill is once again running before they sell their wood. It could be months."

Mr. Longstreet spoke for the first time. "If not longer."

Euphanel looked to Arjan and then back to Zed. "What is this about?"

Zed shook his head. "I don't rightly know. What are you saying, gentlemen?"

"Simply this," Albright began. "We haven't yet decided if we will rebuild."

"You can't be serious," Arjan interjected. "It would be pure waste not to rebuild."

"Not at all, Mr. Vandermark, and I assure you I am very serious. My partner and I own two-thirds of the mill. There are a great number of debts to be paid, and our debtors will not care that the place lies in charred remains—they will expect their money. We will have to consider the most advantageous plan for seeing our obligations fulfilled."

"Well, surely that includes having the mill up and running. You can hardly make money to pay your debts if the mill sits idle," Deborah said, looking to her mother. "I've read that contract. You are under obligation to us, as well. You have pledged to take a certain number of logs and are required to pay us in a timely manner whether the market suffers or not."

"Ah, but this has nothing to do with the market," Stuart countered. "The mill is unable to manufacture lumber. We have not yet come to terms on the costs or ability to rebuild the mill. Until that decision is agreed upon, Vandermark Logging will be forced to stockpile their logs. I've already checked with a lawyer on this matter—a judge, as well. You may feel free to contact one or both. I can give you the information on how to locate them when we conclude this meeting."

"Just how long before you are able to decide about fixin' up the mill?" Arjan asked.

Euphanel could tell by the tone of his voice that he was barely containing his anger. She started to reach out to take hold of his hand, then thought better of it. Rutger never liked to be touched when he was mad. It was probably the same for his brother.

Albright and Longstreet looked at each other and shrugged before turning back to the others. "It is difficult to say. I intend to thoroughly establish the cause for the fire before rebuilding. You see, there is the matter of insurance coverage. The inspectors will want to take a full account of the situation."

"Insurance?" Zed asked. "But I don't have any fire insurance."

"No, you don't, but Mr. Longstreet and I took out our own policy. We had to protect our interests, you understand."

"So you have insurance that will provide for you to rebuild?" Arjan asked.

Again Stuart shrugged as though he were discussing nothing more important than what would be served for supper. "The insurance inspectors will have to decide that matter. They will be delayed, no doubt, due to the storm. A great many fires have arisen in areas damaged by the hurricane. When the inspectors are able to come to Perkinsville and see for themselves what happened, then and only then can we consider rebuilding."

Arjan leaned back in his chair and crossed his arms. "So you want us to sit and do nothing while you wait for your inspection."

"Not at all, Mr. Vandermark. As I said, I expect for you to stockpile your logs for future use."

"But that means we will have to continue paying wages and keeping men employed, even though we won't be bringing in any money."

Albright looked at his fingernails as if something had magically appeared there. "The day-to-day running of your company is hardly my concern." He lifted his gaze to Deborah. "Wouldn't you agree, Miss Vandermark?"

Euphanel saw her daughter stiffen. Deborah returned the man's gaze without difficulty. She opened her mouth to speak, but Euphanel decided it might serve them better to remain silent. She jumped to her feet and held up her hand.

"I'm sorry, but I must put an end to this meeting. I'm afraid we need to see the constable before heading back to the house. We found ourselves vandalized last evening, and it is important we contact the law officials in order to see if they can figure out who might be responsible." She looked to Deborah, hoping she would remain silent. She did.

Stuart and Mr. Longstreet got to their feet, and with this, the others followed suit. Deborah took hold of Euphanel's arm and gave her a light squeeze as if to reassure her.

Arjan looked to Albright and Longstreet. "I reckon the best thing for me is to have a lawyer of our own look into matters." He turned to Zed. "I'll be in touch. You let me know if you need anything."

Zed seemed overwhelmed by the turn the discussion had taken. "I'm sure sorry about this Arjan—Euphanel. I'll do what I can to get the matter straightened out."

Euphanel reached out with her free hand and patted Zed's arm. "I know you will. You've always been a good friend to my family. I know we can trust you to do what's right."

Once they'd spoken to the constable about the attack on their home, the Vandermarks climbed into the wagon and headed out of town. Deborah was furious with the actions of Stuart Albright.

"He's only doing this to punish G.W. and Lizzie. He's punishing me, as well, because he knows that I encouraged Lizzie to leave him at the altar. I suppose this is really all my fault."

"Nonsense," Arjan said. "Ain't nobody's fault but Mr. Albright's and Mr. Longstreet's. Zed isn't a part of this. You saw how upset he was."

"Poor man." Mother met Uncle Arjan's gaze. "I feel so bad for him—for Rachel, too. They are going to suffer tremendously from this."

"I should have known Stuart would try something like this," Deborah muttered. "He said he would punish Lizzie, and now he has."

"I suppose we must tell Lizzie and G.W. what's happened. This certainly will be upsetting to them."

"Now, Nell, you can't hardly keep this from 'em. G.W. is handling the books, and Lizzie knows the kind of man Albright is. They may both expect somethin' like this."

Deborah eased back in the leather carriage seat and frowned. "What if Stuart also had something to do with the attack last night?" The question hung in the air for several moments before her mother turned.

"We can't know that for sure. Like Ralph said—if we didn't see anyone, there's little hope of figuring out who was responsible."

"I can't help but think this is all related," Deborah replied. "Stuart hates us and would stop at nothing to see us pay for what he perceives as our wrongdoings."

"But he wasn't even in town until this morning," Mother reminded.

"She's right," Uncle Arjan threw out. "Can't say he did it when he wasn't even here."

"He didn't have to be here to pay others to do his dirty work. Same with the mill."

"Now be careful what you say, little gal," Arjan replied with a glance over his shoulder. "You can't go accusin' a man without proof."

"Why not? Folks around here weren't at all shy about accusing me of inappropriate behavior. They gossiped and told stories each time Christopher and I worked together. They didn't think it was proper for me to be a doctor; then they didn't feel it was proper for us to court if I was going to insist on being a doctor. It's not right that townfolk can accuse me in such a way, then refuse to listen when we know that Stuart only wishes us ill for what happened with G.W. and Lizzie."

Arjan seemed to understand her anger and gave her a sympathetic nod. "I can see what you mean, but Albright and Longstreet would have no reason to burn their own mill down. They're sufferin' in this, too."

"Not if they have insurance," Deborah replied. "The policy is between the two of them. They will make money whether Mr. Perkins does or not. They can easily take their profits from the insurance and never look back."

"Oh, Arjan, you don't suppose she's right?"

Deborah could see her uncle's face darken. "If she is right," he said, fixing his gaze on the road ahead, "then we're dealin' with men of much worse character than I figured."

"I can't speak for Jael's father," Deborah said, shaking her head, "but Stuart is a demanding man who would have forced a woman into marriage purely to keep from losing his inheritance. He's the very kind of man who would cut his nose off to spite his face . . . or burn his mill in order to make us pay."

Chapter 28

Deborah pored over the contract once again. She chided herself for not having been more thorough in her examination. Especially since she was the one to encourage her family to accept it. Had she been less prideful—less focused on what she perceived as her intelligence in business dealings—then perhaps she would have suggested they go to a lawyer.

"This contract is vague enough that I suppose they can manipulate it however they want," Deborah said, pushing away from the desk.

"It's not like we were used to havin' a contract," Arjan said. "I never wanted one in the first place, but Zed needed it for the bank." Her uncle shook his head. "That wood can't sit on the ground forever—it'll rot. Which may be exactly what Albright wants."

Deborah looked at the office door. "Where are G.W. and Lizzie now?"

"They're helping Sissy bring in the laundry," Mother replied. "Why?"

She drew a deep breath. "I think we need to tell them the truth now. Stuart isn't the kind of man who will keep this a secret. I say we call them in here and simply explain the situation for what it is. But it will be hard on Lizzie. She'll blame herself."

"I don't want her to feel responsible," Mother said.

"Then we need to tell 'em the truth, Euphanel."

Deborah was surprised by her uncle's declaration. Mother looked at him oddly and he continued. "If we try to hide it, they're goin' to feel that we were lyin' to them—even if it was to protect them. To my way of thinkin', that would only serve to make them feel it was their fault."

"How so?" Mother asked.

"Well, I'd figure that if I had nothin' to do with it, folks wouldn't be afraid to discuss it with me."

"He's right, Mother. You know that G.W. would rather be dealt with openly."

Mother nodded. "I'll go get them." She rose slowly and hesitated. "I know that God will give us direction. I'm not going to let Mr. Albright's underhanded actions take my sight from God's faithfulness."

With that, she walked from the office. Deborah looked to her uncle. "She's right, you know." She smiled ever so slightly. "I'm sure the devil uses these kinds of matters to steal our hope. Perhaps we just need to look at this in a different way."

"What do you mean?" her uncle asked.

Deborah picked up the ledger. "First, we need to cut our costs."

"My first suggestion would be to get rid of the workers, but I can't very well produce logs without loggers."

"What if we speak to the employees? If we explain the situation, maybe some sort of arrangement can be made."

"Possibly," Arjan agreed.

Mother returned with G.W. and Lizzie. Their expressions told Deborah that they knew the news wasn't going to be good. Deborah got up from behind the desk and motioned G.W. to take his regular place. She moved quietly to the side of the room and remained standing. Lizzie crossed to stand beside her.

"What is this about?" she whispered.

"Trouble with the business."

Lizzie frowned but said nothing more as Uncle Arjan began. "We called you here to let you know what we learned in the meeting with Mr. Perkins." He paused and seemed to think about what to say next. "Mr. Albright and Mr. Longstreet have returned."

"I should have come with you," G.W. said, looking apprehensive. "I can tell this isn't going to be what I want to hear."

"Well, it's not exactly what any of us wanted, but facts being what they are—it can't be helped. The mill may not rebuild for a time. There was some sort of insurance policy held by Longstreet and Albright, and until the company can come out and assess the details of the fire, apparently nothing can be done."

"So we cease production or find another buyer—is that it?" G.W. asked.

Arjan glanced at Mother and then to Deborah before he answered. "It's not that simple. Apparently our contract requires that we stay in production, and that we can only sell to the Perkinsville mill. Since that mill is temporarily out of operation, we must stockpile our logs."

"For how long?" G.W. asked.

"For as long as it takes them to make a decision," Uncle Arjan answered.

"I don't understand." G.W. fixed his gaze on Deborah. "There's something you aren't telling us."

"Not at all," Mother said. "That's why you're here. The business arrangements have been complicated not only by the fire, but by the arrival of Mr. Albright and Mr. Longstreet."

He frowned. "What have they got to do with this?"

Deborah took hold of Lizzie's hand. "They now own the majority of the company. They have say over whether the mill gets rebuilt. They have the only insurance on the property and will obviously be the ones who hold the responsibility of paying the debts against the mill."

"And Stuart warned us that he would get back at us," Lizzie murmured.

For a moment, the room went silent. G.W.'s expression changed to one of anger. He looked to his uncle. "This is Albright's idea?"

Arjan nodded. "He says they've had a lawyer look into it—a judge, too. They can force us to continue working in order to have the log quota available if and when they need them. We can't sell to anyone else."

"That's hardly fair," Lizzie said, shaking her head. "If they can't take the logs, then they are breaking their part of the contract."

"That's what I presumed," Deborah declared, "but apparently the wording leaves it open to question."

"We can't keep paying our workers if we aren't getting paid," G.W. said. "How are we supposed to run a business if we don't have money coming in?"

Lizzie was growing more upset by the minute. Deborah turned to her sister-in-law and smiled. "We have some ideas. Why don't you go sit beside Mother?"

Lizzie hesitated only a moment, then did exactly as Deborah suggested. Mother took hold of her hand and patted it reassuringly. "Please don't fret."

"This is outrageous. I'm gonna go give Albright a piece of my mind," G.W. said, getting to his feet.

Deborah stepped forward. "Not until you hear me out."

Everyone looked at her in surprise. Deborah looked to Uncle Arjan, who nodded.

Reluctantly, G.W. took his seat. "All right. Get to it."

"Look, we know that Stuart Albright holds this family a grudge." She gave careful thought to her words. "But that problem won't help us accomplish what we need to do. God will avenge any wrongs done to us, and we need to look to Him to direct our steps."

"Deborah's right," Arjan said. "We've started thinkin' of some ways to handle the situation. First, I think we can all agree that we need to hold on to as much of our money as possible."

"That will mean letting our workers go," G.W. said. "How are we supposed to produce without workers?"

"We talked briefly about that," Deborah said, hoping her words wouldn't make G.W. feel they had planned things out behind his back. "That's why we needed you here. What if we ask the men to work mainly for room and board with the promise that we will pay them in full within a certain time?"

"How can we be sure to meet that time frame?" G.W. asked.

Deborah gave a slight shrug. "The question of the mill can't remain unanswered forever. We can get our own lawyer to help us."

"That's gonna take money we don't have to spare." G.W. practically growled the words.

"My father!" Lizzie declared. "Father would help us with the contract issues, and he wouldn't expect pay. He said when he left that if there was anything at all he could do to help, he would, because it would give him a good excuse to come see us." She fixed her husband with a smile. "He hasn't yet seen the twins."

"That's true," G.W. said, sounding a little more hopeful.

"We can also step up the turpentine production. They've been after us for months to give them more trees," Arjan said. "I think if we double their acreage, we can meet our loan payments and have a little money left for other needs—maybe even a bit of pay for the men."

"But the best of the summer is over and spring is months away." G.W. shook his head. "They can do the fall and winter scraping, but I don't know if it will do us much good."

"All we can do is try," Arjan declared. "We can speak to the turpentiners and get their opinion on the matter. Let's call the boys in and have a meeting here at the house tomorrow. It'll be Saturday, and we can give those who stay the rest of the day off and reconcile with those who want to go."

"I think that's a good idea," Mother said. "Will you go and bring them in?"

Arjan nodded. "I will. That way I can secure the camp before I head back."

G.W. reached for the ledger. "I'll see if I can find ways to save us more money."

Deborah went to his side. "I'll help you. If we put our heads together, we can come up with something that will help."

The loggers listened as Arjan detailed the problems at hand. Mother and Sissy had put together a magnificent dinner, and now everyone remained at the table, trying to figure out their futures.

"Look, I know some of you have families, so stayin' on with us probably isn't possible. There will be no hard feelings if you have to quit. The rest of you will have a place to sleep and three meals a day. We'll see to your injuries and keep a detailed record of the pay owed you.

"If possible, we'll have a little money each week for you. It might only be script, but it will be something. We won't work to exceed our planned production, either. We'll just do what's necessary and nothing more. We've been performing at the level designated by Mr. Perkins for when the mill expansion was complete. As G.W. pointed out to me, we can cut production down to what was required for this phase."

"Mr. Vandermark?"

"Yes, Jake?"

Jake pushed back his chair a bit. "I have what may sound like a strange question, but I hope you'll hear me out."

Arjan raised a brow. "All right."

"Well, I'm just wonderin'—Vandermark Loggin' owns a lot of land that's already been harvested. Now, I know you have young trees growin' as replacements, but that will be some time—if ever—before they're ready to cut."

"Go on," Arjan encouraged.

"Is there any chance you might consider sellin' off some of that land for farmin' and ranchin'? I, for one, wouldn't mind takin' some of my pay in acreage."

G.W. got to his feet, and Deborah was afraid for a moment that he would be wholly against the idea. "That's something we overlooked," he said, quite enthused. "I think it would be a great idea. We could sell or trade off pieces of the unproductive acres and bank the money for our future needs, as well as maybe trade some acreage for wages."

"Who of you here would be of a mind to take acreage?" Arjan asked.

"I wouldn't be able to live without some money," Warren replied, "but I'd sure be interested. I always wanted to have a few acres—nothin' big."

"It wouldn't be large pieces," G.W. countered. "Probably more like ten- or twenty-acre parcels, at the most."

"I like the sound of that," Warren said, looking to Jake. "That was a good suggestion, whistle punk. You'll be fellin' trees before you know it."

"We will continue to work out the details of how we can make this situation work," Arjan continued, "and let you fellas know what's expected. However, if you need to quit us, I'd like for you to come talk to me in the office."

He sat down and motioned to Mother. "Now, if you don't mind, I'll have another slice of pie."

Chapter 29

October 1886

With October's arrival came the devastating news that Deborah had feared. Indianola, Texas, had not only suffered the brunt of the hurricane's forces, but it had been, for all purposes, destroyed. First, the storm itself had sent tidal floods and heavy winds. The newspaper account Uncle Arjan brought her reported that many people had tried to gather in the Signal Station, which was thought to be the strongest of buildings. However, as the water rose, the building began to rock. People, fearing for their lives, abandoned the place and hurried in the rising water to find shelter. The Signal Officer, a Mr. Reed, was charting the weather changes and remained behind to set the anemometer. The act proved to be fatal. A signal lamp set fire to the building and burned not only him, but an unidentified doctor. The fire didn't kill them, however.

They drowned as the water swept through the town and engulfed everything.

Deborah felt numb as she lowered the paper to her lap. Her mother and uncle sat beside her, waiting for her to say something. She looked at them, shaking her head. No words would come. Surely the unidentified doctor wasn't Christopher.

"We heard the news in town," her mother began. "Then I read it for myself in the paper. They say that over twenty-five people were lost in the Indianola area. Victoria sustained incredible damage, as well. We came home as quickly as we could to give you the news."

"But that doesn't mean the doc was there," her uncle began. "It could be he was able to get out of Indianola before the storm hit."

"And go where?" Deborah murmured. She looked at them both. "I need to be alone." She got to her feet, the paper fluttering to the floor of the porch.

Without another word, she walked deep into the woods that she had always loved, her place of refuge. Even as a young girl she had come here to pray and seek God's comfort when things were difficult. But there was no comfort to be had today. She could hardly form words of prayer.

"Oh, God," she prayed, "Oh, God, please . . . please let Christopher be all right. I cannot bear the thought that he might be dead."

Speaking the words aloud seemed to drain her of any pretense of strength. Deborah fell to her knees sobbing. "I cannot bear this, Lord. It's too much." She buried her face in her hands. All of her life, she had relied upon her intelligence to reason away complications and sorrows. She'd always found a way to make sense of things, in some capacity or another. To find some measure of solace.

But there was no solace to be had in this.

She remained on the damp forest ground for a long while. Easing back against one of the longleaf pines, she pulled her knees to her chest and hugged them close. She felt empty inside. Maybe this was a sign that Christopher truly was dead.

Deborah couldn't get the words "unidentified doctor" out of her head. Surely, if the newspaper reporter had been able to learn the identity of the signal officer, the townsfolk could have told him the name of the doctor, as well. Unless, of course, that doctor had arrived in town only the week before.

A gentle breeze filtered through the trees and touched her damp face. Deborah lifted her gaze skyward, watching the gentle sway of the pines. Their lofty branches made a green canopy, allowing just enough light through to cast streams of illumination here and there.

"Are you with me, Father? I feel so alone." A rustling in the brush nearby caused Deborah to take note, but she didn't move.

A feral sow with her piglets came onto the path. The hog froze in step and stared at her as if trying to ascertain the threat. Deborah did nothing but return the stare. If the tusked animal charged her, Deborah would most likely suffer a fatal injury. Maybe that would be God's mercy. Maybe Christopher was dead, and God knew the pain would be too much for her to endure. The hog snorted and the piglets came running to her side.

Deborah closed her eyes as if accepting her fate. There was no need to be afraid or to prepare for a fight for which she had no strength. If this truly was to be the end of her life, she wanted to face it without fear. She drew a deep breath.

I give my life to you, God. I have nothing left—no strength of my own.

When she opened her eyes again, the sow had moved on. Deborah could only see the hind ends of the piglets as they headed deeper into the woods with their mother. There was neither relief nor regret in the moment. It simply was as it was—nothing more, nothing less.

Deborah got to her feet and began to walk once again. She pushed into the heavier stand of pines, into areas where the trails narrowed and the brush had not been burned away. The drought had kept them from doing all of their normal winter burns the year before and only minimal work had been accomplished. This left them with a higher threat of fire, but the longleafs were strong. Fire actually stimulated their growth, so long as the temperatures of the flames weren't too intense.

If I were a longleaf pine, Deborah thought, *I could surely withstand this fire.*

But even the pines would be reduced to stubble if the fire burned hot enough. There was always a point at which any living thing could be killed.

She knew she should be aware of her surroundings—snakes and other Piney Woods rooters could harm her. Deborah tried to focus on the ground and the path ahead, but her mind imagined horrific scenes—collapsed, burned rubble and flooded streets. Images of the dead laid out side by side, waiting in their eternal rest for someone to take them home.

Tears anew blurred her eyes. *I feel no hope. No hope.*

The words seemed to pace themselves to the beat of her steps. *No hope. No hope. No hope.* Despair poured over Deborah, leaving her breathless. She spied a stand of trees where the forest grass was not too deep and moved across the opening. Without being mindful of the ground, she collapsed and closed her eyes.

No hope. Oh, God, do not leave me without hope.

Deborah awoke some hours later. She had no idea of the time, but the light was greatly diminished and an uneasy silence hung over the woods. Getting to her feet, Deborah brushed off pine needles and dried grass.

For a moment, she couldn't remember why she'd come here, and then the memories came rushing back. Christopher might be lost to her forever. He might be dead or injured . . . or if he was alive, not even care that she suffered. No, surely he could never be that cruel. Not the Christopher she knew.

Deborah looked around to get her bearings, then spied the path that would lead back to the house. Her mother would be worried by now. They might even be looking for her. Deborah had never intended to be gone for so long. Despite her sorrow and confusion, she didn't want to add to her family's worries.

She lifted her skirt to avoid tripping over it as she maneuvered through an area of fallen branches. Once back on the path, Deborah let out a long sigh. "I feel so weak now, but maybe that's the point," she murmured. As a human being—especially a woman—her strength was quite limited. These were the times, she could very nearly hear her mother say, when God's strength was sufficient to carry her through.

"But how, when I don't know what to do? How foolish to think myself so full of wisdom and knowledge that I would never make the same mistakes—endure the same hardships—that others might face."

Perhaps the best thing to do would be to go back East and live with Aunt Wilhelmina. It would be getting cold up north, but she could be there before the first snows set in. Aunt Wilhelmina would happily welcome her back—she had said as much on many occasions. Perhaps her aunt could also help Deborah find a doctor who might be willing to train her. Philadelphia was a very progressive town. Surely there were equally progressive physicians.

The robust scent of the earth and pine wafted on the air, reminding Deborah of how much she loved this area. It wouldn't be easy to leave again. It wouldn't be easy to say good-bye to her family.

"And this time I won't have Lizzie and Jael with me in Philadelphia." The thought momentarily gave her pause. Could she live happily without her friends and family? Aunt Wilhelmina was a dear, to be sure, but she was aging and quite self-focused. She had spent much of her life on her own, after being widowed at a young age. Because her husband had left her a small fortune, her aunt had lived quite comfortably, doing exactly what pleased her. She had no children, offering instead her love and kindness to her sisters' children. That was how Deborah had come to benefit and, hopefully, would be blessed again.

If I return to Philadelphia and offer to work, she will, no doubt, tell me it isn't necessary. However, if I work, I can afford to send money back to Mother and Uncle Arjan.

She frowned. Mother would never allow for her to tell Aunt Wilhelmina of their problems. Money issues were simply not spoken of in such a manner. It was one thing for an aunt to offer her riches to spoil a much-beloved niece, but entirely another for that niece to bring the intimate details of the family's struggles to her aunt's attention.

Staring ahead as the trail widened once again to the main road, Deborah felt defeat threatening her meager plans. Her mother would want to keep her from leaving—G.W. and Uncle Arjan, too. Lizzie would never understand and would certainly beg her to stay. And then there were the twins. They were so precious, and Deborah couldn't imagine living so far away. "If I can't convince myself—how can I hope to convince my family?"

The light was fading fast. Quickening her pace, Deborah put aside her concerns. She would figure out the details of her trip and what she would tell her aunt after she announced the matter to her family. She needed for them to believe that this was something she was doing out of a desire to complete her medical training. And in truth, that was part of her reasoning. They didn't need to know that she also wanted to go to escape her memories and relieve the burden of an extra mouth to feed.

But what of Christopher? How could she ever know for sure what had happened to him? Could she perhaps write to his mother in Kansas City? Did Mr. Perkins have the address there? She would check with him tomorrow—or better still, she'd go to the doctor's office and look through Christopher's papers. Having a plan in mind gave her a moment of courage.

As the house came in sight, Deborah wasn't surprised to see her mother standing on the porch with a lantern in hand.

"I'm here," Deborah called as she stepped into the clearing. "I'm all right."

"Oh, Deborah. I was so worried. We all were. Where have you been?" Mother declared, putting the lantern on the post. She hurried down the steps.

"I am sorry. The news about Indianola was just so overwhelming," she admitted. "I tried to pray and I guess I fell asleep."

"Oh, child, did you not think of the dangers?" Mother embraced her, and for a moment Deborah found comfort there. It was easy to imagine she was a child again—safe and secure. Her father would round the corner of the house any moment to announce that it was time for supper and evening devotions.

She pulled back, fighting tears. "I never meant to grieve you," Deborah told her mother.

"I know, just as I never wanted to grieve you with the news

from Indianola. I realize you're very worried for Dr. Clayton. We mustn't give up hope, however."

Deborah shook her head. "I've searched deep inside myself and found that place empty."

"Oh, darling, your hope doesn't come from within—not in the sense of self, anyway. It comes from God alone. If not, then it will crumble and blow as dust to the wind. You have only to fix your sights on Jesus. Remember the words of the psalmist.: 'Why art thou cast down, O my soul? and why art thou disquieted in me? Hope thou in God: for I shall yet praise him for the help of his countenance.' You will find your strength in Him, Deborah."

She nodded, knowing her mother's words were true. "It just seems that He is so far away."

Her mother cupped Deborah's chin. "He isn't. He promised He'd never leave you. Perhaps you are simply afraid to trust—afraid to hope."

Deborah nodded. "Does that make me an awful person? I love God with all my heart, but I feel so weak—so tired."

"You aren't awful at all," Mother said, smiling. "Everyone is afraid at one time or another. If not afraid, then perhaps nagged with doubt. But God will take away your fear and doubt. When you look for Him, you will find Him there waiting, as He has always been."

"And I can count on Him to direct my path," she murmured.

"Of course," her mother said. "The Bible even tells us we can make our plans, but that we need to put our faith in God to direct our ways. You have trusted Him far too long to let doubt control your heart."

Her mother was right, but God still seemed distant—not really gone, just standing afar. Maybe He was just waiting for Deborah to catch up or ask for help—like Father used to do when they would go for walks and she would tire. If the trek was too exhausting, she would beg her father to come and carry her. He always did. She wondered if her heavenly Father would carry her now.

"I've been thinking I'd like to complete my medical training. I want to go back East to live with Aunt Wilhelmina and attend classes. I've saved some money and can purchase my own train ticket."

"Oh, Deborah . . . please don't go. I missed you so much when you were gone before."

"But it would be a good thing, and when I complete my studies, I could come back here or to Lufkin. I wouldn't live far away. I love this land. I am at home here."

"Then why leave it?"

In the muted light of the lantern, Deborah could see her mother's worried expression. This wasn't how she'd wanted things to go. "We can talk about this later. I'm starved. Can I help with supper?"

"It's all ready, but we delayed eating to wait for you; we figured to send out the men soon to look for you. Everyone will be so glad to see you've returned."

Making their way up the steps, Mother put her arm around Deborah's shoulders. "I'll be praying God will give you peace and help you through this difficult time. I love you, and I only want the best for you. He wants the best for you, too. Never forget that."

They joined the others in the house. Most of the men were assembled in the front room and Uncle Arjan seemed to be instructing them.

"She's back!" G.W. said, leaping to his feet. He hardly limped at all as he crossed the room to take hold of her. "Where have you been? We've been worried about you."

"I . . . fell asleep."

"What were you thinking?" G.W.'s tone was quite stern.

"I obviously wasn't keeping a clear mind," Deborah said. "Now stop fretting, big brother. I'm fine." She forced herself to take strength in the moment. So long as she put her mind on the worry she'd caused others, perhaps she could keep her own concerns at bay.

"Oh, Deborah!" Lizzie exclaimed, coming into the room.

Turning just as Lizzie embraced her, Deborah felt guilt drive away her fears for Christopher. "I'm so sorry to have worried all of you." She hugged Lizzie and pulled away to face the others. "Please forgive me."

"We're just glad you're unharmed," Uncle Arjan said. His smile assured her that all was forgiven.

"Let's go eat," Mother said, putting her arm around Lizzie. "If I recall, Sissy has made us a wonderful dessert. She wouldn't tell me what it was, but said it was something new and quite delicious. But first, we must get through the main meal."

"That won't be a problem, Miz Vandermark," Warren declared. Several of the other loggers agreed and followed her and Lizzie toward the dining room.

Arjan gave G.W. a slap on the shoulder and grinned. "Maybe we should harness that little sister of yours. That might keep her out of trouble." He winked at Deborah.

Deborah heard someone laugh from behind her and turned to find Jake. "So you think this is funny?" She narrowed her eyes and feigned anger. "I'm going to tell Sissy not to give you any dessert."

"You wouldn't," he said, grinning impishly. "I thought I was your favorite punk."

She rolled her eyes. "I have no favorites."

"Well, that's not . . ." Jake's eyes widened and the words seemed to stick in his throat. Deborah thought he looked as if he'd seen a ghost.

"What's wrong with you?" she asked.

Deborah heard her uncle give a whistle. She couldn't imagine what had stirred such a reaction. Whirling on her heel, she felt as if the wind had been knocked from her. Standing in the doorway was Christopher.

"Deborah." He spoke her name like a prayer.

It was all Deborah heard. The room closed in and went dark as she felt strong arms wrap around her from behind. After that she knew nothing more.

Jake lifted the unconscious Deborah in his arms and shook his head at the man who rushed forward. "I've got her."

The doctor's gaze narrowed. "Not if I have anything to say about it."

Arjan stepped between them and took Deborah from Jake's arms. Jake immediately missed the scent of her hair and the softness of her in his arms. He stepped back, but his gaze never left Dr. Clayton's face. There was an unspoken challenge between them, but Jake had a feeling that wasn't enough. Deborah thought she was in love with this man, but Jake had a plan to change all of that.

He couldn't let the doc just come back from the dead and steal the woman he planned to marry.

Chapter 30

Deborah opened her eyes to find Christopher sitting beside her. He looked pounds thinner and far more careworn. Was that a scar along his left eye? She shook her head, not quite trusting her eyes. Reaching up, she touched his beard-stubbled face.

"Are you really here?"

"Yes." He pulled her up into his arms and crushed her against him.

Deborah could scarcely draw a breath, but she didn't care. She clung to Christopher as if he were the only thing that would save her from certain death. There were no words—no other thoughts. They were the only two people in the universe, and this moment was all they had.

She didn't want him to ever let go of her. If this were merely a dream, Deborah never wanted to wake up. The warmth of his embrace left little doubt that it was all real. Christopher had returned to her.

Reluctantly, Deborah pulled away to look deeply into Christopher's eyes. "I thought you were dead."

"I very nearly was," he replied. He touched her cheek and trailed his finger along her jaw.

Tears formed in her eyes, blurring her vision. Deborah closed her eyes and felt the tears trail down her cheeks.

"Don't cry, sweetheart. It's all over—it's behind us."

She opened her eyes. "When you left, I understood that your brother needed you. But I needed you, too, and I didn't understand how you could so easily cast me aside."

"There was nothing easy in leaving you. You were all I could think of—even at the worst of the storm. I wanted only to live in order to get back to you. I will always love you." He lowered his mouth to hers and kissed her gently.

Deborah wanted the moment to go on forever. She didn't care about the propriety of the situation or that she was sitting on her mother's bed, embracing the man she loved. None of that mattered.

He took hold of her face as he pulled away. "I thought so often of doing that."

"Where have you been?" she asked in a whisper. "Why didn't you let me know you were all right?"

"I wanted to, believe me. I was hurt for a time—my brother, too. They took me south to Corpus, and I couldn't send word to you."

"I read just today that the signal man in Indianola died. He drowned with an unidentified doctor. I was so afraid it was you. I didn't even want to go on living."

"I'm so sorry. I came as soon as I could." He smoothed back her hair. "My brother was much worse off than I was. After I started to heal, I worked to help him. Calvin gradually recovered."

"Were there many injuries?" she asked. "Were you in Indianola when the storm hit?"

He nodded. "Yes to both questions. We had no real warning. We knew a storm was moving in, but some of the old-timers didn't think it would be all that bad. They mostly sat around, telling stories of the hurricane that had wreaked havoc in the seventies. We had figured to leave, but the sheriff told me it wasn't a good idea to try and travel with a hurricane bearing down, so we decided to take shelter and wait it out."

"I read about the floodwaters and the fire."

"The water came in so quickly—it was like nothing I'd ever seen before. The winds were so fierce, you couldn't hear the words of the person standing next to you." He shook his head. "Then the fire spread, destroying everything it touched. We were forced from the building. Into the flooded streets. Into the heart of the storm." He shuddered.

Deborah hugged him close. "I'm so very sorry."

"I nearly lost my hold on Calvin," he continued as if he hadn't heard her. Deborah released him while he went on. "We were being swept into a fierce current. It had a terrible pull that we tried hard to fight. I managed to get hold of a post of some sort. I held fast to it and to Calvin while the water kept rising. It was a nightmare."

"But you're safe now," she said, gently stroking his arm. "You're safe."

He looked at her blankly for a moment, then drew a deep breath. "I'm here with you. I should never have gone."

"Your brother needed you. I understood."

"I'm sorry that I handled things so badly." He hung his head. "There have been far too many secrets between us, and I have to be honest with you now. It might cost me—it might take you from me—but I cannot lie to you anymore."

"I have my secrets, too," she replied. "You may well not want me after you hear them."

He looked at her in disbelief. "There is nothing you could say that would ever make that possible."

She cocked her head slightly and smiled for the first time since she'd awakened. "And yet you think it possible for me to stop wanting you?"

This made him drop his hold and lower his head. "You don't know the truth of my past. It's not something I've borne very well."

Deborah took hold of his hands. "Let me bear it with you, then. Start with your brother. You said he was injured, but you didn't speak of the charges against him. What was the outcome of his trial?"

"He was acquitted. A witness came forward and defended Calvin's actions. He made it clear my brother had no choice in the matter. It was kill or be killed."

"And where is Calvin now?"

"I sent him back to Kansas City," Christopher replied matter-of-factly, pulling his hands from hers. "He had a broken wrist and badly injured leg. Even so, he's promised to seek employment and help our mother. He seems to be a changed man."

"Perhaps this ordeal opened his eyes."

Christopher lifted his gaze. "Perhaps. I suppose only time will tell."

"And what else must I know?" she asked.

He drew a deep breath. "My name."

"But I already know that."

He shook his head. "No. You know what I changed it to."

She looked at him oddly. She had imagined that he would tell her his mother had been married before—that he didn't share the same father as his brothers and sisters. "What are you saying?"

"I wasn't born with the last name of Clayton. It's actually my middle name. My mother named me Christopher Clayton . . . Kelleher. I dropped the Kelleher to keep people from realizing that I am Irish."

Confusion swirled through her thoughts. "But why?"

"Why? Because the Irish are hated in many places. My father and mother worked hard to disassociate themselves from the prejudices and conflicts, but it followed them no matter where they went. The accident that nearly took my father's life was a fight between the Irish workers and the non-Irish. The attitudes and actions against those of Irish ancestry were not so different as what we've seen here in the South with the blacks."

"I'm truly sorry, Christopher. I had no idea."

"When I went east to study medicine, I decided that I would go by Clayton. That was still my name, and it could be associated with the English if questions arose. After all, I also shared some English ancestry."

"And did it work?" she asked.

"It did. I felt like a liar, but it worked. I never figured it would matter much in the long run. I didn't have an Irish brogue, so I believed I could forever bury the truth. I told my mother and siblings that I was going to call myself Christopher Clayton and that any correspondence should be addressed accordingly. My father was livid. He disowned me and told me to never again darken his doorstep. Then he was injured in the fight that killed some of his friends. It killed his spirit and left him without hope."

She reached up to touch his face. "I don't care if you're Irish or Indian or anything else. I love you. I never knew how dearly until you left me."

Deborah's mother came into the room with a basin. "How is she?"

Christopher eased away from Deborah. "She's much better. I shouldn't have shocked her with my return that way."

"Do you feel up to some supper, Deborah?" Mother put the basin on the dresser. "If not, I could bring you something here."

"I can come to the table. In fact, I feel quite well—almost as if the world has suddenly righted itself." She paused and looked past Christopher to where her mother stood. "Mother, how do you feel about Irish people?"

"Irish? Why do you ask a question like that? The Irish are fine folks. We've had dear friends who were Irish."

Deborah grinned. "It's not important right now. I just wondered."

The special dessert turned out to be a most amazing chocolate cake that Sissy said was made entirely without flour or cornmeal. The cake was then drenched in a buttery brown sugar sauce and topped with whipped cream. There wasn't so much as a crumb left after everyone pushed back from the table.

"That was a mighty fine meal," Uncle Arjan said, giving Sissy a nod. "Especially that cake. Mighty fine."

Sissy laughed and got to her feet. "I's glad you enjoyed it. Much more pickin' at the plate, and I won't even have to wash it."

Mother began gathering the dishes, and Deborah started to do likewise. "Oh no," she told Deborah. "You go spend time with Dr. Clayton."

"Thank you very much for having me to supper," Christopher replied. "And thank you for freeing Deborah from her chores." He turned and smiled at her. "Would you care to take a walk?"

"It's already dark and gettin' a bit chilled out there," Uncle Arjan declared. "Maybe you'd prefer to sit on the porch? I'm sure we can find something to do elsewhere—can't we, boys?"

The rest of the men chuckled and got up from the table. All but Jake. He didn't seem at all happy about this new arrangement. Deborah allowed Christopher to help her from her chair while the others shuffled out of the room.

Deborah looked to Christopher and smiled. "Let me get my wrap."

They made their way to the front porch swing. Deborah enjoyed Christopher's arm around her and leaned closer.

"When I thought I might never see you again," he said, "I came to realize how important you were to me. I had always dreamed of the kind of woman who could share my life—my desire to help people. When I came here and met you, it seemed that you fulfilled all of my hopes for a wife. I didn't ask you to court me without giving it great consideration."

Deborah straightened and looked at him. "And I didn't accept without great consideration."

He laughed. "You said yes before the words were hardly out of my mouth."

"That's not true, Christopher Clayton Kelleher." She stopped and smiled. "I like the sound of that. Anyway, you are completely mistaken. As I recall, we discussed your family and your age before I ever agreed to court you. Oh, and we talked about your willingness to marry a female doctor."

He shrugged. "I'm still pondering that one."

She elbowed him and got to her feet. "Well, I suppose you can ponder that alone, because I plan to go back East and finish my medical training." She gave him a coy smile. "Unless, of course, you know some other way to remedy the matter."

"I might have some ideas," he said in a low, husky voice.

His tone caused Deborah to feel weak in the knees. Goodness, but this man could set her all a-flutter. He held out his hand, and she again sat beside him.

"The past doesn't matter," she said, looking into his eyes. "I'd much rather think about where we go from here."

"Where would you like to go?"

She smiled. "Well, I'd like our courtship to be reinstated, for one."

He shook his head. "I've no interest in that." He took hold of her hand. "I'd rather we begin our engagement."

Deborah felt her breath catch. Had he really just proposed? "Say that again," she whispered.

He smiled. "Would you marry me, Miss Vandermark?"

"I know you two wanted some privacy," Jake Wythe said, coming up the porch steps, "but I figure this is important enough to interrupt."

Frustrated, Deborah pulled back from Christopher's hold. "What is it, Jake?"

"I heard the doc propose to you."

"What business is that of yours?" Christopher asked.

"I want to propose, as well."

Deborah looked at him in surprise. "I beg your pardon?"

Jake smiled. "You heard me. I want to marry you, Miss Deborah. I know you care for me—maybe not exactly the same way you do the doc, but I figure we deserve a chance to explore your feelings for me before you go runnin' off to marry him."

"I think you've misjudged me, Jake. I do care about you, but . . ." She fell silent, unsure of what to say. She could feel Christopher tense. The last thing she wanted was a fight.

"Doc left you, without even speakin' to ya face-to-face. Just because he finally figured out what he wants doesn't mean you should just fall into his lap. He was unkind to you, and you deserve better."

Deborah got to her feet and Christopher was quick to follow. "He had his reasons for leaving me," she said, putting herself between the two men. "I don't need to explain them to you. I've never led you on or given you reason to think that I held more affection for you than I do. Please don't ruin this happy occasion for me."

Jake's expression fell. "I don't want you to ever be unhappy. Especially not on account of me."

"I'm sorry to hurt you, but I cannot accept your proposal. I've already accepted Christopher's. I accepted the night he asked me to court him. He held my heart then—just as he does now."

The younger man's shoulders slumped, and he shook his head. "Ain't hardly fair. I just figure out that I'm in love with you, and you go and agree to marry someone else. You ought to at least give me a chance."

Deborah felt saddened by the obvious pain she'd inflicted. She wanted to tell Jake she thought some young woman would be lucky to have him as a husband, but she knew it wouldn't ease his hurt.

She was grateful that Christopher remained silent. "I'm sorry, Jake. I'm going to marry Christopher." Her statement was firm, yet she tried hard to keep the timbre of her voice gentle.

"I reckon I can't change your mind right now," Jake said, lifting his head. "But that don't mean I can't try to change it between now and the weddin'."

Christopher put his hands on Deborah's arms in a most possessive manner. "I believe you've out-stayed your welcome, Mr. Wythe. The lady has made it quite clear what her intentions are."

Jake fixed his gaze on Christopher for a moment, then returned it to Deborah. "I guess only time will tell that for certain."

He walked back down the porch steps and disappeared around the corner of the house. Fearing that Christopher would want to follow him and teach him a lesson or two, Deborah decided to distract him the only way she knew how. Turning in his arms, she smiled.

"Now, where were we? Oh yes—you had proposed marriage. I accept. Now I think it would be quite appropriate for us to share a kiss."

Christopher's anger seemed to fade. He pulled her close. "I think I can manage that."

She grinned. "Indeed, I believe you can."

His lips on hers left her heart aglow in a blaze of passion and the promise of what tomorrow would yet bring.

Turn the page to enjoy

some of Tracie's family recipes,

featured in this book!

Lemon Cornmeal Cake

1 cup yellow cornmeal
2 cups all-purpose flour
2 teaspoons baking powder
½ teaspoon baking soda
¼ teaspoon salt
1 cup butter, softened
1 ¾ cups sugar
(can substitute Splenda)
1 Tablespoon grated lemon zest
¼ cup lemon juice
4 eggs
1 cup buttermilk

Glaze

1 cup sugar
(can substitute Splenda)
⅓ cup lemon juice

Heat oven to 325°F. Grease and flour a 9 x 13 or Bundt cake pan.

Sift together flour, cornmeal, baking powder, soda, and salt. Set aside. In a separate bowl, beat butter and sugar until creamy. Add lemon zest and juice mix. Beat four eggs together, then add to mixture. Blend in flour mixture and buttermilk until batter is smooth. Pour into pan. Bake 1 hour.

For glaze, mix sugar and lemon juice and brush onto warm cake. Let cool and serve.

Rhubarb Cobbler

Filling

1 ½ cups sugar
½ teaspoon cinnamon
4 cups rhubarb, chopped
1 ½ cups water
2 Tablespoons butter

Topping

1 cup flour
½ cup sugar
1 ½ teaspoons baking powder
¼ teaspoon salt
¼ cup butter
6 Tablespoons milk
⅓ cup chopped pecans

In a saucepan combine 1 ½ cups sugar and cinnamon. Add rhubarb and water. Cook and stir until mixture boils; reduce heat and cook 5 minutes. Stir in 2 Tbsp. butter. Pour into a greased baking dish.

For topping, mix flour, ½ cup sugar, baking powder, and salt. Cut in ¼ cup butter; stir in milk and pecans. Spoon dollops onto hot filling.

Bake at 400 degrees for 25–30 min.

Garmelia Edgar 9-3-2012

EMBERS *of* LOVE

STRIKING A MATCH, BOOK 1

EMBERS *of* LOVE

TRACIE PETERSON

BETHANY HOUSE PUBLISHERS

Minneapolis, Minnesota

Embers of Love

Cover design by Jennifer Parker
Cover photography by Kevin White Photography, Minneapolis

Scripture quotations are from the King James Version of the Bible.

Published by Bethany House Publishers
11400 Hampshire Avenue South
Bloomington, Minnesota 55438

Bethany House Publishers is a division of
Baker Publishing Group, Grand Rapids, Michigan.

Printed in the United States of America

Library of Congress Cataloging-in-Publication Data

Peterson, Tracie.
Embers of love / Tracie Peterson.
p. cm. — (Striking a match ; bk. 1)
ISBN 978-0-7642-0819-5 (hardcover : alk. paper) — ISBN 978-0-7642-0612-2 (pbk.) — ISBN 978-0-7642-0820-1 (pbk. large-print)
I. Title.
PS3566.E7717E48 2010
813'.54—dc22

2010015874

To Judy Miller

Your friendship has blessed me
in so many ways.
I pray God gives you strength
to manage the days to come.

Books by Tracie Peterson

www.traciepeterson.com

A Slender Thread • *What She Left for Me* • *Where My Heart Belongs*

SONG OF ALASKA
Dawn's Prelude • *Morning's Refrain* • *Twilight's Serenade*

ALASKAN QUEST
Summer of the Midnight Sun
Under the Northern Lights • *Whispers of Winter*
Alaskan Quest (3 in 1)

BRIDES OF GALLATIN COUNTY
A Promise to Believe In • *A Love to Last Forever*
A Dream to Call My Own

THE BROADMOOR LEGACY*
A Daughter's Inheritance • *An Unexpected Love*
A Surrendered Heart

BELLS OF LOWELL*
Daughter of the Loom • *A Fragile Design* • *These Tangled Threads*

LIGHTS OF LOWELL*
A Tapestry of Hope • *A Love Woven True* • *The Pattern of Her Heart*

DESERT ROSES
Shadows of the Canyon • *Across the Years* • *Beneath a Harvest Sky*

HEIRS OF MONTANA
Land of My Heart • *The Coming Storm*
To Dream Anew • *The Hope Within*

LADIES OF LIBERTY
A Lady of High Regard • *A Lady of Hidden Intent*
A Lady of Secret Devotion

RIBBONS OF STEEL**
Distant Dreams • *A Hope Beyond* • *A Promise for Tomorrow*

WESTWARD CHRONICLES
A Shelter of Hope • *Hidden in a Whisper* • *A Veiled Reflection*

YUKON QUEST
Treasures of the North • *Ashes and Ice* • *Rivers of Gold*

*with Judith Miller **with Judith Pella

Tracie Peterson is the author of over eighty novels, both historical and contemporary. Her avid research resonates in her stories, as seen in her bestselling Heirs of Montana and Alaskan Quest series. Tracie and her family make their home in Montana.

Visit Tracie's Web site at *www.traciepeterson.com*.
Visit Tracie's blog at *www.writespassage.blogspot.com*.

Chapter 1

Philadelphia—June 1885

"I won't let you go through with this," Deborah Vandermark declared. She clasped her best friend's gloved hands. "Even something this drastic will not win your mother's respect, and it certainly won't soften her heart with love."

Elizabeth Decker—known as Lizzie to her dearest friends—shook her head. "You don't understand. If I don't go through with this, I'll have to return home with her."

"Nonsense," Deborah replied. "You can come home with me. My brother is waiting at the train station—or will be in another half hour. There's no reason to remain here. You're of age, and my guess is that even your father will approve."

"Simply one more thing my mother would blame him for."

Deborah squeezed her friend's hand. "Lizzie, your parents are divorced and your father is capable of dealing with this. They live in different towns. They needn't ever speak to each other again—and even if they do, it won't change how you feel about Stuart. Don't let your concerns about everyone else be the reason you go into a loveless marriage."

Lizzie walked over to the window and gently removed her wedding veil, revealing carefully coiffed blond hair. With that one simple action, Deborah took hope that her friend was finally starting to see reason.

"Oh, Deborah, how I can stop things *now*? Everyone is seated and waiting for a wedding. And what of Stuart? He doesn't deserve such ill treatment."

"Stuart doesn't love you any more than you love him. This is all some sort of game to him. You are simply a beautiful ornament for him to add to his life."

"Just as my mother has always said. Men do not marry because of love."

"That isn't entirely true, and you know it," Deborah countered. "Many men marry for love. My father, for one."

"But if I walk away, then Mother wins this battle." Lizzie shook her head. "I can't believe I'm saying these things . . . and after I fought so hard for this day."

"Marriage and romance isn't a war—at least it shouldn't be," Deborah replied. "You speak of the fight to get to the altar, not of the hope, joy, and love that should have brought you there. You don't want to marry Stuart Albright. You're only doing this to upset your mother."

Lizzie bit her lip. "It's not just that. I have to prove to her that I can make my own choices. She's so steeped in her battles for women's rights. She cares about the treatment of every woman in America—except for me."

Deborah joined her friend at the window. "Perhaps that's true, but I care about you, Lizzie. And it's not too late to stop this marriage. You can walk away—run away. You can leave now with me."

"I can't. If I don't marry Stuart, Mother will expect me to return home with her and involve myself in the suffragette fight. She'll drag me from one rally to another. Not only that, but I'll have to offer some sort of explanation to Stuart and his family—to my parents—to Jael and the rest of the congregation."

"Jael knows you're making a mistake. She's the only other friend we have here in Philadelphia. She'll be back any minute and we'll simply explain that you've come to your senses."

"How is running away from a promise coming to my senses?"

Deborah wanted to shake Lizzie until some semblance of reason formed in her brain. Instead, she took hold of her slender shoulders. "It is when the promise was falsely made. You don't continue with a lie just because you were the one who started it. Your mother's love will not be won this way. Your mother doesn't understand what she has lost. She doesn't see your value for who you are. You don't have to go home with her. As I've already said, you can come with me."

Lizzie looked at her oddly. "What would I do in Texas?"

Deborah tapped the side of her cheek considering the question. "There's plenty to do. You can stay with my family. We don't have the luxuries that we've known here in Philadelphia, but there's no reason we can't make the best of it. You can share my room, just like we did while attending college."

"But how would I explain this to my family—to the guests?"

Joy surged through Deborah. Now it was just a matter of helping Lizzie reason through the details. "We'll let your father handle it. He will understand completely."

"But I've already signed the church records."

"No vows have been said. The preacher has not officiated any ceremony."

"And what of Stuart?"

Stuart Albright had a reputation for getting what he wanted. He had been seeking Lizzie's hand for the past two years, and in order to spite her suffragette mother, Lizzie had finally agreed to the wedding. Deborah knew he wouldn't take kindly to being publicly humiliated, but on the other hand, she honestly didn't believe he loved Lizzie.

"Perhaps your father will have an idea. Let me get him." The church bells chimed the hour, and Deborah knew their time was up. "I'll be right back."

Carefully maneuvering in her cream and pink silk gown, Deborah made her way into the hall. Just then Jael Longstreet returned, her red curls bouncing very nearly to her waist.

"The church is full and everyone is waiting. Why is Lizzie not ready?"

"Because she's not going through with it," Deborah announced.

Jael's eyes widened and she clapped her gloved hands together. "Oh, won't this make for a scandal."

"Don't take such joy in it, Jael. This has been very hard for Lizzie. I'm going to take her to Texas with me. You go wait with her. I'm going to find her father."

Near the church's foyer she spied Mr. Decker. He was pacing rather nervously, tugging at the starched cuff of his sleeve. When he caught sight of Deborah, he halted and squared his shoulders.

"Are we ready?" he asked, beaming a smile.

"Not exactly." Deborah cautiously looked past him toward the church sanctuary. "Would you please follow me?"

"Of course. Is there a problem?"

Deborah waited to speak until they were back in the tiny room where Lizzie was waiting with Jael. "Something was wrong, but now we are trying to make it right." Deborah left Mr. Decker's side and went to Lizzie. "Your daughter doesn't want to go through with this wedding."

They had no way of knowing how Mr. Decker would take the news, but his broad smile was not at all what Deborah had expected.

"I'm so glad, Lizzie. I know you don't love him, and it gave me real concern."

Lizzie took several halting steps toward her father. "How did you know?"

"It was quite evident that you were doing this only to assert yourself. I could clearly tell during our supper last night that you and Stuart shared little affection for each other. Then after he left and your mother began railing at you regarding the marriage, you never once mentioned love."

"Stuart has pursued me quite diligently," Lizzie said. "He has lavished me with gifts and attention. I'm sure he must care for me, but I do not love him. That much is true."

"Oh, my sweet girl, that man does not love you," her father said, taking her small hands into his. "I believe he has been using you as much as you have been using him."

"How, Father?"

Decker shrugged. "He likely believes you would benefit his political and business ambitions. A beautiful wife who possesses all the social graces always does."

"Then he will not willingly let me go," Lizzie said.

"Oh, don't worry about him," Jael interjected. "He'll survive."

"But I feel cruel."

The sorrow in Lizzie's tone only strengthened Deborah's resolve. "Mr. Decker, my brother G. W. is waiting at the train station for me to join him as soon as the wedding has concluded. We are to journey back to Texas, as I believe I told you last night."

He nodded. "I remember."

"My thought—that is, if you approve—is to take Lizzie with me. My brother will not mind, and my mother will relish having another young lady in the household. Lizzie can stay with us as long as she likes."

"That would be a good solution, Lizzie," Mr. Decker said, turning back to his daughter. "Texas will put enough distance between you and the Albrights so that I can smooth things over. Your mother will be upset that you didn't tell her good-bye, but I suggest you two slip out of the church right now." He reached into his vest pocket and pulled out a leather wallet. "I will give you all the money I have on me. It should be enough to see you through for quite a while. If you need more, simply write to me."

Lizzie took the money he handed her. "But, Father, what if—"

He put his finger to her lips. "There is no time for further questioning. Leave now, and I will explain to the congregation that you have taken ill and we are postponing the ceremony. Once I've had an opportunity to speak to Mr. Albright and your mother privately, I will explain that the wedding is permanently canceled."

Deborah reached out for her friend's hand. "Come on. We can slip out the back door."

"But what of my clothes? I can hardly remain in my wedding satin."

Deborah considered the situation. "We are the same size and we shared our clothes all the time while attending university. There's no need for much finery where we're headed, so I'm sure to have suitable attire for us both."

"Besides, your steamers are packed for the wedding trip. I can simply have them forwarded to you when the time is right," her father added.

Deborah smiled. "There, it's resolved."

Lizzie's father leaned forward and kissed her soundly on the cheek. "Go. Go quickly. Miss Longstreet and I will stall for as long as we can." He looked to Deborah. "Where can I write to Lizzie?"

"Address letters to her in care of Deborah Vandermark in Perkinsville, Texas. There will be no problem in receiving correspondence there. It's a tiny town. Once she arrives, everyone will know her."

G. W. Vandermark was uncertain what to think when his sister and a satin-clad bride approached him at the train station. Nearly everyone in the depot stared at the two as they approached.

An older woman behind him commented to her friend, "How ridiculous. What bride wears her gown for such a trip? Why, it will be covered with soot in no time." She came alongside G. W. and looked at him. "Do you know them?" she asked as the girls walked toward him.

"I reckon I do," he replied. "At least I know the dark-haired one." He stepped forward, ignoring the old woman's grunt of disapproval.

Deborah put down a small carpetbag before throwing herself into G. W.'s arms. "I've missed you so much."

"Looks like you grew up while you were away. I can see I'm gonna have to beat the boys off to keep them from hangin' all over you."

"Oh, nonsense. You're the one to worry over. Just look at you, all duded up." She pulled back with a grin. "Come meet my dear friend."

G. W. glanced to where the young bride waited and tipped his hat. "Lookin' for a wedding?" he asked in a lazy drawl. He'd never seen anything like her; she was the prettiest gal he'd ever laid sight on. Her blue-eyed gaze locked onto his face and G. W. could not look away. She was like one of those fancy store-bought dolls with gold curls and smooth white skin.

"Lizzie, this is my brother G. W. Vandermark. G. W., this is Miss Elizabeth Decker."

G. W. tipped his hat again. "Howdy."

"We have a problem. Lizzie—Miss Decker—needs to travel west with us. She cannot go through with the wedding."

"Is that a fact?" His mind raced with thoughts of all the complications that had just been created. It was typical of his little sister to stir up a nest of hornets.

"I suggested she come to Texas with us. Her father is even now explaining the situation to her mother and Mr. Albright."

G. W. checked his watch. He had a hundred questions but knew they would have to board the train now or wait for the next one. Unable to figure out what he should do, he pulled at his tie. He hated dressing up, but for the trip east to retrieve his sister, he had promised his mother he'd wear the new store-bought clothes. Unfortunately, the black wool sack suit was layered with a stiff long-sleeved shirt, and the June heat was nearly unbearable. Not to mention the collar was about to strangle him. G. W. was tempted to remove the offending pieces, but noted the gentlemen around him were wearing theirs. It was a good thing he'd decided against wearing the waistcoat.

"I don't guess I understand, but I suppose you ought to give me your bag," he said, trying to figure out what they should do. "Oh, wait. Miss Decker's gonna need a ticket."

The young woman reached into her reticule and pulled out a

wad of cash. G. W. smiled, took several bills, and handed the rest back to her.

"This'll be enough," he said and made his way to the ticket agent. What in the world had Deborah gotten herself into this time? Showing up at a train station with a woman in her bridal gown was unusual, even for his sister. There were bound to be further consequences, but trouble seemed to follow his sister. Well, maybe not trouble so much as . . . disruption. As he made his way back, he could see that the folks around were still gawking and pointing at the young bride-to-be.

"I have all our tickets now," G. W. announced. "So you wanna tell me what this is about?"

"Look, G. W., I can explain once we're on our way," Deborah said, pushing him and Lizzie forward. "Now, help Lizzie onto the train. This dress is cumbersome, and she may well fall on her face if you don't assist her. I can get my own bag."

G. W. shrugged and picked up his case, then took Lizzie's arm. "Miss Decker, it's this way." He didn't wait for her comment, but instead headed to the platform and the waiting train.

"Congratulations," the conductor offered as G. W. and Lizzie approached. "My, but you two make a handsome couple."

G. W. looked to Lizzie, who was blushing red. He thought to offer the man an explanation, then just nodded and helped Lizzie up the steps to the passenger car.

They showed their tickets to a waiting porter. "Bettin' it was a mighty fine weddin'," the porter declared, taking the bag from Deborah. He bore a smile that ran from ear to ear. His dark skin appeared even darker against his white coat.

"It was the best I've been to in a long time," Deborah told him. The man nodded and secured their bags just as the conductor called the final board.

Once they were settled in, G. W. couldn't help but notice that all heads had turned to watch them. Smiles were plastered on every face, and without warning, one man began to applaud. This caused the entire car to begin clapping.

"I wish I could melt under the seat," Lizzie said, tucking her head. "I'm so sorry."

"It can't be helped," Deborah said, patting Lizzie's hand. "Once we make our first stop for the night, you can change clothes."

G. W. felt sorry for her. No doubt she was completely offended at the idea of being married to a backwoods bumpkin who could barely read, even if he was wearing a thirty-dollar suit bought in Houston. He offered her a smile, but she couldn't see it since her gaze was fixed on the floor.

"So why don't you tell me what's goin' on and why you two showed up at the station in your weddin' duds," he said as the train pulled out.

"It's a truly complicated story, but we have a long trip ahead of us, so here goes," Deborah began. "Elizabeth—you can call her Lizzie, as she hates the name Elizabeth." She looked to her friend as if for confirmation. Lizzie nodded. "Lizzie had to escape."

G. W. felt a sense of confusion. "Escape? From what?"

"Well, you see, she was only doing this . . ." Deborah gestured toward the bridal gown. "That is, she wasn't in love." G. W. would have laughed had she not remained fixed with a serious expression.

Deborah stopped short and shook her head. She sat back and folded her hands. "Wait. Maybe I should start from the beginning."

"That's generally best," G. W. said.

"Elizabeth and I attended classes together at the university in Philadelphia and shared lodging. She's been my closest confidante for these last few years. I'm sure you remember me telling you about her when I was home for the summer two years ago."

"Sure I do," G. W. replied, though he was sure she never mentioned how beautiful this woman was.

"Well, Lizzie's like family to me. She has a sad past—a tragic one."

"Oh, Deborah, do not make it sound so melodramatic." Lizzie gave a quick glance around as if to see who else might be listening. "Our appearance is bad enough. Let us keep it simple." She looked directly at G. W. "My parents divorced some years ago. My father has remarried and my mother is working for the cause of women's rights and feels men are unnecessary in her life."

"And because of that," Deborah went on, "Lizzie found herself at odds with her mother's plans for her future. One thing led to another, and she began a courtship with Stuart Albright."

G. W. listened to his sister go on about the sorry state of Lizzie's relationship with Mr. Albright. Apparently the man was a bore and not the least bit in love with the golden-haired beauty. But how he could keep from loving her was beyond G. W.'s ability to reason. She looked like an angel. Who wouldn't want her for a wife?

"Though she didn't love Mr. Albright, Lizzie felt she had no recourse but to go through with the wedding. That is, until just a little while ago, when she finally admitted that she didn't want to be married. Her father agreed with her and with my idea that she should come to Texas with us."

"And what of your groom?"

"I didn't feel that I could . . ." Lizzie began to offer before Deborah could speak again. "Well . . . you see . . . he's not one to take bad news easily. I was, quite frankly, afraid. Call me a coward if you must, but that's the simple truth."

G. W. shook his head. "I wouldn't be one to call you a coward, Miss Lizzie. I don't rightly know you well enough."

"Well, she's no coward," Deborah announced. "She's very brave, in fact, to put an end to this farce before it became final."

"So she's just gonna live with us?" G. W. asked.

Lizzie blushed again and looked out the window. Deborah nodded. "She needs time and distance so she can better think of what she'd like to do next. Her father will be in touch with her."

"Don't seem like her father will be the problem," G. W. said. "What about that mother of hers? What about her groom? He don't seem like the kind of guy to take to this kind of thing."

"Maybe not, but he won't know where she is." Deborah turned to Lizzie. "Once you're settled in with us, we'll see to it that no one can harm you. Never fear."

"It may be a moot point to worry ourselves anyway," Lizzie replied. "After all, what man would want to chase after a woman who has clearly rejected him?"

G. W. laughed. "If she looked like you, I know I wouldn't let her get away."

Lizzie's mouth dropped open. G. W. might have roared in laughter, but he felt pretty sure it would only serve to offend her further. Leaning back in his seat, he pushed his hat down over his eyes. He needed to have a think, and it would be just as well if the ladies thought him to be sleeping.

Of course, he'd much rather spend his time looking at Lizzie Decker. My, but she was a fine figure of a woman. She was all genteel-like. In fact, she reminded him of the stories his ma had told about the Georgian women before the war. Ma had been every bit as genteel before going west with their pa. She said Texas took the elegance right out of a lady, but Pa always said she was still the most elegant woman he knew.

G. W. frowned at the thought of his pa. Three years had passed since the logging accident that took Rutger Vandermark's life. G. W. had been right there when a huge pine log had crushed his father. The memory never faded. It was only made worse by the fact that G. W. blamed himself for the accident.

G. W. had relived the day of the accident over and over at least a thousand times. The guilt ate him alive and, try as he might, he couldn't shake off the horror of his father's mangled body. He'd been killed instantly by the two thousand–pound log, so at least there had been no suffering. But neither was there time for good-byes or to tell him how much G. W. loved him—how he needed him to live.

There was just no time.

Chapter 2

On the final leg of their journey nearly two weeks later, Deborah found G. W.'s general state of mind to be worrisome. "I don't know why he frets so—the worst is behind us," she confided to Lizzie. The train car shifted and pitched right, and Deborah braced to keep from slamming into her friend.

The Houston East and West Texas train, affectionately called "the Rabbit" because of its tendency to jump the narrow gauge track, was not at all a pleasant experience. Having connected from another line in Nacogdoches, they were riding the Rabbit into the heart of the Piney Woods. Deborah would have just as soon ridden horseback, but she knew Lizzie was not experienced.

Paul Bremond, well known among Houston businessmen, had a vision to create a rail line from Houston to Shreveport, Louisiana, and the HE&WT was the reality of that dream. Poor Mr. Bremond had died just the month before, unable to live long enough to see his railroad completed. Folks had chided him for the narrow gauge creation, telling him he would rue the day, as standard gauge lines were bound to take over the country. But Mr. Bremond had continued with the line and now it was rumored that by next year, it would be complete.

Deborah thought it sad that the man had worked so hard for his dream, only to die before it was ever realized. Of course, sometimes she felt the same might happen to her. The only problem was, she wasn't entirely sure what her dream might truly be.

"This train ride is so uncomfortable," Lizzie declared, squirming. "I can't imagine people using this as a main means of transportation."

A smile crossed Deborah's face. "They don't. Well, that's not exactly right. The railroad is the main means for bringing supplies into the Piney Woods region. However, it is expensive and most folks never travel more than twenty miles from home—if that."

"I can certainly understand why," she replied, gripping the armrest.

"Most would stay whether the train was a luxurious ride or not." Deborah looked at her brother's empty seat and continued. "Take G. W., for example. He loves Texas, and the only reason he ventured out was to escort me back and forth. Oh, he goes occasionally to Houston or Lufkin for supplies, but he has no desire to leave the area. He loves his forest and the people here."

Lizzie shook her head. "Seems a mundane existence."

"I suppose to some." Deborah looked out the window and noticed several dilapidated houses. "Some don't get a chance to choose. Folks here are far from rich. Most work for sawmill or logging companies. Some raise cattle and cotton, others farm. But the war was very hard on the South, you must remember."

Her friend turned and put her hand on Deborah's arm. "I'm sorry. I didn't mean to offend."

"Oh, Lizzie, you could never offend me. But you must prepare yourself for somewhat of a shock. Perkinsville is not Philadelphia. Many of the people who will be your neighbors have had very little education. They can't read and write much. They really don't understand why it's important, but my hope is to show them. I truly want to encourage education in our area."

"Is there no school?"

Deborah thought of the tiny school. "There is, but education is not valued—hard work is. The important things of life take on a different appearance in Perkinsville. Here, folks count themselves lucky to have a roof over their heads—never mind a floor."

"What do you mean?" Lizzie appeared to forget about the roughness of their ride.

"Many folks have only dirt for floors—although it's the cleanest dirt you will find." She laughed. "It's always strange to see women sweeping their earthen floors. Mama told me that she used to do the same until Papa put in a wood floor for her. She said my uncle and father worked day and night for months to put together enough scrap lumber. She cherished it until they moved into the new house shortly before Papa died."

"What happened to your father, Deborah?"

"He was killed when a log rolled onto him."

"A log? How could that kill a man?"

Deborah pointed at the passing trees. "See those? They're shortleaf pines. They are much like the pines we saw in the East. We log longleaf pine."

"Isn't one pine tree pretty much like another?"

The question was innocent enough, but Deborah laughed. "Hardly. Stick around for a while, and you'll learn the difference soon enough."

"But what happened to your father?"

"G. W. and my brother Rob were helping Father bring the week's harvest to the rail. They were pole rolling logs onto the train cars. That's where they hook the mules up on one side of the railcar and run a series of chains and cables to the log they are bringing up on the other side. Several sturdy poles are positioned so that when the mules are driven forward, the log rolls up onto the train car. Usually it works very well, but this time the chain snapped and the log rolled back onto my father. It weighed about a ton, and he couldn't get out of the way in time."

"A ton? That's hard to imagine."

"This particular log was a huge butt log—one taken from the very base of the tree." Deborah looked once again to the passing scenery. She hadn't been home when her father was killed. Word came to her through her beloved Aunt Wilhelmina—the same woman who was responsible for seeing that Deborah received an education.

"My father's skull was crushed, and he died immediately. Mama said he knew the dangers and would have wanted it that way. A quick death was always desired over a painful lingering. . . . I was traveling with my aunt at the time, and we didn't get word until nearly a month after the accident. By the time I learned of his death, school was nearly ready to begin again, and my father was long past buried."

Lizzie nodded. "That was the year we met."

"Yes. And what a godsend that was."

"But, Deborah, you've never talked much about this before. Why?"

She considered Lizzie's question for a moment. "I suppose because of the pain in remembering. But I also learned that G. W. blamed himself for our father's death, and I suppose I buried it deep within to hide from both his pain and my own."

"I'm so sorry, Deborah." Lizzie frowned. "And what of your other brother—Rob? Does he blame himself, as well?"

"No. Rob was injured. The mules pulling the logs got scared when the chain whipped back. They took off, out of control. Rob got a good beating as they dragged him. G. W. blames himself for the accident because he couldn't hold the log back. He felt he should have added more support. Mama said it could have happened to anyone. Others agreed—after all, they weren't working alone. By this time, Papa and Uncle Arjan had hired another five men to help them."

"Were they hurt, too?"

"No, just Papa and Rob."

"I hardly see why G. W. would blame himself—especially if even your mother doesn't."

"I can blame myself without anyone else needin' to help me," G. W. said from behind them.

Deborah watched Lizzie look away in embarrassment. "Yes, but it still doesn't make you right," she told her brother. She was never one to keep such thoughts to herself.

"Doesn't make me wrong, either," he answered, taking his seat across from Lizzie. He folded his arms against his chest and fixed his gaze on Deborah.

She could see the pain in his blue eyes. "No, it just makes you stubborn."

"Deborah!" Lizzie gasped. "Don't be so harsh."

G. W. seemed surprised by her sudden support. He nodded with a smug look of satisfaction. "Yeah, don't be so harsh."

Deborah rolled her eyes and shook her head. "I'm not about to coddle him, Lizzie, and don't you dare, either. He doesn't need that from us. The accident wasn't his fault, and if he's too bullheaded to see the truth for himself, then I say it's our job to help convince him." Silence descended like a heavy mantle over them. No one seemed willing to challenge Deborah's comment or to continue with the conversation.

After several moments, G. W. finally spoke up. "We'll be stopping in about twenty minutes." He cast a quick look outside. "Unless the Rabbit jumps the tracks."

"Oh, you don't really think it would, do you?" Lizzie asked, her hand going to her throat.

He shrugged. "It's been known to happen, but it shouldn't. Not the way we're pokin' along. I swear I could have walked from Nacogdoches faster."

And with that, the tension broke and G. W. seemed to relax. Deborah closed her eyes and whispered a prayer for him. Her mother had said very little about his continued sadness, but Deborah hoped she could find time when they could be alone so that she could talk to him. She had to convince him to let go of this guilt.

In her no-nonsense way, Deborah added such matters mentally to the list of things she already planned to see to once they returned home. She was soon to take the helm as bookkeeper and manager of the Vandermark Logging Company. It was her obligation, now that she'd completed her education. She had made a promise to her family—a promise driven by her love of learning. She remembered long talks with her father.

"I'm going to learn all that I can to help the family," she'd told him. *"I want to make things easier for you. I can't very well log, but I can handle the books."*

She could very nearly recollect her father's smile and feel his pride in her. *"You do that, darlin'. You'll be mighty helpful to me."*

Deborah had studied as hard as possible, always keeping the image of her family before her. She might not have the stamina for heavy labor, but anything that required reasoning was right in keeping with her abilities. Her family needed her, and it was for that reason she felt she could put aside her own desires. More important—she didn't allow for any desire that wouldn't benefit her kin. It would only muddy the waters, and Deborah needed to stay clear on what her duties were.

She kept her eyes closed, pondering the future and pushing aside her concerns. She found bookkeeping hopelessly boring. Truth be told, she had preferred her biology and botany classes.

If she'd had her choice, Deborah would have remained in school for a time longer. She gave a sigh. What possible good could come from fretting over it now? Women were not expected to attend college, nor were they truly accepted as scholars. But her love of knowledge was something no one could take from her. Deborah cherished reading new books, exploring new worlds and cultures. Her intellect, however, was nothing to wear as a badge of honor. Men were offended by her, and women, intimidated. In truth, she believed it was more that the men felt stupid and the women were afraid to admit that they, too, would like to learn. But it didn't matter. Her family needed her now, and there was some comfort in that. Well, maybe not exactly comfort.

Father God, she prayed silently, *I don't know why you made me just this way. Is it wrong that I long for something more?*

Perkinsville had been built alongside the railroad to accommodate the loading of lumber and unloading of supplies. It was,

Deborah said, a typical sawmill company town—whatever that meant. Lizzie wasn't at all familiar with such a thing and definitely didn't know what to expect. Everything, in her eyes, looked hopelessly dirty. The day was unbearably warm, and Lizzie was glad that she'd listened to Deborah regarding her attire. They had stopped at a secondhand shop in Nacogdoches and purchased lightweight blouses and skirts. G. W. had long ago replaced his wool suit with a simple shirt and trousers, and Lizzie thought he seemed far more relaxed, although he carried a coat with him and donned it as propriety demanded.

Lizzie dabbed at her forehead with her handkerchief as Deborah showed her about the town. Philadelphia could be hot and humid, as well, but it lacked the same heaviness she felt here in the South. She longed for a bath, or perhaps a quick plunge—clothes and all—into the nearby pond. When she mentioned this Deborah laughed.

"That's the mill pond. We used to swim there on occasion, but now it's much too busy and Mr. Perkins has asked folks to keep their children out for their own safety. The mill is dependent upon the pond." Lizzie followed Deborah's gaze. "They unload the logs from the train and dump them there. Later they use a series of conveyors and chains called a jack ladder to pull the logs into the sawmill."

Lizzie spotted the smoke belching from the stacks. "With the damp air and thick smoke, I can't imagine living here."

"Usually there's a breeze to move it out. We arrived on a still day, and that tends to make things worse."

"My mother would say it serves me right," Lizzie murmured.

"That's really the first time you've mentioned her since leaving the wedding." Deborah eyed her thoughtfully for a moment. "I haven't wanted to pry, but how are you feeling toward her?"

"To be honest, I've actually found myself concerned for Mother. I know she had great plans for me prior to my wedding announcement and, no doubt, had figured out some way to use me for her purposes even after I married Stuart."

"And what of Stuart?"

Lizzie grew thoughtful. "I feel guilty for having embarrassed him so publicly." She paused for a moment. "My main thoughts are for Mother, however. I suppose now that we've arrived, I should send her a letter. She must surely be worried. Is there a post office here?"

"Of course, right over here." Deborah continued the tour. "Then this is the depot and commissary. There are many things housed under this one roof," Deborah explained. "The pharmacy is here, the post office and paymaster for the sawmill, plus it is the main source of supplies. The commissary itself is quite large and contains most everything you could ever need." She smiled. "Yet like I said before, it's hardly Philadelphia." She glanced around. "I can't imagine what's keeping Rob and G. W."

G. W. had gone off looking for their brother. Rob was supposed to meet them at the station with the wagon, but so far he'd not shown himself. Lizzie hoped he'd arrive soon. She wasn't sure how much of the heat she could stand. She looked at the unpainted buildings and dirt roads. *What in the world have I gotten myself into?*

Deborah chatted on as if the heat didn't bother her in the least. "Across the street just there is the boardinghouse for whites. On the other side of the tracks is the black boardinghouse and quarters where the blacks live. In the South, you will find that the color of your skin determines a great deal. Folks around here try to be tolerant, but many cannot put the issue aside. And it's not just in dealing with the blacks. Mr. Perkins hates Mexicans and Indians. He won't even allow them to live or work here."

"And why is that?"

"Something to do with the past and his family. I believe they were injured or killed by people of those races. Folks around here always have a reason for hating others—that way it seems more acceptable to them."

"I suppose it isn't easy. Being a different color isn't exactly something you can hide," Lizzie commented. "The town is so small," she said, casting her gaze back to the commissary. "Is this the only store?"

"Very nearly. This is a company town, owned and operated by the Perkins family. They own the sawmill and arranged for most everything you see. Mr. Perkins is a very nice man, so folks here count themselves blessed. Some towns suffer at the hands of cruel masters. Here the people are treated quite well. Prices are not overly inflated and people can be paid in cash upon proof of an emergency. Oh, and they pay out cash at Christmas and Texas Independence Day—March the second. Some folks are suggesting it be changed to America's Independence Day, but like I said, many of the citizens are still feeling rather hostile toward the northern states."

"I'm not sure I understand what you said regarding money. Aren't the people otherwise paid?"

Deborah smiled. "Not in cash. They're paid with company tokens that they can exchange for goods. Payment for rent and medical needs is taken out of their salaries. They even tithe in tokens."

Lizzie had never heard of such a thing. "But how then can they save up money or invest for their future?"

Her friend shook her head. "They can't. They have no future but this town. They are essentially owned by the company."

"But that's slavery, and Mr. Lincoln abolished that during the war."

"Don't talk about Mr. Lincoln too loud down here. Folks won't take too kindly to it." Deborah motioned to the commissary. "Let's step inside. It's much too warm to stand out here in the sun. G. W. will know where to find us."

Lizzie followed her up the wooden steps, avoiding the splintered rail. Three large dogs were resting near the door and looked up only long enough to ascertain whether Deborah and Lizzie were a threat before putting their heads back down.

The screen door moaned as Deborah pulled it open. Lizzie stepped inside, taking a moment to allow her eyes to adjust to the darker interior. The walls were stacked to the ceiling with shelved goods. Rows of tables and display cases offered everything from razors to shoes to writing paper. Across the store in the far corner were shelves lined with canned goods and sacks of rice, beans, and cornmeal. Each was clearly stamped, along with the weight.

"Let's see if they have anything cold to drink. Mr. Perkins brings ice in from time to time." They made their way across the rough-hewn floor to the counter, where an older man was busy folding fabric.

"Mr. Greeley, it's good to see you again," Deborah began.

The man looked up and studied the two women for a moment. "Miss Deborah?"

"It's me," she replied, laughing. "All grown up, as Mama would say."

He put aside his material and gave them his full attention. "I knew you were expected. Your mama has been tellin' everyone about you comin' home."

"Just came in on the train. G. W.'s gone to find Rob. He was supposed to be here with the wagon since we didn't want to wait for the log train."

"Are you home for good?" He looked at Lizzie. "Oh, where are my manners? Introduce me to your friend."

"This is Miss Elizabeth Decker. We attended school together. She will be staying with us for a while."

"Miss Decker, you are like a ray of sunshine. Menfolk down here will be happy to see another female. It's a pleasure to make your acquaintance."

"Likewise," she said, uncertain if the nod of her head was the proper greeting.

Deborah didn't give her time to consider the matter further. "We were hoping you might have something cold to drink."

"I surely do. Mrs. Greeley made two pitchers of lemonade, as well as some sweet tea. Which do you prefer?"

"Oh, lemonade would surely be perfect," Deborah declared.

"Why don't you two have a seat, and I'll bring it right out to you."

Deborah nodded and led Lizzie to an area just beyond the counter, where several small tables and chairs had been positioned. "The men often gather here for coffee and checkers. Sometimes they even have a meeting or two."

Lizzie took a seat on the obviously handmade chair. She worried that the unfinished wood would snag her skirt, but noted that Deborah seemed to give it little thought. Deborah had been right; this was quite different from what she had known back East.

"As you can see, the store has an ample supply of cloth goods, foods, and household supplies. My mother wrote to tell me that they recently opened a hardware store across the street to handle some of the larger tools and building materials. Down the street is the church and school. There's a livery and blacksmith, as well as a new doctor's office and infirmary. According to my mother, Mrs. Perkins finally convinced Mr. Perkins to hire a quality doctor since a great many women have died from childbed fever or in childbirth itself."

"How sad that they should have died when such progress has been made. Remember the lecture we heard just before graduation? Mrs. Lyman was the speaker."

Deborah nodded. "Yes, I know she was especially encouraged that medicine was making abundant improvements, especially in women's needs. But a doctor will be very valuable to the men in this community, as well. There are frequent accidents. A doctor will be a blessing."

"Here you go, ladies." Mr. Greeley reappeared with two glasses of lemonade.

Lizzie immediately sampled hers and smiled. It was just right—not too tart. "It's very good."

"Mrs. Greeley will be pleased to know you enjoyed it."

"Just put it on our account, please," Deborah instructed.

"Oh no, Miss Deborah. This one is on the house. We're just pleased as can be to have you home. Bet your mama is fairly dancin' a jig. She's talked of nothing but your return."

Lizzie marveled at the easy manner in which they fell into conversation. There were no formalities, yet there was a certain genteel respect that she found rather comforting.

"I finally found him," G. W. declared as he and another man bounded into the commissary. Lizzie looked up just as Rob Vandermark caught sight of her. He grinned from ear to ear and stepped forward in three bold strides to take hold of her hand. Bowing low, he drew her fingers to his lips.

"Why, if you aren't the purtiest gal! Hair the color of corn silk and eyes bluer than a summer sky."

"This is my brother Rob," Deborah announced. "He's the poet in the family."

Lizzie nodded, but found herself at a loss for words. Rob seemed more than a little delighted as he turned to face his sister.

"For once you've brought me somethin' worth my time," he declared, then looked back at Lizzie and gave her a wink.

G. W. frowned and Deborah shook her head. "Rob is also the Romeo of the family."

"She calls me that all the time," Rob said, laughing. He tucked his thumbs in his suspenders. "Guess she can't help it, what with havin' such a handsome brother. Can't fault me for lookin' for my Juliet."

Lizzie could scarcely take it all in at once. Rob was rather like a whirlwind compared to G. W.'s soft-spoken, easygoing manner.

"Rob, this is Miss Elizabeth Decker. Lizzie to her friends."

"Miss Lizzie," he said, turning back to her with a beaming smile. "I certainly hope we will be very good friends."

Chapter 3

Deborah found her homecoming bittersweet. The longing for home and family had nearly consumed her in Philadelphia, mixed with an equal measure of regret. Well, maybe not so much regret as concern.

And yet that wasn't exactly right, either.

A fear of things changing—of losing something precious.

Education had been an escape from the loneliness and isolation she'd known in childhood. It had given her purpose and a sense of being able to help those she loved. But because no one else in her family desired an education, Deborah felt alone.

Living miles from any real town, Deborah had grown up with only her mother and their cook, Sissy, for female company. Later, she had a girlfriend or two at school, but they never thought or felt the same way she did. Their idea of fun was sharing new quilt patterns or parading around, vying for the attention of boys. Deborah wanted to talk about books she'd read or what was going on in the world. Unfortunately, the only ones talking about current events were the men, and they had no interest in discussing the news with the female gender. Truth be told, the men paid her little attention until she blossomed into a teenager, and by then, her heart was far more desirous of learning than loving.

"Mama!" Deborah cried, jumping from the wagon as G. W. drew it to a stop. She ran the distance to her mother's open arms. Two big hounds bayed a greeting and dashed across the porch to welcome her.

"Jasper! Decatur!" Deborah lavished attention on the dogs before turning to her mother. "Where's Lula?"

"She's had another litter of pups." Her mother motioned her to turn around in a circle. "Oh, just look at you," her mother whispered. Taking hold of Deborah's face, she shook her head. "You are even prettier than you were the last time I saw you. I'll bet you have the tiniest waist in the county." She gave a quick glance past Deborah. "You boys will have your hands full keeping order with the men who come a-callin'."

"Mama, I missed you so much." Deborah hugged her mother close. It wasn't a lie. If she could have had her mother with her back East, she would have done so. "So tell me what has changed."

Her mother laughed. "I'm older and a little more gray, and the house is a little more worn. Guess we both are."

Euphanel Vandermark was not known for her great beauty, although Deborah thought her a pretty woman. She was instead known for her strength, honesty, and integrity. People knew when they made an arrangement with Mrs. Vandermark that she would keep her word.

Standing several inches shorter than Deborah's five-foot-six-inch frame, Euphanel Vandermark was a petite but formidable force. Uncle Arjan often teased her about being a hurricane, but Mama took no offense at such a statement. Since their father's death, Deborah and her brothers had seen their mother triple her efforts at efficiency and productivity, but never at the expense of her beliefs. Her faith in God was her mainstay, and from that foundation, she would never be moved.

"You don't look a bit older," Deborah declared. "Papa used to say you never grew older, just more beautiful."

Her mother's expression softened. "He did say that quite a bit, didn't he?"

"And with good reason." Deborah turned and motioned to Lizzie. "I have someone for you to meet, Mama. I hope you won't mind, but I've brought a friend home with me." Deborah reached out to Lizzie. "This is Elizabeth Decker. Call her Lizzie. She's the young woman I roomed with—the one I often wrote you about." Jasper and Decatur sniffed around the stranger as if to ascertain her acceptability.

"I would recognize her anywhere," Mother said. "You are just as beautiful as Deborah described. We'll be pleased to have your company."

"Thank you." Lizzie exchanged a look with Deborah, then turned back to the older woman. "I hope I might be useful to you."

Deborah's mother laughed heartily. "You are a guest, and you needn't be anything else. Come along inside. I'm sure you want to freshen up. Deborah, take Lizzie on upstairs. I'll bring warm water to your room. The boys will carry up your trunks, and later, when you're ready, I'll make sure you get a bite to eat."

"Mother, we're hardly invalids. We can join the family for supper."

"I know how exhausting that trip can be," Mother replied. "I wouldn't want you to feel that you had to sit at the table and share conversation with the rest of us."

"There's plenty of time to wash up and rest a bit before supper," Deborah assured her. "I've been looking forward to sitting down to a family meal; please don't deny me that privilege."

"That makes two of us. No one cooks like you and Sissy," G. W. said as he passed by with one of Deborah's trunks hoisted on his shoulder. "What in the world do you have packed in here, little sister? More friends? It weighs a ton."

She grinned. "You could say that. It's full of books."

He shook his head. "Most females would be fillin' their steamers with gowns and pretty doodads, but not my sister. She brings back books."

Deborah waited until Rob followed after with two of the suitcases before turning to her mother. "Mama, there's a heaviness about G. W., and I'm not speaking of the books. From time to time, we managed to get him to smile, but he's just not his old self."

"If you got him to smile at all, I'd say that was a great accomplishment. He's changed since your father died, and though I've tried to talk to him, I think he worries that if he says too much to me, it will only serve to bring me sorrow."

Deborah looked to her friend. "We shall do what we can to encourage him, won't we, Lizzie?"

The blonde seemed taken by surprise, but nodded. "Of course."

After a supper of corn bread, beans with thick pieces of pork, and spicy rice and tomatoes, Deborah settled into a porch rocker alongside her mother. She was glad that Lizzie had chosen to retire early and that the boys were elsewhere discussing business with Uncle Arjan.

"I hadn't realized how much I missed your cooking."

Mother smiled. "I'm sure you had fancier meals back East."

"Maybe fancier—but not better. We certainly had more beef than we eat here. People were absolutely amazed that we should eat so little beef when our state is known for its cattle."

"Known for it because we ship them north and east," Euphanel said with a chuckle. "Still, if they were here to see this place for themselves, they would understand. It's hard enough to keep other things, much less beef, from spoiling."

"That's what I would tell them. I explained about the large number of wild hogs and how much easier it is to salt and cure, or even smoke pork, than it is with beef."

Silence descended and Deborah shifted uneasily in her chair. How was it that she could be so happy to be somewhere, and so miserable at the same time?

"So you want to tell me what's wrong?" her mother asked.

The night air was full of sounds, magnified by the heaviness of the air. "Nothing is wrong," Deborah replied.

When her mother didn't say anything more, Deborah turned. "I suppose I'm worried about G. W. He blames himself for Papa's death."

Mother swatted at a mosquito on her arm. "He does. I've talked to that boy until my throat was raw, but he still won't listen. Arjan says that in time he'll come to accept that the accident wasn't his fault. I can only hope he's right."

"Me too." Deborah glanced at her mother with a grin. "Maybe Lizzie can help him."

"Don't you be matchmakin' for your brother," her mother warned. "Nothing good ever comes out of putting your nose in other folks' business. If the good Lord intends those two to fall for each other, He'll work out the details."

"But if G. W. could strike a match, it would take his mind off of Papa."

"Let G. W. determine that matter. The only matches you need to strike are ones for the kerosene lamps." Her mother's tone was firm, but not harsh.

"Yes, ma'am," Deborah said, reverting to childhood politeness.

"Now, tell me what else is goin' on in that head of yours. You seemed mighty preoccupied tonight at supper."

"Well, I am tired. The trip is not for the faint of heart, to be certain. I'm also anxious to get started with the bookkeeping and such. I know Uncle Arjan said it's going to take some time to get things recorded properly. A lot of what I need to put down on paper is registered only in his head."

Mother gave a light laugh. "Arjan has a good mind for such things, but I keep sayin' that if something happens to him, we won't none of us know what's going on. I think he's more relieved than I am to have you take over the office."

Deborah looked out across the darkness. Occasionally fireflies winked their light, but otherwise the velvety blackness remained unbroken. "It feels strange—coming home after being gone so long."

"You're no longer a child." Euphanel gazed at her daughter. "Something happens to us when we cross that threshold to womanhood."

Deborah considered that a moment. "Everything seems different, and yet nothing has changed."

"You've changed."

She startled at her mother's words. "I'm still the same old Deborah."

Her mother shook her head. "Hardly that. You are a woman now. While many would have called you one before, there can be no doubt about it now. You have tasted the world and its delights—traveled to see so many exciting things. You walked beyond your own gate, as my mother would say. It opens your heart and mind to so much that you didn't know before."

"I suppose so," Deborah admitted.

"It was what made life so difficult for me when I first came to Texas as a young bride," her mother continued. "I had walked beyond my gate, and I knew what the world could offer. Your father brought me here in 1858. His dreams fueled his desire for a new life here, but my dreams were wrapped up in him. Texas seemed a terrible desolation to me—at least until your grandma and grandpa came west during the war. I kept thinking of all that I'd known in Georgia. Now you will think of all that you knew back East."

Deborah shrugged. "But while I was back East, all I could think about was Texas. I honestly missed my family and home. But . . ."

"But?"

She heaved a heavy sigh and looked at her mother. "I almost feel like a stranger in returning. Does that sound odd to you?"

"Not at all. I remember when I accompanied my parents back to Georgia just before my grandmother passed on. Let me think now . . . you were just a little girl of eight—maybe nine."

"I was nine and heartbroken that you left me to accompany them," Deborah said. "I was afraid you might never return."

"It was hard to leave you here—the boys, too—but I knew it would be a hard trip for a child to endure. The South had suffered so much during the war and frankly I was afraid of what we might face." She paused for a long pregnant silence. "I was right to be afraid. Nothing was the same. It broke my heart to see the changes, and I was glad to return to Texas. That's when I realized, however, that my heart had changed—this was home now. There was something bittersweet in that realization."

"I think I'm going to miss my classes a great deal, but not the city. I prefer the quiet, easygoing pace I find here. There is a frantic spirit in the East that seems to devour everyone in its path. I will miss hours of reading and educating myself to new cultures and ideas, but I will be happy for the peace. And for the comfort that comes in knowing that people know you, recognize you, have a history with you."

"You needn't stop learning just because you're back in Angelina County," her mother chided.

Deborah couldn't suppress a yawn. "I suppose you're right."

"I'm also right in suggesting that you need to go to bed. I want you and Lizzie to sleep as long as you can in the morning. Don't you even think about getting out of bed before eight."

"Yes, ma'am." She grinned. "I doubt you could rouse me before then." Deborah got to her feet. "At least it's cooled off enough for sleeping."

"Oh, I forgot to mention that Mr. and Mrs. Perkins are coming to dinner tomorrow night. There's some sort of business to discuss with Arjan, so you'll probably want to be available for that. The girls are coming, too, so you can introduce Lizzie to them."

"Maybe with all the ladies at the table, G. W. will have more to think of than his misplaced guilt."

Her mother nodded and slapped at another mosquito. "Perhaps, but you let G. W. make his own choices. Nothing's worse than being thrown into the arms of a person you'd just as soon avoid. From what you've told me, your friend Lizzie's situation should have proven that, if nothing else. G. W.'s heart will lead him to love when the time is right."

"I just hope he's not too focused on what isn't true, and misses what is."

Her mother got to her feet and embraced Deborah. "Then we'll just have to pray that his mind is clear."

Lizzie studied the small room from the edge of her bed. Deborah had warned her that things would be different, but it felt as if she'd stepped into another world completely. The walls had been papered with a delicate print of violet sprigs entwined with white ribbons, while a simple braided rug adorned the oak floor between the two iron-framed beds. Homemade muslin curtains hung at the windows and decidedly feminine quilts covered the beds.

The door slowly opened and Deborah peered around it into the room. "Oh, I was afraid you were already asleep."

"I thought about it," Lizzie admitted. "I'm very tired, but I wanted to make sure everything was all right with your family. I mean, what with me coming unannounced."

Deborah entered the room and closed the door behind her. "Of course it's all right. Mother is delighted to have you here." She began to undress. "I wouldn't be surprised, however, if she doesn't have you canning and working in the garden before noon tomorrow. I told her you wanted to learn how to be more self-sufficient, domestically speaking."

Lizzie smiled. "I'm glad. Do you know that I've never had to cook for myself? I can honestly say that I would like to learn."

"Then you've come to the right place. My mother is a wonderful cook and a superb teacher. She learned a lot from Sissy, and I'm sure together they will be more than delighted to help you."

"Was Sissy a slave?"

Deborah nodded and pulled pins from her long dark hair. "She was, but she and Mother were close and she came here when my grandparents came to stay with us during the war. My mother hired her on to work at our house when my grandparents went back to Georgia after the war. I doubt Mama would have hired anyone, but Sissy was sickly and needed help. She was too proud for charity, so my mother suggested Sissy teach her to cook. That way, Mother did a lot of the work, while Sissy recovered her health. It worked well."

"Your mother is such a gracious lady. She seems so innocent at times—yet so knowledgeable."

"She's not highly educated. She attended school until she married my father when she was sixteen. But she always loved learning and regretted to a degree that she could not continue her education. Of course, women were even less encouraged to seek out schooling back then than they are now."

"Still, she seems very happy with her house and family. I wish my own mother might have shared such thinking. I can't help but imagine what life might have been like had she enjoyed her domestic duties."

Deborah discarded her blouse and skirt and stretched before releasing the hooks on her corset. "But perhaps you wouldn't be the dear woman I know and love now. Mother always says there's no sense fretting over what might have been, since it can't ever be."

"She's no doubt right about that," Lizzie admitted. "Your mother seems very wise."

"It's a wisdom borne of experience." Deborah pulled a nightgown over her head.

Lizzie said nothing for several minutes, then gave a sigh. "I suppose then, in time, it shall come to each of us."

Deborah looked at her oddly as she came to her bedside. "What shall?"

"Wisdom," Lizzie answered. "Wisdom borne of experience."

"I suppose it shall, but it will have to wait until I get some sleep. Mother said she didn't even want to hear us rousing before eight. I assured her I could very easily yield to her request."

Lizzie laughed. "What a chore! But as a guest, I suppose I have no choice." She eased back onto the bed. "Tomorrow I shall begin my new life as an East Texas woman."

Deborah laughed. "Then Texas be warned."

Chapter 4

Rachel and Zed Perkins arrived the following evening with daughters Annabeth and Maybelle. Both shared their father's fair complexion and red hair. They were pretty girls, with trim waists and lovely blue eyes, but Deborah found their general silliness overwhelmed their virtues.

The real treat of the evening was the unexpected guest that Zed and Rachel introduced as the new company doctor. Christopher Clayton was a handsome and witty man who hailed from Kansas City, but he had studied medicine at Bellevue Hospital Medical College in New York City.

"Dr. Clayton, we are certainly happy to have you join the community," Deborah's mother declared as Sissy placed a large platter on the table. A succulent ham, complete with a molasses glaze, wafted a tantalizing aroma into the air. She hurried back to the kitchen and brought out another platter with two large baked chickens.

"Sissy, come join us and meet the new doctor."

The woman smiled. "I gots too much to do, but I's pleased to make your acquaintance."

Dr. Clayton nodded. "As am I, to make yours."

Sissy gave a little curtsy that she reserved for strangers and headed back to the kitchen. Mother lost little time explaining to the doctor. "Sissy's a good friend, and I hired her to work so she could help her family."

He seemed to understand her discomfort. "You needn't explain to me, Mrs. Vandermark. I'm just grateful to share such fine company and food."

"You haven't even tasted it yet," Deborah teased.

He studied her for a moment, as if appraising her features. His scrutiny made Deborah feel uncomfortable.

"I think I shall enjoy living here," Dr. Clayton replied. He glanced around the table. "Beautiful ladies for company, delectable food for nourishment, and intelligent conversation with the gentlemen. Who could ask for more?"

Deborah frowned. "Perhaps you could have intelligent conversations with the ladies, and the men could be admired for their beauty."

Rob laughed out loud and the Perkins girls giggled uncontrollably. Dr. Clayton, however, nodded in agreement. "Why not?"

She could see the response was not offered in jest. Dr. Clayton seemed to genuinely agree that the idea was possible. Deborah couldn't help but throw him a smile.

"Do you have a family, Doctor?" Deborah's mother asked.

"If you mean am I married, then the answer is no. I do have a family, however. I am the oldest of fifteen children. My mother and father reside in Kansas City."

"Fifteen children," Mrs. Perkins said, shaking her head. "Goodness! And I thought my five were plenty to keep a woman busy."

"My mother is indeed a busy woman. She was made even more so, I'm sorry to say, when my father was left crippled after an accident in the rail yard."

"How tragic," the woman replied. "I often worry after Zed at the sawmill, although he's not nearly so busy with the day-to-day running as he used to be. But I am concerned for my sons. Injuries happen all the time."

"Well, that's why we brought in a doctor, Mrs. Perkins," Zed told his wife. "So you would stop fretting so much."

Everyone chuckled at this. Sissy placed the last bowl of food on the table and stood aside with folded hands as was her traditional signal that it was time to pray. Deborah bowed her head, finding even this simple reminder of home to be a blessing.

Grace was offered by Uncle Arjan and conversation was put aside to focus instead on fried okra, rice and beans, and of course the promise of dessert. Deborah smiled appreciatively at the sight of her mother's buttermilk biscuits. How she'd missed the food of her childhood.

The conversation picked up a bit after the eating began. Once their initial hunger had abated, folks began to discuss the issues of the day between bites. Deborah listened with great interest as Mrs. Perkins addressed her desire for a larger school.

"I believe with the growing number of children in our community, it would serve us well to build a school separate from the church. I've been after Mr. Perkins for some time now to consider the matter. The schoolmaster agrees it is a much needed project."

"I think that would be grand," Euphanel Vandermark replied.

Deborah knew her mother's longtime friendship with Rachel Perkins often had the women seeing eye-to-eye on town matters. "Education has long suffered in this area."

"Too many folks associate free school with the Reconstructionists and their impositions on our society," Mr. Perkins stated.

Mrs. Perkins nodded. "People are inclined to cut off their noses to spite their faces. Still, I think if we offered a nicely built school with quality desks and good books, educating children through the eighth grade would be no problem at all."

"Rachel is good about spending my money before I make it," Zed Perkins said, laughing.

"Aren't all women?" Rob questioned with a wink at Lizzie. "It's because they're so pretty, though, that we don't seem to mind too much." He smiled at the Perkins sisters, causing them to flush and giggle all the more.

"Why not take them beyond eighth grade?" Deborah asked.

Everyone looked at her for a moment, and then Annabeth shrugged. "Not many folks are even interested in education beyond that point."

Mrs. Perkins nodded and looked to Deborah. "It's true. I doubt there's much of an interest. It's hard enough to get the people around here to spare their children for six years of education, much less eight. I'm hopeful, however, that we can make it more appealing."

Deborah held her tongue. No sense in appearing too confrontational on her first full day back. If the last four years away had taught her anything, it was that sometimes it was best to watch and listen. Popping a piece of buttered biscuit into her mouth, Deborah closed her eyes and savored the flavor. It was just as good as she remembered.

"Miss Vandermark, you have an expression that suggests pure euphoria."

Deborah's eyes snapped open to find Dr. Clayton watching her. Actually, everyone was now watching her. Apparently Dr. Clayton's comment had interested them all. She fought her embarrassment and swallowed.

"My mother makes the best biscuits in the county—probably even the state, although I've not attempted to verify that fact."

Dr. Clayton grinned. "I would agree." He turned toward Deborah's mother. "I've never eaten anything quite so delectable. If my mother had made biscuits half so well, I might never have left home."

"Why, aren't you just the kindest man to say so," her mother declared. "I shall have to make sure you get an extra large piece of pie for dessert."

"Hey, just hold on a second. You know I love your biscuits, Ma. I tell you all the time," Rob threw out from the opposite end of the table. Everyone laughed at this, and Euphanel nodded.

"You shall have a large piece of pie, as well. I happen to know it's your favorite—egg custard."

Rob grinned and pushed his plate back. "Why didn't you say so? I could have just skipped the rest of this food and started there."

His mother laughed. "That is exactly why I didn't tell you about the pie."

The meal passed amicably with conversations about the locals and even some of the concerns in areas around the county. Deborah enjoyed it, although she found herself more an observer than participant. She wasn't exactly sure why, but a sense of reflection seemed to hold her captive.

With each absence from home, Deborah had found the differences more noticeable. But she also found the precious things more poignant, as well. Little things, like the creaking sound of her mother's rocker on the porch as she snapped beans; the warmth of a dog curled up at the foot of her bed; even the wonderful scent of the pines mingled with woodsmoke. Each memory could bring a smile to her face. Deborah was bound to her birthplace in a way that she couldn't quite explain. She had once tried to write about it for a school paper but found herself doing a poor job. Her teacher had chided her for being "dreamy and childish" in her declaration that, "Nothing will ever comfort me quite as much as the scents of my mother's lavender sachet, strong coffee brewing, and freshly cut wood." Deborah felt sorry for the professor. He would never understand the way she felt.

She couldn't help but notice G. W.'s silence. He focused on his meal, nodded in acknowledgment from time to time, but otherwise shared very little of his thoughts. Deborah had hoped that one of the young women might have attracted his attention, but upon reacquainting herself with nineteen-year-old Annabeth and seventeen-year-old Maybelle, Deborah was just as happy that G. W. was preoccupied. What ninnies those two turned out to be! One minute they were giggling and blushing, the next they were staring wide-eyed at the handsome doctor.

Lizzie seemed to be enjoying herself. Mrs. Perkins had very nearly assaulted Deborah's friend with questions about her background and how the two women had met. Lizzie didn't seem to mind, however, and took each question in stride.

"So you were both attending university in Philadelphia?" Dr. Clayton asked.

Deborah nodded, but it was Lizzie who answered. "Deborah was my dearest friend and always shall be. She kept me from giving up when our studies turned difficult."

"And what studies were those?" he asked.

"It was that wretched biology class," Lizzie said with a shudder. "Seems like just yesterday. I spent more time confused than in understanding. I had fully planned to give up my attempts to understand cells, but Deborah began tutoring me, and before I knew it, the class was concluded and I had managed to get a passing grade. But just barely."

Dr. Clayton smiled and turned to Deborah. "And what of you? Did you enjoy the class?"

Again Lizzie jumped in. "She most certainly did. One of the professors tried to interest her in the women's medical school."

Deborah found all eyes turned to her and gave a weak laugh. "Then I could have opened an infirmary in the logging office."

Her mother's gaze seemed fixed upon her, and Deborah felt the need to move the conversation elsewhere. "Lizzie is quite gifted in the arts. She plays piano and sings, and has the most amazing talent with watercolors."

"All very useless skills for real life," Lizzie added.

"Not at all, Miss Decker!" Rachel Perkins's excitement got the best of her. "We suffer for entertainment in these parts. It would be marvelous to plan an evening where you could sing and play for us." She turned to her husband. "Don't you think such an event would be popular? Why, the folks would simply love it."

"I believe she's right," Zed Perkins replied. "We will depend upon you, Miss Decker."

Lizzie threw Deborah a rather panicked look, but Deborah was simply glad to have the conversation turned elsewhere. The last thing she wanted to do was answer any more questions regarding her own interests.

After pie was served and praise issued with the devouring, the men wandered outside to the porch to discuss business. Mrs. Perkins and the girls settled in the living room with Lizzie, while Deborah helped her mother serve coffee. She could hear the men's muffled discussion through the open windows but paid it little attention.

To think too long on such matters only made Deborah wish for the classrooms she'd left behind. She enjoyed a rousing discussion of politics and business. Too bad a woman would be considered out of place to position herself with the men rather than to gossip with the ladies.

"I do wish we could have taken a stroll," Annabeth declared. "It seems the perfect night for such a thing. The moon is nearly full."

Mother shook her head. "I'm afraid it would be dangerous. We've had trouble with the Piney Woods rooters."

Lizzie looked at Deborah for an explanation. Deborah leaned closer. "Wild hogs."

"Very dangerous animals indeed," Mrs. Perkins said as she lifted her coffee cup. "Many a man has been desperately wounded by those beasts."

"By a pig?" Lizzie asked.

The Perkins sisters burst into laughter. "Oh my dear," their mother interjected, "they aren't merely pigs. These are feral animals—razorbacks that roam the woods at night. They are smart and can outthink a normal man. They are mean and ill-tempered, with fierce tusks that can tear you to ribbons."

Deborah could see that Lizzie was notably impressed. "There are a great many dangers no matter where you live. We had our share of desperate beasts in Philadelphia, as well," Deborah offered. "Most were two legged and wore trousers, however."

Mother met her gaze and smiled. "I'm sure your experience here helped to keep you safer back there. However, I'm very glad to have you home now."

"Have you a beau, Miss Vandermark?" Annabeth asked innocently.

For a moment, the question took Deborah by surprise. "I hadn't the time for such things. I needed to get my education so that I could come back to Perkinsville and help my family. It was what my father wished for." Deborah saw Mother frown, but continued. "As I understand from Uncle Arjan, we need to totally modernize our methods of doing business. I'm going to see to it that this happens in an orderly fashion."

"Oh, I would hate to have to work," Maybelle said, fanning herself furiously. "Just the thought of trying to add up numbers and keep track of orders . . . Goodness, but you are more—oh, what's the word I want? Well, I suppose *industrious* would do. You're more industrious than I, what with your interests in things related to business."

Deborah knew that the comment was a veiled insult. What Maybelle really seemed to be inferring was that Deborah was less womanly—more masculine in her concerns. But again, Deborah held back. There was certainly nothing positive to be gained by cutting Maybelle Perkins down a peg or two.

"Oh, we simply must tell them about the new gowns we have ordered," Annabeth said, as if to cover up for her sister's indiscretion. "Mother ordered us new dresses from France. Isn't that exciting?"

"To be certain," Lizzie answered with a sympathetic glance at Deborah. "Of course, there aren't quite as many grand occasions to wear them as we enjoyed in Philadelphia, I suppose."

Deborah appreciated her friend's effort, but didn't wish for the Perkinses to dislike Lizzie. She smiled and patted her friend's hand. "I hope we shall see your new gowns at the Christmas dance, perhaps?"

The girls tried unsuccessfully to suppress their excitement. "That is our desire, as well. Mother was assured they will reach us in plenty of time." Annabeth's volume was increasing with her enthusiasm. "My gown is lavender, and Maybelle has one of iced blue. I am positively delirious at the thought of actually wearing the gown for the first time."

Mother lifted the china pot. "I'm sure it will be an occasion to remember. Now, would anyone care for more coffee?"

"None for me," Mrs. Perkins replied. "In fact, I'm afraid the hour has slipped Mr. Perkins's attention. We should be making our way back. I've so enjoyed our evening."

Deborah watched her mother replace the pot and offer Mrs. Perkins a gracious smile. "As have we. I'm so glad you were able to talk Mr. Perkins into bringing us a doctor. The community will benefit from such generosity."

"Well, there's still Mrs. Foster to deal with," Rachel Perkins said in a conspiratorial tone.

Deborah's mother nodded. "She's served the area as healer and midwife for a very long time. She will, no doubt, be put off at such modernizing."

"But with all of the deaths we've suffered over the last few years—especially with our women," Mrs. Perkins replied, "I hardly think we can do anything else. Perhaps it's her age, but Margaret Foster is clearly unable to deal with the needs of our town." The two Perkins girls bobbed their heads in agreement. When their mother got to her feet, the sisters followed suit.

"Do come see me when you are next in town," Mrs. Perkins told Deborah's mother. She turned then to Deborah and Lizzie. "You are also welcome. It's so pleasant to have good friends drop by for a visit."

"Thank you, Rachel. I'm sure we will take you up on the offer very soon," Mother replied.

They departed, and Deborah was relieved to see them go. She thought the nonsensical Perkins sisters absolutely exhausting. "And to think I considered encouraging G. W. to take up with one of them."

"What was that?" Lizzie asked.

Deborah shook her head. "Nothing much. Just glad to see this evening come to an end. Did you enjoy yourself?"

"I found it all very fascinating." Lizzie looped her arm through Deborah's. "Your family all seem to genuinely enjoy one another's company. What a concept."

Deborah laughed and squeezed Lizzie's arm. "At times we are less congenial, but for the most part we are quite companionable."

"I wish I might have known the same in my family."

Her wistful tone caused Deborah to stop. "You can be a part of my family now. We shall love you as our own. And who knows—maybe one day you will truly be a part of it. I do, after all, have two unmarried brothers."

Lizzie laughed and playfully nudged Deborah with her elbow. "Yes, and one seems to constantly notice my every move like a child with a new puppy, while the other has no interest whatsoever. Hardly encouraging."

Deborah joined in her friend's laughter. "Well, take heart, Miss Decker. Your visit has only begun. Who is to say what will happen in the days to come?"

Chapter 5

Christopher Clayton frowned as he caught sight of the unpacked crates. He felt he'd been unloading supplies all morning. When Zed Perkins hired him to be the new company doctor, Christopher had given him a long list of things that would be needed for a proper medical facility. As far as he could tell, Mr. Perkins had purchased everything he'd requested. Now it was his job to find a place for each article.

Another task would be to figure out how to keep the dust and soot from coating everything. Christopher was a firm believer that fresh air was healthy and helped to promote healing; however, the air quality in this town would not always be beneficial. If the wind was blowing just right, it appeared that Perkinsville could escape the worst of it. But if the day was calm, folks just had to endure the smoke and soot put out by the sawmill chimneys.

He ran a finger along the windowsill and shook his head at the collection of blackened dirt. He would have to figure out something that could be done. Perhaps if he tacked up material across the windows? It would have to have a very fine weave to hold out the damaging elements while still allowing fresh air. Wiping his finger on his already dirt-stained trousers, Christopher turned back to the job at hand.

He was generally pleased with the arrangements Mr. Perkins had made. The man had built the facility to the doctor's suggested specifications. While most of the houses here were of unfinished wood, the new doctor's office and infirmary was a stark white. Christopher had made a firm requirement that everything be whitewashed for easy cleaning. It stood out in the tiny town just as Christopher had hoped it would.

The front door opened into a small waiting area, and behind that was a private office that led into the examination room. Beyond the examination room was the infirmary. There were four cots and a washstand in this room, with a back entrance that allowed for easy access from the mill. The thought had been that should a terrible accident arise, it would allow for a wounded man to be brought in without making a scene.

A side door off the infirmary led to Dr. Clayton's private quarters. There he had a small kitchen, living room, and bedroom. It was nothing fancy, but neither did it need to be. Christopher was quite content.

"Hello?" A knock followed the female voice.

"I'm in the back," he called in reply. He hoped fervently that it wouldn't be a patient in need, for he wasn't ready to set up shop just yet.

Deborah Vandermark marched through the doorway with a plate extended in front of her. She looked rather like one of the wise men presenting his treasure to the Christ child. "I have come bearing a gift," she announced.

He smiled. "I can see that."

She returned his smile, and he very much liked the way it seemed to spark a fire in her dark brown eyes. "Mother made fresh doughnuts and instructed me to bring you a batch straightaway. I rode the train into town when they brought a load of wood."

He took the plate from her and put it on a nearby table. "Well, that was most kind of you. You will have to thank your mother for me."

"I will. It looks like I caught you at a bad time," she said, glancing around the messy room. "Might I help? The train won't be heading back for another hour."

"I couldn't let you spend your day laboring over this mess." He reached absentmindedly for one of the doughnuts and had it in his mouth almost before he realized it. The pastry practically melted on his tongue. "Oh, this is delicious."

Deborah turned and smiled. "My mother makes the best in the county."

"Along with biscuits?"

She laughed. "And many other things. So what is all of this? If you don't mind my asking."

"Not at all." He moved to where she stood. "This box has medical supplies. I ordered them from Mr. Perkins. The next crate holds many of my personal books and medical journals, and the others . . . well, I haven't opened them yet so I'm not exactly sure what they hold."

"I presume you will have an office?"

He nodded. "The small room you came through on your way

back here—the one with the bookshelves—will be my office. This is the examination room. Through that door over there is the infirmary, where I can care for long-term patients. Mr. Perkins had the entire structure built according to my suggestions."

"And are you pleased?"

"Very much so. Mr. Perkins also ordered the equipment I asked for. I was rather surprised to find most everything waiting and ready. He even managed to get this examination table for me." Christopher put his hand to the metal table.

Deborah reached into the crate of books. "Why don't I start by putting the books on the shelves? You can organize them at a later date, but at least it will get them out of the box."

"Thank you. It's most kind of you to help."

"I'm just nosy, that's all," she said in a teasing tone. "I love to read. Books are simply irresistible to me. I think I shall miss the libraries back East most of all."

"I gather your love of literature is rather unusual around here."

Deborah took up several large books. "Sadly, that is true. Folks leave school at an early age in order to work or marry. Reading is a luxury and books are a novelty. So, too, is having a doctor. You do realize that you might not be well received at first." She didn't wait for an answer but trotted the books to the office.

When she returned Christopher couldn't help but ask, "Why is that?"

"Margaret Foster has taken care of folks around here for as long as I can remember. She's a widow with three grown sons."

Again she headed off with more books, then quickly returned. Christopher admired her petite form as she bent to pick up additional medical tomes. "And she's the reason I won't be accepted?"

"Partly. People can be very odd. Mrs. Foster is superstitious, and she's convinced a lot of other folks to see things the way she does."

Deborah straightened and smiled. "But she didn't have to try that hard. Superstition walks hand in hand with ignorance."

"I've found that to be true," he replied, nodding. "But somehow I don't think that's a concern with you."

"Hardly."

Christopher laughed. "So what is a concern of yours?"

She shrugged and stopped to consider his question. "There are a great many things that concern me. My family's welfare is probably at the top of the list. Helping the people of this community is another."

"I heard someone say that your father passed away a few years ago."

"Nearly three. He was killed in a logging accident." Her expression sobered. "It was very hard on my family. We were all extremely close. We still are."

"I can well imagine. My own father was injured . . . in an accident." He hesitated. "It nearly claimed his life, but instead left him crippled and my mother struggling to support my siblings."

"Oh my, and you're the oldest of fifteen," Deborah said, shifting the books. "How in the world does she do it?"

He was touched by her concern. "Only the five youngest are still at home. The rest of us do what we can to help." The conversation suddenly made him feel self-conscious. "It seems your family is good about helping one another."

"Oh, they are. Uncle Arjan and my father were brothers, and when Papa died, my uncle felt it was important to see to Mama's needs. The boys inherited Papa's land and business—that's the way the law works down here. Everyone agreed, however, that Mama will never want."

"How was it that you ended up going to college?"

"The blessings of a wealthy aunt—one of my mother's sisters.

My folks needed me to learn what I could in order to help the business. My brothers weren't interested in an education. You'll see that about most folks. However, I hope that will change around here. I believe most people are ignorant of the possibilities."

"And you intend to show them?"

"I hope to. I want them to see how beneficial an education can be. There are some very hardworking people in this community. Education simply hasn't been something that was valued."

"How do you propose to help them change their minds?" he asked, intrigued by this little powerhouse of a woman.

"Mainly by example, I suppose. I'd like to show them how pleasant it can be to simply enjoy a good book—to be able to read the Bible for themselves. To better understand science, medicine. If they understand what you are able to do for them, Dr. Clayton, they will be more open to accepting you." She headed back to the office once more with an armload of books.

Christopher picked up several books and followed her. He waited until she'd secured the books on the shelf. "You really don't have to keep doing this." He placed his books beside hers.

She eyed him intently for a moment. "Are you too proud to accept help?"

He rubbed his bearded chin. "Not at all."

"Then what?"

He liked her spunk. "The books can wait, actually. If you truly want to be useful, I need to get the examination office set up first."

Deborah dusted off her hands and headed back to the other room. "Very well. Let's get to work. They'll sound the whistle when the train is ready to head back up the line."

Helping Dr. Clayton set up his examination office was a great diversion for Deborah. She found it fascinating to unpack his medical equipment and listen to his reasons for placement. When she came upon a collection of medical journals, Deborah couldn't help but thumb through a couple of them.

"These look quite interesting."

"If you're of a mind to read them, be my guest. Just bring them back."

She looked up to see if he was serious. His expression assured her he was. "I would like that very much."

"You may feel free to borrow any of my books, as well."

Deborah hugged the journals to her breast. "Do you always lend your books?"

"Never," he said, turning back to a crate he'd been emptying.

Deborah thought about this for several seconds and was about to extend an invitation to him to utilize her book collection when someone called out from the open back door.

"Doc, you in there?"

"I am," Dr. Clayton announced. He moved to the door and welcomed in a man and woman.

Deborah didn't know the couple, but she knew their type. They were dirt poor, ill-kempt, and probably had no more than six years of education between them. The woman looked tired and was clearly with child. Her face was edged with lines and her hair was stringy and dirty. Neither the man nor woman looked as if they'd had a bath in a week of Sundays.

"I'm Dr. Clayton. What can I do for you?"

The man held up his hand. "I'm John. My wife here wanted me to see you. My hand is hurtin' me something fierce."

"What did you do to it?" Dr. Clayton led the man to the examination table and drew up a chair. "Just sit here and rest your hand on the table."

The doctor went to a bowl of water and washed his hands.

Deborah saw him pour something onto his hands before taking up a clean towel. He then took up a brown bottle and another clean towel.

Deborah could see the man's hand had swollen to nearly double the normal size and was clearly inflamed. A jagged cut oozed green-tinged fluid. She watched as Dr. Clayton took the matter in stride.

"How did you injure your hand?"

"Cut it at work. Didn't seem that bad. Miz Foster put a poultice on it, but it don't seem to be any better."

The doctor continued his exam. "When was that?"

Deborah couldn't help drawing closer to see what was happening. The woman stepped forward, as well. "He cut it near a week ago. Ain't been right since. Cain't work with it like that."

"Now, Sally," he said, throwing her a grin. "You stop your frettin'. I came here like you asked."

"And it's a good thing," Dr. Clayton announced. "You'll be lucky if you don't lose that hand."

"What?" The man was clearly stunned.

"It's desperately infected. I'm afraid this will be quite painful. Miss Vandermark, would you please bring over a basin and my scalpel set?"

Deborah didn't even question him. She hurried to do his bidding, rather excited to be of some help. The procedure that followed was not at all pleasant. Without so much as an injection of morphine to kill the pain, Dr. Clayton cleaned the hand and applied the knife. The infection shot from the wound, filling the room with a hideous smell.

Unmoved by the situation, Deborah continued to follow the doctor's instructions, handing him the supplies he needed to treat the infected hand.

"This town doesn't seem to overly concern itself with cleanliness. You cannot have a wound of this magnitude and not pay heed to keeping it clean."

The man and woman exchanged a look. The woman frowned. "Miz Foster said to keep the poultice on. She told us not to wash it at all—said the herbs would draw it until the moon was full. It was a full moon last night, and we took off the bandages."

"Well, apparently she was wrong," Dr. Clayton said. He looked to Deborah. "Is this some of that superstitious nonsense you told me about?"

She nodded as the doctor continued to clean the hand. The man was clearly in horrible pain, but though his face paled, he said nothing. She fanned away the flies that hovered and prayed that God would intercede to heal the wound.

"I'll need to see you first thing in the morning," Dr. Clayton told the man.

"Cain't." He barely breathed the word. "Gotta be at the mill."

Dr. Clayton straightened. "If you do what I tell you to, I might be able to save your hand. If you don't, I can guarantee you that you will lose it."

"John, you cain't lose your hand." The woman's voice was edged with hysteria. "You cain't work without a hand."

Deborah reached out to touch the woman's arm. "Dr. Clayton is a good man. He'll do what he can, but you have to be willing to do your part. Mr. Perkins trusts him, and you should, too." She knew that most everyone thought fondly of the sawmill owner. "He looked far and wide to find a doctor as well trained as Dr. Clayton. He wouldn't allow your care to just anyone."

"She's right, Sally." A fine line of perspiration edged the man's upper lip. "Doc, will you let Mr. Perkins know that you told me to come here in the morning?"

"I will speak with him as soon as we've finished. Now this wound needs to drain." He instructed Sally as to what she needed to do. "Do exactly as I've told you, understand?"

She nodded. Deborah felt sorry for the woman and patted her hand. "You did the right thing in coming here. Dr. Clayton will do everything he can."

Once the couple was gone, Dr. Clayton turned to Deborah. "You handled that well."

She shrugged. "I just wanted to help."

"You definitely did that."

The train whistle sounded in the distance and Deborah realized she would need to go. She quickly washed her hands. "Things are starting to look a whole lot better in here, but I need to go. Thanks for the loan of the journals." She gathered up the three magazines that she'd set aside to take with her. "I'll have them back soon."

"Please thank your mother for the doughnuts."

"I'm sure there will be other offerings as people get used to the idea of having a regular doctor. You'll find folks around here can be very friendly once they feel safe with you."

She wanted to tell him how much she admired his skills but held back. Instead, she just smiled and headed for the door. "Mama also wanted you to know that you're always welcome at the house. Come anytime for supper—or any other meal, for that matter."

Deborah didn't wait for an answer but headed out across the dirt road and made her way to where the little engine waited.

"Come on up," the fireman said, extending his hand.

Deborah gathered her skirts, careful not to damage the journals, and made the stretch to reach the first step. She grabbed the grimy rail and pulled herself up. George steadied her as she finally made it into the engine compartment. The engineer, an older man named Jack, tipped a finger to his cap and gave the whistle another short blast.

"I figured you'd come back with all sorts of girly geegaws," George told her. "Told Jack we probably wouldn't have room for it all."

She smiled. "I'm not much of a shopper, George." She held up the journals. "More of a reader."

"Never learned myself." He turned back to his job of loading the firebox as Jack put the train in motion. "Never saw a need. Guess you can read enough for all of us."

Deborah shook her head. "You ought to learn, George. You'd be surprised how much fun it can be. I could even help you if you'd like."

He laughed. "Won't help in gettin' the steam up, so I don't reckon I need it."

She looked out the window and sighed. Ignorance seemed the answer to all things uncomfortable or challenging.

Lord, she prayed, *I know you brought me back here to help my family. I want to help them. I love them. But there's so much more out there, beyond my little world in Perkinsville, Texas. . . .*

Chapter 6

After church on Sunday, the congregation gathered outside under the shady box elders and hickories and held a picnic lunch. Everyone brought something to share, and soon the atmosphere was quite merry. Lizzie had never experienced anything like it. Gone were the pretenses and worries of social status. Even the Perkins family blended with the lowliest mill worker and his family.

The contrast in clothing was evident. The members of the poorer families were dressed simply in garments that had seen a great deal of wear. Many of the outfits bore patches and stains, but it was the best they could offer. People from more affluent families wore stylish outfits that looked store-bought and new, compared to the outfits of their less wealthy neighbors. The Vandermarks fell in between, neither too fashionable nor too unkempt. Lizzie now understood why Deborah had traded most of her beautiful gowns for simpler fare at the secondhand shop in Nacogdoches. Yet even now, as Deborah approached in a lovely gown with yellow flowers set against a cream-colored background, she looked radiant—almost elegant. Everyone seemed happy to see her and stopped her frequently to bid her welcome home or to ask about her travels.

At last Deborah managed to separate herself and closed the distance to Lizzie, who was filling her plate. "G. W. is all alone, and I want you to help me keep him from stewing and fretting."

Lizzie met Deborah's determined expression. "What can I do?" She turned back to the table and took a piece of corn bread.

"Just go talk to him. He tends to get moody at these gatherings because he doesn't want to have to talk to anyone about anything. Just sit with him and keep him from thinking on Papa's death."

Lizzie took up a piece of fried chicken and looked to her friend in confusion. "And how am I supposed to do that? I can hardly keep a man from thinking about what he chooses."

"If you talk to him about other things, he'll have to keep his mind elsewhere." Deborah took hold of Lizzie's arm and pulled her in the direction of the creek. "He's over here."

Barely keeping her plate balanced, Lizzie fought to keep up with Deborah. She didn't think this was a good idea, but it didn't appear she had a choice in the matter.

"G. W., Lizzie doesn't have anyone to talk to. I told her she could come sit with you," Deborah said, releasing her friend as they approached G. W.

He sat with his back to a tree, a plate of food uneaten in his lap. Lizzie could tell that he wasn't in a mood for company, but he was too much of a gentleman to say so.

"I can go if it's too much of a bother," she said softly.

He shook his head. "That's all right."

Deborah smiled. "I told you it would be fine." She lifted her skirt and whirled off in the opposite direction. "I'll be back after a bit."

"I really am sorry," Lizzie told him.

G. W. shrugged. "I know what she's up to. So long as you know it, too, then we won't be duped."

She looked at the ground and then to her plate, wondering how she was going to sit without dumping her food. G. W. seemed to understand her predicament and put his own plate aside. He was on his feet assisting her before Lizzie could ask for help.

"Thank you. I was rather perplexed for the moment." She smiled and settled the plate of food on her lap.

They sat in silence for several minutes. Lizzie nibbled at her chicken while G. W. stared out at the muddy waters, lost in thought. She couldn't help but wonder what was going through his mind. How could she possibly impose her own interests upon him? Whether Deborah liked it or not, Lizzie knew there was only one topic of conversation that would help G. W.

"If I'm not causing you even more pain, I wonder if you might tell me about your father's accident. Deborah tells me the anniversary of his death is coming up."

G. W. looked at her in surprise. For a moment, Lizzie wasn't at all sure he would even remain at her side, much less speak. Finally, however, he exhaled a long breath.

"Three years next month," he said as if she'd asked for confirmation. "But it seems like just yesterday." He started at the beginning and filled in the details that Lizzie hadn't known.

"The work is unpredictable," he told her after reliving the accident in detail. "Any time you combine sharp tools, animals, and human error, you're bound to have trouble."

"It sounds like logging is a very dangerous industry," Lizzie said. "Did your father realize just how dangerous it was when he started this business?"

G. W. gave a brief laugh. "He knew. He'd been around it in Georgia. My father and uncle had honestly planned to come here and plant cotton, but loggin' seemed a necessary way to start."

"Why?"

"The good farmin' ground was taken by the time they arrived. The land they were able to get was all wooded. They figured they could log the forests, get the lumber to the nearby towns, and clear their land at the same time. They were fixin' to clear out enough of the forest to plant cotton, but it never worked out that way. The loggin' proved to be a valuable means of gainin' an income. Pretty soon they were buyin' more forest land, and Vandermark Logging became a permanent operation. It was actually my father's pride and joy. He loved the work he did."

"So they chose their profession, even knowing the dangers. That's true bravery, in my mind," Lizzie said casually. "It amazes me that a man, knowing the possibility of death lingered just around the corner, would continue to put his hand to a task."

"It was Pa's way of earning a livin' for his family. He always said he got along well with the Piney Woods. I reckon he could have done something else. He was a smart enough man."

"Obviously. Just as you are. Look at how successful the logging industry has proven to be. Why, I heard Deborah say that eastern investors are all over the place looking for land to buy so they can be a part of this success. Your father had great insight."

G. W. nodded. "I suppose you could say that. He knew the yellow pine was good wood, even though a lot of folks didn't care for it. He had a way of doin' the right thing, at the right time. Too bad I didn't."

"Why do you say that?" Lizzie watched the play of emotions in his expression.

"If I had been like him—knowin' what to do at the right time—Pa might be alive today."

"Maybe he should have trained you better," she suggested.

"There's no call to say that. Pa was a good teacher. Like I said, he was smart. He taught me and Rob real good."

"Well, I suppose I'm confused." She gave him an innocent smile, hoping he wouldn't realize the trap she'd put in place. "If your father was smart and trained you well, and if he knew all of the dangers about the business, but continued to log anyway—how can his death possibly be your fault?"

G. W. opened his mouth to speak, then closed it. He looked at her for a moment and shook his head. "You book-learned women sure have a way of confusin' a guy."

"Maybe it's not as confusing as you think. I'm just suggesting that accidents have a way of happening, no matter how smart or careful people might be. You know the risks in your job. Your uncle and brother know them, too, yet all of you go out to work every day. Your father knew the risks and even had a choice to do something else. He chose to stay with logging." She smiled. "I think maybe it's time to consider that his death was simply one of those risks he was willing to take."

"Well, here you are," Rob declared as he joined the twosome. "I've been lookin' pert-near everywhere for you."

Lizzie held G. W.'s gaze for a moment longer, then cast a glance toward his brother. "Your sister brought me here, and it's so much cooler here in the shade that I couldn't help but linger. I'm afraid I've been talking your brother's ear off."

Rob plopped down on the ground in front of Lizzie. "You can

talk my ear off anytime you like." He grinned. "I reckon that would suit me just fine."

Deborah saw Rob heading over to join G. W. and Lizzie and frowned, wishing it were her instead. She'd been swarmed by people all afternoon. Most folks wanted to welcome her back, but others were would-be suitors who seemed quite bold in rekindling previous acquaintances.

"Miss Deborah, I wonder iffen you'd like to take a walk with me," Sam Huebner asked.

She looked up at the tall, lanky man. She'd known Sam for just about as long as anyone. His folks had been good friends with hers. "Hello, Sam. How are you?"

His smile broadened. "So you remember me."

"Of course I remember you. You've hung around my brothers and worked for my family nigh on forever." She noticed his brother working to spark an interest with one of the Perkins girls and nodded in that direction. "Looks like Stephen is sweet on Annabeth Perkins."

Sam followed her gaze. "He's got rocks for brains. Ain't no chance of courtin' her, and he knows it."

"Well, I suppose a man can dream." She turned back to Sam. "What of you? Have you settled down and married?"

He turned red and shook his head. "No, ma'am. Wouldn't be here talkin' to you iffen I had."

Deborah spied her mother approaching from behind Sam. "Well, don't worry, Sam," she said, moving to the side. "One of these days the right gal will come along. If you'll excuse me now, it looks like my mother needs me."

She was glad to hurry away before he could say anything else.

When she reached her mother, Deborah couldn't help but grin. "You saved my life."

"What in the world are you talking about?"

Linking their arms, Deborah walked with her mother toward the tables of food. "Sam just asked me to take a walk with him. I needed an excuse not to go."

"But why? Sam's a nice boy. You might have enjoyed a walk."

Deborah shook her head. "I don't think so. He can't even read."

"You would reject a man's love because he couldn't read? Your father couldn't read very well, and yet I loved him."

Deborah felt chastised. "I'm sorry, Mama. I didn't mean it to sound like that." She let go of her mother's arm. "I just . . . well, it's so hard sometimes." She looked around the gathering of people. "I wish I could explain it."

Her mother smiled and reached out to smooth back an errant strand of hair from Deborah's face. "Why don't you try?"

"I'm glad to be home—truly I am."

"But . . ."

"But . . . I don't really know. Things feel different, yet they're the same. I feel different, yet I'm the same."

Mother shook her head. "Nothing stays the same. It might have some of the same appearances, but changes are always taking place. The town's grown a bit. There are new buildings and people. The mill has expanded. You're older and, hopefully, wiser. You're more educated and have experienced more than you had two years ago."

"I know, and maybe that's part of the problem," she said, feeling like such a snob for even continuing. "Mama, I loved learning. I love reading and writing. I love books that teach me new things.

I want to discuss those things with others, but this isn't exactly the place to find someone of a like mind."

"Oh, sweetheart, I completely understand."

"Do you really? Because I'm not sure I do. I feel horrible for it. It sounds like I think myself better than others, but that's not it at all."

"Of course not," her mother agreed. "Just because you have one interest and someone else has another doesn't mean either one of you is better. Zed Perkins knows how to run a sawmill. Jack knows how to engineer a train. You can't drive a train. Does that make Jack better than you—worse than you?"

Deborah shook her head. "But I'm afraid that when it comes to courting, it will be a problem. Not that I have time for that." She ignored her mother's frown. "Mama, when Sam suggested a walk all I could think about was how I could never marry someone like him. I know that's horrible, and I'm sorry." She looked at her mother in desperation. "Please don't hate me, but I'm not sure I could fall in love with a man who didn't have an education."

Her mother reached out to pat her cheek. "Darling, when the right man comes along all of these things will fall into place. Don't fret over it. No one is asking you to marry Sam. The important thing to keep in mind is whether or not you're like-minded when it comes to God. Being unequally yoked can certainly pertain to other things, but spiritually, it is a never-ending battle that no married couple should have to endure. You need a man who first and foremost loves God."

"A man who loves God and is intelligent," Deborah said. "Of course, he should be thoughtful and kind, as well."

Her mother laughed. "And it wouldn't hurt if he was handsome, too. Maybe even well off."

Deborah grinned. "Well, if we're making a list, we might as well add it all."

Mother gave her a hug and released her. "I'm glad you're home. I missed your sense of humor and open frankness. Just don't fret over what you can't change. Folks here are just glad to be working and have a roof over their heads. Reading and writing isn't something they miss."

"Maybe not, but maybe that's only because they never had it to begin with," Deborah replied. "They don't know what they're missing."

Her mother nodded. "Sometimes that's the best way to get by. I find it a lot easier to be content when I'm not pondering the things I miss."

"Like Papa?"

"Yes," her mother said with a sigh. "He was my best friend, and it's hard to lose that. I know he's in a better place, but sometimes I'm lonely."

Deborah didn't know what to say. She longed to be able to say something that would give her mother just the right sense of assurance, but truth be told, Deborah felt completely unable to help. What did she know of losing a mate—a best friend of nearly thirty years?

Finally she put her arm around her mother's shoulders and simply held her close. Sometimes, words simply had no power to help.

Chapter 7

July 1885

The weeks of June slipped into July, and as the heat grew more intense, Deborah's efforts to set up the Vandermark Logging office did, too. She had decided the best way to get organized was to actually have an office. In the past, Uncle Arjan had just carried a ledger around with him to the logging site and then back to his small cabin just a few yards behind the main house. Now, however, Deborah believed the size of their organization merited a place for everything and everything in its place.

There was a sewing room on the ground floor of the Vandermark house that would work quite well. With her mother's enthusiastic encouragement, Deborah arranged for her brothers to move the sewing things upstairs to the storage room, where she and Lizzie could fix it up properly. There would always be mending and sewing to see to, but Mother said they could tend to it on the second floor as well as on the first.

Still, Deborah knew it was a sacrifice. The upstairs was much warmer in the summer, and while they saved most of their major sewing projects for the cooler winter months, it would still be less than ideal. Maybe in the future she could encourage her uncle and brothers to build a separate cabin for the office.

With Lizzie's help, the office took shape quickly. Deborah arranged a small desk, several chairs, and bookshelves, along with other things she would need. Now that she was settled, the trick was to interpret her uncle's chicken-scratch notes. Often she found a few figures and a name without any other comment. Deborah was hard-pressed to know exactly what they meant, but she gradually began to recognize his style.

She was just finishing tallies on May's figures when her uncle and Mr. Perkins showed up at the door of the office. Uncle Arjan looked rather perplexed.

"Sorry to bother you, Deborah, but Mr. Perkins has some papers for us to look over."

"Good to see you, Mr. Perkins. Come in," Deborah said, putting down her pen. "Pull up a chair and tell me what you need."

"I told Arjan that I wanted someone in the family to read over this contract. One copy is for you and one's for me. I need to have it signed to take with me when I go to Houston on Friday."

"A contract?" Most everything related to the business had always been done on a handshake. Contracts had never been needed among friends.

Mr. Perkins looked rather embarrassed as he handed her the papers. "I know what you're thinking, but it's not my idea. The bank wants me to give them proof that I have a steady supply of logs pledged for production at the sawmill. I'm getting signatures from all my major providers."

Deborah began reading over the contract. "But why?" she asked without thinking. She glanced up and smiled. "If you don't mind my asking."

The older man shook his head. "Not at all. Like I said, I know this comes as a surprise. Here's the situation: I want to double the size of the mill."

"Double?" She looked at her uncle. "Would that mean we would have to double our output, and double the number of employees, as well?"

"It would definitely mean adding people," her uncle replied.

Mr. Perkins moved forward. "See, I need to get a pledge of so many logs so I can project our board feet. This becomes a sort of collateral for the bank. They will see the contract agreements as a promise of production and your agreement to sell only to me, and in turn they can feel safe in loaning me the money I need for the expansion."

Deborah couldn't begin to imagine what that would do to the size of their small community. "I suppose you will have to bring in additional stores and housing for the workers, as well."

"Yes indeed. I'll be adding at least another ten houses right away, with plans for twenty more. Now that we have the new doctor—not that folks will go see him—" he muttered under his breath, "the missus wants me to think about bringing in a full-time preacher and maybe build a regular icehouse."

"All of those things would be very nice, especially with additional workers." Deborah looked at the papers again, and then to her uncle. "Has Mr. Perkins gone over the numbers with you?"

Uncle Arjan nodded. "He did."

"And are you in agreement with that number?" She glanced

down to look at the figures once more. "It says here that you'll provide logs with a potential of ten thousand board feet a day until the mill's first phase of additions is complete. After that, you'll increase to fifteen thousand, and after phase two and the completion of all additions, you'll increase to at least twenty thousand board feet a day, with bonuses paid if you go over your quota. Oh, and it's all to be paid in cash rather than script."

"Yes, that's always been our agreement. As for the amount of wood, I think we can do that, so long as we get in a good crew of workers," Uncle Arjan told her.

"And you'll have a few months to get them trained," Mr. Perkins added. "Once I get my loan, I intend to see the work completed by Christmas at the latest. That will give you a full five months to hire and train your men."

"I'm comfortable with that," Uncle Arjan declared.

Deborah worked some figures on paper for a moment. "So eventually you will need to provide something like between twenty-seven and thirty-five trees a day by the time the mill is doubled. Is that correct?"

Uncle Arjan laughed. "I told you she was the smart one in the family."

"What about these figures on what you'll pay Vandermark Logging?" Deborah asked Mr. Perkins. "Shouldn't there be an allowance for escalation, should the price of lumber go up?"

"She is the smart one," Mr. Perkins agreed. "I'm sorry I didn't think of that myself. Shows that my mind was purely on my own gain, and for that, I apologize. Why don't we figure a percentage that will be acceptable to both of us?"

"A figure based on increases of more than five percent in finished lumber prices could trigger the escalation clause. If the prices bottom out, we would revert to the original base price. That base price, however, could not be allowed to drop—at least not without new negotiations. If we have to pledge to provide a specific amount of board feet and take penalties if we fail to meet our quota, then you must, in turn, pledge to pay for the wood even if the market suffers. There should also be a clause that allows for acts of God—fire, hurricanes, and such."

"That's only fair," Mr. Perkins granted. "Write that in. I'll sign off on it."

They haggled over figures for another few minutes before Deborah was finally satisfied. Mr. Perkins reached out to shake her hand. "Your family will benefit greatly from you handling their affairs." He turned to Uncle Arjan. "Don't let her get away from you."

"I don't intend to," her uncle agreed.

She felt a mixture of emotions at his words. It wasn't that she didn't want to benefit her family, but with each passing day, Deborah had the distinct feeling that she had backed herself into a corner. She remembered one of her professors once saying, "Be careful of making yourself irreplaceable and indispensable, lest you find that you are."

"You'll be providing half my supply." Mr. Perkins patted her shoulder. "Your pa sure would have been proud."

Deborah nodded. "He would have been." She finished adjusting the terms of the document on one set of papers and handed the paper to her uncle. Dipping her pen in the ink, she passed that to him, as well. "You should both initial where each of the changes are listed and sign on the last page."

Uncle Arjan took the pen and did just that. He let Deborah blot the signature then handed the contract back to Mr. Perkins. "Looks like I'd better hire me some men."

Mr. Perkins initialed and signed while Deborah adjusted the

second copy of the contract. Once all of the signatures were in place, Zed Perkins handed Arjan his copy. "I'll be in touch as soon as I get back from Houston. I don't think we're going to have any problem now. I have four other small operations agreeing to provide wood, so the bankers can easily see that I'll have the wherewithal to furnish what I say I can. It was good to do business with you, Miss Deborah."

She smiled. "Likewise."

Uncle Arjan left momentarily to walk Mr. Perkins to the door, then returned to the office. Deborah looked up and smiled. "Guess you have your work cut out for you now."

"Well, my first order of business is to assign you a salary. You earned your keep today."

She shook her head. "I didn't take on this job expecting to be paid. Father wanted me to do this job. I benefit from the prosperity of the company—same as you. I don't need a salary."

"I can't say that I ever recall your father thinkin' you needed to work at anything. Leastwise, he never told me."

"That can't be right. We used to talk about it all the time. He knew I couldn't very well log, but he said many times that everyone in the family needed to pull their weight. So he allowed me to go to school."

"I don't suppose I know about that. Your pa talked about how proud he was of your ability to think—especially for a woman."

She grinned. "That sounds like him."

"And he loved to indulge you. But, anyway, everyone needs some spending money," Uncle Arjan countered. "What say you let me pay you a dollar a day? If you find you need more money than that—say you want to buy something special—just come and see me. Agreed?"

Deborah considered it for a moment and nodded. "Very well."

She got up and kissed her uncle on the cheek. "You are awfully good to me—to Mama, too. I want you to know how much I appreciate that."

His face reddened slightly. "You and your mama mean the world to me—the boys, too. Wouldn't expect anyone else to take care of you."

"Even so, I'm grateful. Mama's peace of mind is important to me. I know she's come to depend on you and the boys a great deal. Hopefully, by taking this job, I can pay you back in a small way."

He laughed and gave her shoulders a squeeze. "Little gal, you are more than payin' me back by what you did here today. You know how this business works, and you know how the world works because of all that schoolin'. You benefited us all today, and I'm right proud of you. Just wait until I tell your brothers. They'll be dancing a jig."

"I doubt G. W. will dance a jig anytime soon." She frowned and looked up at her uncle. "Have you ever talked to him about Papa's death?"

Uncle Arjan grew thoughtful. "I've tried. He knows I don't hold him responsible. Doesn't change the fact that the boy holds himself in that place."

"I know. Mama said she worries about him for that very reason. I keep praying for him, but I sure wish I could do something to encourage him—get his mind off the fact that the anniversary of the accident is coming up."

"He's got to come through this himself, Deborah. You can't force a man to make peace with his own self. Give him time. He'll come around sooner or later."

But Deborah wasn't at all convinced that he would.

Lizzie brought Deborah a glass of lemonade and plopped down on a chair opposite her. "Goodness, but it's hot down here."

Deborah laughed. "Yes, and this is only July. Just wait for August."

"I can't imagine it getting any worse." Lizzie dabbed her damp forehead with the edge of her apron.

"I suppose Mama had you busy in the garden all morning?"

"Only for a little while. She was worried about me and the heat, so she wouldn't let me work for long. I tell you, I feel positively useless to you all. I really shouldn't have come."

Sampling the lemonade, Deborah nearly choked. "What? Why are you saying that?"

Lizzie shrugged. "It's just that everyone has their duties and tasks—everyone but me, that is. I'm just living here and eating your food and doing nothing. Your mother wouldn't even take money from me for my keep."

"I'm sure she wouldn't," Deborah replied with a grin. "Goodness, but she would never want it said that she charged a guest."

"But I wasn't thinking of it that way. I just wanted to help out."

"Don't fret about it. Mother is glad you came. She said there is nothing she can imagine worse than marrying a man you do not love. One of her sisters did that and it proved to be nothing but misery. Mama often uses Aunt Alva as an example."

"Why did she marry a man she didn't love?"

"To help the family. Her husband was from Holland and had a great deal of wealth. When he told her they would live there instead of America, she was very unhappy. Mama says her letters are always full of sorrow."

"How sad."

"Exactly so. Which is why it's good that you are here and not back in Philadelphia, playing the role of Mrs. Stuart Albright and sending *me* letters full of sorrow."

Lizzie shuddered at the thought. "Even the Texas heat is worth enduring to avoid that. I do wish, however, that Father would write. I can't help but wonder how Mother took the news. I'd imagine she was quite humiliated."

"Or extremely happy," Deborah offered. "After all, she's the one who believes women needn't marry or otherwise have a man in their affairs. She might have been miffed at first, but she's probably greatly satisfied by now."

"I just hope she isn't too mad. You know how awful she can be when she gets spiteful. Her tirades can be worse than a child's. I'm glad to have the distance between us." Lizzie watched as Deborah downed the lemonade. "Would you like more?" she asked.

"No, I'm fine. I need to get back to work on these ledgers. Some of this," she waved to a pile of papers, "is quite confusing. I feel I should have schooled in some foreign language just to interpret it, but I don't know which one might have helped."

Lizzie smiled. "Well, before you get back to work, maybe you can help me with this problem of feeling useless. Might there be some sort of job I could take on? Something I could do to benefit the family?"

"Goodness, no," Deborah said. "They really don't look highly on women working in these parts. It's different for me because this is my family. For you, however, it would be scandalous."

"I know my talents are few, but there must be something. What about taking in washing?"

"And see men's unmentionables?" Deborah asked in mock horror. "We'd get six weeks of sermons on women of low character from the Bible, only to be punctuated by the preacher standing at the front of the congregation letting a bit of salt run through his hands to remind us of poor Lot's wife. I can just hear it now." Deborah cleared her throat and lowered the timbre of her voice:

" 'Women are to be protected and sheltered from the unpleasant things of life. When they stray from such protection, they give themselves over to the influence of Jezebel, Delilah, and Sapphira. Let us remember this, and tremble.' "

Lizzie couldn't help giggling. "You really do that quite well. Perhaps you should take up preaching."

Deborah rolled her eyes. "That is a whole other set of sermons. Truth be told," she said, settling her gaze on Lizzie, "I agree for the most part. I think that in fighting against the boundaries set before us, often we forsake the good that could be had. I rather like the idea of being sheltered and protected from certain things. Other things . . . well, I suppose I would like to see some matters changed. But I don't want it enough to raise the ruckus your mother does."

"Me either," Lizzie agreed. "The very thought of going to jail for something like the cause of women voting is appalling."

"Well, I don't think you'll have to worry about that down here—at least not for a while. Anyway, I wouldn't worry about having nothing to do. My mother is good about keeping folks busy. I heard her mention that the Texas blacks are just about ready for picking."

"Texas blacks?"

"Grapes. You'll find that every month there is something new to harvest around here, and my mother has recipes for it all. I wouldn't fret about being idle. Once you get accustomed to the heat, you'll be busy enough."

Lizzie reached to take the glass. "Are you sure you won't have another?"

Deborah shook her head. "No. I'd probably just spill it all over everything, and then all my hard work would be for naught. Please tell Mama thanks for me."

"I will."

Lizzie bounded out the door just in time to run headlong into G. W. He reached out to take hold of her, but Lizzie still managed to fall against his chest and step on his foot. He continued to hold on to her as she regained her balance.

"I'm so sorry, G. W. I wasn't expecting anyone to be here. Your mother was out in the garden and . . . well, I just didn't think."

"No harm done. Are you all right?"

"I'm fine." She looked up and smiled. "How about you? Did I crush your foot?"

"A little bitty thing like you?" His drawl was thick and more pronounced.

She laughed. "If I keep eating fried green tomatoes and ham steaks, I won't be little for long. Gracious, but your Mama can cook."

"She sure can. I'm sure if you ask, she'll learn ya."

"When I was in town, Mrs. Greeley told me a girl has to be able to cook a decent meal in order to catch a decent man," Lizzie said without thinking.

G. W. surprised her by laughing out loud. "Miss Lizzie, you could do nothing but burn water and still catch a man."

Deborah appeared in the doorway. "What's all the fuss? A person can't even hear themselves think with all this noise."

Lizzie felt her face grow hot. "I . . . well . . . I came rushing out the door . . . and . . ."

"She threw herself at me—plain and simple," G. W. said, still grinning.

Deborah shrugged. "Well, it's about time someone did. You need a wife, G. W. Now, if you'll both excuse me, I have work to do.

Maybe you two could take your courting outside." She closed the door, leaving G. W. and Lizzie to stare in stunned silence.

Finally, Lizzie gathered her wits and hurried away. *After all this time*, she thought, *you would think I'd be used to Deborah's outspoken ways. But just when I think she can't surprise me any more, she goes and says something like that.*

Chapter 8

Euphanel Vandermark was always at her chores long before anyone else came downstairs. She liked this time of day, when the house was cool and quiet. She could pray and seek God's direction for her life. She would put on a pot of coffee, then start the bacon to fry. While it cooked, she would cut potatoes or mix corn dodgers. Once the bacon was cooked, she'd pull it from the cast-iron skillet and put the potatoes or dodgers into the grease. By this time, she would have asked special blessings on all of her children and kin and would be ready to go down her list of praises. With the coffee perking and the food set aside, she would go out to the hen house to feed the chickens and gather eggs.

It was the way she'd lived her life most every morning for the last twenty-some years. At forty-three, she felt well seasoned in the duties of motherhood and keeping house. Having married at sixteen, Euphanel had spent far more of her life married with children of her own than alone. She supposed that's why it was so hard now to be a widow with children who no longer needed her as they once had. Oh, they still enjoyed her cooking and were grateful to have the cleaning done, but there were no bedtime stories with little ones or moments of lingering in the arms of her man.

She pushed aside the sad thoughts and opened the gate to the chicken yard. She threw out some feed as she called, "Chick, chick, chick. Come along, little chicks."

With the hens and their broods busy eating, Euphanel could quickly gather the eggs—what there were to gather. The hens were laying light, no doubt because of the heat. She made her way toward the house with Decatur and Jasper now at her side. Dottie, the larger of the two milk cows, lowed miserably as if to remind her that she was in need of Euphanel's attention even if no one else was.

"Don't you worry, Dottie girl. Sissy will be here soon." This drew the attention of the other cow, which seemed to think it necessary to join in. Euphanel laughed. "Now, Dorothy, you just keep Dottie company, and we'll see you both in a few minutes." The dogs looked up hopefully at the sound of her voice. Euphanel shifted her basket and leaned down to give Jasper a rub behind the ears. "Yes, you'll be taken care of, as well."

By the time she arrived in the kitchen, Euphanel was surprised to find Lizzie and Deborah setting the table.

"Boys will be right down," Deborah told her mother. "Any sign of Uncle Arjan?"

"I didn't even think to look," she replied, putting the basket of eggs on the counter. "Guess my mind was otherwise occupied."

"I'm sure he'll be here soon," Deborah said. "He'll smell the coffee and bacon and that will bring him running."

Euphanel laughed. "It always has in the past."

"Can I do something?" Lizzie questioned, looking ever so hopeful.

"Absolutely. Come on over here. You wipe off these eggs and I'll go get the few we had left from yesterday. We'll fry up a batch for breakfast and then mix up some flapjacks."

Lizzie began the cleaning process while Euphanel fetched the additional eggs. How merry it was to have the girls with her in the kitchen. In a few moments, the boys had joined them, and by the time the flapjacks were done and the eggs fried, Arjan had made his way to the house, as well.

"We have a lot of work to do today, boys," he declared. "Better pack us a big lunch, Nel."

Arjan was the only one besides Rutger who had ever called her by the nickname. She smiled and placed a platter of flapjacks in front of him. "Don't I always?"

He grinned up at her. "I thought yesterday's was just a mite on the small side."

Euphanel met his teasing expression and cocked a brow. "I thought you looked like you were wasting away."

He laughed and leaned back to pat his ample but well-muscled midsection. "Glad you noticed."

They all chuckled at this as Euphanel took her place at the table for prayer. Bowing, she couldn't help but remember when Rutger had started the tradition. Shortly after they'd arrived in Texas, he'd gathered her and his brother to the breakfast table one morning and announced that it was about time they got their priorities straight.

"We need to be startin' and endin' the day in His presence," her husband had begun, *"and we need to be mindful of our heavenly Father*

throughout the day. It's the only way to get through, and I'm convinced we've been rather poor in this."

No one had questioned Rutger's decision. Euphanel smiled to herself. Her broad-shouldered husband had a way of commanding respect without ever raising his voice. She'd only seen him mad twice in his life, and both times were more than justified—once when a feisty mule had kicked him square in the head, and the other when a wild hog had cornered her. Rutger had seen red both times, but once the trouble was behind them, he had calmed down just as quick.

"Gotta get glad in the same clothes I got mad in," he used to say. *"Might as well be quick about it."*

"Mother?" Deborah called.

Euphanel looked up rather sheepishly as she realized the prayer had ended. "Amen."

She was about to offer some excuse when Sissy bustled into the dining room. "It be a glorious day. The Lord is good and the world rightly declares it."

"The Lord is good," Euphanel replied. "Good to see you feeling so fit this morning. I was worried about your hip."

"Bah, my hip ain't gonna stop me." The older woman gave her leg a slap. "I'm too ornery to let the devil catch hold of me."

Euphanel added food to her plate. "I'll be out to help you in just a few minutes."

"You take yor time, Miz Euphanel. Ain't no bother to me," Sissy declared. "I heard Miz Dottie and Miz Dorothy callin' for me." She chuckled and took up the clean milk pails. "We'll have ourselves a little time of praisin' the good Lord."

"You do that," Euphanel said. "The girls love to hear you sing."

The black woman made her way outside, leaving everyone

in the room feeling more lighthearted. Deborah was the first to comment.

"I swear that woman is the best medicine. If you could bottle her and sell her to people, you'd make a fortune."

Her daughter was right, Euphanel thought. Sissy always had a way of making folks feel better. It was almost impossible to stay troubled or discouraged when she was around.

Euphanel ate her breakfast quickly and made a mental list of all that she wanted to accomplish that day. She had plenty of gardening to tend to and canning to do. She had laundry and mending, meals to fix, and she still hoped to get some cleaning done upstairs.

First, however, the cows needed milking. Sissy would have already started with Dottie, but poor Dorothy would be beside herself if Euphanel didn't make haste.

"Mother, Lizzie and I can fix the lunches," Deborah offered as Euphanel got to her feet.

"That would be a great help to me," she said. "That way I can get right out to help milk."

"Could I learn how to milk the cow?" Lizzie asked.

"You sure you want to learn?" Rob asked in disbelief.

Lizzie nodded and looked to Euphanel for an answer. "I need to start learning useful skills. I might know about art and music, but I haven't had an opportunity to use my knowledge here."

Euphanel smiled. "Of course you can come and learn how to milk a cow. I'll be happy to teach you most anything. Just remember, though, when the heat of the day is upon us, I want you to take it easy."

"I promise I will." Lizzie set aside her napkin and got up from the table. Looking to Deborah, she asked, "Can you handle packing the lunches by yourself?"

"Of course. Go on and enjoy your new experience."

"And don't get yourself stepped on—Dorothy's real bad about that," Rob declared.

G. W. nodded and added, "And watch the bucket—she likes to kick it over."

Euphanel held out her hand to Lizzie. "Come along. I'll show you all the tricks."

Several hours later, after seeing her friend busily occupied with Mother and Sissy in the kitchen, Deborah announced she was going to Perkinsville.

"I have some journals to return to Dr. Clayton," she told her mother. "Is there anything I can bring back from the store?"

"Sissy can go with you and get the supplies we talked about," her mother replied. "I don't like you going all that way by yourself."

Deborah didn't argue with her mother. It wouldn't have done any good. It was probably best that her mother never know about the many times she'd walked unescorted through the city streets of Philadelphia. Probably wise, too, that she not mention the times she'd attended evening functions unaccompanied.

"I'll hitch the wagon," Sissy said, pulling off her apron.

It was also wise not to argue with Sissy. The woman might be fifty years old and shorter than Deborah, but she was a powerful opponent if the situation arose.

"I'll be back soon, Lizzie. Is there anything in particular I can bring you?"

"A letter from my father would be nice," Lizzie said, looking up from a bowl of green beans.

Deborah knew her friend longed for news. It had already been several weeks, and still no word. "I'll do what I can," she promised.

Sissy had the team harnessed and ready to go in no time at all.

Matthew and Mark were two of the sweetest Morgans ever trained. Their temperament even allowed for them to be ridden from time to time, although it was usually bareback.

Deborah climbed up on the wagon and sat down beside Sissy. "You wanna take the reins?" Sissy asked.

"It's been awhile, but there's no time like the present to get back in practice." She clucked her tongue. "Walk on, Matthew. Walk on, Mark."

The day was warm, and the building clouds threatened of storms to come. Deborah hadn't noticed them until they were nearly to Perkinsville or she might have stayed home. Texas thunderstorms were not to be ignored.

"Looks like we may have rain," she told Sissy.

"Yes, Miz Deborah, I do believe we will. Guess we'll get a soakin' on our way back."

"Unless we wait it out here," Deborah said. "You've got friends to visit, don't you?"

"Shore I do, but yor mama don't pay me to visit."

Deborah laughed as a loud rumble of thunder sounded. "I don't think Mama would want us out in this storm. I have things to do myself. I'll meet you back here at the store after the storm has passed." She handed the reins to Sissy and stepped down from the wagon. "Why don't you go visit first, and then when the storm lets up, you can get our shopping done. That way, we won't have supplies getting wet in the wagon."

"I reckon that be best," Sissy said.

Deborah smiled. "I'm sure it is." She hurried off in the direction of the doctor's office, careful to keep the journals close in case it started to rain. She'd just reached the door of the office waiting room when the first large drops started to fall.

Opening the door, she called out. "Hello? Are you here, Dr. Clayton?"

He immediately appeared from the opposite doorway. "Well, hello. What brings you here today?"

Lightning flashed and Deborah hurried to close the door behind her. "I brought back your journals."

"And did you enjoy them?" he asked with a smile.

"Actually, I did. I was hoping to maybe borrow another." She held out the collection.

He took them and motioned her to step into the office. "Help yourself, but I have to ask: Was there anything in particular that you found appealing?"

Deborah headed to the stack of journals on the bookshelf. "I was rather fascinated by the article on Dr. Robert Koch."

The doctor's face lit up. "He discovered the tuberculosis bacillus, and his work on cholera has been highly discussed."

"Yes. That's the very man," Deborah replied, quite excited. She jumped at the boom of thunder. "The storm caught me by surprise. Our cook, Sissy, came with me to town, and I'm afraid we'll be stuck here until the storm passes."

"Well, why don't you wait here with me? We can discuss the article."

"I wouldn't want to keep you from your work . . . and folks might think it strange for me to be here." She considered leaving, then shook her head. "Let them think what they will."

He chuckled and rubbed his bearded chin. "By all means, have a seat. Free time is all I seem to have." He motioned for her to take a chair.

She frowned. "Why do you say that?"

"Because it's true." He sat at his desk and leaned back to stretch his arms behind his head. "I have all the time in the world—it's patients I don't have. Not one person this week, and only one in the weeks before."

"I was hopeful that word would get around regarding your good work with John Stevens. His hand is healing well."

"It would seem Mrs. Foster's word holds more weight. She's got the town stirred up, believing that if they come to me for help, it's going to offend the spirits or some such nonsense. Mr. Perkins is quite beside himself. He's hired me and pays me a good salary, and here I sit idle."

"Give them time," Deborah advised. "I'll be sure to say good things about you and encourage others to do the same. Many of the folks here are uneducated and steeped in superstitions and traditions. It's always a headache for the preacher, too."

"I suppose I was expecting folks to be grateful to have a doctor."

"Maybe they're afraid they can't afford it," she offered.

"Mr. Perkins takes fees out of the mill workers' wages each week for their doctor and hospital needs. They're entitled to my services."

She shrugged. "Like I said, it will most likely take time. The people around here have to come to terms with change. It's always hard for them. In the meanwhile, Mr. Perkins is doubling the size of his mill and hiring a great many new people. Maybe they'll be able to bring in folks from outside the area who won't be so superstitious."

Dr. Clayton looked unconvinced. "I have no patience for ignorance."

"Neither do I, but I find that often the only way to get folks to see things right is to give them an example. John's hand is a good one. In time, word will get around that it was your handiwork, and not Mrs. Foster's poultice, that did the trick."

Rain hitting the window drew her attention and a brilliant flash of lightning filled the room. The boom of the thunder came nearly on top of it. "I do hope the men working outside got to safety."

"Seems we can use the rain," Dr. Clayton offered.

"Yes, I suppose we should be grateful for that." She brushed imaginary lint from her brown skirt. "Dr. Clayton . . ."

"Call me Christopher," he suggested. "We are friends after all."

She looked at him for a moment and saw a glint of amusement in his expression. "It would be scandalous if I were to do so. You're new to the community. I didn't grow up with you around. And you're my elder."

"I'm not that old. I've yet to start using a cane, and I still hear quite well."

Deborah giggled. "It would be inappropriate. I can just hear the reprimands. Why, the preacher would probably be informed on his next visit, and I'd be called before the congregation to repent of my sinful ways."

He leaned forward and crossed his arms. "Well, I suppose I can't have that. Still, couldn't you call me Christopher in private?"

"I don't think it would be wise. I might become too comfortable and blurt it out accidentally." She sobered. "There are a lot of rules for young women—for any woman, actually. I wouldn't want to stir up trouble after just arriving home. To be honest, I think people are looking for something they can point at."

"What do you mean?" he asked.

Deborah went to the window. The rumble of thunder seemed to be growing less frequent. "I know I'm being watched carefully by those who knew me before. They will want to see that I didn't pick up any bad habits while attending school in the East. They don't really value education."

"Why is that?"

"No one can afford the luxury of it," she replied. "Children are needed to help earn a living, so school for them is usually done by the eighth grade—if they get to attend that long. Adults have no time for pleasures like reading. Even so, few can read—especially among the men. When I went off to school, folks were mixed on how they felt about it. Some thought I was lucky and wished me well. Others frowned on it and said I was sure to be ruined by the ways of the world."

"You don't look too ruined to me," he said with a chuckle.

Deborah studied him and found she liked the way tiny lines formed at his eyes when he laughed. He was a handsome man—perhaps Dr. Clayton would find a woman here in Perkinsville and marry. Maybe it would even be one of Mr. Perkins's daughters. They had certainly enjoyed his company when they'd been at the Vandermark house for supper.

She put aside such thoughts. "It will be scandal enough that I'm here. Of course, the storm will be my excuse. I brought back your periodicals and took refuge until the rain let up."

"What of when you brought me doughnuts?"

"I was doing the good Christian thing in greeting a new neighbor. I stayed to help, because anyone would have done likewise. But mark my words: Someone will have seen me come here today and make a comment about it later. Hopefully it won't cause harm to your reputation."

He laughed and shook his head. "I doubt anything could harm it more than Mrs. Foster's warnings."

Margaret Foster was raising a ruckus when Deborah entered the store a short time later. The rain had let up and folks had started to come out again. The store was the most common gathering spot; even the men would come after their shifts to hear the latest gossip and news.

"He ain't got no right to be forcing a doctor on this town. I've been doctoring folks for thirty years," Mrs. Foster railed. "A good many of those right here."

Deborah spotted Sissy and made her way across the store. Deborah could only hope the supplies were paid for and Sissy was ready to go. The last thing she wanted was to get into a confrontation with Mrs. Foster herself. The woman had never approved of Deborah.

"She been like this since I got here," Sissy whispered. "Been tellin' the world—leastwise, the part that will listen—that Perkinsville got no need of no doctor."

Deborah watched Mrs. Foster corner Helen Greeley and Olivia Huebner. "That book-learned man ain't gonna know how to treat the ailments we got here in Texas. He ain't even from Texas."

Leaning toward Sissy, Deborah asked, "Are you finished with the shopping?"

"Shore 'nuf. I got myself over here soon as the storm passed. Everything's sittin' on the porch, waitin' to be loaded. Mr. Greeley said he'd come put it in the wagon."

"Maybe we could just do that ourselves. He seems busy with—"

"Deborah Vandermark! What sort of rudeness did you learn back East that you stand over there whisperin'?"

She forced a smile. "Why hello, Mrs. Foster. How are you?"

The woman scowled as she made her way across the room. She pointed a crooked finger at Deborah. "I heard tell you was there when that man commenced to cuttin' on poor John Stevens' hand."

"I was, indeed," Deborah replied, nodding. Mrs. Huebner and Mrs. Greeley made themselves scarce as they hurried into the back room. "The hand was horribly infected."

"It were healin'," Mrs. Foster countered. "It didn't need to be cut open."

"It was swollen to twice the normal size."

"'Course it were. The poisons were gatherin'. They woulda burst out and drained if it'd been left alone."

"Nevertheless, it was hurting him, and the doctor did a fine job of cleaning out the infection. I hear that John is able to use it again."

The older woman screwed up her face. "Ain't 'cause of that doctor. You'd do well to steer clear of him. He's gonna be nothin' but trouble, and them that keeps company with him ain't gonna have nothin' but bad luck."

"I don't believe in luck, bad or good, Mrs. Foster. I only count on the Lord for my well-being. He's more than able to see me through." With that, Deborah took hold of Sissy's arm. "We'd best get the purchases back to Mama. She'll be waiting for us."

Chapter 9

To everyone's delight, the fierce heat of summer cooled a bit, making the days much more bearable. Lizzie adjusted easily to life in Texas. The world of logging yellow pine fascinated her. It wasn't long before she was identifying a variety of trees and vegetation, not to mention snakes and insects. She would have happily done without the latter, but the Vandermarks assured her she'd be better off for knowing what was poisonous and what wasn't.

The days seemed to pass quickly as Lizzie immersed herself in household chores. She liked learning to work with her hands and was becoming a fair cook. She found baking to be her favorite. The men in the family particularly seemed to enjoy those treats, so she supposed the attention she got added to her pleasure in the task. How very different this family was from the one she'd grown up with. Here, folks didn't mind teasing or being challenged on habits or thoughts. The Vandermarks seemed quite open, in fact, to discussing most anything. In Lizzie's experience, families rarely spoke about anything except the causes of the day. She had vague recollections of conversations with her father, but the years and distance between them had faded the memories.

There was still no word from her father and that discouraged her. Lizzie just told herself he would write when he could. At least she hoped he would. He had told her that he'd hated not being a part of her life.

"If you hated it so much," she had asked him the night before her wedding, "then why didn't you come back?"

He had looked so troubled by her question that Lizzie immediately wanted to take her words back. But she didn't. His response was a feeble attempt to rectify the matter.

"I didn't want to make life more difficult for you," he had replied.

He needn't have worried. Her mother made it difficult enough for all of them. Lizzie had felt like a burden—a strange but unique possession that had to be maintained but wasn't really desired. It wasn't until she got older that her mother actually began to see some value in her. She had great plans for Lizzie to get an education and show the world that women could accomplish important things. Lizzie, however, had little interest in school. She had barely passed her classes at the university.

Lizzie found her true calling being with the Vandermarks and learning how to run a household. *This is how life should have been,* she thought. She bent over the washtub and began scrubbing at one of Euphanel's blouses. Perhaps if she'd had siblings and parents who'd remained together, it might have been this way for her. Instead, there had been nothing but fighting and misery in her youth. Her mother had left Lizzie to an indifferent upbringing by nannies while she went out to save the world. At night, she would return to rant and regale Lizzie and her father with a list of injustices that women were forced to suffer. Lizzie had followed her father's example and learned to say little in response.

A dull ache in her neck caused Lizzie to abandon the wash for a moment. She stretched and tried to work out the knot in her tired muscles. She wasn't having much luck when, to her surprise, G. W. appeared.

"Can I help with that?" He didn't wait for her response, but brushed her hands aside and began to massage her shoulders.

Lizzie didn't know what to think for a moment. The warmth of his hands seemed to permeate the thin cotton of her blouse. Ordinarily, she would never have allowed a man to touch her so intimately.

"Is this helping?" he asked softly.

She gave the slightest nod, certain that if she opened her mouth to speak she would make a fool of herself. Lizzie felt mesmerized by the rhythmic kneading of his hands on her shoulders and neck. She felt her stomach do a flip and her pulse quicken as the strokes softened to a gentle rub.

She pulled away rather abruptly and turned to face him. "Thank you. What are you doing home at this hour?"

He stared at her for a moment, and Lizzie almost felt as if she couldn't breathe. What was happening to her? Maybe she was working too hard and the heat was worse than she thought.

"I had to come pick up another ax. We broke two today."

She could see that for some odd reason, he was perplexed. Maybe touching her had also affected him. The idea rather pleased her, and she didn't want to say anything to change the feeling of the moment.

"I want to tell you that I've been thinkin' on what you said the day of the church social. About Pa knowin' the risks and takin' 'em anyway. I know you're right, 'cause like you said, I do the same." He shook his head and looked toward the sky. "I reckon I couldn't have stopped the accident—not if God said it was Pa's time to go home."

Lizzie nodded. "No one could."

"And a single man couldn't very well hold back a log that size—not with the chain broke and all."

"I'm glad you can see the truth of it," she whispered.

He cast his gaze back on her face. "You're a right smart gal, Miss Lizzie. I think maybe now I can start puttin' Pa's death behind me."

She smiled and without thinking, reached out to touch his arm. "I do hope so. I know your family has been very concerned for you. I've been concerned, as well."

"You have?"

"Yes."

He put his hand on top of hers and held it in place for a moment. Lizzie's knees trembled, and when G. W. brought her hand up to his lips, she thought she might well faint. "Thank you for caring about me."

She could only nod. As he released her and turned to head off toward the barn, Lizzie let out the breath she hadn't even known she'd been holding. For a moment she felt as if the blood rushed to her head as she gulped in another breath. She wasn't entirely sure what had just happened, but there was little doubt that it was important.

Later that evening after supper, G. W. sought Lizzie out once again. She was alone in the dining room, repositioning the tablecloth and lamps, when he found her. He couldn't begin to understand the way she made him feel. He'd been sweet on girls before, but this was the first time he'd actually thought about spending the rest of his life with someone.

"I was wonderin' if you'd like to sit with me on the porch before it gets too dark."

Lizzie seemed startled by his question. Her blue eyes seemed to grow the size of saucers and her mouth was open, but no words were coming out.

"I suppose that was a little bit forward of me," he said, trying to think of how to smooth the awkwardness over.

She shook her head and put aside the lamp. "I'd like it very much."

G. W. couldn't help but grin. "I would, too."

They made their way out to the porch. G. W. had no idea where the others had gone. Sissy had returned to her home just before supper, and he knew Uncle Arjan had gone back to his cabin. Otherwise, there was no telling. No one was here on the porch at the moment, and that was really all he cared about.

Taking a seat in one of the rockers, Lizzie appeared a picture of the prim and proper lady. In the soft twilight, G. W. thought she looked almost angelic, with her pretty blond hair fixed just so atop her head.

For a moment he stood rather nervously, not knowing what to do. Finally, he cleared his throat and took a seat beside her. "I thought . . . well, that is . . . I was hopin' you might tell me about yourself."

Lizzie focused on her folded hands. "There really isn't a lot to tell. I'm an only child, and my parents divorced when I was eleven."

"That must have been really hard," he said, trying hard to weigh each word before he spoke.

"It was," she said in a wistful manner. "My parents' relationship had always been strained, but to see them divided . . . well, it was heartbreaking for me. I used to cry myself to sleep every night."

"I'm sorry," he said, almost regretting that he'd brought up the subject. "I shouldn't have asked about something so unpleasant."

She looked at him and a slight smile touched her lips. "I believe I could tell you most anything, Mr. Vandermark."

"G. W. Please call me G. W."

"What does that stand for?"

It was his turn to be uncomfortable. "Promise you won't laugh?"

"I would never laugh at a person's name."

"My people are from Holland. I got named traditional-like. As a firstborn son, I was named for my father's father. His name was Gijsbert Willem Vandermark. Folks called him Gijs."

"Keys?"

"It's spelled with a G. I didn't like it much, so I made folks call me G. W."

"I think it's a fine name, and quite wonderful that you were named after your grandfather," she assured him. "I was named after one of my mother's women's suffrage heroines. Elizabeth Cady Stanton. I actually hate the name—hence the use of Lizzie."

"I like Lizzie better," he agreed. "So why did your folks divorce?"

She grew thoughtful, and for a moment, G. W. worried that she wouldn't answer him. Had he asked too intimate a question? Maybe she never spoke to anyone about such matters. He'd never thought to ask Deborah.

"My mother was always swayed by causes. She loved the temperance movement and it just seemed to flow naturally into women's suffrage. I seldom saw her, but I loved her fiercely. Maybe I loved her more because she was so absent in my life. I could pretend she was the mother I wanted her to be, even if she wasn't present. I was raised by a long list of nannies who would endure Mother's rantings for only so long, then leave the job. Eventually, she arranged for me to attend boarding school—but that was after the divorce."

"What about your pa?"

"When I was little, my father would come to see me every evening after I'd been given supper. He would read me a story and ask me about my day. Sometimes he would even dance with me." She smiled sadly. "I cherish the memories—what few I have. Until the day before the wedding, I hadn't seen him for nearly a decade."

"Why not?"

"Mother. She became so obsessed with her cause, she felt he corrupted her by marrying her. Funny . . . most women would have felt just the opposite. After a great deal of fighting, he finally left. I didn't see him again because my mother refused to allow him to visit. Once I asked if I might go see him, as he and his new wife had moved to another state by that time. She was livid and accused me of being a traitor to her. Her anger kept me from ever mentioning it again."

"I'm sure sorry for what you went through."

Lizzie glanced back at her hands. "I'm sorry that you had to witness my shameful attempt to get back at her. I didn't really want to marry Stuart, as much as I wanted to prove to my mother that I could make my own decisions. It was terrible of me, and I can only hope he will forgive me."

"So you really didn't love him?" G. W. knew this was what Deborah had said, but he was never quite certain of Lizzie's feelings.

"No, I didn't love him. He was everything I knew my mother would hate. He was overbearing and particular about what I could do and where I should go. He was quite opinionated about politics and deeply resented the women's movement. Oh, he was charming, but I knew he only wanted to marry me because of my appearance and what it would mean to his political career."

G. W. shook his head. "Seems like he owns as much shame for that weddin' as you."

"I suppose so. But my own guilt keeps me from thinking about his responsibility in the matter."

"A man ought not act in such a way."

"Neither should a woman." Lizzie looked up rather hesitantly. "I let the wounds of the past keep me from good judgment. I don't intend to make that mistake again."

He was about to comment when Rob came flying out the front door calling his name.

"I'm right here. You don't have to be yellin'." He got to his feet. "What's wrong?"

Rob turned abruptly, nearly falling off the porch. "Well, I didn't see you there. Nothin' wrong. Uncle Arjan sent me to fetch you. He wants to go over some plans for tomorra."

Lizzie stood. "I should go inside anyway. I'm afraid the mosquitoes are having quite a feast on me."

G. W. nodded, regretful that their conversation should end so soon. "Thank you for speakin' with me."

She smiled, then turned to head into the house. "Any time, G. W."

He felt awash in pure joy at the sound of his name on her lips. Feeling just a little taller, he punched Rob on the arm and grinned. "You heard her. Any time."

Chapter 10

August 1885

After being in Perkinsville for almost two months, strolling among the houses and people as he was doing just now, Christopher Clayton had come to an understanding of why the community had lost so many women to childbed fever. The answer was quite simple: Margaret Foster. The woman was the driving force behind healing and medicinal treatments, yet she had no use for soap and water or any other means of fighting bacteria. She went from patient to patient without ever washing her hands, much less her instruments. She was passionate about her cures and tonics, but again, he doubted they were prepared with cleanliness in mind.

He had tried to approach the woman, hoping to explain and offer at least some small bit of advice to combat the dangerous situation. "You know, they are making great strides in medicine,"

Christopher said one morning after coming face-to-face with the midwife at the commissary. "With the discovery of various bacteria and how they cause illness, we've learned that keeping our hands and instruments clean is of the utmost importance."

Margaret Foster's lips curled into what could only be described as a snarl to reply, "I ain't got no use for city medicine."

"But it's not just useful for the city," he countered with a smile. It was hard to maintain a civil attitude with such hatred staring him in the face, but Christopher put his best skills to work. "Mrs. Foster, I respect what you have been able to do for the community. But the truth is, it's been documented that childbed fever decreases considerably with proper cleaning techniques. I would be happy to discuss the matter with you, as a colleague."

"I ain't no colleague," she nearly growled. "Whatever that is. I don't need your book learnin' to heal folks around here. You'd do well to leave this town before someone—like me—puts a curse on you."

It was there that Christopher did the wrong thing. He laughed. Apparently no one had ever laughed at Margaret Foster's threat of a curse. "Madam, I do not believe in curses."

"You'll believe it soon enough," she said. She muttered a string of words so quickly that Christopher had to strain to make sense of them. It was something to do with bad luck following him like a wounded hound or some such nonsense. She stormed off then, leaving him to wonder why she held him in such contempt. He wondered still.

Crossing Third Street, he saw Deborah Vandermark exit the commissary. Christopher couldn't help but call out to her. Perhaps she was in town to borrow additional medical journals. He'd recently received several in a package from his mother.

"Miss Vandermark!"

Deborah looked across the street and saw him. He waved and she did likewise. "I have new journals," he declared, closing the distance between them.

"How tempting," she replied. "I will have to keep that in mind for my next trip into town. Right now, I'm afraid the workload at home is more than I can keep up with. There's been no time for pleasure reading."

"Just know that they are available whenever you'd like to borrow them."

"So are you coming from a house call?" she asked, nodding toward his medical bag.

Christopher had decided to carry the bag with him when he went for his walks around town. That way people would get used to seeing him with it and perhaps realize he was the doctor. As it was, he doubted that he'd been able to meet more than a handful of citizens. He was a stranger to most.

"No, I just always take it with me in case there is a need."

"I suppose that makes good sense."

He chuckled. "Not really. Folks around here still don't want anything to do with me. I suppose they all know that Mrs. Foster put a curse on me."

Deborah laughed. "There aren't many who haven't had one of Mrs. Foster's curses imposed on their peace of mind."

"You?" he asked.

She nodded. "Once when I was quite young, I took some papaws from her yard. She ran after me with a broom yelling for all the world that with the setting sun, I would bear the thief's curse. Of course, I never knew exactly what that was. Mama heard about the situation and made me return with a batch of cookies and an apology. Mrs. Foster took the curse off and that was the end of that. I've avoided messing with Mrs. Foster ever since."

"That's no doubt for the best. Still, it seems most folks around here are afraid of her."

Deborah looked past him toward the row of houses. "People fear what they don't understand. In your case, medicine is a great mystery. Talk of things like bacteria and internal disorders makes no sense to them. You might as well be speaking a foreign language."

"But there's so much good that could be done. Women needn't die in childbirth. Men needn't die from injuries. Poor Mr. Perkins is beside himself. Here he is, taking money from the workers and giving me a good salary, and I'm doing nothing."

Deborah put her hand up to block the sun. "It's not for a lack of trying, though. Mr. Perkins knows you've made yourself available. He knows that you are willing to work at the task he's hired you to do. You must hold on to the belief that time will change things."

With the sun bearing down on them, Christopher motioned to the shade of the commissary porch. "Perhaps you'd be more comfortable if we got out of the sun."

Deborah glanced around and nodded. "I'm actually waiting for my mother. She's gathering the mail and seeing the paymaster."

They made their way to the porch bench, where Deborah took a seat while Christopher remained standing. Her simple blue calico gown accentuated her trim waist and black hair, but it was her intelligence that continued to draw his admiration.

"So I presume your family is of Dutch ancestry with a name like Vandermark," Christopher began. "Yet you have ebony hair and dark eyes."

She glanced around and leaned toward him as if to share a great secret. "My mother's side of the family had Spanish ancestry, as well as Dutch. I'm told that I take after my mother's grandmother." She eased back and grinned. "I just don't say that too openly around here. There is still a fair amount of negativity toward Mexico and Spain."

"Yet I've noticed that Mr. Perkins hires people of color for the sawmill work."

"You will find that to be true in most of the mills around here. Workers are workers. If the men can be trained and prove capable, they are kept on. A lot of former slaves came here to work because Mr. Perkins has a reputation for being fair. My family has also hired former slaves for the logging business."

"And what of your cook, Sissy? Was she also a slave?"

Deborah nodded. "She was with my mother's family from birth. When the war came my grandparents thought to remain in Georgia. Things just got worse, however, and when the Emancipation was issued, my mother's family took the matter seriously, much to their neighbor's displeasure. Grandma and Grandpa told their slaves they were free to go. Someone set fire to their fields the next night. It nearly took down the house. They were worried about how much worse things would get, so they decided to board up the house and come stay with Mama and Papa.

"Sissy loved my mother and asked my grandparents if they might consider letting her accompany them to Texas. They did, and Sissy has been with Mother ever since."

"And does she live with you?"

"No," Deborah said, trying to adjust the ribbon in her hair. "She fell in love and married a man named George Jackson who works for us as a logger. They have a family and their oldest son, David, works for my family, as well. They have a house just north of town."

The ribbon came free and Deborah's black hair rippled down across her shoulder. "Goodness, but my hair can be a nuisance. Sometimes I think I should cut it all off."

"No!" he responded rather enthusiastically. Deborah looked up in surprise, and Christopher laughed nervously to cover his excited reply. "I would hate to see you do that. I once treated a woman who needed to cut her hair following weeks of sickness and fever. The hair was hopelessly matted and falling out anyway, so she had it cut short. She was so miserable."

"Well, it can be wretched with a mass of hair to contend with, too." She managed to adjust the ribbon and pull the hair back up off her neck. "Especially in the heat."

For a few minutes, neither one said anything else. Christopher thought of asking Deborah about the work she was doing for her family or maybe about her schooling back East, but he suddenly felt self-conscious as two young women made their way up the porch steps to the commissary. One was Mrs. Stevens; the other, he didn't recognize.

"Hello, Sally," Deborah called out. "Dinah." She turned to Christopher. "You both know Dr. Clayton—don't you?" The women turned rather shyly and nodded toward Christopher.

"Afternoon ladies," he said. "How are you feeling, Mrs. Stevens?"

"Tired," she replied. "Guess I've got about another month before the baby gets here." She put a hand to her belly and nodded to the girl at her side. She couldn't have been more than seventeen or eighteen. "We're both tired."

Deborah turned to Christopher. "This is Dinah Wolcott."

He smiled. "Are you expecting, as well?"

The sallow-faced girl nodded and pushed stringy blond hair from her face. "Gonna have a young'un, come next year."

"Well, congratulations. I'm sure your husband is delighted."

Deborah turned to Christopher. "Her husband works for Vandermark Logging." She smiled back at the young woman. "I'm sure Dr. Clayton will be able to help you when your time comes."

The two young women exchanged a look. "Mrs. Foster's been seeing to us," Sally Stevens replied. "She said . . . well, that men got no good reason to be tendin' women in a family way."

"Bah," Deborah said. "Women back East have men deliver their babies all the time. You know, there have been quite a few cases of childbed deaths in this area. Mrs. Perkins was quite upset at the number of young women passing on during delivery. That was one of the biggest reasons she brought in Dr. Clayton."

Sally's eyes widened. "You don't suppose there's a curse on this town—do you?"

Deborah shook her head. "I don't believe God works that way. The Bible says Jesus became a curse for us—it also says that by His stripes we are healed. I think God has better plans for us than cursing us with dead babies and mamas. Just think about it. I know having a new doctor can be rather frightening, but I assure you Dr. Clayton is a knowledgeable man. Of course, I don't have to tell you, Mrs. Stevens, since he saved your husband's hand."

She looked at the wood planks of the porch floor. "Miz Foster says it were her poultice that did the cure."

Christopher started to comment, but Deborah got to her feet. "Mrs. Foster would, no doubt, say that, but you know as well as I do that your husband was in great pain when he came to the doctor. We both saw that hand. It wasn't getting better—it was much worse than when Mrs. Foster began treating it. Wasn't it?"

Sally Stevens nodded very slowly. "I reckon it was. I don't rightly know what to believe. Mrs. Foster said my John could have lost his hand what with the doctor cuttin' on it and all."

"Mrs. Foster is just afraid that word will get around that her poultice didn't help. I mean no disrespect to the woman, but you two must understand that for all her experience, she's just a human being and she will make mistakes. Doctors make them too, but they have so much more training and understanding of the human body. I want you to really think about it, Sally. You too, Dinah. The lives of your babies, as well as your own life, might very well depend upon such reasoning. Don't be afraid."

The women murmured something Christopher couldn't quite make out, then nodded toward him and Deborah and hurried into the store. He looked at Deborah, who was fussing with her rolled-up sleeves by this time.

"I appreciate your support," he said softly.

Deborah glanced up and shook her head. "I hope they'll listen. I would certainly hate to see more deaths in childbirth."

"If Mrs. Foster would just listen to reason and sterilize her equipment and wash before and after tending to patients, it would help a great deal. I'm not opposed to herbal treatments and using nature for medicinal purposes, but it's well-founded that thorough cleaning can terminate the growth of bacteria and save lives."

"Well, I'm sure word will get around of what I said and I'll receive another curse," Deborah said with a grin.

He chuckled at the delight in her expression. "I'm still scandalized to know that you would steal from anyone."

"I learned my lesson, Dr. Clayton. I haven't stolen since. A green switch to my backside sealed the deal for me. I'm living a completely righteous existence now."

Mrs. Vandermark came from the commissary just then, carrying several letters and a basket containing a variety of articles. Dr. Clayton offered to take the basket, but she waved him off.

"Thank you, but we have to get on home and the wagon is just over there in the shade. It's good to see you again, Dr. Clayton. Do you think you could join us this evening for dinner? I figure if I don't ask, you won't just show up."

"It hardly seems right to just drop by unannounced."

"Around here, we don't stand on such concerns," Mrs. Vandermark replied. "I told you we wanted to see you joining us regularly, yet you haven't been out since nearly a month ago. So will you join us this evening?"

He couldn't think of anything he'd like better. "I would love to. May I bring something to help with the feast?"

She laughed. "Nothing but yourself."

Deborah reached past him to take the basket from her mother. "We'll see you tonight then, Dr. Clayton. I'll take this now, Mother. Goodness, but it must weigh twenty pounds. What all do you have in here?"

Her mother laughed. "Only a small portion of what I needed. They're bringing the rest by train when the supplies come in. Good day, Dr. Clayton. Dinner will be on at six."

He watched them leave and felt a genuine loss in their going. The Vandermarks were among his few friends in Perkinsville. He especially enjoyed his conversations with Deborah, but knew it was probably just as well that she lived well out of reach. He had to remain focused. If he strayed from his purpose, others would suffer.

Chapter 11

Lizzie had never expected to see Stuart Albright again, yet here he was standing in the Vandermark living room. He pinned her with a stare that might have withered her had Deborah and G. W. not been standing at her side. A few feet away from Stuart, her mother, Harriet Decker, was conversing with Euphanel. It was all like a very bad dream.

Rob sauntered into the room casually after bringing the two visitors by wagon from Perkinsville. He just happened to be in town on one of his many Saturday evening courtships when someone from the boardinghouse had announced there were folks looking for the Vandermarks.

"It's wonderful to get to meet you," Euphanel told Harriet Decker. "Your daughter has spoken of you on many occasions."

"Elizabeth is a thoughtless young woman," her mother replied. "She has left us these many weeks worrying after her well-being." With a quick glance around the simple room, the woman added, "And I see for myself it was with good cause."

"Mother, there is no need for rudeness," Lizzie interjected, trying her best to ignore Stuart's continued glare. "Mrs. Vandermark and her family have been quite good to me. I have very much enjoyed living here with them."

"Oh, the pleasure's been ours, Lizzie. You are a great help to us," Euphanel said.

"And you are an incredible teacher. Did you know, Mother, that Mrs. Vandermark has won awards for her canned goods? She's been teaching me, and I find it all so very fascinating."

"Well, that's enough of that," her mother replied. "We've come to take you home."

Lizzie stiffened and looked to Deborah first and then G. W. "But I'm perfectly happy here."

"But you have a husband who is not perfectly happy for you to remain here," her mother said as she crossed the distance to where Lizzie stood. "You shamed this family by running away as you did. We were able to cover it up with the excuse that you were ill and needed to come west to take the cure, but now you need to return home."

Lizzie shook her head. "No. I'm of age, and I choose to remain in Texas. And I hardly know why you call Mr. Albright my husband. We are not married. As you recall, I left before the ceremony."

"But not before signing the papers," Stuart declared. "It matters not that the traditions of religiosity were not performed. You are, by law, my wife."

She would have laughed had Stuart's expression not silenced her with its intensity. Married? How could it be? She had of course signed the papers given to her prior to the ceremony. They had been witnessed, and the minister had said that . . . that . . . Oh, what was it he had said? Something about it not being official until he joined them in the sight of God and man. Deborah and her father had both been convinced she wasn't bound in any legal manner.

"I can see we've taken you by surprise," her mother remarked. "See there, Mr. Albright. She didn't run away as your wife. She simply had bridal nerves and thought herself still free to do as she pleased." Her mother looked back to where Lizzie stood. "You know how I feel about marriage. I didn't want you to marry in the first place. I saw no use in it. However, you're married now, and that changes everything."

Lizzie stumbled backward and might have fallen had G. W. not shot out his hand to take hold of her. Stuart's eyes narrowed. He had always been very possessive of her—it was one of the things that drove her mother into fits and one of the reasons Lizzie had chosen to marry him.

"I cannot be married to you," she said in a barely audible voice. "I made no vow."

"Your vow was your signature. Now we must return to Philadelphia. I have work to do. My father is also quite anxious that I assist him with his legislative affairs, as well as our family investments."

"I won't go," she said, shaking her head slowly. She looked at Euphanel and then Deborah. "I don't want to go."

"You needn't go if you do not want to," Deborah said matter-of-factly. "Honestly, this is the most preposterous thing I've ever heard." She stepped in front of Stuart. "Why would you wish to be married to a woman who doesn't love you?"

He laughed and Lizzie felt her knees grow weak. "Frankly, I have no love for her, either. In time, she will grow comfortable with my presence, and I shall enjoy being seen with her on my arm." He sobered slightly. "In time I might even become fond of her."

"And this is the life you want for your daughter, Mrs. Decker?" Deborah asked. "You would desire her to live in misery—to be used as ornamentation by this man?"

Lizzie saw her mother's face contort. "As women, we will always be used by men. We might as well be the ones to decide who that man will be. My daughter gave her word. I care far more about her keeping her word than about whether or not she made a poor choice of masters."

Lizzie could bear it no longer. "I can hardly believe that you, of all people, would say such a thing. I thought you believed women superior to men! I thought you said women had no need to be chained to a husband—they needed only to expand their minds with education and use them, in turn, to better their lives."

Mrs. Decker looked taken aback for a moment, but it was Stuart who spoke. "I believe the choice was already made. This argument is a moot point. You are my wife, and you will return with me to Philadelphia."

Deborah's mother stepped forward in an attempt to calm the waters. "Why don't we have some coffee or tea? We can all think better if we sit down and try to relax a bit. No doubt you two are very tired. You've been traveling for days, and we know how uncomfortable the train trip here can be."

"I have no desire to take coffee or tea," Stuart replied.

"Then you can return to Perkinsville," G. W. said casually. "I'll escort you back."

Stuart looked at him in disgust. "Excuse me?"

"My brother is offering to take you back to the boardinghouse in Perkinsville," Deborah interjected. "That way Mrs. Decker and Lizzie can have a bit of a discussion over coffee."

"Elizabeth doesn't drink coffee," her mother declared.

"Oh, yes I do," Lizzie said, feeling ever so daring to voice her new vice. It made her feel only marginally back in control. "Furthermore, I'm tired. I had no idea that you would be here. I've been up since four this morning helping with chores and making jam. I am ready now to retire for the evening. I'm sorry if this is a problem for either of you, but I will speak to you more about it tomorrow."

With that she turned and left, hoping—really praying—that no one would try to stop her. When she reached the stairs, she felt a surge of triumph. Deborah and Euphanel were busily commenting on how Stuart and Mrs. Decker could return in the morning as early as they liked, or perhaps prefer to meet at church.

"We always attend church, if possible. We'd be happy to have you here for dinner afterward," Euphanel told them.

Lizzie shook her head and continued to make good her escape. She could scarcely draw a breath. How could it be that she'd had no word of warning from her father? Perhaps he didn't know her mother's plans—after all, they were no longer civil to each other and didn't even live in the same state.

Throwing herself across the small bed, Lizzie wanted to cry. What if Stuart spoke the truth? What if she truly was married to the man? The very thought chilled her to the bone. He'd make her miserable for leaving him at the altar.

The door to the room opened and Deborah stepped inside. Her expression was a mixture of sympathy and determination. "Are you all right, Lizzie?"

"How can I be?" She made the effort to sit up, but what she really wanted was to crawl under the bed instead. "I cannot believe he followed me here. I can't believe Mother came here, either. What is happening? Has the world come to an end and someone failed to notify me?"

Deborah sat opposite Lizzie on the edge of her own quilt-covered bed. "Mother has managed to ease tensions for the moment. She invited them to join us here after church tomorrow. That will give us time to consider what is to be done."

"But what *is* to be done? Stuart says that I'm legally wed to him. I don't see how that can possibly be."

"I don't, either," Deborah said thoughtfully. "I don't know a great deal about the law, but perhaps I can speak with Dr. Clayton before church tomorrow. He might have some knowledge."

"If only my father were here, we could ask him," Lizzie said sadly. "Oh, and my life was just starting to settle into place. I was actually happy."

Deborah nodded. "So was G. W. I don't think this will brook well with him at all. Did you see the way Mr. Albright looked at him when he kept you from falling backward?"

"I did. That's Stuart's way. He cannot tolerate any other man touching me or speaking to me overly long. Oh, Deborah, I simply cannot bear this. Why is this happening?"

"I don't know, but I firmly believe all things happen for a reason."

"Yes, but this is for a very bad reason. Of that, I'm sure." Lizzie got up and began pulling pins from her blond hair. "I don't wish Stuart ill—I never did. I'm sure that Father would have made that clear to him."

"It's not your father who puzzles me," Deborah said, following Lizzie's example. She crossed the room to where they shared the simple dressing table and placed her hairpins in a decorative ebony box. "What is your mother doing here? She should have been quite happy that you didn't marry. It would have given her a great story to tell her suffragette friends. She could have gone on and on about how you finally came to your senses, realizing no woman needs a man to make her complete."

Lizzie picked up her brush and began to run it through the long waves of hair. "That's right. I cannot imagine her caring one whit about Stuart's feelings, and obviously she doesn't care about mine." She grew thoughtful. "What is she doing here?"

"We shall have to figure that out." Deborah picked up her own brush. "But in the meantime, I don't think you should fret. Let's send a telegram to your father. Perhaps with his connections he can advise you best on the matter."

Lizzie gave a heavy sigh. "I certainly hope he can. I don't want to find myself Mrs. Stuart Albright."

Sunday dinner at the Vandermark house was an unusually serious event. Rob and Uncle Arjan sat on either side of Stuart and occasionally made comments to him, while Deborah made sure that Lizzie was sandwiched between herself and Uncle Arjan.

A last-minute addition was Dr. Clayton. Deborah had thought it a good idea to include him. It gave their side a man of learning to balance against Stuart Albright. At least that was her thought on the situation.

Lizzie was too nervous to eat and pushed her food around the plate so much that Deborah wanted to take away her fork and spoon. Instead, she launched into comments about the sermon that day, hoping it would draw the focus away from the underlying tension in the room.

"I am quite frustrated with the sermon this morning," Deborah began. "I know the preacher meant for us to take away the lesson of what God's people can do when they come together, but I think there are serious issues with the story that did not get discussed."

"Such as what?" her mother asked, immediately realizing Deborah's intent.

"Well, in reading through chapter nineteen of Judges, I found myself completely at odds with the entire matter. You have a man who is a Levite. That was supposed to mean great things in those days. They were faithful when the rest of Israel fell down to worship the golden calf during Moses' absence. They were blessed because of it. They were appointed to be rabbis and teachers of Israel. The Lord was their inheritance, rather than lands and properties."

She could see from their expressions that Stuart and Lizzie's mother had no more understanding of the topic than did the dogs sleeping on the front porch.

"So you have this Levite and he has a concubine, which in those days was, if I understand correctly, an acceptable position as a second wife. Although she couldn't be endowed, so her children couldn't inherit. At least, I think that's what the rabbi told me."

"You spoke with a rabbi? But you aren't Jewish," Harriet Decker said in surprise.

"Our Deborah believes it's important to get to the heart of the matter and understand a situation—or in this case, a Bible story—from all angles," her uncle explained.

Deborah nodded. "I went to a synagogue in Philadelphia after reading this book the first time. The rabbi, a very forward-thinking man, explained several things to me. In fact, he was the one who taught me about the Levites. Anyway, so you have this man and his wife and she plays the harlot or, as the rabbi told me, the Hebrew word is *zanah*. And while its primary definition is whore or participating as a whore, it can also mean to dislike—to hate. He said it is entirely possible that the woman hadn't committed adultery but had merely fought with her husband. They could simply have had a fight, and she went home to her father's house. This could explain why the husband doesn't require her to be stoned. It would also allow for why her father let her stay with him—he surely wouldn't have done so if she were an adulterous woman." Deborah tapped her finger to her chin.

Dr. Clayton joined in. "The fact that the man goes after her, yet stays to eat, drink, and make merry with her father suggests to me that he was not at all in ill spirits. The fact that, as you say, he did not go there to have her put to death says to me that he was of a mind to put the matter behind him. I tend to think there's great possibility in your thoughts on *zanah*, meaning that there was some sort of fight and they were angry with each other."

Deborah nodded. "Even so, here's this man—this Levite. He's supposed to be knowledgeable and a strong man of God. So let's say she was at her worst and he did the honorable thing by forgiving her. As far as I can see, that's where his merits end."

"How so, Deborah?" her mother questioned.

It was almost comical the way Harriet Decker stared at them while Stuart kept his gaze on the plate in front of him. He said nothing, but his irritation was evident by the way he mutilated his food.

"The Levite has so little regard for the safety and well-being of his wife. Even if he did consider her nothing more than property, as many did, you would have thought he would want to protect his property."

"That's right," Dr. Clayton said. "Yet he leaves late in the day and heads into territory that he knows will be a problem. He has made no provision for their lodging."

"Oh, but he has food for the donkeys and for the people," G. W. interjected. "I remember the preacher saying that."

"Yes, he had food," Deborah agreed. "But he made no other provision. Not for safety, not for lodging, and certainly not for the welfare of his wife. So an old man finally shows up, well after they'd given up hope of finding a place to stay, and he takes them in. The Bible says they were 'making their hearts merry' when these horrible men show up at the door demanding to have carnal knowledge of the Levite."

"I say, this is the most inappropriate conversation I've ever been forced to endure," Stuart Albright declared. "I would never allow a young woman of my family to speak as you do." He looked to Arjan. "Is this how women act in Texas? If so, I'm glad to get my wife out of here before she can be further corrupted."

Arjan looked at him hard. "Deborah is sharing Scripture and talkin' about understanding God's Word. There's nothin' wrong with that, as far as I can see."

"It's completely unacceptable." Stuart threw down his napkin. "She's talking of adultery and men . . . well, I will not repeat the matter. Suffice it to say I cannot and will not sit by and allow my wife to be a part of such conversation. Elizabeth, go pack your things."

Deborah had never seen Uncle Arjan truly angry, but the muscles in his neck tightened and his eyes narrowed over Stuart Albright's outburst.

"Son," Uncle Arjan began slowly, "this is the Vandermark house. My sister-in-law is the lady of the house, and it's entirely up to her to say who stays and who goes. But to my way of thinkin', you're the one who should leave. Unless, of course, you can make yourself civil."

For a moment, no one said anything. To her surprise, it was Lizzie's mother who defused the situation. "Mr. Albright, I must say it is the height of rudeness that we should chastise our hostess and her family for the topic of conversation that they choose. In fact, I find the subject quite interesting."

Stuart looked at her strangely for a moment, but Harriet simply patted his hand. Deborah, too, found her behavior confusing.

"Would anyone care for dessert?" Deborah's mother asked. "I find difficult questions go down better when accompanied by pecan pie."

"Sure sounds good to me," G. W. replied.

Rob and Uncle Arjan nodded, while Dr. Clayton patted his stomach. "I think I can find room," he declared.

Stuart said nothing. He fixed Deborah with an icy stare, made only more chilling by the blue of his eyes. He was cold and harsh. His stare told her clearly that he did not approve of her or her intellectual discussion of the Bible. It was almost as if he were trying to will her into silence.

Better men than you have tried, Mr. Albright. The thought made her smile.

"So now, what was your question, little gal?" Uncle Arjan asked.

Deborah met her uncle's amused expression. It was almost as if he could read her thoughts. "The men come with their demands of . . . unmentionable evil." She looked at Stuart. "Is my word choice better?"

He refused to answer but instead folded his arms against his chest. Deborah smiled sweetly. "I suppose I can understand how disturbing the Bible can be." She turned back to her uncle. "The men want their way, and the host and the Levite, wanting no part of that evil, offer instead the man's virgin—Oh, should I not use that word?" She again looked to Stuart for an answer.

Lizzie gave an unladylike snort that she quickly covered with a coughing fit. G. W. offered her a glass of water, further irritating Mr. Albright. Deborah decided she was being too difficult and drew a deep breath. "I do apologize, Mr. Albright. I tend to let my temper get the best of me from time to time, but there is no call for me to take it out on you. Now, where was I?"

"You were about to mention that the host offered his virginal daughter and the Levite's concubine to the evil men instead," Dr. Clayton threw out.

Deborah gave him a smile. "Of course. So for whatever reason, they reject the virgin and take the concubine. They do all manner of evil to her throughout the night. God alone knows what that poor woman must have had to suffer. And the story doesn't stop there."

"It does give a person a mite to ponder," Uncle Arjan said between bites of pie.

"You should ask the preacher about it," G. W. suggested.

"I did," Deborah said, looking hard at Stuart Albright. "He said my mind was a wonder, and that for a woman I thought entirely too much. He said that God knew what He was doing by putting it in the Bible, and that men of God would understand it, and women needn't worry about it."

Dr. Clayton managed to draw her gaze from the smug expression of Mr. Albright. "I'm a man of God, and I don't believe I understand it."

"Neither do I," her uncle agreed. "Seems to me it's a hard story to understand."

"If your own minister will not reveal its mysteries," Mrs. Decker began, "then perhaps it is best we leave it as an example of the thoughtlessness of men toward women. I will definitely remember this story and use it as an example of how women have been treated throughout the ages."

"I hardly believe that was God's purpose in the story, Mother." Lizzie said, much to Stuart's displeasure.

"You can hardly know what God was thinking," Stuart said

firmly. "Now, if you don't mind, and with your permission, Mrs. Vandermark, I would like for my wife to pack her things so that we can make our way to Philadelphia."

Deborah started to comment, but her mother spoke instead. "Mr. Albright, I am a woman of reason. It is my understanding that Lizzie is of age and capable of making her own decisions. She is of the belief that the marriage did not take place, and therefore she is not your wife." Albright started to speak, but Mother held up her hand. "However, even if she is your wife, and I'm not saying that she is, she is still able to decide for herself if she will continue being your bride. There are alternatives that would rectify the situation either way."

"Of all the nonsense." Stuart got to his feet. "Mrs. Decker, let us speak with the legal officials in town. I'm certain we can accomplish more there than here."

Mrs. Decker nodded and got to her feet. "I believe you may be right in that. Elizabeth, I want you to come to town and stay with us that we might be able to speak with you privately."

"There's nothing anyone can say to me that I would not allow these good people to hear," Lizzie replied.

"Well, there is much I would say to you, and frankly, I believe it very rude to bring strangers into such intimate conversation. It only serves to make both parties uncomfortable."

"I doubt anyone would be all that uncomfortable, Mother. And these are not strangers to me." She exchanged a smile with Deborah's mother.

Deborah was proud of Lizzie. It took a great deal of courage to stand her ground in the face of her mother's demands.

"Very well. Perhaps we shall speak of it tomorrow."

Deborah's mother walked out with Mr. Albright and Mrs. Decker, leaving the others to consider all that had just happened.

"I'm so sorry," Lizzie said. "I never meant to bring this on you all."

"Y'all," G. W. said with a smile. "If you're gonna be a Texan, you ought to learn to speak like one."

This brought chuckles from the table, but to Deborah's surprise, Dr. Clayton's expression remained serious.

"Are you all right? Is something wrong?" she asked.

He nodded. "I'm fine, and yes, something is wrong. I'm afraid I shall be thinking long and hard about Judges nineteen and twenty." He smiled. "And I agree with the preacher—at least in part. Your mind is a wonder."

Deborah didn't even think before elbowing him soundly as she might have done one of her brothers. Realizing what she'd done, she covered her mouth with her hands. Her uncle and brothers dissolved into laughter, while Dr. Clayton looked at her in surprise.

"You have to watch yourself with her," Rob warned. "That's why we won't sit beside her. We've had sore ribs too many times."

Deborah shook her head and lowered her hands. "I'm so very sorry. I never meant—"

He put a finger to her lips and grinned. "You are forgiven, but you really should learn to control that temper of yours."

Her eyes widened, but she said nothing. Instead she put the Bible aside and picked up her fork as Dr. Clayton went back to eating.

"We should definitely keep him around," G. W. said, smiling. "I've never seen anybody be able to shut her up like that."

Chapter 12

A week later, Mr. Perkins stood at the front of the small church with preacher Artemus Shattuck at his side. "As you know," he began, "Brother Shattuck has been riding the circuit to speak to us every other Sunday. I'm happy to announce that he has agreed to become our regular minister and move here to Perkinsville."

The congregation murmured and nodded approvingly. Brother Shattuck smiled and bobbed his head in return. G. W. thought it a fine idea to have a regular preacher, although he couldn't help but wonder how Deborah would feel. She had often commented that Brother Shattuck had admonished her on more than one occasion that she should marry, saying her husband would explain the biblical things she didn't understand.

"Let's pray and be dismissed," Brother Shattuck announced after shaking hands with Mr. Perkins.

G. W. bowed his head and found that his focus of prayer was once again for Lizzie's safety and security. He had unexpectedly fallen hard for this young woman. She had been a quiet strength in his life these past few weeks, for when he needed to talk about his father and the accident, she was there for him. Little by little, he had found that his memories had lost their power and God was healing his pain.

He also found himself praying that God would take Stuart Albright and Mrs. Decker back to Philadelphia or any place but Perkinsville, Texas. He didn't like Albright, his bossy way of dealing with folks, and the claim he had on Lizzie.

"Amen. Now go with the Lord's blessings," Brother Shattuck declared.

Casting a quick side glance, G. W. saw Deborah slip away, leaving Lizzie to remain in the family pew. He wasn't about to desert her and leave her to the likes of Albright, so he offered her his arm as they exited their seats. Lizzie took hold of him and smiled. "I thought the sermon quite interesting today."

G. W. nodded. "Preacher definitely gets all fired up for the Lord. That's a good way to be."

"I agree. Although I'm not sure what Deborah will think about him becoming the regular pastor."

"She'll get used to it. It's him I feel sorry for," G. W. said with a grin. "My sister isn't likely to let him off easily."

Lizzie laughed softly. "No. I'm sure she won't."

They shook hands with Brother Shattuck and G. W. thanked him for answering God's call. They were just making their way down the steps when Mr. Perkins approached with a couple of strangers.

"Excuse me, G. W., but I want you to meet Mr. Wright and Mr. Bishop of Buffalo, New York. These gentlemen have come to Perkinsville to observe our logging and milling industry."

Lizzie patted G. W.'s arm. "I'm going to go speak with Mrs. Greeley for a moment."

He reluctantly watched her go, then turned his attention back to the trio. The men extended their hands and G. W. obliged with a firm shake. "G. W. Vandermark," he declared. "Glad to meet you." But he eyed them cautiously.

Lately, there had been more and more visitors from the East showing up to buy property and start new sawmills. Logging in East Texas was becoming something akin to a gold rush of sorts. Where once yellow pine had been considered too full of resin for practical use, it now was finding more public approval. Especially as eastern white pine became scarcer. Eastern investors were like bloodhounds, sniffing out a profit to be made.

"I was hoping I might persuade you to take these gentlemen with you for a visit around some of the logging sites. I know you have a decent camp where they might stay and learn about the industry."

"I don't know. That takes me away from my work," G. W. answered. The last thing he wanted to do was play nursemaid to a couple of society fellas.

The man introduced as Mr. Wright spoke up. "I assure you, Mr. Vandermark, we won't be any problem. We are quite happy to sleep outdoors and enjoy God's nature. We aren't without our own skills in the woods. We both grew up in forested areas. What we'd like to do is see how your operation differs from those we've been a part of in the past."

G. W. could see that Mr. Perkins had his mind made up that he should somehow be the one to show these men around. He decided to oblige him, for Perkins was his family's oldest and dearest friend in the area.

"I suppose they can come along. They can ride the train out and back."

"I had in mind that you might actually show them the full extent of your property and operations. They'll even hire out some of the livery horses," Perkins explained. "And, of course, you will be subsidized for the time away from production."

"That's quite right. We are prepared to pay you a fee for acting as our guide and informant. We truly seek to learn all that we can from this trip," Mr. Bishop said. A quick glance to his companion had both men nodding.

G. W. felt there was no choice. "Have 'em come in the mornin'. We'll leave after breakfast and ride north to where we're cuttin'. I hope you fellas brought a sturdy pair of shoes. You'll need 'em."

"We have, indeed," Mr. Wright answered.

G. W. caught sight of Lizzie. Mrs. Greeley was bidding her good-bye, and Stuart Albright had maneuvered beside her, no doubt to harass her about leaving Perkinsville with him. The very thought that she might actually be married to the man gave G. W. a sick feeling in his gut. Surely it wasn't true. He didn't want to be pining over a married woman.

He thought of Lizzie declaring to all of them that she didn't consider herself married—that she'd made no pledge to God and therefore the signed paper meant nothing. But the law of the land could say otherwise, he supposed. He couldn't help but hope Lizzie's father would write soon to tell them the matter was resolved in her favor. She and Deborah had sent Mr. Decker a telegram immediately after Stuart had arrived, and then they had followed that up with a letter supplying all the details of the situation. They were all anxiously awaiting a response.

A thought came to mind as Perkins and the gentlemen turned to go. G. W. couldn't help but be concerned about the problems that might occur in his absence. "Mr. Perkins, I think it might be a right friendly gesture if you were to include Mr. Albright. He's a fella from Philadelphia who also invests," he offered as explanation to the two strangers. "Let me call him over." G. W. turned. "Mr. Albright."

Stuart Albright looked up, none too pleased at the disruption. Lizzie quickly slipped away and G. W. motioned the man forward. "Join us. Mr. Perkins has something to say."

Albright closed the distance, a scowl edging his face. "Mr. Perkins, gentlemen," he said with a brief nod of his head.

"Mr. Albright, these are two business associates from Buffalo, New York," Zed began. "They've come to investigate the logging industry, and G. W. plans to take them along tomorrow to see the Vandermark operations. We thought you might like to go along."

"No, I have other business," Albright answered.

"You aren't by any chance related to Garrison Albright, the legislator and railroad baron?" Mr. Wright questioned.

Stuart seemed to take interest in the man. "I am his son."

"Well, this is indeed a pleasure, and how fortuitous!" Mr. Wright said, looking to Mr. Bishop. "We are working even now on an arrangement that will include your father's interests, as well as your family friend, President Cleveland. You should definitely join us, as we hope to convince them both to invest in Texas lumber."

Albright considered this new information for a moment while Mr. Bishop jumped in with additional news. "We have already toured several operations around Orange and saw the mills at Beaumont. We are happy to say we've bought several parcels of forested acreage at very reasonable prices and hope to do so in this area, as well."

G. W. was none too happy to hear that but held his tongue. He thought Albright looked rather uncomfortable at this open conversation, as he seemed to hurry its conclusion. "Thank you for the offer. I will be happy to go," he agreed. "How long will we be?"

"Plan on several days—maybe a week," G. W. replied. He hadn't thought to take the men out for more than a few days, but keeping Albright away from Lizzie was uppermost in his mind. He looked to Zed Perkins. "You may need to outfit Mr. Albright. I doubt he brought anything but dress shoes and suits."

Zed patted Stuart on the back. "Not to worry. We've got everything you need at the commissary. We can just slip in the back door and take the supplies you'll need since you'll be leaving quite early tomorrow morning." He looked to G. W. for confirmation. "I think the Lord will understand, and since no money will change hands, we won't be guilty of commerce on the Lord's Day."

G. W. took that moment to exit the conversation while Mr. Perkins continued to speak to the trio of Eastern investors. He wasn't entirely sure why Perkins felt so compelled to accommodate the men.

"Unless he's thinkin' to sell out," G. W. muttered. But no, the man had been working with the bank in Houston to arrange a loan. Expansion was already taking place. He wouldn't sell out now—there was no reason for it. Still, he seemed awfully happy to attend to strangers who could very well prove to be his competition.

"Why, hello there, G. W." Annabeth Perkins practically gasped the words, trying overly hard to play the prim and proper southern belle. "I do declare it's a hot day, don't you think? Even with the rain threatenin', it hasn't cooled." She batted her eyelashes and opened her fan. Waving it back and forth in a lazy, unhurried manner, she smiled. "You aren't too warm, are you?"

"I'm just fine. Thanks for askin'."

"How do you like my new dress?" she asked.

He glanced at the blue-and-white-striped arrangement. "It's nice."

She frowned. "It's silk. Don't you think it's beautiful?"

He fingered his collar where it rubbed him just as wrong as Annabeth Perkins did. "I don't think much on such things. I'll bet my sister would discuss it with you."

"Your sister is much too unconventional." Annabeth simpered. "Honestly, you would think she didn't enjoy the company of her own gender. I swear she spends more time in discussion with the town doctor than anyone. She isn't sick, is she?"

"Of course not. They just have a lot in common, what with their book learnin'."

"That's my point exactly. She's not acting very ladylike. Going away to finishing school would have been one thing—but she attended the university. That's entirely another matter."

G. W. frowned. "Why don't you talk to her about it? Maybe she can help you understand. Now, if you'll excuse me." Before she could stop him, G. W. hurried around the corner of the church and made his way to the wagon. He paused as he approached the back of the church and heard recognizable voices.

"I think it's a good thing you're going along," Harriet Decker was saying. "You can get information and keep an eye on that ghastly bumpkin. If he's with you, he won't be attempting to woo my daughter."

"You mean, my wife."

"Call her what you will. I'll have better luck working on Elizabeth if he's out of the picture. She'll come to her senses in time."

"And what if she doesn't?" Stuart Albright questioned.

G. W. frowned as Mrs. Decker answered. "Just leave it to me. She'll do what she's told, and then everyone will benefit."

"I hope you're right. We've already wasted a lot of time down here. I'm anxious to return to Philadelphia."

"As am I. I have no desire to spend my days in this backwoods town. There isn't a decent meal to be had. Goodness, but if I see one more piece of ham or pork, I might very well throw the entire thing across the room. Come along now. Let us return to the boardinghouse before it starts to rain."

Backing away slowly, G. W. considered what he'd heard. He waited for several minutes before he approached the back of the church. Albright and Mrs. Decker were gone, much to his relief.

He made his way to the wagon and found his uncle already preparing for the trip home. "You look like you've been suckin' on a sour persimmon," Arjan declared.

"I overheard something that gave me concern," G. W. replied, climbing up to sit beside his uncle for a moment. "Zed Perkins wants me to take some investors out tomorrow to the campsite and then escort them around the area—maybe for as long as a week. I didn't want to do it, but he didn't give me much choice. And they're payin' for it."

Uncle Arjan nodded. "Guess we can make it through. I just arranged to hire a couple of new men."

"I convinced Mr. Perkins to include Stuart Albright so I could keep him away from Lizzie for a time. Turns out, he knows the men who've come. They're actually workin' with his pa and the President of the United States."

"And that's what you overheard?"

"No. They said that much outright." G. W. leaned closer. "I just heard Mrs. Decker talkin' to Albright, though. She was sayin' something about how she was gonna work on Lizzie to convince her to leave with 'em. Said it would benefit them all."

"That's a curious thing," his uncle replied.

"It concerns me somethin' fierce. I cain't hardly be in two places at one time, but I'm hopin' folks at home will look out for Lizzie. Her ma don't seem to hold much affection for her, and I worry about what she has planned."

"You'd do well to share your thoughts with Deborah. She'll see to Lizzie. She'll get your ma's help and Sissy's, too, if need be. They won't allow Miz Decker to take liberties, even if Lizzie is her daughter."

"Seems to me some folks treat their kin worse than they do strangers," G. W. said, shaking his head. "Just don't seem right."

"It ain't, to be sure," Uncle Arjan agreed. "Here come our ladies."

G. W. jumped down from the wagon and assisted his mother up to Uncle Arjan. By the time he got to the back of the wagon, Rob was handing up Lizzie and telling her how pretty she looked and saying something about her being brighter than the sun.

Deborah rolled her eyes to the heavens and settled her gaze on G. W. "You look tired. Are you all right?"

"I reckon I am," he replied and then helped her into the wagon. He leaned close and whispered, "I wouldn't mind a few words in private with you later on."

Deborah turned to eye him curiously but said nothing. She gave him a nod and turned her attention to Lizzie and Rob. G. W. admired his little sister greatly. She was very smart when it came to seeing beyond the surface of things. He hoped she would have some idea of what was going on with Albright and Mrs. Decker.

Later that night, after hearing G. W.'s concerns regarding Stuart and Mrs. Decker, Deborah returned to her bedroom and confronted Lizzie.

"Do you have any idea what it might mean?"

Lizzie shook her head. "I honestly don't. Mother can be quite manipulative when she has something to gain. There must be some benefit, but for the life of me, I can't imagine what it is. And then there's Stuart. I can't see Mother having anything that would help him. His family is wealthy and well connected."

"Well, despite that, it sounds as though your mother plans to impose herself upon us and make certain you listen to her every thought on the matter. I will do what I can to help you, but I'm not entirely sure what you need me to do."

Lizzie shrugged. "I'm not sure I know myself. I suppose it would be good if you could help me to avoid being alone with her overly much. I know she'll want some privacy with me, and that's fine. I can tolerate her haranguing me for a short while, but then I simply lose my patience. I don't want to make this matter worse than it already is."

Deborah considered her words for a moment. "If you were to leave first thing in the morning with my mother and go grape picking, then you wouldn't be available to your mother."

"We can hardly go pick grapes every day until my mother leaves," Lizzie countered.

Laughing, Deborah pulled down the quilt and sheet and slipped into her bed. "You don't know my mother very well. She'll find something for you to be picking for as long as you need."

Lizzie sat down on the edge of her bed. "I can't avoid my mother forever. I shall simply have to stand up to her and be the brave and strong woman she raised me to be. It's not like she can force me to leave. Your brothers and uncle would never allow for that."

"Especially not G. W." She paused. "I think you've completely won his heart."

Her friend flushed. "I think he's won mine, as well, but this matter of whether or not I'm legally married to Stuart is a problem we cannot ignore. Oh, I do wish Father would write."

"Don't worry. In time, he will. Until then, we shall simply do what we can to avoid confrontation. If that means picking grapes, pecans, papaws, or any number of other things, then that's what we'll do." Deborah smiled. "You have the advantage here."

"And what would that advantage be?"

"We have time and the Lord. Both will be to our benefit."

Chapter 13

Harriet Decker sat prim and regal as if she were a queen holding court. Dressed from head to toe in a severely cut navy blue suit, she looked every bit the righteous matriarch. Deborah could see why she intimidated her daughter. Lizzie's nature was far more lighthearted compared to the stout woman whose serious expression demanded solemnity.

Sipping the tea Deborah's mother had served, Mrs. Decker finally got to the point of her visit. "I do not pretend to be happy about my journey here. However, I found it most necessary, given the legalities of the matter at hand."

"And what legalities are those, Mother? Did you ask Father to check into the situation, or are we relying solely on the word of Stuart?"

Her mother frowned. "Your father has no need to be consulted in this matter. I was aghast to have him make an appearance at the wedding. It was an embarrassment."

Deborah watched Lizzie fix her mother with an emotionless stare. "He's my father. He had as much right to be there as you did."

"He had nothing to do with your upbringing. There was no reason for him to be there, although I'm sure he enjoyed making me feel uncomfortable."

Lizzie put down her cup and turned to Deborah and then to Euphanel. "At my mother's insistence, my father had little in the way of visitation. Those few times he did attempt to see me, she was cruel and made the situation quite difficult."

"How dare you lie? And with me sitting right here. I was not cruel or difficult. Your father wasn't interested in visiting you. He found another woman with whom to take his comfort and had little to do with either of us after that."

"You drove him away and then faulted him for taking comfort with someone else. I hardly consider that fair."

Mrs. Decker stiffened. "I can see that you understand nothing of what really happened."

"It would seem that the past is not nearly as important as the present," Deborah's mother interjected with a smile. She picked up the tray of grape tarts and extended them toward Harriet Decker. "Would you care for another?"

For a moment, Deborah thought Mrs. Decker would refuse, but from the woman's expression, she'd very much enjoyed the first two. She reached for the tart and continued. "I completely agree with Mrs. Vandermark. It is the present that holds the key to your future, and your future is with Stuart Albright."

"I'm sorry, but I don't feel the same way," Lizzie replied. "I do not love him, Mother, and realize now I was only marrying him to prove to you once and for all that I could make my own choices. Now I'm doing that again. I'm making my choice not to become his wife."

"But you are already his wife—at least on paper."

"I spoke with Dr. Clayton, who is a learned man," Deborah interjected. "He suggests that if Lizzie's signature does indeed bind her in marriage, an annulment would be quite easy to secure, given that the marriage was never consummated."

"But Stuart does not wish for an annulment. He is quite willing to forgive your flight and move forward in the marriage. The Albright family represents the very best in society and politics. They are dear friends of President Grover Cleveland and can offer Elizabeth introduction into the best places in society."

Lizzie frowned. "But none of that interests me. Honestly, Mother, until I came here to Angelina County, I wasn't sure what did interest me. Now I know. This place is exactly what I was searching for all along."

"You are better than this place." Mrs. Decker looked to Deborah's mother. "I have no issue with the fact that you have chosen this way of living for yourself, but my daughter was hardly raised to do menial labor. Why, look at her hands! They're horribly stained."

"We all have stained hands," Euphanel replied. "We've been pickin' grapes and puttin' up jam. Stains are just an unfortunate part of the process. Getting dirty is a part of life here in Texas."

"Which is exactly my point. Your daughter may have been raised to such an existence, but mine was not. Elizabeth was raised to see the value in being an independent woman—in thinking for herself."

"Yet you condemn me for that very thing, Mother. How is it

you can speak of such qualities as admirable and valuable in one breath and fault me for them in another?"

Mrs. Decker eyed her daughter for a moment and tried her best to soften her stern expression. "Elizabeth, I do not fault you for wanting to stand on your own two feet, but you hardly have the skills needed to do so in this land."

"I beg to differ with you," Deborah's mother said. "Lizzie is quite capable. She has eased my work load considerably. Whatever else might be true, Lizzie lacking skill is not an issue here. She learns quickly and seems to genuinely enjoy working with her hands."

"I do," Lizzie agreed. "I find this work to be satisfying. There is something quite noble—and dare I say it matches perfectly with your suffragette beliefs of providing for one's self and family. The average woman here in East Texas must be mistress of many skills. Not only is she needed to serve alongside the men, but she is primarily responsible for the benefit and well-being of her family. She must plant gardens and reap the harvest. She must prepare foods that can last through the year so that her family will not be in need. She must tend to the sewing and mending."

"These are hardly duties that will make a difference in the world," Mrs. Decker said rather haughtily. "I raised you for something better."

Lizzie shook her head. "I thought you raised me to be a good woman—to make choices that would make me happy no matter what society said. You once told me, 'While society may scorn me for my decision, my conscience rewards me in full.' Well, Mother, my conscience rewards me for making this choice."

Mrs. Decker turned red, and Deborah briefly wondered if the woman had stopped breathing. She looked quite angry and turned to Deborah's mother. "I do wonder if you would excuse me to speak in private with my daughter."

"I have no desire to speak with you in private, Mother. Not if you have come to harangue me. I will not be Stuart's wife, and I will not return to Philadelphia. The matter is settled. You cannot convince me to do otherwise."

"I have never been so insulted. You are in such a state of mind that you cannot even be civil with your own mother."

Lizzie got to her feet. "I have been nothing but civil. You and Stuart arrived here uninvited and proceeded to argue against what I want in life. You tell me I'm a rebel and a disappointment, all the while insulting the things I've come to love. Furthermore, I fail to understand why you are suddenly in support of my marrying Stuart. You have no respect for marriage—you've said so on many occasions."

"That was before," Mrs. Decker replied, seeming to regain control of her emotions. "You are the type of young woman who needs a man to help guide her. You are not as self-sufficient as you would like to believe. Your mind simply does not work in the same way as a woman of more worldly understanding."

"Excuse me?" Lizzie looked at her mother in disbelief. "You have long told me women are not only equal to men but superior in many ways. Now you tell me that I am the exception? That I need a man because my mind is too frail to possibly retain concepts important to living on my own? Well, perhaps you are right, but understand this: I will not be wife to Stuart Albright. I might very well take a husband, but it will not be anyone's choice but my own."

With that, she stormed off, leaving her mother to stare after her in gape-mouthed surprise. Without warning, Mrs. Decker turned to Deborah. "I blame you for this. Elizabeth would never have done this without your encouragement."

Deborah nodded. "I think perhaps you might be right, and for that, I congratulate myself. Lizzie would have been most miserable married to Stuart Albright. She deserves to find true love and happiness, and I believe perhaps here she has done exactly that."

"With that backwoods bumpkin brother of yours?" Mrs. Decker asked, her voice rising ever so slightly to emphasize the insulting words. "You can hardly expect me to be overjoyed at the prospect of that."

"Mrs. Decker." Euphanel put aside her cup and saucer. "I cannot allow you to come into my home and insult my son. G. W. is a good man with a loving heart and strong work ethic. Your daughter could do far worse."

"Equally, she could do far better. I do not say these things to insult your family but rather to point out the truth. My daughter is educated and refined."

"But you also said she needed a man to guide her," Euphanel countered. "It seems to me you have different standards for different women. Either we are all intelligent and capable or we are not."

Mrs. Decker was momentarily taken aback. After a long silence she regained control. "Elizabeth was not born to this life of hard work and sorrows. She would never be able to withstand this difficult environment, nor could she possibly respect a man such as your son."

Deborah sipped her tea to avoid betraying the way Mrs. Decker's words reminded her of her own heart. She had said and thought similar things. She knew that an uneducated man—a man who couldn't read or understand the concepts of science and world history—would never be of interest to her.

"I don't believe your daughter is that shallow," Deborah's mother replied, furthering Deborah's own guilt. "A good woman would look beyond the surface of things that could easily be changed and reflect instead upon the heart. A good woman would be far more interested in whether her husband loves her and is willing to treat her with the same love and respect as Christ had for the church. I believe Lizzie understands a great deal. She is hardly the kind of person who would refuse a man simply because he lacked education or social standing."

Deborah wanted to agree, but the words stuck in her throat. She felt strongly about the very things her mother spoke out against. What kind of woman did that make her? She wanted—no, needed—to have a man to match her intelligence and love of learning. She needed to know that he valued education and that he would want to see their children educated.

East Texas was full of people who were smart enough in the ways of everyday life. There were truly good, admirable people who had no more than a few years of home education. There were loving, kind, gentle folks who couldn't read more than a few words, who would never write letters or read a variety of literature. Deborah loved many people who fit that description. Most of her family would definitely fall into that category. But when it came to considering a husband—someone with whom she would spend every day of her life—Deborah knew she longed for something more.

Her heart sank. Maybe she was destined to spend the rest of her life alone.

"I don't expect either of you to understand the problems that this can cause," Mrs. Decker stated, drawing Deborah's attention once more. "The Albrights are powerful people. They could cause a great many problems for Elizabeth if she refuses to honor her word. They will not appreciate their son being shamed in this way."

"Do you suggest they mean to harm her?" Deborah asked.

Mrs. Decker met her gaze. "It is possible."

"Then Stuart can't possibly love her."

"Love is not the only thing of importance here," Mrs. Decker replied. "As I said, I don't expect you to understand, but I do. I know what this could mean to Elizabeth's future—perhaps even to mine. I will not see my causes suffer simply because my daughter could not keep her word."

Deborah didn't know how to respond. She supposed it was possible that powerful people like the Albrights could cause harm to Lizzie. She didn't know to what extent they could reach her here in Texas under the protection of G. W. and the rest of the family, but she wasn't a fool. Stuart Albright already struck her as a man to keep under a careful watch. Perhaps there was more at stake here than she'd first thought.

G. W. introduced the work crew to the visitors he'd brought. Rob was busy harnessing the mules but took a moment to shake hands with Mr. Wright and Mr. Bishop. He nodded to Stuart Albright, then turned to his brother. "We've got more damaged seedlings. Looks like the rooters were at it again."

"The rooters?" Mr. Bishop asked.

"Feral hogs," G. W. explained. "They have a particular fondness for the pine when it's in a young state. He pointed to a tree that had gone undamaged. "Over there, you'll see what I'm talkin' about."

He crossed to where the new pine stood. Long grasslike needles had showered down to settle around the seedling stem that was only some twenty inches tall. It looked rather like a clump of grass from afar. "These young trees are quite tender, and apparently very tasty. We are trying to save 'em so that we'll always have trees to harvest. They can stay in this small state for seven or so years. During that time, they're quite vulnerable."

"Can't something be done to corral or kill the beasts? What about fencing?" Mr. Bishop asked.

"Folks around here don't take well to fences. As you probably saw on your ride out here, animals pretty much run where they will. They graze on the forest grass at will. If we were to put in a fence or even set up traps, it would cause a lot of hard feelings in the community."

"It hardly matters what other people want," Albright piped up. "This is your land, is it not?"

"It's ours alright, but we try to be good neighbors, as well. Open grazin' is the law of the land."

"It really isn't all that critical," Mr. Bishop added. "The point of logging this area is to bring in the wood and move on."

"Cut out and get out," G. W. muttered.

"That's right. There's no concern to us about replanting. It simply takes too much effort to cultivate and care for a new crop of trees, as proven by your comment regarding these wild hogs. The cost would not be worth the effort," Mr. Wright declared. Mr. Bishop nodded.

"Well," G. W. said in a slow drawl, "isn't that part of the reason you've come west for your lumber? You've stripped out the forests back East and now find that there's little there to profit you?"

Albright narrowed his eyes. "That seems a rather opinionated thing to say."

"It's true, isn't it? I've heard that over and over. Nobody wanted yellow pine for the longest time. It wasn't until after the war that folks outside of Texas even started givin' it much of a look. Now with shortages of other woods, they're suddenly interested. I'm not tryin' to be overly opinionated, as you suggest. Just statin' the facts."

"It is true that the forests in the East and around the Great Lakes are seeing a great depletion," Mr. Bishop said thoughtfully. "But by coming here and utilizing the yellow pine, we can give those forests a chance to grow again. I hardly see a problem in that. By the time we are able to harvest the Texas wood, it may well be time to start to work again on the white pine."

"Well, I happen to believe that God called us to be good stewards of the land," G. W. replied. "My father told me that it was important to cultivate it and allow for the replenishin' of what we took from it. So that's why it's important to me to see these seedlings protected." He squared his shoulders and looked each man in the eye. "Now if you'll follow me, I'll show you some of the work we're doing today."

Chapter 14

Deborah drove Mrs. Decker back to Perkinsville with a reluctant Lizzie at her side. The day was uncomfortably hot, and word had come that severe storms on the coast might be headed their way. With the heaviness of the afternoon, Deborah thought the rain might actually benefit them—release the tension. Too bad there wasn't something equally beneficial to relieve the tension of Lizzie's situation.

"I would appreciate it if you would at least grant me the decency of accompanying me to the boardinghouse," Lizzie's mother stated as Deborah pulled the wagon to a stop near the commissary. "There are a few things I'd like to speak to you about—in private."

Lizzie sighed. "I suppose if I refuse, you'll just continue to nag me about it." She got down from the wagon and looked back up to Deborah. "I'm sorry about this. Do you mind waiting?"

Mrs. Decker gave a huff and looked away. It was clear she didn't like her daughter seeking someone else's approval before agreeing to see her mother alone.

"Not at all. Mother sent some grape tarts for Dr. Clayton. I'll just go deliver them. I'll meet you back here at the wagon." Deborah took her brown skirt in one hand and secured a hold on the wagon with the other as she climbed down. Together, she and Lizzie assisted Mrs. Decker from her perch.

"I won't be long," Lizzie promised.

Deborah lifted the basket of tarts from the wagon and made her way down the dirt street to the doctor's quarters. The air was thick with soot from the mill. With very little wind, the smoke seemed to blanket everything. It only added to her anxiety.

Knocking at the waiting room door, Deborah felt a sense of relief when Dr. Clayton opened it. He smiled and stepped back. "Well, this is a pleasant surprise."

"More so than you know. Mother has sent her black grape tarts," Deborah said, holding up the basket. "They are quite delicious."

He closed the door. "I must say were it not for your mother, I might never get a decent meal." He paused for a moment and shook his head. "No, that isn't exactly true. Mrs. Perkins has me to the house at least once a week. The preacher and I share their table and hear all of the latest gossip about the town. Annabeth and Maybelle Perkins are better than having a newspaper's society page."

Deborah nodded. "I know that to be true." She pulled the plate of cloth-covered tarts from the basket and placed them on a small table by the door.

Dr. Clayton seemed to immediately sense her mood. "Something is wrong."

She met his gaze. "That's putting it mildly."

"Does this have to do with Mr. Albright and Lizzie's mother?"

"Mostly it has to do with Mrs. Decker. She has no consideration for Lizzie's desires whatsoever. She came to visit and went on and on all morning. Even at lunch, which Mother graciously invited her to, Mrs. Decker made everyone miserable. I couldn't wait until I could suggest I drive her back to town.

"Lizzie accompanied me and on our journey here, her mother berated us both until I very nearly thought I'd push her from the wagon bench." Deborah looked away. "I wouldn't really have done it, of course, but she just keeps insisting that Lizzie is married to Stuart Albright and that she should remain so! Furthermore, she's insisting that Lizzie leave with them when Stuart returns from observing the logging operations with G. W."

The doctor motioned to one of the chairs. "Why don't you sit and tell me all about it? Did you mention to Lizzie the possibility of getting an annulment?"

"I did. She said that if her father finds out that she truly is legally married, then she will journey to Houston or wherever necessary and arrange an annulment."

"So why this degree of contention?"

"I can't really put my finger on the exact problem. Mrs. Decker is clearly up to something, but I can't figure out what that might be. Lizzie is quite clueless, as well. There seems to be some reason Mrs. Decker stands behind this marriage—even though she's divorced herself. But I'm ranting, and that's hardly fair." She forced a smile. "How are things coming along for you here?"

"Miserably. I have managed to see one patient, but otherwise, it's remained as quiet as a graveyard."

Just then the door burst open, nearly startling Deborah out of her skin. She saw the worried expression of Jeren Perkins and knew something must be horribly wrong.

"They're bringing an injured man from the mill. There was an accident with one of the saws. He's nearly cut off his arm, and he's bleeding profusely."

Dr. Clayton got to his feet and motioned to the exam room. "Tell them to bring him through the side door. It will be quicker that way. Miss Vandermark, I'd appreciate your help. You know where everything is in the exam room, and I'll need someone who can work fast to help me."

"Of course," she said, feeling a surge of excitement.

The doctor went immediately to wash up, and Deborah opened the side door to admit the men. She had presumed Jeren had exaggerated the degree of injury, but as the men rushed into the examination room, she could see for herself that he had not.

Butch Foster's clothes were drenched in blood, despite the fact that someone had thought to tie a tourniquet just above where the arm had been cut. The man was pale and unconscious, not offering so much as a moan when the men placed him on the metal table.

Dr. Clayton motioned Deborah to his side. "Hold his arm."

Deborah frowned. "But I haven't washed."

"We can't save that part anyway. Hold on to it while I cut away the remaining piece. All we can hope to do is stop the bleeding and keep the man from infection." He worked quickly, freeing the arm from the man's body. Deborah stood rather dumbstruck for a moment, not knowing what to do. She looked down at the arm, then back to Dr. Clayton.

"Put it in the spare washbasin," Dr. Clayton instructed.

She did as he told her, washed up, and hurried back to the table to see what she might do to help. The men who had brought Mr. Foster in had backed away from the scene, keeping their distance from the injured man. Dr. Clayton was already busy examining the oozing stump and cleaning out pieces of debris. Time seemed to stand still, yet Deborah knew the minutes were flashing by. When

Lizzie called out from the front room, Deborah had nearly forgotten all about her. The medical emergency had consumed her focus. She glanced at the clock and realized it had already been an hour.

"I'm in here helping the doctor, Lizzie."

Her friend came to the entrance. "What's happened?"

"Mr. Foster lost an arm at the mill. The doctor's trying to get the wound cleaned and cauterized so that he won't bleed to death."

Dr. Clayton stopped and looked at Deborah with a frown. "Mr. Foster? As in a relative of Mrs. Margaret Foster—the very one who cursed me?"

"The same. This is one of her sons."

He shook his head and went back to work.

"Lizzie, if you don't mind—I'm going to be a while. Why don't you take the train back? They'll be returning shortly, and you can hitch a ride in the engine. Let Mother know what's happened and tell her I'll be home later."

Her friend hesitated but finally nodded. "I'll do that."

The train whistle blasted and Deborah motioned her toward the door. "Hurry or you'll miss your ride."

As Lizzie left, Mr. Perkins showed up, anxious to know of Butch's status. "Will he live?" he asked.

"I don't know," Dr. Clayton replied. "He's lost a lot of blood and infection is bound to set in. I'll do what I can to ward it off, but there's no guarantee."

Mr. Perkins nodded and then seemed to notice Deborah. "This is no place for you! Why are you here?"

"I asked her to stay," Dr. Clayton told him. "She helped me set up the examination room and knew where my instruments were. She also has proven herself to have a strong stomach and stable nature in the face of such matters."

Mr. Perkins looked to the men who'd brought Butch to the

doctor. "Why don't you men get on back to the mill? You too, Jeren. I'll stay and see what happens."

"Do you want me to go find Mrs. Foster?" Jeren asked.

"No," Dr. Clayton replied before Mr. Perkins could speak. "Not yet. I don't need to have a distraught mother hanging over my shoulder. She has little use for me as it is."

"You heard him. Go on with you now." Mr. Perkins inclined his head. "See to things at the mill."

Jeren nodded and took the two men with him as he left. Deborah couldn't help but wonder what would happen when Mrs. Foster did learn of her son's condition. If Dr. Clayton could save him, this might turn out to be the very thing that would change Mrs. Foster's mind about him. Mother always said that God worked in mysterious ways, and Deborah supposed losing an arm might well be one of the strangest she'd seen.

"He was a good man," Mr. Perkins said, coming alongside the table. "Hard worker. I hate to see this happen to him."

"If he lives, he'll have a long recovery," Dr. Clayton told Perkins. "He'll have to learn to do for himself all over again—this time without two hands. He certainly won't be able to work at the mill."

"No, I don't suppose so. Not unless I could find something for him to do that required only one arm."

"His balance will be off, and the pain will be excruciating for a long time. Of course, that's only if he can somehow recover from the blood loss." Dr. Clayton stood back and eyed the patient in serious contemplation. "He's a fighter; I'll say that for him. I would have expected to lose a lesser man by this point."

"Well, I think I'd best go find Mrs. Foster, now that you have things under control. She won't take kindly to being left in the dark about this."

"She won't take kindly to me treating her son," Dr. Clayton declared with a shake of his head. "She won't like that at all."

Mr. Perkins rubbed his finger and thumb over his graying reddish mustache. "Hopefully you've saved the boy's life. She can't fault you for that."

But Deborah knew she would. Mrs. Foster's superstitions would cause her to believe that her son's recovery had been jinxed by Dr. Clayton's interference. She went to the cupboard for more bandages. She would need to stay with Dr. Clayton and explain the good he'd done to Mrs. Foster. The older woman would never listen to the doctor, but she might well be willing to hear Deborah and Mr. Perkins.

Mr. Perkins lingered a moment longer, as if he had something else to say. He shook his head instead and headed for the door. "I'll be back."

"Oh, how I wish this weren't her son." The doctor began to wrap the stump, shaking his head the entire time.

"Dr. Clayton," Deborah began. He didn't seem to hear her, so she broke with protocol. "Christopher." He looked at her. "You've done good work here. He would have died by now if you hadn't interceded. Mrs. Foster will have to realize that sooner or later. She might resent the fact that she wasn't allowed to care for Butch immediately, but in time she'll understand that this was for the best."

"If he lives," he replied. "The man is barely alive. The shock alone may kill him."

"I know." Evidence of the blood and trauma surrounded them.

From Dr. Clayton's earlier instructions, Deborah knew that she'd find warm water in the stove receptacle in his kitchen. "I'm going to clean him up a little."

Dr. Clayton met her gaze and nodded after a moment. "Thank you. That's a good idea. There are towels in the cupboard over there," he said and pointed. "I'll wrap up the dismembered arm before Mrs. Foster arrives."

Deborah nodded and hurried to see to her tasks. Once Mr. Perkins found Mrs. Foster, it wouldn't take any time at all for her to make her way to the office. Deborah returned with the water and retrieved two towels before going to work to remove the blood that had matted on the man's chest and neck. She had just managed to clean Butch's face and neck when Mrs. Foster came screaming into the house.

With something akin to a wounded animal's cry, she crossed the room and all but threw herself upon her son's bloodied chest.

"Git away from him. Git, I say!"

Backing away, Deborah put the towel aside. "Mrs. Foster, Dr. Clayton has managed to stop the bleeding."

"Bah! Git away from him. You have no right. No right at all." She straightened and noted the missing arm. "You done cut off his arm." It was more accusation than declaration. Her face screwed up and she began to wail. "Oh, you done took away his manhood."

"Mrs. Foster, the accident at the mill did that," Deborah interjected before Dr. Clayton could speak. "Didn't Mr. Perkins tell you what happened?"

Margaret Foster rocked back and forth, hugging Butch's good arm to her breast. "Oh, my boy. My boy."

Dr. Clayton exchanged a glance with Deborah. She could see his growing frustration. Just then Mrs. Foster let go of Butch's arm and pointed a gnarled finger at Dr. Clayton. "You've done your worst, but I'll save him yet. He ain't stayin' here. I'll be back to take him home."

"You can't move him, Mrs. Foster. He's lost too much blood already. If you move him, he'll start bleeding again," Dr. Clayton argued.

She fixed him with an angry stare. "I know what I'm doin'. You just want him here so you can finish him off. The devil is using you to try to hurt me, but I won't let him. I'll fix you with a spell that you'll never throw off." She stormed out the door, leaving Deborah and Dr. Clayton in stunned silence.

The silence didn't last, however. Dr. Clayton had clearly reached his limit of patience with the old woman's nonsense. "Of all the ridiculous, absolutely stupid . . . argh." He turned away, muttering.

"I've spent half my life learning medicine, studying and working to be the best doctor possible, and now this backwoods witch comes to undo everything. She'll be the death of this man."

"You've performed to the best of your abilities," Deborah reminded him. "Whatever she chooses to do and whatever happens to Butch—it won't be your fault."

"That hardly matters!" His voice grew louder in his anger. "A reasonable person would understand the danger of the situation. If this were your brother, I could make your mother understand the need to leave him here."

"You certainly could, but she would be just as upset as Mrs. Foster. You cannot change a mother's desperation to save her child. Mrs. Foster might calm down by the time she returns."

Dr. Clayton looked at her in disbelief. "Neither one of us believes that. She won't listen to reason. It's impossible to imagine that woman calming for any reason, but especially in a situation like this. She hates me. She's made my life a nightmare. She's maligned me and spoken against me." He began to pace, flailing his arms as he walked. "She thinks her ways are the only way. She doesn't believe in book-learned medicine."

"It's hard for—"

"And no matter how I work to prove myself, I have no chance with these people."

His tirade continued, the volume of his voice growing. Without thinking, she went to where the pitcher of clean water stood beside the washbasin. She drew a deep breath.

"She has no desire to understand what I can do for this community. I can't even talk to someone on the street without them fearing it will get back to Mrs. Foster and she'll put a curse on them. A cur—!"

In one smooth move Deborah turned. She didn't say a word, but instead swung the pitcher forward and allowed the contents to hit Christopher Clayton full in the face. He stopped in midstep, his jaw dropping in surprise.

As water trickled down, dampening his bloodstained shirt and coat, Deborah offered him a sheepish smile. Dr. Clayton's shoulders relaxed along with his expression. "I suppose I deserved that. I don't often lose my temper, but when I do . . . Well, I'll just leave it at that."

She shrugged. "I completely understand. You might well have to do the same for me one day."

He grinned. "I'll remember to keep the pitcher handy."

Hours later, Christopher sat in the silence of his bedroom. Mrs. Foster had arrived with a half-dozen male relatives and directed them to take Butch back to his home. He had tried to reason with the woman one more time, but she wouldn't hear any of it. Christopher gave up.

"His blood is on your hands now," he declared. "If your son dies, Mrs. Foster, it will be because of your poor judgment."

But she hadn't heard him, or if she had, she didn't care. No doubt she didn't believe his words. Christopher ran his hand through his hair and sighed. Why could these people not understand the good he could do? He had a great deal to offer, and if he wasn't allowed to do his job, Perkins would have no choice but to get rid of him. Then he would have left his mother and father, his siblings, and his life in Kansas City for nothing.

He shook his head. "God, did I misunderstand your direction? Did I fail to hear correctly?" He sighed. "What am I supposed to do, God? Please . . . show me the way."

Chapter 15

On their third night in the woods, G. W.'s companions seemed only interested in the amount of liquor they had left. Each evening, they had made a habit of sharing what they said was extremely expensive, smooth whiskey. They'd offered G. W. a drink each time, and each time he had refused. Had he any say on the matter, the men wouldn't have brought liquor into his camp at all. He'd seen the results of alcohol around logging, and it usually resulted in someone getting hurt.

Stuart Albright seemed rather amused by G. W.'s abstinence. He spoke of it several times, but always G. W. maintained his calm and refused to comment. He certainly didn't owe Albright an explanation. What G. W. chose to do with his evening was no one's business.

Taking up a cup of strong coffee, G. W. walked away from the fire to think. He'd been watching Stuart Albright and trying his best to figure out what the man was about. The trio of easterners had discussed a great many ideas regarding logging. Apparently they were all in agreement that it would behoove them to buy up many thousands of acres of prime forest while the prices were still low. The idea grieved G. W.—this was his home, and the idea of eastern businessmen buying up the land really disturbed him.

They wouldn't relocate to Texas; it was the mentality of "cut out and get out," as Wright and Bishop had mentioned more than once. Use the resources until they're gone, and then move on. There was no concern about what would be left behind in their destructive wake. G. W. remembered his father saying years ago that they were guardians of the land. That God had given mankind the earth to tend and care. Stripping the land of trees hardly seemed a good way to do either.

He finished off his coffee and headed back to the center of camp. To his surprise, Stuart Albright seemed to be waiting for him. He was sitting by the fire with a book, and when G. W. approached, he quickly pocketed the thin volume and stood.

"So, Mr. Vandermark, it's my understanding that your family has been in Texas since before the Southern states seceded, causing the war."

G. W. figured the man hoped to goad him into some sort of political argument. "That's true enough."

"Why did they choose to come here?" Albright asked.

"My father believed it was a good place to live," G. W. stated. Albright pulled out a cigar and offered it to G. W., but he shook his head and continued speaking. "There was a mighty push for settlin' this land."

"If you have people living upon the land, it's much harder for someone to come in and take it away." He clipped the end of the cigar and drew a stick from the fire to light it. "It was not that long ago we were fighting Mexico for this very place."

"So are you figurin' to settle in Texas?"

Albright drew on the cigar for a moment. "I hardly think so, although I'm not against the idea of investing. I see the potential, just as Mr. Wright and Mr. Bishop suggest. There is a great amount of virgin forest to be harvested. It could prove advantageous."

"For whom?" G. W. asked. "I don't see that layin' waste to the land is going to help the folks who stay behind."

The man shrugged. "People will find other uses for the land. This seems to be hardy soil. Surely they can plant and raise crops or increase their herds and produce cattle for market. It's a narrow view to believe the land is only good for one thing."

"So you'd cut down all the trees and move on—leave the land to be cleaned up by someone else?"

"Probably." Albright's disinterest in the subject was clear. "So what of you? Will you stay after the logging is finished?"

"If I have any say about it, the loggin' will never be done. I hope to pass this down to my children."

"And you actually believe that is possible?"

"Of course it's possible. My pa passed it to me and my brother." G. W. decided to turn the tables on Albright. "So do you think your father and the president are gonna be impressed with what your friends are seein' here?"

"I can hardly speak for either man. They will consider the profit to be made, and that alone will influence their decision. My father has a knack for such things. He's always been able to see the future potential of a product or industry. He was born into money, but it was nothing like the vast fortune he's created."

"I think my father did the same thing here. When he arrived, he and his brother bought what acreage they could. It wasn't much, but they continued to add to it, takin' in small pieces of land as they became available. It wasn't long before they could buy up bigger ones."

"Was it always their thought to manage the land rather than harvest it?"

G. W. thought back to the days when his father had still been alive. The old sadness seemed to drape him like a wet blanket. How he wished his father were still here. He would be able to set Albright straight.

"My pa was a very wise man," G. W. finally replied. "He couldn't read or write well, but he had wisdom that few can boast. He loved God and his family—this land, too. All he ever wanted was to provide a good place to live for his kin and to honor God with whatever he did."

Albright said nothing for several minutes. When he did speak up, his question took G. W. by surprise. "How old are you?"

"Twenty-six." G. W. couldn't imagine why the man wanted to know, but didn't question him.

"I'm twenty-five. I've been college educated and have worked for my father's business, just as you have worked for yours. The differences between us, however, are great. You are a man of the land. I dare say you probably can't even read."

"I can," G. W. countered in a defensive tone. "Not well, but I can read some."

The younger man considered this a moment and drew several puffs on the cigar. "Well, it's not of any real concern. Andrew Johnson was illiterate when he was a child, and he became president. Anything is possible, I suppose." He flicked the rest of his cigar in the fire as Rob approached them.

G. W. had no idea where Albright had planned to go with

the conversation, but he seemed to be lost in his thoughts as Rob joined them.

"I'm bushed," Rob declared. "Headin' to bed."

"I reckon we all ought to do the same," G. W. replied. "I'm pretty tuckered myself."

Rob nodded and yawned. "See you in the mornin'."

G. W. returned his tin cup to its spot beside the coffee pot, then took up a lantern and lit it before kicking dirt into the fire to put it out. He thought about all the things he would like to ask Albright—things that might explain why he wanted to marry Lizzie. Or why he insisted the marriage was legal. He'd never been one to stick his nose in other folks's business, but this time it really stuck in his craw. He didn't want to see Lizzie hurt by this man.

"It must be hard on your pa, havin' you gone all this time," G. W. threw out.

"Not at all. He has plenty of employees to see to what is necessary. He's far too busy trying to influence the president to worry about my absence."

"What's he tryin' to influence the president about?"

The casual question seemed to take Albright by surprise. "Mostly he's working to get legislation passed that will support the various causes of women's rights. He's a fan of the suffragette movement."

G. W. considered this for a moment. "Must make him popular with Lizzie's ma."

Albright gave a laugh. "Indeed it does. She was quite glad to see her daughter wed to a family who could benefit her beloved cause."

Well, at least that gave Harriet Decker a reason to push the marriage forward. But what was Albright's reasoning? He clearly didn't love Lizzie. In fact, as best G. W. could figure, Lizzie rather annoyed him.

He wanted to ask Albright outright as to why he had really come. Why was it he wanted to impose this sham of a marriage on a woman who clearly wanted nothing to do with him? But instead, he motioned with the lantern. "Guess we'd better turn in."

G. W. didn't wait for Albright's approval. He started walking to where they had set up tents. Wright, Bishop, and Albright shared the larger of four tents while G. W., Uncle Arjan, and Rob shared a smaller tent positioned away from the easterners. The other two tents held the other Vandermark employees. They only spent the night out in the forest like this when they were working on a deadline for extra product.

Pausing by Albright's tent, G. W. waited for the man to say something dismissive, but he simply ducked into the lighted tent without a word. Wright and Bishop welcomed him with the offer of a drink.

G. W. had plans to move his visitors deeper into the Vandermark holdings in the morning. He wanted to show them some of the differences in the trees available for harvest, as well as the hardwoods that were intermingled among the pines. Mostly, however, he wanted to finish this journey and get back home to Lizzie. He missed her and could no longer deny his feelings for her. He wanted to tell her how he felt—to tell her that he didn't care about the mess with Albright, that he'd wait for her. Of course, there was a chance she didn't feel the same way, but he didn't think that was the case.

Rob and Uncle Arjan seemed to be waiting for him when G. W. entered the tent. They looked at him rather expectantly. G. W. secured the tent flap and crawled over to his bedroll.

"Guess we'll be parting company in the morning," G. W. said.

"Saw you talkin' with Albright," Uncle Arjan commented. "Did the man have anything of value to share?"

G. W. nodded. "Said his pa is working to get some laws in place that Mrs. Decker likes. Laws that help her cause."

Uncle Arjan nodded. "So that's why she's come to persuade Lizzie to go back with them."

G. W. unfastened his bedroll. "I figure it that way. But I still cain't understand how Albright stands to benefit. Guess maybe in time that will come clear, too." He crawled on top of the blanket and stretched out. It felt good to lie down and rest. His body ached from the day of work. With a sigh, he closed his eyes and put his thoughts on the pretty little blonde at home.

❧

The night passed much too quickly, and before he knew it, G. W. was being roused by his uncle. "Time to get up."

He yawned and stretched. It was already getting light, and from the wafting aroma in the air, one of the men was already frying up some smoked ham. G. W. gathered his things and considered which direction they would head. He'd just as soon take the men back to Perkinsville, but he knew that Mr. Perkins intended them to see just how far the Vandermark holdings extended. Apparently there was discussion about them buying land just to the east of his family's property line, and Mr. Perkins thought it would be good for the men to see exactly what the lay of the land was and how it could best benefit them.

They ate a quick breakfast, then started packing for the trip just as the train whistle sounded. Most of the men would spend the morning loading logs, while Sissy's husband, George, and son David would continue felling trees.

G. W. secured their provisions on two of the pack mules, while

Rob saddled the horse Stuart Albright was riding. Mr. Wright and Mr. Bishop held true to their word and seemed quite capable. They tended their own mounts, while Stuart Albright waited impatiently for Rob to finish.

"How much longer do you plan for us to stay out here?" Albright asked when G. W. came to saddle his own horse.

"I figure we'll be back next Monday. Why?"

Albright seemed to consider this a moment. "I was thinking I might take the train back to your house. Mrs. Decker and Elizabeth must surely be ready to return to Philadelphia."

G. W. stopped what he was doing and looked hard at Albright. "Lizzie's got no plans to go back to Philadelphia. She's told you that several times. Why do you keep insistin' on it?"

The expression on Albright's face clearly proved he'd been taken by surprise, but his tone bore no hint of such feelings. "She's my wife."

"She don't see it that way."

Annoyance crossed Albright's expression. "It really doesn't matter how she sees it. It's the truth of the matter."

G. W. shrugged, trying his best to hold his temper. "Seems to me a man oughta care about what a woman thinks when it comes to somethin' as important as marriage." He stared Albright in the eye. "Lizzie's got a good head on her shoulders, and I think she can decide for herself what she wants. It's obviously not bein' married to you, so maybe you should just stop tryin' to force the issue."

Albright reddened. "Stay away from her, Vandermark. She's my wife, and she will return to Philadelphia with me."

"If I were a bettin' man," G. W. said, allowing himself the slightest hint of a grin, "I'd take a wager on it that you're wrong."

Rob and Uncle Arjan came up just then, and G. W. left Albright to decide what he'd do next. G. W. hated the thought of the man returning home to harass Lizzie, but there was really nothing he could do to stop him.

"They're settin' up to start loadin' logs," Arjan told his nephew. "I guess we'll see you back to home when you finish your job with these men."

G. W. nodded and was starting to say something when George Jackson came running—waving his arms in the air. "Come quick. David's done cut himself bad."

Gone was any concern about Albright. The men made their way to where David was moaning in pain. Uncle Arjan squatted down to see how bad the wound was. Blood had drenched the young man's trousers.

"We started too low, I reckon. Ax just seemed to bounce back off the trunk and hit David instead."

The lower trunks of the older pines were hardened from resin deposits, making the cutting sometimes perilous. The men hated trying to fell them at a low level for this very reason, but the rule was to cut no higher than the diameter was thick. Arjan motioned to Rob. "Get some help. Let's get him loaded on the train and get him to the doctor."

Rob raced off just as Mr. Wright and Mr. Bishop came to see what the commotion was all about. G. W. straightened. "David's taken a bad blow to his leg. We're gonna get him to town, where the doc can stitch him up and tend him."

"Is there anything we can do?" Mr. Wright asked.

G. W. appreciated the man's concern. "No. Just stay out of the way."

The men nodded as Rob returned with several of the other loggers. Once Arjan had tied off the wound to cut down the bleeding, the men made quick work of lifting David and carrying him to the train.

"George, you go along with him. Sissy should have you there to tell her what happened."

George nodded and wiped his bloody hands against his bibbed overalls. " 'Preciate that, Mr. Arjan. I'll be back soon as I see to him."

"Just take the rest of the day, George. I won't dock your pay," Uncle Arjan assured him. "Now, hurry."

George looked like he wanted to say something more, but instead, he gave a slow nod and made his way to the train. G. W. looked to Wright and Bishop. "We should be headin' out, too."

He left them and went to where the horses waited. Albright stood by his mount, looking bored with the entire matter. He held up his left hand, studying his fingernails for a moment. "I don't suppose I understand all the fuss. The man is a Negro, is he not?"

G. W. stopped in his tracks and looked hard at Albright. "What does that have to do with anything?"

Albright shrugged. "It just seems to me that given it's only a Negro and not a white man, you wouldn't make such an ordeal over the matter."

It was clear by Albright's expression that he was trying to irritate G. W. further. No doubt it was payback for G. W.'s earlier conversation regarding Lizzie. He stepped forward, his nose nearly touching Albright's. "I'm gonna forget you said that."

"Why? I meant every word. There are thousands of freed blacks who could easily take his job. Why expend the money and time on a man who was obviously too stupid to keep himself from harm?"

G. W.'s jaw tightened. He wanted so much to punch the man square in the nose. He forced himself to take a step back. "You can think what you like. But just keep in mind, that man bleeds red, just like you're gonna if you don't keep your thoughts to yourself."

Albright gave G. W. a rather sardonic smile and turned away.

G. W. was glad the man had not replied. It had taken every bit of his self-control to keep from acting upon his anger. He could hear his mother telling him, *"The Bible says 'Be ye angry, and sin not.'"* Those words often helped G. W. keep his actions under control. But would it really be a sin, he wondered, if he hit Albright? The man clearly deserved worse than that. Wasn't there such a thing as righteous anger?

Chapter 16

Lizzie found herself constantly thinking of G. W. and Stuart while they were off on the Vandermark property. They'd been gone for a week, and she hoped fervently that when they returned, Stuart would declare that he was mistaken—that they weren't married at all.

She gave a sigh and put away the last of the dried supper dishes. After learning what had happened to David, Lizzie found it hard not to fret about the men. What if some other tragedy had befallen them? What if G. W. were somehow harmed? Lizzie knew she had no claim on G. W. He had appeared kind and considerate of her, and definitely seemed to enjoy her company. But she had no reason to expect more.

"Is there a specific reason for that frown, or is it just life in general?"

Lizzie jumped and snapped her head up as if her neck were a springboard. "I beg your pardon?"

Deborah smiled. "I saw your frown and couldn't help but wonder what caused it. I know you're disappointed that G. W. hasn't returned, but maybe it's something more?"

"There's certainly enough to frown about," Lizzie said. She looked around the kitchen to make certain she'd put everything away.

Deborah came to her and took hold of her hands. Giving Lizzie a squeeze, she lowered her voice. "I know you miss him. I'm sure he misses you, as well."

"Oh, Deborah, am I so obvious with my pining? I feel like a schoolgirl all over again."

"I think you've hidden your feelings well. Although I would be remiss if I didn't tell you that Mother suspects. She has mentioned several times how wonderful it would be to have you in the family. She really likes you." Deborah let go her hold and gave Lizzie a wink. "I suppose I should be jealous."

"Hardly. Look at the mess my life has become. I may or may not be bound in marriage to one man, but I love another."

"Do you truly love him?" Deborah asked. She clapped her hands together. "I had hardly dared to hope!"

Lizzie leaned back against the counter. "For all the good it does me. Oh, why hasn't Father responded to our letter or telegram? I'm starting to fear that something terrible has happened to him. Oh, Deborah, what if he's met with an accident?"

"Stop it. You mustn't worry about your father. He's probably doing what he can to get to the bottom of all of this. You must give him time to work out the details. I'm sure that when he's able to offer you counsel, he will."

"I know you're probably right, but I thought we would have heard something by now. It's so hard to wait."

"At least we haven't had to deal with Mr. Albright or your mother much this week."

"Mother was none too happy with me when I accompanied her back to the boardinghouse." Lizzie drew up her apron hem and wiped perspiration from her forehead. "I know she expected to badger me into submission, but I found the strength to stand my ground. I told her specifically that I would not be forced to return to Philadelphia. She told me I was selfish and needed to consider the feelings of others."

"She should take her own advice," Deborah said, shaking her head. "I mean the woman no disrespect, but she honestly irritates my patience."

Lizzie smiled. "I told you so. Remember all the times I'd return from our visits and rant about Mother's demands?"

Deborah nodded. "I do, and I feel sorry for you." She leaned back against the doorframe. "I'm glad I could share my family with you. Now you can see what I was talking about, as well."

They both heard the back screen door open and turned. "G. W.!" Deborah exclaimed. "Well, aren't you a sight for sore eyes. We thought maybe you'd decided to make the woods your permanent home."

He looked weary but managed a smile and gave Lizzie a nod before addressing his sister. "I wanted to deliver Albright and the other fellas to town before I came home. Took a bit longer than I figured, as Mr. Perkins wanted to jaw a bit about the trip."

"Have you eaten?" Lizzie asked. "I could warm something up for you."

"No, Mrs. Perkins fed me." He patted his stomach. "Ain't near as good as what I get here, but it filled me up. Right now, all I really want is to go to bed."

"What about a warm bath?" Deborah asked. "Lizzie and I will bring you hot water."

He considered that for a moment, then shook his head. "Sounds tempting, but I washed up outside. I'll save that for another night." He crossed the room. "I'll see you both at breakfast."

"You'd best let Mama know you're back. She'll have a fit if you don't."

He nodded at Deborah's comment and kept walking. Lizzie watched him go, wishing she could have had more time with him. She had missed his company—their quiet evenings on the porch together, their occasional walks.

The clock in the dining room chimed the hour. Nine o'clock. Deborah seemed surprised by this. "I guess we all should be getting to bed. Morning will come early enough."

Lizzie nodded and gave another sigh. At least G. W. was home, safe and sound. She might have to contend with her mother and Stuart on the morrow, but worrying over that could wait.

G. W. stumbled into the kitchen well past breakfast. "Why didn't anybody wake me?" He plopped down at the kitchen table, nearly upsetting a pan of cooling corn bread.

His mother eyed him for a moment, then poured a cup of coffee and placed it in front of him. "Because Arjan said you were to be allowed to sleep. He figured you'd earned a day off since you'd been squiring those men around."

He downed the hot coffee, hardly even noticing the burn, and held the cup out for a refill. "Thanks, it's mighty good. Could I maybe have another?"

His mother grinned. "You know you can have a whole pot if you want." She went to pour more coffee while Lizzie surprised him with a big plate of food.

"We saved breakfast for you. Would you like me to cook you up some eggs to go along with this?"

He looked at the thick ham steak, fried potatoes, and slices of fresh tomato. "I guess a couple of eggs would top this off just right."

She laughed. "Just a couple?"

"Well, maybe half a dozen," he admitted. "Scrambled up fluffy like you made the last time I was home."

Lizzie blushed, and G. W. couldn't help but grin. She was the prettiest gal he'd ever known, and he knew she cared for him. Who would've thought it possible that a city girl all educated like Lizzie could fall for someone like him?

Deborah came into the kitchen and spied G. W. at the table. "I thought I heard you."

"How's the office work coming?" he asked.

"Not too bad. I feel I'm gaining a better understanding of things." She went to pour herself a cup of coffee. "I don't know how Uncle Arjan kept track of it before, but it's all recorded now." She sipped the coffee and smiled. "This is really good."

"Lizzie made it," her mother replied. "She's learned so fast, she'll have me all but replaced in the kitchen."

"Hardly that," Lizzie countered. "I may have mastered coffee, but I still have a great deal to learn. You saw my dinner rolls. They were terrible."

"Well, all things come with practice. We don't use flour as much as cornmeal around here, and yeast breads are always harder to master." She turned to her son. "While Lizzie makes your eggs, maybe you could tell us how the trip went. Are those men going to invest in forested lands nearby?"

G. W. cut a piece of the ham steak. "I believe that's their plan. They marveled at how inexpensive property is around here. Wish I had a bunch of extra money—I'd buy it all up for Vandermark and keep the greedy easterners out."

"Your father said the same thing during the influx of people right after the war. That was the one and only time he borrowed money to buy land. Paid it off as quick as he could, too. But at least we were able to increase the holdings."

"Do you think we should borrow and buy land again?" Deborah asked her brother. "I mean, you did just sign the new contract with Mr. Perkins."

"It's a thought, but we've also got to hire new men. It's all gonna take money. Speaking of men—how's David doing? I feel bad for not askin' last night."

Lizzie placed the eggs in front of him and answered before anyone else could. "Dr. Clayton was just here yesterday. He said David's injury was healing well."

"That's a relief. It looked like a nasty cut."

Mother nodded. "It was bad enough. I suggested Sissy stay home to take care of him until he's able to be up and around. She sent word with George that she figures to be back tomorrow."

"I'm glad you gave her the time off, though I doubt they can afford it," G. W. said, digging in to the eggs.

"Arjan said we could manage to pay her anyway, and David, too. I was glad for that," Mother stated. "They need every bit of money they can get."

"Should I pay them all in cash instead of half company script?" Deborah questioned.

"You certainly could, but Sissy told me that script is just fine. She doesn't like me paying her without her being here to work. She thinks it's charity. I suppose she'd think herself unreasonable to demand cash."

Deborah exchanged a look with her brother. "Like Sissy would ever demand anything."

G. W. shook his head. "Ain't charity. They're good folks. They've been here for this family when others walked away—too busy to help or just didn't care. George and David dug Pa's grave and Sissy prepared his body."

Mother nodded and replenished the coffee in G. W.'s cup once more. "Exactly my thinking." She gathered up several baskets and headed for the back door. "I'll let Lizzie take care of you. I have a garden to tend to."

"Wait, Ma. Is there anything you need me to do for you here at the house?" G. W. questioned. "You know I can't just sit around."

She thought for a moment. "Well, you and Rob have been promising to build me a place to store food, and the lumber is out there waiting. You could sure enough get to work on it, if you absolutely needed something to do."

"I'll get to it after breakfast." He waited until his mother had gone, then addressed Lizzie. "If you don't have anything better to do, you could always keep me company."

She looked hesitant. "Stuart and my mother will no doubt be out here to see me today. Stuart has never been one to wait, if he's of a mind to do something."

"I figured as much, but if you're busy helping me, they can't very well expect you to parlor sit with them."

Deborah put her cup aside. "He's right, you know. Let them come. If you're busy out back helping G. W., they'll either have to wait for you to finish up or come out there to find you. Either way, you won't have to be alone with them."

"I don't know how much help I'll be, but I'd very much like to try," Lizzie said, giving G. W. a shy smile.

"I just hope the two of you will talk about your future and stop this nonsense," Deborah declared, heading for the door. "Honestly, when two people are as gone over each other as you two, they should be planning a wedding—not a food shed."

True to Lizzie's prediction, Stuart Albright and Mrs. Decker showed up just before noon. Deborah heard her mother invite them to lunch. They accepted, though they sounded more irritated than grateful and immediately asked about Lizzie.

"She's working outside," Deborah's mother explained. "She'll be in for lunch, however, so why don't you just make yourselves comfortable? I'll get the meal on the table and let you know when things are ready." She turned at the sound of Deborah coming into the room.

"Ah, Deborah, we have company."

Deborah looked at the well-dressed and now rather tanned Stuart Albright. His blue eyes seemed even more piercing set within the bronzed skin of his face. Mrs. Decker was dressed very properly in a suit of light gray linen and seemed ill at ease. "I trust you had a pleasant journey out here?"

"It was tolerable," Mrs. Decker answered. "The roads leave much to be desired. They certainly aren't the quality of those in the East."

"I'm sure they aren't," Deborah replied and turned to Mother. "Do you need any help in the kitchen?"

"That would be very nice. Mrs. Decker and Mr. Albright

have agreed to stay for lunch, so please set two extra places at the table."

"I'd be happy to." Deborah turned to their guests. "If you'll excuse me."

She was glad to slip away and not have to make small talk. While they both were quite capable of intellectual discussion, Deborah found that she would rather have a long talk with just about any of her neighbors. They might be uneducated, but at least they were genuine.

"Maybe I'm not such a snob after all," she murmured. There were clearly worse things than lacking the ability to read and write.

When Mother could no longer delay dinner, she sent Deborah to retrieve G. W. and Lizzie. Deborah found them out by the summer kitchen laboring over a sufficiently sized A-framed structure. G. W. had smartly positioned it under a thick stand of pines that would shelter it from the sun.

"It's time to eat," she announced. "But be warned. We have dinner guests."

"My mother and Stuart?" Lizzie asked.

"Yes, and as usual, neither seems to be in good spirits."

Lizzie looked from Deborah to G. W. "I'm truly sorry. I have encouraged Mother to go back home, but she will not consider it." She gave G. W. a shy glance. "But I'm going to telegraph Father again. If I don't get a reply, I'll go to wherever I have to in order to see a lawyer."

Deborah put an arm around Lizzie's shoulders. "Hopefully, it won't come to that."

They washed up and walked slowly—almost ceremonially—toward the house. Deborah led the way into the dining room from the kitchen. Lizzie followed and G. W. brought up the rear. It was easy to see that Stuart was less than pleased to see G. W.

"Please be seated," Mother encouraged. G. W. pulled out a chair for Lizzie at the end of the table and took the seat beside her. Albright was clearly annoyed but said nothing as he took his place across from G. W.

Mother offered grace and encouraged everyone to dig in. It was clear that Mrs. Decker was used to being served and still hadn't gotten comfortable with this informal style of eating. She managed the serving spoon rather clumsily, as if to make a special point to everyone of how ill at ease she truly was.

Deborah had to practically bite her tongue to keep from commenting. She was trying hard not to let her anger and frustration get away from her, for she knew she shouldn't disrespect her elders. But what about when those elders didn't deserve respect? What about when those in authority—even parents—chose to do sinful, wrong things? But then, was it a sin for a mother to force her grown daughter to return home with a man she believed was her child's husband?

"How did it go with the A-frame?" Mother asked G. W. She turned to Harriet, explaining, "G. W. is building me a place where I can store food."

"We're pretty much finished. With Lizzie's help, it went quite fast. I just have to pack it with pine straw now."

Stuart looked aghast. "You were helping him?"

Lizzie nodded. "It was great fun. I'd never helped build anything before."

"And well you shouldn't have," Albright countered. "I can hardly believe you would impose men's labor upon a lady of such delicate nature."

G. W. put his fork down and looked hard at the man. "I didn't impose anything on Lizzie. She's the one who insisted on helpin' me."

Albright was unmoved. "That was only because she was being polite. She surely never expected you to take her up on such an outlandish offer."

G. W. turned to Lizzie. "Is that true? Were you just offerin' to be polite?"

"Goodness, no," Lizzie countered. "Stuart, I do wish you would stop trying to determine what I meant by my actions. You really know very little about me. I enjoy hard work. It makes me feel useful. You ought to try it sometime."

Deborah nearly choked on her corn bread. She wanted to burst out laughing but bowed her head as if contemplating her meal.

"Elizabeth!" Mrs. Decker set her napkin down. "That was most uncalled for. Stuart is merely concerned about your well-being. He's trying to protect you, since no one else seems to take such matters into consideration."

"My well-being was never compromised," Lizzie replied. "Furthermore, Stuart has no reason to concern himself with anything at all related to me."

"You are acting disgracefully!" Her mother's face turned red with fury. "As a woman who considers herself a Christian, you would do well to remember what the Bible says about wedded women obeying their husbands."

"Were there any currently wedded women at this table, you might have a valid argument," Deborah interjected. "However, I was under the impression that you did not hold with such beliefs. I remember a discussion we once had about that portion of the Bible. Didn't you tell me that you rejected that belief as something that was reserved only for the times in which it had been written?"

"Deborah, I'm sure you misunderstood Mrs. Decker," her mother said before the other woman could reply. "No one would pretend that the Bible can be picked apart in such a manner. To suggest that some things are true for us while others have no purpose seems quite blasphemous."

"She did not misunderstand me; neither do I misunderstand her now," Harriet Decker replied. She leveled a fierce scowl at Deborah. "My affairs with Elizabeth are not your concern. I would appreciate receiving the respect I deserve. Please stay out of the discussion."

Deborah started to reply, but her mother stepped in. "Mrs. Decker, our daughters are grown women. They have every right to speak up on the issues at hand—especially since this is my home, and I allow for such behavior. I also thought from things Lizzie had told me that you were in support of women speaking their minds."

"Well . . . I never said that . . . I mean . . ." Harriet looked uncomfortably at Stuart and then her daughter.

Lizzie met her mother's gaze. "I suppose this entire situation came about because I was following your instruction. You have told me over and over that a young woman should be allowed to work alongside a man—to earn the same pay—to have the same say. Honestly, Mother, you cannot hold to one set of beliefs for yourself and pin another on me."

Deborah knew it had been hard for Lizzie to stand up for herself, but she was getting better and better at it with each passing day. Her mother was a hypocrite—that could not be denied. The trouble was, Deborah knew there had to be some beneficial reason for Harriet Decker to act in such a manner. The woman had never wanted Lizzie to marry. She had wanted Lizzie to join her cause. She had specifically sent Lizzie to the university hoping she might become a physician or scientific genius—anything that would smack in the faces of polite society's paradigm for the weaker gender.

No, the woman was definitely up to something. There had to be a reason for her actions and attitude. Harriet Decker was not a person to do a thing without it benefiting herself at some point.

If Deborah and Lizzie could just figure out what that advantage was, perhaps they could sway her to their side by offering an even better prize.

It was worth a try.

Chapter 17

As September neared, the temperatures lowered in a surprising manner and summer eased into a gentle, more bearable season. With the change came word that Butch Foster had succumbed to his wounds. His death sent a wave of dissatisfaction and grief throughout the community. Questions began to arise. Was it Dr. Clayton's fault? Had his scientific methods killed Butch? Was Margaret Foster right about the doctor's inability to help them?

Deborah heard the rumors while shopping in the commissary and was frustrated that people should blame Dr. Clayton. Butch's wounds had been massive; to lose a limb and bleed out as much as he had were reason enough to die. Throwing caution and protocol to the wind, Deborah left her shopping basket with the promise to return and went in search of Dr. Clayton. No doubt he'd already heard the news and the awful things that were being said about him.

"I figured he wouldn't survive," the doctor told Deborah. "But to tell the truth, I don't know that he would have made it had he remained here with me."

Deborah's voice was barely a whisper. "You should be aware that Mrs. Foster is blaming you."

He frowned and toyed with a bottle of carbolic acid. "I figured as much."

Deborah immediately regretted bringing it up. "I'm sorry. I know it hasn't been easy for you here." She sighed. "It hasn't been easy for me, either, and I love this place and the people."

He looked at her oddly for a moment. "How is it that you love it so? You're an educated woman who loves learning. You seem completely out of place here."

She smiled. "I am. I miss attending school. For me, it was like having my eyes opened for the first time. Life here . . . well, it just is. And for most of my life, I've been content."

"But not now?"

Deborah considered his question for a moment. "I'm content with knowing that I'm doing what is required of me." She shook her head. "I should reword that. It was never required, nor even expected. Unless of course you count the fact that I expected it of myself."

"How so?"

"I've always felt my family needed me to gain as much knowledge as possible. The world is changing so fast, and the days of a handshake agreement are rapidly fading. Mr. Perkins is even requiring a contract from my family. Without the skill I've learned, I fear Vandermark Logging would be victim to all manner of scheming."

"I suppose I can understand that. You're good to help your family in such a way."

She shrugged. "I suppose so, but it still grieves me to see things as they are. I wish my brothers valued education more. I wish my father had valued it for them. Perhaps they would have been the ones to attend school instead of me."

"That would have been a grave injustice for you."

She met his smile and nodded. "I think so, too. But on the other hand, perhaps it would not have awakened such desires within me."

Dr. Clayton put down the bottle and crossed his arms. "What do you mean?"

Deborah hadn't meant to get into such a conversation, but now she found herself baring all of her secrets with ease. "I feel like a hypocrite—like a society snob."

He laughed, taking her by surprise. "I find that hard to believe. There isn't anything in the leastwise snobbish about you."

She moved to the window. "Yes there is. I'm sorry to say it, but it's true. I look at the people here differently now. When I first went away to school, it was after I'd completed eighth grade. Mother arranged for me to attend a ladies finishing school in Houston. I was quite excited. It was there that I learned French and fine sewing. I learned how to properly instruct household staff and arrange a dinner party." She turned and faced him. "All the things a proper young lady should know. I came back here wondering how in the world I would ever find use for such things, but I felt confident that I would. I even imagined marrying one of the young men I'd grown up around. Then I heard about some of the colleges and universities back East allowing women to attend. The very thought stirred something inside my mind."

"How did your folks feel about it?"

"I think at first they were worried about my going so far away, but when I reminded them that my aunt would be less than a mile away, it calmed them. Then, after attending a year of classes, I found myself awakening to another world. I knew that I could help my family with the business. I stayed in school, learning all that I could, always knowing that I would one day return here and do what I could to help my loved ones."

"And how do you feel about it now?"

Deborah considered the question for a moment. "I know I'm doing the right thing. They were very much in need of my abilities. You should have seen the mess." She laughed, remembering all the scraps of scribbled notes her uncle had given her. "It's in order now, and they have a new contract that will ensure they have work for years to come. I think things are looking up."

At that there was a knock on the front door and a man called out. "Doc? You in here?"

It was Zed Perkins. Deborah recognized his voice and frowned. Had there been another accident? She followed Dr. Clayton into the front waiting area.

Mr. Perkins nodded at her but turned his attention to Dr. Clayton. "I was hoping to have a word with you."

Deborah pushed down a feeling of uneasiness. She could see by the look on Mr. Perkins's face that something wasn't right. "If you don't mind, I'll pick out a couple of your journals to read and be on my way."

Dr. Clayton nodded and Deborah smiled at Mr. Perkins. "I hope your family is well."

"They are, Miss Deborah. Thanks for asking. How about your family?"

"They, too, are doing well, thank you." She turned and without another word slipped into the doctor's office. She could hear Mr.

Perkins begin to speak, and although she picked up a journal to glance through, it was his words she focused on.

"I'm sorry to come here, Doc, but there's been some trouble. As you've probably heard, Miz Foster's son died."

"I had heard," Dr. Clayton replied.

"Well, it's got folks riled up."

Deborah had feared it would be like this. She had hoped Dr. Clayton could escape the ire of her community.

"My guess is that Mrs. Foster is behind the rumors I've heard."

"True enough, Doc, but the fact is, there's talk about me getting rid of you."

Deborah stiffened and forgot about the journal. The very idea of the townspeople listening to Mrs. Foster rather than accepting the truth was more than she could stand. She could barely refrain from rushing back into the waiting room to speak her mind.

"Butch Foster most likely died from loss of blood and infection," Dr. Clayton replied. "I honestly didn't expect him to survive. Wounds of that nature are life-threatening. Still, Mrs. Foster should never have moved him. I'm sure she wasn't overly worried about cleanliness, and it would have acerbated his condition."

"I don't doubt that, Doc, but . . . well, folks are easily swayed in this community. Especially by one like Miz Foster."

"With her superstitious nonsense, no doubt."

"Doesn't much matter, Doc. I'm not at all sure what should be done. Folks aren't comin' to see you like I'd hoped. It seems they only come for care if there's no other choice. Still, I know it's not your fault."

"What is it you want me to do? I can leave, if that's what you've come to suggest."

Deborah leaned closer to hear the response. For a moment, she wasn't sure if Mr. Perkins would answer. Finally, he spoke in a slow, even tone. "I suppose I was hoping you might have a suggestion."

Silence hung in the air and Deborah wanted nothing more than to interject her own thoughts on the matter. She was ready to rejoin the men when Dr. Clayton replied.

"I guess the best thing we can do is pray about it."

Pray? When people were spreading lies and speaking ill of a good man? Surely there was something more. They should call a town meeting or send someone to reprimand Mrs. Foster. Of course, the poor woman was suffering the loss of her son, but that still didn't give a person the right to lie about someone else.

"I think you're right, Doc. God has His hand on the situation. I tend to react too quickly and not spend enough time considering what the Lord would have me do."

"It's easy enough to forget to seek Him first."

"Well, I need to get back to the mill. I don't plan to let folks dictate decisions to me, but I want you to know that it probably won't be easy for you in the days to come."

Deborah heard Dr. Clayton chuckle. "It hasn't been easy yet—might as well not expect it to change now."

She waited until she heard Mr. Perkins leave before marching into the waiting room. "Pray?" she asked, her voice a little louder than necessary. "You want to *pray* about it?"

He shrugged. "Seemed like the right thing to say and do. I can hardly change people's minds by myself."

"But that woman is out there spreading lies about you. You can't just sit idly by and allow for that. She's made enough trouble already."

He looked at her for a moment, then headed toward the office. "I can't force people to like me. Nor can I force them to believe me."

Deborah followed on his heels. "This is utterly ridiculous. Mrs.

Foster is maligning your name and reputation. You've done nothing but serve this community in an admirable and professional manner. It's not your fault that she's full of ignorance."

Dr. Clayton made his way into the examination room, and she marched right behind him. When he said nothing, she continued. Her anger was getting the best of her, but it didn't matter. "You have a right to defend yourself."

"It would hardly change people's minds if I did."

"It might," she declared. "You don't know what might convince them."

"That's true, but more important, I do know that losing my temper won't help."

Deborah couldn't believe his calm. She wanted to shake him. "Mrs. Foster will turn this entire town against you, Dr. Clayton. She will poison the minds of the people and scare them with her threat of curses. It's not right, and I intend to see that it stops," she said, waving her arms in the air for emphasis. "This challenge should not go unmet."

Dr. Clayton turned away from her and walked to the washstand. Without warning, he picked up the pitcher and turned to face her. "Do you need my help?"

Deborah looked at the pitcher and then to Christopher Clayton's face. She immediately felt foolish for her outrage. A sense of embarrassment washed over her.

"I'm sorry. I suppose I am rather out of line."

He grinned. "I appreciate your defense of me. I doubt anyone else would offer me such support. You are a formidable opponent, Miss Vandermark, and if any one person could rectify the situation, I believe it would be you. However, I am coming to see more and more the value of prayer."

She nodded. "You humble me, Doctor. I do apologize for losing my temper. I hate ignorance."

"As do I," he agreed. He replaced the pitcher on the washstand. "More than you will ever know."

Later Deborah accompanied her mother to the Foster residence. The run-down, unpainted house seemed dark and ominous, and the yard was nothing but dirt and dried-out herb patches. It was an appropriate setting for viewing the dead. Deborah was convinced little of life had existed in this place for some time. Mrs. Foster lived her life steeped in superstitions. The living water of Christ had no place among her elixirs and potions.

"I don't imagine Mrs. Foster will be too happy to see me," Deborah whispered to her mother. "I was there when Dr. Clayton worked on Butch."

"I know, but I think it's good that you've come. By staying away, you would only give her reason to believe herself right," Mother replied. "This way, you will come face-to-face with her accusations and dispel them."

"I can hardly raise a fuss in the middle of the viewing."

"I didn't expect you to raise a fuss," Mother said with a hint of a smile. "I think your very presence will offer an attitude of innocence."

They approached the front step and encountered Sadie Foster, wife of Mrs. Foster's oldest son, Matthew. Mother reached out to take hold of Sadie's hands. "I'm sorry for your family's loss."

Sadie nodded. "Thank ya kindly. Ma Foster will appreciate your comin'."

"We brought a corn bread casserole—two in fact," Deborah's mother told the young woman. "They're in the wagon if you want to send someone to fetch them."

"I'll do that. Thanks again."

Deborah followed her mother into the darkened house. Candles had been lit throughout to reveal the somber setting. Butch had been laid out in the front room, coins on his eyes and a cloth tied around his face to keep his mouth from falling open. The air was heavy—putrid from death and decay.

Dressed in patched trousers and a too-small coat, Butch scarcely resembled the robust man he'd once been. Deborah noticed the clock on the wall had been stopped, in keeping with the superstitious traditions. The family believed that it was important to stop all of the clocks in the household lest they stop on their own, foreshadowing another death in the family.

Likewise, the mirrors were covered and the stairs were roped off. If a step were to squeak under the weight of any person while the dead body was still in the house, the Fosters believed that someone in the family would die within the year.

Mrs. Foster caught sight of them and approached with a look of displeasure. Deborah told herself it was just her state of grief that caused such an expression.

"Margaret, I am so very sorry for your loss. I know your grief is great, and I've been praying for you," Euphanel said.

"It's true," Mrs. Foster replied. "I ain't hardly myself, and the loss of Butch is more than I can bear."

"Deborah and I want you to know that if there's anything we can do to help, we are here for you."

The older woman looked at Deborah and scowled. "Ain't nothing that one can do to help. She was with that butcher when he cut away my boy's arm."

Her mother squeezed Deborah's arm but looked at Margaret Foster. "Sawmills are such dangerous places. No one could have known that blade would break loose and sever poor Butch's arm. The loss is great, and he will be missed."

Deborah admired the way her mother chose to respond. Mrs. Foster was clearly at a loss for words. She nodded and turned to look at her son's displayed body.

"The loss," she finally murmured, "is one that should be avenged."

Chapter 18

September 1885

Lizzie knew the time to confront Stuart could no longer be delayed. G. W. had shared what he'd learned from Stuart on their trip through the Vandermark forests, and Lizzie felt she finally had some idea of why her mother so adamantly accepted the marriage. If Stuart's father had a way to help further her mother's suffragette cause, she would push for Lizzie to do whatever was needed. Never mind whether or not Lizzie loved the man.

I've been so foolish, Lizzie thought. *It was childish to act out against Mother, and I've only managed to create a mess for myself.* She sighed. The sooner she talked to Stuart, the better.

Making her way to the front room after supper, Lizzie braced herself for the job at hand. She had already told G. W. of her plans—Deborah, too. Now, she just needed the gumption to see it through.

"We'd like to leave tomorrow," her mother was telling Mrs. Vandermark as Lizzie entered the room. She looked up. "That is, if Elizabeth will stop this nonsense and pack her things."

Rather than confront her mother's comment, Lizzie fixed her gaze on Stuart. "I'd like to have a word with you. Would you join me outside?"

He smiled and his blue eyes seemed to spark to life. "Of course."

"Finally," Lizzie's mother grumbled. "Now perhaps we will be able to go home."

Lizzie frowned as she made her way to the porch. The warm glow of light spilled out from the open living room windows. Having no desire to be overheard by the people in the house, Lizzie stepped to the opposite side. It was a little darker there, but she would still be able to see Stuart's face. That was important to her right now. If he lied to her, she hoped she'd see it in his expression.

"I want to know the truth," she began. "No more of this nonsense. I do not intend to return with you and Mother. I want to know what you stand to gain by imposing this marriage on me."

Stuart looked stunned. He put a hand to his chest. "You wound me. You were the one who accepted my proposal. You planned the wedding quite enthusiastically, as I recall."

"I was wrong to do so," Lizzie replied. "I was wrong to agree to marry you. I could never love you, and a marriage without love would be a nightmare for both of us."

"What convinces you that you can't learn to love me? Is it that Vandermark man? Do you fancy yourself in love with him?" His words were edged with a tone of sarcasm. Instead of a jealous sweetheart, he sounded like a displeased father.

"This isn't about G. W. I decided not to marry you before ever meeting the man. This is about us."

"Well, it should be, but it isn't." He stepped toward her, lowering his voice. "Elizabeth, I have watched you these last few days. You are clearly infatuated with G. W. Vandermark. I've tried to be patient about it, but no more. You are my wife, and you must return home with me."

Lizzie narrowed her eyes and cocked her head ever so slightly to the right. "Why? Tell me now what you stand to gain. Why is it that you need me to return with you as your wife?"

Stuart looked surprised and then turned his head aside rather quickly, and Lizzie knew he was preparing to concoct some sort of story. "I want the truth, Stuart. If you lie to me, I'll know it."

"Oh? And what makes you so sure?"

"God." She gave him a look of confidence that she didn't quite feel. "I have come to believe He will give me an understanding of whether you speak truth or lies."

He laughed, but his expression revealed that Stuart wasn't quite sure of the situation. For a moment, she feared he might turn for the house, but he held himself fast. She waited for him to speak, praying he would just drop the façade and speak openly. The silence became an unbearable discomfort. Lizzie knew this was his way of controlling the situation, but she wasn't about to let him have the upper hand.

"Very well. You will not speak honestly to me, so I will bid you good night—and good-bye. I am going to ask Mrs. Vandermark to refuse you and Mother as further company in this house." With that, she pushed past him and headed for the door.

He reached out with one quick move to take hold of her arm. "Wait."

She stopped in midstep. "Release me, and I will stay."

Stuart let go of her, and Lizzie quickly maneuvered away from him. She backed against the porch railing and waited for him to speak. He seemed to consider his words carefully.

"You are correct. I stand to gain from this union, but so do you. You will have everything a woman could want. I will lavish you with gowns and jewelry. I will buy you a large house in the most fashionable district of Philadelphia. And if not Philadelphia, then New York. You will be free to do as you please. You will have a carriage at your disposal and servants to see to your every need. You may entertain and hold parties, spend your days shopping and visiting your friends—whatever you like." He paused and took a step toward her. "Elizabeth, I know you do not love me, but in time you might come to a measure of affection for me."

"And you would want this kind of marriage? A loveless one, built only on the hope that I might come to have affection for you one day?"

"I need this marriage," he answered, clearly more quickly than he'd intended. His discomfort was obvious.

Lizzie pounced on his error in judgment. "Why?"

"It's enough that you know I do," he replied.

"No, it's not." She folded her arms. "It's not nearly enough. I need the truth, Stuart."

He made a sound that reminded Lizzie of an animal in pain. "You are the most infuriating woman."

"Be that as it may, I require the truth."

He studied her for several minutes. His shoulders seemed to slump a bit. "Very well. My father has required I marry in order to receive money left to me by my grandfather. There, are you happy?"

"I did not expect to be happy with your answer, Stuart. I knew you were using me; I just couldn't imagine what you stood to gain. Now I understand. But why . . . me?"

"Your beauty, your education, your social skills—they all fit perfectly into what my father mandates my wife should be. To gain my fortune, he must approve. And he's chosen you, Elizabeth."

"But what of my mother? What is her part in this? Have you promised her some vast fortune?"

"No. She's been promised something entirely different."

"And that would be . . . ?" She let her voice trail off and waited while he shifted his weight and looked away.

"She will get political help."

It was just as G. W. had told her. "You mean her cause will get political support, don't you?"

"Yes. Now that you have the truth, just as you required, it's time to put this nonsense behind us and return to Philadelphia."

"I have no intention of returning to Philadelphia. I plan to obtain an annulment."

"No!" He stepped forward. "You have no grounds."

"I believe we both have grounds. We were false with each other—that alone seems worthy of a judge's willingness to end this fraudulent relationship."

"I won't stand for it. My father won't, either. Remember, you're dealing with men of power."

Lizzie shook her head. "I'm not afraid of you or your father. And, for once in my life, I'm not afraid of my mother, either. I have people here who love me. I will not be forced to do as you say, simply because it's your desire."

Stuart stepped forward and roughly grabbed her shoulders. Giving her a slight shake, he scowled. "You'll do exactly as I say. I have your signature, and that is enough. I will lie or cheat to see that this marriage remains intact. Do you understand?"

Lizzie felt the old sensation of helplessness return. What if Stuart had the power necessary to keep her in the marriage?

"In time, you'll come to see that I'm right—that this is the best way for both of us. You'll see that the life I'm offering you is all that a woman could want. I will deny you nothing."

"Only love," she whispered.

"What?" He looked as if she'd hit him in the face.

"You say you'll deny me nothing, but you are denying me the thing that matters most. You're denying me love."

"I can give you love, Elizabeth. I promise you that." He crushed her lips with his own. Lizzie fought against his hold but knew she was no match for his strength. She tried to cry out, but his mouth against hers muffled the sound.

Just as quickly as he had begun, Stuart pulled away. It was then that she saw G. W. had taken hold of the man. In one fluid motion, he twisted Stuart around and punched him square in the nose. Stuart lost his balance and fell backward with a loud thump.

Lizzie wanted to cheer. Instead, she came to G. W.'s side as Stuart picked himself up off the porch floor. She took hold of G. W.'s arm just in case he had thoughts of continuing the fight.

"I think it's time for you and Mother to leave," she said in a soft, but firm, tone. She looked to G. W. "Would you mind getting the door?"

He quickly complied, leading her into the house. Lizzie noted the stunned expression of her mother and addressed her immediately.

"Mother, Stuart has explained your arrangements with him regarding our marriage. I realize your cause is more important to you than I am, but I refuse to be used in this manner."

Her mother stared back at her with openmouthed surprise. For a moment, she was struck speechless, but then her wits returned. Getting to her feet, she pointed a finger at Lizzie.

"You are an ungrateful wretch of a child. No doubt this is the influence of your new friends, but I will not tolerate the selfishness.

You will do as you're told. I will not see my cause suffer because of your unwillingness to aid us."

"Aid you?" Lizzie exchanged a glance with G. W. "You mean sacrifice my life and happiness for you. This is far more than simply 'aiding.' You require my entire being—my all."

"And what if I do? It's no more or less than I've given."

"But you forget, Mother—this is your cause, not mine."

"Women's rights should be the issue of every female in this country," Harriet countered. "How can we hope to convince the men who run this country if we cannot even rally our sisters to the cause?"

Lizzie shrugged. "I have no idea, nor am I overly concerned about it. I will not sacrifice my happiness for a political scheme." By this time, Stuart had come to stand only a few feet away. She turned to him. "Nor will I sacrifice for the sake of your inheritance."

"This is completely unreasonable," her mother said. "You have no idea the harm you are causing."

Shaking her head, Lizzie looked at them with great sadness in her heart. She was nothing more than a pawn in their game. "You have no idea the harm you've already caused."

"I'm proud of you," Deborah declared when Lizzie finished revealing the evening's conversation. "And I would have dearly loved to have seen G. W. put Stuart Albright in his place."

"It wasn't as satisfying as you might have imagined."

Deborah could hear the sadness in her friend's tone. "Look, it will be all right. We'll go see the lawyer in Lufkin, and if he can't help, then we'll go to Houston. We'll get your annulment and that will be the end of it."

Lizzie shook her head. "I know I threatened Stuart I'd do so, but the truth is, I have very little money left. And without Father's help, I have no way to get any more."

"You leave that to us," Deborah replied. "I'm certain everyone in this family will want to give you whatever you need."

"I can't take advantage of you in that way. I need to find work that will pay me."

"Nonsense. Don't let your pride stand in the way. Besides, I can easily train you to assist me. As we add more employees and more expenses, I'll need the help."

"I suppose I could try it," Lizzie said with a shrug, "but if it doesn't work out, then I'll have to search for something else."

Deborah smiled. "It will work out. You'll see."

Chapter 19

Deborah looked at the town constable the next day and then to the sign posted on a barricade in the middle of the dirt road. The entry into Perkinsville was clearly blocked by the crudely constructed warning: *Quarantine.* She applied the wagon brake and questioned the man standing at its base.

"Ralph, what in the world has happened here?"

He tipped his hat in greeting, then announced, "It's typhoid, Miss Deborah. I can't let anyone in or out—Dr. Clayton's orders."

She looked to her mother. "I suppose we aren't going to be able to trade at the commissary."

"Ralph, is there much sickness?" Euphanel asked.

"The Fosters came down with it first, and most everyone who

lives near them." The younger man pushed his hat back. "Looks to be bad."

"And your family, Ralph? Caroline, the boys?" Mother asked.

"They're fine . . . for now. Thanks for askin', Miz Vandermark."

Deborah thought of Dr. Clayton. He would be overwhelmed with work. "Is there anything we can do to help? I could stay here and assist Dr. Clayton."

"No, Miss Deborah, I cain't let you in. Dr. Clayton said you might suggest such a thing, but I was to turn you away."

She felt her cheeks flush. Dr. Clayton had presumed to know how she would respond. Worse still, he'd told Ralph about it. Her mother seemed to sense her embarrassment and moved the conversation on.

"What about supplies, Ralph? Does the doctor have everything he needs? We can always bring things to you and leave them here."

"Right now everything seems to be under control. Doc says we need to see how far this has spread before we'll really know what's needed."

Deborah suddenly remembered Lizzie's mother. "What of Mrs. Decker and Mr. Albright? Did they leave on the morning train?"

"No one was allowed to board the train. They're still here, quarantined with the rest of the folks."

"Oh dear," Mother said, shaking her head. "That will not bode well with them."

"No, ma'am," Ralph agreed. "They tried earlier to head out your way, and I had to turn them back. That Mr. Albright wasn't at all happy."

"I'm sure he wasn't," Deborah muttered.

"Well, I suppose you'd best turn the wagon around, Deborah.

Ralph, you let the doctor know that we'll check back. If he needs anything—or if you need anything—we'd be happy to help."

"I'd appreciate it if you'd send word to my family. Tell Caroline to hold up at the house and not let anyone in or out. No sense in risking it."

"We'll stop by there on our way home," Mother assured. "Take care of yourself, Ralph."

"You, too, Miz Vandermark, Miss Deborah." He tipped his hat again.

Deborah released the brake and turned the horses in a tight circle.

"I do hope this will pass quickly."

Deborah saw the worry in her mother's expression. "Dr. Clayton is a good doctor, Mama."

"Yes, but typhoid is quite dangerous. I've seen these epidemics before."

She wished she had words to comfort her mother. Deborah knew something about typhoid. William Wood Gerhard of Philadelphia had established typhoid as a specific disease in 1837. She had attended a lecture at the university dealing with various diseases, and Gerhard had been mentioned with great pride.

Typhoid was now known to be spread through fecal-contaminated water and milk, as well as a general lack of cleanliness from person to person. Deborah remembered that the prominent markers of the disease were fever and diarrhea. There were four main stages of the illness, and each one had its miseries.

"You are worried, aren't you?"

Deborah turned to face her mother. "I remember hearing a lecture about typhoid and the many dangers for those stricken."

Her mother nodded. "It will be weeks before we know the full effect."

"I was just thinking on that. At least four weeks are needed to let the disease run its course, right?"

"Yes, at least."

"The people have been so afraid to use Dr. Clayton's services," Deborah said thoughtfully. "I suppose they will have to let him help them now."

"Perhaps this is the very thing necessary to bring the people to their senses," Mother replied. "Although it's a hard lesson to endure, people often have to come to the end of their own self-sufficiency in order to trust someone else."

"Just like we sometimes have to come to our lowest point in order to trust God."

"Exactly like that. We are very stubborn children at times, and acknowledging our need of God is difficult. It makes us feel helpless—out of control. Little do folks realize that when we put God in charge, only then do we find true confidence and liberty from worry. Maybe the townsfolk will see the same thing with Dr. Clayton. They will come to trust him when they come to the end of their own abilities."

Deborah knew her mother was right. "So long as they don't blame him for the typhoid. I've seen folks do that, as well. Blame their caregivers for the very ailment they help them with. Still, Dr. Clayton has often mentioned Mrs. Foster's lack of hand washing and keeping wounds clean. I suppose it's possible that she's the cause of this epidemic."

"There's no real way of knowing, so there's no sense in accusing her. It won't change the situation now."

"Perhaps not, but if she could understand that it was her unwillingness to listen to Dr. Clayton's advice that caused this sickness, maybe she would gain a desire to change. I don't doubt at all that Mrs.

Foster knows a good deal about healing, but with the discovery of bacteria and the cause of diseases, her methods are antiquated."

"I'm sure you're right, but I'd say nothing about it for now. It would serve Dr. Clayton better to simply treat the sick and prove himself capable of helping turn this situation to good."

"He'll have no one to help him," Deborah murmured, not really meaning to speak the words aloud.

Mother patted her leg. "He'll have God, Deborah. You told me he's a man who fears the Lord and prays. God will not abandon him to face this on his own."

"I know, but I fear that with so many folks suffering, he'll have to work alone. He will risk his own health, and that could leave us without a doctor."

"Then we must pray for him more than ever," her mother suggested.

"That's the hardest part," Deborah said, shaking her head. "It seems so little."

"But it's not. You are petitioning the King of all things for help." Mother smiled. "God knows what Dr. Clayton faces physically and spiritually."

"But Mrs. Foster is responsible for turning the people against Dr. Clayton."

"And God is able to change that, as well." Euphanel grasped Deborah's hand. "God is in control, Deborah. Let Him change hearts, for you cannot."

Lizzie was anxious for G. W. and the other men to return from logging. Word had been sent by Mr. Perkins that the mill was running at a very limited capacity, since more and more of the men had fallen ill. So far the Vandermark employees and family were faring well, and Arjan wanted to use the time to work ahead on cutting trees. The logs could sit and wait until they were needed—a sort of insurance against problems that might yet befall them.

Everyday activities went on much as they always had, with exception to their weekly trips into town. Lizzie thought of her mother and Stuart. Had they succumbed to typhoid? For all of her frustration with the duo, she could not wish them ill and found herself praying for their health and safety frequently throughout the day.

Putting another kettle of water to boil, Lizzie checked the clock again. G. W. should be home within the half hour. She hurried to pour a cooled pan of water into a pitcher for use. Deborah had insisted that they boil all water and milk—apparently it helped to kill any typhoid bacteria. It seemed a lot of fuss since none of them were showing signs of the illness, but Lizzie knew Deborah was far more learned about such things and complied without complaining. If it kept them well, it would be worth the extra work. She would be devastated if G. W. took ill.

It amazed her that she'd grown to love this man so dearly. He was nothing like the man she'd imagined herself marrying, yet he understood her as no one had before—not even Deborah. He admired her artistic abilities but also encouraged her to learn new skills. He also offered her laughter and joy, things that had been sorely missing in her life until now.

"Have the men returned?" Deborah asked as she strode into the kitchen.

"I don't think so. Since the train isn't running, I can't always hear them when they get in. I suppose they should be back soon, however." Lizzie turned her attention to the oven and pulled out a large pan of creamed ham and potatoes. "Supper's ready."

"It smells wonderful," Deborah said, going to the back door.

She looked outside for a moment, then turned back to her friend. "I wish I knew how things were going in town."

"I know. I do, too. I was just wondering if Mother or Stuart had taken sick."

Deborah nodded. "I know. I thought of them, too. Hopefully, Dr. Clayton will have warned everyone to boil their water and wash thoroughly."

"Is there nothing else that can be done?"

"Not that I'm aware." Deborah took down plates from the cupboard. "Even amongst scientists, there are arguments and debates on how best to manage sickness. I suppose Mother is right in saying that it's all in God's hands. We can only watch and wait."

The unmistakable sound of the men drifted through the windows. They were bringing the mules in, and it would only be a short time before they'd come to the house, expecting their supper.

"I guess we'd best get a move on," Lizzie said. "Gracious, just listen to me. I'm sounding more and more like a Texan."

Deborah laughed and headed to the dining room while Lizzie began cutting the corn bread. She found a great sense of satisfaction in her routine here, and hopefully tonight she would find herself sitting beside G. W. on the porch after supper. She shivered slightly at the thought. She hoped he would ask her to marry him soon. They both knew it was an implied desire, but the question had never been posed.

She frowned as a thought came to mind. Perhaps G. W. wouldn't ask for her hand until the annulment was secured. She supposed that was only right. He was a gentleman, and a good Christian man. He wouldn't want to besmirch her reputation.

Putting such matters aside, Lizzie squared her shoulders and stacked the corn bread on a plate. No matter what happened, things were better here than they'd ever been in Philadelphia. God would see her through. She had to trust that He had made a way through for all of them.

ꕥ

G. W. finished washing his face and hands. He took the towel and dried off, then drew a comb from his pocket and smoothed back his damp hair.

"You sure are gone over Miss Lizzie," Rob teased him. "I ain't never known you to worry overmuch about your looks."

"No one could ever fuss as much as you do," his brother countered.

Rob shrugged. "I have my reputation to uphold, don't ya know. The ladies expect me to look my best."

G. W. laughed and put the comb back in his pocket. "You're gonna have to pick just one of 'em and settle down soon. Ain't good for a man to be alone—God himself said as much."

"I'm hardly alone, big brother. 'Cept for now, maybe. What with the quarantine, I can hardly head to town for my usual sparkin'." He frowned. "Sure hope things are going good for folks."

"I do, too," G. W. replied, heading to the house. "But right now, I'm hopin' even more that supper's hot and waitin' on the table."

He bounded up the steps and into the house. The pleasant aroma of coffee and ham filled the air. Much to his satisfaction, he found Lizzie watching him from the corner of the kitchen.

"You look like the cat that stole the cream," she teased.

G. W. shrugged. "I feel more like the cat whose stomach is so empty it's pressin' against his backbone."

"Mercy, that can't be good. We'll have to see to that. Can't be having you suffer such misery."

He fixed her with a wicked grin. "Feedin' me won't put me out of my misery, but I don't guess it will hurt me, neither."

Her cheeks flushed, but she didn't look away. "Hopefully, we can ease your suffering in every way—one of these days. Soon."

"That's what I'm a-countin' on," he replied. "And what I'm prayin' on."

Sooner or later, he was going to make this woman his wife. He'd wait for as long as it took.

Chapter 20

Christopher looked down at the ailing Mrs. Foster. He put a hand to her head and could feel that the fever had not yet abated. She was still desperately ill, and worse yet, she knew it. That was the trouble of having knowledge of sickness and disease. Mrs. Foster knew the seriousness of her ailments, and by the looks of it, she was not only in misery and pain but also gravely afraid.

He listened for a moment to her heartbeat. The woman opened her eyes and focused her dazed expression on him. "I'm dyin', ain't I?"

"Nonsense. You just rest, Mrs. Foster. You're doing a bit better, but this is going to have to run its course. Can you take some water?"

She gave a weak nod. He lifted her shoulders and brought a glass to her parched lips. "Not too much at a time. Just sip it."

To his surprise, she did exactly as he told her. "I figure God is punishin' me for my pride," she said as he placed her back on the pillow.

"How is that, Mrs. Foster?"

She put a hand to her stomach and moaned softly. "My pride," she finally continued, "ain't no excuse for how I acted toward you."

He smiled. The third week of the disease was often marked by delirium—perhaps her confession was nothing more than that. "You just need to rest. Soon you'll be back on your feet."

Christopher realized with great relief that he held this woman no malice. For all her ill treatment toward him, she was a suffering soul who needed his help. Whether her change in attitude was due to the illness or a contrite heart, Christopher wanted only to see her recover.

"Is the whole town sick with the typhoid?"

"Quite a few of them are. Some seem to have escaped the worst of it." He blotted her forehead with a damp cloth, then straightened. "I need to go see to the rest of your family, but I'll be back to check on you tonight."

She nodded weakly. Christopher gathered his medical bag and went into the next room to check on Sadie and Matthew. Both were quite ill and into their second week of the sickness. Marked by a rosy rash on their abdomens and bearing high fevers, neither was able to get up from bed without help. Two girls, no more than twelve or thirteen, had been called upon to assist with chamber pots and give water and medicine. Children seemed to have easier cases of the disease or often escaped it altogether. No one knew why. Still more confusing was why some took the disease and died, while others bore the misery and recovered with few complications.

But mysteries such as this had drawn Christopher to medicine in the first place. Treating symptoms and searching for new remedies were always a challenge. But losing lives was a price Christopher refused to pay.

He finished tending the Fosters and moved on to the next family. One by one, Christopher made the rounds to all of the cabins, finishing just after two in the afternoon. He had been forced to expand the quarantine area to include the black town across the railroad tracks. Thankfully, the train was still running, although it couldn't stop in the restricted area. Supplies were brought in on the train and set beside the tracks, just outside of town. Once this was done, the train had to move on before Dr. Clayton could send men to retrieve the goods. At least this way, they continued receiving medical supplies and food.

Walking toward the depot, Christopher suppressed a yawn. His muscles ached and he longed for a good night's sleep. The epidemic was far from over, however, and rest would have to wait.

"Dr. Clayton!"

He looked up and focused his bleary gaze toward the sound. Deborah Vandermark stood just beyond the makeshift quarantine fence. He gave a wave and smiled. He was greatly relieved to see that she'd not succumbed to the disease. He ambled toward the roped boundary, stopping about fifteen feet from the line.

"How are you doing?" she asked.

"Not as bad as I could be. There are still some folks who haven't come down sick."

Deborah frowned. "I wish I could come and help you. You look awful."

He chuckled. "Well, thanks for the compliment."

"You know I meant no insult. It's just that you need help, and no one is qualified to give it."

"The risk is too big. Besides, God is seeing me through."

Deborah glanced toward the boardinghouse. "Have you seen Mrs. Decker and Mr. Albright? Are they sick?"

"They seem fine. Folks at the boardinghouse haven't come down ill. They're nearly a quarantine unto themselves."

"Mrs. O'Neal is a very capable housekeeper. I'm sure she's heeded all the warnings and suggestions you've offered."

"So far, it would appear that way. The few residents who are there seem healthy," Christopher replied. "Although none are too happy about having to be imprisoned."

"They'd like it a whole lot less if they came down sick."

"That's true enough. So how's your family?"

"We're all fine. I've been boiling the water and milk and making everyone wash until their fingers are pruned." She smiled. "I've never seen the boys with such clean hands."

He could well imagine Deborah standing over her brothers with a threatening glare. "And your mother is fine?"

"Yes, she's always been the healthiest of us all." Deborah looked past him to the town. "We heard there were a couple of deaths."

Christopher nodded. "Sadly enough, we lost Mr. Downs and one of the Foster cousins. Amelia."

"Do you think there will be additional deaths?"

He shrugged. "It's hard to say. Some folks are recovering. Mrs. Foster has been terribly ill, but I believe she's turned the corner. I think another day or two will show her greatly improved."

"Perhaps this will take some of the bitterness from her."

"She did tell me this morning that she thought this was punishment for her pride," Christopher replied. "I suppose only time will tell as to whether she changes her ways. Her son Matthew and his wife are very sick. I worry that Sadie might not make it."

Deborah looked as though she wanted to say something more, but she remained silent. He knew she was frustrated she couldn't assist him, and he would have loved to have had her help. But he was simply unwilling to risk exposing her to this dreadful disease.

"Well, I need to get on over to the depot, Miss Vandermark. They've brought in a new shipment of supplies."

"Do you have everything you need? Is there anything we can make for you?"

He considered the matter for a moment. "No, I think at this point I have all I need. Mrs. Perkins sends over food for me to eat—when I get a chance."

"You must take care of yourself, Dr. Clayton. We'd be in a dire situation without your healing care."

He smiled. "A few weeks back, I couldn't beg patients to come see me."

"Mother said it often takes a situation like this to change the hearts and minds of a community. It's sad, but maybe now folks can see how important a doctor is to this town."

"Yes, perhaps you're right . . . but then I must hold myself partially responsible for this epidemic."

She frowned and shook her head. "How can that be?"

"I prayed for God to cause the people to put aside their fears and prejudices and allow me to help them. I suppose I should have been more careful with my request, as I didn't stipulate how I would like to see that change accomplished."

Deborah shrugged. "God's ways are often a mystery. You need to trust that He has heard your prayers and answered them by His design—not so much with typhoid, but with your ability to be the one who can help these folks."

"I suppose you're right." Christopher took out his pocket watch and noted the time. "I need to go. Please give my regards to your family and send word if anyone falls ill."

"I will. And Dr. Clayton, I will be praying for you—for your safety in the midst of this work."

She sounded so concerned that he couldn't help but smile. "Never fear, I will wash my hands and wipe down everything . . . twice."

ꕥ

Deborah returned home, feeling only marginally better. She was relieved to finally see Dr. Clayton, but it did little to allay her fears. He looked terribly tired. How long could he go on like this?

"Oh, Lord," she prayed as she sat down to attend the logging books, "please send someone to help him with this sickness. Don't leave him to face this on his own. There are so many to care for." She considered the possibility of sneaking back to town. Perhaps if she crossed the quarantine line by coming through the back side of town through the woods, Dr. Clayton would have no choice but to accept her help. "Once I'm in there, he can hardly send me away. Oh, show me what to do, Lord."

"Deborah? Did you say something?" Her mother came to the office door. "I thought I heard you call."

"I was just praying. I saw Dr. Clayton in town. He looks exhausted, and I was asking God to send someone to help. The doctor won't allow me to assist him, for fear I'd take ill."

"I'm glad for that." Her mother looked at her sternly. "There's nothing to be gained by even one more person getting sick."

"But I know about the precautions. The things I've read and heard about avoiding typhoid are quite simple: Bacteria are spread because of a lack of cleanliness. I would pay attention to such things whether here or in town."

Her mother smiled sadly. "I know you care about Dr. Clayton, but I'm sure the Lord will watch over him. Please promise me you won't put yourself at risk."

Deborah looked up in surprise. "What do you mean?"

"I know you well enough, Deborah. Do not think to slip into town unnoticed. We need you here. Promise me you'll do as the doctor asked."

How did her mother know her heart so well? Deborah might have laughed had the situation not been so serious. "You always know exactly what I'm thinking. I can't fool you at all."

Mother shook her head. "That's no promise."

Deborah drew a deep breath. "But what if that's where God wants me, Mother?"

"If God wanted you there, He would have had you in town when the quarantine was set in place. Remember—this hardly took Him by surprise."

It was a reasonable argument, and Deborah knew that her mother desired only to keep her from harm. She offered her mother a smile. "I promise I won't sneak into town and cross the quarantine line." She thought for a moment and then added, "Unless Dr. Clayton specifically requests me to come."

"Thank you. I'm sure if he asks for your help that I can rest assured the worst is passed and you will not be at risk."

Deborah waited until her mother left the room, then glanced heavenward. "So if you cannot send me to help him, please send someone else. Someone who understands medicine and who will be willing to listen to Dr. Clayton's instruction."

Chapter 21

I have a surprise for everyone," G. W. announced days later as he bounded into the dining room, leather suitcase in hand.

"You're back!" Deborah exclaimed, looking up from the table, as did the others.

"You're late for supper," Mother said with a look of concern. "Did you have trouble in Lufkin? Is something wrong?"

Lizzie eyed him carefully, then let her gaze settle on the leather case. "You took a suitcase just to buy saw blades?"

He laughed and placed the baggage against the wall. "Nothing is wrong. In fact, I would say things are finally lookin' up." He stepped aside, and Brian Decker entered the room, hat in hand.

"Hello, Daughter."

Lizzie gave a squeal and jumped to her feet. "Father!" She ran to him and wrapped herself in his arms. "I can't believe you're here." The hat fell to the floor as he embraced her.

"He was in Lufkin, where I was buying supplies." G. W. explained. "He was fixin' to find you when he overheard my name while I was talking with the storekeeper. God worked it all together for good."

"Oh, indeed He did." Lizzie pulled back. "Why have I not heard from you before now?"

"I've been quite busy. You gave me an assignment, as you'll remember." He kissed her on the head. "And I could hardly come to you or even write until I had accomplished the task."

"Accomplished? Do you mean you have an answer for me?" Lizzie's voice was so hopeful, and G. W. found himself feeling much the same.

"Goodness, Lizzie, let your poor father join us at the table," Mother declared. She motioned for the man to take the seat to her left. "I'm Euphanel Vandermark."

"It's a pleasure to meet you, Mrs. Vandermark. I presume you're Deborah's mother."

"Yes, and you've met my son G. W. This is my younger son, Rob, and my brother-in-law, Arjan Vandermark."

"Good to meet you all." He shook hands with Rob and Arjan before taking a chair.

Euphanel passed him a plate of greens. "We've already prayed, so please dig in."

"But first tell us the news," Lizzie said, slipping into the seat beside her father. "I cannot bear not knowing what you've learned."

"Then let me put your mind at ease." He pulled some papers from inside his coat. "When I received your telegram, I went immediately to Philadelphia to visit a good friend there who happens to be a judge."

"And?" Lizzie leaned forward in anticipation.

"You, my dear, are a free woman. The marriage was not completed."

Lizzie fell back against her chair with a heavy sigh. "Oh, thank you. Thank the Lord."

"The judge said that it wasn't a concern, but he thought it might relieve your mind if we went ahead and arranged an annulment. So we did. These are the papers that will confirm it." He handed them to Lizzie. "Now your mother and Mr. Albright will be no further threat to you."

Lizzie looked to G. W. His heart swelled. She was his. Well, she would be. He picked up the platter of ham steaks and gave himself a double portion.

"I never expected you to come here, Father," Lizzie said gratefully. "Not only because of the distance and expense, but the typhoid outbreak."

"Yes, G. W. told me about the quarantine, but since we weren't going into Perkinsville, we had no difficulty getting here. I was relieved to know you were all unharmed. Typhoid is a terrible disease."

"It is, indeed. We've already lost eight people," G. W.'s mother said sadly. "But we've got a wonderful doctor in town, and hopefully most of the folks are on the mend. Thankfully, no one's taken sick at the boardinghouse where Mrs. Decker and Mr. Albright are staying."

Mr. Decker nodded and took a bowl of grits from his daughter's hand. "That is good news. I'm sure the delay in returning east has been a hardship on Lizzie's mother. There is to be a big suffragette rally in New York City. I know she had planned to attend."

"That's right—she was supposed to speak at one of the affairs. She will be greatly dismayed." Lizzie sighed.

"I think given your father's news," Deborah said, picking up her coffee cup, "the rally will be the least of her concerns."

Lizzie nodded. "Especially in light of what she stood to gain."

"What are you talking about?" Lizzie's father asked.

"Stuart told me he needed to marry me in order to receive an inheritance from his grandfather. Mother, in turn, was promised a helpful vote for her cause if she helped to ensure I honored the marriage."

Her father shook his head in disgust. "I am sorry for that. Your mother has forgotten the importance of love and honor."

Lizzie reached over and squeezed her father's hand. "But you never have."

G. W. was moved by Lizzie's tenderness. Although she had spent more time in her mother's company, he sensed her relationship with her father was much closer.

The rest of the meal passed in catching up on news from the East and sharing about life in Texas. G. W. had already spent a good deal of time talking with Mr. Decker and found the man's company quite enjoyable. Now, however, he longed for time alone with Lizzie. He had an important question to ask her, and now that everything was settled regarding her questionable marriage to Mr. Albright, he wanted to waste no time.

"Miss Lizzie," he said, putting his napkin on the table, "I was wonderin' if you'd take a little walk with me?"

She smiled at G. W. and nodded. "I'd like that very much." She got to her feet. "Let me fetch my shawl." She hurried from the room.

G. W. met his mother's smile as she began to clear the table. Mr. Decker eyed him with a knowing grin. "I suppose," he said as G. W. headed for the front door, "you'll be discussing that matter we talked about in Lufkin."

G. W. returned his grin. "Yes, sir."

Mr. Decker seemed more than pleased. "Good luck."

G. W. knew he'd not rely on luck. His love for Lizzie would be all he needed. He found her waiting by the front door. "Ready?"

She nodded and fixed her gaze on his face. "I've been ready for a long time."

He linked arms with her and opened the door. "Me too."

Lizzie pulled her shawl closer. The air was slightly chilled. The dampness made things cooler and also seemed to enhance the noises of the night. They didn't walk far from the house before G. W. turned to face her. Taking hold of her arms, he pulled her close.

"I don't want to waste any time," he murmured before capturing her lips in a long and passionate kiss.

Lizzie melted against him and wrapped her arms around his neck. He drew her even closer, and she felt her heart skip a beat. *This is what it feels like to truly lose your heart to someone,* she thought. Not only was he physically attractive and a wonderful kisser, but she loved G. W.'s sense of humor, his concern for family and community, his integrity.

"I know I'm rushing things here," he said, "but Deborah is right. I need a wife."

"Just any wife?" Lizzie asked with a teasing frown.

"Hardly," he replied, his lazy grin spreading. "I want you."

She felt a tremor go through her entire frame. "And I want you," she managed to whisper.

"So will you marry me?"

She simply nodded, unable to find the words. Tears came unbidden and slid down her cheeks. She hoped it was too dark for G. W. to see them, but he seemed to know instinctively that they were there. Reaching up, he gently drew his finger across her cheek.

"Don't cry."

"I'm . . . it's just . . . I'm happy. When I think of all I could have lost—knowing true happiness and love . . . well, I can't even speak the thoughts that come to mind."

He took her face in his hands. "Lizzie, life here in Texas won't be easy, as you've already seen for yourself. It ain't gonna be like the life you had back East."

"I know, but I don't care. I like working alongside your mother and sister. I know I have a lot to learn, but I will endeavor to make you a good wife."

"You're already perfect for me." He brushed his lips upon hers in a brief kiss. "I told your father on the trip from Lufkin that I couldn't ever love another woman as much as I love you."

"You spoke to my father about this?" She couldn't contain her surprise. "What did he have to say about it?" They walked back toward the house. From the light glowing from the windows, Lizzie could see the happiness on G. W.'s face.

"I asked him for his blessing, and he gave it. He could tell that my love for you was real."

Lizzie smiled, imagining her father's thoughts as he sat through dinner, knowing what G. W. intended to ask her. Her smile faded, however, as she thought of her mother and Stuart. No doubt they would do whatever they could to stop the wedding.

"Can we marry right away?" she asked. "I mean, could we marry tomorrow?"

He laughed heartily and twirled her in circle. "You are a bold one—exactly what I need."

She felt her cheeks grow hot. She realized too late how forward—almost risqué—her comment sounded. "I . . . well, it's just that . . ." Lizzie knew there was no sense in trying to explain and lowered her head.

"Darlin', don't you go gettin' all red-faced and shy. We can marry right this minute, if you can find us a preacher. You won't get any argument out of me. It's been sheer torture to spend all this time so close to you and not be able to . . . well . . ." It was his turn to look embarrassed.

Lizzie could only giggle. She put her hand to her mouth as he threw her a questioning look.

"So you think this is funny, do you?"

She nodded and giggled all the more. G. W. smiled and took hold of her once again. Pulling her tight against him, he locked her in an iron embrace. "I'll give you something to giggle about. I've been wantin' to tickle you since you first showed up. First it was because you never smiled—you always seemed so serious. Then I just wanted your smile to be because of me."

Lizzie tried to twist in his arms, but he held her fast. When he ran his fingers lightly under her chin and down the side of her neck, it wasn't giggling that Lizzie thought of. She sighed and her knees nearly buckled.

"So do you suppose," she whispered, "there might be a preacher nearby?"

G. W. halted and gazed deep into her eyes before roaring with laughter. In one quick move, he threw her over his shoulder and marched toward the house. "You go pack. We'll take the train to Lufkin tomorra."

"Put me down before someone sees us," Lizzie protested, pounding against G. W.'s back with her fist. "G. W.!"

He only laughed all the more. "I like a gal with some fight in her. Lizzie Decker, you're gonna be the joy of my life."

She relaxed against him and smiled to herself. G. W. pulled her from his shoulder and cradled her in his arms as he climbed the steps to the porch. When he reached the top, he put her down. Shaking his head, he put her at arm's length.

His voice was a hoarse whisper. "You'd best go along now before I kiss you again."

ꕥ

Deborah awaited Lizzie's return to their room. She was hoping that G. W. would propose to her friend, and when Lizzie walked, or rather floated, into the room, Deborah was certain the question had been asked and approved.

"So when's the wedding?"

Lizzie gave a sigh. "Tomorrow we're going to take the train to Lufkin."

"Leave it to G. W. to waste no time."

Her friend flushed. "It was a mutually agreed upon idea."

Deborah couldn't help but laugh. "Spoken like a true daughter of a suffragette. Stand up for your rights, and all that."

Lizzie plopped down on the side of her bed. "Oh, Deborah, I've never been so happy. G. W. is everything I could ever want in a husband. He's perfect. So kind. So smart. So gentle."

"Goodness, but you sound completely daft over him." Deborah shook her head. "Well, I suppose it's a good thing you brought your own wedding gown."

"Oh, I don't plan to get married to him in that dress," Lizzie said. "I'm a simple Texas woman now—not an eastern socialite."

"That doesn't mean you can't dress beautifully for your wedding day." Deborah smiled. "Although I'm sure G. W. won't care what you wear so long as you say 'I do' when the preacher asks if you'll pledge your life to him."

Lizzie smiled and nodded. "I'm so happy, Deborah. I want to cry and laugh all at the same time. It's like all of my dreams came true in a single moment." She looked to her friend. "I even get to be your sister and be a part of a real family who loves each other. I've wanted brothers and sisters all of my life, and now I'll have them."

Deborah laughed and threw a pillow at the dreamy-eyed girl. "And you'll see just how ornery siblings can be. All of this time I've just been being nice to you because you were a guest."

"Well, so long as I get to marry G. W., you can treat me any way you like."

Deborah rolled her eyes and got to her feet. "Guess we'd better get packed."

"We?"

"Of course. Do you think I'm going to send you off to Lufkin without a maid of honor? Goodness, you'll probably have the whole lot of us. Mother would never want to miss seeing her son get married, and Rob and Uncle Arjan will enjoy a day in the big city . . . well, as big as it comes this close to Perkinsville."

"Oh, do you really think they'll join us? That will be wonderful!"

"Wild pigs couldn't keep them from coming." Deborah paused and looked at Lizzie. "Who could have imagined when we ran away from your sham wedding in Philadelphia that you were actually running away to find true love?"

Lizzie met her gaze and a sob caught in her throat as she began to speak. "You told me . . . God would work out all of the details. And now He has." She started to cry and Deborah immediately came to her side.

"He always will," she told her friend. "He is always faithful." She thought of Dr. Clayton just then and realized that God would be faithful to him, as well. She needn't worry about whether or not the doctor would have help. God could and would provide whatever was necessary to get the job done.

"Come on," she said, pulling away from Lizzie. "We've got work to do."

Chapter 22

The wedding was a rushed affair, but everyone involved enjoyed the event. The bride vacillated between looking as though she might faint and nervously giggling through most of the ceremony. The groom, on the other hand, grinned like the cat that had found his way into the cream crock.

Deborah couldn't have been more pleased for her dear friend and brother. She found that the very idea of Lizzie being with her in Texas made the life she'd chosen more bearable. It wasn't that she didn't want to be there with her family; she'd just grown accustomed to spending her days reading and learning while at the university. Now that part of her life was over.

"The train is finally coming into the station," G. W. announced. "Guess the Rabbit didn't jump the tracks this time."

Deborah smiled and nodded. She made her way to Lizzie and hugged her close. "I'll see you in a few days."

Lizzie and G. W. had opted to remain in Lufkin for a few days of privacy, while the others would journey through the night to reach home. Deborah released her friend and turned to go as the train conductor approached them.

"Word's come that there's a bad storm brewing just off the coast," he announced. "Looks to be a hurricane comin' in."

Deborah frowned, while her uncle pressed the inquiry. "When did you get word?"

"Just came over the telegraph. One of the ships brought news to Houston, and they've sent out wires along the track."

Uncle Arjan looked at Deborah's mother and shook his head. "Might be we should stay put. No tellin' how fast that storm's movin' in or which direction it'll take." He turned to the other men. "I've seen them come on fast and furious. You don't want to be on the Rabbit when it hits."

"I agree," G. W. said. "Why don't you take rooms at the hotel? I know it's an added expense, but it'll be for the best."

"That seems wise." Mother looked quite grim. "Sissy will know what's happened if she gets word about the storm. She won't fret, and she'll see to the animals."

Lizzie was wringing her hands, so Deborah went to her side to reassure her. "Don't look so worried. These storms occur from time to time—especially in the late summer and fall. There's nothing you can do to keep them from coming, so we simply prepare for them the best we can."

"I've never been in a hurricane, but I've read about the destruction they can cause."

Deborah could remember some very bad storms in the past but certainly didn't want to give her friend undue fright. She believed they were far enough inland that any damage would be lessened considerably—at least she hoped so. "The best thing is to use good judgment. Traveling home just now would not be prudent to say the least." She thought of the folks in Perkinsville. Deborah excused herself. "Lizzie, I'll be right back."

She hurried over to where the engineer was just starting to climb back aboard. "Excuse me. Do you know if the folks in Perkinsville were warned?"

He stepped back down and turned to face her. "Yes, miss. We've left word at every town on our way. Of course, Perkinsville is in quarantine, but they got the message. I blasted the train whistle until the depot master came to see what the trouble was." He smiled from behind a thick mustache. "They'd been wired and were already making preparations."

She nodded, relieved. Her mother came to stand beside her. "Is something wrong, Deborah? I saw you hurry over here."

She met Mother's gentle expression. "No. I wanted to make sure the folks in Perkinsville had been warned about the storm. The engineer assured me he told the depot master and said plans were already being made to assure their safety."

Mother put her arm around Deborah and hugged her close. "Don't worry. Folks there know what to do. I'm sure they'll keep Dr. Clayton apprised."

She looked at her mother rather surprised. "I care about everyone there, not just Dr. Clayton."

"I know that, but I also realize you have a special . . . fondness for him."

Deborah didn't want her mother to think there was something more between her and the doctor than there was. "Dr. Clayton is just a good friend, Mother. I appreciate his intellect, and he doesn't seem to mind that as a woman, I like to expand my knowledge. Don't believe there to be anything more than that."

Her mother laughed. "You are such a goose sometimes. Come along. The fellas are taking our things over to the hotel. Hopefully they've got room for all of us."

She wasn't sure what her mother had meant. Was she implying that Deborah's worries were unfounded—that of course she knew the doctor was only a friend? Or was she suggesting that Deborah was a goose for trying to make her believe something other than the truth?

But that is *the truth.* Deborah rejoined Lizzie and together they walked to where Uncle Arjan waited for them. *What in the world did Mother mean? But if I ask, she's only going to know that I'm troubled by her statement and that, in turn, might lead her to believe that I do feel something more for Dr. Clayton.* Mother and Lizzie took hold of Uncle Arjan's arms, while Deborah followed rather absentmindedly behind.

Surely Mother didn't suspect that there were romantic feelings between her and Dr. Clayton. He was a nice man—quite handsome and very intelligent. She did enjoy the time she spent with him, but she wasn't sweet on him. Or was she? *Oh, grief and nonsense, what should I do?*

Her concern was quickly dismissed when a powerful grip took hold of her arm and pulled her violently to the side of the road. Deborah felt herself falling just as a freight wagon barreled around the corner behind her. She landed with a thud against the firm, lean frame of the man who'd rescued her, then quickly scrambled up to regain her legs.

"I am so sorry," she said, dusting off her skirt.

"Deborah, are you all right?" her mother's frantic voice sounded from behind. "Oh goodness, look at your gloves."

She saw how dirty her gloves were and quickly tucked them into the folds of her skirt. *Funny that we should worry about gloves at a time like this*, she thought.

Looking up, Deborah caught sight of her hero. He was tall—probably about G. W.'s height—and dressed in the unmistakable style of a ranch hand. Throwing her a lazy smile, he shrugged.

"Afternoon, miss."

Deborah laughed as Uncle Arjan extended a hand toward the cowboy. "Thank you, son. We're very grateful for what you just did."

"Did you not see the wagon, Deborah?" her mother questioned.

"I'm afraid I was daydreaming." She smiled at the stranger. "I'm Deborah Vandermark. Thank you for your assistance . . . and the soft landing."

He grinned and slapped his leg. "You're certainly welcome. I hope you're no worse for the venture."

Deborah tested her weight on each foot and flexed her arms. "I seem to be completely unscathed."

"Are you sure, Deborah?" Lizzie asked, her expression one of grave concern. "I thought for certain that wagon would knock you to the ground. I was just looking back to say something to you when I saw him come bearing toward you."

"I'm fine, truly I am. Thanks to Mr. . . ." Deborah looked at the man. "I do not know your name."

"Jacob Francis Wythe. Though my friends just call me Slim."

"Thank you, Mr. Wythe, for saving my daughter. Would you care to join us for supper tonight so that we can thank you properly? We're hoping to take rooms at the hotel and would be happy to have you dine with us this evening," Mother said.

The man's dusty face lit up, although his expression sobered. "I'd be honored, ma'am. But you know, it's not necessary."

Something in the way he added the latter didn't sound quite as sincere. Perhaps he was afraid of missing a good meal.

"I know it isn't necessary, but it's exactly what I'd like to do. I know Deborah's brothers will want to meet you and thank you, as well."

Mr. Wythe picked up his hat and slapped it against his leg, causing a cloud of dust to rise. "I'd be happy to join you, ma'am."

"Let's say about five-thirty; would that be all right?"

"Yes, Miz Vandermark. I'll be there." Casting a quick glance at Deborah, he planted the hat on his head, then tipped it to her and to the other two women. "Thank you kindly."

Deborah watched him saunter off as though he'd just taken first place at the county fair. She couldn't help but giggle.

Mother looked at her and shook her head. "What in the world is so funny? You could have been killed! You know a town this size is no place to lose your thoughts."

Taking the admonition in stride, Deborah nodded and looped her arm with her mother's. "I know. It was pure foolishness. I won't do it again, but . . . it did introduce us to that nice cowboy."

Mother rolled her eyes while Lizzie laughed out loud. Uncle Arjan shook his head. "There are easier ways to meet suitors, Niece. If I were you, I'd try a church social next time or maybe a house raisin'."

"I wasn't thinking of courtship, Uncle. I thought perhaps we could buy some beef—that's all."

At the hotel, they found the men had secured rooms for everyone. Rob and Arjan would share a room, as would Lizzie and G. W. Mother and Deborah would be together, and Mr. Decker would have a room of his own.

"Your room is upstairs and just to the left. There's a washroom across the hall," G. W. said, handing Mother the key. "We'll bring up the bags."

Mother nodded and led the way. "After all that excitement, I'm ready to rest for a bit."

"Excitement?" G. W. asked.

Deborah shook her head. "I'm sure Lizzie will tell you all about it. It starts out rather bad but ends with the possibility of negotiating the purchase of beef." She gave her brother a wink. "Who knows what might happen next?"

The bad weather pushed in with frightening speed. Thick, heavy rain clouds built to the southeast and seemed to boil and churn with great fury as they made their way north. Deborah prayed that the damage would be minimal, then altered the prayer to ask that there be no damage at all. Hurricanes generally played out most of their strength on the coast, and she was determined not to ruin the evening fretting over what might or might not come.

Supper was a rather somber affair, dominated by talk of the upcoming storm. Deborah toyed with her fried chicken. The meal was delicious, but she couldn't help but be intrigued by the man sitting opposite her. There was something about Mr. Wythe that captured her attention.

"So where are you from, Mr. Wythe?" Mother asked.

"Please, ma'am, could you not call me that? If you don't like Slim, how about Jake?"

She smiled. "Very well. Jake."

"I'm from up Dallas way, ma'am. My father has a spread up there."

"And what brings you to Lufkin?" Uncle Arjan asked.

"My aunt. She was up visiting my mama—her sister. I escorted her home and was planning to head back tomorrow. I guess I'll see what's happening with the storm before I get too devoted to the idea."

Arjan nodded. "That would be wise. So you'll stay with your aunt?"

"Yes, sir. She's by herself, so having me here during the storm could be useful."

Mother exchanged a look with Deborah. "I wish we'd known about your aunt. I would happily have had her join us here tonight."

"She was much too tired, ma'am. The trip was hard on her. Wore her out."

"I can understand that," Mother replied. "The trip up here this morning had me dreading the ride home. Our little narrow gauge to Perkinsville isn't exactly a smooth ride."

"That's understating it considerably," G. W. said with a grin.

"So what brought you folks to Lufkin?"

"G. W. and Lizzie were married this afternoon," Deborah said before anyone else could reply. She liked it when he fixed his blue eyes on her.

"A wedding, eh? So tonight we should give them a shivaree."

"I think the storm will provide all the wedding night interference needed," G. W. replied. Lizzie was turning three shades of red, and Deborah couldn't help but grin. She looked down at the table so that Lizzie couldn't see her response.

"Have you lived in Texas long?" Mother asked.

"All my life. I was born on the ranch." Jake fixed a smile on Lizzie and then on Deborah before looking back at Euphanel. "But I don't reckon the ladies are nearly as pretty up there as they are down this way."

"You are sweet to say so." Mother shook her head as if amused.

"Have you lived on the ranch all of your life?" Lizzie questioned.

He nodded. "For most of it. I was a few years at the Agricultural and Mechanical College of Texas."

"You attended college?" Deborah asked in surprise. Everyone looked at her as though she'd insulted the young man, and indeed, it was starting to sound that way to Deborah, as well. "I would have thought the ranch would have kept you much too busy to go away to school," she quickly added.

"My folks wanted me to be the first in the family to have a college education," he said proudly.

"I find that admirable," Mother interjected. "I'm sure your studies have benefited you, even in ranch life."

"Yes, ma'am. I learned a lot of mathematics. Got some military training, too."

"Military?" G. W. questioned.

"Yup. They require all the students to participate in the Corps of Cadets. My pa fought in the War Between the States and figured it would do me well to have some experience. My ma would just as soon there be no more wars."

Mother glanced at G. W. and Rob before replying, "I feel the same way. So tell us about your folks. Were they born here, as well?"

"Yes, ma'am. My granddaddy came to Texas in 1840. My pa was born the next year. We're Texan, through and through."

They heard the first drops of rain hit the small window behind the table. Deborah glanced over her shoulder and wondered again how bad the storm might be. The upstairs windows had all been shuttered against the weather, but a few of the downstairs windows were open to let in the night air. The hotel manager now moved through the dining room, closing these down.

"Sorry, folks, but the wind is pickin' up and will soon have the place drenched."

Most diners appeared unconcerned. They noted the situation, then went back to their conversation and food.

Deborah braved a glance at Jake and found him watching her. He smiled in a sympathetic manner. "Are you worried, Miss Deborah?"

"Concerned, but not overly worried. How about you?"

"Not for myself, but for my aunt. I should probably excuse myself." He got up and pulled the linen napkin free from where he'd tucked it into his shirt.

"Please give your aunt our best," Mother said. "I hope she'll forgive the oversight of not inviting her to join us. Perhaps another time."

He nodded. "I'll let her know." He started to leave, then paused. Looking directly at Deborah, he asked, "Will you be stayin' in town long?"

"It's doubtful," Uncle Arjan replied before Deborah could answer. "We have a loggin' business to get back to, and this storm could be wreakin' havoc on our livelihood. We'll head out as soon as it's safe to go."

"Well then, if I don't see you again, it was a pleasure." He smiled at each person then looked back to Deborah and winked. "Watch out for freight wagons."

She smiled. "I assure you, I won't make that mistake again. I'm normally quite capable of taking care of myself."

He headed to the door but called over his shoulder, "I don't doubt that for a minute."

That night, as the rain fell hard against the windows, Deborah enjoyed her mother's attention and conversation. With long determined strokes, Mother brushed Deborah's thick dark hair, just as she had long ago. There was something so very comforting in the action.

"He was certainly a charming young man," Mother began. "I think he was quite smitten with you."

"Oh, I hope not," Deborah admitted. "Although he was very kind. I certainly owe him my life. That wagon wasn't slowing for anyone."

"And he's educated. Perhaps there might be a future with him. I wouldn't be surprised at all if he makes it down to Perkinsville for a visit."

Deborah hadn't expected this from her mother. "First you talk of Dr. Clayton and me, and now Mr. Wythe. Goodness, but you sound as though you're trying to get rid of me, and I've only just returned."

Mother stopped and came around to face her. "I would never want to get rid of you, but you will find someone and fall in love one day. I think either of those men might be suitable choices."

Deborah shook her head and got to her feet. "I don't. Neither would be willing to remain in Perkinsville. I know for a fact that Dr. Clayton is only doing this to help his family. As for Mr. Wythe—well, he no doubt wishes to continue with the family ranch, and that's near Dallas."

"What are you saying, exactly?" Mother looked at her oddly. "You surely don't mean to suggest that you have to remain in Perkinsville for the rest of your life."

"Well, coming home only proved to me how much my skills were needed. Mother, you have no idea what a mess I found in the books. People owed us money and we owed them, and it was completely mixed up as to who was to receive what. Proper billings hadn't gone out. The only person who knew for sure what was going on was Uncle Arjan, and he kept most of the information in his head. That wasn't useful to anyone."

"He knew very well how to run this business, and don't you suggest otherwise."

Mother's stern response surprised Deborah. "I didn't mean to say he didn't. It was just that . . . well, while he knows what he's doing, no one else really had an understanding of it. What would happen if he died . . . like Father?"

Her mother frowned. "I don't think I could survive that."

Deborah hadn't expected that response but continued. "Exactly. None of us could have survived it easily. We would have had to talk to nearly everyone who'd done business with us to discover what we owed them and what they owed us. And we could only hope they didn't cheat us."

Mother reached out to touch Deborah's face. "I know you've always wanted to help, but I will not stand by and let you tie yourself to the business, forsaking happiness. I couldn't bear it if you fell in love and turned it away because you felt obligated to the family. We can always hire a bookkeeper, Deborah. True love is more difficult to find."

She considered her mother's remark for a moment. The idea of being needed by her family had always driven Deborah to learn—to excel in her studies. For certain, she loved knowledge, but there had always been that desire to better her family's situation. She had convinced herself over the years that she might somehow be able to guide them into a better life.

"I don't know what to say, Mother. I won't lie to you and tell you that I haven't believed it necessary to return and help you all. It was Papa's hope that I could attend school and help Vandermark Logging."

"Where did you get that idea, Deborah?" her mother asked.

"Your father wanted only for you to have the things you desired. He never wanted you to work or labor over anything."

"What are you saying?" Deborah whispered.

Mother looked at her oddly. "Did you only go to school because you thought your father wanted you to?"

Deborah felt an unwelcomed sensation run through her body. It was like suddenly realizing she'd been taken for a fool. "I thought I was needed."

"You are, darling," her mother replied. "But not at the price of your own happiness. You weren't made to be alone in this world." She smiled. "Not with a face like yours. Not with a heart like yours. Your aunt Alva sacrificed love for her family, and I won't see you do the same. Your father always used to say that there was a very lucky man out there somewhere who was going to be quite blessed to take you as his wife."

Deborah forced a smile. Her mother couldn't possibly understand her confusion, and to press for further answers might only serve to upset her. "I can just hear him saying that." Thoughts of her father were bittersweet. "I miss him . . . especially at times like this, with the storm. He always used to make me feel so safe when I was little. I would curl up on his lap and he'd wrap those big arms around me and hold me close. Nothing scared me then. I knew any harmful thing would have to come through him to get me."

Her mother smiled sadly. "He loved you—loved all of us dearly. He was taken from us too soon, but I know he's in a better place."

Deborah wrapped her arms around her mother. "I'm sorry if I made you sad or caused you to worry about me. Let's forget it for now. I'm happy to be right where I am. I don't want to think about leaving again. Not for a long, long while."

ꕥ

Lizzie knocked on her father's door and hoped he wouldn't mind the disturbance. She'd had so little time alone with him and wanted to talk to him before he returned home to his other family.

He opened the door and looked confused. "Is something wrong, Lizzie?"

"Not at all. I just wanted to speak to you for a few minutes."

He nodded. "Come in, but I have to tell you, a bride should be with her groom on their wedding night."

She entered the small room and smiled. "I'll have the rest of my life with G. W. I just wanted a few moments with you. I can't bear that you'll be leaving so soon."

"Well, I know I've only arrived here, but I've already been gone from home for over a month. First with my time in Philadelphia—then my travel here." He smiled. "I've missed you, Lizzie. I missed all of what might have been."

She swallowed down her grief. "I know that, Father. Mother always said you were much too busy to be bothered, but I always hoped that wasn't true."

"It was never true." He reached out to touch her face. "You were my pride and joy then and you remain so now. I only wanted the best for you, and I'm sorry that I didn't work harder to keep you with me. I was convinced it would be better for you in the long run if you stayed with your mother. Convinced, too, that a strife-filled house was no home. That's the reason I left as easily as I did."

"I know," Lizzie said, placing her hand atop his. "I always knew."

He nodded very slowly. "I prayed you would. Just as I pray now that you will never know such pain and separation. You have a good man in G. W. He loves you and he will move mountains to see you happy."

She smiled. "You've moved the only mountain in our way. I'm very blessed." She leaned up on tiptoe and kissed his cheek. "I love you, Father."

Chapter 23

"Looks like the house and barns bore the storm well," G. W. announced, sizing up the scene as they disembarked the train. The dogs caught sight of them and came running and howling.

"I do hope there wasn't any damage to the logging site," Deborah heard her mother tell Uncle Arjan amidst the baying of the dogs.

"Nothing we cain't handle, I'm sure," he replied. "The boys and I will get right over there and see what the situation looks like. Don't hold supper for us." Arjan looked to Rob and G. W. "Boys, fetch the horses." G. W. nodded, then gave Lizzie a quick kiss despite his brother's teasing.

"You two are upsettin' the dogs." Rob reached down to scratch the nearest hound behind the ears. "There now, don't be frettin', Decatur. They'll soon grow tired of each other."

"Hardly," G. W. said, winking at his wife. Lizzie blushed and looked away.

Sissy greeted them at the door with a big smile on her face. "Shore glad to see ya'll back safe. Blowed up quite a bit 'round here, but we held on tight."

"And how's David?" Mother asked.

"He be doin' fine, jest fine. 'Nother few days, and he be back to work."

Deborah waited until the men had gone to announce she was heading to town. "I want to see how things are going with the quarantine."

"Oh, quarantine done been lifted, Miss Deborah."

"That's wonderful news!" Deborah turned to Lizzie. "Do you want to come with me?"

"No, I'm weary from the train and have no desire to see Mother and Stuart just yet. You go ahead. If you don't mind, I'm going to go upstairs and move my things."

Mother nodded and turned to Deborah. "I don't like you driving into town by yourself."

"Iffen you like, Miz Euphanel, I ken ride into town with Miss Deborah."

Mother smiled and cast a quick glance at Deborah. "I would like that very much. Let me prepare a grocery list, and you can fetch what we need."

"I already done started one," Sissy said, laughing. "It be all up here." She tapped her head.

Deborah hurried upstairs to retrieve Dr. Clayton's medical journals. She was quite anxious to know how he was faring now that the quarantine had been lifted. Surely it meant that most everyone was on the mend.

She noticed that Lizzie was packing her things and felt a

momentary sense of loss. Mother had insisted Lizzie and G. W. take the big downstairs bedroom that had once been hers to share with Father.

"I'm going to miss you," Deborah said, clutching the journals. "It won't be the same without you. Still, I suppose G. W. would be rather unwilling to let you stay here."

Lizzie gave a little laugh. "G. W. wouldn't be the only one. You make a great friend, but I prefer rooming with my husband."

"You both seem so happy."

"Oh, we are. I never imagined it could be like this, Deborah." She seemed to glow with the joy that bubbled from within. "I'll happily live here the rest of my life."

"You won't miss Philadelphia?"

Lizzie looked at her as if she'd lost her mind. "There is nothing there to miss. You were one of the only friends I had. Mother certainly will have no use for me now." She sat down on the bed. "But you know . . . she never did. I was only a pawn in her chess game for women's rights. It makes me so sad, especially now that I'm a part of your family and know how it could have been." She paused. "It must have been hard to leave them and go away to school."

"I suppose it was at first, but of course, I was doing it for them. I knew I'd be back here one day."

Lizzie frowned. "What do you mean? I thought you went to school because you loved learning."

"Oh, I do. Don't get me wrong." Deborah held up the journals as if for proof. "I love to study, even now. Medicine is particularly fascinating."

"Or is it the doctor who fascinates you?"

Deborah found she couldn't reply. When she found her voice she simply mumbled, "Sissy's waiting on me. I'll be back before you know it."

She hurried from the room before Lizzie could comment further. Why would her best friend assume something was going on between her and Dr. Clayton? Was it possible for feelings to develop without a person realizing it?

If she lost her heart to someone like Dr. Clayton, it would interfere with her plans to help her family. He'd already encouraged her to study medicine, and while Deborah liked the idea, she still felt she couldn't let it take her away from the family's logging business.

There was no other choice. She would have to distance herself from Dr. Clayton . . . and from reading his medical journals.

On the ride into town she contemplated how best to handle the matter. Perhaps she'd just tell Dr. Clayton that with the increase of work the logging company had taken on, there would be no time for reading. She frowned.

I can't lie to him. It wouldn't be right. I've been able to talk to him about most everything. I'll just tell him the truth.

Sissy looked at Deborah and narrowed her dark eyes. "You shore look upset about somethin'. You comin' down sick?"

"No, I was just thinking about the work that needs to be done." At least that wasn't a lie. "I'm fine, honestly."

"Uh-huh."

Deborah had never been able to fool the older woman, so with a sigh, Deborah gave Sissy a hint of a smile. "I guess I'm just trying to figure out where life is taking me. I want to do what's pleasing to God, but I'm starting to wonder exactly what it is He wants me to do."

Sissy nodded. "Jest ask Him, child. He's faithful."

"I guess part of the problem is, I thought I knew what He wanted. All of my life, I've seen the lack of education keep Father and the boys from making a better way for themselves. So many people around here can't read—they have so little. I just wanted to help my family. Maybe I was wrong."

"Helpin' folks is good—ain't never knowed it to be wrong. You folks always done well enough, Miss Deborah."

"But I want so much more for them."

"Mebbe they didn't want more. Could be they were jest happy with life like it was."

Deborah thought about that for a few minutes. Perhaps Sissy was right. It was possible that Deborah, in her travels and education, had imposed her own dreams over those of her parents. But didn't everyone want a better life?

The question warred within her. Her father had always seemed happy enough. Rutger Vandermark was not known for complaining. Maybe that was because he had little to complain about.

Still, as good as that thought was, Deborah felt a sense of confusion. Since becoming old enough to think about others before herself, she had been driven to help her family find better success. She had thought it was up to her to learn whatever was necessary to help them further the business. Was it possible she had wasted her life seeking the wrong thing?

Sissy hummed an old hymn and kept the horse moving down the road. She seemed quite content, yet Deborah considered the woman's life difficult. Most white folks looked down on the people of color. The war had scarred and damaged the country. Even for the slaves who had been freed, Deborah saw fear and desperation. Everything they'd known for generations had been stripped from them. It wasn't so different from when they had been captured and forced into slavery to begin with.

The slaves had been set free, but it wasn't a true freedom. Even Sissy chose to come west to continue working for the Vandermarks. It was a comfort, Deborah had heard the older woman say. A comfort to have an understanding of the folks you were working with. Life had changed so little for Sissy, as was true of many blacks.

Deborah shook her head, but Sissy didn't seem to notice. "Are you happy, Sissy?"

"Gracious—I'm blessed through and through, Miss Deborah. Why you ask?"

Deborah shrugged. "I just wondered. You always seem happy." She smiled. "It encourages me."

Sissy laughed. "It be the joy of the Lord. Never forget God's joy, Miss Deborah."

Nodding, Deborah found herself longing for the confidence and happiness that Sissy had found in God. She supposed that Sissy's situation had left her with few choices. She could forsake God, thinking Him cruel for allowing her oppression, or she could turn to God for strength.

Sissy began humming again and then broke into song. " 'There is a balm in Gilead, to make the wounded whole; there is a balm in Gilead, to heal the sin sick soul. Sometimes I feels discouraged, and think my work's in vain, but then the Holy Spirit revives my soul again. Oh, there is a balm in Gilead . . .' "

She stopped and gave Deborah a big smile. "God always knows what dis old woman needs. Hard times or good," she said, as if reading Deborah's questioning mind, "He be a balm to my soul."

"But do you find yourself longing for more?"

Sissy chuckled. "Folks can always be longin' for more, Miss Deborah. It's the learnin' to be content what gets the soul through. Whether there be more or less—the Lord is my strength."

Ten minutes later, they arrived at the edge of town. It was good to see the bustling activity that suggested Perkinsville was very nearly back to normal. Deborah climbed down from the wagon almost before Sissy had brought it to a stop.

"I'll meet you back here shortly. I promise I won't be long." Sissy nodded and set the brake.

Deborah hurried down the still-muddy road and made her way to Dr. Clayton's. There were several people waiting outside the establishment, and a half dozen more greeted her when she entered.

Deborah greeted each person before approaching the office door. She peered inside but found no one. Slipping into the room, she closed the door behind her. No doubt Dr. Clayton was busy with a patient. She'd just write him a note and leave the journals.

Sitting at the desk, Deborah quickly located some paper and took up the ink pen. She thought for a moment on what she'd say, then began to write. She'd gotten no further than "Dear Dr. Clayton" when the examination room door opened and the man himself accompanied Sally Stevens from the room. In her arms was a small infant.

Dr. Clayton's face lit up when he spied her. "Miss Vandermark. This is a pleasant surprise."

Sally turned and smiled at Deborah. She held the sleeping baby up for Deborah to see. "Come meet my daughter Matilda. Doc says she's perfect."

Deborah got up from the desk and came to where Sally stood. "Oh, she's beautiful. I'm so happy for you."

"I was afraid John might be disappointed that she wasn't a boy, but he said he's mighty pleased."

"And how could he not be?" Dr. Clayton said. "Now, Sally, you remember what I told you about keeping things clean."

"I will. You can count on that." She looked to Deborah. "You'll let your mama know 'bout Matilda, won'tcha?"

"Of course." Deborah knew it wouldn't have taken any longer than attending church on Sunday for everyone to be caught up on the happenings of this small community, but she'd share the news just the same.

Sally left the office and Dr. Clayton turned to Deborah. "What brings you here?"

"I brought back your journals. I was just leaving you a note."

"Do you want to look through the stack and see what's there that you haven't already read?"

"No thank you. I've decided to put medicine aside and focus on my job." As he opened his mouth to respond, she hurried to change the subject. "What happened with the typhoid epidemic? Did we lose more folks?"

His expression revealed he wished to return to the subject of her decision, but he addressed her question instead. "We had two more deaths, for a total of ten. Everyone is on the mend now, and hopefully there won't be another outbreak. Folks have started following my instructions on cleanliness and boiling water."

"Good. I'm so glad to hear that. I don't suppose you'll ever convince Mrs. Foster, but at least others can see the good of it."

"On the contrary." He opened the examination room door and revealed Margaret Foster wiping down the exam table. "Mrs. Foster has become a great asset. Once she recovered, she began to work with me."

Deborah tried not to look too surprised, but she couldn't imagine the two people working together. "Hello, Mrs. Foster," she managed to say when the older woman made her way over.

"Afternoon. Your family escape the typhoid?"

"Yes, ma'am. We're all doing just fine. I must say, I never expected to find you working with Dr. Clayton."

The woman nodded. "God done a work in me, to be sure. My pride nearly cost me my life—other folks, too. Now I've mended my ways. Helpin' here is my way of makin' it up to the doctor."

"Like I told you before, Mrs. Foster, your apology was enough. Please call the next patient." Dr. Clayton turned to Deborah. "So as you can see, I'm doing much better than the last time we spoke."

"I've been praying that God would send someone to assist you." Deborah held further comments about never imagining it would be Margaret Foster who'd answer that need.

"Well, He certainly did that. Now, however, I'd best get back to work. As you saw out front, folks are making up for lost time." He grinned and escorted her to the side door. "It'll be easier to go this way."

Deborah turned to meet his gaze. She felt a strange emptiness at his dismissal. He obviously didn't need her—not that she'd expected that he did. "I'm glad folks have come around to seeing the good you have to offer."

He smiled. "Me too. I hated sitting around, taking Mr. Perkins's money without earning it. Guess those days are behind me."

As Mrs. Foster brought in another patient, Deborah knew there would be no opportunity to speak her mind. She supposed it wasn't really necessary that Dr. Clayton understand her situation. After all, he seemed perfectly content to work on without her.

She bid him farewell and made her way back to the commissary without so much as a backward glance. *I'm doing the right thing,* she told herself. *The necessary thing.* Then why did it leave her feeling so uncomfortable?

Sissy was already waiting in the wagon when Deborah climbed up. Neither made a comment as Sissy guided the horses toward the road home.

"Wait! Deborah Vandermark, don't you even think to leave without first speaking to me."

It was Harriet Decker. The woman was positively huffing and puffing like a steam engine as she bounded out from the boardinghouse. She came to a stop on Deborah's side of the wagon.

"Come down here immediately," the woman ordered.

Deborah looked at Sissy. "Excuse me." Climbing down, Deborah wondered exactly what she should say to the woman. She didn't have long to contemplate, however.

"I've heard the most appalling rumor—that my Elizabeth ran off and married your brother. Is it true?"

"It is." Deborah said nothing more, feeling the need to guard her words.

"She's already married to Mr. Albright! She cannot give herself to another." The woman's voice seemed edged with hysteria.

"She is not married to Mr. Albright," Deborah replied. "Mr. Decker arrived a short time back. He announced that he'd checked into the matter, and there was no real marriage. He secured Lizzie an annulment, just to satisfy any further protests, and that left her free to marry my brother."

"This is preposterous!" Harriet waggled a finger in Deborah's face. "This will not be tolerated."

Deborah shrugged. "Lizzie and G. W. are man and wife. The ceremony was legally completed in Lufkin and witnessed by the family. Your ex-husband even gave Lizzie away, so you see it was all done properly . . . this time."

Something between a moan and a wail broke from Mrs. Decker's lips. "I cannot believe how he goes out of his way to do me harm. You have no idea what you've done."

"Lizzie is the one who has stood up for herself and made her own way—just as you've always suggested she should. Now if you'll excuse me, I need to make my way home before the light is gone." Deborah stepped up and seated herself in the wagon.

"This isn't the end of the matter," Harriet Decker called out. "Mr. Albright will never allow for this."

"Mr. Albright will need to take it up with Lizzie's husband, then. Good day, Mrs. Decker."

Sissy snapped the lines and the horses continued past the boardinghouse. Deborah shook her head. Mrs. Decker wasn't known to back down from a fight, and this time would surely be no exception.

Chapter 24

Lizzie had known her mother would waste little time before making a scene at the Vandermark house. After Deborah reported their encounter in Perkinsville, Lizzie had steeled herself for what was sure to come next. When her mother and Stuart arrived the next day, Lizzie invited them into the front room as if nothing were amiss. She allowed her mother to be the one to bring up the topic. Which, of course, she did.

"I want to hear the truth from your own lips," her mother began.

"The truth of what?" Lizzie questioned, as if genuinely taken off guard.

Her mother's face turned several shades of red before she very nearly exploded her declaration. "You know perfectly well what I'm talking about. The matter of you marrying the Vandermark man while already being married to Mr. Albright."

"Oh. Well, the truth of that is quite simple. Stuart and I were never legally bound. Father checked into it and discussed it with some of the best legal minds in Philadelphia. Even so, he figured you might feel better if a formal annulment was filed. He did just that. I have copies of the papers, if you'd like to see them."

"Where is your father? I'd like to take this up with him. No doubt this is all part of some underhanded scheme of his. Legalities are never resolved so easily, and certainly not in a manner to benefit a woman."

"We parted in Lufkin after the storm passed through. He needed to get back to his family. He said you could contact him once you returned home if you had questions."

"You are a selfish girl. You have no idea what harm you've caused." Lizzie's mother turned to Stuart. "What of your father? Can he come to our aid? Can this situation be reversed?"

Stuart narrowed his eyes as he looked hard at Lizzie. "I would not have it reversed, madam. I do not want the leavings of another man."

Lizzie felt her cheeks grow hot, but she held her tongue. She was glad G. W. was away working; otherwise Stuart might well have suffered a broken jaw.

"Oh, this is most outrageous. You had no thought except for yourself. I cannot believe you would cause so much suffering, Elizabeth Cady Decker."

"Vandermark."

Her mother's eyes narrowed. "I don't care what you call yourself; you had a marriage first to Mr. Albright."

"And he clearly does not want me. He said so himself. Not that he has a choice in the matter." She smiled and got to her feet. "I suppose now you will want to return home?"

Mother stood, as did Stuart. "Stuart, I am sorry that you had to come all this way and lose important time with your business dealings. I know you needed to marry in order to receive your inheritance. Perhaps you will find another suitable prospect—someone who does not care about love. As for me, I could not marry for anything less."

"You'll have a lot less when I get done with you and your beloved Mr. Vandermark," Stuart stated matter-of-factly. "You think this to be over and done, but I assure you, I'm not one to stand for such treatment. You gave your word to me—accepted my proposal and planned a wedding with me. I will not forgive you for making me the fool." He picked up his hat and headed for the door.

Fear washed over Lizzie as Stuart's threat began to sink in. Her mother only gave her a smug look.

"You should have known better than to insult a man of means," her mother said. "You have sown the wind, and now you will surely reap the whirlwind."

Deborah sat beside her mother, while Rob and G. W. sat to the left with Lizzie. Uncle Arjan had said that it was important they all be at the gathering and give their honest opinions, but as of yet, Deborah wasn't at all sure what this was about.

"After careful consideration," Uncle Arjan began, "I decided to call this meetin'. I already talked to your mother about this, and we're in agreement. However, we won't move forward if there are any objections from you."

"Objections about what?" G. W. asked. "This isn't makin' a whole lot of sense."

Arjan gave a small chuckle. "I s'pose I am backin' into this rather than just going headlong. This is the situation: In order to build the company and expand the business to meet Mr. Perkins's contract, I'm of a mind to take out a loan. It's not somethin' I've considered lightly, but I think it's necessary. We need new equipment, extra mules, and workers. We'll need to work fast, too. My thought is to secure the loan, usin' the land as collateral. The risk is minimal to us, given that we have the contract with Perkins. However, should something happen to Perkins, I believe we'll have little trouble selling the wood to other mills."

G. W. nodded and looked to Rob. "Makes sense to me. What about you?"

"Sounds good."

Mother took that moment to speak up. "I believe this is what your father would have wanted. He had hopes of expandin' the business."

Uncle Arjan nodded. "There are other considerations, too. The house could use some repairs and expandin'. We'll have to work those things in as time allows or hire someone to help."

"I think it sounds like a good idea," Deborah offered. This expansion would keep her working harder than ever.

G. W. leaned back in his chair and crossed his arms. "Seems we're all in agreement. So what's next?"

"I'm thinkin' to go to Houston. I've already had word from a bank there. We shouldn't have any trouble gettin' the loan."

"When will you go?" Deborah asked.

"I figured to leave on Saturday. I can meet with the bank folks on Monday and set home that night if everything is worked out."

"They'll probably want to see a copy of our contract with Mr. Perkins," Deborah said thoughtfully. "I'll have that ready for you."

"They'll want the deed to the land, too," G. W. added.

"Your mother has already provided it," Uncle Arjan replied.

"Will you bring some new workers back with you? We've had a hard time with David not well enough to work, and like you said, when we go to cuttin' even more trees, we're gonna need extra help," G. W. said.

"I 'spect to bring at least five men back with me. They'll need a place to live, and your mother suggested we could bunk 'em at my cabin temporarily. It'll be a bit snug, but I think it will work out until we can help 'em get another place to stay. If they're family men, I'll speak to Zed about what's available in town."

"I prefer family men," Mother interjected. "They're more reliable—not so likely to go drink away their wages."

"If the weather holds and don't get too cold, they could use the tents," G. W. suggested.

"That's a good idea," Uncle Arjan said, nodding. "The other issue at hand is the growing problems we're having with the rooters. The razorbacks are startin' to be a real nuisance, eatin' the young trees and destroying any new growth."

"We've been thinkin' about ways to stop them, but it just ain't that easy," G. W. added. "Can't lay traps or somebody's livestock is likely to walk right into them."

"Can't fence, neither," Rob added. "You know how folks feel about that 'round here."

"Still, we have to find a way to protect the new growth," Deborah said, giving it serious thought. "When I was in school, I attended several lectures that discussed the idea of replanting. I realize most logging companies like to clear the land and move on, but we've always thought differently. This is our home."

"Our living, too," Mother agreed. "Your father always said it was important to be a good steward of the land."

"Are there other options for getting rid of the rooters?" Lizzie asked. "I mean, what about just shooting them and using the meat to feed the crew?"

"That's a good idea, but the rooters are mostly out at night. It would be tricky to have someone hunt them," Uncle Arjan replied.

"I think we should ask around and see what other folks are doin'," G. W. suggested.

"Dinner's on the table," Sissy announced from the hall.

Mother rose. "Thank you, Sissy. I suggest we head in to lunch."

Deborah got to her feet and the others followed suit. "Uncle Arjan could easily explore the matter while he's in Houston. Other logging industries must be dealing with the same problem. There might already be a ready solution."

"It's worth tryin'," her uncle agreed.

Christopher Clayton took a seat toward the back of the church and suppressed a yawn. He'd been called to deliver a baby in the middle of the night and this, added to the busy week he'd already endured, had left him exhausted.

Brother Shattuck stepped to the front of the church with a troubled expression. "Brothers and sisters, I've had some sad news come to me this morning. Apparently a group of troublemakers attacked a black man last night down by the mill pond. No one knows who the men were, but I suppose we can imagine why they felt the need to do this man harm. It comes as no surprise to anyone here that many whites hold a great deal of animosity toward those of a differing color."

Christopher wondered why he hadn't been informed or called upon to help the man. He had often been summoned across the tracks to treat the people of color. With Brother Shattuck's next statement, however, it became clear as to why the doctor had been unnecessary.

"The man died as a result of his injuries. He wasn't even discovered until an hour ago. He was a good man—a man with a family, just like many of the men in this congregation—but others decided he didn't deserve to live."

He moved down from the pulpit and came to stand directly in front of the pews. "I can hardly believe that civilized men would act in such a manner. There's not a man in this community who doesn't know sorrow and death, and in knowing such miseries, should not willingly give them to another. I'm more saddened than I can say."

There was a low murmuring in the congregation and the man beside Christopher elbowed him sharply. "Preacher ought to mind his own business and talk about the Scriptures." The woman beside him nodded in agreement.

The man to Christopher's left leaned forward. "Somebody ought to teach that preacher some manners."

Suddenly, Christopher felt wide awake.

"This country suffered a terrible division over slavery, among other issues," the preacher continued. "Like a family at odds with one another, this nation fought a war that left many without their fathers, sons, husbands, and brothers. They're mourning in the black church today, and our community faces dealing with the murder of Mr. Samuel Davis."

"Samuel?" Mrs. Vandermark stood in shock. "He used to work for us. Who would do such a thing?" She buried her face in her hands and began to weep.

Deborah came to her side and put an arm around her mother. "Brother Shattuck, is there something we can do to get justice for this man?"

"Justice?" someone questioned from behind Christopher. He turned to find an older man scowling. "Justice was probably already done served. Folks don't put others to death for no reason."

"That's right!" the man beside Christopher bellowed. "Sins of the fathers revisited on the children. That's in the Good Book."

Brother Shattuck's sorrow turned to disbelief. "Listen to yourself! That isn't what's happening here."

"My guess is that man committed a crime." This came from the man at Christopher's left.

"Then the law should have been summoned to deal with the situation," the pastor replied.

In a matter of moments, the entire church erupted in conflicting opinions. Christopher saw Deborah lead her mother from the church and followed after them. They'd barely stepped outside when Deborah's mother collapsed. Christopher stepped forward quickly and caught her before she fainted to the ground.

"Mother!" Deborah reached for her mother's hand.

"She'll be all right. She's had a bit of a shock. Where's your wagon?"

"Just over there," Deborah said as she pointed. "I'll lead the way."

Christopher followed her and gently eased Mrs. Vandermark onto the wagon bed. She rallied as Deborah tapped her hand.

"Mother, are you all right?"

"Oh, what's happened?" She struggled to sit up, but Christopher held her back.

"Take it easy. You fainted."

She looked up at him and shook her head. "How embarrassing." Her expression changed as she appeared to remember the reason. "Oh, poor Samuel. His wife must be beside herself. Two little children and no father. What in the world caused those men to kill him?"

Christopher met her tear-filled eyes. "I couldn't say."

"Hate," Deborah whispered. "That's what made them kill."

Christopher felt a chill run down his spine. No doubt she was right. He'd seen such things before and had hoped to never see them again. For a moment an unpleasant memory came to mind. Hate had been at the very heart of that horrendous moment from his past. Hate had very nearly taken a life then . . . just as it had taken Samuel Davis.

Chapter 25

October 1885

Deborah wasn't surprised that her mother insisted on helping Miriam Davis and her two young sons. Mother's compassion extended to everyone, but especially to those who had no means to help themselves. Not only was it fitting to help the widow and orphans as the Bible commanded, but Mother viewed former employees as extended family—even if their skin was the color of ebony.

"Did you remember the green beans?" Mother asked. Deborah helped her mother get up into the wagon.

"Yes, ma'am. Ten quarts, just like you said." Deborah hiked the skirt of her dark blue gingham dress and climbed up beside her mother. The early morning air had a hint of chill to it, but Deborah didn't expect it to last for long. The afternoons were still warm and sunny, sometimes hot. She loved this time of year. The hardwoods were starting to turn colors; the promise of things to come.

Sadly, she couldn't help but wonder if Samuel's death was also foretelling the future. Back East, she had seen ugliness directed toward many people—not only those whose skin was a different color. There had been many problems with hatred and prejudice toward the Irish and Jews, just to name two groups. Here in Texas, there was more than just a disliking of the Negroes—whites were quite negative toward the Mexicans, as well. In fact, Mr. Perkins wouldn't even hire those of Mexican or Indian blood. His grandparents had suffered under the Mexican government and Comanches had killed other members of his family years earlier.

"Do you suppose we'll see more killings?" Deborah asked as they drove to the Davis home. "A great many people around here seem to feel free to overlook what's happened."

"I hope there won't be further conflict. Arjan plans to speak to Zed about puttin' some additional men out to guard the area. Some old hatreds have stirred up since he hired new people to work at the sawmill. Sometimes it seems the war took place just yesterday."

Deborah focused on the road ahead. "I don't suppose folks will ever be willing to completely forget."

"And maybe they shouldn't, lest we repeat the wrongs. However, forgiving the past is important. My parents held slaves, and so did their folks before them. It's not something I'm proud of, but it's a fact. When Mr. Lincoln called for an end to slavery, my family complied. They believed that the law of the land was to be obeyed. They didn't agree with secession, but it caused them to face much ridicule and anger from their neighbors."

"But that war was about so much more than just slavery," Deborah countered. "I heard an esteemed statesman in Philadelphia. He spoke of the war as if it were really the final steps of our country's battle to become a nation. Until the war, we were simply a collection of individual states without a cohesiveness to join together as one. States' rights were always considered more important than that of the nation as a whole. The fight was also about bringing us together as one."

"Sometimes you have to tear down to build up," Mother replied. "But I don't like seein' where the bitterness has taken us. There will always be those who consider themselves better than their brothers, but the very idea of takin' a life because a person looks different—has a different manner of speaking or religion—that's just wrong. How can good Christian people act like that?"

Deborah shrugged. "Maybe because we aren't really as good as we'd like to think. Being a Christian doesn't mean we are perfect. Besides, don't forget slavery is discussed in the Bible. Many people used that as an argument to support and defend it."

"But now a woman is without a husband and her children without a father—and for what reason?"

Mother brought the wagon to a stop in front of the Davis home. There were several older women gathered near the open front door, while small children played in the dirt. Deborah helped her mother from the wagon, then went to the back to unload the goods they'd brought.

"Afternoon, Miz Vandermark," one of the women greeted.

Deborah heard her mother respond and ask after Miriam Davis. She was surprised when Dr. Clayton came from the house. He spoke momentarily to one of the women before spying her. He gave a brief wave and made his way to where she stood.

"Is someone ill?"

He nodded. "Mrs. Davis. She was expecting another baby, but sadly, she lost it. Poor woman was hysterical. I gave her something to make her sleep."

"First Samuel, and then a child." Deborah looked toward the house and thought of the family that lived there. She knew what it was to lose a father—the void could never be filled. She turned back to find Dr. Clayton watching her with such intensity that it caused her to tremble. "We . . . ah . . ." She waved her hand over the end of the wagon. "Mother wanted to bring the family some supplies."

"I'll help you carry them inside," he said.

Mother joined them. "Dr. Clayton, how good to see you. I hear that Miriam has suffered a miscarriage. Is she going to be all right?"

The doctor lifted a box of canned goods. "I believe she'll make a physical recovery, but she is devastated over the losses she's suffered. I was just telling Miss Vandermark that I gave Miriam something to help her sleep."

"That's for the best, I'm sure," Mother replied. "Is it all right if I go inside and speak with her sister?"

"Of course."

Mother led the way, while Deborah and Dr. Clayton followed behind with their loads. Inside, the cabin smelled of pork grease, tobacco, and death. In the corner, an old black woman sat and puffed on a pipe while keeping watch over Samuel Davis's body. Deborah nodded to the woman as they passed by.

Placing the box on the rickety dining table, Deborah took a moment to look around the cabin. It was terribly small—hardly big enough for one, much less four. The furnishings were mostly homemade and poorly constructed.

Miriam's sister Ruby came from the back room. Her eyes were red-rimmed, and she bowed her head as Deborah's mother took hold of her arm and spoke in a low, comforting voice.

"Ruby, we've brought some canned goods, cornmeal, sugar, and a couple of hams. I wanted to make sure the family had plenty to eat during this sad time."

"Oh, Miz Vandermark, what we gonna do without Samuel?"

"Don't fret. Now isn't the time. Miriam needs you to be strong for her." The younger woman nodded and began to sob as Mother embraced her.

"Why don't you take me to Miriam," Mother said, drawing Ruby with her toward the bedroom. "I know she's sleepin', but I just want to look in on her."

"I'll get the other boxes," Dr. Clayton told Deborah in a whisper.

Several of the women who'd been outside came in and gathered round the old woman. Deborah felt uneasy, almost like an intruder as a couple of the women began to wail. "I'll go with you."

He nodded and allowed her to go through the door first. Once outside, Deborah drew a deep breath of the fresh air and looked to Dr. Clayton. "Thank you for your help. If you need to get back, however, I can manage."

"Nonsense. I don't mind at all. In fact, I can get these last two boxes. Why don't you just wait here." It was more a command than a question. He hoisted one box on top of the other and headed back into the house.

Deborah leaned against the wagon bed and cast a quick glance around the yard. The children were still playing in the dirt, avoiding the awkward sorrow inside. The two Davis children, Jonathan and Saul, were among them. She thought to go and speak with them, but Dr. Clayton was returning.

"Thanks again," she told him. He smiled and she felt her stomach give a flip. The feeling took her by surprise. *What in the world is wrong with me?* She struggled for a moment to think of something to say.

Blurting out the first thing that came to mind, Deborah tried hard to push aside her discomfort. "Do you have any idea how we might trap wild hogs?"

Dr. Clayton looked at her oddly for a moment, stroking his chin as if truly considering the question. "I can't say that I've ever had to deal with wild hogs." His brows rose as he cocked his head to one side. "I don't think I've ever known anyone who wanted to trap a wild hog . . . until now."

Deborah looked to the ground. "I suppose it's just been on my mind. We're having trouble with the razorbacks eating the young pines. We were just talking about it and looking for ways to deal with them."

"What about fencing off your land?"

"No, that won't work. It's too expensive for one thing, but for another, folks around here despise fences. They want their cattle to graze freely. Fencing the land would only make enemies, and in time, folks would simply pull the fences down."

"I see. And I suppose you couldn't just fence small areas of these young trees? Maybe even around each small tree?"

"I suppose it's a thought," Deborah replied. "Very labor intensive, but possible. We talked about traps, but of course, with other animals moving through the area, it's too dangerous."

"That makes sense, but what of creating some sort of trap that would allow only something the size of the rooters to enter? Fix it in such a way that they couldn't get back out once they were inside. It would only contain them, not harm them."

"Is there such a trap?"

"I believe so. Your brothers are handy with tools—they might even build one of their own."

Deborah heard her mother's voice and turned to see her coming from the house. Mother reached out to take Dr. Clayton's hand. "Thank you for helping Deborah with the boxes."

Dr. Clayton put his hand over Mother's. "It wasn't a problem at all. Are you doing well? You look a bit tired."

"I am. This grief has kept me from sleeping at night."

"I could give you something to help," he offered.

She shook her head. "No, I use the time to pray. I figure if the good Lord wants me to sleep, He'll bring it about." She smiled and patted his arm. "I hoped that we might meet up with you while in town. I wanted to invite you to join us for supper tonight. Can you make it?"

"I believe I can." He looked at Deborah. "Perhaps we can talk to your brothers about building those pens."

Mother glanced to Deborah and then back to Dr. Clayton. "Pens?"

"For the rooters," Deborah explained. "Dr. Clayton has an idea of trapping them in a pen—something only big enough for them."

"And even if it caught other animals, it wouldn't harm them. Of course, the rooters might if they got inside with them. It's not without its dangers."

"We can discuss it over supper," Mother said. "I think Arjan would like to hear your ideas."

Christopher eased back from the Vandermark table and patted his stomach. "I must say, of all the folks who've blessed me with a meal, you offer the best. Just don't let it get around, or I might have to go back to cooking for myself."

"No, we'd simply have to have you here for supper every night," Mrs. Vandermark declared.

Christopher glanced across the table at Deborah. She was

beginning to captivate his thoughts in a most unexpected way. Several times a day, she would come to mind. He tried to tell himself that it was only because of her interest in medicine and how he thought she should be trained as a physician. But he knew better. It wouldn't be hard to lose his heart to her. Perhaps he already had.

"Doctor?"

He looked at Mrs. Vandermark in surprise. "I'm sorry. I was just thinking of other things. The meal was incredible. I've never had such delicious pecan pie. I'd love to send my mother the recipe. It's not as heavily sweet as the one she makes. I actually prefer it."

"I'd be happy to send her the recipe. It's one I brought with me when I moved to Texas. It goes way back in our family. Speaking of which, I don't believe I know much about your family. You came here from Kansas City, is that correct?"

Christopher drew a deep breath and nodded. "I did. My mother and father live there still with five of the children at home."

"That's right. I seem to recall there were fifteen children in your family."

"Yes. I'm the oldest."

"Goodness, but I can't imagine how your mother could even get through the day."

Laughing, Christopher easily remembered those times. "She is extremely efficient—much like you, Mrs. Vandermark. I have no doubt you'd handle it in easy order."

"You are sweet to say so," she replied. "Why don't you and the boys go discuss buildin' the pens now? Deborah can bring you more coffee."

Rob got to his feet. "I think Dr. Clayton's idea is a good one. I already have some ideas about how we can do it."

Christopher thought to excuse himself from the gathering, but a part of him didn't want to leave. He had come to enjoy this family.

They reminded him of home and of all that he was working for. His gaze settled on Deborah once again. He was treading dangerous waters. He'd come here with one purpose—to make money for his family. He needed to keep to his plan.

Chapter 26

November 1885

"I hope these traps work," Rob told G. W. as they secured the last of the makeshift pens. They pounded stakes to fix it to the ground, then adjusted the door.

"Should do just fine, long as the rooters go for the bait."

Rob pulled out a bucket of slop and poured it inside the pen. "Can't imagine them passing up a treat like this." He laughed and threw the bucket into the back of the wagon. "That makes six pens. Guess we'll see what happens in the mornin'."

Decatur and Jasper looked up from where they'd been lazing under a tall pine. At the sight of the boys loading their tools into the wagon, the two hounds got to their feet and stretched. The sun had dropped below the trees, and the damp air took on a chill that made everyone long for the warmth of home.

"So who you gonna take to the Christmas dance?" G. W. asked his brother. They climbed onto the wagon seat, and G. W. picked up the reins.

"Haven't decided if I'm takin' anybody. You take someone, then you gotta dance with them most of the night. I ain't got my fix on one gal just yet, so I may not ask anyone."

"That's gonna break many a heart," G. W. said, laughing. He reached for the brake as Decatur got wind of something and bounded off in the opposite direction, barking. Jasper followed suit.

"Guess they got the scent of a rabbit," Rob suggested.

"Rabbit stew would be a nice change of pace. What say we put off headin' home for a bit and follow after 'em?"

Rob nodded and grabbed his rifle. "Sounds good to me."

G. W. secured the reins, grabbed his own rifle, and jumped from the wagon. He couldn't think of anything he liked quite as much as his mother's baked rabbit stew. Just the thought made his stomach rumble.

The two men took off in the direction of the dogs, following the baying as Decatur and Jasper led them deeper into the woods. Just as they neared a freshly cleared area, the baying changed to more of a bellowing bark.

"I don't think it's a rabbit they're after," G. W. said as they slowed. "Maybe they've treed a cougar."

"Most of 'em have gone west—at least that's what Uncle Arjan says."

"I know, but it ain't impossible for them to still be around. One was spotted north of here just a couple months back."

Rob nodded, and G. W. pointed. "There they are."

They saw the two dogs had something backed up against the steep creek bank. Without warning, the animal charged, and the brothers could now see it was a razorback—by the look of its size, a male. Jasper quickly jumped out of the way, but Decatur wasn't so lucky. The hog took him by surprise and dragged the dog to the ground in a vicious attack. Blood spurted from Decatur's neck as the tusks dug in.

G. W. and Rob closed the distance to the ruckus. Rob fired his gun over the hog's head but found it did nothing to deter the beast. Jasper tried to join in the fight, but the hog simply knocked him out of the way. Yipping in pain, Jasper got up and charged again.

Rob yelled and fired the rifle, while G. W. called to Jasper and Decatur. Jasper came, although reluctantly, while Decatur was still locked in combat. Rob took careful aim and fired at the rooter. The animal moved, however, and the bullet just glanced off the thick shoulder hide. Even so, it caught the hog's attention, and it quickly abandoned its attack and ran for a brushy thicket upstream.

G. W. rushed to Decatur, while Rob chased after the rooter for a short distance. G.W could see that while the dog was still alive, he was mortally wounded. They would have to finish him off; otherwise, he'd suffer.

"Sorry, boy," G. W. said, reaching down to stroke the hound's bloody face. "You've been a good friend." Decatur whimpered in pain, and G. W. lost little time putting a bullet in the animal. It brought tears to his eyes to kill such a good companion. Jasper began to howl mournfully.

Rob walked back, shoulders slumped. "I lost track of him. I heard the shot and figured you had to put Decatur down."

"Yeah," G. W. said, shaking his head.

Rob handed him his rifle. "I'll carry him back to the wagon. We can bury him at home. If we leave him here, that rooter will just dig him up."

G. W. nodded. "You're right. Let's go."

After a week, the traps proved to be a good investment. They had captured more than ten rooters, and the family shared the meat among the Vandermark workers. Deborah was deeply sorrowed at the loss of Decatur but certainly no more than Jasper and Lula. They seemed to mope around, seeking far more attention than they had before the death.

"I suppose animals mourn as do we humans," Deborah told Lizzie as they sat together on the porch. "Still, it seems so sad. They can't understand or be comforted by mere words."

"I think they're comforted, just the same," Lizzie said as she stroked Jasper's long silky ears. He placed his head in her lap and rested there while the ladies conversed.

"I wish the train would come. I'm so excited about going to Houston, I can hardly stand the wait," Deborah said, getting up again to look down the tracks. They were waiting for the southbound log train in order to catch the Houston East and West Texas line in Perkinsville. It had been determined that since Arjan had secured the loan for the Vandermark expansion, G. W. and Rob would escort Lizzie and Deborah to Houston, where they could buy extensive supplies for the business. If the Rabbit kept any kind of schedule, they'd be bound for Houston before nightfall and hopefully settling into their hotel sometime the next morning.

For Deborah's part, she hoped to buy a crate of books to keep her busy during long evenings. She didn't know how she could feel so lonely in a house full of people, but she often did.

"I hear the whistle," Lizzie declared, jumping to her feet. "G. W., the train is coming!"

She went inside the house and called again. Deborah could

hear her brothers respond and reached down to pick up her valise. Mother came from the house to bid her good-bye.

"Are you sure you won't come with us?" Deborah asked. "We'll have a great time."

Mother smiled and shook her head. "No, Arjan and I have a lot to do. We need to get that pork smoked, and I have to make sausage and soap."

Deborah frowned. "Maybe I should stay."

"Nonsense. I've hired Miriam and Ruby to help Sissy and me. They need the money, and the work will help keep their minds occupied."

Reaching out, Deborah hugged her mother close. "I know they'll appreciate your kindness."

The train chugged slowly to a stop aside the Vandermark property. The small siding train wasn't all that powerful, but it got the job of hauling logs to Perkinsville done in good order. Jack waved from the engine compartment.

"Come on, boys! Train's a-waitin'," Mother called.

G. W. and Rob came from the house carrying the rest of the suitcases. Two trunks were already by the rails. They made quick work of loading the bags, then assisted Lizzie and Deborah into the engine before they climbed atop one of the log cars.

"Let's go!" G. W. called out. They all waved to Mother. "We'll be back as soon as possible."

"Be careful. I love you all." Mother returned their waves.

In Perkinsville, Lizzie found a letter waiting for her. She held it up to Deborah. "It's from Mother."

"Well, open it and see what she has to say," Deborah encouraged. "Perhaps she's accepted the idea of you marrying G. W."

"I seriously doubt that." Lizzie opened the missive and scanned the lines of script. "It's just as I thought. She's telling me how I have solely managed to undermine the suffragette cause—delaying the vote for years, maybe even decades."

"You are such a powerful foe," Deborah said, smiling.

Lizzie continued. "She said that Stuart's father was giving serious consideration to pursuing the matter of my annulment, but . . ." She stopped speaking and looked up in surprise, "Stuart has married."

"Oh, that is good news." Deborah leaned closer and glanced down at the letter. "Does she say who he wed?"

Lizzie nodded in surprise. "Yes. He married Jael."

"Our Jael?" She was the only other real friend that Lizzie and Deborah had known in Philadelphia.

"Yes. Listen." Lizzie turned her attention to the letter. "Mother says, 'He returned home a heartbroken man, and when Jael learned of your treachery, she eagerly sought to offer him comfort. The two were quietly married a short time later. Stuart's father not only welcomed the match, he praised his son for the union. I hope you realize what you've lost.'"

Lizzie looked up. "I cannot believe Jael would marry such a man. She never cared all that much for Stuart."

"I thought, in fact," Deborah said, putting her finger to the side of her temple, "she was in love with Ernest Remington."

"I did, too. She told me the night before my wedding to Stuart that she fully intended that theirs would be the next wedding to take place. She seemed quite convinced."

"Apparently things have changed."

Deborah shook her head slowly. "This will certainly complicate our friendship with her."

"To say the least."

Houston had grown at a rapid rate and looked nothing like Deborah remembered. Now boasting nearly ten thousand residents, the town had blossomed into a bustling city to rival some of those back East. Of course, it had a long way to go to match Philadelphia, but it was well on its way.

The foursome settled into a small but elegantly appointed hotel. It was determined that in order to save money, the ladies would share a room and the brothers would take another. G. W. looked less than pleased at the arrangement but said nothing.

The train trip had been anything but restful, so rather than strike out for the day, everyone in the party decided a brief nap might serve them well. G. W. and Rob, however, changed their minds and came to tell the girls their plans.

"We're goin' over to the bank," G. W. said. "I need to make sure there are no problems with our credit so we can get started right away in buyin' the equipment."

Deborah barely suppressed a yawn. "When will you return?"

"Before evenin'. You and Lizzie sit tight," G. W. instructed. "This is no place for you to go off gallivantin'. We'll be back in time to take you to supper. If you get hungry before then, you can get a meal downstairs."

"Very well," Deborah said, though she already had in mind that after she and Lizzie rested, they might visit some of the nearby shops. She appreciated G. W.'s protective nature, but honestly, she saw nothing to fear. There were hundreds of people walking about on the street. A person would have to be a fool to accost another, for surely half of those present would come to the aid of the afflicted person.

G. W. kissed Lizzie quite soundly before giving Deborah a questioning look. "Are you sure you don't want to bunk in with Rob?"

Deborah laughed, much to Lizzie's apparent embarrassment. "He snores. Lizzie doesn't."

G. W. nodded. "Don't I know it."

After the men had gone, Deborah and Lizzie stretched out in the bed. They dozed comfortably for nearly two hours, and when Deborah rose, she found Lizzie standing at the window.

"Is something wrong?"

Lizzie turned and smiled. "No, silly. I just wanted to see what was out there. You know, for as large as Houston is, it still seems rather primitive."

Deborah straightened the covers and sat on the end of the bed in order to secure her boots. "I'm sure the shops will still have a better selection than we can get at home."

Lizzie came to her. "You aren't thinking of going out, are you? G. W. said—"

"I know what he said, but I'm a grown woman. I fared for myself just fine in Philadelphia, and I will fare for myself fine in Houston. Remember—I once attended finishing school here. Of course, that was quite a few years ago and the town has changed a great deal, but I can't imagine there being a problem. You will come with me, won't you?"

"I shouldn't," Lizzie said. "G. W. wouldn't like it at all."

"He's too protective of you."

Lizzie looked at Deborah for a moment, then sat down beside her. "I've been longing to tell you something."

"What is it?"

Lizzie's cheeks reddened. "I believe I'm with child."

Deborah let out a squeal of joy and grabbed Lizzie to hug her. "Oh, what happy news! No wonder G. W. doesn't want you to go out on your own."

"G. W. doesn't know yet. I wanted to surprise him at supper.

Hopefully, he'll forgive me for telling you first, but I wanted you to help me surprise him."

Deborah nodded. "To be sure, I will. We should talk to the hotel manager and ask about a suitable restaurant. Tonight must be very special. Come on. We can go shopping tomorrow. For now, we need to prepare. We'll probably need a long-handled broom."

Lizzie looked at Deborah in confusion. "Whatever for?"

"To sweep G. W. off the ceiling after he hears the news." They giggled, pressing their heads together like two little girls with a secret. Then Deborah straightened and sobered just a bit. "Of course, we might also take smelling salts with us . . . just in case."

CHAPTER 27

With the arrangements made for a special supper, Deborah found that they still had plenty of time to explore the shops near the hotel. She convinced Lizzie to join her but knew her friend was feeling uncomfortable as they ventured outside.

"G. W. isn't going to like this, Deborah."

"Once he sees that we've returned unscathed, everything will be fine. He should have seen us in Philadelphia."

Lizzie shook her head. "No. No, he would never have approved of that. We were rather . . . reckless at times."

Deborah grinned. "I suppose so, but we weren't as wild as some. Oh look, the shop across the street carries fabric. Let's go explore."

They maneuvered across the busy street narrowly avoiding

several carriages before reaching the other side. Deborah pulled Lizzie into the shop.

"Welcome, my dears," an older woman greeted them. "Are you looking for anything particular today?"

"We need some material for making diapers and baby clothes," Deborah announced.

The woman nodded and led them to a stack of flannel. "This is the best for making diapers."

"How much do you suppose we should purchase?" Lizzie asked.

"Well, ten yards will make you a little more than a dozen diapers," the woman told them. "You'll want at least two dozen diapers available to you, and if you can afford it, I highly recommend three dozen."

"That sounds good. We'll take enough for three dozen," Deborah said, then looked to Lizzie. "Does that sound good to you?"

"I can't imagine a baby ever needing so many diapers, but if you say so," she replied, looking at the woman as if for confirmation.

"Believe me, you'll be glad for them," the saleswoman assured her. "Now, come this way, and I'll show you some wonderful fabric for little gowns."

They spent half an hour picking out material and another twenty minutes in choosing buttons and trims. They ordered the things to be delivered to the hotel and then continued down the street, glancing in store windows as they went. Turning onto one of the side streets, Deborah pointed to a millinery shop.

"Oh, look there—just beyond that small alleyway." She led the way. "Let's go inside. That little straw hat would be perfect for Mother."

"We've already been gone for some time," Lizzie said, glancing back down the street in the direction they'd just come. "Don't you suppose we should go back?"

"It's just now four o'clock. We can take another half hour, at least." Deborah entered the shop and quickly forgot about the time.

By the time they exited, the sun was beginning to set in the west. "I suppose we'd better go back," Deborah said, shifting the hatbox to her left hand. She looped her arm through Lizzie's. "After all, we want to get you all dressed up for dinner. No sense in making such a wonderful announcement looking all shoddy."

"I look shoddy?" Lizzie questioned in horror. She looked down at her gown.

"No, silly. You look just fine. I was only teasing you. Come on."

They had reached the alley when a man dressed in a sorry-looking black suit came hurrying out. He plunged between them as though trying to get past. Without warning he turned and slammed Lizzie backward. She stumbled into the wall of the building, while the man reached for Deborah. Realizing he meant no good, she swung the hatbox hard against his arm. Her action momentarily stunned the man.

"Unhand me," Deborah demanded. Perhaps the man was drunk. Perhaps he was a thief. Either way, she wasn't going to stand for him molesting them. She went to Lizzie and took hold of her arm.

The man rushed at them and grabbed at Deborah's waist for her chatelaine. "Give me your money!"

Lizzie screamed for help, but Deborah knew she would have to defend them as best she could until help arrived. She tried again to knock the man out of the way with the hatbox, but this time he was ready for her. He ripped the parcel from her and tossed it to the ground.

In one motion, Deborah hiked her skirts and kicked the man

hard in the shins. She then turned and pushed Lizzie toward the street. "Get help!"

The ruffian took hold of Deborah and swung her back against the hard brick wall. The action infuriated Deborah, and she kicked him again, but this time her skirts wrapped around her legs, deflecting the blow. Doubling her fist, she sent a punch into the man's face with all the force she could muster. Pain coursed through her hand and up her arm. Hitting someone wasn't nearly as easy as her brothers made it look.

"I'll teach you a lesson you won't soon forget." The man gave a growl and reached out to twist Deborah's right arm to her side.

Frantic to maintain some sort of control, Deborah screamed and pummeled the man with her left hand. He took the first blow in the shoulder and grunted, but still refused to let her go. She doubled her efforts with the second attack, but this time he ducked. To Deborah's surprise, however, her fist connected with another man—her would-be rescuer.

The man let go of Deborah and whirled around to face this new adversary. Deborah hurried to the opening of the alley, where Lizzie awaited her. By now a couple of cowhands had come to their rescue, as well, with a police officer following close behind. The thief didn't stand a chance to escape.

Once the man was manacled and taken away, Deborah turned to thank her original rescuer. To her surprise, it was none other than Mr. Wythe. He beamed her a smile and pointed to his reddened eye.

"You pack quite a wallop, Miss Vandermark."

"Mr. Wythe! What are you doing here?"

"I'm in Houston selling bulls for breeding. I recognized your sister-in-law and was crossin' the street to say hello when she started hollerin' for help."

"Oh, am I ever glad you were here," Deborah replied. "Imagine—someone trying to rob us in broad daylight!"

"Well, it's not exactly that," he said, waving a hand to the twilight skies. "Can I escort you ladies somewhere?"

"We're at the hotel just around the corner and down a block." Deborah looked to Lizzie. "You weren't hurt, were you?"

"No, just scared."

Deborah nodded. "Me too."

Jake laughed. "You didn't look scared. You looked mad."

"I was that, too. I tend to get angry when I'm afraid."

He took hold of Lizzie's arm and then reached for Deborah. "I'll keep that in mind for the future."

He led them toward the hotel, talking all the while about his new purchases and the affairs of the ranch since he'd last encountered them.

"I never figured to see you two here. I did, however, give some thought to stopping off in Perkinsville on the way back north." He threw Deborah a grin.

The comment took her off guard. She wasn't at all certain what to say, so she changed the subject. "Seems you've become my guardian angel once again, Mr. Wythe. I thank you for the help."

"No problem. What, if you don't mind my askin', were you two doing out unescorted anyways? Houston can be kinda rough."

Deborah tried not to sound offended. "I hadn't expected trouble. I attended finishing school here some years ago and . . . I was remiss in considering the changes."

He nodded, looking as though he were pondering a great mystery. "I suppose you were well protected back then."

Deborah couldn't deny that fact. She was never allowed to go anywhere without the escort of someone from the finishing school. "So how long will you be in Houston?"

"I leave tomorrow. I've been here for a week already. I found a prime bull and some great heifers. I plan to strengthen our herd when I get back home."

By now, they'd reached the hotel and Deborah motioned Lizzie inside. Her friend paused, however. "Mr. Wythe, would you care to join us for supper?"

Deborah held her breath. She had hoped they could get by without having to explain their trouble to G. W. and Rob. Neither would be happy with her.

"It would be a pleasure, ma'am, but I'm afraid I can't." He looked to Deborah and boldly gave her a wink. "Although I'm mighty tempted."

Deborah looked away quickly. She tugged on Lizzie's arm. "That is a pity, Mr. Wythe, but we do understand. We'll bid you good day, and thank you once again."

He gave a little bow and chuckled. "You are welcome, Miss Vandermark, and don't be surprised if I don't turn up for a visit one of these days."

She nodded uncomfortably and hurried Lizzie up the steps to the hotel. Inside, she finally let out the breath she'd been holding. "Lizzie, what were you thinking inviting him to supper? We can't let G. W. and Rob know what happened. If they saw Mr. Wythe and he mentioned the situation he found us in—why, we'd never hear the end of it."

"I don't imagine we deserve to hear the end of it," Lizzie said. Deborah continued pulling her up the stairs. "G. W. would want to know."

"Well, as my mama used to say, 'Wantin' and gettin' are two entirely different things.'"

They reached their room without further mishap. Deborah unlocked the door and all but pushed Lizzie into the room. It wasn't until they were inside with the lock secured that Deborah let down her guard.

"I was afraid G. W. and Rob might return and find us out there. Now we can just pretend that nothing happened."

"They're going to know we went out. The fabric will be delivered in the morning."

Deborah looked around the room. "Oh bother—I forgot about the hat I purchased. I suppose it's lost forever." She frowned and began taking the pins from her own hat. "It was such a lovely hat, too. I suppose it's a small price to pay." She looked at Lizzie's doubtful expression. "I don't mind them knowing about our outing, as much as what beset us during that time. Still, if it doesn't come up, there's no sense causing them to worry. Now, let's put it aside and talk about what you're going to wear tonight. You have a big announcement to make."

G. W. had never seen his wife looking more radiant unless it was the day they'd married. Tonight she seemed to even outshine that glorious event. She and Deborah kept their heads together through a good portion of the meal, but finally as dessert was served, they seemed less preoccupied.

"This chocolate cake is delicious," Deborah said casually. "I think I would very much like the recipe. Do you suppose the cook would let us have it?"

Her brothers shrugged. Rob stuffed another bite into his mouth and nodded. "It is mighty fine."

"Don't speak with your mouth full," Deborah chided.

"She's startin' to sound more like Ma every day," Rob said with a frown.

"Speaking of mothers . . ." Deborah let the words trail off and looked to Lizzie.

"What about them?" G. W. looked perplexed.

Deborah elbowed Lizzie. "Go ahead."

G. W. frowned. "Does this have to do with that letter your ma sent?"

Lizzie shook her head. "No. Not in the least. I . . . well . . ." She looked at Deborah before turning back to her husband. "We're going to have a baby."

Nothing could have surprised him more. G. W. looked at Lizzie and then Deborah. Maybe he'd misunderstood. He glanced at Rob, who by this time was grinning from ear to ear. He punched G. W.'s arm.

"Well, if that ain't something. Congratulations there, big brother."

G. W.'s gaze was locked with Lizzie's. She smiled ever so slightly—almost shyly. "A baby? For sure?"

She nodded. "I've been pretty certain for a while now, but I wanted to wait. I hope you aren't displeased. It is rather soon."

"I couldn't be happier." G. W. leaned over toward Lizzie and kissed her gently on the cheek. "A baby."

"Why, hello there."

G. W. looked up to see Mr. Wythe. He was grinning and holding a battered hatbox. "Mr. Wythe. It's a surprise to see you."

"I just dropped by to bring this to Miss Vandermark. The clerk at the desk said you were in here havin' supper, so I thought instead of leave it with him, I'd deliver it personally."

G. W. was confused. "How did you know we were staying here?" Just then he noticed the younger man's black eye. "What in the world happened to you?"

Wythe put his hand to his face. "Your little sister packs a wallop. That's what happened to me."

A feeling of dread washed over G. W. He looked to Deborah for an explanation. "You have something to say?"

She clamped her lips together and shook her head. G. W. then looked to Lizzie. "What's this all about?"

"You mean you didn't tell your brothers what happened?" Mr. Wythe asked Deborah.

"I didn't see the need," she said in a rather curt manner. "After all, no harm was done."

"Except for Mr. Wythe's eye," Rob threw out. "That's quite a shiner."

"It was an accident," Deborah declared.

"Yeah, the man she intended to hit ducked. I just happened to be behind him."

"I guess you'd better have a seat, Mr. Wythe, and tell us the whole story. I'm not likely to get it out of my sister anytime soon."

The man laughed. "Wish I could stay, but fact is, I've got other business to tend to. Like I said earlier, I just wanted to drop this off." He handed the hatbox to G. W. "I hope you'll excuse me now."

G. W. got to his feet. "Thank you for your . . . Well, I'm sure you were probably very helpful. Knowing my sister, I can only imagine what mighta happened. Of course, she was supposed to be safely asleep here at the hotel, but somehow I get the feelin' that wasn't how she spent her afternoon."

Mr. Wythe gave a chuckle. "I'll leave it to her to tell. Evenin' to y'all."

G. W. didn't even wait until Wythe had departed the dining room. He turned to Deborah and Lizzie. "Somebody better start talkin'."

Deborah shrugged. "We went shopping."

"We? You mean Lizzie went, too?"

She glanced at the now-empty dessert plate. "I did."

"I thought we had an agreement." G. W. shook his head. "What happened?"

"It wasn't our fault," Deborah began. "We were walking back to the hotel when a man tried to get my money."

"Deborah hit him and actually was faring pretty well when Mr. Wythe came along," Lizzie added.

G. W. shook his head. "It ain't safe for a lady to walk around unescorted down here. Please promise me you won't go out alone again."

Lizzie put her hand atop his forearm and nodded. "I promise."

As they walked back to their rooms, Deborah took G. W. aside. "I'm really sorry. I know you're mad at me, but I'm asking you to forgive me."

G. W. eyed her for a moment. "I don't know what I would do if something happened to one of you. You're the smartest one of us, yet sometimes you don't use the sense the good Lord gave you."

"You're absolutely right," Deborah agreed. "I suppose I get in my mind that I can do a thing without the help of anyone else. I'm sorry. It won't happen again. I promise." She squeezed his arm. "Please forgive me."

"Of course I forgive you." He smiled and led her to the room. "We'll knock on your door in the mornin' when it's time to go down for breakfast. Then we'll take you out shoppin'."

Deborah stretched up on tiptoe and G. W. bent down for her to kiss his cheek. "Good night, brother of mine."

G. W. waited as she opened the door. He peaked in at Lizzie and motioned her to the door. Lizzie stepped into the hallway with him, and after a quick glance down the hallway, she wrapped her arms around him. G. W. pulled her close and lifted her face to meet his. He felt her melt against him as he kissed her.

"I'm so happy," he declared.

"I was worried that you'd think it too soon," Lizzie said, pulling back just a bit.

"God's timing is never too soon or too late. This baby will be right on time." He grinned and kissed her once more on the forehead. "I'm gonna miss you tonight."

He released his hold on her and she stepped back. "No more than I'll miss you." She opened the hotel room door and paused. "Maybe I can convince Deborah to share Rob's room. I'll start working on her tonight."

G. W. laughed and waited until she'd closed the door. Maybe they should just splurge on an extra room.

Chapter 28

Christopher was surprised and concerned to find Euphanel Vandermark sitting in his waiting room when he finished with one of his patients. He reached out to help her up from her chair.

"Are you ill?"

She shifted her basket to her left hand and reached in with her right. "Not at all, Dr. Clayton. I've come with a plate of cookies and an invitation."

He eyed the gift and couldn't suppress a smile. "What a pleasant surprise. Now, what is it you're inviting me to?"

"Thanksgiving dinner. I hope you haven't already made other arrangements."

"Not at all. I would love to share your table. Is there something I can bring?"

"Just yourself," Euphanel replied. "I know the family will be delighted to see you. Especially Deborah."

He considered her comment for a moment. Deborah had been on his mind a great deal lately, almost against his will.

"I understand she's in Houston."

She nodded. "They're due back the day before Thanksgiving. Sissy and I have already started workin' on the arrangements. She'll be with her own family and friends for the day, but we'll get much of the work out of the way the day before. I wanted to arrange it so that Deborah and Lizzie didn't feel obligated to jump right in and work."

He smiled and reached under the cloth to sample a cookie. "I'm sure they'll want to help, no matter how much you've managed to set in place." He bit into the cookie and found a wealth of spices and nuts. "Mmm, this is wonderful."

"I'm glad you like them. They go well with coffee. They're a pumpkin nut cookie that Sissy created. Our family is quite fond of them."

"I can see why."

"Well, I should let you get back to work," Euphanel said, turning for the door.

"I'm not exactly overwhelmed at the moment."

She stopped and looked at him over her shoulder. "Is there somethin' on your mind?"

He was taken by surprise. "Why do you ask?"

Euphanel turned and her expression reminded him very much of his own mother. "You just seem to . . . well, you seem deep in thought."

Christopher acknowledged her perception, but he wasn't all that comfortable in sharing the truth. "I just appreciate your kindness. I miss my family, and you've helped to fill that void by allowing me to be a part of yours."

"And, of course, there's Deborah."

He looked at her and shook his head. "What do you mean?"

Euphanel looked thoughtful. "I suppose I shouldn't say anything. After all, I've only got my own intuition to go on." She shrugged. "But in my opinion, it's obvious the two of you were meant for each other."

Stunned, he felt his eyes widen. "I . . . well . . . Deborah is a wonderful young woman."

"She is that, and I believe she thinks you a wonderful man. You have a great deal in common."

Christopher didn't know what to say. How could he explain to Deborah's mother that he had lost his heart to her daughter but intended to do nothing about it?

"You know, Dr. Clayton, if you don't put your claim to her, someone else will."

He frowned. "It isn't that easy."

"And why not? Have I misunderstood how you feel about her?" She fixed him with a puzzled look. "Do you plan to go through life alone?"

"Not at all. But there is the matter of my family. My father is unable to work. My mother cannot earn enough to properly care for the family. There are a lot of mouths to feed and bodies to clothe. Without my help, they wouldn't be able to make it very well."

"And you think this would be a problem for Deborah? Why, she would fully support you in such a matter. She's doin' much the same for her own family—only we aren't in as great a need."

"But without a wife and children of my own, all of my extra money can go back to them. A wife would eventually want and need things of her own. Children would most certainly come along, and they, too, would have needs."

"Still, it would be a shame to let true love pass you by. There has to be a way to have both. My guess is that you could probably ask Deborah to wait for you, and she would."

He couldn't help but grin. "You truly think she cares for me that much?"

"I do, but like you, she has it in her mind that she must sacrifice herself for us. It's nonsense, but still, it's her belief. You see, she went away to school to help the family. Had I realized what her deepest heartfelt thoughts were on the matter, I might have refused her."

"But why?" Mrs. Vandermark's comment truly confused him.

"Because she's wrong. Her efforts have benefited us, no doubt about it. I greatly appreciate her desire to improve our business arrangements and handle them efficiently. However, in speaking with her recently, she left me with the impression that she believes she can't marry and risk leavin' us. I told her she was wrong. Perhaps if you give her something more to consider, her opinions will change."

"But it might be years before I could actually wed," he replied.

"All the more reason to secure her hand." Euphanel smiled and resumed her walk toward the door. "Pray about it, Dr. Clayton. I think you'd make a wonderful son-in-law."

Deborah felt a sense of peace and happiness wash over her as her family gathered to celebrate all that God had done for them. Thanksgiving was not taken lightly in this family. Not only was it a time to celebrate a good year of harvest, but it had always been a celebration of God's goodness. For as long as Deborah had memory, she had shared in the family tradition of naming the thing or things she was most grateful for. Each member of the family would tell about the blessings of the year and how God had answered prayers. Mother even encouraged them to keep a journal about it and then share the biggest blessings at the table.

This year was certainly no exception. With the table nearly bowing from the plates heaped high with food, Mother turned to Arjan and nodded. He stood and cleared his throat. "As you know, your father started this time of sharing on Thanksgivin'. I have been blessed to be a part of this family and carry on that tradition."

Deborah glanced at Lizzie. She'd not yet told Mother and Uncle Arjan about the baby. G. W. had suggested she wait and deliver the news during their dinner. Deborah felt almost giddy with delight. They'd had such a wonderful time in Houston, shopping for the baby's needs, as well as Lizzie's. Deborah couldn't help but wish she might also bear a child one day.

Of course, I would need a husband first, she told herself. She glanced across the table to where Dr. Clayton sat. He seemed to be watching her and offered a bit of a smile before turning his attention back to Arjan.

Deborah felt her heart skip a beat. *Goodness, but what is wrong with me? I find myself unnerved by the silliest things.*

She looked up and found Mother getting to her feet as Arjan took a seat.

"I'm so thankful for all of you. My children have always been a delight to me, but now I have the joy of adding another daughter to the family. What a blessing Lizzie has been to me. Deborah, you have also blessed me with your love and care for this family. Even though it's never been your burden to take on, I want you to know that I appreciate and understand your efforts. That said, however, you must also know that I will never stand by and allow for you to let life pass you by."

Surprise must have clearly registered on Deborah's face, because Mother paused. Reaching out, she gently touched Deborah's shoulder. "Don't be so shocked by my words. It's not like I'm sendin' you away." She gave Deborah a squeeze, then went back to reciting her list of blessings.

Deborah could scarcely concentrate on the words. She couldn't imagine what had caused Mother to say those things. It hardly seemed appropriate. What must Dr. Clayton think?

"I have so much to be thankful for, and perhaps one of the sweetest gifts is that God has clearly mended my heart. I was devastated to lose your father, but over the years, I have felt release from that pain. I believe part of it came in G. W. learnin' to forgive himself for what he saw as his role in Rutger's death." She looked at her elder son. "You have to know how hard it was for me to watch you suffer. Seein' you now, having learned to let go of the past and move forward, has been a healing to me."

G. W. bowed his head. "I didn't know how it hurt you. I'm sorry, Mama."

"Don't be. You were simply dealin' with your own grief. How can I fault you for that?" She turned to Rob. "You have always been a bit of a wild one, but I find your love of life has helped to pull me along through my mourning."

He smiled, but Deborah was taken aback to see tears in Rob's eyes. It wasn't often that either of her brothers showed their emotions.

"Dr. Clayton, I'm thankful for you, as well. This community desperately needed a real doctor. You came at just the right time. You are precious to this family, and I hope you will be around for years and years to come."

She turned to Arjan. "Last, but definitely not least—Arjan,

I'm very thankful for you. You have honored me by joinin' with my children to ensure my safety, protection, and well-being."

"You all are my family," Arjan said. "You won't never be without a home or meal, so long as I have anything to say about it."

Mother nodded and took her seat. It was Deborah's turn. Getting to her feet, she thought of all the things that had blessed her.

"I'm thankful for so much. I love . . . all . . . of you." She stumbled over the words, realizing she'd included Dr. Clayton. Hoping no one would make too much of the matter, she quickly hurried on with her statement. "I have been blessed by each one of you in so many ways. I am grateful to have a sister in Lizzie. We have long been friends, but now we are family. I'm blessed by my brothers, who, although they can be a bit bossy and overbearing, love me and only want the best for me. I'm blessed by my education and the life experiences I've had. I am completely thankful for you, Uncle Arjan. Your love and kindness to this family have truly sustained us all."

She paused and turned to her mother. For a moment, her mother looked years younger. Perhaps it was the veil of grief being lifted from her. Maybe it was just the presence of the Lord and the blessing of fellowship. Deborah reached out to take her mother's hand and kiss it.

"I am more thankful for you, Mother, than I have words to say. You have been a constant in my life—an inspiration to me. I thank God for you every day."

She turned back to the table of people. "I, too, am grateful for Dr. Clayton. I'm thankful for his friendship and the way he has shared his knowledge with me." She continued at a rapid pace. "I'm thankful to be home again. I love this place—I love Texas. I'm blessed to be back where I belong."

Taking her seat, she tried not to think about the man sitting opposite her. She tried not to think about his broad shoulders and gentle face. She tried not to remember the times when he'd caused her to feel weak in the knees. She tried . . . but wasn't really making much progress. It wasn't until Lizzie took her turn and announced her pregnancy that pandemonium set upon them, and Deborah could actually consider something besides Dr. Clayton.

When Christopher's moment to speak arrived, he wasn't quite sure what to say. There was a great deal he was thankful for, but speaking it aloud was hard. "I love my family," he began, "and I'm grateful for them. Like Deborah, I'm thankful for my education and also for the friendship you all have shown me since my arrival. I am thankful for this meal, to be sure, and figure you'll be thankful if I keep my comments to a minimum so that we can eat."

Everyone laughed and Christopher took his seat, fearing he might embarrass himself if he remained standing to say more.

G. W. was quick and to the point when he declared his greatest blessings were his wife and unborn child. He spoke of his happiness and the knowledge that God had truly brought it all about. Then Rob stood and told them he was glad they had avoided the typhoid. Everyone nodded, knowing that this alone had been a huge blessing for them.

"I'm thankful, too, that I've never been punched in the eye by Deborah. I've seen what that can do."

Mother cocked a brow. "What are you talkin' about?"

Deborah looked as though she'd like to melt under the table. Christopher waited for Rob's explanation with great curiosity.

"When we were in Houston, it seems little sister decided to go out on her own. She met with trouble, and Mr. Wythe . . ." He paused and looked directly at his mother. "You remember Mr. Wythe, the man who pulled Deborah out of the path of the freighter?"

Mother nodded. "I remember him well." She looked at Deborah while Rob continued.

"Anyway, Mr. Wythe showed up to rescue her once again when a man accosted her and Lizzie."

"Oh my! Is this true?"

Deborah nodded. "It wasn't my best decision."

"Well, she was wallopin' the guy when Mr. Wythe showed up to help her. But it seems the robber ducked and Mr. Wythe took Deborah's blow to the face. Anyway, I wouldn't be surprised if Mr. Wythe don't show up for a visit. I think he's rather sweet on Deborah."

"I hope you won't take another chance like that again," Uncle Arjan declared.

Deborah gave a quick look in Christopher's direction. She blushed and nodded. "No, sir. I don't intend to."

Christopher found himself almost more troubled by Rob's comments about Mr. Wythe than the assault. After all, though Deborah was safe from the man who would have hurt her, she apparently wasn't free from this Mr. Wythe.

He remembered Euphanel's warning about someone else making a claim on Deborah. It seemed there was already a potential suitor. He didn't like the way this news made him feel. It was stealing his Thanksgiving joy and peace. Maybe he should have a talk with Deborah about his feelings. At least that way, he could be the first one to bring up the subject.

Frowning, he shook his head. But what subject was he going to bring up, exactly? Courtship? Marriage? The very thought left him struggling to concentrate.

Chapter 29

December 1885

The Christmas dance was only a week away, and Deborah couldn't help but feel uncomfortable. She had been asked to accompany no fewer than five different would-be suitors and had turned them all down. At this point, she wasn't sure she even wanted to attend the dance. Not to mention that Dr. Clayton wasn't among the five who'd asked her to attend. Not that it mattered. Or did it?

"It shouldn't," she told herself. But lately, Deborah wasn't convinced that her heart was listening to her.

"Brought the mail," Rob announced, striding into the room. He gave the stack a toss to her desk. "It looks like Vandermark Logging is startin' to exchange lots of letters with folks. I ain't never seen so much mail."

"Hopefully it won't just be a bunch of bills," Deborah said, glancing through the missives. It took her by surprise to see the decidedly feminine script of her friend Jael Longstreet.

"No, she's an Albright now," Deborah remembered.

Rob raised a brow. "What did you say?"

Deborah opened the letter. "Nothing of importance. I was just noticing a letter from a friend." She glanced at the opening line and smiled. Jael was worried she had somehow broken the most important rule of friendship—never steal a girlfriend's man.

"I'm heading out to the logging site. I'm sure the boys are missing me," Rob said with a grin. "After all, I do more work than any of 'em."

"It's a surprise, then, that Uncle Arjan sent you to town for the new saw blades and axes."

Rob just laughed. "He knows I'm the best at gettin' a good price, too. I can barter better'n anyone."

"Well, get on with you now. It won't stay light forever."

Once Rob closed the office door, she began to read the letter.

> *I never imagined myself married to Stuart, but there are circumstances that brought about this arrangement. One day I will explain. I hope that Lizzie isn't angry with me. I took it upon myself to believe that since she rejected Stuart at the altar, and then again in Texas, she couldn't possibly remain attached. I pray this is so. I would never have wanted to hurt her.*

Perhaps the biggest surprise came toward the end of the letter. Jael wrote of her father's desire to come west and check into the Texas lumber industry. If he did make a trip to Texas, she intended to accompany him. She was certain that Stuart wouldn't mind, and she would simply love to see Deborah and Lizzie.

Deborah finished reading the letter and pondered the situation.

Jael never spoke of loving Stuart. Never once mentioned anything that suggested the two had enjoyed a whirlwind romance. Jael also never said a word about Ernest Remington, her previous beau. It was all very curious.

A knock sounded on the office door and Lizzie came in. "I thought I'd come and see what I could do to help you. Your mother and Sissy seem to have the kitchen under control."

"I was hoping you'd stop by," Deborah said, motioning to a straight-back chair. "Come sit here and read this letter from Jael."

"Jael? Goodness, I never expected to hear from her." Lizzie swept into the room, wearing a simple gown of dark pumpkin. Orange wasn't a color Deborah had ever cared for in clothes, but with Lizzie's coloring, the dress looked quite lovely.

"So what does she have to say?" Lizzie asked as she took her place beside Deborah.

"Here. I'll let you read it for yourself. The news is rather interesting."

Lizzie took the single sheet of paper and scanned it quickly. She looked up and met Deborah's gaze. "I can't imagine what kind of circumstances could come about to cause Jael to give up her interest in Mr. Remington for Stuart."

"I couldn't either. I thought maybe it was something his father wanted, but she also hints that things are not good between the Albright men."

Lizzie nodded and handed the letter back to Deborah. "It doesn't surprise me."

"It would be nice to see her here in Texas, however." Deborah tucked the letter into her desk drawer. "I'm surprised by the entire matter, however. I thought perhaps your mother had erred in reporting the marriage, but obviously that's not the case. I simply cannot imagine the two of them together."

"Nor can I. I thought about the situation for quite some time, and it makes little sense on Jael's part. I can well understand why Stuart did it—he was desperate to get his inheritance. But Jael always had more sense than that. I don't know what could have happened to make her do this." Lizzie's expression was one of worry. "I hope her father didn't force her to marry him."

"Maybe since Jael was the only child still at home and with her mother's passing, her father felt it necessary to see her wed." Deborah began to thumb through the other letters. "If she does come for a visit, we shall have to clarify the matter."

"I agree."

Seeing nothing that couldn't wait, Deborah set aside the mail to take up the balance sheet she'd been working on earlier. "I guess we can begin with this," she told Lizzie. "Although I don't know why you're even bothering with office work now that you're expecting. You have more than enough to occupy yourself in making baby clothes and preparing for this wondrous event."

Lizzie looked rather embarrassed. "I'm afraid I know very little about childbirth. Remember—while you were studying biology, I was learning about European art."

"I know the medical information—at least the portion I could find in books; but you would do better to talk to Mother about the experience. She's done this three times; I'm sure she'll have all the answers you need."

"I feel silly being a grown woman and not knowing. My mother was so remiss in teaching me much of anything that had to do with being a wife and mother. If left to her example for guidance, I'm sure poor G. W. would never have wanted me."

Deborah laughed. "That's hardly possible. G. W. would have loved you no matter. I've never seen two people more smitten."

"And what of you, Deborah?" Lizzie's expression turned quite serious. "When do you plan to open your heart to someone?"

"I . . . I hardly know how to reply." Deborah abandoned her place at the desk and moved to close the office door. Rather than return to her seat, however, she strode to the window and gazed out at the overcast December day.

"What's the matter?" Lizzie questioned. "You've never had any trouble speaking your mind before."

"I know. I've always been able to talk to you or Mother, but this time I feel a bit tongue-tied." She turned and met Lizzie's inquiring expression. "I had honestly figured to stay here—remain single and help my family. Mother is totally opposed to that idea, but all of these years, I thought it was what she and Father wanted. Having me handle the office freed up the men to take their needed places in the forest. Mother and Sissy were then able to handle the animals and the kitchen, and of course now that you're here, they certainly don't need me for household chores. Well, at least not as much." Deborah smiled for a brief moment, then frowned.

"I suppose I'm uncertain as to what I should do. I've planned for one thing all of my life and now that thing seems . . . well . . ."

"To have disappeared?" Lizzie asked.

"No. It's more like it never existed at all. It's as if I invented something in my mind that had no physical substance. Like a child creating an imaginary friend."

She sat down beside Lizzie and gave a sigh. "I feel confused by the entire matter. Mother wants me to marry and start a family. She says she's not, but it's like she's trying to get rid of me."

"Oh, Deborah, that isn't even possible. Your mother has always held a special place in her heart for you. However, I know she's concerned that you would let life and love pass you by, in favor of what you consider duty."

"She said that?"

Lizzie nodded and reached out to take hold of Deborah's hand. "You must understand: She only wants good things for you. She is proud of your intelligence. Proud of the things you've accomplished. She wants you to live life in a way that pleases God, of course. But she also wants it to please you."

"And she believes marriage would be pleasing to me?"

"Who can say? I know she sees the interest young men are taking, and she wants you to feel the liberty of sharing your heart."

Deborah started to reply when they heard a commotion outside. It sounded like Rob calling for help. Getting to her feet, Deborah headed for the office door. "I hope no one is hurt."

She made her way outside as the driver pulled back hard to bring the team to a stop and Rob rose up from the wagon seat. Lizzie came to her side, and it wasn't long before Mother and Sissy were there, as well.

"Come quick!" Rob yelled. "It's G. W.!"

Lizzie swayed and reached for the porch post. "No!" She started for the wagon, but Deborah grabbed hold of her. "You wait here and let me see how bad it is."

Mother and Sissy were already at the wagon. Deborah heard them ask if anyone had gone for the doctor and knew it must be very bad. Lizzie seemed to sense this, too.

"I'll wait," she said, "but please hurry."

Deborah nodded and ran to the wagon. The sight there was not one she had anticipated. For a moment, she thought she might very well swoon. She steadied herself against the edge of the wagon and noted the blood that had soaked through to the wagon bed.

"Rob, what happened?" Mother asked, staring down at her unconscious son.

"He climbed up to top a tree. Somethin' went wrong and the

tree snapped and G. W. fell. A branch impaled his leg. I was just heading out to join them when I spied Klem here driving the wagon like there was no tomorra."

Deborah didn't wait for her mother to comment. She took charge without even thinking. "We need to get him inside. Mother, it would be best to lay him out on the dining room table."

Mother looked at her for only a moment and nodded. "Rob, can you and Klem manage him?"

"We'll do it," Rob assured her. "You just hold the door for us."

"I'll fetch an oilcloth for the table," Sissy said. She was gone before Deborah could so much as comment. She looked to the porch and could see that Lizzie was crying.

"Lizzie, go help Sissy. We're going to need clean towels, bandages, and hot water—lots of it."

Deborah didn't wait to see if Lizzie did as she bid. She turned to her mother as Rob and Klem worked to move G. W. "Mother, this isn't good. He may well bleed to death. I'll do what I can if you'll allow me to. I've observed several procedures and assisted Dr. Clayton. Hopefully, I can do the preliminary things before he gets here."

Her mother took hold of her arm. "Do whatever you can to save him, Deborah. Tell me how I can help."

Deborah drew her mother toward the house. "I'll need your good sewing shears and some tweezers." She noted the piece of tree branch protruding from G. W.'s leg along with bone. It wasn't a simple fracture. Fortunately, someone had strapped a belt around his upper thigh. "We may need some pliers, and get some of the soft soap and melt it in a pan of hot water. After it's melted, cut it with half again as much cold water so as not to burn the skin. We're going to have to clean that wound and see just how bad things really are." She began rolling up her sleeves as she walked toward the house. She could only pray that something she'd learned could now benefit her brother.

By the time the men had G. W. laid out on the table the way Deborah thought most beneficial, her brother had still not regained consciousness. It wasn't a good sign. Neither was the shallowness of his breathing. It was entirely possible he'd broken some ribs and punctured his lung.

The women worked together to cut away G. W.'s trousers. They were hopelessly caked with blood and mud, with numerous jagged tears. Deborah motioned to Rob. He came without hesitation.

"I don't know if the doctor will be able to save his leg. He's got a bad break and he's lost a lot of blood. The wounds are multiple and severe. You may need to lend support to Lizzie. She needs to be careful in her condition."

"You can count on me, Sis. I'll try to keep watch over her. Is there anything I can do to help G. W.?" His worried gaze never left G. W.'s lifeless body. "I shouldn'ta been so slow gettin' back. This might not have happened if I'd been there."

"Stop it. We don't have time for such thoughts. It might not only have happened, but it could have involved both of you," Mother declared.

Lizzie seemed in a daze as she reached out to touch G. W.'s brow. "Please don't leave me," she whispered against his ear.

"He's not going anywhere, if I have anything to say about it. Mother, is the soap and water ready?"

"Just about. Sissy said she'd bring it."

Deborah nodded. "We need to clean the debris from the wound, but in a way that minimizes the bleeding. We won't remove the larger pieces. Dr. Clayton will see to that."

Sissy arrived with the soap concoction and helped Deborah to pour part of it over the leg. G. W. didn't stir or even moan, furthering

Deborah's concern. But she was glad he didn't have to consciously endure the pain.

"We're going to need more light. Please bring several lamps so that we can see better." She hadn't issued the order to anyone in particular, but Mother and Sissy hurried to get them.

Deborah bent over her brother's leg and soaked up some of the dirt and blood with a towel. She then poured additional water over the wound and repeated the process. The flow of blood was stymied by the belt around G. W.'s thigh. The only problem, however, was that cutting off the blood flow for too long would only lead to killing the limb. She toyed with the idea of releasing the belt a bit to allow the blood to circulate through the undamaged vessels. It would also show her whether or not the artery had been severed. If it had, there wasn't much hope of G. W. keeping his leg.

When the lamps were in place, Deborah looked at her mother. "I'm going to loosen the belt to see how bad the bleeding is. Hopefully I'll be able to tell if the artery is pierced. Meanwhile, can you and Sissy strip off his shirt? We need to see what damage was done to his ribs. He's not breathing well."

Everyone went into motion at once. Deborah handled the belt and was relieved when no bright red blood spurted from the wound. Blood oozed from the wounds, but to her surprise it wasn't all that bad. She tried not to think about the fact that G. W. might very well not have much blood left. She opted instead to get back to cleaning the debris. She would leave the belt loosened so long as the bleeding didn't increase.

"Mother," she said suddenly, having a great idea, "do you still have that magnifying glass of Father's?"

"I do." She nodded and headed off without Deborah saying another word. When she returned, Deborah instructed her to hold it over the wounds so she could see better to clean the lacerations.

With meticulous care, she began pulling splintered wood and bits of rock and dirt from the wound. She had worked for maybe thirty minutes when Uncle Arjan rushed into the room.

"Doctor's here."

Deborah straightened. "I've been doing what I could to clean out the debris. I've left the bigger pieces in place for you, in case they caused the bleeding to increase. He seems to be breathing in a shallow manner."

Dr. Clayton nodded and immediately opened his medical bag. Deborah saw that he'd brought a much larger case than he usually carried.

"You keep picking out the small pieces while I listen to his lungs."

Deborah focused back in on her work. She put aside the fact that this was her brother. Such reminders wouldn't serve her well. If anything, it would only cause her to lose her focus.

Dr. Clayton listened to G. W.'s breathing for several moments. "Perhaps a small collapse, but air is moving well." He continued to check G. W. for further wounds. "Arjan told me what happened," he said to Deborah. "Has he regained consciousness since the fall?"

"No, not since they brought him here," she answered.

They both looked to Rob, who shook his head. He turned to Klem. "What about it?"

"Ain't come awake since he fell," Klem told them. "Not so much as a grunt."

Dr. Clayton pulled a large bottle of carbolic acid from his bag. "Hopefully the bleeding helped to clear away some of the fragments."

Deborah pointed to the pan of soapy water. "I used that to clean away the dirt and some of the caked blood. It's Mother's soft soap and warm water."

He nodded while pouring the soapy liquid over the site. Straightening, he then used a liberal amount of the carbolic acid over his scalpel and probes. "Deborah, hold his legs steady, and Arjan, grab his shoulders. I don't expect him to move, but you can never tell."

He noted the belt. "It was good thinking to control the blood flow. I'm going to check the break and situation of the tree piece, and then we'll get to work on seeing if we can save the leg." He looked at Deborah and smiled. "Ready to assist me?"

She nodded. "Just tell me what to do."

Chapter 30

G. W.'s recovery was doubtful the first few hours. His fever soared and his unconscious state was broken only by an occasional moan. Further examination revealed several broken ribs and concern that his back may have been damaged in the fall. The discoloration and bruising were of grave concern.

Deborah remained at G. W.'s side as much as possible as the hours moved into days. Mother and Lizzie were there, as well. The three women took turns cooling G. W.'s feverish body with wet rags. In addition, Deborah helped Dr. Clayton tend to the leg wounds. A makeshift splint was fashioned to hold the bone in place. It was far from ideal, but with the need to watch the wounds for infection, it was the best they could do at the present.

When G. W. finally showed signs of response, Dr. Clayton

started to worry about the degree of injury he'd sustained. "His neurological reactions are slow. However, I'm not overly worried at this point. I think there may be a great deal of swelling along the spinal column, and hopefully that will reduce in time."

Deborah knew how serious the situation might be. Her brother could be left paralyzed. She doubted Mother and Lizzie understood the matter's gravity. Exchanging a look with Dr. Clayton, his expression told her that it was best they kept such thoughts between the two of them. Sometimes knowledge could be the enemy—especially where emotions were concerned. They would know soon enough if G. W. had the ability to move his legs.

"When do you suppose he'll awaken?" Mother asked hopefully.

"I can't really say. We'll know more with each passing day. We need to keep hoping and praying. The fever is down, and the leg looks good. I'm not seeing any infection, but he could still have trouble. We'll just keep watching it closely."

"I'll come again in the morning," Dr. Clayton said as he gathered his things.

"Thank you so much for all you've done," Mother told him. She handed him an envelope. "Tuck this away for later. Maybe it will help your family." He glanced at it for a minute, then put it in his coat pocket. "Deborah," her mother continued, "why don't you take Dr. Clayton to the kitchen and get him a plate of food to take home with him?"

"I will, Mother." She looked to Dr. Clayton, wondering if this would be to his liking. He smiled and opened the door for her.

Deborah made her way through the house knowing that the good doctor wouldn't be far behind. She picked up one of the oil lamps from the front room and carried it to the kitchen as they went.

"Sissy's gone home for the evening, but she kept a plate warming for you on the stove. If you'd rather just sit down and eat it here, I can get you some hot coffee, as well."

He smiled. "Can you sit with me?"

She felt taken aback for a moment. Nevertheless, she nodded and motioned to the small kitchen table. "I've already eaten, but I'll share your company. Why don't we just stay in here rather than go into the dining room?"

"I'd like that." He took a seat while Deborah gathered a cup and the coffee pot. "This is most likely strong. It's been sitting there since supper." She poured a cup and put it in front of him.

Returning the pot to the stove, Deborah next grabbed the towel-covered plate that Sissy had left for the doctor. She removed the cloth and placed the food in front of Dr. Clayton. "I'll bring the silver."

"This looks delicious," he commented.

"It was," Deborah replied, laughing. "Sissy made the most delicious ham loaf with black grape glaze. I think you're going to like it."

She returned with the silverware and a linen cloth, then took the seat opposite him. "I know you're worried about G. W."

"I am, but it serves your family no good to say so. His unconscious state is a mixed blessing and curse. The longer he remains asleep, the more rest his body will get. If he has broken his back or caused grave injury to the spine, such rest will be best. On the other hand, his unconscious state doesn't bode well for injury that may have been done to the brain."

Deborah nodded. "I wish I could have done more for him."

"You helped him a great deal, as did the men at the logging camp. Stopping the blood flow and getting him help as soon as possible were the best things they could have done. You were wise to start cleaning the wound and get him set out on the table. It made a good surgery room."

"There is so much I don't know. So much I wish I did."

"So why not learn?"

She looked at him and shook her head. "Women doctors are hardly tolerated down here. Healers are one thing, and midwives are obviously expected to be women. However, there is little acceptance of women getting an education in any field. Certainly not medicine."

His right brow rose. "And this would stop you?"

"Well, I certainly can't go traipsing off to the university again. Philadelphia allows for women doctors, but the time away from here would be difficult for my family. Especially now." She shook her head. "Goodness, but now G. W. is incapacitated and Lizzie is expecting a baby. There are just too many responsibilities."

"So why leave? Why not stay here and train with me?"

She looked at him in surprise. "I . . . uh . . . don't know what to say."

He laughed and reached for a piece of corn bread. "You could say yes. You could even say that the idea fills you with great joy, because the company would be so agreeable."

Deborah could hardly draw a breath. She felt an overwhelming rush of emotions. Dr. Clayton became quite serious—all hint of humor fading from his expression. He watched her face intently, leaving Deborah unable to look away.

"I'm the only one around here who truly knows the potential you display. I'm one of the very few who recognize your intelligence as something special—something valuable. Others tell you how astounded they are with your ability to think, when what they really mean is that you confuse them. I tell you I'm impressed because I am. I can appreciate what you have to give—what you can yet learn."

Deborah tucked her hands under the table to keep Dr. Clayton from seeing how they were trembling. The very thought of spending hours each day with him caused her to feel rather dizzy. Was this what love was all about? Had she fallen in love with Dr. Clayton?

Maybe I'm just infatuated with the idea of becoming a doctor. She frowned. Maybe that's all it was for him, as well. She knew he had concerns about helping his family, just as she had. Maybe he was actually hoping to train a replacement.

She opened her mouth to comment when Mother came rushing into the room. "Oh, I'm so glad you're still here. It's G. W." Tears were streaming down her face.

Deborah jumped to her feet. "What's wrong?"

Her mother laughed and wiped at her tears. "He's awake."

There was no talk of the missed Christmas dance. Deborah hadn't truly cared about the event to begin with, and now that G. W. was painfully recovering, she had even less interest. Nothing more was said about her learning to become a doctor under Christopher Clayton's tutelage. She began to think perhaps his comments had simply been offered to give her something to concentrate on besides her brother's uncertain future.

As the holidays approached, the atmosphere in the house lightened and cheered. Mother wasn't decorating in her usual holiday fashion, but Sissy still worked to bake many of their favorite treats. The delicate aroma of warm yeast breads and fruitcake filled the air, and visitors were on hand daily to sample the fare. Most came to see how G. W. was doing and even to bring an occasional Christmas gift. Lizzie spent her days nursing her husband and quietly making baby clothes. She seemed almost hesitant to discuss G. W.'s condition with Deborah, for fear of somehow calling disaster upon them.

Mother invited Dr. Clayton to join them for Christmas dinner, but an unexpected baby delivery kept him in Perkinsville. Deborah regretted that he couldn't join them, but she enjoyed her family nevertheless.

As the New Year came and went, Deborah found herself growing more and more restless. Everyone was busy with their own interests and duties; Sissy was very nearly managing all of the chores while Mother helped Lizzie to tend to G. W. when needed. Otherwise, Mother was often off visiting Miriam or speaking to Mr. Perkins on behalf of the townsfolk. The acts of violence against the black folks had increased, and Mother felt quite passionate about helping put an end to such things.

Rains affected production in the logging camp as January progressed. Rob and Arjan were often found in discussion at the kitchen table. Uncle Arjan had hired five men prior to Christmas, and now he was considering arranging for at least two more employees. Added to this, the turpentine company in Beaumont had come to negotiate a deal to harvest resin from the pines prior to their cutting. It was a fascinating turn of events that promised more money for nothing more than allowing their workers to come in and set up their process in forested areas that were not scheduled to be cut for months.

Deborah tried to keep herself busy with the logging books. She faithfully recorded the information of each new employee and arranged their pay in script and cash as Uncle Arjan dictated. In the back of her mind, however, she continued to think of what Dr. Clayton had said. Could it be possible for her to learn medicine and use it to benefit her community?

Deciding to check on G. W. and give Lizzie a break, Deborah left her office work and went to the couple's bedroom. The door was open, and she could see that G. W. had just finished lunch. She smiled and gave him a wave.

"May I come in and visit?"

G. W. grunted a reply, but Deborah wasn't at all sure whether it was in the affirmative or negative. She decided to take it as an invitation, however. Lizzie removed his dinner tray and smiled.

"His leg is aching something fierce today."

"So why are you smiling?"

Tears came unbidden to Lizzie's eyes. "He's able to feel it."

Deborah immediately understood. The swelling to his spine was lessening. "I'm not glad he's hurting, just glad he's feeling." She looked at her brother. "You are quite fortunate, you know."

"So folks keep tellin' me." He sounded less than convinced.

"Why don't you go take a rest, Lizzie? You can lie down in my bedroom. Your old bed is still there. I'll sit with G. W. for a time."

"Yes, go on. I want to sleep anyway, so after I get rid of Deborah I'll take a bit of a rest myself," G. W. declared.

Lizzie hesitated only a moment. "I think I will. I'm sure G. W. will enjoy talking to you. Just come fetch me if he needs somethin'."

Deborah laughed. "There you go again, sounding like a Texan. Next thing you know you'll be drawlin'."

They both laughed at this. Deborah took a seat beside her brother's bed and studied his face for a moment. He was healing on the outside, but he still seemed troubled. Perhaps it was nothing more than his boredom with recuperation.

"So you seem rather . . . well, unhappy?" Deborah half commented, half asked.

"You'd be unhappy, too, if you were facing an uncertain future." His tone was harsh, but Deborah didn't take offense.

"Even the doc can't tell me how long I'll be laid up or if I'll ever recover enough to go back to workin'. If I can't work, how in the world can I support my family? It ain't like there's a lot of jobs for cripples."

Deborah nodded but refused to pity him. "I suppose you're right. I can't see you climbing trees again. Certainly no time soon."

"Exactly. I tried to explain that to Uncle Arjan, and he just kept saying, 'You'll be back in time.'" G. W.'s hard façade seemed to soften just a bit. "We both know that ain't true, but he can't bring himself to say it."

"So what if you had another job to do—one you could even do while you were sick in bed?"

He looked at her as if she'd gone crazy. "And what would that be?"

"What if I trained you to take over the office?"

"I can't read and write well enough for that. I'm not so bad with figures, but even there I don't have the same kind of learnin' you have."

"And I suppose you aren't willing to be taught?" She looked at him quizzically and shrugged. "Maybe you think such things are a waste of time?"

"Hardly. But I'm not so smart as you."

Deborah shook her head. "That's nonsense. You aren't as formally educated as I am, but you are definitely as smart—if not smarter. I could teach you to read and write, as well as keep the books. G. W., it would give you something to fall back on if the worst is realized."

He considered this for several long minutes. Deborah said nothing, allowing him to ponder his words. He was a proud man, but hopefully not too proud to allow himself to be taught.

"I guess I never thought about learnin' anything more. Didn't seem practical."

She could understand that and nodded. "There wasn't time. Father needed you and Rob to join him in the camp. That's why I thought I could best serve the family by going to school and learning all that I could to benefit the business. I always thought that's what Father wanted me to do. Now I realize he was just giving in to my desires. He thought it was what I wanted."

G. W. met her gaze. "But it ain't?"

She drew a deep breath and let it out slowly. "I don't think it is. G. W., I convinced myself that this was what was expected of me. So I gave up any other thought and turned my mind to it."

"And now?"

"Now I see that this could be the perfect answer to your situation. The office and books have to be kept in order. The business end of logging is just as critical as the physical labor, especially now with the turpentine arrangement."

"I reckon I can see that well enough." He frowned and fixed her with an intent expression. "And you really think you could teach me?"

Deborah wanted to shout for joy. The question assured her that G. W. was willing to put his mind to this new venture. "I know I can. You have a quick ability to reason and learn. You figure things out on your own all the time. Now you'll simply have me to help you understand what's what. Not to mention you already have a strong foundation. You can read some, and you know your letters and numbers. I think the rest will come quite easily."

"You sure about this?"

She nodded and got to her feet. "Why don't we get started?"

"I was going to take a nap," he protested.

Deborah laughed. "You can take a nap in twenty minutes."

Christopher didn't know quite what to think when Deborah showed up at his office. It had been nearly a week since he'd been to the Vandermark house, and he worried that perhaps G. W. had taken an unexpected turn.

"Is something wrong?" he asked when she knocked on his open door.

"I suppose you are the only one who can help me determine the answer to that."

He looked at her for a moment, then motioned to the chair. "Have a seat. What can I do for you? Are you ill?" She certainly didn't look sick. She looked radiant, the rich dark green of her gown reminiscent of the surrounding forests.

"I want a straight answer, Dr. Clayton. I don't want you worrying about hurting my feelings or causing me pain. Just a simple yes or no will do."

"I will happily give it, if you will just ask the question." He sat down. "I'm still not very good at figuring out a person's unspoken thoughts. Especially those of a woman."

She folded her hands precisely and nodded. "Very well. Were you serious about training me to assist you?"

Christopher couldn't have been more pleased. He knew the matter was quite complicated, given his family situation and all, but at least this way . . . this way he could spend time with her. If not every day, then at least every week. Looking up, he found her staring at him—waiting for his response. She looked almost like a patient preparing for bad news. He couldn't resist making her wait for an answer as she had done with him.

"No. I cannot say that I was at all serious about training an assistant."

Her eyes widened and her cheeks reddened. She lowered her gaze and seemed to consider this for a moment. "I thought perhaps as much." She looked up, trying hard to appear as though she had her emotions under control. "Very well." Getting to her feet, she headed for the door.

"Don't you want to know my reasons?"

She turned and shook her head. "I think I know well enough. You were simply trying to take my mind off of G. W.'s serious condition."

"Not at all." He got to his feet and came to stand just inches from her. Without asking permission, he took hold of her hand. "I can't train you to simply be my assistant. You are much too intelligent for that. I want to teach you to be a doctor in your own right."

Her mouth dropped open and her eyes widened. *My, but she has the loveliest dark eyes*. She was speechless, which only managed to elicit a chuckle from Christopher.

"So . . . let me . . . let me get this straight. You are willing to train me to be a physician?"

"I am."

"And what will you expect in return?"

The question surprised him. He grinned. "I hadn't really thought of that, but I suppose you can work here to earn your training. That is, if you can spare the time from home."

"And that's all?"

He looked at her and dropped hold of her hand. "Did you expect there to be something more? Perhaps you thought I'd force you to court me? I'm really not that kind of man at all."

Her face flushed scarlet again. "I . . . well, not exactly." She turned her gaze to the floor.

Christopher couldn't help himself. He reached out to touch her sleeve. "I would want to court you only if you truly desired it. I wouldn't want you to spend your time doing such a serious thing unless you could honestly see yourself one day becoming my wife."

Her head snapped up. "You would marry a woman doctor?"

He tilted back his head and roared with laughter. "That's all that you're concerned about? I mention marrying me, and you're only worried about being a woman doctor?"

She shook her head and looked befuddled. "I suppose I didn't think about it that way. Goodness, but you have a way of setting me off balance. A part of me feels like laughing and another part like crying."

"Should I get the water pitcher?" he asked quite seriously.

Deborah immediately calmed and began to smile. "So let me get this straight: You want to teach me to become a doctor *and* you want to court me?"

"That sounds about right. Of course, there is something you need to know, something that might change your mind on the entire matter."

She frowned. "And what would that be?"

"My family. They need me, Miss Vandermark. My father cannot work and my mother can barely earn enough for food. I am sending very nearly every penny I make back to them. Until my siblings are able to help or the younger ones grow up, I cannot think of marrying anyone." He again saw her surprise and added, "Not that I'm proposing. I'm simply asking you to . . . well, commit to waiting?"

She considered his words for a moment. "I think that very wise of you, Dr. Clayton. Your family is obviously in need of your help." She smiled. "It only serves to make me fonder of the idea. I will bide my time."

"But you must agree to stop calling me Dr. Clayton. It makes me feel very old."

She giggled. "But you are old. And your years have made you oh so wise."

He rolled his eyes. "I'm not that old. I'm only thirty."

"Hmm, I suppose that isn't so very old." She cocked her head slightly and smiled. "Christopher Clayton, I would be happy to learn all that I can from you."

He felt the embers of love that had been smoldering within him spark a flame. This woman was simple and complex, all at the same time. How was that even possible?

He gently took hold of her face. Her dark eyes seemed to drink him in. "And I shall be very happy to teach you all that I can."

Turn the page to enjoy

a family recipe from Tracie Peterson,

featured in this book!

Black Grape Tarts

4 cups black grapes
2 Tablespoons cornstarch
1 teaspoon of lemon juice
¾ cup brown sugar
2 Tablespoons butter

Cut grapes in half and pull out seeds. (Or for the old fashioned way: push hulls from skins and set skins aside. Cook hulls until mushy and seeds come free, then strain to get rid of seeds and add pulp and skins back and cook until the skins are tender.) Cook grapes over medium heat until the skins are tender.

Take off the heat and add brown sugar, cornstarch, butter, and lemon juice. Pour into tart crusts. Bake for 20 minutes at 365° F or until the crust is brown.

Sweet Dough Pie Crust

(for tarts—do this ahead of time in order to chill)

4 cups of all-purpose flour
½ cup butter
¼ cup sugar
⅔ cup cold water

Mix dry ingredients, then add butter and mix. It will be crumbly. Add water until dough sticks together.

Divide dough and shape in a flattened ball. Wrap and chill 3–4 hours.

Roll out and use large drinking glass to cut circle that will fit into cupcake pans or mini-muffin pan. Form your tart crust in the cupcake pans. Poke a few holes into the raw dough with a fork to vent and prevent puffing.